ALISON WEIR is the top-selling female historian (and the fifth-bestselling historian overall) in the United Kingdom, and has sold over 2.7 million books worldwide. She has published seventeen history books, including *The Six Wives of Henry VIII*, *The Princes in the Tower*, *Elizabeth the Queen*, *Eleanor of Aquitaine*, *Henry VIII: King and Court*, *Katherine Swynford*, *The Lady in the Tower* and *Elizabeth of York*. Alison has also published six historical novels, including *Innocent Traitor* and *The Lady Elizabeth*. Her latest biography is *The Lost Tudor Princess*, about Margaret Douglas, Countess of Lennox. *Anne Boleyn: A King's Obsession* is the second in her series of novels about the wives of Henry VIII, which began with the *Sunday Times* bestseller *Katherine of Aragon: The True Queen*. Alison is a Fellow of the Royal Society of Arts and Sciences and an Honorary Life Patron of Historic Royal Palaces, and is married with two adult children.

By Alison Weir

The Six Tudor Queens series
Katherine of Aragon: The True Queen
Anne Boleyn: A King's Obsession

Six Tudor Queens Digital Shorts
Writing a New Story
Arthur: Prince of the Roses
The Blackened Heart

Fiction
Innocent Traitor
The Lady Elizabeth
The Captive Queen
A Dangerous Inheritance
The Marriage Game

Quick Reads
Traitors of the Tower

Non-fiction
Britain's Royal Families: The Complete Genealogy
The Six Wives of Henry VIII
The Princes in the Tower
Lancaster and York: The Wars of the Roses
Children of England: The Heirs of King Henry VIII 1547–1558
Elizabeth the Queen
Eleanor of Aquitaine
Henry VIII: King and Court
Mary Queen of Scots and the Murder of Lord Darnley
Isabella: She-Wolf of France, Queen of England
Katherine Swynford: The Story of John of Gaunt and
His Scandalous Duchess
The Lady in the Tower: The Fall of Anne Boleyn
Mary Boleyn: 'The Great and Infamous Whore'
Elizabeth of York: The First Tudor Queen
The Lost Tudor Princess

As co-author
The Ring and the Crown: A History of Royal Weddings, 1066–2011

ALISON WEIR

SIX TUDOR QUEENS

ANNE BOLEYN
A KING'S OBSESSION

REVIEW

First published in Great Britain in 2017
by HEADLINE REVIEW
An imprint of HEADLINE PUBLISHING GROUP

1

Cataloguing in Publication Data is available from the British Library

ISBN 978 1 4722 2762 1 (Hardback)
ISBN 978 1 4722 2763 8 (Trade paperback)

Typeset in Garamond MT by Avon DataSet Ltd, Bidford-on-Avon, Warwickshire

Printed and bound in Great Britain by Clays Ltd, St Ives plc

HEADLINE PUBLISHING GROUP
An Hachette UK Company
Carmelite House
50 Victoria Embankment
London EC4Y 0DZ

www.headline.co.uk
www.hachette.co.uk

SIX TUDOR QUEENS

ANNE BOLEYN
A KING'S OBSESSION

1512

EUROPE

Maximilian I	m.	**Mary**	**Ferdinand II**	m.	**Isabella I**
Holy Roman Emperor		of Burgundy	King of Aragon		Queen of Castile
b.1459		1457–82	b.1452		b.1451

Juan	m.	**Margaret**	**Juana**	m.	**Philip**	**Katherine**	m.
Prince of Asturias		of Austria	b.1479		of Habsburg	of Aragon	
1478–1497		b.1480			b.1478	b.1485	

| **Eleanor** | **Charles** |
| b.1499 | b.1500 |

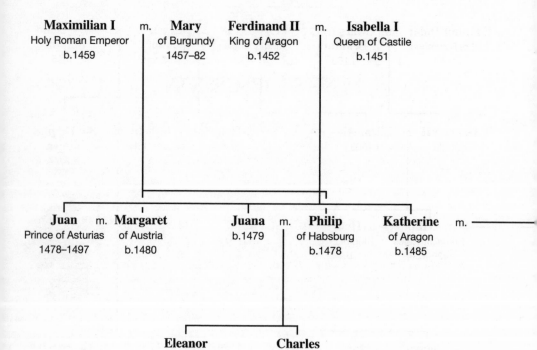

ENGLAND

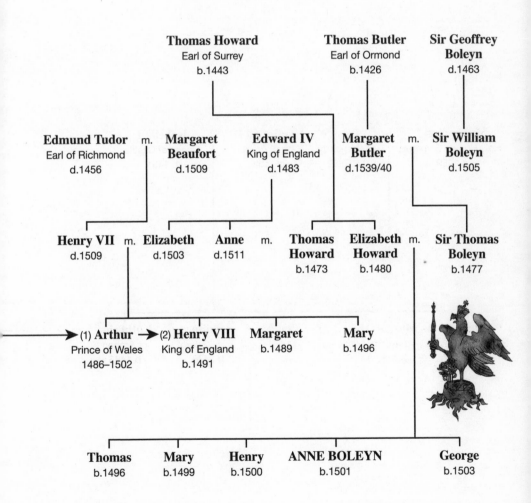

Thomas Howard
Earl of Surrey
b.1443

Thomas Butler
Earl of Ormond
b.1426

Sir Geoffrey Boleyn
d.1463

Edmund Tudor
Earl of Richmond
d.1456

m.

Margaret Beaufort
d.1509

Edward IV
King of England
d.1483

Margaret Butler
d.1539/40

m.

Sir William Boleyn
d.1505

Henry VII
d.1509

m.

Elizabeth
d.1503

Anne
d.1511

m.

Thomas Howard
b.1473

Elizabeth Howard
b.1480

m.

Sir Thomas Boleyn
b.1477

➤ **(1) Arthur** ➤ **(2) Henry VIII**
Prince of Wales   King of England
1486–1502   b.1491

Margaret
b.1489

Mary
b.1496

Thomas
b.1496

Mary
b.1499

Henry
b.1500

ANNE BOLEYN
b.1501

George
b.1503

To Rankin, my wonderful husband, and Julian,
my brilliant literary agent, without whom none of my books
would be possible.

Who list her hunt, I put him out of doubt,
As well as I may spend his time in vain.
And graven with diamonds in letters plain
There is written her fair neck round about:
Noli me tangere, for Caesar's I am,
And wild for to hold, though I seem tame.

(Sir Thomas Wyatt)

'. . . Verily,
I swear, 'tis better to be lowly born
And range with humble livers in content,
Than to be perk'd up in a glistering grief,
And wear a golden sorrow.'

(William Shakespeare, *King Henry VIII*, Act 2, Scene 3)

Part One

'Not of Ordinary Clay'

Chapter 1

1512

Her skin *was* rather sallow, Anne thought as she studied herself in the silver mirror, and she had too many moles, but at least her face was a fashionable oval. At eleven she had no womanly figure to speak of, but that hopefully would change in the next year or so. Mary, after all, was already buxom at thirteen.

She drew back, considering herself. People had often said, within her hearing, that Mary was the more beautiful of the two Boleyn sisters. Yet they were both brunettes, with long glossy hair, high cheekbones and pointed chins, and both slender and graceful, for the deportment fit for royal courts had been drummed into them. So what was it that made a girl beautiful? What made the arrangement of Mary's features better than hers? It had begun to bother Anne, now that she was growing up and was constantly being enjoined to prepare herself for a glorious future in which royal favour and a wealthy husband of rank loomed large.

Maybe it was the moles and the sallow skin. The sallowness could be rectified by a lotion of powdered egg whites and alum. At least she had a pretty mouth, and the black eyes that her Grandmother Butler always said were her best feature.

'And you know already how to use them for effect, child.' Anne had not quite understood what that meant, but then Grandmother was Irish and a little fey and often said some startling things. Everyone tolerated it because she had been a great heiress and one of the chief sources of the family fortunes.

Anne propped up the mirror on a chest and twirled in front of it. She did look good in the green gown, which made her waist seem so slender. The dark colour became her too. The only thing that was wrong was the cut of the sleeves, which were tight to the wrist and did not cover the deformity of which she was always so painfully aware. She was forever curling it into her palm, the little finger of her right hand, so that none should see the tiny extra nail. If only she could have a gown with hanging sleeves that would cover it! But Mother said it was foolish to worry about such a little thing. It was not a little thing to Anne, and it had loomed larger than ever since the day when Mary, bested in one of their interminable arguments, had called it a witch's mark.

Anne pushed the hateful memory aside. She would not dwell on it on this beautiful late-summer day. She had a free hour before her lesson with the chaplain, and was determined to waste not a minute of it. In a trice she had summoned her maid, changed into her everyday worsted, descended the stairs and crossed the stone drawbridge across the castle moat; then she picked up her skirts and ran through the gardens into the meadows by the River Eden, where she loved to wander.

From here she had a grand view of moated Hever Castle, her family's seat, and the lush wooded Kentish countryside that cradled it. But of greater interest was the sight of her beloved brother George lying sprawled in the grass, twanging his lute, his dark brown hair tousled, his clothes crumpled.

'They are looking for you indoors,' she told him, kneeling down. 'You should be at your books. You'll be beaten if you don't go back.'

George grinned up at her. 'I had an idea for a song. Listen!'

He played well for a boy of nine, and his composition had the sophistication one would have expected from someone far older. He was gifted, this brother of hers. He could make his mark as a musician if he did not carve out a career at court, as their father expected.

They had always been close, Anne and George. They looked alike and thought alike.

'I know, I know – I can't spend my days making music and writing poetry,' he sighed, mimicking Father's voice.

'Much good it would do you! And in the end you would not be satisfied. It would never be enough for you. So stop playing truant. Father Davy is livid.'

For all her mock reproof, she felt sorry for George. She knew how deeply it gnawed at him, being the youngest of three sons. It was sixteen-year-old Thomas who would inherit Hever and all their father's lands and wealth – and it was Thomas who, to George's envy, had been sent to the household of the mighty Duke of Buckingham at nearby Penshurst to learn courtly manners and the martial arts, which would befit him for the glorious future that awaited him. And then there was clever Henry, twelve years old and destined for the university at Oxford, since Father had decided to dedicate him to the Church – and save himself the burden of having to provide for him. There had been other sons too, but they slept in St Peter's Church, to their mother's great grief. Anne had never got used to the appalling sight of her tiny dead siblings lying in their cradles, all decked out in macabre finery, to receive the final prayers and farewells of their family.

Lady Boleyn doted on George, her youngest, more than she did on Thomas and Henry. But in George's breast there burned a fierce resentment against his older brothers. Unlike them, he must make his own way in the world. Father reminded him of it often.

Given her rivalry with Mary, and George's envy of their older brothers, Anne often felt that it was a case of her and George, the two youngest Boleyns, against the world. Because she did not have looks and he was not the heir, they had pulled together since they were very little. Some took them for twins.

'Come on!' she commanded, pulling him up, and together they raced back to the castle.

Father Davy was waiting for them as they sped across the courtyard and tumbled into Father's new entrance hall. Their tutor was a rotund little man with a merry face and cheeks rosy as apples.

'Ah, you've deigned to grace us with your presence,' he said to George. 'And mightily timely too, for we've just had word that your father is expected home this evening, and we wouldn't want to greet him with the news that you're in disgrace, would we?'

'No, Father Davy.' George was trying to look contrite.

'Mistress Anne, you may join us,' Father Davy said. 'You can set an example to this young knave.'

'Where's Mary?' George asked, rolling his eyes.

'Reading,' said Father Davy. 'I have given her a book on kings and queens. It will improve her mind.' It was no secret that he had almost given up on Mary.

Anne followed them into the private parlour used by the family in the evenings, and sat down at the oak table. She knew she was fortunate, being a girl, to receive a good education. Father had very advanced ideas, but then he was always concerned that his children should do well in life – which, of course, would reflect favourably on him. Accomplished in foreign tongues himself – which was why he had been away these last weeks at the court of the Regent of the Netherlands at Mechlin in the Duchy of Burgundy – he was particularly anxious that his sons and daughters become proficient too.

Anne struggled with French, despite excelling at everything else. Mary was good at French, but dismal in all other respects. Anne could compose passable poetry and songs, thanks to Father Davy being a famous composer of church music and a gifted teacher. Mary battled, murdering her lute; it did not help that she was tone deaf. Anne danced gracefully; Mary galumphed about the floor. Anne sang like a lark; Mary's voice was flat. But Mary had the looks, everyone said, so it didn't matter that she was an idiot. Most men would not see beyond her beauty and the dowry Father could give her. Thus it did not matter that, when the time for lessons arrived, she was rarely to be found.

Most of the daughters of the local gentry in the Boleyns' circle could barely wield a pen, Anne reflected, as her quill traced her graceful Italianate hand across the paper. Today's exercise was composing a letter in French, which was a challenge, but she was determined to persevere. She enjoyed learning for its own sake, and revelled in the praise Father Davy lavished on her.

From the kitchens nearby they could hear a great clatter and commotion. The household was preparing for the return of its master, and Mother would be giving orders and inspecting the cooking pots, much to the cook's ill-concealed annoyance. There would be a feast tonight, Anne thought happily.

*

Dressed in the new green gown, Anne stole a peep at the great hall, where the tables had been beautifully laid with snowy-white linen. The best silver was set out on the high table above the great gilt salt, with polished pewter on the lower trestles set at right angles to it. Banks of greenery trailed along the centre of the boards, interspersed with candles and ewers of wine. Hever was a small castle, and the hall not large compared to some she had seen, but it was sufficiently grand for an up-and-coming diplomat and favourite of the King, with its great stone fireplace and imposing carved screen. The early evening sunshine cast a golden glow through the tall windows set high in the thick walls, reflecting its jewel-like glints on the impressive display of family plate on the buffet and the expensive wall hangings. Father liked to impress his neighbours with his wealth. They were all coming tonight: the Wyatts from Allington, the Sackvilles from Buckhurst Park and the Hautes from Ightham Mote.

Normally the family dined in the parlour, seated at the long polished table. It was a cosy room, its walls adorned with wainscots of oak and painted friezes, and hung with another of the costly tapestries of which Father was inordinately proud. But that was all familiar and common-place; feasting in the great hall was an occasion, and Anne was impatient for it to begin.

Father was home, and she had been summoned to see him in his study before dinner. There he sat, in his high carved chair, nodding as she made her curtsey: the man who had dominated her life for as long as she could remember, whose lightest word was law to his family and servants, and to whom Anne and her brothers and sister had been brought up to render unconditional obedience. When she and Mary married, their husbands would take over his role. It had been drummed into them both that women were weak creatures and should always be subject to the wise dominion of men.

When Sir Thomas Boleyn was at home, the household revolved around him, but that was a rare occurrence. When he was not abroad using the diplomatic skills that had so endeared him to King Henry, he was usually at court, building on his reputation as a jouster and courtier and all-round good fellow. At thirty-four, he was still a handsome and agile man, and sat a horse superbly. He was outstandingly learned – it seemed to his children that he knew everything – and even the great Dutch scholar Erasmus had dedicated two books to him. Thanks to these virtues he had risen high and fast in royal service, becoming one of King Henry's best friends and jousting partners, and never tired of reminding everyone of it. He had been knighted at the King's coronation, three years earlier, and then appointed Esquire of the Body to the monarch.

'It is a most sought-after post,' he was prone to boasting, 'for it brings me into daily contact with the King. I enjoy great influence. I have His Grace's ear.' He would gleefully expand on the patronage he was in a position to exercise. Anne understood that there were many people who wanted Sir Thomas Boleyn to ask the King for favours, and that they were ready to pay him a lot of money to do that.

She was pleased to see Father's pugnacious face broaden into a wolfish smile as she rose from her curtsey. 'I have some good news,' he said. 'The Regent Margaret was most interested to hear of your accomplishments and has offered to take you into her household as one of her eighteen maids-of-honour. It is a signal favour, much sought after.'

'Me, sir?' Anne echoed. 'Surely Mary . . . ?'

'I know, it is highly unusual for the younger sister to be advanced before the elder, and Mary speaks good French. But,' and he gave Anne a calculating look, 'I believe that *you* have what it takes to succeed at court and be a credit to me. Besides, I have other plans for Mary. And the Regent specially asked for you.'

Anne felt excitement bubbling up.

'When am I to go, sir?' she breathed, envisaging the glorious palaces, the fine gowns, the glittering lords and ladies, the Regent smiling as she made her obeisance with everyone looking on.

'Next spring,' her father said, and the bubble burst. That was *months* away. 'There will be many preparations to make. Your mother will know what is required. I'd rather it be you than the Devil who makes work for idle hands.' He and Mother barely spoke to each other unless they had to.

'You must work hard at your French,' he went on. 'You will complete your education at the court of Burgundy. There is no finer place, for it offers many opportunities for a young girl of good birth, and is universally well regarded. You will be well placed to attract a marriage that will advance the interests of our family. I hope you appreciate your good fortune.'

'Oh, yes, sir!' Anne exclaimed. It was almost too much to take in.

'I would remind you that the competition for places in the Regent's household is fierce, and there are many who are ready to offer substantial financial inducements to secure the honour of an appointment for their daughters. Each one of her *filles d'honneur* must know how to dress fashionably, be accomplished at dancing and singing, and be able to entertain her mistress and important visitors with witty conversation – and she must understand how to conduct herself when in attendance on the Regent in public and on state occasions.' Father leaned forward in his chair, his rugged face intent. 'It was for such an opportunity as this that I provided you and Mary with a good education, although much Mary has profited from it. But you, Anne . . . you will shine. And I have no doubt that the considerable outlay required of me to provide you with suitable court attire will be well spent.'

'Yes, Father. Thank you, Father.'

'You may go. It's nearly time for dinner.'

Anne sped upstairs, still buzzing with excitement, to the chamber she shared with Mary, whom she found fastening around her neck the gold pendant in the shape of a bull that she always wore on important occasions. The girls had been given one each by their father; the bull was his family's heraldic emblem, and a pun on its name.

Mary leaned into the mirror. Her black eyes, with their alluring slant, were watching Anne's reflection.

Anne was savouring her news, wondering how to break it to Mary with maximum impact. She could no longer contain herself. 'I'm going to court!' she announced.

Mary swung round, shock and fury in her face. '*You?*' she shrilled. 'But – but *I* am the elder.'

'Father knows that, but the Regent asked for me.'

'The Regent?'

'I am summoned to the court of the Netherlands to serve her. It is a great honour to be asked. Father said so.'

'But what of *me*?' Mary's lovely face was flushed with outrage. 'Am I not to go too?'

'No. Father said he has other plans for you.'

'What plans?' Mary hissed.

'I don't know. He didn't say. Why don't you ask him?'

'I will! He cannot pass me over like this.'

But he had. Anne hugged that delicious knowledge to herself. For the first time in her life, it felt good to be the younger and less beautiful sister.

Elizabeth Howard, Lady Boleyn, unravelled the bolt of tawny velvet and held it up against Anne.

'It suits you,' she said. The mercer standing respectfully at her side beamed. 'We'll have this one, and the good black, the yellow damask and the crimson tinsel. Pray send your bill, Master Johnson.'

'Very good, my lady, very good,' the merchant replied, gathering up the fabrics that had been rejected and withdrawing from the parlour.

'I'm glad the Regent gave us good notice,' Mother said. 'It allows us time to get these gowns made up. You should be grateful that your father has made such generous provision for you.' She tilted her daughter's chin upwards and smiled at her. 'You have fine eyes, and innate grace,' she said. 'You will do well and make me proud.' Anne's heart was full. She loved her mother more than anyone else in the world.

Elizabeth Howard herself was dark in colouring, but her long Howard face was rounded with generous lips and fine eyes. In youth she had been a celebrated beauty, and the poet laureate, Master Skelton, had dedicated verses to her, likening her charms to those of the gorgeous Cressida of Troy. It was Mother's little conceit. Her great conceit was her pride in her aristocratic lineage. She let no one forget that she came of the noble House of Howard, and it was no secret that, had her family not been in royal disfavour at the time, plain Thomas Boleyn, as he then was, could never have aspired to marry her, even though his grandsire was the Earl of Ormond. But with her father stripped of his titles and not long released from the Tower for fighting on the wrong side in the battle that had put the late King Henry on the throne, her chances of making a decent marriage had been slender; and so she had permitted herself to be tied to a young and ambitious man whose recent ancestors had been in *trade*.

But thanks to that, the Boleyns were rich. By dint of their business acumen and by marrying wealthy heiresses, they had steadily acquired wealth and lands. Anne's great-grandfather, Sir Geoffrey, had been a mercer like the fellow who had recently departed with his wares, but he had risen to be Lord Mayor of London and been knighted. That was the way one made good in the world, and it was new and able men such as the Boleyns, rather than the old nobility, who were now favoured by the young King Henry.

But for all that Father had done – and was still doing – to make himself a suitable husband in the eyes of his high-and-mighty in-laws, there was no doubt in anyone's mind, even her children's, that Mother had married beneath her.

'You will be the equal of any of the other maids,' she said to Anne now. 'You can be justly proud of your Howard ancestry. Remember, we Howards are descended from King Edward Longshanks and from all the English monarchs back to William the Conqueror, so you have royal blood in your veins and must be worthy of it.'

'Yes, Mother,' Anne said, bobbing a curtsey. She walked slowly back to her bedchamber, thinking on what Lady Boleyn had said. She was deeply proud of her heritage, especially now that the Howards had been rehabilitated and were firmly back in favour at court. In the long gallery she paused before a portrait of Grandfather Howard, the Earl of Surrey. She was in awe of this just and honest aristocrat, the head of the family, and of his son, whose picture was further along – Uncle Thomas, her mother's brother, a stern-faced, no-nonsense soldier and courtier. She had only a few memories of his wife, the aunt for whom she herself had been named, but she could never forget that the late

Princess Anne of York had been daughter to King Edward IV and sister to the present King's mother. It made King Henry her own cousin, in a sort of way.

Anne had long been aware that any love her parents might have had for each other in the beginning had long since died, for they avoided each other as much as possible. It was easy to understand why Mother looked down on Father. What was more difficult to comprehend was why Father treated Mother, that highly prized bride, with ill-disguised contempt.

It disturbed Anne that Mother had once been compared to the Trojan beauty Cressida. For, having pledged her undying love for Prince Troilus, Cressida, cruelly captured by the Greeks, had treacherously betrayed him with the heroic Diomedes. Father Davy had read them the story when they had studied the Greek myths.

'Her name has become a byword for a faithless woman,' the good friar had said. Anne stifled a gasp. Clearly he did not know what Skelton had written of her mother. The five of them – Tom and Henry had been at home then – had looked at one another, appalled.

Yet Anne had never heard of any hint of a blemish on Mother's reputation. Lady Boleyn presided over her household with competent authority, and preferred country life to the teeming existence of the court, although she did sometimes go there when needed as an occasional lady-in-waiting to Queen Katherine.

At home Anne and Mary helped Mother in her still room, where they made comfits and jams while she distilled sweet waters or prepared medicines and poultices from the herbs they had gathered in the gardens.

'It is essential that you both learn the skills that will enable you to run a great house,' she was always reminding them. 'A lady should keep her servants busy not only by precept, but by example.' But if Anne might happen to glance up from what she was doing, she would occasionally surprise Mother with her hands idle, a faraway look on her face and a tune playing on her smiling lips, as if she had withdrawn into a secret life. And again she would wonder if her mother had a lover.

*

12

The months that she had envisaged dragging sped by. Expensive tutors were engaged to give her and Mary advanced instruction in singing and dancing, skills that Anne acquired easily and enjoyed.

'Bravo!' cried the tutor, as she twirled and leapt and skipped in *branles*, farandoles and *basse* dances. It came easily to her, as if she had been born to it. Mary, who was all arms and legs at awkward angles, would glower at her. Father had not revealed what his plans for Mary were, and Anne now doubted that he had any, while Mary's angry jealousy simmered and often bubbled over. Thrown together as the sisters were, it did not make for a peaceful existence.

Sir Thomas, however, was impervious. Anne was to go into the world as his ambassador, a walking testimonial to his greatness. If there was any talent that might be useful at court, she was to acquire it. Father Davy was deputed to enhance her musical skills.

'You have a true voice,' he said, and Anne thrilled to hear it, for his praise was never won lightly.

He also encouraged Anne and George's love of poetry. The two of them would sit together for hours composing and transcribing verses and binding them into books. Father Davy told Anne she had a rare talent for it, especially for a woman. He refrained from remarking on how Mary thought that cow rhymed with low.

In these months in which her wardrobe was being prepared, Anne became an expert embroiderer. She made biliments to edge necklines and hoods, quilted sleeves and pouches, and decorated her lawn nightrails in bright scarlets and greens. She discovered the pleasure of enhancing her clothes with novel details: a border here, a contrasting colour there, and – always – long hanging sleeves to hide her extra nail. Her nurse, Mrs Orchard, a plump, motherly soul who had been with her since birth and was to accompany her as chaperone on her journey, did all the plain sewing, stitching and hemming under-smocks and petticoats. As the weeks went by, the pile of finished garments stowed in Anne's new travelling chest grew and grew.

In the autumn, Father returned to the court of the Netherlands, leaving Mother in charge of the preparations for Anne's departure.

'Remember,' he said to Anne before he left, 'your task is to perfect the attributes that will secure you a good marriage. I have had you educated to that purpose, and to instil virtue.' Father was very zealous on virtue. He was always warning his daughters of the dire consequences – mostly for him – if they fell from it. They were his assets – his jewels, as he liked to put it – and their success was essential to him.

In these last months at Hever, Anne found herself resenting the dull routine. She longed for her escape into the glamorous world of courts. She and Mary found their chief excitement in putting on their best gowns and, escorted by a groom and a maid, riding the three miles into nearby Edenbridge for the market that was held there every Thursday, just to show off their finery. When they were not at lessons or sewing, they played cards, or visited the houses of neighbours with their mother – and fought constantly over silly things until Lady Boleyn lost patience and sent them to their rooms to cool down.

Their existence was dominated by the unchanging round of the seasons. That autumn of 1512 was heralded as usual by Michaelmas, soon followed by Harvest-tide, when St Peter's Church by the castle was filled with ears of wheat and hymns of thanksgiving. That was the grease season, when all the local gentry went hunting. Father had ensured that Anne and Mary were both competent horsewomen, and they were allowed to participate in the chase or go hawking in the company of their neighbours. In the evenings they savoured the rich game from their bag, served on thick bread trenchers saturated with meat juices.

On wet days they took their exercise in the long gallery above the great hall, a new-fangled improvement to the castle that Father had decided he must have. Up and down his daughters walked, past the pictures and hangings that adorned the walls, bickering and gossiping and occasionally slapping and pinching each other.

As autumn fell, fires and braziers were lit, and the castle was filled with the sweet aroma of beeswax candles. The three young Boleyns played cards, dice and chess in the flickering light, or teased each other with riddles, before tumbling into their feather beds. On many nights Anne lay awake, with the damask bed curtains pulled back and the moonlight glinting on the diamond-paned windows, imagining the glittering life to come in the magnificent court that lay miles across the sea in another land.

Hard on the heels of All Souls, when the nights were dark and ghosts were said to walk in the woodland that faced the castle, came the season of Advent, followed by the Christmas and Twelfth Night celebrations. Before Anne knew it, it was Candlemas, then Lady Day – and soon it would be May Day, when she and Mary always observed the ancient custom of rising early to bring in the May blossoms.

With the May came Father, back from the Netherlands.

It was time, at last, for her to depart.

Chapter 2

1513–1514

Anne found the sea voyage exhilarating; she stood on the deck, bracing herself against the brisk spring breeze and the choppiness of the waves, and watched the chalk cliffs of Dover receding into the distance. She kept thinking of Father's last proud embrace, Mother's tearful kiss, Mary not bothering to hide her jealousy, and George – bless him – struggling not to cry. She had almost cried herself, knowing that she would miss them all, especially Mother and George. She allowed herself a brief moment of sadness, then turned resolutely to Sir John Broughton, a knight of Westmorland with whom her father had become acquainted at court. Sir John was travelling to Bruges on business, and had offered to extend his journey so that he could escort her to Mechlin. He was about thirty, fresh-faced, with curly red hair and a broad northern accent.

'I am honoured to have charge of such a charming young lady,' he had said, bowing, then he'd helped Anne and Mrs Orchard to mount their horses, given instructions to the grooms responsible for the wagon bearing their luggage, and led them over the drawbridge and away to the south. Throughout the journey to the coast he had been the epitome of courtesy and good company, selecting the best inns at which to lodge overnight, demanding the choicest food, and entertaining the two ladies with witty stories. The weather had been fine and they had made excellent progress. At Dover Sir John had commandeered good cabins for Anne and Mrs Orchard in the ship that was to take them across the English Channel, and he had accompanied them whenever they took the air on deck.

From her father and Sir John, Anne had learned a great deal about the lady she was soon to serve. Margaret of Austria was the only daughter of the Holy Roman Emperor Maximilian – a wily old fox if ever there was one, her father had said – by his late wife Mary, the Duchess of Burgundy. It was through their marriage that the Burgundian Netherlands had come to the House of Habsburg. Margaret had once had a brother, the Archduke Philip, a young man of such beauty that he had been known as Philip the Handsome.

'He married the Queen of Castile, but he died young, and Queen Juana, who had loved him fiercely, went mad with grief and was deemed unfit to rule,' Sir John explained as they sat at dinner at the captain's table in his oak-panelled dining room in the sterncastle. 'Her father, King Ferdinand of Aragon, took over the government of Castile in her name, and the Emperor appointed the Archduchess Margaret, Duchess of Savoy, as his regent in Burgundy and the Netherlands, in Philip's place, and entrusted her with the upbringing of Juana's children, including her heir, the Infante Charles of Spain, although in Burgundy they call him the Archduke. You will meet them soon, I'm sure.'

'What happened to Queen Juana?' Anne asked, her curiosity piqued by this sad tale.

Sir John frowned. 'There are many tales about her. It is said that she refused to give up her husband's body for burial, dragging it around Spain with her for months and ordering her servants to open the coffin so that she could gaze on the corpse and kiss and embrace it. In the end they forced her to relinquish it so that it could be interred, and she was sent to a convent to be cared for by the nuns.'

Anne shuddered. You would have to be mad to do such horrible things. They were the stuff of nightmares.

'I feel sorry for her children,' she said, sipping her wine. 'Do you think she will ever get better?'

Sir John frowned again. 'There are reports that she is not even ill, but was shunted aside so that her father could seize power in Castile. With Juana shut away and her son only thirteen, there is no one else to rule that kingdom.'

'But that's dreadful!' Anne cried. 'If she is not mad, then she should be restored to her throne. Surely her own father would not treat her so terribly.'

'When kingdoms are at stake, Mistress Anne, human feelings count for nothing,' Sir John observed. 'But Queen Juana might well be mad, as most people think.'

'God send that she is,' Anne said. 'It is better for her not to be aware that she has lost her husband, her children and her crown.'

'She is still queen. When he is of age, her son will become joint monarch with her.'

'How I pity her.' Anne laid down her knife and rose to her feet. She did not want to hear any more about tragic Queen Juana or the ruthlessness of kings.

Thanks to the frisky wind, the crossing passed quickly, and soon they were sailing along the Zwin Channel to Bruges. Anne was agog to see the bustling city with its wondrous churches, its soaring belfry in the vast market square, its pretty canals and tall red-brick houses, so unlike the timbered thatched cottages of England. In the busy streets, well-dressed merchants jostled with foreigners of all nations, and there was a general air of prosperity. She was surprised when Sir John told her that Bruges was a dying port.

'The Zwin Channel is silting up. Soon this prosperity will dwindle.'

She stared at him. 'What will happen to these people?'

'They are resourceful. They will find a way to preserve their valuable trading links, especially with England. And Bruges is famous for its art – there are many great painters working here. Did you know that William Caxton published the first printed book in this city?'

'Did he?' There were several books from Caxton's London press at Hever; she had read them all. Not so long ago, Father Davy had told her, all books had been written by hand. It was a marvellous age she lived in, she thought.

Anne would have loved to linger in Bruges, but Sir John quickly completed his business and said they must press on to Ghent. They travelled on horseback across flat country that seemed strange after the sweeping hills of the Weald of Kent and was criss-crossed by canals and dykes and avenues of tall trees. After Ghent they turned eastwards, and before long they could see a tall tower in the distance.

'That's Mechlin,' Sir John said. 'The capital of Burgundy. And that tower belongs to St Rumbold's Cathedral. You can see it for miles.'

Anne felt a thrill of anticipation. As they drew nearer to the city, myriad spires came into view around the great church, and clusters of red roofs. They were nearly there. In a matter of hours, please God, she would be making her debut at the court of Burgundy and being presented to the Regent.

'I'll be glad of a rest,' Mrs Orchard sighed. 'We've been in the saddle for days, it seems, and now you and I have to go all the way back, Sir John. I hope we find a decent inn tonight, and that Anne gets a fine lodging.' Anne eyed her impatiently. Who wanted to rest when one could be plunging into the pleasures of court life? But then Mrs Orchard was old – she must be at least thirty – and there was grey in her brown hair.

'The Regent is famous for keeping a good house,' Sir John told them. 'You will be well accommodated, Mistress Anne. And you will quickly master French here. It is the language of this court.'

When they had skirted the walls and ridden through the massive gateway of the Winketpoort, Anne saw that Mechlin was much like the other Netherlandish cities she had passed through, with its wide market square, tall houses and magnificent churches. Presently they were clattering along the Korte Maagdenstraat and drawing to a halt before an imposing archway.

'This is the Hof van Savoye, the palace of the Regent,' Sir John said, as the guards waved them through. Anne gasped. They were in a vast rectangular courtyard surrounded by splendid facades on all sides, mostly built in the ubiquitous red brick of the Netherlands; there were graceful open arcades at ground level, tall mullioned windows and a steep pitched roof with dormer rooms.

'The Regent is a great builder.' Sir John pointed to a wing covered in scaffolding and crawling with workmen. 'It will be years before this place is finished.'

'I love it!' Anne breathed. 'I have never seen anything like it.'

'You certainly wouldn't in England,' Sir John agreed, as they dismounted.

An officer wearing black and yellow livery was approaching. Sir John made the introductions and Anne was invited to follow the man, who would take her to her lodgings. It was time to bid farewell to Sir John and Mrs Orchard. Anne was sorry that the moment of parting had come, for she had grown used to Sir John's merry company and come to appreciate his care for her and his wide knowledge of the world. And while she found her nurse's fussing irritating, she was fond of her.

Sir John bowed and kissed her hand. 'May God keep you, Mistress Anne, and send you joy.'

Mrs Orchard hugged her; there were tears in her eyes. 'Take care, my little mistress,' she enjoined. Then they both mounted their horses, Sir John doffed his hat and they disappeared through the gatehouse.

'Come!' the man in livery said, in his heavily accented English. He led Anne into the palace, taking her through chambers of breathtaking magnificence. She gaped. Beside such splendour, Hever was a barn. She understood now why her father was so often away at court. She had never imagined great staircases like these, or galleries filled with such paintings, so lifelike and colourful. Gifted artists had brought Madonnas, saints and angels to life so skilfully that it seemed they might step out of their frames and breathe.

The *filles d'honneur* were accommodated in a dorter on the second floor, within the steep dormer roof. Save for Gerda, a little Dutch maid who had been assigned to attend her, it was empty when Anne arrived and she thankfully threw off her travelling cloak, sinking down on the bed with red woollen hangings that had been assigned her, one of eighteen that lined the long room end-to-end, like a series of wooden boxes. She had been told that she might rest a while and unpack her clothes before someone came to present her to the Regent. But she was too excited to rest. As soon as her baggage had been delivered, she opened her chest and pulled out the yellow gown bordered with black silk, which had been made in the Regent's colours, as a compliment. She had been longing for this moment.

She bade Gerda unlace her travelling gown and help her strip down to her smock. Then she held up her arms so that the square-necked gown could be lifted over her head and laced up at the back. The feel of the silk was sensuous, and she loved the hanging sleeves, and the long court train that from now on would be obligatory. Her hair she left loose, falling to her hips. Now she was ready! She sat there fidgeting, waiting for the summons to her new mistress.

The Archduchess Margaret of Austria, Dowager Duchess of Savoy and Regent of the Netherlands, was entirely unlike the beautiful princess gowned in cloth of gold and laden with jewels Anne had envisaged. As she rose from her curtsey, she was astonished to see that the chair of estate beneath the rich velvet canopy was occupied by a little woman in black swathed in a white widow's wimple and chin barbe – and that this daughter of the mighty Emperor Maximilian had a face that could only be called homely, with unusually full lips and a heavy, pointed jaw.

Those lips were smiling, however, and the next thing that struck Anne was the warmth the Regent exuded.

'Welcome to my court, Mademoiselle Boleyn,' she said, speaking in French, and Anne did her best to reply in the same language, tripping over her tongue as she answered polite questions about her journey and whether she was comfortable in her lodging.

'Admirable!' twinkled the Regent. 'And I am honoured by the colours of your pretty gown. But I think that Monsieur Semmonet will have his work cut out. It is he who will be teaching you how to speak French properly.' Anne blushed as Margaret indicated a middle-aged bearded gentleman in scholar's robes, who bowed when he heard his name.

'Consider my court your home, child,' the Regent went on, still smiling. 'I hope I will treat you in such a way that you shall be quite satisfied with me. Now you may join your fellow *filles d'honneur*.'

Touched and reassured by the warm welcome, Anne went to sit on the floor with the seventeen other fortunate young ladies – many from the greatest families in the land – who had been singled out for the high honour of serving at the court of Burgundy. They were all in their early teens, and all expensively dressed. Some smiled at her, some stared at her gown; a few – she felt – looked haughtily down their noses.

In the dorter that night, they clustered around, gabbling excitedly and indicating that she open her chest and pull out her clothes for their inspection. Some, she was gratified to see, were impressed – others, to her dismay, dismissive.

'*C'est provinciale!*' sneered a tall girl, fingering the crimson tissue, which had been cut in the English fashion.

'*Non, Marie, c'est jolie!*' a blonde maiden with rosy cheeks retorted, smiling at Anne. Marie shrugged.

Soon they lost interest and began chattering in rapid French of things about which Anne knew nothing. She realised that, as the only English girl among them, she would always be a little set apart.

Not that it bothered her too greatly, even in her first few days at Mechlin. There were other young ladies ready to be her friend besides the blonde girl, whose name was Isabeau, and as she worked hard at her French under the vigilant tutelage of Monsieur Semmonet, and grew more fluent, communicating with her peers was easier and she became more accepted.

The tutor – who seemed to have unlimited talents – also schooled Anne and the other *filles d'honneur* in deportment and dancing, and instructed them in manners and the art of conversation, a talent much encouraged by the Regent, who deemed it essential for anyone who wanted to succeed at her court. Every day Monsieur Semmonet would choose a different situation they might encounter, and they would act out their responses in the most courteous way. Anne found herself addressing imaginary princes and discoursing with them on music and painting and poetry. She could hardly imagine it happening.

It was instructive to wait with the other *filles d'honneur* upon the Regent as she sat in council, kneeling unobtrusively in a group on the floor and trying to understand the commands and directives Margaret issued from her seat at the head of the table, or deciphering the advice given her by the worthy, solid men who deferred to her. Clearly they respected her wisdom and judgements. Anne was so keen to learn more about how a woman ruled that she redoubled her efforts to be proficient at French.

After just a week, the Regent sent for her. 'I have written to your father to tell him that I am delighted with you,' she said, 'and to thank him for sending you to me. He could not have given me a present more welcome. I have told him that I find in you so fine a spirit, and such perfect courtesy for a young lady of your years, that I am more beholden to him for sending you than he can be to me for receiving you.'

Anne exhaled in relief and happiness. She had feared she might be admonished for the many small mistakes she had made in trying to do and learn all that was expected of her. To see the Regent smiling so broadly and to be enfolded in her wholesome embrace was more than she could ever have hoped for. She sank to her knees, full of gratitude.

'My pleasure is only to serve your Highness,' she declared with fervour.

How very fortunate she was, not only to be serving a kind and affectionate mistress, but also to have come to a court that led the rest of northern Christendom in manners, art and learning.

'This is a princely school and a place of high culture and advanced civilisation,' Monsieur Semmonet told her and her fellow pupils. 'All scholars are welcome here.' Anne soon discovered that the Regent, who was rarely without a book in her hand, was especially devoted to something called 'the New Learning', which meant the recently re-discovered texts of ancient Greece and Rome. There were ripples of excitement when the famous humanist scholar Erasmus visited Mechlin. Anne was privileged to be in attendance on the Regent that day, and she listened enthralled as this learned man with his ready wit and wise, sensitive face talked about his plan to make pure Latin and Greek translations of the Scriptures. She was stunned to realise that the Bible used in churches was not in its original form. How exciting it would be to read Erasmus's translations and know the truth.

More shocking was his attack on the extent of corruption within the Church, for at home Holy Mother Church was always spoken of with the greatest reverence. Yet to hear Erasmus talk was revelatory. As Anne listened to his passionate exposure of the degeneration of Rome, the avarice of priests and the worldliness of the clergy, she began to see a deal of truth in the great man's criticisms.

In the little leisure time she had, her newborn thirst for knowledge drew her to the Regent's wondrous library, where she and her companions had been permitted the free run of the numerous manuscripts, missals, music books and printed volumes. There were racy tales by Boccaccio, the delightful fables of Aesop, the blushingly erotic poems of Ovid, and heavy works of philosophy by Boethius and Aristotle, among many others. Anne's favourites were the collections of verse expressing devotion and love. She read them avidly. It helped her to write better poems of her own.

She was leafing through a brightly illuminated bestiary one day when her eye caught a pile of books at the other end of the table. The arms of the Regent were stamped on the tooled leather binding. Curious, she got up to see what they were, and discovered, to her astonishment, that they had been written by a woman. She had thought that only men wrote books. But this Christine de Pizan, who had lived over a hundred years ago, had been no milksop maid, and had had some pithy things to say about the way men treated women. Anne's eyes widened when she read: 'Not all men share the opinion that it is bad for women to be educated. But it is very true that many foolish men have claimed this because it displeased them that women knew more than they did.' She had never heard anyone voice such an opinion.

She had been devouring the book for an hour when the Regent walked into the library. She smiled when she saw Anne, who had risen and sketched a hasty curtsey, and took the book from her.

'Ah, Mademoiselle Boleyn. I see that you have discovered my favourite writer.'

'Your Highness, what she writes is extraordinary.'

'You think so?'

'Madame, this Christine de Pizan would have laughed at my father's insistence that men, by the natural law of things, are cleverer than women.' Anne took back the book and opened it at a passage she had marked with a ribbon. '"Just as women's bodies are softer than men's,

24

so their understanding is sharper,"' she read aloud. "'If it were customary to send little girls to school and teach them the same subjects as are taught to boys, they would learn just as fully and would understand the subtleties of all arts and sciences. As for those who state that it is thanks to a woman, the Lady Eve, that man was expelled from paradise, my answer to them would be that man has gained far more through Mary than he ever lost through Eve.'"

Margaret nodded sagely, opening another volume. 'I like the passage where she asks, "How many women are there who, because of their husbands' harshness, spend their weary lives in the bond of marriage in greater suffering than if they were slaves among the Saracens?" Not that my poor late husband was cut of that cloth. But most astonishing of all are her views on female rulers. "The wives of powerful noblemen must be highly knowledgeable about government, and wise – in fact, far wiser than most other such women in power. The knowledge of a noble-woman must be so comprehensive that she can understand everything. Moreover, she must have the courage of a man."'

No wonder the Regent favoured Christine de Pizan's works. They were something that every woman of rank should read – and heed. Was it possible that women really could be the equals of men?

Anne was at her happiest when she was in the company of the Regent, who was so approachable that she found herself asking Margaret for her views on women, the Bible and a hundred other things she had learned about in this exciting new world. Margaret always answered her with humour and wisdom.

'Ah, *la petite* Boleyn, you are right to ask if women should be the equals of men. But it is not often given to women to shape their destiny, or to rule as I do. My late mother-in-law, Queen Isabella of Castile, was a queen in her own right, but hers too was a rare example. It is up to us women to show men that we are just as capable as they are.'

'We could not lead armies into battle, madame,' Isabeau piped up, and the others giggled, but the Regent silenced them by raising her hand. 'Isabella did,' she said. 'She did not fight, of course, but she was an inspiration. And that, ladies, is what we must all aspire to be. We want men to admire us for our courage, our characters and our intellect, not just our beauty.' It thrilled Anne to hear her say this.

She soon discovered why the Regent always wore black.

'Many call her the *Dame de Deuil*,' Gerda said one morning as she was brushing Anne's hair.

'The Lady of Mourning? How sad. But why?'

'It is in perpetual memory of her husband, the Duke of Savoy. He died nine years ago.'

Anne had seen a portrait of him hanging in the palace, a romantic young man with the face of an angel framed with long fair hair. It must have been terrible to lose so beautiful a husband so early. The Regent was only thirty-three.

In the weeks after her arrival, Anne had been surprised to hear Margaret of Austria speak freely to her women of her past. 'Do you know, I was given in marriage three times?' she said to Anne just two days after the conversation with Gerda. They were sewing in her tapestry-hung chamber, the other *filles d'honneur* ranged about, heads bent over their needles. 'I was married in childhood to the Dauphin, and was brought up at the court of France, but when I was eleven they found a better match for him, and so I was annulled and sent home. I was more angry than sad.' She smiled at the memory. 'Then I *was* married, to Juan, Prince of Asturias, the heir to King Ferdinand and Queen Isabella of Spain. He was young and handsome, and I was happy, but he died just months after we were wed, leaving me with child.' A shadow clouded her normally cheerful countenance. 'My little girl died at birth. I had to leave her in Spain when I returned to the Netherlands.'

'I am sorry, madame,' Anne commiserated.

'She is with God,' the Regent said, her voice suddenly brisk. 'He has her safe in His keeping. And I found love again, with my Philibert. He adored me. I helped him rule his duchy of Savoy. I made myself respected throughout Christendom. Alas, we had but two years together – such a short time to be happy. And then he went hunting boar in the sweltering sunshine, got overheated and drank cup after cup of iced water. He died in agony.' She laid down her needlework and gazed into the distance, as if seeing the man who had been lost to her. 'And that, *la petite* Boleyn, is why I have vowed never to remarry. Wherever one loves, one risks loss. Never forget it.'

Erasmus was just one of many guests who enjoyed the Regent's famed hospitality. Often she was joined at table by the artists, men of letters, philosophers and musicians whom she patronised. The evenings were enlivened by concerts of the polyphonic music she loved, or her guests would be treated to a personal tour of her prized collection of paintings by the great master Jan van Eyck – paintings of exceptional richness, colour and beauty. Anne was often present on these occasions, captivated by the sparkling conversation, the exchanges of ideas, the soaring harmonies and the glorious works of art. It was a world she could never have conjured up in her wildest dreams, and it was entrancing to be a part of it. She did not miss her home and family at all – apart, of course, from Mother and George, who wrote to her frequently, lamenting her absence.

Her life was not all ceremony and study. The Regent threw feasts and banquets; she hosted soirées and dances; she loved hunting; she presided over tournaments; and she positively encouraged the play of what she called courtly love.

'It is an essential aspect of chivalry,' she told her *filles d'honneur*. 'You are all of an age to start finding men attractive. One of the reasons your parents placed you at my court is that they hope I will find you good husbands.' Anne could sense a frisson rippling through her companions, and her own excitement building. At twelve years old – old enough now to be wed – she was becoming aware of her budding figure and the admiring glances of the young men of the Regent's court. Already she was learning how to flash her dark eyes, swish her skirt or sway her hips to effect, and beginning to understand the infinite possibilities of dalliance.

She listened avidly as the Regent explained about courtly love.

'It is quite permissible for gentlemen, even married ones, to pay their addresses to you,' she said. 'They may express their devotion and even their passion. It is for you to have mastery over them, and in that sense the title of mistress is an honourable one. But it is never permissible for you to allow any man to go beyond the bounds of propriety. And you must keep your suitor guessing, and at arm's length, for men do not value what is easily obtained. Even the lightest kiss is a great favour, you understand. The greatest jewel you possess is your honour, and no husband wants a wife whose reputation has been besmirched in any way, however fair a face or rich a dowry she has. Never forget it, young ladies!'

'At least we're allowed to kiss them,' a pert girl on Anne's left murmured.

The Regent had heard her. 'No, Etiennette de la Baume, it is up to you when – or *if* – you allow *them* to kiss *you*. A gentlewoman must at all times take care not to forget who she is, or the honour of her family, or their hopes for her future. And it is up to us ladies to rein in and civilise the lusts of men.' She hid a smile at their smothered giggles. 'You may flirt, you may encourage, you may even bestow favours – to a point – but the ultimate prize is your virtue, which is the greatest gift you will bring to your husband.'

Anne had read much of love in the poems and romances she had devoured, but she had never received such salutary and sensible advice. She had thought that men were omnipotent in matters of love and marriage – certainly Father thought he was – but now it seemed that women could be in control, even of men's lusts – a subject of which she knew little. The prospect of enjoying mastery over the opposite sex excited her. All of a sudden she realised that she had unsuspected power within her grasp.

The next time a court gallant bowed and paid her a compliment, she smiled sweetly and turned away, as if it did not matter – although it did, for the young man was handsome. When, later, he engaged her in conversation and then led her out to the dance floor, she looked up from under her dark eyelashes and regarded him as if pearls of wisdom were tumbling from his lips – and then made sure that she danced the next time with someone else. Her evasions seemed to work. The Regent was right – always the gentlemen came back, more ardent than before.

28

She did not look for more than flirtations. She was not yet thirteen, after all. It was just a highly enjoyable and novel game, far removed from the strictures of her father and the dull round of life at Hever. The world was opening out to her, abundant with new ideas and unexpected delights.

Above all, she desired to emulate the mistress she had come to love and revere. She made the Regent's tastes and pleasures her own, in the surety that all the knowledge and talents she was so pleasantly acquiring would befit her to grace any court, as Father had wished. Whenever the Regent praised Anne's dancing skills, the songs she composed, or her skill with a lute, her cup ran over. Above all, she was learning to think independently. Whereas at home she had been expected to accept unquestioningly the wisdom and decrees of her elders, in Mechlin she found that it was permissible, even encouraged, to have ideas of her own, and to think for herself.

She also became aware of the power of display. What you wore sent out important messages to people who mattered, be they princes or suitors. The watchword was magnificence. And so she discovered the joys of further enhancing her limited wardrobe, for new court gowns were dreadfully expensive, which was why Father had provided only six. But with a length of ribbon here and a well-placed jewel there, plus a few strategic stitches to transform the high square neckline into the wider and more revealing French style, which was the height of fashion at the Regent's court, they could be made to look different and eye-catching. It was the way you wore your clothes that mattered. If you stepped out as if you felt beautiful and elegant, others might just believe it.

It was the same with your looks. Anne was fascinated by people's faces. She knew that her own long, narrow face with its pointed chin did not conform to the current ideal of beauty, but she was learning that a charming smile and a ready wit, with that sideways gaze under the eyelashes, had in itself the power to attract.

Anne shared some of her lessons with the Regent's nephews and nieces, the orphaned children of Philip the Handsome and Juana the Mad. She had come to know the eldest, the Archduke Charles, a little

– but only a little, because he was a reserved, self-contained boy, young for his thirteen years, forever ailing of one complaint or another, but always standing on his dignity.

He was the strangest-looking person Anne had ever seen, for in him the pointed Habsburg jaw was so pronounced that he could not close his mouth properly or eat without difficulty. But no one ever mentioned it. The Regent doted on the boy, and fussed over his education. He had the best tutors, who were turning him, Anne thought, into a pious little despot, but it had to be admitted that he was clever, and brilliant at learning foreign tongues. And he was a very important young man indeed, for he was Archduke of Austria by birth and the heir to the kingdoms of Castile and Aragon. He was also too grand to take much notice of an insignificant English *fille d'honneur*, until the day came when Monsieur Semmonet instructed him to practise the pavane with her.

Clearly reluctant, but remembering his manners, the awkward youth bowed before Anne and stretched out his hand. As the musicians began playing, she placed hers in his loose, unwilling grip, and they moved forward at the required stately pace, one step to every two beats, and then sideways.

'There is no need to lift your train, Mademoiselle Anne,' the tutor reproved. 'This is a dance performed at high court ceremonies and even in nunneries on clothing days. It is slow and dignified.'

The Archduke Charles kept sniffing. Anne was sure that he was conveying his disdain for her. She turned to him, furious.

'Does your Highness have a cold? If so, here is my handkerchief.' And she thrust the delicate square of fine linen at him.

The sagging jaw dropped at her presumption. 'I thank you, mademoiselle,' Charles said, in icy tones, taking the handkerchief as if it were a dead rat.

'I pray that your Highness recovers soon,' she replied sweetly. The dance was resumed.

She wondered if he would complain to the Regent of her boldness, yet Margaret of Austria continued to show her as much kindness as was ever her wont. But the Archduke Charles made it clear that he now held Anne in high disfavour, and she saw no point, for her part, in trying to win his friendship – ugly, priggish boy that he was.

That summer and autumn Anne heard of the victories that King Henry and his allies, the Emperor Maximilian and King Ferdinand of Aragon, had won over the French. The names of Tournai and Thérouanne, the towns he had taken, were on all lips, and much mirth was had at the expense of King Louis's troops, who, seeing an English army bearing down on them, had spurred their horses and fled.

'It is aptly called the Battle of the Spurs,' the Regent laughed. '*La petite* Boleyn, you have every reason to be proud of your King and countrymen.'

'Madame, the glory also belongs to the Emperor, your Highness's illustrious father,' Anne said.

Margaret of Austria patted her hand. 'How very kind. Now, ladies, I have a surprise for you. We are to journey to Lille, to meet the victors.'

Anne joined the others in a chorus of eager approval.

Pennants and standards fluttered colourfully in the light October breeze as the Regent's great cavalcade made its stately way westwards from Mechlin to Lille, which could not be far off now. Word had been passed back through the ranks that the Emperor Maximilian and the King of England were waiting to greet Margaret of Austria at Tournai, and would then accompany her to Lille.

The *filles d'honneur* were seated in two gilded chariots, chattering gaily as they rode in the wake of their mistress and the Archduke Charles. Anne was as excited as the rest at the prospect of setting eyes on King Henry, who by all accounts was an extraordinarily handsome and valiant young man. In the opinion of all the young ladies he was a hero too, for trouncing the hated French. The campaigning season was over now, but everyone was sure that next year would see King Louis finally beaten.

The Regent had generously given all her *filles d'honneur* bolts of rich fabrics to make gowns for the occasion. Anne's was a wine-red damask with a raised black velvet pile. She had never owned such a sumptuous gown. Having it made had taken most of her quarter's wages, but it had been worth the outlay.

The gates of Tournai were in sight, and Anne craned her neck to see a great concourse of people and soldiers awaiting them. As they drew nearer, two imposing figures in front caught the eye: both were tall, both had a kingly carriage, and both were magnificently attired in velvet and cloth of gold. The Emperor was immediately recognisable from the portraits the Regent kept of her father – there was the large, high-bridged nose, the firm chin, the haughty mien, the sparse grey locks. Maximilian had an arresting presence, but he looked decrepit beside the man standing next to him. If an artist had wanted to paint a picture of Youth and Age, he could not have found better subjects. For Henry of England was blooming with vitality.

And that, Anne thought, disappointed, was all that could be said for him. He too had a high-bridged nose and firm chin, but his fresh face had little otherwise to recommend it. His eyes were narrow, his mouth prim and ungenerous. He had a mass of reddish hair, broad shoulders and a manly bearing, but had he not been a king, she would not have given him a second glance. Those who had praised him were mere flatterers. Even Father – never given to flights of fancy – had said he was handsome in the sight of ladies, and had spoken nothing but good of him. *He* would – he had done very well at this King's hands, and was accounted his friend.

As the Regent dismounted to be greeted by her father and King Henry, and her ladies and *filles d'honneur* clambered out of their chariots and formed a train behind her, Anne's eyes lighted on the man who stood behind the English monarch. They could have been brothers, for the likeness between them was striking, yet in this face the firm nose, pursed lips and narrow eyes were striking. By his rich dress, this gentleman was a nobleman; where the King was clean-shaven, he had a luxuriant chestnut beard.

'Your Highness, may I present my good friend Charles Brandon, Viscount Lisle?' Anne heard King Henry say, in a surprisingly high-pitched voice. The handsome man stepped forward and bowed low over the Regent's outstretched hand, which she seemed to withdraw with some difficulty. As Lord Lisle rose, his bold eyes met hers and Anne saw her cheeks flush.

The city fathers now came forward to welcome Margaret of Austria. Her delight was unfeigned when they presented her with a set of tapestries depicting scenes from Christine de Pizan's *Book of the City of Ladies*. They could not have chosen a better gift. Anne was eager to see the tapestries when they were unrolled.

Escorted by the Emperor and the King, the Regent rode at the head of her vast company into Tournai as church bells rang out triumphantly and crowds swarmed in the streets. That night there was a lavish feast in the Bishop's Palace. The Regent was seated between the King and Viscount Lisle, and Anne, from her place well below the high table, watched as the handsome lord flirted and laughed with her mistress.

Later, as they were preparing her for bed, Margaret was much animated, singing the praises of the English Viscount.

'Never since my dear Duke died have I ever met a man to whom I felt attracted,' she confided, as her hair was being brushed. 'I feel I am no longer a lady of mourning but a lady with possibilities.'

Anne and her fellow *filles d'honneur* stared at each other, amazed. Their mistress had sworn a vow never to remarry!

The Regent smiled at them. 'I know what you are thinking. But am I not allowed a little pleasure? Think you I do not know the rules of this game of love?'

There was more to it than that, Anne learned. Within two days gossip was rife that Lord Lisle had proposed marriage. The Regent said nothing; she just kept on smiling her secret smile and making out that the whole business was an elaborate play. It was what happened in courts, she said. But seeing her together with Lord Lisle, you would have thought they were lovers in every sense. When he jousted against the King, both of them resplendent in purple velvet trappings, Margaret of Austria gave him her scarf as a favour, rising from her seat on the high stand to bind it to his lance. Then she watched, hand to her mouth, her breathing tense, as the courses were run and the spears broken. In the end a tie was declared; the King and his companions rode around the tiltyard in triumph, doing great reverence to the ladies.

That night Anne was present at the sumptuous banquet hosted by King Henry in honour of the Regent and the Archduke Charles, who – miserable boy – looked as if he would rather be anywhere else. After his aunt frowned at him, he made an effort to be sociable, but it was obvious that King Henry was having to work hard with him.

Course after course was served – there must have been a hundred dishes, Anne reckoned – and the food was wonderful. After the banquet, at a sign from their mistress, Anne and the other young ladies rose with her and danced for the company, stepping out to the sound of vielles, shawms and sackbuts in a stately *basse* dance and then proceeding to a livelier almain, which got the audience tapping their feet and clapping. It was obvious that the Regent was showing off her skills for the benefit of Lord Lisle, but suddenly King Henry was casting off his doublet and shoes and whirling her around in his stockinged feet, leaping like a stag, much to the amusement of his friend and the whole company.

After that, he and Viscount Lisle and several other lords and gentlemen disappeared for a time, and when they returned, wearing gowns and bonnets of cloth of gold, they performed a masquerade, in which they danced and sang. Afterwards, they cast off their outer costumes and distributed them among the ladies. It was King Henry himself who handed his cap to a giggling Anne, who had drunk rather too much of the good Rhenish wine.

'And who are you, fair maiden?' the King asked. He was drunk too. She could smell it on his breath. Close up, he looked younger than his twenty-two years, and his fair skin was rosy and sheened with sweat. His blue eyes glittered in the candlelight. Still she could not perceive what it was that women saw in him.

'Your Grace, I am Anne Boleyn,' she said, executing the elegant curtsey she had now perfected. 'My father, Sir Thomas, serves you as ambassador.' She placed the golden bonnet at a jaunty angle on her head above her pearl-netted caul.

'It becomes you,' the King complimented her. 'Will you do me the pleasure of dancing with me, Mistress Anne?'

Anne curtseyed again, and he led her in a lively *branle*, both of them leaping and kicking as the courtiers formed a circle around them and clapped.

'Bravo!' cried the Regent, who was standing close to Viscount Lisle.

'Bravo, Harry!' echoed the Viscount.

As the music drew to a close, the King bowed, thanked Anne and turned away. Later she saw him dancing with Etiennette de la Baume. She watched as his eyes held Etiennette's, and saw him bend and kiss her on the lips. Anne frowned. Surely this was forbidden? Henry had a wife and queen, and no business to be playing the game of courtly love in this manner.

She thought no more of it, for she herself was swept away into another dance by one of the young officers of the Regent's court, and then by many other gallants, until it was near dawn, when spiced wine and wafers were served to the company, the King bade farewell to his guests, and Anne went unwillingly to bed.

The next morning, after the Regent had risen late and was breakfasting on beef and manchet bread, she fell to discussing with her ladies the events of the previous evening. Lord Lisle featured prominently in her praise of the festivities, and well he might, Anne thought, for she had never left his side. The bells of St Rumbold's might soon be pealing in celebration of a wedding!

'You partnered the King well, Mademoiselle Anne,' the Regent said.

'Thank you, madame.'

The Regent turned to Etiennette. 'You, young lady, overstepped the bounds of propriety. King Henry is a married man.'

Etiennette's pretty face was flaming.

'Some hold that love has nothing to do with marriage,' Margaret of Austria said. 'Since marriages are often arranged, people do look elsewhere for love. It is proper for a married lady to accept the addresses of a knight or suitor, even someone far below her in rank, and some allow that it is permissible for a married man to acknowledge a lady as his mistress. But neither should go further than compliments, dancing, conversation and perhaps holding hands. I trust that is understood,' she said, looking at Etiennette.

'Yes, madame,' the girl whispered.

Later, when they were alone in the dorter, she exhaled in relief.

'I could have lost my position!' she told Anne.

'You should have thought of that before,' Anne said. 'Letting the King kiss you in public was madness. It's your reputation that's at stake, not his.'

'Who do you think you are, Mistress High-and-Mighty?' Etiennette hissed. 'I love him, and he loves me, and what we do is none of your business.'

'He loves you? Tomorrow he will be gone from here, back to England, and you will never see him again.'

'I know.' Etiennette crumpled, her eyes brimming with tears. 'He told me last night that he would always care for me, and that when I marry I should let him know, and he will send me ten thousand crowns for my dowry.'

'How will you explain that to your husband?' Anne retorted.

Etiennette ignored the question. 'I don't care. I love him.'

There was no reasoning with her. She was a silly, deluded girl.

That night, unable to sleep after another day packed with entertainments and a magnificent farewell dinner, Anne became aware of a figure moving stealthily in the gloom of the dorter. Heavens, it looked like a young lad wearing the English King's livery of green and white, although the room was so dark that it was hard to tell what colour it was. Anne concluded that the youth had been smuggled in by one of the *filles d'honneur*, but then the door clicked open, admitting a shaft of moonlight, and in its beam she could see plainly the face of Etiennette de la Baume, dressed up as a page, and determinedly sneaking away – no doubt to meet her royal lover.

Thank God the King would soon be gone. He was to blame. He had no business trying to seduce a young lady of good family; it was unforgivable, especially in one who enjoyed showing himself to the world as a chivalrous knight. How could anyone esteem such a dishonourable man so highly?

*

36

'Lord Lisle took a ring from me,' the Regent said, as she preceded her attendants into her bedchamber after yet another banquet. 'He would not give it back. I told him he was a thief.'

They stared at her.

'It really does seem that the handsome lord means to marry me,' she went on, her tone unusually flat. 'And King Henry is pressing for the match. He has not ceased to remind me of its advantages.'

'But your Highness is not sure?' one of the older women asked.

'No, Jacoba.' Margaret sank down on the bench at the end of her bed. 'In truth, I am in turmoil, not knowing what to do. Our ambassadors tell us there is gossip about this marriage all over Europe. It seems that many have us wed already! People are making wagers about it. It's awful – and embarrassing.'

Anne thought that the Regent should marry the captivating Brandon. They were a well-matched pair, and she had given every appearance of being smitten with him. And it would put an end to the rumours.

'What prevents your Highness from accepting his suit?' asked Jacoba, who was close to their mistress.

'A lot of people do not think it a fit match for me. It is being said that King Henry has made a nobleman out of a stableman. Even Erasmus disapproves – he wrote and told me so. And I do not know what my father the Emperor will say. My marrying an Englishman may preclude my ruling here, and I would not give that up easily.'

'But your Highness loves Lord Lisle?'

Margaret flushed. 'I do not know. I like him very much. He has such grace in his person – I have rarely seen any gentleman who can match him. King Henry urges the match, and warns me that I should decide soon, since he fears that my father may force me into marriage with another. I think he dreads my allying myself with one of England's enemies. But I told him that my father would do no such thing, and promised him only that I would not enter into any other marriage this year. And Lord Lisle has vowed that he will never marry another, but will remain all his life my humble servant. Maybe it was just the play of love; I must not be seduced by words. Now I must to bed. I have much to think about.'

Henry of England went home, the Regent continued to speak fondly of Lord Lisle, and Etiennette emerged subdued but unscathed from her midnight liaison. The months that followed passed pleasantly – and quickly – at the palaces of Mechlin, Lille and the Regent's summer retreat of La Veure near Brussels.

Speculation continued to rage as to whether or not she would marry Lord Lisle – or my lord the Duke of Suffolk, as he now was, having been ennobled after his return to England. Anne kept hoping that they would make a match of it, for the Duke was a jovial fellow, and with such a man at the helm, life at the court of Burgundy would be even more lively and pleasurable than it was already. And he had many eligible young men in his retinue whom he might bring with him. Not that Anne was in any hurry to be wed – she was too busy enjoying herself – but she did love the innocent flirtations that were now so much a part of her life.

She had no wish to end up like Etiennette, whose father had arranged for her to marry a rich old man of sixty-two. Anne had heard Etiennette weeping at night; she had listened to her fruitless protests to the Regent, who had looked sad, but said that she could not override the will of a father. Anne had watched a tearful Etiennette take up quill and paper and write to King Henry, reminding him of his promise to give her a dowry. She had witnessed the girl droop with disappointment as the weeks passed and no reply came.

There was much talk of weddings in the air. The Archduke Charles was now fourteen, and of an age to be married. For six years he had been betrothed to King Henry's sister Mary, who was said to be a great beauty. Much joy she will have of him, Anne thought. He looked as happy as if they had been planning his funeral. But he, like Etiennette, had no choice in the matter. His bride would soon be crossing the sea, as sure as doom, and he must do his duty. God pity the poor princess who must endure such a husband.

They were at La Veure, an exquisite turreted palace surrounded by a lake and a vast hunting park, enjoying the summer sunshine and embroidering Etiennette's beautiful silk wedding gown, when the blow fell.

For some weeks Anne had been hearing talk of a rift between King Henry and his allies, the Emperor and King Ferdinand. She had given it little thought, being more preoccupied with refurbishing her clothes in the latest French style, or discussing love and art with her mistress, or learning the latest dance steps and polishing her French, in which she was now almost fluent.

It did not dawn on her until afterwards that preparations for the Archduke's wedding had come to a standstill. She only realised that something was amiss when Isabeau asked the Regent if the Archduke and his wife would be having their own establishment.

'The Princess is not to come here after all,' Margaret of Austria said, her cheerful face suddenly clouding. 'King Henry has broken her betrothal.'

Two dozen needles were stilled or suspended in mid-air as the ladies and *filles d'honneur* looked up in surprise.

'Apparently His Grace of England feels that his allies have not kept faith with him, but have betrayed him by making peace with the French. He is to make a new treaty with King Louis.'

Anne resumed her stitching. This had little to do with her. She hoped the Regent would not think badly of her for being the subject of a king who had suddenly become unfriendly to the Emperor her father.

Thankfully Margaret continued to treat her with the same affection and kindness she had always shown her. Despite the difference in their ranks and ages, they had become friends; it was a friendship that Anne prized above almost everything else.

But then came the day when the Regent sent for Anne to attend her in the little gallery overlooking the lake. She had a letter in her hand.

'Mademoiselle Anne, I have heard from your father. He has sent two gentlemen to escort you home to England.'

Home to England? It could not be true!

'No, madame!' Anne cried, horrified. Surely the Regent could make Father understand that her place was here, at her court. But Margaret was raising a hand to silence her.

'Let me finish,' she reproved gently. 'Your father has found a new place for you. The Princess Mary is to marry King Louis. Yes, I see you are as shocked as I am. Another young girl being tied to an old husband. Ah, but it is the way of the world, *la petite* Boleyn! And for compensation, the delightful Mary will be Queen of France. You and your sister are to serve her. She has asked for you both, and naturally your father could not refuse. As for me, I will be deeply sad to lose you. But I think you have benefited from your time here, and been happy. Your French is now excellent, and you have a certain polish about you. Your father will be pleased, I know. It is what he sent you to me for. Now all he desires is that you conduct yourself worthily when you go to the French court, and I have no doubt that you will do that very well.'

It was too much to comprehend at once. All Anne could think of was that she was to leave this brilliant court and the mistress she loved. She knew nothing of the Princess Mary, and had no desire to go to France.

The Regent was regarding her with sympathy.

'I had to leave my homeland three times,' she said. 'I was sent to France, to Spain, and then to Savoy. The French court is magnificent. It is famed for its art and its culture. You will like it, I promise you. This is an excellent opportunity for you, being given the chance to serve the Queen of France. Do not despise it. And who knows, maybe one day we will meet again, *ma petite*.' There were tears in the Regent's eyes now; it was obvious that she was putting on a brave face to enable Anne to do as she was bid.

'So, I will write to your father,' she continued briskly, 'and tell him that his request is granted. Now go and make ready. And you also can send him a letter, telling him how pleased you are at your good fortune.'

Anne dragged her footsteps as she made her way back to the dorter. Everything in her path reminded her that she would soon be leaving the glories and familiar sights of this beautiful palace. Worst of all, she would be cut off from the Regent. She wanted to weep and rage at her father. She did not believe that the Princess Mary would have asked for her; why should she ask for someone she had never met? No, Father had boasted of her – and her sister Mary, although Heaven knew why – and the Princess had been persuaded to appoint them maids-of-honour.

The dorter was, mercifully, empty, so she threw herself headlong on her bed and gave herself up to a torrent of tears. Later, when she had cried herself out and washed her face, she wrote, with gritted teeth, to Father. It was hard to be civil to him when he had ruined her life. All she could think of was the inevitable parting from the Regent. How hard it would be not to give way to weeping and to conduct herself as courtesy demanded.

But when the time came to leave, it was Margaret of Austria who wept and could not bear to release Anne from her embrace.

Chapter 3

1515

Anne finally arrived in Paris on a cold day at the beginning of January, weeks later than planned. The delay had been frustrating – she had arrived back at Hever after an arduous journey to find, to her chagrin, that Mary had long departed for the court – but it had been necessary, for Anne's budding figure was beginning to outgrow her fine court gowns, and Mother had decided that some should be altered and some replaced, summoning the tailor and setting Mrs Orchard to work to ensure that her daughter was fittingly attired to serve the Queen of France.

The preparation of her new wardrobe had delayed Anne for a month, and then the bad weather had set in, with storms rendering the English Channel impassable, so she was forced to remain at Hever for Christmas, missing Burgundy, and angry and resentful because her sister was enjoying herself at the French court, having been dispatched from home in time to attend the new Queen Mary's proxy marriage ceremony at Greenwich, her wedding to King Louis at Abbeville and her triumphant entry into Paris.

She missed George. She hadn't seen him or Father, for Sir Thomas had taken George to court for the festivities, in the hope that the King would make the boy one of his pages. And though her older brothers came home for the festive season, back from Penshurst and Oxford, they inhabited worlds too far removed from hers to offer any comfort.

It had been with huge relief that she drew back her curtains on St Stephen's Day and saw that the winds had died down. After that there had been all to do packing her gear and making ready for her journey.

Her brother Hal had been appointed her escort, with two of the Hever grooms to look after the baggage cart.

And now – at last – she was in Paris, a beautiful city that seemed to be abundant with opportunities. As she and Hal rode along the left bank of the River Seine, in company with the guide they had paid to escort them, they could see ahead of them the Île de la Cité with its turreted palace, the soaring Sainte-Chapelle, and the mighty towers of the cathedral of Notre-Dame, their stonework painted in bright colours. The great bells were tolling, their clamour echoed by other city churches.

'Someone important has died,' Hal said, his dark features creasing in a frown.

Paris had spread well beyond its stone walls, but when they entered the old city, Anne found her senses assailed, for it was cramped and noisy, and it stank. She wrinkled her nose, trying to breathe through her mouth as they negotiated their way along streets teeming with people, who all seemed to be in an excitable mood. Passing around a corner, they glimpsed a procession of clergy wearing black robes.

'Something is definitely going on,' Hal declared.

Ahead of them were the towers of the Louvre, the royal palace, but that was not their destination. On approaching Paris, they had been directed to continue southwards to the Hôtel des Tournelles, where they would find the court. Anne could not wait to get there. But when they arrived, the stately building had a deserted, shuttered look about it.

Hal approached a porter lounging by the gatehouse.

'Is the court in residence?' he asked.

'Have you not heard?' the man replied. 'The King is dead. The court has moved away.'

The news hit Anne like a blow. Hal looked at her in dismay.

'Where is the Queen?' he asked.

'Gone into seclusion at the Hôtel de Cluny, across the river.' The man pointed and turned away.

'I'm sorry, little sister,' Hal commiserated, turning to Anne.

Anne's stomach was churning. 'I pray they do not send me home.

Even a widowed queen needs attendants. I wonder what happened to the King.'

'Mary will tell us, no doubt,' her brother said. For once, Anne was looking forward to seeing her sister.

The Hôtel de Cluny was a small medieval palace with fashionable classical embellishments. They were shown into a parlour, as if they had arrived at a religious house, and indeed an atmosphere of piety and silence did seem to cast a pall over everything. It was so quiet. The bustle of the streets seemed a world away.

A young woman entered. It took Anne a moment or so to recognise Mary, whose beauty had flowered in the nineteen months of their separation. Her face was a perfect oval, her eyes doe-like, her mouth a rosebud. The black damask gown and halo-shaped hood became her delicate colouring and dark hair.

Mary held out her hands. 'Thank God you are here,' she said, as Hal embraced her. She turned to Anne and kissed her on both cheeks in the French manner. 'Sister, you have grown so! You are become a lady. Oh, I cannot tell you how relieved I am to see you both. But Hal, you cannot stay long – this is a house of women now. No man may go near Her Highness.' She made a face. 'She has to remain in seclusion for forty days, until it is known that she is not *enceinte* with the King's child. A pretty storm that would stir up, I assure you.'

'Tell us what happened,' Hal said.

'The King died on New Year's Day. They are saying that Her Highness wore him out by making him perform marvels in the marriage bed, but it is not true. He was ill, and she had shown much care for him. The truth is, he defied his doctors and ate foods that were bad for his gout. That brought on the fit of vomiting that killed him. When they told Queen Mary, she fainted. We had all to do to revive her and offer some comfort. She was distraught.'

'Is she *enceinte*?' Hal wanted to know. He had inherited Father's interest in dynastic breeding.

'It is too early to tell, but I think not.'

'Then Louis's cousin, the Dauphin François, will be king.'

44

'He acts as if he is king already,' Mary said.

'I can see why an announcement that Queen Mary is pregnant would cause trouble,' Anne observed.

Mary sank down on a stool. 'It's more complicated than that. The Dauphin's nose was much put out of joint when King Louis married our Princess, seeing his chance of a crown flying out of the window. He even had them spied on in their marriage bed, to see if Louis could sire children. But then – this, you understand, is a man whose brain is in his codpiece – François began to take a blatant interest in Queen Mary, not caring what King Louis might do. She did nothing to encourage it; she does not trust him or even like him, but you should have heard the gossip. The word was that François's mother, Madame Louise, gave him a piece of her mind. She's as ambitious as he is, and minds to see herself ruling France at one remove as the King's mother.'

'He sounds a devil!' Anne cried.

'He is, and if he hears that you have been here, Hal, he'll make something of it. You must go. We dare not compromise the Queen.'

Hal stood up. 'Then I will take my leave, dear sisters. I have to be home for the Hilary term, though I had hoped to spend some time with you both first.'

They said their farewells, then, when Hal had gone to find his horse, Mary took Anne to see Queen Mary.

'I warn you, it's very gloomy in there,' she said. 'But I would not leave her service, the poor unhappy lady. Thank goodness she has been allowed to keep her English attendants – or rather, those of us who weren't sent home after she arrived in France.'

Anne's spirits sank. How she wished herself back at the court of the Regent. Leaving it for the French court had been bad enough; finding herself in a house of mourning was fifty times worse.

'My gown!' she said suddenly, looking down at her skirts; she had worn the wine-red damask for her presentation to the Queen. 'It is not suitable.'

'You can change it later,' Mary said. 'I trust you have a black one.'

She led Anne through an antechamber, opened a door and pulled aside a heavy curtain. The room beyond was in darkness, even though it was full daylight outside. The only illumination came from a few flickering candles. As Anne's eyes accustomed themselves to the dimness, she could see that the windows were shrouded in heavy curtains, blocking all the light, and that the walls and the great mourning bed that dominated the room were hung with black. It felt like being in a tomb.

A ghostly pale figure lay on the bed, swathed in voluminous robes and a nun-like mourning veil and cap, all in white. Around her sat several black-clad maids-of-honour and an older lady, very finely attired, who must surely be the *dame d'honneur* in charge of them. She watched as Anne sank into a deep curtsey.

Queen Mary propped herself up on one elbow, regarding her new maid-of-honour. She had exquisite features, with green eyes, pouting lips, and fair skin like her brother, King Henry; a tendril of flaming red hair had escaped from her cap. She looked younger than her eighteen years, with her slender child's hand extended to be kissed.

'You must be Mistress Anne Boleyn,' she said in English. 'I can see the family likeness.' She smiled. 'Welcome. I am sorry to have to receive you in such sad circumstances.'

'I am sorry for your Highness's tragic loss,' Anne said.

The Queen smiled at her. 'Thank you. It was bad enough losing my kind husband, without having to suffer this incarceration for forty days. How do you like my *deuil blanc*? It is traditional for French queens to wear white mourning. God's blood, I look like a nun. I *feel* like a nun.' The *dame d'honneur* was looking on benignly. Obviously she did not understand English.

'Could your Highness not wear something else in private?' Anne asked.

Mary giggled. 'I like your daring, Mistress Anne! But I dare not, not with Madame Louise bearing down on me unannounced at all hours. And it would look disrespectful to my late husband.' For a moment she looked as if she was going to cry. 'King Louis was very good to me. I miss him.' Her face brightened again. 'You will be glad to be with your sister.'

Anne nodded. It was true, although she knew it would not be long before jealousy reared its malevolent head between her and Mary. It had ever been so. She could feel her sister's eyes on her.

'We are fortunate to be serving your Highness together,' she said.

'But not fortunate to be doing it in this place,' Queen Mary sighed. 'Oh, the time does drag. I am willing the weeks to pass.'

Anne was already willing it too. Yet she had no choice but to take her place alongside her fellow maids-of-honour and ladies-in-waiting and tend to her new mistress.

She soon found that some of the maids were about her own age, and high-spirited, which made life more tolerable. They were kept in check by the *dame d'honneur,* whose name was Madame d'Aumont. Anne soon learned that she was impeccably connected, having once served the saintly Queen Jeanne, King Louis's repudiated first wife, and married one of his most trusted *seigneurs.*

It was hard not to compare young Queen Mary to the Regent Margaret. She seemed a kind girl with a wicked sense of humour and a naturally sunny disposition, but she had none of the Regent's intellectual interests.

King François – for so he was already calling himself – came to see the Queen almost every day. He was just as Anne had imagined him – tall, dark, saturnine and lascivious, with a perpetual shadow of growth on his chin. When he looked at her – or at any woman – it was as if he was seeing her naked. His eyes were lustful, his long nose devilish, his lips sensual. No female was too lowly to escape his interest, and Anne had to stand there and look pleased when he tipped her chin up and told her she was charming, then lowered his gaze to the swell of her breasts. Yet she had to admit to herself that there was a certain attraction about him, which might spell ruin for any gullible lady. But not her!

The Queen's ladies were bursting with gossip about him, but Mary herself, Anne noticed, did not censure them. Instead she took a mischievous pleasure in joining in, knowing that Madame d'Aumont could not understand her.

'They say he is habitually clothed in women,' giggled pale-eyed Lady Elizabeth Grey, sister to the Marquess of Dorset. Florence Hastings blushed all over her pretty face.

47

'He considers whoring a sport on a par with hunting,' the Queen chimed in.

'People say he boasts of his special "*petite bande*" of courtesans, and drinks from many fountains,' Mary Boleyn laughed.

'The word is,' murmured Mary Fiennes, with an impish smirk, 'that he has had spyholes and secret doors made in his palaces, so that he can watch women undressing and making love.'

This was greeted by a chorus of mirth. Anne wondered if the Queen knew that François had spied on her and Louis.

But Mary was warming to their theme. 'I read that Alexander the Great paid attention to women when he had no affairs of state – but King François attends to state affairs when there are no women!' There were more shrieks of laughter.

'God pity his new bride.' Queen Mary shuddered. 'You know he married Louis's daughter Claude last year? She is no match for him, poor little cripple.'

It was plain to all that, for the moment, François's chief interest was in young Queen Mary. His constant concern for her health was transparently a means of asking the question he could not, in propriety, put to her. His mother was as bad – descending on the young widow as she lay in her dark chamber and asking pointed questions. You could not blame them, of course, for upon this crucial matter turned François's likelihood of keeping the crown he had so long coveted.

'I would love to see his face if I told him I was pregnant,' Queen Mary said, after yet another interrogation. Her mischievous streak was surfacing more and more, and one day she could not resist telling François that she had a craving for cherries. 'Sadly they are out of season,' she complained, 'so I shall just have to go without. But I have never fancied anything so much in my life.'

Anne, who was in attendance, was hard put to it to keep a straight face, especially when she saw the King's look of alarm. But then she saw the angry glint in his eyes.

'The Queen has gone too far,' she said to Mary later. 'He looks as if he could be dangerous if provoked.'

'I don't think she realises how perilous it might be to cross him,'

Mary agreed. 'They still speak of a queen of France who took lovers and was found out. She was put in prison and strangled there.'

Anne shuddered. 'We must never leave her alone at any time. We must warn the others.' It was agreed between them all, and Madame d'Aumont, that four of them at least would be in attendance at all times.

François kept returning to the black-hung chamber, oblivious to the fact that his visits were increasingly unwelcome to the Queen.

'I have had enough,' she seethed, after his questions had become a little too personal.

'What will your Highness do?' asked the *dame d'honneur*. She was clearly uneasy about the conduct of her royal master, but nervous of offending him.

'Put an end to his nonsense,' Queen Mary declared.

The next day she sent to ask if the King would visit her. He came with all speed, and Anne was present at their meeting.

'Sire,' the Queen said, 'my forty days of seclusion will soon be at an end, and I am glad to tell you that you are the only possible King of France.'

The sardonic eyes gleamed. François seized her hand and kissed it fervently. 'That is the most welcome news I have ever had in my life, and it is doubly welcome, for not only does it make me a king, but it also means that the lady I admire more than any is free from ties. Marie' – he always used the French form of her name – 'this is no life for you. You are beautiful and made for loving. Why sleep in this miserable bed when I can have you spirited out of here and into mine?'

Anne was shocked at François's boldness. It would never have been tolerated at the Regent's court.

The Queen's eyes widened in outrage. 'Sire, in your delight in your good fortune, you have obviously forgotten that I am a princess born, and mourning my husband.'

'Let me comfort you,' he urged. 'Let me help you to forget your sad loss.'

'That is kind, but I would be left to weep in peace.'

He ignored that. 'I would set you above all other ladies, as your beauty and gentleness deserves,' he declared. He actually had his hand on his heart.

'And what of your charming wife, who is now Queen in my place?'

'*Ma chère*, there are ways of arranging these things. The crown of France looks better on your golden head, as we have all seen. Claude would rather have been a nun than a queen.'

'She loves you, sire. She told me that herself. And she is to have your child.' Mary's panic was becoming evident in her shrill voice and tense posture.

'Popes have been accommodating before,' François told her. He seemed not a whit put out by her resistance. 'Tell me I may wait in hope.'

'Alas, sire, I cannot consent to anything that would harm my honour or that poor, blameless lady. And now, if you would leave me to rest . . .'

When François had gone, reluctantly and still protesting his love as he walked out of the door, Queen Mary controlled herself for a few moments, then burst into furious tears.

'How dare he!' she cried. 'He is unspeakable. I will write to my brother. I will beg him to send for me. I do not know how long I can hold out against this satyr! Bring me pen and paper.'

Thanks to the good offices of Elizabeth Grey and Jane Bourchier, the letter was smuggled out and sent to England by means of friends of their families in Paris, and it was followed by another, and another, for François did not give up. He haunted the black-hung chamber. The citadel must yield: he was determined upon it. Queen Mary put up a brave defence, and although she did nothing to encourage him, and repeatedly rebuffed him, in private she confessed to her ladies that she feared she would not prevail: he was the King, after all.

She was drawn and tense, having spent so many sleepless nights raging against him and bewailing her lot. Inevitably there came a day when her patience snapped.

'Sire, I beg you to leave me alone,' she flared. 'I cannot love you, and I have no wish to be married to you.'

Anne had never heard her speak so plainly to the King before, and the effect was dramatic.

'Then perchance you wish to be married to a prince of my choosing, to France's advantage,' he retorted nastily. The ardent lover had been instantly eclipsed by a dangerous adversary. The Queen gasped, then quickly recovered herself.

'My brother shall hear of this!' she cried.

'By then it may be too late,' François warned, and stalked out.

'He is using me!' the Queen stormed, as her women hastened to console her. Anne and Mary glanced at each other, then looked at their mistress, who was sitting on the bed twisting her rings, utterly distraught.

'How can he do that?' Anne whispered.

'He is threatening to marry Her Highness to England's detriment, in revenge for her rejecting his advances,' Florence murmured.

The Queen nodded. 'It is for the King my brother to dispose of me in marriage, and he has made me a promise,' she said mysteriously. 'I will not be married to some foreign prince. If François did that, King Henry would declare war on him, I am certain of it.'

Anne hated to think of women being forced into marriages they did not welcome. Poor Queen Mary had been made to wed the King of France, and now his successor was trying to compel her to marry someone else. Even the Regent had feared being forced by her father into marriage. It was wrong, surely, that men had the right to make women take husbands against their will. She would never let anyone force her into marriage!

Fortunately King Henry had taken his sister's complaints seriously. Word came that he was sending an embassy to Paris to bring her home.

Hard on the heels of that welcome news came a furious King François.

'Madame, I will not allow the King your brother to marry you to anyone hostile to France.'

Mary glared at him. 'Sire, I have no intention of marrying anyone!'

'You dissemble!' he growled. 'And these English ladies abet you in your scheming. No doubt they smuggle out your letters to England. Well, I will have them replaced by French ladies.'

Anne was torn. Her life in France was tedious, but going home to Hever held little appeal, unless, of course, Father could find her another place at court – any court. She did not want to leave her kind mistress in such peril and distress, yet go she must, it seemed. On the King's orders she and the rest were escorted to a set of chambers in another wing of the Hôtel de Cluny, and left to wait there, comfortably accommodated but under guard, until arrangements could be made for their journey to England. Most were indignant.

'My brother shall hear of this,' sniffed Elizabeth Grey. 'And I shall write to King Henry, who is my cousin. He would not wish me to be treated in this way.'

Mary Fiennes and Jane Bourchier said that they would write to their relatives too. Florence Hastings was all for packing her things and going home at once.

Anne fretted about the Queen. 'Shut in here, we can do nothing to help her,' she lamented.

They were not confined for long. A few days later they were summoned to see Queen Mary, and astonished to find that there were no guards outside their door.

It was a great relief to discover the curtains drawn and the black hangings gone from the Queen's chamber. The walls were now hung with beautiful floral tapestries in rich shades of blue and red, and the room looked so much more cheerful with the hazy February sunlight streaming in. Where the mourning bed had stood there was a chair upholstered in velvet beneath a cloth of estate bearing the royal arms of France and England – the lilies and the leopards – quartered. Here the young Queen was seated, still wearing her white weeds and veil, and in a defiant mood.

'The embassy has arrived,' she told them. 'I have dismissed the guards and the French ladies. You are restored to your places. Let King François complain if he dare! My brother's envoys will answer for me. Now stand around. They will be here soon.' She was in a fever of excitement.

Minutes later, the embassy was announced, and in strode several well-dressed gentlemen in furred gowns. Anne stared at the man who led them. That spade beard, those powerful good looks – it was the Duke of Suffolk! As he bent low over the Queen's hand and she reached out both hers and raised him, Anne saw the look that passed between them.

She was astounded. These two knew each other! And there was that between them which suggested intimacy. Had it been so before Suffolk paid his addresses to the Regent? Anne had heard gossip that had Margaret of Austria still cherishing notions of marrying him. He had sworn to be her servant for always!

'Ladies and gentlemen, I would speak with my lord of Suffolk in private,' the Queen said, her cheeks pink and glowing against her lawn veil. Madame d'Aumont raised her eyebrows, and Anne cast a look at her sister, who widened her eyes expressively. In the outer room they settled to their embroidery under the eagle eye of the *dame d'honneur*, whose stiff manner betrayed just what she thought of her young mistress being closeted alone with a man not related to her. No one spoke, but the maids kept exchanging surreptitious glances, conveying that they had all read the situation correctly.

When Madame d'Aumont visited the privy, a buzz of chatter broke out.

'What was Her Highness thinking of?' Florence Hastings hissed.

'It's plain on her face!'

'Aye, and it's been plain for a long time.'

'Did you not know?' Mary asked Anne. 'It was common knowledge at the English court that the Princess was in love with the Duke.'

'And it was common knowledge in Mechlin that the Regent was thinking of marrying him,' Anne countered. 'He led her on! I saw him.'

'But what of Lady Lisle?' Mary Fiennes put in.

'*Lady Lisle?*' Anne echoed.

'Yes, silly. How else do you think he got his title?'

'I *assumed* the King ennobled him,' Anne flung back, cross at being called silly.

'No,' Jane Bourchier said. 'His betrothed is Viscountess Lisle in her own right, for all she is but ten years old. Two years ago the King consented to my lord of Suffolk contracting himself to her, and using her title in anticipation of their marriage.'

Mary Boleyn giggled. 'By then he had had two wives already.'

Anne's jaw dropped. 'What happened to *them*?'

'The first he divorced. The second died. He is as good as wed to Lady Lisle, so I know not what business he has pursuing any lady, let alone royal ones.'

That a man could be so perfidious – so deceitful! Anne shook her head. How sorry she felt for the Regent, who had been duped by his flattery. Maybe Queen Mary had been duped as well.

Florence made a face. 'Betrothals can be broken. What worries me is Her Highness's lack of respect for the conventions.'

Anne turned to her. 'I admire her. Look what she did today, dismissing those guards and ladies on her own authority. Why should she not receive a man alone? Are all men beasts, that they cannot be trusted?' She was aware that the Duke of Suffolk was not to be trusted – but even he would surely not stoop to molesting a queen.

The others stared at her.

'Maybe it's she who can't be trusted,' Mary giggled, and the tension broke. Anne was about to defend her bold statement when Madame d'Aumont returned and the interminable stitching resumed in silence.

An hour later, they were summoned back by the Queen. She was alone. Her eyes were swollen from weeping, her manner distracted.

'You all know how this King has importuned me,' she said, 'and about his threats to force me into an unwelcome marriage. Well, I had already chosen my future. Before I married King Louis, I had an understanding with my lord of Suffolk that if my husband died, we would be wed, if he could be released from his betrothal. The King my brother knew that I did not wish to marry Louis, and he promised me that I could choose my second husband. He knew who it would be. And yet he has sent my lord here with strict instructions not to marry me, even though he is now free to do so.' She raised her tear-stained face to them, looking distraught. 'I told my lord that my situation was becoming intolerable. I urged him to wed me without delay, but he refused. So I warned him that if he did not, I would retire to a convent.' She was crying now, her shoulders heaving. 'And I will!'

There was nothing that any of them could do. They gave her handkerchiefs, they brought her wine, they murmured words of comfort. And then the Duke of Suffolk was announced, and they had only moments to make her presentable before she hissed that they should leave. They flew through the door just as the Duke was about to enter, and the last thing they heard was him saying, 'My sweet lady, I cannot let you do this . . .'

Anne stood with the other maids-of-honour and Suffolk's two gentlemen under the magnificent vaulting of the chapel of the Hôtel de Cluny and watched as Queen Mary and her Duke were joined in matrimony. Mary was still wearing her white mourning, but this afternoon she would cast it off for a gorgeous gown of black velvet trimmed with gold. The chaplain had been sent by King François, who knew very well that this marriage was being made without King Henry's knowledge or approval, and was no doubt gleefully relishing the prospect of his brother monarch erupting in impotent fury.

A pale beam of March sunlight pierced the jewelled colours of the stained glass and bathed the couple in light. Mary's face was suffused with rapture, and Suffolk was looking at her as if she was the only woman in the world.

Anne dared not think of the Regent's reaction when she heard of this marriage. Margaret of Austria had been abashed enough by the rumours speculating that she might marry Suffolk; how much worse she would feel when the whole of Christendom was gossiping about her being jilted. How could Suffolk look so happy and satisfied with himself when he had treated her so despicably?

'It just goes to prove that a woman can have what she wants if she is clever enough,' Mary Boleyn said, as they left the chapel to help the Queen change.

'Yes, but at what cost?' Florence put in.

'Aye!' Anne said vehemently, thinking of the poor Regent.

'The way they look, it will be worth it,' Mary Fiennes sighed. 'I wish I could get a husband who loves me so well.'

'We will see if King Henry approves,' Anne said, remembering how he had urged the Regent to marry the Duke.

Letters came thundering across the Channel from England. The Queen's face, flushed with love for several days, now registered alarm.

'The King is outraged to hear of my marriage,' she told her ladies. 'He accuses my lord of breaking his promise. He says he will have his head for his presumption.' Her voice broke. She was trembling.

Anne was horrified. Suffolk might be lacking in honour, but he was the King's friend. She had seen them together; they had been like brothers. Surely Henry would never carry out his terrible threat. Mary was his favourite sister, and he loved her. He could not do that to her!

The couple were beset on both sides. King François – the hypocrite, for he had abetted the secret marriage – expressed disapproval at the Queen remarrying so indecently soon after King Louis's death. The French court was apparently reeling from the scandal. All across Europe, the gossips were regaling each other.

Then Cardinal Wolsey, King Henry's chief minister and friend – and by all reports the most powerful man in England after him – used his considerable powers of diplomacy to still the troubled waters. King Henry graciously allowed himself to be mollified: he would forgive the errant pair in return for a punishing fine, paid in instalments over several years. The Queen gaped when she saw the sum mentioned.

'We will be in penury for life!' she cried.

Anne watched as the Duke took her hand and kissed it. 'It will be money well spent,' he said gallantly, 'and it means I get to keep my head.' But he sounded as if he had just eaten something bitter. He should have married the Regent and avoided all this, Anne thought. 'We should be thankful,' he added. 'His Grace promises us a second wedding, with proper celebrations, at Greenwich. And we are going home, my love!'

The maids-of-honour were wondering what was to happen to them, for it was clear that Queen Mary could not now afford to retain them all. Over the next few days, some were summoned home by their families. Anne did not want to be rusticated in England with the Queen, for Mary had said that she and Suffolk would have to live quietly in the country; nor did she and her sister want to go home to Hever, so Anne wrote to Father explaining their dilemma and asking for his help. He was quick to act. Not two weeks had passed before Queen Mary informed them that Queen Claude had honoured them by offering them places in her household.

Anne clapped her hands, enjoying the undisguised envy of her fellow maids-of-honour. Although still pining for the court of Burgundy, she was fired up with excitement. The French court! At last! After weeks of living in the secluded gloom of the Hôtel de Cluny, she could not wait to be back in the world. Joyfully she and Mary packed their chests, as Mary recalled the glories of the Hôtel des Tournelles with its twenty chapels, twelve galleries and beautiful gardens, and the wondrous chateau of Saint-Germain-en-Laye, just outside Paris. And there were other sumptuous palaces too, further south on the River Loire, of which Mary had only heard – Blois, Amboise and Langeais. They would be able to wear their new gowns, which had been laid away while they wore mourning, and dance, and meet noble gentlemen . . . King François, for all his faults, was a young man with a great zest for living, and life at his court would be one long round of pleasure.

King François remembered the courtesy expected of a monarch, and hosted a farewell dinner for Queen Mary at the Hôtel de Cluny. He was at his most charming, and it was as if he had never behaved otherwise towards her. Afterwards there was dancing, and Anne watched as François, dazzling in cloth of silver, led out his royal guest. Queen Claude was not present, being with child, so the Duke of Suffolk danced with the King's sister, Marguerite, Duchesse d'Alençon, a lively, witty lady with the long Valois nose and a wealth of frizzy dark hair.

When Anne saw her own sister in the throng, it was always with a different man. They smiled at each other as they whirled past, skirts billowing. It was strange how well they had got on these past weeks, instead of eternally squabbling in an exhausting game of rivalry. Perhaps the long months of absence had something to do with it, or being thrown together in a difficult situation. Anne was in such a happy mood this evening that she was ready to love even her normally infuriating sister.

Around midnight, she saw Mary dancing with King François. It disconcerted her. Not that she was jealous – he was the last man she wanted to dance with – but she had heard about his lascivious life and his womanising, and witnessed his assault on Queen Mary's virtue. Her sister, she hoped, would be mindful of that.

Anne herself was asked for dance after dance. The young gallants flocked around her, and the evening passed in a whirl of music and laughter. It was not until later that she looked around for Mary and realised there was no sign of her, or the King. Most people were drunk, engrossed in their partners or deep in conversation. The air was rank with the scent of sweat, leftover food and spilt wine. She did not care, for the musicians were striking up again, and yet another young man was bowing before her.

It was not until two o'clock in the morning that she saw King François, urbane as ever, and very drunk. He was sitting on his great chair, toying with a buxom woman on his lap. It was not Mary. Anne looked for her sister in vain, beginning to feel anxiety creeping up on her. It was not like Mary to go to bed and miss an occasion like this.

Damn Mary, giving unnecessary cause for concern when she herself was enjoying this wonderful night! She supposed she ought to go and look for her – but probably she was worrying unnecessarily. Mary was older than she, and could surely look after herself.

Towards dawn, she ascended the stairs to the dorter, tired but exhilarated, surrounded by the excited chatter of the other maids-of-honour. Many had gained admirers, it seemed.

Her bubble of happiness burst when she saw Mary sitting on her bed in the moonlit darkness, weeping uncontrollably. Anne hastened to her, the others clustering around. Some lit candles, some offered handkerchiefs.

'What is wrong?' Anne demanded, feeling guilty for not having sought out her sister earlier.

Mary shook her head, and went on sobbing. She looked utterly distraught. Anne shook her. 'Tell me!'

'He . . . he . . .' she gasped.

'Who?' Anne cried. 'What did he do?'

'The King . . .' Mary burst out in fresh floods of tears.

There was a shocked silence.

'He takes what he wishes,' Florence said in a tone of disgust. 'It is well known.'

Anne put her arm around Mary. She was trembling herself. 'Is this true?'

Mary nodded. 'He . . . forced me,' she whispered through her sobs. 'He was taking me to see a painting. He said it was a work of art such as no one had ever surpassed. But . . . there was no painting. When we got into the gallery where it was supposed to be, he put his arms around me and started kissing me. I did not know what to do. He is the King. I dared not gainsay him!' She gulped. 'Then he said we'd be more private and comfortable elsewhere, and pulled me through a door. It was a . . . bedchamber. I tried to protest, to say that I was a maid and was saving myself for my husband, but he just laughed and said that everyone says that but it means nothing. And then he . . . he pushed me on the bed and . . . Don't ask me to say more.' She hung her head. 'He did things to me I had never heard of.'

'It was rape!' hissed Elizabeth Grey, her eyes blazing, and the others murmured shocked agreement. 'Shame on him!'

Shame on me, Anne thought, distraught, unable to grasp the enormity of what had happened. *If I had gone to look for her, I might have prevented it.*

'I cannot face going to court,' Mary wept. 'Waiting on Queen Claude, I will see him every day, and I could not bear the shame. She will guess!' Her cries rose to a piteous wail. 'She will dismiss me!'

Anne could imagine the scandal, and shrank from the prospect. She held Mary tightly, waiting until the storm had subsided. The others stood round, shaking their heads in concern.

Eventually Mary straightened, her face red and blotched with tears, her hair tousled. She took a deep breath. 'I will see Queen Mary in the morning and ask if I can go home with her.'

That seemed to Anne to be even more fraught with difficulties. 'But what will Father say?' she asked. 'How will you explain it to him? He secures for you one of the most coveted posts to which a girl can aspire, and you turn your back on it!'

'Do you think I wanted this?' Mary flung back. 'It was not my fault!'

Anne knew that, if she had been Mary, she would have stamped on the King's foot, or screamed, or slapped his face, but she refrained from saying it. She would not upset Mary further. Outraged on her sister's behalf, she reflected bitterly that whatever anyone – even the enlightened Christine de Pizan – said, men were still stronger than women and able to take what they wanted. With them it was either brute force or cruel deception. Look at how Suffolk had treated the Regent. And kings did not have to answer to anybody.

'I understand that you cannot face serving Queen Claude,' Anne said, feeling like crying herself, 'but you must think about what you are going to say to Father.'

Mary gave a shuddering sob. 'I don't know. I can't think just now. I'll think in the morning.'

'We have to be up early to ride to Saint-Denis,' Anne reminded her. 'Queen Mary has a long journey ahead.'

'Just leave me alone!' Mary wailed, and lay down, still in her clothes.

Looking at her, defiled and broken, Anne was again swamped with guilt. Why did she not feel sorrier for her? The truth was that Mary could be so exasperating – and stupid. Why go off alone with the King in the first place? But – she pulled herself up – that did not excuse his appalling behaviour. Mary's silliness was as nothing compared with what he had done.

She bent down, contrite, and began unlacing her sister's gown, then fetched her night-rail and helped her into bed.

'Perhaps, Mistress Anne, you understand now why a woman should not be by herself with a man,' Florence said nastily.

*

When they were roused at six, Anne was feeling ragged. She had not slept for racking her brains over what to do about Mary. After the horrifying thought that Mary might be pregnant occurred to her, she'd lain awake torturing herself for being responsible, and worrying about what would happen to her sister, and how a pregnancy could be concealed. She did not dare think what their father would say.

King François arrived promptly at eight o'clock to escort Queen Mary to the great abbey of Saint-Denis, where they would say farewell and she and Suffolk would begin their journey back to England. Anne could hardly look at François, she was so filled with loathing. She was seized with the urge to slap him – it was the least he deserved – but what good would that do? She felt so impotent.

It had been arranged that Anne and Mary were to return to court in the King's train and be presented to their new mistress, Queen Claude. Elegant in black velvet and a jaunty cap that showed off her red hair to advantage, Queen Mary embraced them and bade them farewell.

'I am most appreciative of your good service – and your discretion,' she told them. Flushed with her good fortune, she did not notice that both were subdued and red-eyed.

But now Mary spoke up.

'Your Highness, let me come home with you,' she pleaded. Anne was appalled. This should be kept within the family. Already too many people knew of it.

The Queen frowned. 'What is this? You are going to court to serve Queen Claude.'

'Madame, I cannot,' Mary said, beginning to weep again.

'Why, for Heaven's sake? Do you not realise how fortunate you are?'

Mary swallowed and lowered her voice. 'Madame, you know, better than most, how persistent a certain gentleman can be.' Her voice faltered. 'I dare not stay here at court. My reputation will be compromised.'

The Queen's eyes narrowed. Understanding dawned. 'Has he seduced you?'

'No!' Anne said. But Mary hung her head.

'Take me home, your Highness,' she begged. 'I cannot bear to see him again after last night. Please do not ask me to elaborate. Believe me, I had no choice in the matter.'

'What of Father?' Anne asked. 'He will be furious.'

'You may leave it to me to explain to him,' the Queen said, her tone unusually strident. 'I will vouch for you, Mary. If he is furious with anyone, it should be with that villain. My dear, I am so sorry – and appalled. I can never forgive myself, for you are in my service and have been dishonoured. I should have been more aware.'

'Your Highness understandably has had weighty matters on your mind,' Anne said.

'It was my duty! But we cannot waste time on regrets. I am late already. Mary, have a servant load your baggage.'

'Oh, thank you, your Highness!' Mary cried, before hastily embracing Anne and hurrying away.

'I must go,' the Queen said. 'Mistress Anne, I wish you well at the French court. After what has happened, I don't need to warn you to guard your virtue – it is the most precious jewel you will ever possess.' She smiled sadly, watching Mary's retreating back. 'I think you are wise, and do not need my advice. You would not let any man take advantage of you.'

Anne curtseyed. No, she would never let that happen. No man would have the chance. In fact, she was resolved never to have anything to do with the perfidious, dangerous, bestial creatures. There were so many other things in life to enjoy.

She looked after the departing figure of her sister. Pray God the Queen spoke to Father before he set eyes on Mary.

As the royal retinues prepared to leave Saint-Denis, Anne bade Mary a hurried farewell.

'If you want me to write to Father in your defence, I will do so,' she said, then lowered her voice. 'Your secret is safe with me. I pray there will be no unpleasant consequences.'

'Oh, there could not be,' Mary said, sounding happier now that she was leaving Paris. 'Mary Fiennes told me that the woman has to experience pleasure to conceive, and most certainly I did not.'

Anne was not sure that was true, but she held her peace. 'God keep you,' she said, and kissed Mary. She watched as the great cavalcade rode away northwards, before climbing into the horse litter that was to take her to the Louvre. The world was opening up again, and she was aware of excitement welling up within her, but it was tempered by what had happened to her sister in the very court for which she was now bound.

Chapter 4

1515–1516

Claude of Valois was little more than a child, a delicate-looking girl with a pleasing face and curly chestnut-brown hair. Her eyes squinted disconcertingly in different directions, and she had a pronounced limp, having been crippled from birth. But as the daughter of the late King Louis, and heiress to the duchy of Brittany, she had been a great prize in the royal marriage market, which was why the future King François had made her his bride, the poor girl.

She arrived late for the audience, walking to her chair of estate in as stately fashion as her condition and her uneven gait permitted. The midnight-blue velvet gown embroidered with the lilies of France, its stomacher unlaced over her belly, seemed to weigh her down, but she was all smiles, and the first impression Anne gained was of an innate sweetness of character.

'Welcome, mademoiselle,' the Queen said, looking both at and past her as Anne sank into a deep curtsey. 'You may rise. Is your sister not with you?'

Anne was prepared. 'Your Majesty, she is unwell and has had to return home to England.' She hoped Claude would swallow the lie.

'I am sorry to hear it,' the Queen said. 'I hope it is nothing serious.'

'Madame, I am assured that time and a good rest in the country will effect a cure.'

Claude smiled. 'Well, Mademoiselle Anne, I rejoice to see *you*, for I have heard excellent reports of you. There is always a great clamour when a place becomes vacant in my household, but I liked what I heard of you, as did my mother-in-law, Madame Louise, who noticed you on her visits to Queen Mary. She told me how accomplished you are.'

'It is kind of your Highness to say so,' Anne said. She was aware that the domineering Madame Louise ruled the court, overshadowing Claude, but she could detect no bitterness in the young Queen's demeanour.

'There are three hundred young ladies in my household,' Claude told her. 'You will be in good company. I hope your time here will be happy.'

Anne was thus dismissed. A lady-in-waiting came to take her to her new lodgings – yet another maidens' dorter high up in the eaves, where she would share space with nineteen other girls. It was sweltering in the warm weather. She found herself missing Mary already. It was a daunting prospect, going alone into this vast royal household. But – and she kept her chin up – she would deal with it. And maybe, among those three hundred young ladies, she would find some friends.

'You will wait upon Her Majesty when summoned,' the lady-in-waiting said. 'At other times, you will confine yourself to this dorter or the Queen's chapel, and you may walk in her private gardens with another of the maids, but never unaccompanied. You will not go anywhere else without permission. Is that understood?'

Anne's spirits plummeted. It sounded worse than the Hôtel de Cluny.

'Yes, madame,' she said meekly.

In those first few days, she began, with mounting dismay, to understand the constraints of her new life. But the Queen's strict regimen played to Anne's advantage, for she found that most of her new companions shared her distaste for it, and it made a common bond between them. They were forever devising schemes to circumvent the rules, and soon Anne was joining in with enthusiasm. Many of the young ladies were keen to hear about her time at the court of Burgundy, and grew wistful when she told them of the freedom she had enjoyed. Having heard only rumours, they were agog to learn about the goings-on at the Hôtel de Cluny from someone who had been there. She was grateful that she had worked diligently at her French, for she was now fluent and could converse and gossip with them on equal terms – and she knew they admired her for it. She was quickly accepted into their aristocratic circle, and began to feel that she was among friends.

Queen Claude was kind and affectionate, but that mild exterior concealed a will of steel – and, Anne came to suspect, a desperate unhappiness; and no wonder, given that she was married to that unspeakable lecher. It was no secret that the King dallied with many mistresses – indeed, it was one of the chief topics of conversation among the excitable young women in that teeming household. But Claude – she was a saint – ignored the gossip, or rather the conversations that were suddenly hushed when she appeared. When the King visited her, which was not often, she was sweetness itself to him, but when he had gone – usually all too soon – she could barely hide her sadness.

That she was aware of his constant infidelities, and the lax example he set to his courtiers, was apparent in her imposition of a strict moral code upon her household. Her mission was to protect her maids from predatory men, but it was like living in a nunnery. Anne was told early on that she must follow the Queen's example and conduct herself with modesty and decorum. Her days were governed by a tedious round of prayers, good works, devotional reading and endless sewing. Within a week, she thought she might go mad or die of frustration. There was no talk *here* of the game of love!

The Queen kept nearly always to her apartments. Anne learned that she did not like the court, and disapproved of what went on there.

'She attends when she has to,' one of the maids said, 'but she would far rather be at Amboise or Blois.'

'Away from the court?' Anne asked, dismayed.

'If the King agrees, yes. And usually he does. He has his reasons, of course.' A sly smile accompanied that statement.

You could not blame Claude, Anne reflected. After all, what queen would want the humiliation of seeing her husband parading his mistresses in public, or of other people's pity or derision? *Look at her, poor little misshapen thing; no wonder he strays!*

It felt like being in prison, immured in the Queen's lavishly painted and gilded rooms, which offered every luxury a woman might require but held no attractions for Anne. What good did it do to wear all her gorgeous court gowns, on which Father had outlaid so much money, if no one saw them?

In June, the King led an army into Italy, where he was to aid the state of Venice against an invading Spanish army. After he and his entourage had left, the Louvre became a peaceful place. Madame Louise was acting as regent, since Claude was pregnant, and she largely left the little Queen to her own devices, preferring the stimulating company of her daughter, Marguerite. Free to rest and indulge herself, Claude relaxed her vigilance and, since most temptations had been removed, allowed her maids more freedom. To Anne's relief, they were at last permitted to wander the splendid apartments and galleries, to gaze at the wondrous paintings that were on display there, and to roam the delightful gardens.

They were still expected to be regular at their devotions, and to eschew the romances that Claude believed would lead to their downfall, in favour of the pious works she prescribed, but Anne soon learned the trick of concealing one volume within another, and was able to read books that were quite scandalous by Claude's standards, which she had purloined from the royal library.

Give her some due, the Queen did appreciate that her maids needed to perfect the accomplishments that would enable them to shine at court when in attendance on her, and attract good marriages. She had them practise their deportment, and stressed the importance of being able to make conversation. Anne was quick to build on her natural inclinations and the training from which she had benefited at the Regent's court. She tripped up and down with books balanced on her head, worked on perfecting her curtsey and on new dance steps, and learned how to glide gracefully along as if she had no feet.

It was disconcertingly clear to her that the expensive gowns her father had provided, which were in the English style, looked out of place in Paris, where square necklines were wider and edged in the front with embroidered and bejewelled biliments, and hoods were shaped like halos rather than the gabled style her mother wore. She had heard clucks of disapproval from older ladies, who held that it was indecent for married women to show their hair, the sight of which must be reserved for their husbands, but even the virtuous Claude loved the French hood, so its critics were silenced.

Anne had acquired two velvet beguine hoods in Burgundy, and now she applied her skills to converting them into French ones, which suited her so well. Her gowns she painstakingly adapted, over many hours, into the French mode, slashing the undersleeves so that she could pull puffs of her lawn chemise through them, and arranging the hanging oversleeves on top, making sure that she had made frills at the wrists long enough to cover that hated sixth fingernail. Always she added her own innovative details: interlacing ribbons and paste gems on her bodice, or repeating the biliment at the skirt hem, or wearing a bandeau of silver chain across her forehead, beneath her hood. The effects were striking. Her slender figure was maturing into the lines of womanhood, and so perfectly proportioned that the gowns looked wonderful. Others thought so too, for within a short while her small innovations were being copied, and after a time she realised that women, many even of high rank, were watching her to see what new fashions she was wearing. It was a heady feeling, setting trends in a court that led the world in style, and almost every day she devised some novel detail.

In the summer, as Paris grew hotter and more foul-smelling, Claude began to pine for her beloved chateau of Amboise, but she was nearing her time and dared not risk any form of travel. This was her first child, and she was praying daily that it would be a son, an heir to France, since the Salic Law did not permit the succession of a female to the French throne.

Anne saw the married women in her entourage shake their heads behind the Queen's back, murmuring that being so delicate and crippled did not augur well for a happy confinement. But the birth – which Anne, by virtue of her maiden status, was not permitted to attend – was by all accounts uneventful. It was disappointing that Claude had borne a daughter, but God doubtless had His reasons for that.

The baby was a tiny thing, with the King's Valois features instantly recognisable. She was baptised Louise, as a compliment to his mother and Claude's father, King Louis. The maids-of-honour were entranced by her, and seized every opportunity to pick her up or rock her in her cradle. Anne remained aloof. Babies held little attraction for her, although she supposed it would be different when she had some of her own. But who knew when that would be? She still had no desire to marry – and as for what marriage entailed, she could not bear to think of it. Every time she did, the image of King François forcing himself on Mary came to mind.

A letter had come from Mary, belatedly, as she had expected, knowing her sister. Anne thanked God that Mary was not pregnant. Father had not been pleased to see her, but was mollified when he read Queen Mary's letter, in which she had explained, quite candidly, that his daughter's virtue had nearly been compromised by the French King, but, by the grace of God, she was unscathed. He had swallowed the blatant lie. He'd even written to Anne, warning her to give the King a wide berth. But now poor Mary was condemned to rusticate at Hever until Father bestirred himself to find a husband for her.

The leaves were turning golden when the bells of Paris rang out in joyful cacophony. King François had won a great victory at Marignano, and made himself King of Milan. In one swift swoop he had achieved what King Louis had fought and negotiated for over many years. The people were wild with joy. Everywhere they were singing the new song, '*Victoire au noble roi François!*' Anne could not get it out of her head. Claude was on her knees in ecstasy, thanking God for His manifold blessings and for keeping her husband safe. Madame Louise ordered public celebrations.

'My son has vanquished those whom only Caesar vanquished!' she declared grandly, bursting with pride. 'It was foretold to me that he would gain this victory.'

Claude now gave the order for her household to move south to Amboise. It was during that hundred-mile journey that Anne began to realise how vast France actually was, and how beautiful, with its broad rivers and fields stretching as far as the eye could see. Approaching the lush green valley of the Loire, she was told that they were entering the Garden of France. It was peaceful, fertile countryside with gentle undulating hills, vineyards, orchards, and chateaux that looked as if they belonged in the pages of illuminated manuscripts; and through it all flowed the broad, tranquil river.

The royal chateau of Amboise rose loftily and majestically on the bank of the Loire, dominating the town and surrounded by glorious gardens and terraces with parterres, lattices and colourful pavilions. It was like no palace Anne had ever seen. The more knowledgeable among her companions informed her that it was centuries old, but had been largely rebuilt in the Italian style some years ago.

Claude was a different person – happier, more carefree and more animated – in this place she regarded as her home. She began planning Christmas celebrations such as had never been seen at court, in the hope that François would be with her to share them. He had been brought up at Amboise, and as children he and Claude had played here together. Anne and the other maids and ladies spent hours making wreaths and garlands of evergreens, as great fires crackled in the elegant stone fireplaces and tapestries embroidered with a thousand flowers shielded them from the draughts.

But the King did not return for Christmas; he was still in Milan. He would soon be home, Claude said stoically, and insisted that the celebrations go ahead anyway.

In January, Madame Louise appeared in the Queen's chamber and informed her that François was to make a slow, triumphal progress through Provence on his way north.

'I am going to join him,' she announced. 'God knows how I long to see him.'

'I will go too,' said Claude, happily and without rancour. It was clear that she, the King's wife, was used to playing a supportive role to his mother.

'We will all go, you, me and Marguerite,' Madame Louise declared, and Claude's face lit up. Anne too was excited at the prospect of travelling south. How far away was Provence? How long would it take to get there?

It took them two weeks. The dead of winter was never the best time to travel, but fortunately the weather was unseasonably mild and the roads and tracks were dry. Their route took them from the rich lowlands of the Loire to Bourges, Clermont-Ferrand, Lyon and Grenoble, skirting snow-capped mountains, traversing majestic country where frost-touched vineyards stretched to the far horizon, and finally reaching the verdant, scenic grandeur of Provence itself, with its towering, craggy hills and ancient olive groves. Anne had never dreamed that a land could show so many faces. These southern parts of France were enchanting, a world away from the familiar places she knew.

As they passed between two high mountain ridges and drew nearer to Sisteron, where they were to meet up with the King and his host, her excitement mounted. She saw Claude's plain face transformed with joy when she caught sight of François, the triumphant victor, bearded now and bravely seated on his horse, looking more magnificent than ever and mantled with a new assurance. Anne watched him dismount to embrace his wife, his mother and his sister. Again she felt that overwhelming distaste.

With the other ladies, she followed the King and Queen up to the mighty Citadelle, which guarded the town from its rocky outcrop far above. An air of rejoicing pervaded the press of people in the procession, and Anne was longing for the feasting and dancing to begin. With itching fingers she helped to unpack her mistress's gear and make her ready to grace the court. Then she flew to the dorter at the top of the great tower, where she hurriedly cast off her travelling clothes, washed herself with rose water and donned a gown of plum damask trimmed with black velvet. Her hair she left floating loose down her back, interlaced with tiny sparkling jewels. A glance in the mirror told her that she had never looked more alluring.

King François noticed her. '*La petite* Boleyn! You are enchanting tonight,' he said, as he passed her on his way to his seat on the dais, his gentlemen following, all of them as gaudy as peacocks. He had put on weight during the campaign.

Anne flushed. He was the last man whose attentions she craved, but she lowered her eyes, dipped a curtsey and murmured, 'Thank you, sire,' praying that he would leave her alone.

'It pleases me to see all you young ladies here,' he said, leering at her. 'A court without ladies is like a year without springtime, or a spring without roses.' He moved on, his courtiers following. Her relief was so great, she could have sunk to the floor.

In slow stages the court made its cumbersome way north, the victor of Milan being feted all along the way. It was at Lyon, where François fell in love with the city and insisted on lingering for three months, that Anne attended the Queen on an expedition to the Roman forum of Trajan, high on a hill, with all of Lyon and the broad confluence of the two great rivers, the Rhône and the Saône, spread out below. She stood by the parapet to admire the view. It was a breathtaking sight.

Someone was watching her. An old man was sitting on a ruined wall, a sketchbook in his hand, busily drawing. You could have called him a lion of a man, with his mane of white hair, his strong features and his powerful build. He smiled at her. She had seen him before, in company with the King, and wondered who he was.

'Good day, sir,' she said.

The old man rose to his feet and bowed. 'Madonna. You like my picture?' His voice was heavily accented, and his French appalling.

Anne had never seen such a realistic and beautiful sketch. She drew in her breath as she saw her own likeness in profile. There she was in her grey figured gown with the black biliment and her red and gold hood. The old man had captured her features perfectly. Her nose was a trifle long, but that did not detract from the overall impression.

'You like it?' the old man asked. 'You have a – how you say – interesting face.'

'It's wonderfully accomplished!' Anne exclaimed. 'I have seen many great works of art, in Burgundy and here in France, but this is exceptional. It's me to the life.'

'Then take it,' he said, resuming his seat and beaming at her.

Anne was staggered. 'For me? Oh, you are kind, sir! I shall treasure it. Will you sign it?'

The artist took a stick of charcoal and traced a cipher of three letters, one above the other, a large D with two downward strokes and a slanting L.

'DVL?' she asked, puzzled.

'Leonardo da Vinci at your service, Madonna,' the old man said.

Chapter 5

1516–1519

'You are done with men? You are fifteen!' Jeanne de Lautrec exclaimed. Recently married, she had been extolling the joys of wedlock to the Queen's other ladies, and Anne, growing weary of it, had felt moved to point out that not every woman thought it an ideal estate.

'They call Mademoiselle Anne the ice maiden,' Madame de Langeac jested. They were sitting in the gardens of the chateau of Blois, enjoying the hot July sunshine while sipping lemon juice. Behind them the pinnacled and turreted chateau that François had restored for Claude rose majestically below an azure sky.

'I have had enough of men,' Anne retorted, shuddering inwardly at the memory of a recent infatuation that had turned sour. What a fool she had been to think that the gentleman had had noble intentions! In fact, few of them did, at least in this court. Cloaked and masked gallants thought nothing of climbing over garden walls and waylaying the Queen's maids as darkness fell, forcing their unwelcome attentions on them. They left notes containing indecent proposals and naughty verses. Following the King's example, they molested any lady they fancied with impunity, and some, Anne knew, would not take no for an answer. Several times she had had to slap a gentleman's face, and she had stamped hard on one persistent rascal's foot.

At a feast only last week, she had been seated next to a young chevalier who presented her with wine in a gold cup. It was only when she drained it that she saw inside the bowl the engraved relief of a couple very explicitly enjoying the act of love. She had felt herself growing hot as the young man guffawed loudly at her blushes and shared the joke with his friends, and she had spent the rest of the evening in a state of mortification. She was now beginning to understand why Claude was so strict.

'There is more to life than men!' she declared.

The ladies laughed. 'What can a woman do outside of marriage?' one asked.

'She can learn, she can be creative in many ways, and she can be herself,' Anne told her.

'I could be very creative with a husband with sixty manors and a title!' another scoffed. 'Really, child, you need a man to be anything in this world. Only marriage opens doors to women.'

'I think it closes more doors than it opens,' Anne observed.

She knew she had a name for scorning matters of the heart, but time had not lessened her antipathy to men – in fact, it had only confirmed her poor opinion of them. And now she was angry with herself at falling head over heels for the handsome deceiver who had led her on and then dropped her when it became clear that she would not give herself to him outside wedlock. She, who prided herself on being independent, had behaved so foolishly that she could not now bear to think of it. Instead she had surrounded herself with a protective carapace. Her fellow maids sometimes seemed wary of her strong opinions and barbed wit. Even she did not like the brittle person she had become.

Queen Claude, preoccupied with her little daughter, her philandering husband and her many charitable interests, did not seem to be aware of the jaded views of her maid-of-honour. After all, Anne was just one among three hundred, so why should Claude notice her especially?

Of late, Anne had almost convinced herself that she should be done with the world and enter a convent.

'I am seriously thinking of taking the veil,' she told her companions, even though she knew deep within herself that she was not the stuff of which nuns were made.

'You, a nun?' Madame de Langeac cried. The others laughed.

Someone must have repeated it, because at a court reception later that week, the King himself sought Anne out. She took care to keep her eyes modestly downcast as she rose from her curtsey.

74

'Mademoiselle Anne,' François said, his own eyes alive with humour, 'it is hinted among the court ladies that you desire above all things to be a nun. This I should regret.'

'Sire, it is something I am thinking about seriously,' she told him. 'I hope I will have your blessing.' Let that ward him off, she thought.

'I pray that you will think hard about what you would be giving up,' the King said, and passed on. And, of course, she did think about it, and gradually it dawned on her that she was enjoying life too much to immure herself in a nunnery, and that really it was her desire not to be taken advantage of by men that had driven her to consider such a drastic step. The world had too many pleasures to offer.

From time to time she received letters containing news from home. It was good to hear that George was making himself noticed at King Henry's court; he would shine there, of that Anne was confident.

Their great-grandfather, the old Earl of Ormond, had died. It was hard to feel sorrow, for he had been very ancient, and she had rarely seen him, since he lived in London and had long served at court. Father's tone was almost gleeful as he informed Anne that her grand-mother, the Lady Margaret, had come into a rich inheritance as the late Earl's heir. The old lady's wits had at last deserted her, so he himself was to be in control of it. That will please him mightily, Anne thought.

Father's letters were always full of his achievements and the honours that were being showered on him. He was cock-a-hoop when, early in 1516, he was chosen as one of the four persons who were to bear a canopy over King Henry's baby daughter, the Princess Mary, at her christening at Greenwich Palace. 'It is a high honour indeed,' he wrote, puffed up with pride.

But the following year saw England visited by a terrifying plague called the sweating sickness, which killed within hours. Every time a letter arrived from England, Anne opened it with trembling hands. Not Mother, nor dearest George, the people she loved best in the world, she prayed. But it was not them who died. It was her eldest brother, Thomas, struck down and buried at Penshurst, because the Duke of Buckingham had not thought it safe to transport his body to Hever.

And then came the news that Hal had succumbed too, in plague-ravaged Oxford.

Sorrowing herself, Anne could only imagine what blows these had been for Father, losing his two elder sons. In his letters he was stoical, dwelling more on Mother's grief than his own, but he was a man who would never show his emotions. Anne mourned her brothers, but she had not been close to them, and a part of her could not help rejoicing that George was now the heir. Mercifully God spared him, and Mary.

A year later, Father came to the French court as England's resident ambassador. It had been three years since Anne had seen him, and she knew she had changed immeasurably in that time. What would he think of her now? Would he approve of the woman she had become? She waited in trepidation to find out.

When they met in the Hôtel des Tournelles, in the *galerie des courges*, with its tiled heraldic ceiling and walls painted with green pumpkins, she was struck by how sadly he had aged. His face was as pugnacious as ever, but etched with lines of grief, and his brown hair had turned grey. He greeted her with unusual warmth and looked her up and down with approval.

'You have grown sophisticated in France, Anne,' he said, which was praise indeed.

He had brought her a book, Caxton's edition of the *Morte d'Arthur*, as well as news of her family. The King had noticed George and praised his learning. Mother and Mary were still at Hever, which was no surprise.

'Have you found Mary a husband?' Anne asked.

'Not yet,' Father said, as they strolled along the gallery.

Fortunately, Mary, as the elder daughter, must be married first. Anne was relieved to know that she had some respite, having wondered what plans Father might have for her once he had seen how she had become the accomplished, virtuous and eminently marriageable daughter he had wanted her to be.

'How does His Grace the King?' she asked, quickly changing the subject.

'Never better,' Father replied, 'and in hopes of a son, for Queen Katherine is again with child. It's her sixth. All lost save for the Princess Mary.' He sighed.

'I will pray for her,' Anne said.

She saw him several times after that, when her duties permitted, and found herself growing easier in his company. It seemed that they were seeing each other with new eyes after their long separation; it was almost as if Father was now treating her as an equal.

Sir Thomas had spoken truth when he said that Anne had grown sophisticated. No longer was she overwhelmed by the splendour of the French court, the extravagant, beautiful palaces that François was building, or the open dalliance and debauchery that had once shocked her. These days, if presented with that erotically chased gold cup, she would merely have smiled. She had grown used to seeing lewd books portraying men and women pleasuring each other in different positions – they were common currency at court. And when one lascivious young man informed her that the King's own almoner had felt obliged to apologise to his mistress for having satisfied her only twelve times in one night, she had merely shrugged and endeavoured to look bored. No man would be permitted a prurient thrill at the sight of her shocked reaction to such things. She knew it was said that rarely did any maid or wife leave this court chaste, but no one was going to say it of her!

She was never short of suitors these days. They all told her that she was the fairest and most bewitching of all the lovely women at court, or that she sang like a second Orpheus. She prided herself that there was some truth in it. When she played on the harp, the lute or the rebec, people stopped to listen. She danced, too – how she danced with the hopeful gallants who flocked around her – leaping and gliding with infinite grace and agility, and inventing many new figures and steps. It thrilled her to see them copied, like her clothes, or to hear them named after her.

At eighteen she was a different person from the naïve girl who had come to the French court. Her mirror showed her the same dark-haired woman with the same high cheekbones and pointed chin as the girl in

Master Leonardo's portrait, which she had proudly hung above her bed, and yet there was a knowing quality to her gaze these days, for she had learned that the way a woman used her eyes, to invite conversation or convey a promise of hidden passion, had the power to command the allegiance of many a man.

These days she played the game of love well, taking care to be a vivacious and witty companion, and exercising her charm to the full – but keeping her suitors at arm's length. The protective carapace was still in place. Never would she allow a man to make a fool of her. When she gave her heart, it would be to the man she married, but that was hopefully far in the future. In the meantime, she would enjoy flirting, making jests, sparring with repartee over a glass of wine, and playing cards and dice with her admirers for high stakes. Or she might compete with them at bowls or in the chase. Father could reproach her for nothing.

She was not always at court. Claude still preferred the peace and tranquillity of Amboise and Blois, and retreated there whenever she could. She had a son now, the long-awaited Dauphin François, and a daughter, Charlotte, but her eldest, little Madame Louise, had died aged only two, much mourned by all the ladies.

Anne would have preferred to be at court more, but Amboise had its pleasures. The King had given his beloved Master Leonardo a house and workshop, Le Clos Lucé, near the chateau, and when the great man was in residence, which was increasingly often, for he was growing old and infirm, he welcomed visits from the Queen's entourage, and took delight in demonstrating his many curiosities to them. There was nothing that did not interest him: he was not just an artist, but a man of science, an anatomist and an engineer, and he was endlessly inventive. Anne was amazed to hear him describe a machine that could fly men through the air.

'It is not possible!' she exclaimed.

Leonardo smiled at her. There was an ageless wisdom in the blue eyes under the beetled brows. 'Time will prove you wrong, Madonna,' he twinkled.

He was painting a masterpiece for the King. It was of an Italian woman with a mysterious sideways glance and a half-smile. He had been working on it for months, and was always retouching it or changing details.

'She is beautiful,' Anne told him.

'What is her name?' Isabeau asked.

'She is Monna Lisa Gherardini, a beautiful lady I knew in Italy,' Leonardo said. 'But she is not yet finished.'

On a warm May day in 1519, Anne and three other ladies walked from the chateau of Amboise to Le Clos Lucé, hoping that Leonardo would show them some more of his inventions. But at the door they were met by his servant, who looked at them mournfully.

'Alas, mesdemoiselles, Master Leonardo died yesterday, in the King's own arms,' he told them, a tear trickling down his gnarled cheek.

'No!' Anne cried, stunned. She had known that the old man was failing, but had convinced herself that, with his genius, he would go on for ever. She had grown fond of him, and – she thought – he of her. He had been someone apart from the usual run of mortals, and the world would not see his like again. At that realisation, she wept.

Chapter 6

1520

Anne stood with the other maids and ladies behind the Queen in a vast field in the Vale of Ardres. She was sumptuously dressed in the French fashion, in a low-cut black velvet gown with great slashed sleeves and strings of pearls draped from shoulder to shoulder and looped across her bodice. On her head was a gold-braided French hood, from which hung a black veil. Her pose was demure, but as she stood there in the breeze, tucking a stray tress back under her hood, her avid eyes darted everywhere, taking in the massed crowds of courtiers and the ranks of men-at-arms, all waiting expectantly against a backdrop of colourful silken pavilions.

They had already been waiting for an hour, and still there had come no word that the English King was approaching. King François was in his tent. He would not ride out until his brother monarch was in sight. Anne's eyes were fixed firmly on the horizon.

King Henry was coming now. She could see the banners and hear the trumpets, the tramp of marching men and the hoofbeats, as what seemed like a great army began its advance. And now King François, with his magnificent train, was emerging from the other direction, across ground that had been levelled so that neither monarch should appear to be higher than the other. Cloth of gold dazzled, great jewels sparkled in the sunlight, and proudly caparisoned horses snorted as the two kings doffed their bonnets and saluted each other from their saddles, then dismounted and embraced.

Anne saw that Henry of England had broadened into solid manhood. She watched as he laughed and exchanged courtesies with François, wondering – as she had wondered seven years before – why people praised his beauty, when really, bar a noble profile, he was just a rather ordinary-looking sandy-haired man with a ruddy complexion.

The greetings over, the two sovereigns passed into François's sumptuous cloth-of-gold pavilion, and Anne followed Queen Claude in their wake. She was surprised when she saw Henry's Spanish wife, Queen Katherine, who looked so much older than her husband, and not by any stretch of the imagination the golden beauty whose praises had long been echoing around the courts of Europe. Of course, the loss of many children would account for her sagging figure and sad face. And, being Spanish, she would hardly look happy being obliged to consort with the French, her country's enemies. But there was King François, kissing her hand and doing her all honour – and there, in Queen Katherine's train, was Mary, Anne's sister!

Mary caught Anne's eye and smiled. She looked happy, and Anne guessed that marriage must suit her. Mary had wed in February; her new husband, William Carey, was an important, rising man in King Henry's court – the King's own cousin, no less! Father had hastened home for the wedding, as well he might, for it had taken place in the Chapel Royal at Greenwich Palace, in the presence of the King and Queen themselves. Anne had stayed in France, not wishing to attend the wedding in case Father remembered that he had another marriageable daughter.

There would be time to catch up with Mary's news and gossip later, but now the great glittering throng was moving towards the banqueting tent. Anne caught sight of her former mistress, Queen Mary, walking hand in hand with her husband, Suffolk, and looking radiant. Then she herself was swept along in the crowd.

They were calling this summit meeting the Field of Cloth of Gold, for the field in which it was set was ringed with rich pavilions of silk like fine burnished gold, all hung with marvellous cloths of Arras, and everyone, it seemed, was decked out in yards of the glittering fabric. Few were more gorgeously attired than the ladies attending the three queens, Claude, Katherine and Mary. Anne thought that the English gowns, however gorgeous, looked less becoming than the French ones, and as the days went on she was amused to see her countrywomen hastily adopting the elegant fashions of France. No doubt many a maid had been kept up late, stitching frantically.

The kings had signed an everlasting treaty of friendship, and now it was time for everyone to enjoy seventeen days of indulgent revelry, banqueting, jousting and disports. But no one could have mistaken the undercurrents of rivalry between the two courts.

Father was here, having been in charge of some of the arrangements for the meeting of the kings. Mother was with him. She held Anne closely when they were reunited.

'I cannot believe how you have grown up!' she said. 'You are quite the lady now!'

It pained Anne to see Mother looking older and sadder, still mourning her lost sons, but full of praise for George, and how he was rising in favour at court.

In the short time Anne spent with him, Father said that he had something he wanted to discuss when there was time. God forfend it was not her marriage!

She sought out her sister, and found her at one of the booths set up in the camp by opportunistic traders. This one was selling an array of pastries, and Mary was buying some in company with a girl with slanting eyes and full lips upturned disdainfully above a jutting, determined chin.

Mary grinned when she saw Anne, and they embraced.

'Congratulations on your marriage,' Anne smiled. 'I hear the King himself attended.'

'Yes, we were greatly honoured,' Mary said, a trifle smugly. 'Anne, may I present Jane Parker, Lord Morley's daughter.' She turned to her companion, whose face was transformed by an attractive smile.

'You are also in Queen Katherine's entourage?' Anne asked.

'Yes, as maid-of-honour,' Jane Parker told her. They exchanged a few pleasantries, and then the conversation dwindled. 'You sisters must have much to talk about,' Jane said. 'I will see you later, Mary.' And she took herself off.

Anne and Mary sat in the sun enjoying the pastries and beakers of the free wine that ran from a great gilded fountain outside the English palace, which was a dazzling, temporary affair of canvas, wood and lashings of gold leaf.

'How is married life suiting you?' Anne asked. They were to watch William Carey in the jousts later that afternoon.

'I am content,' Mary said. She had grown sleek and complacent, and it was clear from the way she smiled that her husband adored her. And yet there was a wary look about her today.

'I did not look to find myself back in France,' she said, 'especially with Will.'

Of course Mary feared to encounter her seducer, King François, or risk Will hearing gossip about them. Anne took her sister's hand in a rare gesture of affection. 'You are hardly likely to come face to face with the King amidst all these thousands of people,' she assured her, 'and anyway, that matter is long forgotten. I have never heard anyone mention it at court.'

Mary smiled weakly. She was eager to change the subject. 'We shall have to find you a husband too, Anne, now that I am wed.' There it was again, that eternal rivalry. She had to remind Anne that she had first place as the elder sister.

'I am in no hurry,' Anne said lightly. 'I am too busy enjoying life.'

'Were you hoping to snare some rich French lord and desert us for good?' Mary asked.

'That's what Father wants, and I've had several suitors, but I am determined to marry for love.'

'Then you're a fool! Father will never allow it. But tell me – is there someone?'

Anne laughed. 'No one, I assure you. I await my knight on a charger.'

Mary was silent for a moment. 'Actually, Father has someone in mind.'

Anne swung round and looked sharply at her sister's face. She knew that gleeful, malicious expression of old. Mary knew something Anne did not. She was enjoying this.

'Our great-grandfather's earldom of Ormond has gone to our distant cousin Piers Butler,' she told Anne, 'but Grandmother, as Great-Grandfather's heiress, has contested that – or rather, her lawyers have – and since he came home from France for my wedding, Father, of course, has backed her claim vigorously.'

'Then she is certain to succeed.' Father was an important man now, a Privy councillor and Comptroller of the King's Household. Anne was impatient, wishing that Mary would get to the point. 'But how does this affect me?'

Mary smiled slyly. 'Father wants to settle the dispute by marrying you to Piers Butler's son, James. That way, you will become Countess of Ormond, and his blood will inherit the title. But the condition is that James gets the earldom, not Piers. You'll have to go and live in Ireland,' she added cheerfully.

No! Never! She would refuse. Let them try to force her, and they would see they had a she-cat to contend with! Father should have consulted *her*, the person most concerned.

'Have you met this James Butler?' she asked, consumed with anger.

'I've seen him at court. He's one of the young nobles in the household of Cardinal Wolsey. He's quite attractive. He may even be here in the Cardinal's train. Father says the Cardinal thinks highly of him, and I have heard the King praise him. I see the King quite a lot now that I'm married to one of his gentlemen—'

'You can point him out to me,' Anne said, interrupting Mary's boasting. 'But I *must* see Father now.'

She flew off, half running through crowded pavilions hung with tapestries, along Turkey carpets spread over the ground, until she saw Father and Grandfather Norfolk talking with a portly, fleshy-faced man in red silk robes and cap, with a huge pectoral cross of diamonds and rubies. The great Cardinal Wolsey himself!

Father noticed her at once. 'Come forward, Anne. My lord Cardinal, may I present my daughter, the one whose future we have been discussing.'

Anne curtseyed, barely containing her fury.

'Delightful, delightful,' the Cardinal said, but it was clear that his mind was on their conversation. She was too lowly for his notice.

'We were speaking of you – and here you are,' Norfolk said. 'Come and kiss your old grandsire, child.' He had always been fond of her.

'I gather that you were discussing my marriage with James Butler,' Anne told him. 'Mary informed me of it.' She glared at Father.

'You have cause to rejoice, Mistress Anne,' Wolsey said. 'If the King agrees, this will be a good match for you and for your family.'

'And will the King consent, my lord?' she asked.

'I shall advise him on the matter. He is, shall we say, well disposed.'

Father and Grandfather beamed. Anne knew herself bested. There was no more to be said. Her heart sank. If the King decreed it, she must marry James Butler.

'There he is,' said Will Carey, now divested of his jousting armour and flushed with victory. Anne was growing to like this brother-in-law of hers. He was warm and witty, and had a kind heart, for all his ambition, and he clearly delighted in Mary. 'That's James Butler, over there.'

Anne looked across the tournament ground to the stand where the Cardinal was seated, surrounded by his household. To his left stood a stocky young man of about her own age, dark-haired with a fringe, and personable – at least from this distance.

'You could do a lot worse,' Mary said.

'Yes, but I don't love him and I don't want to go and live in Ireland,' Anne retorted. It was galling that Mary's marriage had brought her a place at court, when she herself was facing exile to a land of bogs and savages, by all accounts – and with a total stranger. Besides, she wanted to stay at the French court.

'I must attend Queen Claude,' she said, and hurried away, not wanting Mary and Will to see how upset she was.

The next day, there was another tournament, graced by the presence of the three queens, each seated on a stage hung with tapestries and furnished with a costly canopy of estate made of pearls. In a heavy gown of cream satin, Anne sat in the row behind Claude, with the other *filles d'honneur*, whose animated chatter went over her head as she faced the bleak prospect of leaving France for a marriage she did not want.

The two kings were riding into the lists now, leading a long procession of knights. James Butler was not among them, but Will Carey was, riding beside a strikingly attractive man with close-cropped golden-brown hair, sensual features and large light-blue eyes. Anne stared at him, captivated. She did not even know his name, but she could not draw her gaze away. Never had a man's appearance moved her so powerfully.

Will and the handsome knight acquitted themselves well, and Anne could see that the latter was high in royal favour, for King Henry, victorious himself in the jousts, was clapping him on the back as they rode out of the lists.

There was a feast that evening, in honour of the winners, and Anne seized the opportunity to ask her sister who the noble knight was. She was determined to make him notice her.

'The one who rode out with Will? That's Sir Henry Norris. He's another of the King's gentlemen, one His Grace favours greatly. He's just married Mary Fiennes – remember, she was with us in the Hôtel de Cluny?'

Lucky, *lucky* Mary Fiennes. 'I do remember,' Anne managed to say. 'I . . . I thought he seemed familiar, but I was mistaken.'

There was no feast the next evening, so Claude dined in private with King François in the chateau of Ardres. Anne, in turmoil at the thought of Sir Henry Norris together with Mary Fiennes, could not face food, and in her downcast mood she was averse to joining the Queen's ladies in their eternal gambling, so she escaped to Claude's private chapel. There, on her knees, she raged at God for dangling before her a future she could never enjoy, and for consigning her to an unwanted marriage and exile from all that she held dear. Was it for this that He had sent her into this world? If so, why had He allowed her to be fitted for a far more glorious destiny than that to which she was doomed? Why had He afforded her a glimpse of what love could be, and then deprived her of all possibility of experiencing it?

As she knelt there weeping, a hand rested on her shoulder, and she looked up, startled, into the concerned face and violet eyes of

Madame Marguerite, Duchesse d'Alençon, King François's sister and the living image of him.

'What is wrong, Mademoiselle Anne?' Marguerite asked. There was about this woman who was so famed for her learning an innate kindliness and warmth.

Anne struggled to her feet and dropped a curtsey.

'Madame, I weep because my father is doing his best to marry me to a man I cannot love, who will carry me off to Ireland to keep company with the snakes.'

Marguerite regarded her with sympathy. 'Alas, it is the fate of women to be disposed of in marriage where men choose. I too was married to a man I could never love, a man whom others sneer at for his illiteracy. They call him oaf, buffoon and worse. It was all for King Louis's advantage. And yet my lord is kindly. I have not done so badly after all.'

'But, madame, do you not want more?' Anne burst out, before she remembered that she was speaking to the King's sister.

Marguerite's face clouded. 'No, I do not,' she said sharply, and Anne was astonished to see tears in her eyes. She remembered hearing talk that the Duchesse was unnaturally close to her brother the King, but had never believed it. Now she wondered.

'Be true to yourself, mademoiselle,' Marguerite said. 'You can refuse this marriage.'

'I intend to,' Anne told her. 'But I fear my father would just ignore me.'

'Stand your ground, *ma chère*. Never let any man, even your father, take advantage of you. That's advice that was given not so long ago by a French princess to her daughter. She even wrote a book about it. You see, women can be strong when they have a will to it. Remember Queen Isabella of Castile? She ruled alongside her husband and rode into battle at the head of her army. Together they drove the Moors from Spain. Isabella's example proves that women can be as capable as men when they set their minds to it. It's just that we are not taught to think for ourselves or question our subjection.'

Marguerite's forthrightness startled Anne out of her self-pity. Here was a woman with a mind like her own. 'I am intrigued by your

Highness's opinions,' she told Marguerite. 'They remind me of the writings of Christine de Pizan, whose works I read at the court of Burgundy. I had long discussions with the Regent Margaret about the status of women in the world. As a sex, we should be stronger, and make the most of our capabilities.'

'Indeed!' Marguerite replied, her face lighting up in surprise. 'Mademoiselle, I am impressed. The Regent is known for her enlightened views. It is refreshing to find one who shares them. *Ma chère*, you must take courage from Christine de Pizan and persist in your refusal. Marriage is founded on mutual consent, and to be forced . . .' To Anne's utter astonishment, the Duchesse burst into tears, sinking to her knees and burying her face in her hands.

'Madame! What is wrong?' Anne cried. 'Here I am, complaining about my lot, when you are so unhappy.' She knelt by Marguerite and stayed there until the older woman's shoulders stopped heaving and her breathing slowed.

'Forgive me,' the Duchesse sniffed. 'I should not be burdening you with my troubles – and you have enough of your own. But I shall go mad if I do not talk to someone. Can I trust you?'

'Of course, madame – I swear it on my life.'

Marguerite paused. It was clear that she was struggling to find words. 'A friend of the King my brother, and a man I admired and trusted . . . No, I cannot say it.' The tears were streaming again, and for a while she could not speak.

'Madame?' Anne whispered.

Marguerite turned a ravaged face to her. 'He has raped me!' she cried out.

Anne drew in her breath and shivered. The word *rape* touched her too nearly. Here was more proof, if she needed it, that men could be beasts. What kind of man would presume to take advantage of his sovereign's own sister, a woman of famed virtue?

'Who is this man?' she asked, outraged.

'I could never tell you – or anyone. I cannot risk being accused of slander.'

'But have you not complained to the King?'

'I doubt he would believe me. He loves me truly, but he would never credit it. You see, when we were young, this man attempted to rape me before. I complained to my brother, but the man denied it vehemently. My brother believed him.' She almost spat the words out. 'He is a man, of course, and all men see women as the descendants of Eve, who led Adam into temptation. Of course, I must have led this man on, even unwittingly!' Her tone was tart. 'And François will think the same if I complain a second time.'

Anne's anger burned fiercely again. How could any woman ever obtain justice for this most foul of crimes if the King of France not only committed it with impunity, but refused to believe that his own sister had been a victim of it? How dare he hold women so cheaply!'

'Madame, in England, I believe, raping the King's sister is treason, and punishable by death.'

Marguerite stood up. 'That is as may be, but it avails me little. In France, the honour of men is paramount – even of men who have no honour! Mademoiselle, speak of this to no one. You did not hear it. I am sorry to have cast my burden on you. And tell your father that you do not consent to the marriage he is planning. Be strong!'

And she was gone, leaving a faint smell of rose water behind her.

The next day a page dressed in Marguerite's livery approached Anne as the Queen's ladies were watching knights running at the ring, practising for yet another tournament.

'Madame the Duchesse requests that you attend upon her, mademoiselle,' the page said, and led Anne back to the chateau of Ardres, where Marguerite had her apartments. The Duchesse, wearing a low-necked gown of brown velvet with wide slashed sleeves, and her dark hair in a snood beneath a jaunty bonnet, was waiting for her in a room flooded with sunshine and crowded with ladies. At Anne's entrance, she laid down her book.

'Mademoiselle Anne!' she cried, stretching out her hands in greeting. Anne regarded her shrewdly, noticing how composed she was. There was no trace of yesterday's distress. Clearly the matter was to be forgotten.

'*Ma chère!*' Marguerite smiled, raising Anne from her curtsey. 'I have a proposition to put to you. The Queen has agreed that, if you wish, you may leave her household and serve me, for I think we agree very well together.'

For a moment, unable to credit her good fortune, Anne could not reply. She was being offered a release from the stultifying routine and rules of Claude's household. It would afford her endless opportunities for intellectual stimulation, and a powerful champion should Father try to force her into marriage with James Butler. And she could remain at court, where Marguerite was firmly established. The oaf of a husband had evidently never asserted himself sufficiently to drag her away to his estates.

She took a breath, controlling her delight and excitement. 'Madame, I will be honoured to serve you,' she said, and curtseyed again.

'Then that is settled. Have your maid prepare your things.'

It was almost like being back at the court of the Regent. Anne revelled in the erudite atmosphere of Marguerite's household, which was accommodated in silken pavilions blazoned with the fleurs-de-lis and red borders of Alençon on a vivid blue ground. She loved the long, intellectual conversations in which the Duchesse liked to engage. It was wonderful to be encouraged once more to write poetry and debate on religion. Above all, it was stimulating to discuss the role of women in society.

'The question is,' Marguerite said one evening, as she and her ladies sat up late after yet another lavish banquet, 'are we women essentially virtuous, or are we – as the moralists see us – over-sexed disciples of Satan, whose chief function is to tempt men into sin?'

'We are naturally virtuous,' one young woman spoke up, 'but men cannot see us that way.'

'They fear us, that is why,' Anne smiled, laying aside her embroidery so that she could concentrate properly on the conversation.

'Very percipient! That is why they want to control us,' Marguerite said. 'But we can confound them with our prudence. It is what made Queen Isabella great, what enables the Regent Margaret to govern so wisely. Prudence is the fount of all virtues. Aristotle said it long ago. What we are enjoying now is the reign of the virtuous woman. We are conquering men with our intellect, our gentler virtues being our strength.'

Anne thrilled to hear her speak so.

'This new learning,' Marguerite went on, 'which we have from the ancient scholars of Greece and Rome, has opened our eyes to the power women wielded in antiquity. Look at Cleopatra. She was the seventh queen of her name. This teaches us that we are not born just to be subordinate to men. Our flesh might be weak – although those who have borne children might deny that – but our hearts and our intellects are strong. I say we can be a match for any man.'

'Bravo!' Anne cried, and several young women clapped.

'It has been argued,' Marguerite continued, 'that men do not oppress women because of some natural law, but because they want to retain their own power and status.'

'My father holds that women are inferior to men because man was created by God first, and is stronger and therefore more important,' a maiden chimed in.

Marguerite smiled. 'Ah, but maybe it was Eve, not Adam, who was deceived. And if you think about it, women were greater than men from the first. Adam means Earth, but the name Eve stands for life. Man was created from dust, yet woman was made from something far purer. God's Creation was perfected when He made woman. Therefore we must celebrate the nobility of women.'

'Do you think these ideas can become widely accepted?' Anne asked.

'They are being debated all over Christendom, particularly in Italy,' Marguerite told her. 'And what happens in Italy often influences the rest of the world. Change will come, have no doubt of it, and we women who have power and rank are the ones who will bring it about. So we must continue the fight.'

Armoured with a new awareness of her own power, Anne confronted her father.

'I do not want to marry James Butler,' she said. 'I feel that a better match could surely be found. And this marriage will be of little advantage to you, sir. Yes, I would be a countess, but what good would that do me, hidden away in the wilds of Ireland? Surely you had me educated for better things?'

Father frowned. 'It will keep the earldom of Ormond in the family.'

'In the *Butler* family. But it will not restore it to the Boleyns, where it rightfully belongs.'

Father frowned, eyeing Anne as if she had suddenly turned into a dangerous beast that needed caging. 'This is a fine to-do,' he said at length. 'Do you want me to look a fool in the eyes of the King and the Cardinal? Your grandsire and I have asked for His Grace's consent to the match – are we now to say we have changed our minds?'

'Is that so very awful?' Anne asked him. 'I imagine that King Henry changes his mind whenever policy requires him to do so; the Cardinal likewise. You could say that you have thought more on the matter and decided that it is not the best solution. Say you want the earldom for yourself. That would make far better sense, sir.' She thought her words might sound less hectoring if she added the 'sir'.

To her surprise, Father was now regarding her with something that looked like respect. She realised that she had probably touched a sensitive spot. He *did* want the earldom for himself.

'I will think on this,' he said finally. 'This meeting comes to an end tomorrow, thank God! It cost a king's ransom and all it has proved is that these sovereigns cordially hate each other. If I get a chance to discuss the matter with your grandsire, I will do so. I doubt it will be easy to gain a moment with the Cardinal. Now mark my words, Anne: if I decide that this marriage must go ahead, and the King agrees, then go ahead it will. But I hear what you say, and will do what is best.'

She left him, light of heart and step. Of course, the decision to withdraw from the negotiations must be his; on no account would he admit that she had swayed him. But she felt confident that the decision he made would be the right one.

At last the great pageant came to an end. After Cardinal Wolsey had celebrated High Mass in the open air before the two courts, and there had been a final farewell feast, there was a magnificent display of fireworks, and all was over. Whether the two kings would stay outward friends was anyone's guess, but they said their farewells warmly enough, and then the splendid sprawling camp broke up, as the royal retinues got down to packing and making their way homewards.

Anne was going back to Paris with Marguerite's household. She had hoped that Father would have some good news for her before she bade farewell, but when the time came for parting, he told her that Cardinal Wolsey had been too busy to see him, so the matter of her marriage would have to be deferred until he returned to England.

'But you think it will be all right?' she asked.

'It will all depend on what the King says,' he replied.

'But you will make a case for me?'

'I am still considering,' he said. He would never admit defeat.

Chapter 7

1522

Serving Madame Marguerite was never dull. Apart from the sparkling conversations and engrossing debates that took place in her sumptuous suites within the King's palaces, there was so much else in which to immerse oneself most satisfyingly. Anne came to like her new mistress enormously: she could see the self-doubt beneath the forceful views, and glimpse the emotional woman behind the witty facade. She understood Marguerite's devotion to her brother, and why people misjudged it. It seemed inconceivable that the Duchesse could feel such adoration for a man whom she admitted would not have lifted a finger to avenge her rape. But Anne knew that she herself would forgive George, if she were in the same position – not that he would ever behave so callously.

She still corresponded often with her brother. He was nineteen and a man now, which was hard to imagine, and hoped for preferment soon. Through Father's good offices and influence, he would surely get it. Anne missed him still. She wondered if he had changed greatly, but in his letters he sounded the same as ever. She hoped that one day he would visit her in Paris.

She had leisure these days to pursue her love of poetry and literature. Marguerite took pleasure in sharing with her ladies the poems, plays and racy short stories she wrote, and encouraged them to emulate her. Anne was impressed to learn that she patronised humanist scholars, and was a great admirer of Erasmus.

'It is wonderful that he is translating the Scriptures,' the Duchesse marvelled. 'He sets a brave example. As I have said to you many times, ladies, the Church is greatly in need of reform.'

Anne was listening avidly. If wise and learned women like Marguerite and the Archduchess Margaret held these views, they should be respected.

'The Church is corrupt!' Marguerite declared. 'There should be more study of the Bible and a return to the pure doctrines of the early Christians. What we need are evangelicals who will spread the word.'

Anne spoke up. 'Madame, a church that encourages people to buy salvation through the sale of indulgences by greedy priests should be reformed. How can the princes of that church – aye, and the Pope himself – justify their wealth and magnificence when they are meant to be emulating our Lord, who was a humble carpenter?'

Marguerite smiled at her approvingly. 'You speak a great truth, mademoiselle. Together we ladies shall change the world!'

In her letters to George, Anne shared her views on reform, and found that he was of the same mind. Maybe more people than she realised were disillusioned with the Church. She wondered if she dared mention it to Father.

He wrote rarely. For over a year he kept Anne waiting for a decision on her marriage. Then, just as she thought she would go mad from not knowing, and was beginning desperately to cast her eye about the court for any young man who might be thought a more suitable match, she received the worst possible news. The Cardinal had told Father that the King was insisting on her marriage taking place. Crushing the letter and throwing it to the floor, Anne erupted in fury against King Henry. How could he justify ruining her future? How dare he treat her as a commodity to be disposed of at his whim?

But England and France were on the brink of war again. Maybe James Butler would cross the Channel to fight and be killed. Perhaps King Henry would be killed, or be so absorbed in the war that he forgot about her marriage. Or maybe she should hurry up and take matters into her own hands, and choose a husband herself. She did not lack for suitors.

She was desperate. As always, she went to consult Marguerite.

'Madame, if you approve a match for me, then surely my father and King Henry must accept it.'

Marguerite shook her head. 'Alas, I cannot. You are an English subject, Anne, for all that you are almost one of us. And . . . I was about to speak to you anyway. *Ma chère*, I am sorry to tell you that you are to leave us. These regrettable hostilities are escalating. Your father has written most apologetically. Apparently, English subjects living in France have been advised to return home as soon as possible. Your parents do not think it fit for you to stay here any longer.'

This was the second time that England's politics had forced Anne to leave a place where she had been happy. It was cruel, cruel!

'No, madame!' she protested. 'I cannot leave France! I love it here. Please write to my father and tell him you command me to stay. He will listen to you.'

Marguerite regarded her sadly. 'I cannot, alas. Staying will place you in a difficult situation. You must leave. I wish it were otherwise, truly.'

There was no point in arguing further. Fighting off tears, Anne went to pack her belongings. She had acquired a lot of clothes during her years at the French court, and there was much to transport home. Father had arranged for her to be escorted back to England by a party of Kentish merchants who were leaving Paris, accompanied by their wives.

'Be strong,' Marguerite said when she bade her farewell. 'And be true to yourself.'

Even King François came to bid her goodbye. 'You have served my wife and my sister well,' he told her. 'I am grateful. It seems strange that you are going home, and that this war is dividing friends. I wish you well. Maybe you will return to France some day. You will always be welcome.' She curtseyed. He was the one thing in France she would *not* miss.

After the great palaces of Paris and the Loire, Hever Castle looked very small and very provincial in the weak February sunlight. But there was George, racing across the drawbridge to greet her and swinging her down from her horse.

'Anne!'

'Oh, my dear George! How good it is to see you!' She could not take her eyes off this tall, bearded stranger. Her grown-up brother was an Adonis, beautiful in face, muscular and elegant.

'You are become a Frenchwoman!' he exclaimed, twirling her round and admiring her attire, as Mother emerged through the gatehouse arch.

'Welcome home!' she cried, hugging Anne tightly. 'Come in, come in, and have something to eat. You must be tired after your long journey.' She sent grooms and ostlers flying to take care of the baggage cart and the horses, as Mrs Orchard hurried forward to clasp her former charge to her ample bosom.

It was so strange to be home, after nine years away. Anne realised, hearing English voices all around her, that she now spoke her native tongue with a French accent. The servants, insular Kentish folk, kept staring at her clothes. Of course, they must look exotic to country people used to sober English fashions.

'Your father is at court,' Mother said, leading them into the parlour, which now seemed small and old-fashioned, 'but he has sent excellent news. He has secured you a place as a maid-of-honour in Queen Katherine's household. You are to go to the court at Greenwich with all speed.'

'That's wonderful news!' Anne cried.

'And I am sent to escort you,' George said, as they seated themselves at the polished oak table and wine and little cakes were brought. Again she was struck by her brother's good looks. No wonder the maids were ogling him.

Going to the English court was some compensation for being banished from the French one, even if it was to serve the sad Spanish Queen. The prospect of being rusticated at Hever had appalled her, after those wonderful years in France, which she could hardly bear to think about right now. It would also be good to spend time with George. She felt cheated at having missed out on the years of their separation.

'What is Queen Katherine like?' she asked.

'Charming, and very kind,' Mother said. 'She is a most pious lady, and good to her servants. Of course, she has suffered tragic losses. Six children she has borne, and only the Princess Mary lives. She dotes on her, as you can imagine. But the King needs a son to succeed him, and there's been no sign of another pregnancy for about four years.'

'Why should the Princess Mary not succeed?' Anne asked.

'Because she is a woman, dear sister,' George replied, pouring more wine. 'Women are not fit to rule – most are emotional, weak creatures.' He ducked as Anne picked up a cushion and swung it in his direction. 'Help!'

'You are being unnecessarily provocative, dear,' Mother said.

'What of Isabella of Spain?' Anne asked. 'What of the Regent Margaret? Wise, successful rulers, both of them. You are behind the times, brother. Give me one good reason why a woman cannot rule.'

'They throw cushions,' George said, smirking. Anne punched him.

'Now stop it, the two of you,' Mother ordered. 'There is much to discuss. Anne, I need to know how well equipped you are for the court. You have sufficient gowns of black or white? No other colours are permitted for those who serve the Queen.'

There was really no time in which to feel homesick for France. No sooner had Anne arrived home than she was packing to leave again. At last all was carefully stowed away in her chests, and she and George were on their way to Greenwich, leaving Mother waving them off wistfully from the drawbridge.

The sprawling red-brick turreted palace nestling by the River Thames reminded Anne of the palaces of the Regent. It blatantly emulated them, having been built for pleasure and display. Over all towered the mighty donjon that housed the royal apartments, and surrounding the palace were lovely gardens.

'The King was born here,' George said, as they rode into the stable courtyard. 'He loves this place.'

Inside, the galleries and rooms were light, thanks to the tall oriel windows that afforded views of the river. The ceiling of the great hall was painted yellow, in keeping with the rest of the brightly coloured decor, which seemed gaudy to eyes used to the sophisticated classical schemes of the French royal chateaux. But the walls were adorned with magnificent tapestries or painted with imposing murals. Fine furniture graced all the chambers, and there were costly Turkey carpets on the rush-matted floors.

George escorted Anne up the stairs of the donjon to the door of the Queen's apartments, where she gave her name to the usher and was announced.

'Good luck!' her brother whispered, backing away, and then she was on her own.

Queen Katherine looked up from her sewing and smiled.

'Welcome, Mistress Anne,' she said, extending her hand to be kissed. She was dressed ornately in rich damask, and her velvet hood was in the traditional gabled English style, with long lappets. It framed a face that was pale, even pasty, and lined with care, but the Queen's expression was sweetness itself.

As Anne rose from her curtsey, she saw that all the other ladies and maids were wearing English hoods covering their hair. She wondered if the Queen might object to the French hood she herself wore, but Katherine said nothing. She was interested only in courteously present-ing Anne to the great ladies of her household, the chief of whom seemed to be the gaunt, aristocratic-looking Countess of Salisbury. Anne soon learned that the Countess and the Queen were great friends.

She quickly settled into the routine of the Queen's household, but she found, to her initial dismay, that it was more like Queen Claude's than Marguerite's. The maids-of-honour were expected to be punctilious in their devotions and charitable deeds. They spent hours sewing altar frontals, copes, or garments for themselves and the poor. But the Queen also loved music and dancing. She was learned, too, and Anne enjoyed the intellectual discussions in her chamber, although she was aware that her new mistress's views were strictly orthodox. There could be no mention of controversial subjects like religious reform or the march of women. Yet Katherine's maids were allowed much more freedom than Claude's, and the young gentlemen of the King's household and Cardinal Wolsey's were even invited into her chamber to make merry with them, all under Katherine's benevolent eye.

The Queen did not stint on praise. Anne was assigned to look after her wardrobe and personal effects, and everything she did was received with a smile and an appreciative thank-you. She found herself warming to Katherine, whom it was impossible not to admire. And the Princess Mary, who was often with her mother, was the most delightful child, graceful, well spoken and entrancing. Within that first week, Anne knew that she had much for which to be grateful in being appointed to the Queen's household.

The English court was far more sober than the French, and one of the first things Anne noticed was the decorum that was observed. Promiscuity was frowned on, and everyone was expected to follow the virtuous examples of the King and Queen. That licence was taken Anne had no doubt, but if so, discretion was the watchword.

She soon realised that she was the focus of attention in the court at large, and supposed it was because she was so very French in every respect: her mode of dress, her manners, her speech, her behaviour. Because of it, she stood out among her peers, and inevitably the men came circling, like moths attracted to a flame. But she would not allow her head to be turned.

'They are calling you St Agnes, for your constant virginity!' Mary giggled as they sat chatting in the lodging in the palace's outer court that had been assigned as a privilege to Will Carey, as one of the King's gentlemen. In these early days, when she knew hardly anyone, Anne often resorted there in her free time, and Mary would serve good wine and marchpane, and tell her all the court gossip. 'They say no one would take you for an Englishwoman, but for a Frenchwoman born. Maybe it is not a good idea to appear thus when we are at war with France.'

'It seems to make no difference,' Anne said. 'I cannot help being what I am. And I doubt that Father would buy me a new wardrobe in the English style. Anyway, I've noticed that some ladies have already copied my gowns.'

Mary shrugged. 'Talking of gowns, we might need to get sewing. Will tells me that there are to be revels for the visit of the Imperial ambassadors. They are coming to arrange the betrothal of the Princess Mary to the Emperor.'

'But she is a child!' Anne thought back to the court of Burgundy and that cold, heavy-jawed, disdainful boy, the Archduke Charles. He was King of Spain and Holy Roman Emperor now – the most powerful man in the world, and he must be all of twenty-two years old. Her heart bled for the exquisite little Princess, to be shackled to such a miserable man. 'He is old enough to be her father! She is only six!'

Yet she understood only too well why the King, who so obviously adored his daughter, could give her in marriage to a man nearly four times her age, luckless little maid. Father would have done the same had an advantageous opportunity arisen.

'She will be empress. It is a glorious marriage for her,' Mary was saying. 'And I imagine that the Queen is delighted. The Emperor is her nephew. Anyway, as I was saying, there is to be a pageant performed before the King and Queen and the ambassadors. Cardinal Wolsey is hosting it at York Place. Do you want to take part? I can put in a word for you.'

'I should love that,' Anne smiled, trying not to think of the poor little Princess.

Two days later, King Henry came to visit his wife and daughter. He was broader and more solid than ever, a big man with a majestic presence and an easy manner, although Anne could imagine, observing his narrow eyes, red hair and prim mouth, that he could be dangerous when provoked. Only last year he had sent his cousin, the Duke of Buckingham, to the scaffold, for allegedly plotting to take the throne; and Penshurst, where her brother Thomas had once served the Duke, had been appropriated by the Crown. Father had been made its keeper – another office to add to the many he already held.

The King bent to kiss the Queen and spoke to her most lovingly. Then Anne was presented to him. While he still held little attraction for her, when he fixed that piercing blue gaze on her she had to acknowledge that there was a certain magnetism about him. It came, she knew, from the authority he wielded, and his considerable talents. There was no doubting that he was highly accomplished. When he tested the Princess on her Latin and French, addressing her in those tongues, he was fluent, and when, later, he played the lute for the Queen and her ladies, and sang one of his own songs, he had everyone rapt.

It was clear that he loved his wife. Anne had not forgotten the incident with Etiennette de la Baume, and no doubt there had been others – kings would be kings, and she had long had the example of the promiscuous, rapacious François before her – but this was a good marriage. Anyone could see that. Even so, there were some ladies present who could not take their eyes off the King, and even some who went out of their way to attract his attention. Anne was certain that this man had only to beckon with his little finger, and half a dozen of them would fall willingly into his arms – and, no doubt, his bed. But he took no notice of them. He was deep in conversation with his womenfolk.

In the ornate stand at the side of the tiltyard, Anne watched the Queen's face as the King, in gleaming armour, on a lavishly trapped white steed, led the contestants into the tournament ground. Katherine was gazing at him as if adoring a saint, and when he wheeled his mount, bowed in the saddle before her and dipped his lance for her favour, she leaned forward eagerly and tied on a scarf bearing the colours of Spain. The Imperial ambassadors, seated between her and Cardinal Wolsey, beamed approvingly. Then, as the King turned away, Anne saw Katherine's expression change. She was staring at the horse's silver trappings, on which the legend 'She has wounded my heart' had been embroidered.

It was probably no more than a device of the game of love that Anne knew so well how to play, but the Queen looked stricken. Then she seemed to recover herself, as the other knights approached the stand and the ladies jostled to bestow their own favours. A gentleman was saluting Anne. She recognised James Butler, smiling at her beneath his visor.

'My chosen lady!' he called.

She did not want his attention, did not want publicly to acknowledge herself his future wife, but she knew it would be churlish to refuse, so with as much grace as she could muster, she attached her handkerchief to his lance, and he rode off happily enough.

The jousts began, and Henry Norris entered the lists. Anne's heart gave a jolt. He was even more beautiful than she remembered – but he was wearing the Fiennes colours as his favour. Her eyes were drawn further along to the stand where many ladies were sitting, and she saw Mary Fiennes among them, cheering her husband on. She had to look away.

James Butler acquitted himself nobly and won a prize, at which he bowed in Anne's direction, showing the world that it was in her honour; but the King excelled all, and emerged victorious to thunderous applause.

When she left the royal stand in the Queen's wake, Anne took care to stay close to Katherine, hoping that James Butler would not come seeking her out. Fortunately, she was able to avoid him in the throng of people crowding into the pavilion where refreshments were being served. The King was there, enlarging expansively and loudly on his exploits, surrounded by the Queen and an admiring crowd of ladies and courtiers. Anne wondered who was supposed to have wounded his heart. He did not look at all wounded. And who would have dared refuse him? Whoever she was, Anne silently applauded her.

That evening, while the King and Queen were dining in private with the ambassadors, Anne was free, so she hastened to Mary's lodging to put the final touches to the costume she was to wear two days hence in the pageant. True to her word, Mary had secured for Anne one of the coveted parts, doubtless through Will Carey's influence.

She was surprised to find Mary downcast and preoccupied. Her sister was making an obvious effort to be cheerful, but in vain.

'I know something's the matter,' Anne said, picking up the heavy white silk gown to finish embroidering it with gold thread.

'I dare not tell you,' Mary muttered.

'Come now, you must,' Anne insisted. 'I will just worry otherwise.'

Mary's dark eyes brimmed with tears. She always could cry beautifully. 'You must promise not to say this to a soul, especially Will,' she blurted out. 'The King is trying to seduce me – and I do not want him!' Now she was sobbing uncontrollably.

'But that's appalling!' Anne cried, as the motto on Henry's trappings suddenly made abhorrent sense. 'You must say no!'

'I have! And he was angry.' Mary dabbed at her eyes. 'It started at Christmas. He paid me compliments, gave me gifts – and I thought he was just flattering me. But then he started to drop hints that he was prepared to be very generous indeed, and last month he gave Will a grant of land. Will was delighted, but I knew it for what it was – an inducement to let me know that I would be well rewarded.'

'I'm glad you said no,' Anne told her. 'But I expect he isn't used to that. Most women are probably flattered by his attentions. He is the King, after all.'

'I think he expected me to submit without a qualm, but I told him that I was a married woman and feared to offend my husband. He said my husband need never know, and that he had had mistresses before without anyone finding out. I said *I* would know, and that I could not betray Will. No one would believe it, Anne – first King François, and now King Henry! Why me?'

'Some might envy you,' Anne observed. 'I wouldn't.'

Mary was scrunching up the fine silk in her agitation. 'I barely avoided ruining my reputation at the French court. I dare not risk it again here. And I don't *want* the King.'

'I can understand that,' Anne agreed. 'Remove the crown and the fine clothes, and you're left with a fairly ordinary man. You should stick to your resolve and keep your distance. Never give him an opportunity to pursue you.'

Mary looked doubtful. 'He is the King – and he is persistent.'

The great double doors swung open, and the wheels squeaked as the pageant car began its cumbersome progress into the hall, pulled by strong men concealed beneath the foliage that adorned it. Its centrepiece, the flimsy wooden green castle into which Anne and seven other ladies had squeezed themselves, began to judder alarmingly, and they were thankful when it came to a stop.

She could hear the voice of a herald announcing: 'Le Chateau Vert!' Beside her, Mary was still sniffing, her eyes having filled with tears when confronted with the three banners that hung from the castle. They depicted three broken hearts, a lady's hand holding a man's heart, and a lady's hand turning a man's heart.

'He has ordered this!' she whispered to Anne. '*He* thinks to turn *my* heart.'

'Come!' the Duchess of Suffolk had commanded, unaware of Mary's distress, and there had been no time for Anne to comfort her sister, or exhort her to stay strong. She knew Mary was weak-hearted, and feared she would not have the courage to stand up to the King. She would have liked to box his ears – and worse – for doing this to Mary, who had suffered enough at the hands of royalty.

They were silent now, awaiting the blare of trumpets that would signal the start of the pageant. They could hear the applause of the diners, the muffled exclamations of surprise and delight – well deserved too, for Master Cornish, the deviser of the pageant, had created a beautiful setting for it. The castle was surrounded by realistic gardens and bushes, and he must have had an army of seamstresses up for nights making the silk flowers that adorned them.

The trumpets sounded, and Anne and the others ladies adjusted their masks, gathered their skirts and burst forth from the castle. They were wearing identical white satin gowns embroidered with Milan-point lace and gold thread, silk cauls and Milanese bonnets of gold encrusted with jewels. Each had embroidered a name on her bonnet. Anne was Perseverance, Mary was Kindness – a name she now regretted choosing, in case it gave the King some encouragement – Jane Parker was Constancy, and the Duchess of Suffolk, out in front, was leading the dancers in the guise of Beauty.

At the high table before them, the Queen sat with the ambassadors, watching the pageant with evident enjoyment. When the ladies had danced, eight masked lords appeared, clad in cloth-of-gold hats and cloaks of blue satin. They too had names: Love, Nobleness, Youth, Devotion, Loyalty, Pleasure, Gentleness and Liberty. The man who led them wore crimson satin sewn with burning flames of gold, on which the name Ardent Desire was emblazoned. It was Master Cornish, not the King, but Anne knew that Henry was among the eight masked dancers, in the guise of Love. The names, the whole theme of the pageant, seemed to symbolise the King's pursuit of her sister.

At the appearance of the lords, the ladies retreated hurriedly into the castle, whereupon the gallant gentlemen rushed the fortress to an explosion of gunfire, which had some of the audience shrieking. Anne and her fellows defended their stronghold with gusto, throwing comfits at the besiegers, or sprinkling them with rose water. They in turn were assaulted with dates, oranges and other fruits, and of course the outcome was inevitable. The men had to win and force the defenders to surrender. Triumphantly they took the ladies by the hand, escorted them down to the floor as prisoners, and led them in a lively circle dance. Anne saw that the King was partnering Mary. She could sense Mary's fear, dancing with her would-be seducer in front of the Queen and the whole court, with people perhaps drawing conclusions as they watched them together. But when the dance came to an end and everyone unmasked themselves, to much merriment and applause, Mary was nowhere to be seen.

For a moment Anne saw the King standing alone frowning, but he was quickly in command of himself, and headed off to host a banquet for his guests in the Queen's apartments.

Anne was one of those who had been excused attendance. Still in her costume, she hurried off to search for Mary, but could not find her. Concerned, she returned to the hall and sought out George to ask if he had seen her. She found him lounging on a bench, and nearly turned back when she saw that he was with Henry Norris and another man. They were all guffawing at some jest, plainly flushed with wine.

'I've lost Mary,' Anne said, trying not to look at Henry Norris. 'She left before the pageant ended. I hope she's all right.'

'Mary can take care of herself,' George said. 'No need to worry.'

Norris was smiling at her. Her eyes met his, which were warm and admiring, and she looked down.

'No matter,' she said, and walked away, her heart pounding.

She fretted about Mary all that night, unable to sleep. In the morning, before the cold cuts, bread and ale were brought to the Queen's dining room for breakfast, she skipped prayers in the chapel and ran to Mary's lodging. There she bumped into Will Carey, who was leaving for the King's apartments.

'I can't stop, Anne, I'm late,' he cried, and sped off.

Anne raced up the stairs.

'Mary!' she called. 'Mary, are you all right?'

The door opened and Mary stood there, looking tragic.

'Thank God you've come,' she said. 'I thought Will would never go.' Then she dissolved into great gulping tears.

'What is it?' Anne cried. 'Is it the King?'

Mary was retching now, bending double and bringing up clear bile, which dripped to the floor. Anne suppressed the urge to recoil. 'Tell me,' she urged.

'He forced me,' Mary moaned. 'While we were dancing in the pageant, he commanded me to wait for him in the little banqueting house by the tennis courts. He said he had to speak to me. I did not want to go, but I was frightened to offend him. I waited ages, and I was frozen when he did come, and then . . . Oh, Anne, it was awful . . . And now I have betrayed Will, even though I didn't want to.'

It beggared belief that two kings had raped Mary. No one, finding out, would ever believe that she had been unwilling. So no one must ever find out.

'Did he hurt you?' Anne asked, putting her arms around her sister.

'No, but he would not take no for an answer, and I dared not fend him off. I felt dirty, soiled – I could not look Will in the face when I got back. But he too wanted his pleasure of me, so I said I was feeling sick, which was true, for I was terrified that he would guess. Oh, Anne, what shall I do? The King wants to see me again tonight!'

'Don't go,' Anne warned her.

'But I dare not refuse. If he can be generous to our family, he can also withdraw his favour, or worse. I *have* to go. Oh, God, why me? Of all the ladies he could pick on.' And she wept again.

'You could tell Father.'

'Are you mad? He thinks little enough of me as it is.'

Anne sat Mary down on the settle. '*I* will tell him how distressed you are.'

'No!'

'Then plead illness. Go home to Hever. Will would understand.'

'I'd have to be ill indeed to do that. He would hate me being away.'

Anne lost patience. 'Then there is nothing for it, unless of course you complain to the Queen.'

Mary looked horrified. 'That's unthinkable. She is a kind lady and I would not hurt her.'

'Well, I can think of nothing else you can do. I don't know what else to say.' Anne felt utterly helpless and angry. 'It's disgraceful that a king who claims to be virtuous, and sets himself up as the living example of chivalry, can so basely abuse his power and get away with it,' she fumed.

Having made Mary take some bread and ale, Anne left her to her maid and went in search of their father. She found him in the office of the Board of the Green Cloth, seated at a large green baize table looking over lists of household accounts.

He looked up. 'Anne! This is a pleasant surprise.'

'Not so pleasant when you hear what I have to say, Father,' she answered in a low voice. 'And it is for your ears only.' She glanced at the two clerks seated at their high desks. Sir Thomas dismissed them.

'Now,' he said, when they were alone, 'what is wrong?'

'The King has forced Mary to become his strumpet,' Anne told him.

'What?' Father was going a nasty puce colour.

'He gave her no choice in the matter. He raped her, to be plain! I thought you should know.'

'How did she allow herself to get into this situation?' Father barked.

'*Allow herself?* I told you, he gave her no choice!' Anne's temper was rising. 'When the King commands, who dares deny him? And of course, he seems prepared to be very generous. Already he has granted land to Will.'

Sir Thomas sank back in his chair, grim-faced. 'It's deplorable – but it can do her no harm,' he said at length, 'or any of us, for that matter. Bessie Blount was his mistress for five years, believe it or not, and bore him a son. She did very well out of it, and made a good marriage.'

'But Mary is already married, and painfully aware that she is cuckolding Will. What will she get out of it except misery and shame?'

'Money, honours, preferment for her family,' Father said, a calculating gleam in his eye.

Anne gaped at him. He would sell his daughter for money?

'We must all make the best of a bad situation,' he told her.

'I thought you would do something to prevent it.' Anne was furious with him.

'Alas, I am as powerless as Mary is. As you say, no one denies the King.'

'I would!' cried Anne defiantly, and left him sitting there, pushing past with an angry swish of her skirts.

Father was looking very pleased with himself. 'I am appointed Treasurer of the Royal Household and Steward of Tonbridge,' he crowed.

He was walking with Anne along the river front at Greenwich, both of them enjoying the first warm afternoon of spring. It had been days before she could bring herself to speak to him after their altercation over Mary, but there was no avoiding him, and gradually she had allowed herself to thaw a little.

'The wages of sin?' she asked. It had been two months now since Mary had succumbed to the King. Will still did not know, and Mary, while resigned to having to endure Henry's attentions, which she conceded were not so bad, was suffering agonies of guilt.

'I hardly think so!' Father snapped, jolted out of his good mood. 'These appointments are rewards for my long service, and my assistance in indicting the Duke of Buckingham. They are no more than anyone would expect a man of my standing to receive. I resent your implication that I got them only because my daughter is bedding with the King!'

'How can you be so complacent?' Anne threw back.

'I can because I must!'

They walked on in silence, aware of the stares of others. Anne fixed her eyes on the river, where myriad boats were bobbing up and down or making their way towards London or Deptford and the sea. There was a stiff breeze and she had to hold on to her hood.

The King had visited the Queen's apartments this morning and singled Anne out. In the weeks since his seduction of Mary, she had barely been able to bring herself to look at him, she hated him so much. Whenever he appeared, she saw not the monarch in his fine robes, but a selfish, lustful man overpowering her sister, without thought for her feelings or the consequences. He was despicable. So when he had noticed her today and asked her how she was settling in, she had responded with the barest of courtesies.

'Well, your Grace.' She'd kept her eyes downcast. If she had looked at him, he would have seen the loathing in them. It was exactly how she had felt seven years before about King François.

There had been a pause.

'I am pleased to hear it,' King Henry had said, and moved away. But later Anne noticed that he kept looking at her. Was it speculation that she read in his eyes? Shame? Good! She hoped he realised that someone knew him for what he was.

She had not, of course, told Father of her coolness to the King. In his eyes, the sun rose and set with Henry Tudor.

'I should tell you that the Cardinal is dragging out the negotiations for your marriage,' Father said now, breaking the silence. 'I don't know what game he's playing, but it's proving impossible to reach any agreement on the terms of the contract. If it's not finalised by the autumn, I'm pulling out.'

Thank God! Anne thought fervently. 'As I have said before, sir, you would do better to demand the earldom of Ormond for yourself.'

'But you are twenty-one and still unwed. Does that not worry you?'

'Not at all,' she told him. 'I have yet to meet the man I want to marry.'

'You mean, minx, the man I want you to marry!' Father growled.

'Let us hope that they are one and the same,' she said. She did so enjoy provoking him.

Chapter 8

1523

Anne had noticed that of all the young gentlemen who frequented the Queen's chamber, none came more often than Harry Percy.

Katherine always made each one of the eager gallants welcome, and looked on indulgently as they talked and flirted with her maids.

'You may entertain your visitors,' she had told Anne. 'Pour wine for them, play for them, dance with them, but behave with propriety. Your parents are doubtless hoping that I will help to secure a good marriage for you.'

Anne had smiled. The negotiations for her proposed marriage to James Butler had finally been abandoned, and she was enjoying a new sense of freedom and hope for the future.

It was on Harry's third visit that Anne realised he was taking a special interest in her. She had noticed him watching her before, and had not paid much attention, but now, as one of the maids struck up a tune on her lute, he was suddenly standing in front of her.

'Mistress Anne, would you do me the honour of dancing with me?' he asked. She looked up into his green eyes, seeing a tall, lanky but personable young man with curly chestnut hair, strong features and a beak of a nose – not handsome in the conventional sense, but honest-faced and deferential in his manner.

'I should be happy to,' she said, accepting his hand and allowing him to lead her into a *basse* dance. When it ended, he asked her for another, and then another, and presently they were sitting on a cushioned seat in one of the tall oriel windows and talking as if they had known each other for years. Anne saw the Queen watching them, and was reassured when she smiled.

Harry told her that he was twenty-one and eldest son to the Earl of

Northumberland. Until a few weeks ago he had been serving in the north as Warden of the Border Marches. Only this spring had he been released from his duties so that he could join the Cardinal's household, where he served his master at table, showing off the carving skills acquired by every gentleman.

'I hope thereby to gain preferment,' he told Anne. 'Like Master Carey, who has done so well. He is my cousin.' She wondered if Will had told Harry that she was unattached and encouraged him to pay court to her.

'I heard that your father was recently honoured with the Order of the Garter,' Harry beamed. 'It is a great accolade, and I am sure it was richly deserved.'

'We are very proud of him,' Anne said, omitting to add, *and he is very proud of himself.*

All the time they were talking, she was becoming aware of how much she liked Harry Percy. While she did not see him ever arousing her passion, she knew without doubt that she could be friends with him, and sensed that he would never let her down. He was too sincere, too genuine – and plainly smitten with her.

At the end of the afternoon, he assured her that, when the Cardinal was next at court, he would seek her out again. Then he bowed and departed, leaving her feeling at once excited and sad to see him go. She had a good feeling about Harry Percy. Being with him felt part of the natural order of things.

He was as good as his word. No sooner had the Cardinal taken up residence again than Harry was there at the Queen's door. And he returned every day, growing ever more ardent. But Anne was determined not to be hurt or made a fool of, or to appear too keen on him. Occasionally she would absent herself and leave him wondering where she was. Later she realised that there had been no need to play hard to get, and that he had been hers from the first.

Gradually, over that enchanted month of May, the carapace she had built around herself broke down, yielding before Harry's kindness and devotion. Their first kiss was stolen in an arbour in the Queen's privy garden, and it felt very sweet.

She knew that she was falling in love with him, but there was more to it than that. She felt more strongly than ever that he was the right man for her. For all his humble devotion, she was well aware that he was heir to one of the greatest and most ancient earldoms in England, and that she could not look for a better match. Beside him, the forbidden allure of Henry Norris had paled.

'Do you know anything about the Percys?' she asked George one day as they watched a bowls match, contriving to sound as if it were merely a matter of general interest.

'They are great lords,' he told her, 'virtually kings in the north.'

That rang true with what Harry had said. His ancestors had come over with the Conqueror. His family had a long and noble history and had married with royalty. She could be my lady the Countess of Northumberland, far outranking her sister! But her motives were not just mercenary. She wanted Harry himself. He had overturned her jaded perceptions of what men were like, and shown her that honour and respect and devotion were not just empty words. She could think of nothing more wonderful than becoming his wife. When Harry confided that he liked her very much, and would say more if he could, her heart had swelled.

George grinned. He knew! 'You could do a lot worse than marry Harry Percy.'

'What do you mean?'

'It's all over the court – how Anne Boleyn loves him.'

Her cheeks were flaming. 'That's my business!' she flared.

'The Queen's ladies do love to gossip,' George smirked. 'And if you will insist on wearing French gowns and drawing attention to yourself, what do you expect?'

'I expect *you* to rebuke them for their idle chatter,' she retorted.

'Oh, I've better things to do with them!' he laughed.

'No doubt!' she said tartly. George's love affairs were notorious in the court. But then he drew her to him and squeezed her affectionately.

'Seriously, I would be delighted if you wed Harry, and there's no doubt that Father would. So go ahead, dear sister, and seize the blessings that life offers you.'

It was June, and the roses in the Queen's garden were in glorious bloom, when Harry led Anne to a bench, plucked a red rose and handed it to her, then dropped on one knee before her. His eyes were afire with feeling.

'I can hide it no longer – I love you, Anne,' he blurted out, as she sat there with her heart beating wildly. 'Will you honour me by becoming my wife?' She looked down into his eager face and saw nothing but true love writ there, and her heart stilled and melted. He was a good man, a kind man, gentle and loyal. He would never hurt or abandon her, never deceive her or force her to do anything she didn't want to do. With him, her future would be secure. How could she have thought, those first days, that she could never love him?

'Oh yes, Harry!' she breathed, and they stole a lingering kiss, hoping that no one had seen them. It left her hungry for more.

'Then we must be betrothed now!' Harry cried, leaping up, and beckoned to two gentlemen sitting on the grass nearby with some of the Queen's maids.

'Sirs! Will you witness our plighting?' he cried.

Anne was startled at his eager haste. She should speak to the Queen first, and to Father, or rather Harry should, but she was swept along by his enthusiasm, and smiled as the two gallants bowed before her. The Queen could not object, surely, and she knew that Father certainly would not. So she had no doubt that she was doing the right thing when she willingly repeated, after Harry, the promise that would bind her to him for life. 'I, Anne Boleyn, plight thee my troth, Henry Percy, to be your wedded wife.'

'I pray you, sirs, do not speak of this to anyone until I give the word,' Harry asked.

The young men promised, and walked off chuckling, wishing them both happiness and good fortune.

Harry squeezed Anne's hand. 'Let us keep this our secret for now, until I tell my father when he comes to court. Then I will speak to yours. We must do everything properly. But Anne, oh my darling Anne, you have made me the happiest man alive!' And he kissed her again, more hungrily this time. It was bliss!

They tried to keep it a secret, but it was hard, since they were almost never alone. The Queen might encourage flirtations, but she was vigilant. At least she could not hear what they said when they sat in 'their' window seat and talked of their future.

'We must have a big wedding, with many guests,' Harry said. 'I want all my kinsfolk and friends to see what a beautiful bride I have won!' He was looking at Anne with such longing that her heart sang. And then his hand reached for hers under cover of her skirts. He even caressed that unsightly extra nail.

One evening, Anne stole away after dinner and met him in the lime walk that led to the Chapel of the Observant Friars, a little way from the palace. The place was deserted, and as they melted into each other's arms, she could hear the brothers chanting Vespers. The King would be hearing the office in the Queen's chapel. They had an hour at most.

He drew her under the shadow of one of the trees and kissed her with passion. She felt desire stir, lively and insistent, but reined herself in. She was the future Countess of Northumberland, soon to be Lady Percy, and must behave as such. So she made a supreme effort gently to disentangle herself, and took Harry's hands.

'I love you,' she told him. 'Dear heart, we do nothing wrong by loving each other, but we must never give any cause to say that we have behaved improperly.'

'I wanted only to kiss you and hold you,' Harry protested.

'And I wanted that too. But I should go back. It cannot be long until our marriage, and then we will have all the time in the world for loving each other.'

'Alas, I cannot wait that long,' he groaned. 'Every day will seem like an eternity. But I respect your wishes, sweetheart. We will go back.'

As she emerged from the shadow of the tree, she saw a man in black standing some way ahead, at the palace end of the lime walk, a stocky man with bullish features. He was looking in her direction, but when he saw her, he turned away. She hoped he hadn't seen her with Harry, but even if he had, their secret betrothal would soon be a secret no more.

As Anne was watching a game of tennis, Mary appeared.

'I need to talk to you,' she murmured, her eyes pink, as if she had been crying. Anne got up and followed her out of the spectators' gallery, and they walked in the gardens, shivering a little in the September chill.

'I'm pregnant,' Mary said. 'It's the King's. There's no way it can be Will's. We haven't . . . well, not for ages. He's always too tired. Oh, God, what am I going to tell him?'

Anne stiffened. 'Maybe the King can advise you. He got you in this mess.'

Mary was crying. 'I told Hal – I mean, the King,' she sniffed. 'He has not summoned me since. I think it is over.'

'Of course it is not over! He has a child for which he is responsible!'

'He will not own it. He told me there is a legal presumption that any child I bear is my husband's, so there is no cause for scandal. But Anne, I never thought to say this – I miss him. I had grown fond of him. There is something about him . . .'

'Whatever it is, it's not honour!' Anne retorted, thinking how lucky she was to have found a man of integrity like Harry. 'Mary, tell me you have asked him for financial support for your child. Don't tell me you've come out of it with nothing!'

Mary's face told her all. 'I know, I know,' she sobbed, as curious courtiers passing by stared. 'But I had no warning. What am I going to say to Will?'

Anne thought rapidly. 'How far along are you?'

'I have missed two courses.'

'Then you had best entice Will to your bed without delay, and let him think the babe has come early. Or you can tell him the truth. After all, you had no choice in the matter. He should be sympathetic.'

'If I was going to tell him, it should have been in the beginning,' Mary wept. 'He might forgive my succumbing to the King, for I was unwilling, but he will not forgive over a year of deceit. No man would.'

'Then you have to live with your secret,' Anne said. 'I'm sorry, that sounds hard, but it's the lesser of two evils.'

'Please don't tell Father about this,' Mary begged.

'Why not? I imagine he'd be delighted to be grandfather to the King's child! You might even outdo the Queen and bear a son. Then you'll see His Grace's interest revive, I'll wager.'

'Bessie Blount bore him a son, whom he acknowledged,' Mary recalled, brightening.

'Yes, and from what I hear, the boy is being brought up like a prince.'

'But if that happened, Will would have to know.'

'Let's meet that when we come to it,' Anne advised. 'Now, if you'll forgive me, I must go to the Queen. I'm on duty at four.' And Harry was coming to see her this afternoon.

Two days later, the Cardinal and his entourage left for York Place, Wolsey's great palace at Westminster, and Anne began counting the hours until she could see Harry again. The time dragged endlessly, and she spent her leisure hours planning her wedding outfit. Oh, to be of noble or royal rank and wear cloth of gold or velvet! But silver tissue would do very well, and it would be lightweight in the warm weather, for assuredly this would be a summer wedding. She would wear her hair loose in token of the virginity she had so carefully preserved, but she could plait the crown and thread some jewels and ribbons into it.

She was happily daydreaming about her wedding one morning, on her way from the maidens' dorter to the Queen's apartments, when a young man who looked familiar stepped out from under an archway.

'Mistress Anne Boleyn?'

'Yes?' She stopped, startled.

'James Melton at your service, mistress.' Of course. Harry's friend, another of Wolsey's young gentlemen. She recalled that he had once accompanied Harry to the Queen's chamber. He was a gaunt-faced fellow, well spoken and wearing riding clothes of good cloth, but glum of countenance. 'I am come from Harry,' he said.

'Oh!' Anne exclaimed, delighted, but James Melton still looked miserable.

'What's wrong?' she asked.

'I would give anything not to be the bearer of this news,' James said.

Panic seized Anne. 'Tell me he is not ill!'

'No, but he has been forbidden to see you.'

All her joy drained away. 'Why?' she faltered, already marshalling indignant protests in her mind.

'I know very little about what has happened, but I believe he is now on his way north. He wrote to me shortly before he left, bidding me tell you that everything has changed between you two.'

'He has forsaken me?' she whimpered.

'On the contrary, Mistress Anne, he is frantic with worry about you, for he has no means of knowing what you have heard, and would not have you think ill of him. He sounded desperate. He begged me not to suffer you in his absence to be married to any other man.'

'Someone has tried to part us,' Anne said, feeling angry tears well up. 'Was it Cardinal Wolsey?'

James nodded. 'I suspect so.'

'Did Harry not stand up for us? I would have done.'

'I know not what happened,' James said, 'but Harry said he was going to see the Bishop of London. He said he feared to do so behind the Cardinal's back for fear of losing his head, but that the Bishop might be able to help him. But if Wolsey had threatened him like that, the King must surely be involved.'

Anne trembled. 'Not necessarily,' she said, trying to reassure herself. 'Everybody knows it was Wolsey who brought Buckingham down. Wolsey is all-powerful. But why did Harry ask to see the Bishop?' Had it been about their betrothal?

'He didn't say, only that it did him no good, because the Bishop told him he had offended grievously. That's another reason why I think the King is involved. You can read Harry's letter for yourself.' He reached into his doublet, brought out a creased sheet of paper and handed it to her. She took it, her hands shaking, feeling cold to her core, and read. There was no more information, but at the end Harry had written: 'Commend me to Mistress Anne. Bid her remember her promise, which none can loose but God only.'

'What can I do?' Her cry was anguished. 'If the King is behind the matter, we are lost.' And she was consumed with white-hot rage against the man who had such power that he could ruin not only her sister's life, but also her own.

James Melton spread his hands helplessly. 'In truth, I do not know. You might ask the Cardinal's gentleman usher, Master Cavendish, what he knows. There's little that escapes him, for he is often in attendance on His Eminence.'

'Take me to York Place!' Anne begged him. 'I am not needed until this evening. I must find out what has happened.

'I dare not,' James said. 'I should not be seen with you. I only risked coming because Harry is my friend.' It was then that Anne understood the seriousness of her situation. It was not only Harry who had given offence.

'I see,' she said. 'Very well, I will go alone.'

'That is madness,' James warned her.

'I don't care!' she cried. 'I don't give a fig for the Cardinal or the King! I want answers! I am going to make them understand that no one trifles with Anne Boleyn!' She was beside herself.

James looked distraught himself. 'All right, Mistress Anne, I will escort you. But do not expect anything good to come out of this foolhardiness.'

They sat silently in the barge as London rolled past them. Anne had brought her maid, for propriety's sake, as the Cardinal naturally presided over a household of men (although Anne had heard it rumoured that he kept his old mistress hidden away in his private chambers, aye, and had children by her).

At Westminster Stairs they alighted and gave their names at the gatehouse of York Place. James was evidently known and liked, and they were waved through.

'I will take you to Master Cavendish,' he said, 'but then I must leave you. My father would kill me if he knew I was doing this.'

'So would mine,' Anne said, tight-lipped, 'but it matters not.'

York Place was massive, a disparate collection of buildings ancient and new, sprawling around gardens and courtyards, and negotiating it was like finding your way through a labyrinth. But James knew it well, and soon he was leading Anne up a privy stair, which led to apartments of such sumptuous splendour that, for all her misery, she gasped. Every available inch of wall and ceiling had been painted or gilded. No wonder so many people envied Wolsey!

They threaded their way through the throng of gentlemen, officials, petitioners and servants who were waiting to see the Cardinal.

'Master Cavendish should be in his office,' James said, knocking at a fine panelled door. But when it opened, it was Wolsey himself who stood framed in the arched doorway. James hurriedly knelt to kiss his ring, which was extended absent-mindedly, for Wolsey was staring at Anne.

'Master Melton,' he said, 'you are a gentleman of great prescience, for you have brought me the young lady I was about to summon. I wonder how that could be.'

James stood up, visibly trembling. Before he could answer, Anne spoke. 'My lord Cardinal, I insisted on coming to see you, and this gentleman reluctantly agreed to escort me.' Everyone was staring at her, but the Cardinal seemed unaware of them.

'Indeed? How very fortunate that he was at hand. James, I will speak with you later.'

James flushed and bowed himself away. Anne felt awful. He had done her a kindness and she had got him into trouble. But she would get him out of it.

'Your Eminence,' she said, 'I do hope you will not think amiss of Master Melton for his goodness to me. He but brought me a letter from Lord Percy. He was puzzled as to what it was about. It was I who, having read the letter, insisted on coming here.'

Wolsey regarded her wearily. She was repelled by his fleshy jowls and red-veined cheeks. She wished that he would take her somewhere they could discuss this matter in private. It was embarrassing having all these people avidly looking on.

'We shall see,' the Cardinal said. 'No doubt you have guessed that I am aware of your pretended precontract to Harry Percy.'

'There was nothing pretended about it, my lord!' Anne bridled.

'Then you are clearly unaware that Lord Percy was betrothed seven years ago to Lady Mary Talbot, the Earl of Shrewsbury's daughter.' He was watching like a great bird of prey to see her reaction.

'I do not believe it,' she said, striving not to betray how shocked she was.

'Then I am sorry for you. The King and I approved the betrothal at the time. It was a most satisfactory arrangement, the parties being of equal rank.'

This was insupportable! How dare this butcher's son imply, in others' hearing, that she, the granddaughter of a duke, if you please, was not fit to mate with the heir to an earldom!

'In the circumstances,' the Cardinal went on, 'it was rash of Lord Percy to promise himself to you. He must have known that his father would not approve.'

'Harry is an honest man!' Anne cried. 'I do not believe he would have gone so far if he was betrothed to another.' But she was remembering his haste to plight his troth to her. Had he naively thought that it could cancel out his earlier precontract?

'You should know, Mistress Anne, that I have discussed the matter with the King, and he is very angry at your presumption. It is his prerogative to consent to the marriages of his nobility.'

Anne said nothing. What *could* she say? If the King had spoken against them, then all was lost. Her world was falling apart around her, and all that was left was a bleak future in which Harry had no part.

'I spoke to Lord Percy,' the Cardinal said. 'I conveyed the King's displeasure.'

She could imagine it. She only hoped that Harry had given a good account of himself.

Wolsey shifted heavily on his feet and fixed his bleary gaze on her. 'It is coming to something, Mistress Anne, when the heir to a great earldom thinks he can with impunity betroth himself to some foolish girl yonder in the court, and so I told the young halfwit.'

Anne seethed to hear herself described as foolish, and in public. *How dare he!* But Wolsey remained oblivious to her anger.

'I told him I marvelled at his folly in so offending His Grace, and I sent for his father, the Earl, who naturally was scandalised and warned the wilful boy that if he did not break this unadvised contract, he would disinherit him for ever.'

That might explain why Harry had gone to see the Bishop of London – or, given that he had not wanted Wolsey to find out, possibly Harry had hoped that the Bishop would find their betrothal good and valid. But of course he had not, he had not . . .

'Are you listening to me, girl?' Wolsey barked. 'I said that the King's Majesty will complain to your father of you, and require him to ensure that you behave yourself in future.'

That would be rich, she thought, coming from a man who had committed rape.

'How have I misbehaved myself?' she asked. 'I have conducted myself with propriety. I knew of no prior betrothal. I had no doubt that my father would approve such a match.'

'Oh, indeed he would!' Wolsey sneered. 'But His Highness intends to marry you to another person, with whom he is already in negotiations. I understand that the matter is almost concluded.'

'Who?' Anne cried. 'Not James Butler?'

'I am not at liberty to say, Mistress Anne. But I do not doubt, if you know what is good for you, that you will be glad of it, and agreeable to what the King arranges.'

'But I gave my promise to Harry!'

Wolsey's eyes narrowed. 'Think you that the King and I know not what we have to do in as weighty a matter as this? Rest assured, you will not see Lord Percy again. He has been commanded in the King's name not to resort to your company, on pain of His Grace's high indignation, and he is to be married to Lady Mary Talbot as soon as it can be arranged. Now be a sensible girl and accept it.'

'But the Queen approved it! She encouraged us!' Anne was frantic.

'The Queen has no power in such matters.' The Cardinal sighed. 'Mistress Anne, you are proving tiresome, and I have pressing business to attend to. It is the King's command that you leave the court, and go home for a season.'

'No!' Anne protested. 'That is grossly unfair!'

'Are you criticising His Grace's judgement?' Wolsey's eyes were like steel. 'Now go.'

'You have not heard the last of me, *my lord* Cardinal!' Anne cried, caution abandoned in her fury, as a hundred faces turned and gaped.

Anne could not have said how she got back to Greenwich. She was too consumed with hatred for the Cardinal and the King for breaking her betrothal and ruining her life. They had not even allowed Harry a chance to say farewell to her. What rankled almost as much was the malicious, contemptuous way Wolsey had spoken to her. It was his revenge, no doubt, for her family having always looked on him with contempt for the upstart he was. How dare he call her a foolish girl! How dare he imply that she was unfit to mate with a Percy! This was not the King's doing so much as Wolsey's. As for the marriage that His Grace was supposed to be planning for her, she did not believe there was one. It was just a ploy to keep her quiet.

Of losing her beloved Harry she dared not think, for that way lay madness. To have had all within her grasp and to have lost it in an instant was more than cruel. Never again to see that beloved face, feel those warm lips on hers, those loving arms around her . . . He had been the one man she could love, the essence of all that was good in his sex. She would never find another like him. No one would love her like he did. When she thought of all their plans, the bright future that would never happen . . . It was more than she could take. A great waterfall of tears was welling.

She had not been missed. It was easy to slip upstairs to the dorter, throw herself on her bed and give way to her grief, weeping her heart out and emitting pitiful cries.

She did not realise anyone had entered the room until a gentle hand touched her shoulder. The Queen herself was standing there with a look of such compassion that Anne's tears fell even faster. Remembering herself, she started to rise, but Katherine bade her stay where she was.

'Tell me what has happened,' she said, sitting on the stool by the bed and taking Anne's hand.

'I am ordered home to Hever, your Grace,' Anne whispered.

'But why?'

'Your Grace will be angry with me if I tell you.' Anne sniffed, choking back tears.

'Your welfare is my concern. You are my maid and I am responsible for you. If aught goes amiss with you, it reflects on me too.'

Anne knew she must tell the Queen the truth, however hard it was. She sat up, composed herself and said, 'Well then, madam, I see I have been very foolish. I entered into a precontract with Harry Percy.'

Katherine looked startled. 'Did your parents know?'

'No, madam. We are in love. We did not think they would disapprove.'

The Queen frowned. 'That was indeed foolish, Mistress Anne. You should know that a precontract is as binding as a marriage, and that you should both have had your parents' permission – and the King's.'

'I know, I know all that.' Anne could not hold back another sob. 'Madam, we did not mean to offend the King, and maybe they would all have been happy with the match, but the Cardinal said no. He called me a foolish girl! And then it turns out that Harry has been betrothed for years to the Earl of Shrewsbury's daughter. They have packed him off up north to marry her. And I am commanded to leave court!' She wrung the Queen's hand. 'Your Grace, I cannot lose Harry – I love him more than life itself – and I do not want to leave your service. Oh what am I to do?' She buried her head in her hands, her shoulders heaving.

'I will speak to the King,' Katherine said. 'But I cannot promise that it will do any good.'

In a fever of hope and suspense, Anne sought out George and told him what had happened. Seeing her tears, he drew her into his arms. He was shaking with anger.

'How dare he!' he raged against Wolsey. 'Wait till Father hears!'

His support was a comfort to Anne. But there was no comfort to be had of the Queen. Katherine did not tell her what the King had said, only that she must go home to Hever.

'When the time is ripe, Mistress Anne, you may be assured of being welcomed back into my household,' she told her.

Anne was barely holding herself together. 'I thank your Grace. You have been very kind. But madam, I have been treated most unjustly, and I have been insulted.' Wolsey would pay for that. 'If ever it lies in my power, I will work the Cardinal as much displeasure as he has done me!'

The Queen stared at her and swallowed. 'I hope that in time you will find it in your heart to forgive him,' she said. 'Now God speed you.'

I will never forgive him! Anne resolved. Head held high, she went on her way. The carapace was firmly back in place.

Chapter 9

1523–1524

Hever was inestimably dull, but Anne was so unhappy that she did not care where she was. The days were all grey, one much the same as another, and she could take no interest in anything. She had been robbed of her future, and her present was unutterably bleak. As for her past, she dared not think of it.

Mrs Orchard offered a shoulder to cry on. Mother encouraged, then begged Anne to have a care for herself, growing increasingly concerned.

'You must pull yourself together,' she urged. 'There's plenty more eels in the pond!'

Father, of course, was at court. She had not seen him since her disgrace, but she knew he was as furious as he had been when Mary confessed that the King had got her with child and abandoned her. He was not angry with Anne, but with that butcher's whelp who had scuppered the brilliant marriage she had planned, and which would have brought Father so much glory. He was on her side, although he could not openly say so at court. The last thing he would do was offend the King.

There had been no more word of the marriage that was supposedly being planned for her. *All lies!* she seethed. She kept going over and over that interview with Wolsey, whose name she could not now bear to utter. She wished, how she wished, that she had given a better account of herself, put the Cardinal in his place, exposed him for what he was. But her moment would come. She did not know when or how, but she and her family would see him brought down. She had vowed it. He would suffer, as he had made her suffer.

It was a sad summer, made sadder still by news of the death of

Queen Claude from a malady caught in childbed. 'Or from her husband!' Mother observed tartly. 'The world knows that satyr has the great pox.' It was news to Anne, but in England people were prone to believing any gossip about King François and the hated French.

All through that dismal winter, Anne could not lift herself out of her depression.

Father arrived home for a week in February, and showed himself unusually sympathetic.

'Don't look so wan, Anne,' he counselled. 'Time heals. We'll find you a good husband yet.'

She smiled weakly, reflecting on how unlucky she had been. She doubted she would ever give her heart again, even if she did wed.

Father went upstairs to slough off the mud from his journey and change his clothes. When he reappeared, he summoned Anne to the parlour, which was gloomy due to the descending dusk outside. He lit two candles, then sat in his great chair by the fire.

'Sit down,' he said, indicating the settle opposite. 'I have something to tell you. Harry Percy is married. The wedding took place last month.'

She bit her lip. She would not cry. But the news that Harry was lost to her irrevocably was the bitterest of blows. She did not know how she would bear it.

'Thank you for telling me,' she said. 'I'd rather have heard it from you than from anyone else.'

Father nodded. 'Mary is coming home to have her child,' he said. 'Will has agreed. The court is no place for a woman in her condition. Your mother will take care of her.' His voice was brusque. They had all colluded in keeping the truth from Will, who was plainly looking forward to the arrival of his child. Anne wondered what he would say if he discovered it was not his, for he loved his wife. Poor Mary. Her deception was a terrible burden to bear.

Anne knew that the King had taken no interest in Mary since learning of her pregnancy, and for a few weeks, when Will was not around, Mary had been tearful and resentful; but as her pregnancy advanced, she had grown absorbed in the coming child, and Anne began to hope that the King had become a distant memory, and that he would not trouble Mary again. Let the world think this child was Will Carey's – and why should it not?

Anne was sent out of the room. It was not fit for an unmarried woman to witness a birth, Mother said, unwittingly twisting the knife by reminding her that she was not married, and probably never would be. She was twenty-three now, and soon she might be too old to snare a husband. Not that it mattered to her any more.

She went downstairs and sat in her mother's office, reading a book. But the words danced before her eyes – she could not concentrate, not when the great miracle of birth was taking place somewhere above her.

She stood up and went to the window. It was a fine April morning, with blossom on the trees and fluffy clouds in the sky. The gardens looked glorious. It was desperately sad not to be sharing their beauty with the man she loved. She realised to her horror that Harry's image was fading and that she could not quite remember what he looked like, or the sound of his voice. It was eight months since she had seen him, and the worst storm of her grief was over. What was left was this pall of sadness, and soon, no doubt, that would pass too, and she would begin to live again, rather than just exist.

A cry echoed through the castle – the unmistakable wail of a newborn. Picking up her skirts Anne raced upstairs.

'Is all well?' she called through the door.

Her mother opened it, a tiny infant swathed in a blanket nestling in the crook of her arm. 'A girl, safely delivered,' she said, 'and Mary had an easy time, thanks be to God. But Anne, look.' She pulled aside the edge of the blanket and the little face was revealed – the very image of the King. The eyes of mother and daughter met.

'There's no point in making a fuss,' Mother said briskly. 'We must all act as if the babe is Will's. Let us pray he does not notice anything amiss.'

A messenger was sent to summon Will from court, and he arrived at Hever within a few hours. Anne and her mother were present when he came into Mary's bedchamber to find his wife propped up on her pillows, the swaddled infant in her arms.

'My darling,' he cried, 'I am so proud of you!' Mary smiled nervously up at him, and eagerly he took the child, gazing at it in awe.

'My little girl!' he cried. 'And she has the Carey looks!' He was unaware of the collective exhalation of relief around him. Of course, Anne thought, the King is his cousin, which would account for the likeness. Mercifully no one had commented on how large for a seven-months child the baby was. Probably Will had no idea how newborns looked.

The infant was called Catherine, in honour of the Queen, and Father came home for the christening, which was held in the church at Hever. Mary recovered quickly from her confinement and became absorbed in her daughter. Motherhood suited her.

Six weeks later, the family were together again, gathered at Framlingham Castle in Suffolk for the funeral of Grandfather Norfolk, who had died at the venerable age of eighty. Neither Anne nor any of the Howard womenfolk attended the lavish obsequies in Thetford Priory, but they were present at the great reception held in the castle afterwards.

It was good to see George again, and to catch up on all the gossip of the court.

'I do wish I could be there,' Anne said wistfully, as they exchanged news over goblets of wine. 'I miss it dreadfully. It is so dull in the country. Have I not been punished enough?'

'I wish you could be there too,' George replied. 'I'm sure you will be soon. Father has influence. He's just been made vice-chamberlain of the Household. The word is he will be chamberlain next. So I doubt you will have long to wait, Anne.'

'Maybe Uncle Norfolk will put in a good word for me,' she said, watching the new Duke, sumptuously attired in a black damask gown lined with sable, receiving the condolences of his guests.

'He will,' George assured her. 'Family is important to him. He sees us as Howards rather than Boleyns.'

'I didn't realise he was fifty – it's late to come into his inheritance.'

'The old martinet has plenty of vigour in him, never fear. He is well thought of by the King, and aims high accordingly.'

'Come.' She drew George over to where their uncle stood.

Thomas Howard looked down at her with his sharp, heavy-lidded eyes. His craggy face with its beak of a nose was drawn with lines of grief, but the thin lips curved in a smile.

'Well, niece, it is a pleasure to see you,' he said. 'We have missed you at court.'

'I wish I could return, my lord uncle,' Anne told him. 'I am sick to the stomach of being exiled to Hever.'

'I could think of worse places to be exiled to,' Norfolk said. 'Be patient, girl. I will speak for you when the time is right.'

And with that Anne had to be content.

That evening, she and George walked along the ramparts of the castle. She thought her brother was quiet, but put it down to sorrow at the loss of their grandfather, whose presence pervaded this place. George paused and she stood silently beside him, looking out on miles of verdant Suffolk countryside.

'Can you keep a secret?' he asked.

'Of course.'

A shadow passed over George's face. 'I am to be married. Father told me today. It was finalised before he left court.'

'Who is the lucky lady?' she asked.

'Jane Parker,' he said, his voice flat.

'She's quite pretty,' she said, 'and her father is very learned.'

'She's passable, if you fancy that type,' George shrugged, 'but I don't like her. Anne, there's something about her – I can't put my finger on it, but it repels me. I wish to God I didn't have to go through with this.'

'I am so sorry,' Anne said.

George sighed deeply. 'Well, I suppose I shall have to do what many men do when they are saddled with wives they cannot love. I shall breed heirs on her and take my pleasure elsewhere.'

She did not doubt that he would. She wondered at herself for being pleased that he would find some comfort in adultery, when she would roundly have condemned it in other men. 'Try to love her, for both your sakes,' she said. 'Your life will be much happier if you do.'

He smiled at her. 'I will try. We haven't been very lucky in love, have we, Anne? Do you still miss Harry Percy?'

'I do. Has he been at court?'

'No, I haven't seen him. If I do, do you want me to say anything?'

'No!' Anne declared. 'That part of my life is over. I can have nothing to say to a married man.' *Truly*, she thought, *I have moved on.* The pain was still there, but it was a dull ache, not a piercing agony, and she often went hours at a stretch without thinking of her lost love.

It was growing dark. She shivered a little in her thin black silk dress.

'Come, let us go in,' she said.

The months dragged on. In November, Anne and her family journeyed to Morley Hall in Norfolk for George's wedding. Lord Morley was a charming host, and a most erudite man, and kind. He made a great fuss of Mary, who was with child again. Jane Parker made a pretty bride in her crimson velvet gown, her long dark hair flowing loose to her waist. The newly wedded pair were a handsome couple, but Anne could tell that George wasn't happy.

There were cheers at the wedding feast when Father stood up and announced that the King had granted George the manor of Grimston in Norfolk as a marriage gift. Anne felt aggrieved. It was not fair. The King had been generous to Father, and now to George. Why could he not show favour to her and recall her to court?

But when they returned to Hever, a letter bearing the Queen's seal was waiting for her. She was to resume her post after Christmas.

Part Two

'A Spirit Worthy of a Crown'

Chapter 10

Anne sat quietly at the far end of the long oak table in the great hall at Eltham Palace, pretending to ignore the group of courtiers nearby. One, a tall, bearded young man with golden eyes and striking good looks, laid down his lute.

'I've written a poem!' he announced.

'Another one?' asked Sir Francis Bryan, who, for his rakishness, was known as the Vicar of Hell. The men ranged around them at the table laughed.

'There's a surprise,' said George. 'Come on, Tom, let's hear it.'

The young man smiled at them diffidently. 'This one is special.' He looked across at where Anne sat, sipping the last of her wine. It was for her, no doubt.

She had known Thomas Wyatt since childhood, for their families were neighbours in Kent, and the young Wyatts, Tom and his sister Margaret, had been regular guests at Hever. In other circumstances she might have loved him. Some ladies would not have thought twice about accepting his suit and becoming his acknowledged mistress. They would enjoy having mastery over so handsome a man, and might even be tempted to become his mistress in the carnal sense. But he was married and, for Anne, forbidden territory. She had rejected all his overtures, yet that had not stopped him from paying court, playing the game in the accepted way. But why should she waste her chances on a man who had nothing to offer her?

She did like him. If only she had not told him that at the outset. Yet, knowing him to have the sensitive soul of a poet, she had been loath to hurt him, because it was plain as day that he loved her. He haunted the palace galleries she frequented; he waylaid her on her way from chapel or the Queen's apartments; he sang beautiful ballads in the Queen's chamber, gazing at her with longing eyes; he passed her notes. 'I love you,' he wrote. 'Be kind to your unworthy but suffering suitor.' And then, of course, there were the endless poems composed for her alone. And all, all she had spurned.

Now he was making another bid for her favour, as he recited his new verses in that deep, musical voice.

> Forget not yet the tried intent
> Of such a truth as I have meant;
> My great travail so gladly spent,
> Forget not yet.

> Forget not yet the great assays,
> The cruel wrong, the scornful ways;
> The painful patience in denials,
> Forget not yet.

> Forget not then thine own approved,
> The which so long hath thee so loved,
> Whose steadfast faith yet never moved;
> Forget not this.

'Bravo!' the others cried. Anne knew that Tom was looking at her, willing her to praise his work, but she merely smiled.

'I must get back to the Queen,' she said, rising.

'Will you be at the revels tonight, Mistress Anne?' he asked, as eager as a lapdog for a crumb of encouragement.

'Of course she will,' Francis Bryan told him. 'How could one of the brightest young stars of the court not be there?'

'I may come,' Anne said, not looking at Tom. Since returning from Hever, she had thrown herself enthusiastically into the life of the court and become the focus of much admiration. Young people seemed drawn to her, and she was now at the heart of a circle of privileged courtiers whose aim was to enjoy themselves to the full while chasing preferment and success.

The Queen had warmly welcomed Anne back into favour.

'I am pleased to see you wearing English fashions,' she told her.

'My French gowns were becoming a little worn,' Anne replied. 'I refurbished some, and made some new ones.' Fortunately, once Father had learned that she was going back to court, he had proved generous with money for material.

The King had noticed the gowns, too.

'I see you are become an Englishwoman again, Mistress Anne,' he'd said, encountering her in a gallery and bowing. 'In truth, since we are at war with France, I was wondering which side you were really on!' And he laughed at his own joke, his gentlemen guffawing with him. She kept her eyes downcast and murmured her thanks, thinking that she had little cause to thank him for anything.

Several times since then she had again noticed him watching her, but always she had avoided his singling her out. She wanted nothing to do with this man who had brought down her sister and allowed the Cardinal to wreck her own life.

In March, Anne was relieved to hear that Mary had been safely delivered of a son, Henry, who, Mother wrote, was unmistakably Will Carey's child. Mary had put her affair with the King firmly behind her, and was now a happy wife and mother. Things had worked out rather well, Anne thought, as she made her way to the Queen's lodging. Relations between her and Mary were warmer these days, now that Mary was fulfilled in the ways that mattered to her. Anne did envy her a little, but she would not have exchanged her sister's life of domesticity for the exciting existence that was now hers.

Standing with the other ladies behind Katherine in the presence chamber at Bridewell Palace in London, Anne could barely contain her excitement, or her triumph. Today, Father was to be ennobled, advanced to the peerage as Viscount Rochford.

This was the latest in a string of honours recently bestowed on him, and it was one to which he was entitled by virtue of Great-Grandfather

Ormond having held the title. But, Anne knew, he believed it was being given to him as compensation for not receiving the earldom of Ormond, which he was still contesting, and – much to his disgust – for the dishonouring of his daughter.

She watched as he entered the chamber and knelt before the King, who placed the mantle of nobility around his shoulders and handed him his Letters Patent. It struck her as incongruous that such pomp should be compensation for the sordid seduction of her sister. 'The wages of sin,' she observed, unthinking. Still she could not see it in any other way.

Immediately the Queen turned round and frowned at her, and she was covered in embarrassment. But there was no time to regret her faux pas, for all eyes were on the little boy who was approaching the throne – the King's bastard son, Henry Fitzroy, come to be ennobled by his father. There were muffled gasps when his titles were announced: Duke of Richmond, Duke of Somerset. The Queen's smile was frozen on her face. It took a moment for Anne to realise that these were royal titles. No wonder there was excited speculation afterwards; no wonder Katherine was unable to hide her outrage. For Anne heard many people expressing the view that His Grace meant to name the boy his heir. And really, who could blame him? The child was beautiful, strong and sturdy: he carried himself like a prince already; and there was no sign of the Queen bearing another child. Nor would there be, Anne was certain. The chamberers of Katherine's household had not had a bloody clout to wash for over a year now. It was common knowledge among her servants.

It was a pity, Anne thought, that the King's bastard daughter could not enjoy his favour. Maybe one day he would arrange a good marriage for her. It was the least he could do.

'Well done!' Anne cried, clapping her hands, as George raised his racquet aloft and whooped in triumph. Beside her in the tennis court, Jane, her sister-in-law, was silent, her face as sour as it had been these past months. Anne wondered what was the matter with her. George was morose in her company, and only became his usual lively self when she was not there.

'Is something amiss?' Anne asked, a trifle tartly, as she and Jane left the viewing gallery and made their way into the gardens, which smelt sweet after a summer shower. Here they waited for George. She was aware of Tom Wyatt shadowing her, a few paces behind, in the press of people.

Jane turned on her a face full of misery. 'You would not believe me if I told you,' she said. 'George can do no wrong in your eyes.'

Anne was startled at the resentment in her voice. 'You have not tried me,' she retorted. 'If my brother is making you unhappy, I may be able to help.' She guessed that George's philandering was the cause of Jane's unhappiness. He was always flirting openly with other women, and there was talk that he had a bastard son. She had taxed him with it, but he had denied it.

'Well I'm sure he'd pay more heed to you than to me,' Jane muttered. 'If only you knew what he's really like.'

'What is he really like?' Anne demanded to know, irritation rising.

'I cannot tell you, for shame,' Jane whispered. Anne wondered what she meant. It must be something very personal and private, and she was not sure she wanted to know. There was no time anyway, for George, a towel around his neck, and his doublet slung over his shoulder, was emerging from the tennis play and waving, and suddenly Jane was no longer there. She had melted into the crowd.

George joined Anne, and Tom was suddenly at her side, asking if she had enjoyed the game. The three of them sat on the grass and shared out sugar comfits and wine, Anne having brought a stoppered flagon with her, which she passed around. She noticed Tom drinking from the place where her lips had been.

George was well aware of Tom's feelings for her, and how she felt about the situation. He deftly diverted Tom with talk of poetry, a subject that interested them both.

'Recite your latest offering, George,' Tom encouraged.

'Not in *your* presence!' George told him. 'I cannot compete with a master. Besides, the stuff I've written lately is rather mournful, and I would not darken this sunny day.'

'Jane was rather mournful after the tennis,' Anne said. 'She as good as said that all is not well between you.'

George shrugged. 'She's right. Who would be happy with a shrew?'

She placed her hand on his. 'Maybe she is shrewish because you are unkind to her, or do not love her enough.'

'She doesn't want me,' he said.

'Oh yes she does. If she did not, she wouldn't be jealous of the kindness between you and me.'

George stared at her. 'But you're my sister!'

'It does not matter,' Anne said. 'She wants you to be as warm to her as you are to me.'

'Then she is asking for the moon.'

Tom gave a morose chuckle. 'I know how she feels.'

'Dear Tom, you are a married man, and you know you cannot have me,' Anne said, as kindly as she could.

'My marriage is not happy either,' he reminded her. She had heard it before, many times. 'My wife thinks nothing of flirting with other men – and worse, if the truth be told.'

'I wish mine would!' George muttered.

'You are not free!' Anne told Tom. 'I am truly sorry that your marriage brings you no happiness, but I cannot be your mistress in any sense. Let us just stay friends, as we always have been.'

'Alas, it is not enough,' Tom lamented. 'George knows.' Clearly George and Tom had confided in each other.

'Bad luck, Tom,' George commiserated. 'Lord Rochford's daughter must be above reproach when she takes a husband.' It was kindly said, but it was a warning nonetheless. George might see most women as fair game, but his sister was another matter entirely.

'I mean no disrespect,' Tom protested. 'I hope you know that, Anne.'

George got to his feet, drained the flagon of its dregs and handed it down to Anne.

'I must go and change,' he said. 'Behave yourselves when I'm gone.' And with a grin he was off, striding across the grass.

Tom leaned across and took Anne's hand. 'I can't help it if I am dazzled by your beauty and your wit,' he told her. 'I would be tied to you for ever in love. I am yours, Anne, whether you want me or not.'

She sighed. 'Tom, it grieves me to have to reject all your talk of love. I am too fond of you to scorn you. But this must stop.'

Tom's handsome face looked so tragic that she could have cried. He had a way of making her feel very special. She could never love him in the way she had loved Harry, but at least he had made her forget Harry. She had learned to live again and enjoy life. If only Tom was single, then she could, would have loved him.

'I have offered you my heart and service. Do not refuse me. At least allow me to live in hope,' he begged.

'What hope can you have?' she asked helplessly.

'Elizabeth might die' – he gave a mirthless laugh – 'or I could divorce her for adultery.'

She stared at him. This was going way beyond the rules of the game. 'Do you know how costly and difficult it is to get a divorce?' she asked. 'You'd have to get the King's consent to an Act of Parliament. As for dying, Elizabeth is twenty-two, the same age as you!'

'I have told her that I want a separation,' Tom revealed. 'I am ready to ask the King about a divorce.' He was in a bullish mood now. 'If he agrees, would you accept me then, Anne?'

She was staggered – and touched – that he would go so far. He seemed so determined. But there was little hope of his succeeding. She could not see his father, Sir Henry Wyatt, approving of his son being divorced, or paying for it. And Tom, she knew, had little money beyond his salary as Sewer Extraordinary to the King.

'Ask me when you are divorced,' she said lightly, smiling.

'Then I will live in hope!' Tom cried, taking her hand and kissing it fervently. 'Give me a token, I pray you!'

'You're still married, Tom!' Anne reproved him, but before she could stop him, he reached across and snatched a black lace that was hanging out of her pocket. Attached to it was a small jewel that she wore as a pendant.

'My token!' he cried. 'A token of the love I know you bear me.'

'No! Give it back!'

Too late, they both became aware that a hush had fallen, and saw the King, at the centre of his entourage of courtiers, staring at them, his expression inscrutable. They scrambled to their feet and made obeisance, as he nodded and walked on.

Tom thrust his trophy into his doublet.

'Give it to me!' Anne insisted.

'No!' he said. 'It is little enough to have of you. I will cherish it.'

She knew herself defeated. 'Very well, keep it. It is of little worth.'

'It is worth all the world to me,' Tom said.

The following evening, when the tables had been cleared and removed, there was dancing in the presence chamber. A consort of musicians in the corner began playing, and the King rose, bowed to the Queen and led her out. The courtiers watched admiringly as the royal pair performed a stately pavane, and then, at the King's signal, they took to the floor themselves. George was among the throng, partnering a blonde girl – Heaven knew where Jane was – and Henry Norris was with his wife Mary. Anne was asked to dance by Sir Nicholas Carew, Master of the Horse and a friend of the King.

'I think we are related,' he told her. 'About three or four generations back, through Lord Hoo.'

'I think everyone at court must be related in some way or other,' Anne replied, as they trod the stately measure. 'Sometimes the court seems like one big family. It's just a matter of degree.'

'I can't say I see it like that,' Sir Nicholas laughed. 'When you hear all the backbiting and see the cut and thrust of the intrigues – it's a cesspit! Actually, that's just like my family!'

She giggled, and then the dance was over, and Tom was before her, craving the pleasure. She let him lead her into an almain.

'You are wearing my jewel!' she reproved him, spying it around his neck through the open collar of his shirt.

'I'm proud to do so,' he answered defiantly. 'It keeps me in remembrance of you – as if I needed any prompting. Besides, no one knows who gave it to me.'

'Only the King and all his gentlemen! They saw you take it.'

Tom grinned. 'I love you when you're angry, Anne. You are looking divine tonight. That gown is superb.'

She twirled her green skirts, pleased with the compliment, unable to feel cross with him for long.

'I cannot stay,' she said. 'After this dance I must attend the Queen. Already she is sitting down. She is unhappy because the Princess Mary is being sent away to Ludlow.'

'Bid me go, then, and straight away I will do so at your commandment. As long as I can look at you from afar, and feast these poor eyes on your beauty.'

She smiled at him, and let him lead her to the Queen, whereupon he bowed to Katherine and withdrew. A row of ladies and maids waited behind the Queen's chair, and Anne joined the end of it, a step down from the dais.

Suddenly the King was standing before her, tall, broad and magnificent in his suit of purple cloth of gold – a confident man in his mid-thirties, with that air of assurance that royal birth and years of ruling had conferred. He bowed in an elegant, courtly fashion that detracted not at all from his majestic dignity, and she sank into a curtsey.

'Will you do me the honour of dancing with me, Mistress Anne?' he asked, looking down at her intensely from his great height. His eyes were blue and piercing. He smelt of fresh herbs – she remembered that from when she had danced with him before, at Lille, in another life.

One did not refuse the King, much as she wanted to. She gave him her hand, bowing her head so that he should not see the hatred and contempt in her eyes. One dance, and that would be it.

'You are very quiet tonight, Mistress Anne,' the King observed, as they set the pace in a *basse* dance. 'Usually, I have noticed, you have a lot to say for yourself.'

'I am a little tired, your Grace,' she said, her manner cool.

He gripped her hand. 'Why won't you ever speak to me?' he growled.

She feigned astonishment. 'I? Sir, it was never my intention to offend you.'

'Every time I speak to you, you do your best to ignore me,' he muttered, with startling fervour. 'At other times you avoid me. Why? Am I not pleasing to you?'

Anne glided around on his arm, startled. She had never dreamed that he had thought of her in any way beyond the ordinary. 'Sir, the King's condescension is pleasing to everyone, including me. I fear you have misunderstood my awe at being in your presence for rudeness, and I am heartily sorry for it.' The words were courteous, yet still she would not bend to him.

'I am relieved to hear that,' he said, looking at her with that inscrutable gaze. 'Yet it is I who am in awe of you. I have been watching you, and admiring you, for some time, fearing to approach you because of your coldness. If you could find it in your heart to be just a little kind, it would be a great happiness to me.'

'Kind to you, sir?' What *did* he mean? 'How could I not be kind to my sovereign?'

'You mistake my meaning,' the King murmured, as they moved closer in the dance. 'I am struck with a dart, Mistress Anne, and I do not know how to tear it out.'

Now there was no mistaking his meaning. Her eyes met his, but she looked away quickly, frantically casting about in her mind for some way to deflect him.

'Sir,' she said, 'since you are married to the Queen, my good mistress, I know not how to answer you.'

'You know well enough how to answer Master Wyatt!' Henry flared.

'He is not the King of England,' she faltered, fearing the consequences of provoking this man. 'And *he* is married too, but I am not afraid of reproving *him* for his pursuit of me. You see, sir, I am jealous of my good name, and I love and fear God. I cannot risk tangling with one who is forbidden to me, however well I think of him.'

The King's eyes narrowed. 'But you are not above dancing with Wyatt.'

'I have known him since childhood, as a friend, sire. I danced with him as a friend.'

His face softened. 'Will you dance with your King as a friend too?'

'Sir, how could I do otherwise, when your Grace has been so generous to my father?'

'I have been glad to show favour to your family, and he has served me well,' Henry said. 'I am prepared to be more generous still.' His meaning was blatant.

Anne stiffened. Mercifully the dance was coming to an end. 'As you were to my sister?' she asked in a low voice, unable to stifle her animosity.

He stared at her. 'I was fond of your sister,' he muttered. 'But these things end . . . It ran its course.'

She gave him a look. 'From what I heard, there was less fondness than force.'

'Anne!' the King said, his eyes blazing with something other than anger. 'Do not let Mary poison your mind against me. She came to me willingly enough.'

'She told me that your Grace gave her no choice.' Oh God, Father would kill her for this – if the King didn't do so first.

Henry's face, rosy from exertion and turmoil, flushed deeper. 'Is that really what she told you? Well, as a gentleman and a knight, I will not gainsay her. But I pray you will not think ill of me for taking only what I believed was offered freely.'

Anne could not allow that to pass. 'Offered so freely that she was distraught and in tears afterwards! I know – I was there.'

The music had stopped. Hastily Anne dropped a curtsey, as the King bowed. She had gone too far, she knew. Her family would be ruined, and she herself irrevocably disgraced. What had she done?

But Henry was regarding her with that intent gaze. 'I pray you, dance with me once more,' he invited. 'I would make things right between us.'

'Sir, forgive my boldness, but there can be no "us", and there is no need to make anything right.'

'Then I will escort you back to your place,' he said in a steely voice, and when they got there, he bowed again and left her.

She waited for the blow to fall. Any moment the order might come for her banishment from court, or even her arrest. Men had been imprisoned – and worse – for lesser offences. Or Father might descend on her like a vengeful angel, demanding to know why he had been dismissed from his offices. Again and again she regretted her renegade tongue.

But nothing of the kind happened, and the next time the King paid the Queen a visit, he smiled at Anne and asked her to play her lute for them.

'You play very well,' he told her, when she had finished.

'Not as well as your Grace,' she said, seeking safety in the correct, the expected, response. And all the while Katherine was smiling at them both, poor deceived woman.

And then it was Christmas, with the usual revelry, a time when good order was turned on its head and all ceremony was forgotten. The King roared with laughter when the Lord of Misrule tapped him with his wand of office and demanded his fee of five pounds – right now, sire! There was a game of Hoodman Blind, when the Master of the Revels, blindfolded, chased the shrieking courtiers through the royal apartments, Anne running with Tom, hand in hand, and hiding behind an arras, with Tom trying to snatch a kiss, and her neatly ducking away. And then there were the disguisings. Anne was astonished one evening when a man wearing an elaborate mask, clad entirely in green, caught her under the kissing bough suspended from a roof beam above the doorway, twisted her round to face him, and kissed her heartily on the lips. She knew, by his large presence and the smell of herbs, that it was the King, but pretended ignorance, breaking away and running off down the deserted galleries until the sounds of merriment had been left far behind and there was not a soul to be seen.

She was just about to retrace her steps, for it was cold here, and she wanted to be back in the warm, enjoying the revelry, when she heard a footfall, and another, growing closer, and there he was, still masked, framed in the archway at the further end of the gallery. She realised that they were entirely alone. Her heart beat furiously as he approached with an air of determination. She did not want this, did not want him as she feared he wanted her. She remembered how King François had raped her sister in a room off a deserted gallery such as this.

'Anne!' Henry said, in that high, imperious voice. 'Do not fear me. I am no rapist, as your sister alleges. For weeks now I have been unable to think of anything but you.' He was standing before her now, the big, powerful man, looking as diffident as a schoolboy. 'I come to you as a supplicant, hoping you will take pity on me.'

She did not want to go through more anxious days worrying that she had offended him, so she kept her voice sweet. 'Sir, I am flattered to receive the attention of so great a king, but in truth I do not know how I can help you.'

Henry pulled off his mask and placed his hands on her shoulders, fixing her with that magnetic gaze that had no power to move her. She could never love him. The essential alchemy that should be between male and female was decidedly absent.

'Anne!' He sounded quite emotional. 'You have cast an enchantment on me. I do not know how to explain it. It seems presumptuous to use the word "love", but I know what I feel. I do not sleep at night; I see only your face before me. I am in torment!'

'Sir!' she cried, shocked that he might think she dabbled in witchcraft. 'I have cast no enchantment! I am your good subject, nothing more.'

For answer, his hands slid down to her waist, and he drew her to him. His hold was strong, and in that moment she understood how it must have been for Mary, and how vulnerable she herself was. 'I want you, Anne,' he murmured in her hair. 'I want to be your servant, and I want you for my mistress.' The passion in his voice alarmed her. 'Venus, that insatiable goddess, has brought me to this pass, but I pray that you, sweetheart, will be kind to me.'

'Sir!' Anne went rigid in his arms, and he let her go, standing back and looking at her with such longing that she almost took pity on him. To think that she, plain Anne Boleyn, had power over this man who held the lives of thousands in his hand. But she did not want him!

What was the right, the proper, answer? Frantically she sought in her mind for a way to deflect his interest without offending him.

'Sir, may I have time to think on this?' she asked at length. 'Your Grace has so overwhelmed me that I do not know what to say to you. Please give me time.'

'Of course,' the King agreed, his face jubilant, for now she was playing the game properly. Except that this was not a game.

Chapter 11

1526

'Declare I dare not' indeed! What was the King about? She had told him, several times now, that she could not love him or be his mistress, as he was married. She had said it in sorrow, in regret, in indignation and in anger – and still he would not take no for an answer. Instead he had bargained that, in return for his promise never to compromise her virtue, she would permit him to acknowledge her publicly as his mistress, and himself as her devoted servant. Thus no one would be offended, he pointed out, with that naive streak that she was learning was as much a part of his character as his imperiousness, his sentimentality and his courtesy.

Still she had said no, and now he had gone too far, wearing that enigmatic motto with the device of a man's heart in flames emblazoned on his trappings of cloth of gold and silver as he thundered into the lists. For all the world to see! Even the Queen was looking at it, her adoring eyes narrowing in a slight frown. Henry had become so importunate lately that some must have noticed his singling Anne out, and it didn't take much perception for someone – not Katherine, God forfend – to put two and two together and make five.

How she held her patience during the jousts she did not know, shivering in her furs in the freezing February weather. She was beginning to feel cornered, and coming to the realisation that decisive action was called for. She was torn between running away – her preferred, instinctive option – or reprimanding her sovereign, which, if she *were* his mistress, as he wanted, she was entitled to do!

But why, she asked herself angrily, should I have to leave court because he can't contain himself? No, she would stay. He would not drive her away. Yet she would not make it easy for him.

There was a commotion in the lists. Francis Bryan had been felled, and blood was spouting from his eye. People, even the King, came running to help. Anne could not bear to look. Poor Bryan! Pleading a headache, she asked the Queen if she might go and lie down, so that she would be nowhere to be seen when the King came with his guests to have supper with his wife.

But she could not lie down for ever. Morning came, as relentless as Fate, and there were duties to be attended to. And there he was, looking like a naughty schoolboy, lying in wait for her in the antechamber to the Queen's rooms. As she paused, startled, to curtsey, he closed the door behind her, leaving them alone. No ushers, no grooms, no maids. He must have dismissed them. She was uncomfortably aware that only yards from the inner door, the Queen was having her breakfast.

'I trust you are recovered, Mistress Anne,' Henry said, taking her hand and kissing it, even the place where that ugly sixth nail grew.

She drew it away. 'I am recovered from my headache, thank you, sir. I have yet to recover from seeing you publicly proclaiming your feelings at the tournament. Truly that was unfair of you. I felt like running away.'

He looked stricken. 'Never do that to me, Anne,' he begged. 'I cannot live without you. I have never been this powerfully attracted to any other woman. Help me, please! Give me *some* crumb of affection.'

'Alas, sir, you are not free, so it would not be proper. How is Francis?'

Henry grimaced. 'His eye cannot be saved, but he will otherwise recover.'

'I am so relieved to hear it. Forgive me, sir, Her Grace is waiting, and I shall get into trouble if I am late. Fare you well!' She pushed open the inner door and almost fled from him.

Mary came up to court in March, leaving her little ones at Hever to be spoiled by their doting grandmother. Anne visited her in Will's lodging; he was waiting on the King, so they could talk freely.

149

This was the first time that Anne had seen Mary since Henry had started paying court, and she suddenly found herself wanting to confide in her. Mary was the one person who would understand her dilemma. But how would she take the news that her former lover was pursuing her sister?

Mary was waxing lyrical about her children, and Anne listened restlessly for a while, then stood up and walked to the fire, stretching out her hands to warm them.

'What is it?' Mary asked. 'You seem agitated.'

'I need to tell you something, Mary,' Anne said. 'The King is trying the same tactics with me as he did with you.'

Mary gaped at her.

'He is becoming very persistent, and I know not how to deter him. He wants me to become his mistress.'

'You mean he wants to bed with you?'

'Of course. I am not so foolish as to think he has a purer motive. For all his fine words, this is all about lust. Believe me, I understand now how it was for you, although he insists you consented.'

'That's not true!' Mary cried out. 'He made me! You saw me afterwards.'

'I told him so. I taxed him with it,' Anne said, sitting down again and taking Mary's hands in hers. 'He still said he believed you were willing, and of course I don't accept that for one moment. But *I* am not willing, and mercifully he has not tried to force me.'

'You are lucky,' Mary said, drawing her hands away and reaching for the tiny smock she was sewing. 'He is the last man you should tangle with.'

Anne looked at her sister, the epitome of domestic contentment. Father still thought that Mary could have done better for herself by holding the King to his responsibilities and asking for money, but at least Mary was happy now. And she herself had learned a salutary lesson from her sister's experience, for it had forewarned her of the King's fickle nature. The woman he pursued today might easily be discarded tomorrow. Anne Boleyn was not going to end up as another abandoned royal mistress.

'I don't encourage him!' she protested. 'I can't fend him off. And then there's Tom Wyatt pressing his suit – and he's married too!'

'You can't really blame Henry, I suppose,' Mary said. 'The Queen is so devout and virtuous, she looks old and she's lost her figure – hardly an enticing prospect.'

It was true, although Anne felt disloyal in agreeing, for Katherine had been kind to her. But the Queen had no joy in life any more, and no sexual allure. Without boasting, Anne knew she had both these things, and must appear delightful to the King in contrast to his wife's piety and solemn dignity.

'Well, he can go and look for someone else to entice him,' she said. 'I'm going to end it.'

But that proved more difficult than she had thought.

One spring evening, Henry invited Anne to walk with him in his privy garden, a place only the privileged entered, and in that small paradise of Nature tamed by man into neat, railed flower beds and gravelled paths, he led her into an exquisite little banqueting house. There, on a table, lay four gold brooches. He presented them to her as if they were votive offerings to a deity. She looked down in dismay at the beautiful pieces lying in their velvet nest: one represented Venus and Cupid, the second a lady holding a heart in her hand, the third a gentleman lying in a lady's lap, and the fourth a lady holding a crown.

She took the meaning in the first three – it was the crown she did not understand.

Henry saw her turning it over in her hand. 'It symbolises aloofness or virginity,' he said, 'which I think is highly apt. It is also symbolic of your holding the love of a king. You do like them?' He was almost boyish in his eagerness.

'They are beautiful, sir,' she said, 'but I am unworthy of them.'

'Nonsense!' he declared. 'Even though they can only be eclipsed by your beauty, they will enhance it. To me, remember, you need no adornment, but I should like you to wear these tokens of my love for you.'

'Then I must wear them in private,' Anne said, 'or people will wonder how I acquired such costly jewels.'

'Let them!' he cried.

'But I dare not,' she protested. 'I'm not sure that I should even accept them, sensible though I am of your Grace's generosity.'

'Oh, but you must, Anne. I commissioned them for you alone. Please wear them, in private if you must, and think of me when you do.'

She sighed inwardly. There was no gainsaying him.

'Very well,' she said. 'Thank you.'

'And will you give me something in return?' Henry asked. 'I beg only for a small token.'

How could she deny it, seeing he had been so generous? She drew a ring from her finger and gave it to him. It was a trifle, of little value, but he kissed it with reverence and pushed it down to the first joint of his little finger.

'I will have it resized,' he said, beaming.

He wore it all the time, but she never wore the brooches. To her, they symbolised something sordid: the price of her body and her virtue. She hoped that Henry, not seeing them, would get the message.

Summer blazed forth in all its golden glory, and still Anne had not succeeded in rejecting the King. The more evasive she became, the more ardent was his pursuit. He had taken care to be discreet, but if he carried his heart on his sleeve like this, the whole world would soon notice. All their trysts had to be snatched in secret, often under cover of darkness. She could not even bring her maid, but she had come to trust Henry. He was always the supplicant, never the conqueror.

'Be mine!' he urged yet again, as he clasped her in his arms. He had summoned her to his bowling alley, deserted in the late evening. 'I want to hold you and love you . . .'

'I cannot love you!' she replied. 'Not only on account of my honour, but also because of the great love I bear the Queen. How could I injure a princess of such great virtue? I live in daily dread of her finding out about . . .' She would not say the word 'us'. It implied collusion.

'She would not know,' Henry hastened to assure her. 'I would act with the utmost discretion.'

'No!' Anne cried, startling the birds roosting in the branches of a nearby tree. She did not want this covert, secretive kind of relationship. She wanted a pure love that she could blazon to the world.

'Please!' Henry's hand stole around her waist, his breath hot in her ear. 'It will not be like that. I will love you and honour you. There is no limit to what I would do for you. You can have whatever you want – riches, houses, jewels – if you will consent to becoming my mistress.'

Anne shook him off and moved away. 'Is that your idea of discretion? Surely your Majesty is jesting, or trying to test me? And to ease you of the trouble of asking me the question again, I beseech your Highness most earnestly to desist and take my refusal in good part. I fear for my soul. I would rather lose my life than my honesty, which will be the greatest and best part of the dowry I shall bring my husband.'

Henry looked as if she had slapped him.

'Well, Mistress Anne,' he said, 'I shall live in hope.'

She rounded on him.

'I understand not, most mighty King, how you should retain such hope. Your wife I cannot be, both in respect of my unworthiness, and also because you have a queen already. Your mistress I will not be! And now, sir, I beg leave to return to my duties.'

'Anne!' groaned Henry. 'Don't do this to me. I am in torment!'

He was like a man possessed – no, he *was* a man possessed. Anne's refusal to sleep with him seemed only to make her infinitely more desirable.

'Why these constant excuses?' he asked plaintively, as they stood by the river at Greenwich one night, in the shadow of the chapel. 'I would not make you do anything against your will, sweetheart, much as I desire you. But if you will consent to be my mistress, and let me be your chosen servant, forsaking all other, then I will respect your virtue and humbly do your will.' Once, Anne could not have imagined Henry Tudor doing anything humbly, but he had surprised her. He was like a puppy, craving a scrap of attention.

And then it came to her. Why not? She knew she was growing warmer towards Henry, simply by dint of getting to know him, and being adored by him. She knew there was much to like about him, and there were many interests they shared: music, art, poetry, sport and stimulating conversation. All of that made her feel kinder towards him, but it was not love, and she could not feel the passion, or anything even approaching it, that he craved of her. And yet being his acknowledged mistress might have its advantages. For the first time since Henry had noticed her, she felt ambition stirring within her. She would have influence, patronage, riches . . . all the things Mary had failed to obtain. And she would not have to give anything in return.

She kept him in suspense for a time as she considered. Then she smiled. 'Sir, I *will* be your mistress, but on two conditions. One is that you do nothing to compromise my honour. The other is that this remains a secret between us, as is proper for a mistress and a servant. I do not want the world thinking I am your whore.'

'Anything, anything, darling,' Henry agreed, tears shining in his eyes. 'You have made me the happiest of men! Let us seal our love with a kiss.' And he bent his lips to hers and kissed her properly for the first time, as if he would devour her. She disengaged herself as soon as she could.

The problem was, Henry would not play the game by the rules. He assumed that Anne was now as ardent as he was, and that she would not mind his constantly trying to kiss or caress her, or even his hand straying to her breast. It was plain to her that the terms on which she had insisted could never satisfy him. She avoided his company as often as she could, but he would not allow it. Always he sought her out. In the end, pleading illness, and praying that the Queen would believe her, she asked if she might have leave to go home to Hever.

Mother was surprised to see her.

'You look well enough to me,' she said, releasing Anne from a welcoming embrace.

'In truth, I am,' Anne admitted, and gave a sketchy account of being pursued by a persistent married suitor.

'I dare not name him, for he is a great lord and could make trouble for me, and for us all,' she said, in response to her mother's probing.

'Then you did the right thing in absenting yourself,' Elizabeth Howard said, looking at her speculatively.

But Anne was not to be left in peace for long. Daily, letters arrived from the King, under cover of a plain seal. He was in torment. Why had she left him? How had he offended her? What was he to do without her? When could he look to see her? It was clear that her absence had only inflamed his ardour the more fiercely.

Hoping to stem the torrent of pleading, she wrote to him, courteous, non-committal letters worded only to cool his passion.

He responded vehemently. Reading them, he said, had caused him great distress, for he did not know whether to interpret them to his advantage or otherwise. He prayed that she would let him know her mind concerning the love between them.

Between us? she thought. It was all on his side.

Of necessity, he must have an answer, he insisted, having for more than a whole year been struck with the dart of love. She had to smile at his courtly way of putting it. Thanks to this new coolness on her part, he continued, he had not known of late whether he was entitled to call her his mistress, for the very name denoted a special love, far removed from common affection. But if it pleased her to be his true, loyal mistress and friend, and give herself up, heart, body and soul, to him – who, he reminded her, had been, and would be, her very loyal servant – he promised her that not only would he then call her his mistress again, but that also he would take her for his *only* mistress, rejecting from his thoughts and affections all others save her.

And she had thought he had dedicated himself to her alone! It sounded very much as if he had been dallying with other ladies as well. Did he think he was doing her an honour?

He had ended by beseeching her to give a definitive answer to what he aptly called his ill-mannered letter, and tell him how far he might trust in her love. He had ended it: 'Written with the hand of him who would willingly remain your H.R.'

She would not reply, she decided. But he wrote again, chiding her for her tardiness, begging her to assure him of her well-being, and enclosing jewels he thought would please her. His tone was abject and

155

pleading. Again she did not respond. In his next letter she detected a hint of irritation at her evasiveness, so she answered that she might return to court in the company of her mother. That prompted an outpouring of joy. But she could not have him assuming that she loved him too much to stay away, so she sent a messenger to say that she had changed her mind and could not come after all, even in her mother's company.

By return, a miserable complaint came winging its way down the leafy lanes to Hever. She was being unduly hard on him. She had not written often enough. It was a long time since he had been assured that she was in good health, so the great affection he felt for her had led him to send again to her, to be the better ascertained of her health and pleasure. He marvelled at her changing her mind about coming to court, seeing he had assured himself that he had never offended her. He thought it small recompense for the great love he bore her to keep him thus distanced from the person he most esteemed in the whole world. 'And if you love me as I trust, this severing of our two selves should cause you some vexation at least. Your absence grieves me greatly, and if I knew that you truly desired it, I would only lament my ill fortune, and regret my great folly.'

She laid down the letter and rested her head back against the settle. She did not love him, or want him as a lover – he should have realised that by now, yet he persisted in his fancy that their feelings were mutual. He really believed it.

She wished she had managed to put him off in the beginning. She thought she might just stay here at Hever and die an old spinster!

By Christmas, Anne felt like climbing the walls with boredom. She had driven her mother to distraction, veering from one mood to another, until in the end Lady Boleyn had insisted that she tell her who was causing all this to-do.

'Nearly every day letters arrive for you! What is going on?'

In the end, Anne told her, unable to contain herself. 'The King is pursuing me. He wants me to be his mistress, and I am trying to fend him off!'

Mother's jaw dropped.

'Tell no one, not even Father. I'll not have him thinking I'm the King's harlot.'

'You think I would? One daughter is enough!' Mother was striding up and down the parlour in agitation. 'It's not right, what the King is doing, and it's not right your being here when you should be serving the Queen. Heaven only knows what she thinks is wrong with you. You could lose your place. And then it will be more difficult to find you a worthy husband. You're nearly twenty-six as it is.'

Anne winced. She did not need to be reminded of that.

'You must return to court,' Mother was saying. '*I* will accompany you, and I will not leave your side.'

'I am most gratified to hear that you are recovered,' Queen Katherine said, as Anne and her mother were announced. Her welcome was warm, and she hastened to assure Anne that she had assigned her only the lightest tasks. She was pleased to see Lady Boleyn too, and willingly agreed that Anne should stay in her father's lodging while her mother was at court.

Mother's presence put paid to Tom Wyatt's hopeful pursuit of Anne. He was playing his lute in a window embrasure when they arrived, and his eyes had filled with joy at the sight of Anne. He jumped up and hurried to greet her, but Lady Boleyn loomed large, for Anne had told her about Tom too, relying on her mother to keep him at bay.

'Why, Thomas Wyatt!' Mother cried. 'How good to see you! How is your dear wife?' At which Tom had rapidly subsided and stammered that Elizabeth was well but preferred to avoid the court.

'She should come more often,' Mother said, and swept Anne away.

The King, of course, was another matter. He was beside himself with joy when he came upon Anne and her mother taking the air in the gardens later that day, but after a courteous greeting, he made the mistake of telling Lady Boleyn that she might leave.

'Your Grace,' Mother replied, 'Anne has told me that you have honoured her with your attentions, and she has also assured me that you are concerned to protect her reputation, so I make no doubt that you will allow me to stay.' She smiled sweetly.

Henry's eyes bored into hers. 'Madam, are you questioning the honour and chivalry of your King?' he asked, in a tone that boded no good.

'Sir, my lady means no offence, but I should like her to stay,' Anne intervened. 'As you have graciously said, you would do anything for me. I am sure your Grace would not wish to see the virtue of one whom you have been pleased to serve as your only mistress compromised by her being alone with a gentleman, even the most chivalrous one.'

His eyes narrowed. 'I will see you later, Anne.' He did not say the word 'alone', but she was sure he meant it.

I think not! she said to herself, and that evening sent word that she had suddenly developed a raging stomach ache.

She had not been back at court two days when an angry Henry caught up with her as she was enjoying a brisk walk along the lime avenue at Greenwich, accompanied by her maid. It was a fine December day, the sun shining, the air crisp.

'Why is Master Wyatt flaunting your jewel?' he demanded to know.

'He took it from me last year,' she said, startled. 'He would not give it back.'

Henry was not mollified. 'I was playing bowls with him just now. The winning cast was mine, but he disputed it. He measured the distance with the lace on your jewel. He almost waved it in my face.'

'Sir, I assure you, I have no feelings for Tom Wyatt beyond friendship. As I told you, he is married. It would be out of the question.' She looked at him pointedly.

Henry gripped her arm. 'You assure me there has been nothing between you? He seems to think otherwise.'

'Let go, sir! You are hurting me. Of course there has been nothing. I have never encouraged him. You yourself saw him steal that jewel.'

Henry let her go. 'Ah, so that was how it was. Forgive me, sweetheart,

I did not mean to doubt you. It's just that you are so precious to me that the thought of your loving another is unbearable.'

'Then all is well,' she said, wishing she dared say that she loved no one.

When she judged it safe, which was as soon as Henry had gone to meet with his Council, she went looking for Tom, and found him near the mews.

'You fool, you stupid fool, flaunting my jewel before the King!' she berated him.

'Then it's true,' he said. 'You love him.' It was an accusation.

'*He* loves *me*, but you must never speak of it. I can't believe you set yourself up as a rival to him.'

'He provoked me,' Wyatt protested. 'He insisted he had won at bowls. When he pointed to the ball, I recognised your ring on his finger, and I was staring at it, and he said, "I tell you, it is mine!" He wasn't referring to the winning ball. I wanted to make it clear to him that you were mine first.'

'I was never yours!' Anne declared, furious. 'You have made it impossible for our friendship to continue.'

'Not so!' Tom argued. 'Hear me out. I said that, if he would give me leave to measure it, I hoped it would be mine, and I took your jewel from my bosom and measured the distance with the lace. I know he recognised it, for he got very angry, and said I might be right, but he had been deceived. And then he stalked off.'

'You both acted like two cocks fighting over a hen!' Anne reproved him. 'And now this farce must end. I pray you, give me my jewel back.'

'No!' Tom protested. 'I love you, Anne – I cannot bear to lose you.'

'You never won me,' she said sadly. 'It could not be.' She held out her hand and reluctantly he laid the trinket in it.

'So you love the King now?' he asked.

'He likes to think so,' she said.

There was sympathy as well as sadness in Tom's eyes. 'You do not have to do this, Anne. It's not worth it.'

'I have no choice. He will not let me go.'

'You know I will always be here for you,' Tom said.
'I know that,' she said, and walked away.

That night, returning to Father's lodging, she found a note waiting for her. Breaking the seal, she saw that it contained just a few lines of verse.

> Who list her hunt, I put him out of doubt,
> As well as I may spend his time in vain.
> And graven with diamonds in letters plain,
> There is written her fair neck round about:
> *Noli me tangere*, for Caesar's I am,
> And wild for to hold, though I seem tame.

Suddenly she was seeing it through a blur of tears.

Chapter 12

1527

'Wyatt has been sent to Italy,' Francis Bryan said, his single eye full of mischief. 'The King has apparently just discovered that he has good diplomatic skills, and a mission has been found for him.' He winked at Anne. They were in the Queen's chamber, where Anne and the other maids were putting the finishing touches to their masque costumes. No fool, Francis, who was close to Henry, had guessed that his master was pursuing her. It was as well that Tom was out of the way. Life would be less complicated.

The King had fallen out with the Emperor, after five years of amity, and was again looking to France for friendship. Anne was delighted, for most of her happiest memories were of her years at the French court, and she was hoping that this new alliance might afford her an opportunity to visit there again. Of course, life had moved on. Poor Claude was dead these three years, and Marguerite had married the King of Navarre, but it would be good to be back, if only for a short while.

Lavish preparations had been made in honour of the French ambassadors who had come to negotiate the marriage of the Princess Mary to the French King's son, which was to seal the new *entente*. Anne was present, in attendance on the Queen, at all the feasts and jousts that were laid on in honour of the visitors. She watched as the King showed off his eleven-year-old daughter, the pretty red-haired child, but small for her age, and skinny, and heard the ambassadors praising her lavishly. Anne knew that the Queen was bitterly unhappy at the prospect of her daughter marrying a French prince, for France and Spain were old enemies and her prejudice was deeply engrained. But she presented a smiling face to the embassy, and played her part faultlessly.

Anne had seen Henry hardly at all, for he had been busy playing host and engrossed in long private talks with the ambassadors. But after a few days she received a note, delivered by an usher in the royal green and white livery. 'Come to the chapel at midnight. I would speak with you. H.R.'

Intrigued, she made her way there after the evening's entertainments ended, thankful that she was not on duty tonight. The challenge would be getting into the maidens' dorter without waking anyone or being quizzed on why she was so late.

The chapel was in darkness, save for the single lamp in the chancel symbolising the presence of God. Anne curtseyed to the crucifix on the altar, then looked around for Henry. He was leaning forward, a dim form in the royal pew above.

'Up here!' he said, and when she had ascended the stairs he embraced her. 'Thank God you came! Come and sit beside me.' He indicated the Queen's chair. 'It's all right. We're alone.'

'What has happened?' she asked, fearing something ominous.

'Anne, I have to talk to you. I am in turmoil, and I do not know whether to rejoice or weep. Monsieur de Grammont, the Bishop of Tarbes, has raised the question of the Princess Mary's legitimacy.'

She was shocked. 'But how can that be, sir? You have been married to the Queen for—'

'Eighteen years,' Henry finished. 'And never did man have such a faithful, virtuous and loving wife. In nearly every respect, Katherine is what a queen should be. But she has failed to bear me a son, and Anne, she is now past the ways of women.' He buried his head in his hands, resting his elbows on the front of the pew. 'What I am about to say to you is in strict confidence, darling, because it touches the Queen too nearly. You must be aware – who is not? – of how much I have agonised over not having a son, and how to resolve the problem of the succession.'

'But sir, your daughter, the Princess, is forward in learning for her years and graced with all the virtues. Why should she not rule after you?'

Henry sighed. 'Don't think I haven't considered it. That's why I sent

162

Mary to Ludlow, to learn how to be a queen. But it galls me, Anne, it eats at me. A woman rule England? It is against Nature for women to wield dominion over men. No man would heed her. And who would lead our armies into battle?'

'The Queen's own mother, Isabella, did in Spain,' Anne pointed out, wondering how the Regent Margaret and Marguerite of Valois would have answered him.

'So Katherine keeps telling me,' he huffed, his hawk-like profile set in stern lines against the flickering torchlight. 'But Anne, this is England, not Spain, and our people would never tolerate it. There was a queen called Matilda, centuries ago, who attempted to rule and became a byword for infamy. Memories are long. I have a bastard son, as you know, but I'm not sure that my subjects would tolerate *his* succeeding me either, although I had come to see it as the only option. But it has just been put to me that my sole legitimate child may well be a bastard too. And if she marries into France, then I might well be the last king of England, for the French will rule here in her name after I am gone. So,' he ended, turning a perplexed face to her, 'you can see why I am in turmoil.'

'I understand very well,' Anne said, feeling – for the first time – some sympathy for him, even if he was wrong about the ability of a woman to rule. 'But why did the Bishop question the Princess's legitimacy?'

Henry sighed. 'On the grounds that, all those years ago, the Pope had no business issuing a dispensation allowing me to marry my brother's widow. The Queen was married to Prince Arthur before, as you know.'

She nodded.

'There were those who expressed doubts at the time, but my Council overruled them, and I was determined to have Katherine for my wife. It was a brilliant marriage alliance, and I loved her. Besides, I was assured, by her and by her father, that she was still a virgin. Arthur was ill when he married her; he died six months later. But, Anne, the good Bishop has directed me to the Book of Leviticus in the Bible, and I have been reading it over and over again, for it warns of the penalty for those who incur God's displeasure by taking their brother's widow to wife. "They shall be childless"! And having only a daughter, I *am* as good as childless. All my sons with Katherine died.'

There were tears in Henry's eyes; he was a bereaved father as well as a sovereign without an heir.

'If the Bishop has these doubts about my marriage, others may too,' he went on. 'God knows I've studied the matter this past week. I've read books till my head ached. I've talked to my confessor. He says I may well be in error, *and* living in sin, and that to avoid God's displeasure I should ask for the advice of the Archbishop of Canterbury and my Council.' He paused, his face that of a tortured soul. 'And so, Anne, I mind to do so, with a view to having my union with the Queen declared incestuous and invalid.'

Anne stifled a gasp. 'Your Grace would go so far? You would divorce such a devout and beloved queen?'

'I must think of my kingdom, Anne, and what will surely ensue if I die leaving no son. There would be civil war, make no bones about it. God knows, I have enough relations of the old Plantagenet royal blood ready to stake their claim, and some of them may not do me the courtesy of waiting till I die.' There was genuine fear in his voice, and anger too. 'I must have a son, Anne, and to do that I need to take another wife.'

Anne was still digesting it all. 'But the Queen? What of her? She will be devastated. She loves you so much.'

'She will understand that these doubts must be resolved, and that I need an heir. But, God help me, I don't know how I am going to face breaking this to her, and for now, Anne, you must say nothing of it to anyone. Katherine has known for some time that all is not well. I have . . . refrained from her bed, not just on account of this new scruple of conscience, although I have been advised by my confessor that I must do so until the matter is settled. She has a disease . . . Well, I will not go into it.'

Suddenly Henry's need for her, his passion, was making more sense to Anne. He had been looking to her for what his wife could no longer give him.

He put his arm around her shoulders and drew her to him. She realised that he was weeping silently.

'Anne, I did not ask you here just to talk about my marriage,' he said at length, and surprised her by sliding down on one knee before her. 'You have said that you will not give yourself to me, and I respect that. But when I am free, will you marry me?'

This was the last thing she had expected, and it threw her utterly. When Henry had spoken of remarrying, she had assumed that he meant some foreign princess who could bring him political advantages and a large dowry. Kings did not marry the likes of her, who had neither.

He was looking up at her yearningly, tears in his eyes. 'Maybe I should not have spoken at this time, since I am not yet free, but Anne, I love you truly, I am mad for you, and I can think of no woman I would rather marry.' He seized her hands and kissed them. 'Tell me I may hope!'

'I am not worthy,' she said, unable to grasp the enormity of what they were discussing. 'I am a commoner.'

'You have the soul of an angel and a spirit worthy of a crown,' Henry enthused, rising back into his seat and taking her hands. 'None could deny it. My own grandmother was a commoner. My grandfather, King Edward, married her for love. There was a lot of fuss, of course. The nobility resented her, and said she was not worthy, but she proved a good queen – as you will, my darling, I have no doubt of it. You are not of ordinary clay.'

Anne's heart was pounding furiously as the realisation dawned that Henry really did want to make her queen, and that it was not such an outrageous proposition as she imagined.

'Besides,' he said, grinning, 'it seems that the only way I can win you is by marrying you.'

A thought struck her. 'Sir, these doubts you have – they are not on account of me, I trust?'

'No, Anne. I have asked myself that. But had I never met or loved you, I would still have them, and still be wanting an annulment. I have to provide for the succession. It is my duty as king.'

She still could not think clearly. Was she dreaming this? But no, here was Henry, big and ardent, his hands warm on hers.

They were becoming clearer now, the implications of marrying the King. Every material thing she wanted would be hers. The advantages to her family would be immeasurable. The Boleyns would be the highest family in the land. Seeing Father's reaction alone would be worth accepting Henry's proposal! Her children and descendants would rule England . . .

But she would have to take the man with the king. She had never wished in her heart to choose him, and still did not want him in that way. She was not in love with him, and she knew there would be less freedom in marriage to him than with a lesser man who was more agreeable to her. Marrying the King would set them both on a controversial course, and there were sure to be obstacles to be overcome. But her pride was welling up – pride in herself and in her family. A Percy had considered her worthy, and Plantagenet blood ran in her veins. Why should she not aspire to a crown?

A distant bell struck, and she heard the watchman's cry: 'One o'clock and all's well!'

'It's late, sir,' she said. 'I must go to bed. I beg you, do not think me insensible of the high honour you do me in asking me to be your wife and Queen. In truth, my mind cannot quite compass it. I pray you, grant me time in which to consider, for this is not a matter to be undertaken lightly.'

'Take all the time you need, sweetheart,' Henry murmured, and drew her into his arms, pressing his lips on hers. This time she did not resist.

Anne realised that she would have no peace from Henry if she remained at court, so she asked the Queen for permission to absent herself, pleading illness again, and rode home with her mother to Hever. In her hand she clutched a folded piece of paper that an anguished Henry had pressed into her palm before she left. On it, he had written:

O my heart, and O my heart,
My heart it is so sore,
Since I must needs from my love depart,
And know no cause wherefore.

Hot on her heels came a letter begging her to return. It plunged her into perplexity. All she had to say was yes, and the riches of the kingdom would be hers, and the power. But *could* she take the man as well as the crown? More importantly, could she betray the good mistress who had never shown her anything but kindness? Katherine was greatly loved, and of royal birth; Anne would be widely condemned for supplanting her. And in the face of opposition, would Henry hold true to her, or would he bend like a reed in the storm?

She did not have to say yes. She had said no so often that it had become a habit, and she no longer feared Henry's reaction. But he was going to seek an annulment anyway, and if he took another wife, why should it not be her?

She thought about the strong women who had influenced her. The Regent had used her power wisely, and it came to Anne that, if she became queen, she might be able to use hers for the good of others, as well as for herself and her family. She might be able to introduce more enlightened religious beliefs into England, and show by example that women could wield power for the common good.

It was too great a decision to make under pressure, yet she did not want Henry to be offended by her failure to leap at the glorious future he had offered her. She must impress on him that she really did need time to think.

An idea came to her. Taking Mrs Orchard and a groom, she rode into Tonbridge, the nearest town, and paid a visit to a goldsmith who had made various pieces for her parents.

'I want a jewel, in solid gold, fashioned as a solitary damsel in a ship tossed by a tempest. Could you do that?' she asked, as Mrs Orchard eyed her suspiciously. The nurse knew of old when Anne was hiding something, and had fished continuously to find out what it was.

'It is for an admirer,' Anne teased her.

167

'That's a fine sum to be paying out, when he should be the one giving presents!' Mrs Orchard sniffed.

The goldsmith, however, was delighted with the commission, and a week later an exquisite brooch, exactly as Anne had envisaged, was delivered to Hever. She sent it to Henry with an affectionate note, hoping he would understand the allusion to her predicament: how she was tossed in turmoil on troubled waters, fearing that she might be overcome by the tempest and praying that her boat would take a safe course.

The jewel provoked a passionate reaction from Henry, reassuring her that henceforth his heart would be dedicated to her alone, and desiring fervently that his body could be as well. 'God can bring it to pass if it pleases Him,' he declared, adding that he was entreating the Almighty every day to bring that about. 'I wish the time short until we shall see each other again,' he ended, signing himself 'the secretary who in heart, body and will is your loyal and most assured servant. H. *autre ne cherche* R.'

Henry the King seeks no other. And around Anne's initials the King had drawn a heart.

It was that little symbol which made her mind up. It struck a chord in her own heart, and made her believe that yes, in time she might come to love him, even if it was not the kind of passionate love that she had tasted so briefly. In the meantime, she would settle for power instead. It was as great an aphrodisiac as Norris's dazzling smile. She knew now that she very much wanted to be queen.

She wrote to Henry in humble and loving vein: she would be honoured to accept his proposal of marriage.

The first response she had was a letter from Father. 'I have received the most joyful and unexpected news, from the King himself!' he wrote. 'Nothing could have been more welcome to me!' Anne knew what this would mean to Father. He was an ambitious man, but even he had never dreamed of such advancement. The prospect of being father of the next Queen of England and, God willing, grandsire to a future monarch would bring him and his family more wealth, power, fame and honour than he had ever craved.

Anne knocked at her mother's door, took a deep breath and opened it. This would be the first time she spoke her news out loud, and doing that would make it feel more real.

'Mother,' she ventured. Elizabeth Howard was sitting on the bed, sorting her embroidery silks. She looked up.

'Yes?'

Anne grasped her hands. 'Mother, I have wonderful news, but before I say anything, you must swear to keep it a secret for now.'

'What is it?' Mother stood up, the silks abandoned.

'The King is to be divorced. He has asked me to be his next Queen, and I have accepted.'

Mother gasped then cried out in amazement and hugged her fiercely.

'I can't believe it!' she said, again and again. 'My daughter – the Queen of England! Does your father know?'

'He does. The King told him, and he is overjoyed. Mother, your grandson will be a king! Think of it! And George will be thrilled!' She paused. 'I'm not sure how Mary will take it.' Thankfully Mary was at court, so she would not have to confront that problem immediately. She remembered that moment of jealousy when she first confided in her sister about the King's advances. Always they had competed with each other, and now Mary could never hope to match Anne's great good fortune.

'What happens now?' Mother asked excitedly, pouring them some wine to celebrate.

Anne explained that the King was taking immediate steps to procure an annulment of his marriage.

'Discretion is the order of the day,' she added, 'so I shall stay here for a while. Hopefully a decision will be given soon.'

'I shall pray for it,' Mother said, 'although I do feel sorry for the poor Queen. She is blameless in all this. It will come hard to her.'

'The King will provide handsomely for her, I am sure,' Anne said, feeling guilty about Katherine. But, she reminded herself, this was not her fault. No one could help it if the Queen's marriage wasn't valid, or that the King had a duty to assure the succession: unfair as it was, it was something that Katherine would have to accept.

Suddenly there was a frantic knock on the parlour door and the steward burst in without waiting for a response. 'My lady – the King is here! He's just riding down the hill!'

As her mother leapt up, screaming at the man to go and welcome him, and to bring more wine, and order the cook to bestir himself to make a good dinner – and not to forget the best silver – Anne jumped to her feet, aware that she was wearing only an old green gown, and had not even bound up her hair. Quickly, her heart pounding, she smoothed her skirts, dragged a comb through her long locks, and sped through the entrance hall into the courtyard. Through the gatehouse arch she could see the King, garbed in his riding clothes and boots, already clattering across the drawbridge, with just four mounted gentlemen and four Yeomen of the Guard in attendance. The steward was bowing low, and Mother was curtseying behind him.

The King dismounted and raised her.

'Greetings, Lady Boleyn! We were hunting in the neighbourhood – I'm staying over at Penshurst – and I thought it would be pleasant to pay you a visit.'

'We are truly honoured, your Grace, but I fear that, not expecting you, we have little to offer in the way of hospitality.'

'No matter!' Henry beamed. 'Some light refreshment and a walk around these glorious gardens would please me mightily. It will be good to be among friends and free for a short time from the cares of state.'

His eyes were drawn to Anne, waiting by the castle entrance, and in them, as she made her obeisance, she could read only jubilation.

'Darling!' he cried, striding forward, raising her up and kissing her on the mouth. 'It does my heart good to see you. I trust you are in health?'

'I am very well, your Grace,' she said, aware of him eyeing the plain gown, and Mother staring at them. 'Forgive our lack of ceremony.'

'You look charming,' he murmured as they entered the castle and Anne led Henry and his companions to the parlour, where a fresh ewer of wine was already waiting.

'You will stay to dine, sir?' Mother fluttered.

'I will not trouble you, Lady Boleyn, but thank you.' He accepted the goblet of wine.

'The Queen is looking forward to your return,' he said to Anne, looking at her hopefully.

'That is most gracious of her,' she replied. 'Please do me the service of telling her that my trouble is a little amended. I will return to court as soon as I am able.'

There was a silence.

'Your Grace, Anne must have the honour of showing you the gardens,' Mother said.

Henry drained his goblet. 'That would be most pleasant.'

'I will summon Mrs Orchard,' Anne said.

They walked out into the warm May air, past the Yeomen of the Guard, who had stationed themselves outside the gatehouse. One left his post and followed them at a discreet distance, keeping step with an agog Mrs Orchard, who definitely was putting two and two together and coming up with an enormous sum.

As soon as they were out of earshot of anyone, Henry turned to Anne.

'Your letter made me weep. I had not felt so joyful in all my life. Thank you, my own darling, for making me the happiest of men.' He seized her hand and kissed it, then tucked it under his arm.

They walked along the banks of the Eden, and then Anne led Henry to her favourite spot in the meadow, where they sat on the grass.

'It's at times like these that I wish I wasn't a king, but a simple country gentleman,' Henry mused, chewing on a stalk. 'This, not the vanities of my court, is the real England.'

'You would miss it, sir,' Anne teased. 'It can be very boring here. Trust me, I know.'

'Then come to court and be with me.'

'I should not – not right now.' She paused. 'Is there any news?'

Henry grinned. 'Yes, sweetheart. Things are moving. In his capacity as Papal legate, the Cardinal has secretly convened an ecclesiastical court at Westminster. Archbishop Warham is presiding, and we've assembled a host of bishops and canon lawyers. I was summoned last week, and asked to account for having knowingly taken to wife my brother's widow. I admitted the charge, confessed my doubts of conscience, and asked for a decision to be given on my case. I should hear soon. And then, dearest Anne, we can be married!'

She hoped his optimism was justified. She did not dare let her excitement run away with her. But in a few short weeks she might be queen! She could see herself seated in Westminster Abbey, feel the weight of the crown on her head. The prospect was an exhilarating one, and still not quite believable.

'I am glad to hear that the Cardinal supports Your Grace.'

'He does now.'

'What do you mean, Sir?'

Henry's eyes narrowed. 'When I first told him that I wanted an annulment, and asked for his wise opinion in the matter, he fell to his knees and tried every persuasion to the contrary.'

Anne drew in her breath. Wolsey again, trying to ruin her future as he had ruined it before!

'But I talked to him,' Henry assured her. 'He is of a different opinion now.'

She fervently hoped so. She would not let that butcher's dog stand in the way of her advancement. But if he secured a divorce for Henry, she would forgive him all.

'Has Your Grace spoken to the Queen?'

'Not yet,' Henry replied. 'I am awaiting the outcome of this hearing.' She sensed he was reluctant to broach the matter with Katherine.

'I will pray for a good outcome,' she said.

'You have no idea how hard I have been praying,' Henry told her. 'I long for the time when we can be together – really together.' He leaned forward, cupped her chin in his hands and kissed her long and lovingly.

'We should go back,' she said, breaking away and getting to her feet, then remembering to whom she was speaking. 'That is, if Your Grace pleases.'

'It does not please me, Anne. Having to leave you is sheer torment. But you are right. Let us return to your mother. She will be wondering what has happened to us.'

'I think she might have guessed!' Anne laughed.

*

Henry's letters all spoke of his pain at being parted from her, and they were beautiful and moving – the kind of letters a woman would cherish, were she in love with the sender. Anne read them dispassionately, pleased that she could inspire such devotion in a man so powerful, but they only made her wonder how she would find ways to keep his passion alive. A man might stand only so much elusiveness before he stopped coming back for more.

But then there arrived a letter that reassured her.

'My mistress and my friend,' Henry had written, 'I and my heart commit ourselves into your hands, beseeching you to hold us in your good favour, and that your affection may not be by absence diminished. The longer the days are, the farther off is the sun, and the hotter; so it is with our love, for we are far apart, yet it nevertheless keeps its fervency, at least on my part, hoping that it does on yours. Your absence would be intolerable to me, were it not for the firm hope that I have of your ever-enduring affection.' And to put her in mind of him, he had enclosed his picture set in a bracelet. 'I am wishing myself in their place, when it should please you,' he ended, and signed himself her loyal servant and friend.

The siege had been raised. It was the first letter in which he had not begged her to be his. It was suddenly clear that her consenting to marry him had wrought a great change in their relations. Of course! If she was going to be his Queen, she must not be tainted by any breath of scandal, nor risk an illicit pregnancy. So he was keeping his promise to respect her honour and wait until he could lawfully enjoy her. From now on, it would not be her who had the power to bring to fruition all Henry's desires: that lay with God – and the men gathered at Westminster.

Henry's next letter was despondent. The commissioners had said that they were not competent to judge his case. He had therefore consulted his Privy Council, who had agreed that there was good cause for scruple and advised him to approach the Pope for a decision on his marriage.

Anne's shoulders sagged in disappointment when she read this.

Applying to Rome would surely take months, even if the Pope was willing speedily to oblige the King.

Far worse news followed. Early in June, Henry wrote to say that Rome had been savagely sacked by mercenary troops of the Emperor, who was then campaigning elsewhere in Italy. Lacking a commander, they had surged unchecked into the city and unleashed an orgy of violence and murder that had raged for days.

'I will not upset you with details of their atrocities,' Henry wrote, 'for they were unspeakable. Those brutes even desecrated St Peter's itself.' The Pope had been forced to take refuge in the Castel Sant'Angelo, and was now a virtual prisoner of the Emperor Charles, Queen Katherine's nephew, who was willing to exploit a situation that had delivered the Holy Father into his 'protection'. And that, Anne realised, her spirits plummeting, meant that, for the present, a favourable decision on Henry's case was as unlikely to be forthcoming as a man flying to the moon, especially if the Emperor learned that he wanted to marry her. She remembered him as an insufferable youth who had hated her for her presumption.

She felt helpless, and when George, now the King's cup-bearer, came home for a brief visit later that month, she poured out her frustration.

'Couldn't the Cardinal, as Papal legate, just declare the marriage invalid?' she cried.

George shook his head. 'Father says the Emperor is all-powerful. If provoked – and Wolsey dissolving the marriage on his own authority might be seen as provocation – Charles might declare war. No, dear sister, there is nothing for it but to have patience.'

'Maybe I should return to court.'

'I would not advise it right now. The King's "Great Matter" – as they are calling it – is now as notorious as if it had been proclaimed by the town crier. His Grace had to command the Lord Mayor of London to order the people to cease spreading rumours, on pain of his high displeasure, but it won't stop them. Father said the clamour has reached such a pitch that the Cardinal felt it prudent to inform all our ambassadors of the truth.'

'Is my name being spoken?' Anne asked, alarmed. It was not meant to happen this way. She had anticipated a speedy, amicable divorce followed by a joyous wedding.

'Not yet.' Brother and sister stared at each other, knowing that it soon would be.

'Does Mary know that the King wants to marry me?'

George grimaced. 'Yes. Father told her.'

'I can tell from your reaction that she was not best pleased.'

George shrugged. 'She doesn't want the King. She just can't bear the idea of your being queen!'

'She's the least of my worries. I can't be dealing with her jealousy at this time.'

Anne could not settle to anything, she was so agitated. Her mother tried to calm her, assuring her that all would be well in the end.

'But you don't know that!' she flared.

'No, but I trust in the goodness of God,' Mother declared. 'Now stop this fretting and help me in my still room.'

At the end of June, Henry rode down from Greenwich Palace. Anne was relieved to lay eyes on his small cavalcade approaching, delighted to see him for once. He must have news!

'Your brother told me that you were disconsolate, darling,' he said, embracing her tenderly after her mother had left them alone together in the parlour. 'You must not worry. The situation in Italy is volatile and could change at any moment. I put my trust in his Holiness. I have been a good son of the Church.'

Anne had hoped for something more tangible, but she forced a smile. 'I know. I have read your Grace's book defending the sacraments that Martin Luther denied.'

'Indeed?' He looked pleased. 'The Pope was so grateful, he conferred on me the title Defender of the Faith. So I am hopeful that he will look favourably on my suit.'

He sat down and accepted one of the little marmalade cakes Anne offered. 'Quince is my favourite,' he told her appreciatively, pulling her to him and kissing her hungrily. 'Anne, you *will* be mine and you *will* be queen, never doubt it!'

She kissed him back, then disengaged herself. Henry let her go reluctantly. His eyes alighted on her illuminated prayer book on the table.

'This is beautiful,' he remarked, turning the pages until he came upon a vivid picture of Christ, the Man of Sorrow, pierced with wounds and crowned with thorns.

'Darling, I meant what I just said.' And he reached for her pen, dipped it in the inkpot, and bent to the page. 'If your remembrance be according to my affection, I shall not be forgotten in your daily prayers, for I am yours, Henry R., for ever,' he wrote.

She could do no less. Taking the pen from him, she added her own inscription at the bottom of the opposite leaf: 'By daily proof you shall me find to be to you both loving and kind.'

'Anne!' Henry murmured, his voice thick with desire. 'You are the sweetest, loveliest mistress, and I am blessed indeed!'

No sooner had the King departed for Greenwich than Father came home, bringing with him Uncle Norfolk. As Mother flapped off to stir the servants to preparing a fine repast, the Duke took Father's chair at the head of the parlour table and fixed his gimlet gaze on Anne.

'Niece, we have reason to believe that the Cardinal is not to be trusted. He does the King's bidding in this Great Matter, but his heart is not in it. Even if the King's suit is successful, Wolsey means to marry him to a French princess.'

'He would not presume so far!' Anne cried.

'He has been presuming thus far for years,' Father said, grim-faced. 'He runs this kingdom.'

'While we, the nobility, who should be the King's natural counsellors, are kept from enjoying the power that should be ours by right of birth,' Uncle Norfolk growled. 'I've always said it – this upstart butcher's whelp is a pernicious influence.'

Father nodded. 'When I was made Lord Rochford, I was forced to resign my post as treasurer without any financial compensation. I blame Wolsey. He hates our family. He sees us as a threat, and will do anything he can to bring us down.'

'I have no cause to love him either,' Anne said. 'I cannot forgive his breaking my precontract with Harry Percy. And he had the gall to call me a foolish girl in front of his household. It was doubly an insult, coming from one so low-born.'

'He will soon have cause to regret it,' Norfolk assured her. 'We have long been searching for a means to deprive him of the King's favour, and we are here today to ask for your help.' He leaned forward, steepling his hands on the table. 'Seeing the great affection that the King bears you, and the influence you enjoy, you would be the perfect instrument to help us topple the Cardinal. What say you?'

Anne did not hesitate. 'I am ready!' she declared. 'The King would be far better off ruling this realm, and securing a divorce, without the interference of Wolsey.' That long-ago insult still rankled. Revenge would be sweet.

Later, over supper, which Mother caused to be served with much ceremony in the great hall, Father revealed that he and Uncle Norfolk, with many nobles and lords of the Council, had been urging the King to send the Cardinal to France to enlist the support of King François.

'The French King might be willing to persuade the Pope to extend Wolsey's legatine powers, which would enable him to adjudicate on the King's case,' he said, spearing some beef on his fork. 'But our intent and purpose is to get Wolsey out of the way, so that we might have leisure to undermine him in the King's eyes in his absence.'

'What we want you to do is persuade the King to send the Cardinal to France,' Norfolk added. 'Can you do that?'

'I can, and I will,' she said.

That very night, she wrote to Henry. Soon afterwards he informed her that Wolsey had departed for France. It was time to go back to court.

Anne found Greenwich buzzing with gossip and speculation about the Great Matter.

The Queen welcomed her warmly, asking after her health and saying how glad she was to see her. She was so kind, so solicitous, that Anne was again stirred by guilt, knowing what would soon befall her gracious mistress. Katherine looked more drawn, more lined, than when she had seen her last. Did she know what was going on? Anne wondered.

Henry sent her a message. She was to come to the lime walk near the friary at eleven o'clock. When she arrived, wrapped in a hooded cloak, for all the warmth of the June night, he enveloped her in his arms.

'Anne! Anne! Thank God! It's been hell here. I have missed you more than I can tell you.'

She tried to respond to his kisses with a similar fervency. But soon he drew apart, looking troubled.

'What is wrong?' she asked, panicking a little.

Henry sighed. 'Tomorrow I am going to speak to the Queen. I have to, or she'll hear about our matter from someone else.'

'Tomorrow? Sir, I'm waiting on her in the morning. I don't think I should be there.'

She couldn't face seeing what this would do to Katherine.

'Don't worry, darling. I won't mention you. This is between the Queen and me.'

All morning Anne found it hard to face the Queen or meet her eye. She was filled with dread for her, and with such heavy guilt that no amount of rationalising could dissipate it.

Henry arrived at ten o'clock.

'Leave us,' he commanded. Anne found herself trembling. When the ladies began busying themselves in the bedchamber, she strained to listen to what was happening next door, but all she could hear was the murmur of Henry's voice.

Then she heard a howl that made her blood freeze.

It was the Queen, wailing, her words one long, unintelligible lament.

When they heard the outer door slam, Anne hung back as the other ladies ran to their mistress, urging her to have a care to herself and steadying her with a cup of wine. Katherine gulped it down. She was shaking uncontrollably.

'His conscience is troubling him,' she whispered. 'He wants to end our marriage. He fears that it is an offence to God.'

There was a chorus of disbelief. Surely not! His Grace had been misled by those who should know better. All would be well in the end. Anne could not speak, for she knew that all would not be well for Katherine ever again.

'No,' the Queen whispered. 'He spoke of taking another wife.'

They burst out in outrage at that.

Katherine rested her head back on the chair. 'This is the Cardinal's doing. He hates me and Spain, and he has never forgiven my nephew the Emperor for not making him pope.'

She drew herself up in her chair, more composed now. 'Whatever they say, my marriage to the King is good and valid.' It sounded like a battle cry. 'The Pope himself sanctioned it. My duty now is to persuade my husband that he is in error, and I will do it, so help me God!'

Her ladies applauded her resolve, and as she thanked them for their loyalty and their love, Anne found herself fighting back tears. Katherine smiled at her. 'I am all right now, Mistress Anne,' she said, taking her hand and squeezing it. Anne understood in that moment how Judas Iscariot had felt.

Later, Anne looked for Henry and found him in his garden, unusually morose and feeling very sorry for himself.

'The Queen was very distressed after you had gone,' she told him.

He grimaced. 'She was in great grief, as I had feared. I told her I wanted only to resolve the doubts raised by the Bishop of Tarbes, and that everything should be done for the best, but it did not help. All she kept saying was that she was my true wife.'

'Give her time,' Anne soothed him. 'She must come to accept it.'

Henry swallowed. 'I am not so sure. When I saw her this afternoon, she told me she had no doubts at all that our marriage was lawful, and that I was wrong to question it.'

'If the Pope rules against her, she will have to accept it.'

Henry shook his head. 'Anne, she means to fight me.'

'You have a strong case.'

'Yes, which is why I am confident that I will win it. By the saints, I hate this unpleasantness. It's not my fault that the Pope was in error.' His tone was plaintive.

'Did you mention me to her?'

'God, no! I want to keep you out of it until the Pope has spoken. I have not mentioned you even to Wolsey. No, Anne, until this matter is resolved, I mean to show that all is well between me and the Queen. I want to be judged in a favourable light, for I fear that Katherine might incite the Emperor to war if she feels she is being treated unjustly. Bear with me in this. I know how to handle her.'

You're afraid of her, Anne realised.

'Be of good cheer,' Henry urged, squeezing her hand. 'Most people at court support me. Archbishop Warham is lukewarm – he's old and he hates change – but he told Wolsey that, however the Queen might take it, the Pope's judgement must be followed. Anne, I am absolutely convinced that I am right to pursue this annulment. And I am absolutely determined to marry you, whoever opposes me.' His eyes were dark with passion. 'I am mad for you. But right now, you must go home.'

Chapter 13

1527

It felt strange to be at Beaulieu, a house in Essex that her family had once owned, and which she remembered visiting as a child, when it had been much smaller. But Father had sold it to the King while she was in France, and now it was a great palace faced with fashionable red bricks, with a fountain playing in the courtyard and glorious jewelled glass in the windows.

Henry seemed to have abandoned all discretion in summoning her here. She had only been gone from court for five weeks, and little could have changed in that time. She was astonished when as soon as she arrived she was escorted to the King's privy chamber and he embraced her in front of all his gentlemen. Seeing her expression, he was bullish.

'I have done with subterfuge, Anne! My love for you is an honourable thing, and I would show the world how greatly I hold you in esteem. No harm shall come to your reputation. The world shall see that you are virtuous, beyond reproach and' – he lowered his voice – 'fit to be my Queen.'

He pressed into her hands a small silver casket, in which nestled an emerald ring and other costly jewels, and she smiled, murmuring her thanks. She was aware of the scrutiny of the men in attendance, whose attention was meant to be focused on their cards, dice and music-making. The handsome Sir Henry Norris was among them. For a brief moment, their eyes met, and Anne felt herself blush. She quickly looked away.

Henry invited her to walk with him in his privy garden. As soon as they were outdoors, she told him how disconcerted she had been to find that the sole topic of conversation in the inn where she and her father had lodged on the way had been the Great Matter.

'People were saying they could not believe that your Grace would ever carry so wicked a project into effect. The women, in particular, spoke out in the Queen's favour. They said that you sought to be rid of her purely for your own pleasure.'

Henry waved a dismissive hand. 'They are ignorant fools, and impertinent to be questioning their King. Sweetheart, I did not bring you here to speak of a few disloyal subjects. I would be private with you for a space before I lose you to the Queen.' He bent and kissed her mouth, drawing her to him, his golden beard rough against her cheek. She twined her arms around his neck, wishing she could feel something of what she had felt for Harry or Norris. For all that she wanted the crown, at times like these, which brought home to her the price of it, she felt as if she was being swept along in a current she could not dam.

She hastened to visit Mary in the lodging she shared with Will. She wanted to warn her that the secret would soon be out. But Mary's reception was cold.

'What business is it of mine?' she sniffed. 'You're welcome to him.'

'There will be a scandal,' Anne told her.

'You made your bed, now lie on it!' Jealousy blazed in Mary's eyes. 'If you think I'm going to bow the knee to you as queen . . .'

'I didn't come to argue,' Anne said. 'I don't want any bad feeling between us over this. I didn't take the King from you.'

'You came to queen it over me!' Mary was implacable.

Anne tried again. 'At least let me see the children.'

'They're asleep. Good night.' And Mary shut the door.

Katherine was going about with a determined smile on her face, but the smile slipped a little when Anne kept absenting herself from her duties. The King would not take no for an answer. She must come hunting with him every day. She must join him in his gallery to make music. She must watch him play tennis. He said that if the Queen knew that it was his pleasure, she would not complain. Nor did she, for at first she

182

clearly did not know that Anne meant anything to Henry; and even when her ladies must have informed her, she showed no displeasure, but accepted what was happening in good part, with – Anne thought – exceptional patience.

'She probably thinks I am merely another Bessie Blount and will be discarded in due course,' Anne said to George over supper in his lodging one evening. It was cramped, but it had two rooms and a privy, and best of all, it was near the King's apartments. The closer to the King, the more privileged the courtier.

'Already there is speculation that you are far more than that,' he told her. 'The world is full of rumours. Imaginations are running riot.'

'What are they saying about me?'

George snorted, and swigged back his wine. 'Only that the King fancies you so much that good order and everything has flown out the window! Most think, predictably, that you are the cause of his doubts about his marriage.'

'He assures me that is not so.'

'No, but what does it look like?'

Almost overnight, Anne found herself in a position of great influence. She was thrilled when a young clerk approached her with a request for a post at court and pressed a bag of gold coins into her hand. She had great satisfaction in persuading Henry to grant him a place in the Lord Steward's office – not that it had been difficult, for he could refuse her nothing – and the man was so grateful. He was the first of many courtiers who fawned on her, seeking her patronage because they knew she had the King's ear. This, her first taste of real power, was a heady experience. It gave her a new confidence, for it was gratifying to be able to fulfil others' expectations and thus secure their loyalty, which would be invaluable when she was raised to queenship.

The King showered her with gifts: jewels, bolts of rich velvets and damask silk, lap dogs, fine wines . . . Dressed in such finery, she looked like a queen. Within two weeks of her arrival at court, rumours were circulating that the King meant to marry her. That provoked an excited swell of gossip, not all of it approving.

When she ran into her sister in a gallery, Mary swept a mocking curtsey. 'My, aren't we fine,' she sneered. 'You should hear what they're saying about you.'

'One day soon you'll sing a different song!' Anne called after her departing back.

The court was one thing – the King's pleasure was too respected there for resentment to spill over into open protest – but England at large was another. Anne was horrified when, riding out to the hunt with Henry, with the Queen there too, people spat at her and shouted out their outrage that she should dare presume to supplant good Queen Katherine.

'Whore!' they shouted. 'Witch! Adulteress!' The women were worse than the men. It was frightening, and Anne's cheeks burned with the unjustness of it. And for all his angry commands, bawled from the saddle, there was nothing the King could do to still the voices. There were always others ahead to shout more abuse. But when Katherine rode by, they cried: 'Victory over your enemies!'

Henry and Anne rode on stony-faced. Anne had never dreamed that this divorce would arouse such opposition.

The Queen must have heard the speculation and the heckling, but when they got back to Beaulieu, she remained courteous to Anne, if a little distant. She only ever made one gentle thrust. Henry, somewhat naively, seemed to think it perfectly acceptable for his wife and his mistress to join him in a game of cards. Anne did not want to join in, but he insisted. When she won, drawing a king, which scored high, Katherine smiled at her and said, 'My lady Anne, you have the good luck to stop at a king – but you are like the others: you will have all or none.'

Henry glowered at her. Anne flushed, but she could say nothing. She sat there feeling intensely embarrassed, resentment and anger mounting. It was unfair of Katherine to taunt her publicly, especially as Anne had tried to fend off Henry's courtship. Now everyone within earshot was staring at her, or whispering, knowing looks in their eyes. Her pride revolted. What did they think she was, the King's whore? She felt her cheeks flushing.

To her relief, the Queen rose, begged Henry's leave and retired to bed. Anne glared after her. The sympathy she had felt for Katherine, the ever-present guilt, had dissipated. Katherine was her enemy, and would bring her down without a qualm if she could.

She turned to Henry.

'Did I deserve that?' she flared.

'No, but let be, Anne,' he said. 'The Queen is fighting a battle she cannot win. I have enough to trouble me as it is. This afternoon my sister shouted at me. She told me she supported the Queen and would leave the court if I insisted on having you here with me. I told her she could go, and she stormed out without even a curtsey.' He looked injured at the memory.

'She hates me, doesn't she?' Anne seethed. 'She swept past me yesterday holding her nose, as if there was a bad smell.'

'I won't have her hold me to ransom like that,' Henry growled, upset because he loved his sister. 'Thank God Suffolk supports us. He'll talk some sense into her.'

Throughout August, Anne, her father, her uncle of Norfolk and their friends, who now included the Duke of Suffolk, took advantage of the Cardinal's absence in France. Anne arranged for her father and the two dukes to sup with the King every night, and over the dinner table they dropped hint after subtle hint that, far from working to secure an annulment, Wolsey might actually be doing his best to prevent the Pope granting one. Henry was sceptical, but no matter – a doubt had been planted in his mind.

At one supper, Sir Henry Norris was present, seated next to Anne, who was all too aware of his physical nearness.

Henry explained, 'I have invited Sir Henry to join us, darling, because henceforth he will act as go-between for us. As Groom of the Stool and head of my Privy Chamber, he will guide you while you establish your position at court, and he is utterly trustworthy.'

'It is an honour, sir,' Norris said warmly, smiling at Anne. And there it was again, that sense of recognition, and she found herself hardly able to look away. For a brief moment there had been a frisson of attraction between them, and she was certain that he had felt it too.

Henry was chatting on, oblivious to the momentous thing that was happening to her. The poets wrote of love at first sight, which she had often dismissed as a mere literary conceit, but now she knew. It did not matter that she was barely acquainted with Norris; there was no doubt in her mind that love was what she had felt for him from the first, or that he was everything she wanted. His looks, his strong body and beautiful hands, his courtesy, his smile – they proclaimed what he was.

But he was married, and she had promised to wed the King. For a mad moment she thought she would tell Henry that she could not go through with it, could not face the uproar or the opprobrium. But even if she did, Norris was not free – and Henry would never accept it.

The men were laughing and she remembered where she was. Quickly she picked up the gist of the jest and joined in.

She sensed Norris watching her, and when the conversation turned to hunting, a favourite topic of Henry's, she smiled at him.

'You have been at court long, Sir Henry?'

He fixed those wondrous light blue eyes on her. 'Please call me Norris, Mistress Anne,' he invited. 'Everyone else does. Yes, my family have had long associations with the court. I came here in my youth and was fortunate to be honoured with the friendship of the King, who has generously bestowed on me many offices. I've served in his Privy Chamber for ten years, and was made head of it last year.'

All the time they were talking, Anne was acutely aware that something else was happening between them, something they could never acknowledge.

'And what do your duties encompass?'

'I am in charge of the twelve gentlemen of the King's Privy Chamber. We are all especially privileged, for we have the right of entry to His Grace's private chambers; we look after his personal needs and provide him with daily companionship.'

'Then you must be in positions of great power.'

'We are, Mistress Anne, but I hope we do not abuse it.'

'And the Cardinal – he resents this power.' It was not a question.

'It stands to reason,' murmured Father, sitting the other side of Anne, as the King and the dukes rattled on about bloodstock. 'Those in the Privy Chamber are able to advise and influence His Grace, control access to his presence, and exercise patronage. The Cardinal fears that. As Lord Chancellor, he can control the Privy Council but not the Privy Chamber. He has tried twice to *reform* the Privy Chamber, as he put it – which meant flushing out those who had too much influence.'

'Some were invited back,' Norris smiled. 'I need not say that the Cardinal is not very popular in the Privy Chamber.'

'And you are in charge,' Anne said, avoiding his gaze. Father must not suspect anything.

'Norris is the most highly trusted man in the court,' Father said. 'He has the confidence of the King, and, if I may say it, could be accounted one of his closest friends.'

Norris bowed his head. 'I have that honour,' he said modestly.

'And the King has given him a fine house at Greenwich.' Anne had a fleeting vision of herself and Norris tucked away there, far from the court and their duties and obligations. What joy that would have been!

Father was asking after Norris's children. He had three. She could not bear to think about them, the living proof of his intimacy with his wife.

'I know you will be a friend to my daughter,' Father was saying.

'I will do all in my power to support her, my lord,' Norris promised. There was no doubting his sincerity – or the warmth with which he said it.

The Queen was fighting back.

'She won't even listen to me!' Henry complained, when they were alone later that night after the others had left. 'She insists that the dispensation allowing us to marry was infallible, and that she was never Arthur's wife properly anyway, so Leviticus is irrelevant.'

'Is that true?' Anne asked, feeling increasingly resentful towards Katherine, who would not face reality and stand aside.

Henry stared gloomily into the empty fireplace. 'My father was assured that her marriage to my brother was never consummated, and – well, to be plain, Anne, I was a virgin when we wed, and I would not have known the difference. I believed her – she is a woman of integrity and virtue. But now I wonder: was it that she, being innocent – as I have no doubt she was – did not understand what was meant to happen, or thought it hadn't happened when it had? They did spend seven nights together.'

'Or she lied, because she still wanted to be Queen of England.'

'I don't think so,' Henry said, flushing a little. It irritated her that he still held Katherine in high esteem and recoiled from any criticism of her. *He* could criticise, but no one else was supposed to! And that, she suspected, was because Katherine was still his Queen, still his wife. *But she has no right!* she fumed inwardly.

'That bar in Leviticus is not qualified,' she said. 'A man may not marry his brother's wife. It's as simple as that, and no pope can sanction it.'

'Katherine argues that Leviticus would only apply if she had borne Arthur a child. She cites a text in Deuteronomy that requires a man to marry his brother's widow, but she's wrong. It doesn't apply to Christians.'

'She is grasping at straws.'

Life was unfair, she knew, but this was especially unfair. There was Katherine, who had no right to be queen, winning sympathy all round; and there was she, who had lived a blameless life, being cursed whenever she went abroad in the streets, and vilified now throughout Christendom – oh yes, she had heard the talk. Most people saw her as a Jezebel who had ousted a virtuous wife, and yet who was the more virtuous of the two? Katherine, who had lived in sin for eighteen years, or herself, who had jealously guarded her virginity and never given the King any encouragement? So it was hard nowadays to feel anything but resentment towards Katherine, for all her kindness.

'Cheer up, darling,' Henry said, pulling her into his arms. 'We will win through. My case is sound. I trust, by the Cardinal's diligence, shortly to be rid of this trouble.'

'And I trust that your trust is not misplaced,' Anne said, accepting his kiss.

'Come on, sweetheart, Wolsey is a good friend and a consummate politician – he will secure this annulment for me, and we'll be joyfully receiving him at his homecoming.' And he bent his head, greatly daring, and pressed his lips to her breast where it swelled above the stiff square neckline of her gown. She let him go so far, but it was only when she thought of Norris that she found some pleasure in it.

It was September, and the air was turning cool. A masque was to be performed in the great hall, and Anne had put on a low-cut gown of white damask and threaded jewels through her hair, which she wore loose. It was long enough to sit on, and Henry loved to see it in all its glory. The Queen said nothing when Anne appeared, glittering in her finery, to attend her with a host of other maids and ladies, but Katherine's particular friends, Lady Salisbury, Lady Willoughby and Lady Parr, eyed her disapprovingly. She ignored them, dragons all of them, and was gratified to see that Henry could not take his eyes off her. She was aware, too, of another pair of eyes looking on admiringly, but when she glanced at Norris, he turned and spoke to another gentleman.

The masque was to portray the legend of Narcissus and Echo. Henry himself showed Anne to her chair, which had been placed to the right of the dais where he and the Queen were to watch the performance. But at that moment an usher approached.

'Your Grace, my lord Cardinal is returned from France and waits outside, wishing to know where he should come,' he announced. Henry's face lit up in anticipation of the news Wolsey brought.

Where he should come? What did he think the King was? A lackey? Anne's blood boiled. Here was her chance to discredit Wolsey, and demonstrate her own power.

'I must go to him,' Henry said, beginning to rise.

Anne summoned her courage and turned to the usher. 'Where else should the Cardinal come? Tell him he may come here, where the King is!' Katherine raised her eyebrows in astonishment. Everyone was staring at Anne. Let them! People must see that she enjoyed more influence with the King than the great Cardinal did.

'Yes, indeed,' Henry said, frowning, and nodded to the usher.

When Wolsey came into the hall, bowed low and made his way to the dais, Anne moved to Henry's side. Father, Norfolk and Suffolk were looking on triumphantly; they would be pleased with her. She could see the dismay in the Cardinal's face, the flash of anger at her presumption. He would not call her a foolish girl now!

She knew, from his manner and the way his shoulders were bowed, that his mission had been a failure. She was aware of Henry stiffening next to her, of the testy pace of his breathing. He knew it too.

It was becoming increasingly difficult to fend off Henry's advances. With no end to the waiting in sight, the Pope still in thrall to the Emperor and Wolsey apparently helpless, he was growing more and more frustrated.

'This delay is killing me!' he complained. 'Be kind to me, Anne! A man has needs, you know.'

'And what needs do you expect me to satisfy?' she teased him. 'You said you would respect my virtue.'

Fine words, but they had not stopped him from summoning her late at night to his privy chamber to be alone with her after his gentlemen had gone to bed. Norris always fetched her and escorted her to the secret stair that led up to the King's most private apartments. It was torment for her, to have him take her to the King, and torment for him too, she suspected.

It was not just her inclination but her prudence that decided her to put a stop to these visits. She must not give Henry the opportunity to press his attentions. Who knew how long it would be before his self-control gave way?

'This is unwise,' she told him one night, when he grew particularly insistent, biting her neck, his hand cupping her breast.

'Why?' he gasped, face flushed, hair tousled. 'I need you! I love you, Anne.'

She drew away. 'Being alone with you is wrong.'

'Norris would never talk.'

'But *I* feel it is wrong. Henry' – for this she now called him in the privacy of his chamber – 'until your annulment is in sight, I do not feel it is right for me to be at court. I want to go home to Hever.'

'No!' he cried. 'Don't leave me!'

'Think of what it is like for me,' she pleaded. 'I am the butt of continual gossip. Some think I am your whore! My position here is anomalous, and until the future is clearer, it is better for me to stay away.' *And if I am at Hever, I won't have to see the man I love daily. And you will spur Wolsey more forcibly into getting you what you want.*

Henry groaned and clasped her to him. 'I don't think I can bear being without you.' He was almost sobbing.

'You can visit me, as you did before,' she said.

'It is not enough. It is never enough!'

'Please grant me leave to go. It grieves me to leave you, but it is for the best. The gossip will die down and my reputation will be saved.'

'Very well,' Henry sighed. 'But this time you must write to me, often. No tardiness like before.'

'I will, I promise,' Anne said, and kissed him. He responded almost violently, every sinew expressing his longing, and she had all to do to fend him off.

Absence did indeed make a man grow fonder – if that were possible. Henry's letters betrayed a new depth of passion. When Anne perceived the increasing intensity of his feelings, she knew she had done the right thing in leaving court.

He was desperate for her. He wrote often of his need for her. In her replies, she never referred to any intimacies, for fear of further inflaming his ardour. She tried instead to express the devotion she could not feel, and pretended a great desire to see an end to their separation.

Henry wrote that he had sounded out his beloved friend Sir Thomas More on his Great Matter. More, Anne knew, was a lawyer of integrity and a renowned scholar, and his opinion would carry great weight throughout Christendom – but he had said he believed the King's marriage to be good and valid.

'I will not press him, for the sake of our friendship,' Henry wrote. 'But I wish he had felt he could support me in my just cause.'

Anne wondered how strong opposition to the Great Matter really was. When the time came, would people like More feel the need to speak out? And what damage might that do to the King's case?

*

The worst thing about being at Hever was the frosty atmosphere. Mary was there with her children for a holiday in the country, and still she could not forgive Anne for snaring the King who had abandoned her. Henry's name hung between the sisters, not to be mentioned without rancour. It did not matter that he had finished with Mary long before he began pursuing Anne: Anne was made to feel as if she had stolen him.

It was Mary who shot the worst barb.

'The King says he is troubled in his conscience because he took to wife his brother's widow,' she said out of the blue one evening, after Mother had retired and as she and Anne sat sewing in chilly silence in the parlour.

'Yes, that is the basis of his case,' Anne said, forcing herself to patience, because surely Mary knew that? The whole world did!

Mary appeared to be considering something, and it occurred to Anne that she was enjoying this.

'What's your point?' she challenged.

'I was wondering if he felt the same scruple about marrying his mistress's sister?' Mary gave her a nasty little smile.

Anne was about to utter a pithy retort when, to her horror, it dawned on her that Mary was right. There must indeed be as absolute a barrier to her marriage to Henry as there was to Henry's union with Katherine. They were equally incestuous.

It was as well that she had never given way to Henry's desires.

This was truly terrible, for such a barrier might prove insurmountable. And if the truth about Henry's relations with Mary, and the child she had borne him, was revealed, he would stand exposed as a hypocrite, and no one would believe that his Great Matter had sprung from a scruple of conscience. They would say it had been driven by lust.

'Cat got your tongue?' Mary provoked her.

Anne was desperate to refute the argument, whatever the truth of the matter. 'I'm sure a bar applies only if the parties are married,' she said. '*You* were not married to the King.'

Mary shrugged. 'Don't worry, I won't say anything. It's more than my life's worth to have Will finding out about the King and me.'

Anne was near to tears. 'Aren't things difficult enough without you making them worse?'

'It's better to know now than later. Maybe the King can get a dispensation that's sounder than the last one.'

Anne swallowed. Asking the Pope for another dispensation – aside from all the other complications – would be tantamount to conceding that the first one was tenable.

Oh, God, was there no end to the obstacles that were being placed in her way?

'You don't love him, do you?' Mary challenged. 'You just want to be queen.'

'My being queen will benefit us all, even you!' Anne flared.

'Yes, but you want all the glory,' Mary riposted. 'You want to see us all making obeisance to you.'

'In your case, I shall look forward to it!' Anne retorted.

She wrote urgently to Henry, and was relieved to receive a speedy response. Yes, he agreed there was cause for concern, but a Papal dispensation allowing their union would put matters to rights. He was sending his secretary, Dr Knight, on a secret mission to Rome to ask for one that allowed him to wed the sister of a woman with whom he had bedded. Dr Knight was also going to ask the Pope for a general commission that would give Wolsey, as Papal legate, the authority to rule on the Great Matter. 'I am absolutely resolved to satisfy my conscience,' Henry wrote.

Thank God that this new dispensation was to be kept a secret. Henry had immediately grasped the implications. He had even promised that, if Pope Clement granted him an annulment, he would declare war on the Emperor to secure the freedom of the Holy Father. And to make things easier for Clement, and bring the whole business to a speedy resolution, Wolsey had helpfully sent two draft dispensations, one annulling the first marriage, the other authorising a second, to which the Pope need only affix his signature and seal. It all sounded hopeful.

Chapter 14

1528

In the depths of a snowy January, a letter arrived from the King. Anne read it as she strode out, wrapped in furs, across the white-carpeted meadows. He would have come himself, he wrote, but the bad weather precluded it. So far, he had paid her five visits, the last before Christmas, and it had been clear that time and distance had only given a spur to his ardour. She had taken care that her mother was never out of earshot, much to Henry's frustration.

He had sent her good news. England and France had together declared war on the Emperor. Better still, the Pope had escaped from Rome to Orvieto, and had issued a confidential dispensation enabling Henry to marry whichever woman he liked, even his mother, daughter or sister, provided his first marriage was declared unlawful. Clement had also granted Wolsey a general commission to try the King's case, but not to pass judgement.

'His Holiness is terrified of the Emperor,' Henry wrote. 'He has secretly urged me to take matters into my own hands, have Wolsey pronounce a divorce, and then marry again; and he assures me he will confirm the second marriage, and so judgement will be passed to the satisfaction of the whole world — as long as no one guesses that the idea came from him. But I have the future stability of the succession to consider. Our marriage must be indisputably valid.'

Anne agreed that this was a perilous course to take. She was beginning to distrust this Pope. Why should God's Vicar on Earth fear a mortal prince? And how fitted to pronounce on the King's case was a pontiff who advised such subterfuges and permitted such unpardonable excesses in the Church?

As soon as the snow cleared, Henry rode down to Hever.

'Things are moving!' he told Anne excitedly, before he had even swung himself down from his horse. 'Wolsey has asked the Pope to send another legate, Cardinal Campeggio, to try my case with him.'

She could not contain her frustration. 'He is stalling.'

'Darling,' Henry protested, pulling her into a cold embrace, 'Wolsey is the most able of my ministers. He's the only man capable of securing an annulment.'

'Is that what he tells you? Henry, he is stalling.'

'I'll not believe it.' Henry looked injured. 'Anne, I have come all this way to see you, and I do not want to waste time arguing. I know you have little love for Wolsey, but you are being unreasonable.'

'He knows that the Pope is reluctant to give judgement in your favour for fear of offending the Emperor. He must also know that any cardinal coming from Rome will do the Pope's bidding and delay a decision. And that will suit my lord Cardinal very well, because the last thing he wants to see is me with a crown on my head!'

'I don't think so,' Henry said, looking perplexed. 'Wolsey bombards my envoys in Rome daily with instructions, promises, threats and inducements. No one has worked more tirelessly in this matter.'

'Yes, but to what end? And you cannot see it! When I think of all you have done for him, the wealth you have showered on him, the offices, the palaces finer than yours . . .' She left the sentence unfinished.

Henry was looking disgruntled. Having sown the seeds of discontent over the past weeks, in her letters and face to face, Anne knew that he was at last growing resentful of Wolsey's power and wealth.

'He has promised me an annulment, and I will hold him to it. We shall see if he keeps his promise. Then will you be satisfied?'

'I shall be forever grateful to him,' Anne declared, realising that she had gone far enough, and that it was now time to lighten the mood. She smiled. 'Our bitch has whelped. Would your Grace like to see the pups? You are very welcome to your pick of them.'

She led Henry into the hall, where Venus, Father's mastiff bitch, was lying in a basket by the fire with her offspring gambolling around her.

Mary's children were playing with them, and Anne bade them bow to the King. She saw Henry's eyes light on Catherine and recognition dawn. He bent down.

'Don't be afraid of me, little maid.' Catherine smiled shyly. It was like looking at Henry in miniature.

'I'm not afraid!' piped up Hal. Henry ruffled his hair.

'You're a fine pair,' he said, looking wistful. 'When I come again, I will bring you gifts.'

'We're going to give His Grace a gift, aren't we?' Anne told her niece and nephew. 'Which puppy shall he have?'

'Vulcan!' cried Hal.

'Saturn,' said Catherine.

'I'll have Saturn,' Henry said. Catherine gathered up the wriggling little dog and laid it in his arms. 'Thank you, sweeting,' he told her.

His eyes met Anne's above his daughter's head. They were full of tears. *Give me children like these*, they were pleading.

At the end of January, the King's chaplain, Edward Foxe, and Stephen Gardiner, a doctor of civil and canon law, called on Anne at Hever.

'Mistress Anne, we bring you news and a letter from the King,' Foxe explained, when refreshments had been served. 'We are on our way to Rome to persuade the Pope to send Cardinal Campeggio as legate. His Holiness refused, you know, but Cardinal Wolsey has asked us to add our arguments to his, and repeat without ceasing that His Majesty cannot do otherwise than separate from the Queen. If all else fails, we are to do our best to excite fear in the Pope.'

It was apparent, after Anne had conversed with Foxe and the stern-faced Gardiner for only a short while, that both were formidable advocates. If anyone could succeed with this vacillating Pope, it was these two determined clerics.

They did not stay long. They had to get to Dover to catch tomorrow's tide.

'I wish you well,' she told them. 'You have a long journey ahead of you. God speed – and bring me back good news.'

When they had gone, she opened Henry's letter. He too was

optimistic. He trusted, by the diligence of Dr Foxe and Dr Gardiner, that shortly he and she would have their desired end, which would be more to his heart's ease than any other thing in the world. It was signed: 'With the hand of him which desires as much to be yours as you do to have him. H.R.'

As usual, in the face of his devotion, she felt guilty. She had tried not to think of Norris during these months at Hever, but he had kept invading her thoughts. If only she could feel the same powerful attraction for Henry.

Soon afterwards, Henry wrote to say that, by careful manoeuvring, the Cardinal was trying to resolve the feud between her father and Piers Butler over the earldom of Ormond, hoping to persuade Piers to resign it in favour of Father. Even if Wolsey *was* seeking to placate the enmity of the Boleyns, it was good news, and Father would be elated at the prospect of being a belted earl.

Henry had suggested that a note of thanks to Wolsey would be appropriate, so Anne clenched her teeth and wrote one, thanking him for his wisdom and diligence in endeavouring to bring about the King's divorce.

> To me, it will be the greatest wealth that can come to any creature. When I am queen, you shall see what I can imagine to do you pleasure, and you shall find me the gladdest woman in the world to do it. And next to the King's Grace, you shall have my love unfeignedly through my life.

It was all lies, and it went against her principles to send it, but she must not let Henry think she was vindictive. The time would come when he would see the truth.

In March, Henry invited Anne and her mother to stay as his guests at Windsor Castle. They found him with only his riding household and a handful of attendants, but George was there, and Norris. Anne tried hard not to keep looking Norris's way, but there came a day when she entered the royal library in search of a book and found him there alone. For a long moment they looked into each other's eyes. There could be no mistaking his feelings now. His gaze held hers, but when he opened his mouth to speak, she laid a finger to her lips. Some things were better left unsaid. It was enough to know that her feelings were reciprocated. Without a word, she smiled and made herself walk out of the door.

The weather was fair, and every afternoon Henry took Anne hunting or hawking. They covered many miles, not returning until late in the evening, when a hearty supper would be served to them. In the mornings they went walking in Windsor Great Park, and Henry told her about a murdered forester called Herne the Hunter, whose antlered ghost was said to walk these woodlands. 'If you venture out at midnight you might see it,' he teased her.

'That's why I'm making sure I walk here in the mornings!' she laughed.

'Anne, I miss you dreadfully when you're not here,' Henry said. 'Come to Greenwich with me.'

It struck her that it was time to exercise a little vigilance on Wolsey.

'Very well,' she agreed. 'I will.'

Henry's eyes were shining. 'You mean I don't have to beg?'

'Not at all. I should like to come very much.'

As soon as she arrived at Greenwich, there was a scramble to pay court to her. People clearly expected that she would soon be queen, and so they vied for her favours and her patronage. And no one was more fawning and obsequious than Wolsey. Eager to please his master and ingratiate himself, he entertained Henry and Anne to great feasts and lavish banquets at York Place. It was gratifying to see the mighty Cardinal almost tripping over his red robes to pay homage to her.

No longer was she to serve the Queen. Henry knew it would be unpleasant for both of them, and assigned Anne a lodging off the tiltyard gallery. It was one normally allocated to the most favoured courtiers, and he had had it furnished with fine tapestries, a carved tester bed and a wealth of silverware. It was wonderful to have her very own apartment, and the leisure to enjoy it.

'It is but a foretaste of what you will have in the fullness of time,' Henry promised.

Now she could entertain her friends in private, and pass the time making music, writing poetry, playing cards or gossiping. George came nearly every day, and sometimes he brought Jane too, but she clearly felt ill at ease among the ladies and gentlemen, many of them self-seekers, who crowded Anne's chamber in search of good pastimes, witty conversation and favours from the King. Anne was relieved when she stopped coming.

Early in May, Henry appeared at her door. 'Dr Foxe is returned from Rome.' And there the good doctor was, right behind him.

'Welcome!' Anne greeted him, trying not to let her hopes surge too high. 'Have you brought us good news?'

'Your Grace, Mistress Anne, it is not quite what we had hoped, but his Holiness *has* agreed to send Cardinal Campeggio to England to try the case with Cardinal Wolsey. Yet we could not persuade him to grant a commission empowering Cardinal Wolsey to give judgement. Nevertheless, sir, we both feel optimistic, given the goodwill of his Holiness towards your Grace.'

'That's wonderful news!' Anne cried. 'Thank you, Dr Foxe, thank you!'

Henry grabbed Anne's hand and led them to the Cardinal, eager to tell him the news.

'Excellent, excellent!' Wolsey said, eyeing Anne nervously.

But then Foxe spoke up. 'There is one cause for concern, your Grace. His Holiness has heard rumours that Mistress Anne – forgive me, mistress – is with child, and he feels she may not be worthy to be queen.'

'That's a wicked lie!' Anne protested.

Henry's expression was thunderous. 'By God, I won't have you slandered so! My lord Cardinal, you will write to the Pope now and inform him that he has been labouring under a vile misapprehension. You will stress Mistress Anne's excellent virtue, her constant virginity, her chastity, her wisdom, her descent of noble and regal blood, her good manners, her youth and her apparent aptness to bear children. You will tell him that these are the grounds on which my desire is founded, and the qualities for which Mistress Anne is held in esteem here.'

Wolsey nodded fervent agreement. 'I will write immediately, sir,' he promised. 'The world shall know the truth about Mistress Anne.' And he bowed in her direction.

But the world – at least that portion of it in England – appeared instead to be paying heed to a mad nun in Kent, who was making wild prophecies and proclaiming that she had seen holy visions.

'This tiresome woman rants against me in public,' an irritated Henry told Anne. 'She's a lunatic, but she draws large crowds wherever she goes. Now, the authorities inform me, she has predicted that, if I put away my lawful wife, as she calls Katherine, I shall no longer be king of this realm and shall die a villain's death.' He shrugged. 'It beggars belief!'

Anne was alarmed. 'Henry, if ignorant people are giving credence to her fantasies, you should take action against her.'

'Sweetheart, she is a harmless madwoman,' he said. 'Just ignore her.'

That summer, the dreaded sweating sickness once again broke out in London, infecting people with alarming speed. It was the disease that had carried off Anne's older brothers eleven years before. She had been in France then, and had not experienced the horrors of an epidemic such as this. She was gripped with fear that, at any moment, she might be struck down with the sweat; that she might wake in the morning feeling well, but be dead by dinner time. Any little symptom – feeling overheated, which was natural in this sweltering May, or a little breathless – assumed a sinister significance. Some said that getting a physician to bleed you helped; Henry swore by a concoction of herbs in treacle. But Anne had no faith in either. When it came down to it, there was nothing you could do to protect yourself, save avoiding contact with those who were stricken.

She was disturbed to hear that some were saying that this visitation was a judgement of God on the King for putting away his lawful Queen. But Henry was having none of it.

'They might also say that it is a judgement on me for living in sin with her!' he growled. 'Do not fret, sweetheart.'

Anne was present when Henry was informed that the number of reported cases of the sweat in London had soared to forty thousand. She watched the colour drain from his face. For all his courage – this was the man who had sought glory on the battlefields of France – he had an inordinate fear of illness, and no wonder, given that he had no son to succeed him.

'We must leave Greenwich,' he said, his voice hoarse with fear. 'The court must remove tomorrow.'

He was debating with himself where best to go, and which parts of the country were safest, when word came that the sweat had invaded the royal household itself. Two servants had sickened – and Sir Henry Norris.

Anne began trembling violently. No! Norris must not die! God could not be so cruel. She strove to calm herself.

'Dear God, not Norris!' Henry lamented. 'The best of my gentlemen, God save him! I will pray for him.' He crossed himself and Anne fervently followed suit. 'That settles it,' Henry went on. 'We'll leave today. I'll give the order to break up the court. Darling, you are shaking – do not fear, I beg of you. We will go to Waltham in Essex, where I have a small house. We'll be safe there – it's a long way from the contagion.'

'What of the Queen?' Anne asked.

'She must come too. I cannot send her away at a time like this. Remember, until judgement is given, I must be seen to be cherishing her as my wife.' He shouted for his grooms. 'We will take only a small retinue,' he told Anne.

It would not be easy, she thought, living in close proximity to Katherine, although the Queen had continued to show herself courteous, if distant. And it would be a challenge concealing her fears for Norris. At least Henry would be kept informed of his progress.

At Waltham she found herself accommodated with the Queen's ladies, none of whom had a kind word to say to her these days. And Henry, to her dismay, seemed to be spending most of his time with

Katherine – when he was not closeted away experimenting with remedies for the sweat. She suspected that he was storing up credit with God, just in case his marriage was found valid – which it wouldn't be, of course; but she was seeing a different side to Henry right now, and was coming to realise how much he really did fear divine disapproval.

Wolsey, who had had the sweat before and was immune, wrote frequently. Norris, mercifully, was recovering, for which Anne gave secret heartfelt thanks. All affairs of state saving the Great Matter were being held in suspension while the sickness raged, but the Cardinal had enough to keep him busy late into the night.

'Write to Wolsey, darling,' Henry urged late one evening, when Katherine had gone to bed and they were snatching a quiet hour together in his privy chamber. 'Let him know how grateful you are for his diligence.'

Dutifully, Anne wrote, the insincere words of thanks dripping from her pen.

'I had hoped,' Henry said, when she had finished and given it to him to read, 'to have heard that Cardinal Campeggio had reached France by now.' He added a postscript, saying as much to Wolsey.

'I warned you,' Anne said. 'Campeggio will not be in any hurry. They are all hoping that you will tire of me and forget about an annulment.'

'Darling, that is just not true,' Henry said, taking her hands. 'His Holiness would not send a legate all this way unless he means to give a favourable judgement. It is only right that my case gets a fair hearing, and that the legates are seen to be weighing the evidence. You must stop imagining the worst.'

'I will try,' she sighed. 'I cannot help being anxious.' She leaned forward and kissed him lightly on the lips. 'There is a matter I wish to discuss with you.'

Henry subsided into his chair and gave her a rueful grin. 'I had hoped to make the most of our time alone together, but go ahead.'

'It will not take long,' Anne smiled. 'You will have heard that the Abbess of Wilton died.'

'Yes. It's a rich and fashionable nunnery, and the nobility send their daughters there, so there's been much ado about choosing a successor. The community supports the election of the Prioress, Dame Isabel Jordan. The Cardinal is in favour, and I dare say I shall approve it.'

Anne already knew that Wolsey was backing the Prioress. She had learned that earlier in the day when Will Carey had come to see her. His sister Eleanor was a nun at Wilton, and both he and Mary were hoping that Anne would exert influence on her behalf. Anne had smiled to herself. For all her jealousy, Mary was quite prepared to use her to get what she wanted. Yet it was chiefly the chance to score one over Wolsey that had made Anne determined to secure the appointment of Dame Eleanor. It would be an effective way of demonstrating her ascendancy over her enemy.

'Your Grace may not be aware that Master Carey's sister Eleanor is a nun at Wilton,' Anne said now. 'I think she would be a far more suitable choice. She is young and learned, and much liked. The Prioress may have many qualities, but she is too old. If it were known that your Grace preferred Dame Eleanor, the convent would vote accordingly.'

Henry considered. 'I will think on this,' he promised.

'Thank you, sir,' Anne replied. 'That would make me so happy.' And she held out her arms to him.

She was delighted to hear that Henry had written to Wolsey expressing his wishes in the matter of Wilton Abbey, and even more gratified to hear that the Cardinal had promised to push for Dame Eleanor's election. But her elation was short-lived. No sooner had she heard the good news than one of her two maids came running to say that the other had the sweat.

Henry was distraught. He ordered Anne to leave Waltham immediately for his manor of Byfleet in Surrey, in case she herself was infected. He would not even kiss her goodbye, or take her in his arms. She left, head held high, concealing her hurt. On the journey, huddled in a litter, a scented kerchief tied around the lower part of her face to ward off infection, she assured herself that it was not because he did not love her, but because he could take no chances with his own health. Indeed, she soon learned that he had abandoned Waltham and fled to Hunsdon House the day after she left.

At Byfleet, alone and in fear, she could not stop crying. The signs were there – Henry had sent her away, having all but returned to Katherine. No doubt Wolsey had got at him, pricking his ever-tender conscience. But soon Henry began bombarding her with letters begging her to send word that she continued well. He also informed her that George had contracted the sweat, but by God's mercy had recovered and was going home to Grimston as soon as he was able. She was desperately relieved to hear that, and that there was not a single sick soul at Hunsdon.

In response, she poured out her fears, of the sweat, of losing Henry to it, and about the Cardinal working against her. Henry was quick to allay them with brave words.

One thing may comfort you, for they say that few women get this malady, and no one at court has died of it. So I implore you, my entirely beloved, to have no fear at all, nor let my absence upset you, for wherever I may be, I am yours. One must sometimes submit to ill fortune, but comfort yourself, take courage, and banish this anxiety as far as you can, and then I trust soon to make us exult in its dismissal. No more for the present, for lack of time, but that I wish you in my arms, that I might a little relieve your useless and vain thoughts.

Written with the hand of him who is, and always will be,
Your ImHRmutable.

There were cases of the sweat in Surrey, he had warned her, so it was advisable for her to leave Byfleet and go home. She had her maid pack up her gear once more, and departed for Hever.

There she found her father, who had returned when the court was broken up. He sent her straight to her bedchamber and ordered her to stay there, lest she infect him, Mother, or Mary and the children, who were staying with them. She went meekly enough. It was a wise precaution.

The next morning, Mary pushed a letter from Will under Anne's door. Anne seethed when she read it. Will had been in attendance when the King opened a letter from Cardinal Wolsey and exploded with anger, for Wolsey had begged him to abandon all thoughts of his nullity suit, for fear of God's wrath.

He used terrible words, saying he would have given a thousand Wolseys for one Anne Boleyn. He said that no other than God should take her from him.

Anne was incandescent. Henry must now see that Wolsey was working against them. Here was proof, if ever he needed it! Maybe he would heed her more now, and not dismiss her real concerns as womanish fancies.

She laid down the letter, her hand trembling with anger, and opened the door to get the tray of food that had been left outside. Cold slices of venison, manchet bread, thickly buttered, and a beaker of ale. She did not fancy any of it; she was in too much turmoil to eat and her head was aching a little. She sat down and picked up her Book of Hours, an exquisite illuminated manuscript in vibrant colours. It had always brought her comfort, ever since she had bought it in the Netherlands, and after reading a few pages she did feel more positive. She would triumph in the end, she vowed it! And in anticipation of that, she took her pen and wrote at the bottom of one page, '*Le temps viendra*. The time will come!' Then she added her name, so that anyone finding the inscription in years to come would know who had written it. By then she would either be famous or forgotten.

The headache was becoming more oppressive, and there was a niggling pain near her heart. And then, suddenly, she was pouring with sweat, and knew what ailed her.

She cried out, again and again, and there was Mother, fearlessly wrapping her in blankets.

'You have to sweat it out, Anne,' she exhorted. Out in the gallery, Mary was wailing about her children. But all Anne could think of was that she was going to die, very soon, and die a virgin, without ever knowing the joy of love's consummation.

Half an hour later, she could not have cared.

Through her delirium, she heard voices.

'The King must be informed!'

'Should we call the chaplain?'

'Oh, my poor, poor child!'

They came to her through a feverish haze, in which she convulsed in violent sweats. Her whole body seemed to be in pain, and the worst of it was an intense feeling of agitation. Consciousness came and went, and when she did wake, her thoughts were in turmoil. She was aware that she had the sweat, and could remember hearing someone say that a sufferer could be merry at dinner and dead at supper, and that only those who survived the first twenty-four hours could hope to live. Terrified, she tried to prepare for death.

But God was not ready for her. In the night, her fever subsided and the sweating eased. At dawn, she awoke to find Mother sitting beside her, telling her rosary beads.

'Praise be to God, you are better!' she cried, as Anne stretched out a hand to her. Mother's cheeks were smeared with tears and there were dark circles under her eyes.

'I have been up all night watching,' she told Anne. 'Your father also has the sweat, but not so badly. He will recover.' She sagged, exhausted, in her chair.

'That's a relief,' Anne murmured, too weak to say much. 'The King . . .'

'We sent to inform him that you were ill. Before I go and lie down, I must send another letter to say you are restored to us.' Elizabeth Howard caressed Anne's cheek. 'I am so very thankful to see you looking yourself again. I was in terror, fearing we would lose you.'

Anne laid her hand over her mother's. 'God, I think, has spared me for a reason.'

Having sent the maids scurrying to change Anne's sheets, sponge her down and put on a clean night-rail, Mother was fast asleep when the

King's own physician, Dr Butts, arrived an hour later. It was Mary who sanctioned his admittance to the castle, the drawbridge having been raised to stop the sweat from spreading, and showed him up to Anne's room.

'Mistress Anne, I rejoice to find you so much better,' Butts greeted her. She had met him before and admired his urbane, reassuring manner and his great learning. He asked her several questions about her illness, then smiled. 'You need no medicine, Mistress Anne, but I have brought you a tonic.' And he handed her a letter bearing the royal seal.

'I will examine my lord your father,' he said, and discreetly withdrew.

Weakly, Anne tore open the letter. Henry had written in a frenzy. The sudden news had been the worst he could have received. It had shocked him to hear that the sweat had visited the person he esteemed more than all the world, whose health he desired as much as his own. He would willingly have borne half of her malady to have her healed. She had to smile at that. Half! It was typical of Henry to shy away even figuratively from illness.

Frantic, he had wanted to send Dr Chambers, his chief physician, but Chambers had been away, tending to the sick. Fortunately Dr Butts had been at hand. If he restored Anne to health, Henry would hold him even more closely in his affection. She must be governed by Butts's advice in all things, and then he could trust to see her again, which would be to him a more sovereign remedy than all the precious stones in the world. He had once more drawn a heart around her initials, writing them between his own at the end.

Father and Anne were out of bed and resting in the parlour when the news came that Will Carey had died of the sweat. The end had come with deadly swiftness; he had ailed only three hours before.

Mary was inconsolable. 'He was only thirty-two!' she wailed. 'What will I do now? Where will I go?'

Anne suspected that Mary's grief was more for herself and the lost prospect of a brilliant future than for the man she had married. She wondered if her sister had truly loved Will. They had got on well – it was as much as could be said for many marriages. She felt deeply saddened herself, for she had liked her brother-in-law.

A friend of Will's wrote to Mary. He had been with her husband at the end, and recounted how, at the last, Will had begged Cardinal Wolsey to look with favour on his sister, Dame Eleanor. Never mind Wolsey! Anne thought. *I* will see that his wish is honoured.

The weeks of her convalescence passed, and soon she was her old self again. Yet still she lingered at Hever, for it was high summer, the sweat was still raging, and the King was always on the move – and no doubt Katherine was doing her best to make him forget about a divorce. But Anne knew from his loving letters that that would never happen.

It was soon clear that Will's death had left Mary destitute and in debt. The lands granted to him by the King had passed to Will's son, Henry, a stolid, defiant three-year-old, who was forever rampaging around the castle on his hobby horse, wielding a wooden sword, much to his grandfather's annoyance. William's offices, with their income, had reverted to the King.

'I have nowhere to live!' Mary wept. 'Will's lodging at court has been assigned to someone else. Maybe,' she looked hopefully at Father, sniffing loudly, 'I could remain here.'

'No,' he said. 'Your place is with your husband's family. I gave Will a handsome enough dowry.'

'But I have nothing left from my marriage settlement, and Will died intestate. You know that, Father!'

But he was implacable, and all the more testy because of his recent illness. 'My responsibility towards you, daughter, ended when I gave you to William Carey! You can't stay here. His parents should support you, and I suggest that you write to them without delay and make arrangements to travel down to – where is it? – Wiltshire.'

Mary rocked in misery. 'But I don't want to live in Wiltshire – and I hardly know them!'

Anne put an arm around her. 'Father, you are being rather harsh,' she reproved. 'Don't you think so, Mother?'

Mother looked up from her sewing. 'Your father is right,' she muttered. 'Mary cannot stay here.' Anne was surprised at her reaction. It seemed that she was as unsympathetic as Father.

'Do as you're told, Mary, and write that letter,' Father barked.

Mary stumbled off, sobbing, to her chamber. It struck Anne that Father's affection for his children lasted only as long as they were useful to him. Mary was poor and nearing thirty. She would find it hard to secure a worthy husband, and could end up being at Father's charge for good. But however annoying and pathetic Mary could be, she was his daughter. And with that thought, Anne rose and hurried up to her chamber to write to Henry.

Two days later there arrived at Hever a royal messenger with a great haunch of venison, a gift from the King. There was a letter too.

'The cause of my writing at this time, good sweetheart,' Anne read, 'is to ask after your good health and prosperity, praying God, if it be His pleasure, to bring us together soon, for I promise you I long for it. And seeing my darling is absent, I am sending you some flesh, representing my name – hart's flesh for Henry – anticipating that soon, God willing, you will enjoy some of mine, which I would were now.' Anne shook her head, smiling at his boldness. And then she was filled with gratitude towards him, because he had instructed his secretary to write to Father informing him of his opinion of his treatment of Mary. 'For surely,' Henry had written, 'it cannot stand with his honour, but that he must take in his natural daughter in her extreme necessity. No more to you at this time, my own darling, although I wish we were together of an evening. With the hand of yours, H.R.'

When he read the secretary's letter, Father's face turned a dangerous shade of red, and he glared at Anne, it being obvious who was behind this. But he knew himself bested. With very poor grace, he told Mary that he had reconsidered and, out of pity, would let her stay at Hever. Mary flung her arms around him and thanked him profusely, but he was cold, pushing her away, and Anne began to realise that Mary might have done better with the Careys, for it would be like a penance living in a house where she was not welcome.

Again Anne wrote to Henry, explaining Mary's unhappy situation.

By return, he agreed to pay Mary the substantial annuity of £100 that had formerly been paid to Will Carey.

Mary's face, when she heard, was transformed. No longer was she the grieving widow: she was a woman of means.

She rounded on her parents, and even on Anne. 'You all said I came out of it with nothing! That I let the King use me and asked for nothing in return! But he has not forgotten me! He had no obligation to assign that allowance to me. But he remembers that he has a daughter. This is for her – and for me, and little Harry. It will afford us a comfortable income, and will spare us from living here in bondage!'

'It's thanks to me that you have that allowance,' Anne pointed out, hurt.

'You live here only because the King commands it!' Father snarled. 'Being at charge for you was not my chief objection to your staying. Do you not realise that you are a living reminder of something this family would prefer to forget? That there are many out to destroy your sister, looking for ways to do so, and if they got one hint that you had bedded with the King, or one glimpse of the child that is him to the life, they would use it against her. Having you out of sight in Wiltshire would have been the best solution.' He turned to Anne. 'And you, my fine lady, would have done better not to have meddled.'

'I did what I thought was right,' Anne countered. 'And so did His Grace! Will you question his wisdom?'

Father threw her a look that told her exactly what he thought of His Grace's wisdom, but he said no more, and presently life at Hever returned to a semblance of normality. That was disrupted when the King informed Anne that he had granted her the wardship of young Henry Carey.

'But he is *my* son!' Mary shouted. 'Isn't the King enough for you?'

'I did not ask for this!' Anne cried.

'Quiet, both of you!' Father growled. 'Mary, you ought to know that when the heir to landed estates is left fatherless, he becomes a ward of the King, and the King can grant that wardship to anyone he pleases. In this case His Grace has made a wise choice, for Anne is high in favour and can secure great advantages for the boy.'

'But he's *my* child!' Mary protested. 'She shall not have him!'

'I won't take him away,' Anne hastened to assure her. 'He can stay with you and all will be as it was before. When he is older, I will find him good tutors, so that he will be well educated. You cannot object to that. Look upon me as a kind of godmother, who will always have a care for his interests.'

Mary subsided. 'You will consult me in everything?'

'I will,' Anne promised.

She did not really want the responsibility of her nephew. She was more preoccupied with the election at Wilton Abbey, and ready to take up the cudgels on behalf of Eleanor Carey. At the very least, it showed Mary that she had the Carey family interests at heart, and indeed Mary softened towards her when she saw how determined Anne was to honour Will's dying wish.

But Wolsey, damn him, had got there before her. Henry wrote to say that the Cardinal had sent a commissioner to Wilton to examine the candidates to assess their suitability for the office of abbess. Dame Eleanor had confessed to having had two children by different priests; she even admitted she had recently left her convent for a time to live in sin with a servant of Lord Willoughby. Anne was horrified, for these revelations would surely reflect on her own reputation. How her enemies would love pointing the finger, jeering that she had pressed for the election of a whore. Wolsey must be laughing.

Henry, thank God, was being reasonable. To do Anne pleasure – for he knew very well that she would not brook Wolsey's candidate winning the election – he had commanded that neither Eleanor Carey nor Isabel Jordan should be abbess. 'I would not, for all the gold in the world, clog your conscience or mine to make Dame Eleanor ruler of that house.' Instead, he had decreed that the office should go to someone of good character. She would not argue with that. She wondered if Will had known that his sister had led such an immoral life.

The sweating sickness was slowly abating. Henry told Anne she should judge whether the air at Hever was best for her, but he hoped it would not be long before he saw her again.

Anne thought she should leave it a little longer before returning to court. She still tired easily in the wake of her illness, and did not feel up to battling off Henry's advances.

She was furious to hear from him that the Cardinal had taken it upon himself to force the election of Dame Isabel Jordan. Henry had spoken severely to Wolsey about his presumption, and Anne could well imagine how scorching that reprimand had been. The Cardinal had made a grovelling apology, and the very next day there arrived at Hever a letter begging forgiveness and a rich gift of jewels for Anne. The election was declared null, and the matter left in abeyance. She had won!

Chapter 15

1528

The King had returned to Greenwich, for the sweat had died down. George, now back at court, appeared at Hever, bursting with news.

'I am appointed a gentleman of the Privy Chamber!' he announced. Anne and Mother hugged him, and Father clapped him on the back. 'You have done well to rise so high at only twenty-five, my son,' he said.

'The King has asked me to give you this, Anne' – George handed her a letter – 'and to warn you that there is much gossip about you.'

Anne broke the seal. 'Darling,' she read, 'I am not a little perplexed with such things as your brother shall tell you, and I pray you give him full credence. That I trusted shortly to see you is better known in London than it is here at court, whereof I marvel. Someone has been indiscreet, but I trust that in future our meetings shall not depend upon other men's light handling. Written with the hand of him that longs to be yours, H.R.'

She shrugged. 'I suppose such gossip is only to be expected. With the legate coming from Rome, there is bound to be talk.'

That night, after an enormous celebratory dinner, Anne and George sat up in the parlour catching up on their news.

'How is Jane?' Anne asked.

'She is enjoying being back at court,' George said. She could sense his evasion.

'How are you and Jane?' she persisted. She had long known that theirs was not a happy marriage.

'We see as little of each other as possible,' George admitted, his expression darkening. 'If you want the truth, we cordially hate each other – and sometimes not even cordially.'

'But why? She's comely enough.'

'Her beauty is only skin deep. Anne, she was brought up without any bridle. Her father seems to have been so immersed in his books that he neglected to instil in her the importance of virtue. She has betrayed me with several men, following her lust and filthy pleasure, without any wifely loyalty.'

Anne was shocked. 'She has actually committed adultery?'

George snorted, his handsome features twisted in contempt. 'Yes, if you want it plain! She dreads neither God nor falling from grace. Her behaviour is vicious.' He downed the dregs of his wine and helped himself to more. 'But I am as much to blame, I and my great appetite for women. Believe me, Anne, I have not been chaste.'

'The whole court knows that,' she said gently.

'They don't know it all,' he muttered.

'What are you trying to tell me?'

George looked stricken. Long moments passed before he spoke. 'Anne, I am consumed with guilt. I must talk to someone, and you're the only person I can trust – and yet if I tell you what torments me, you will hate me.'

'I could never hate you,' Anne declared. 'Tell me!'

He hesitated, not looking her in the eye. 'It's as if I want to devour women; it's all I think about, day and night. I'm out of control, and powerless to change. I've – I've even forced widows and deflowered maidens. They are all one to me.' His voice was strangled.

Anne was shaken to the core. Her own brother, whom she loved like a second self, was confessing to rape, the crime she most abhorred – it was beyond comprehension. No wonder Jane had looked elsewhere!

'You should have more control!' she hissed at him, leaping up and slapping his face hard. 'Have you no respect for women?'

'I can't help it.' George looked utterly wretched. His cheek was red from the slap. 'It's my nature, and sometimes I hate myself for it. But I can't love Jane anyway. There's a rottenness in her. She . . . she wanted to watch me with one of my paramours.'

'By all the saints!' Anne cried. 'What's the matter with you both? George, these excesses won't do you any good. Do you want to get the pox? You should look to your wife, and put an end to her misconduct. Stop forcing yourself on other women! I can think of few worse things a man can do. Have you any idea of the hurt and damage it does? Look at Mary, our sister!'

George hung his head. 'I will try, Anne. Honestly I will.'

He held out his hand, but she would not take it.

'I'm going to bed,' she snapped, and left him.

She did not sleep that night, but lay wakeful, trying to come to terms with the knowledge that her beloved brother was the kind of man she most despised. By the morning she knew that, even though she was bitterly, devastatingly, disappointed in him, she could never stop loving him. They were too close for that.

By the middle of August, Anne was back in her apartment off the tiltyard at Greenwich. Henry came to her immediately, and embraced her as if he would never let her go.

'Darling! You cannot know what a health it is to me to see you looking so well,' he told her. 'I thank God every day for restoring you to me.'

'And I thank Him that your Grace was spared,' she replied.

'He ever favours the righteous,' Henry observed, finally relinquishing her. 'I hope soon to hear news of Cardinal Campeggio's arrival in England. Apparently he was delayed by illness, and then, of course, he was unable to come because of the sweating sickness. But I trust he will soon be here – and then, sweetheart, we will see an end to this vexatious waiting.'

Anne desperately hoped so. She wanted an end to all the uncertainty and speculation too.

'It has been eighteen months now since you asked me to marry you,' she recalled. 'I never thought to wait so long.'

'And it is three years since I fell in love with you,' Henry murmured, caressing her hair and tilting up her chin so that he could kiss her. 'But take heart – all will soon be well.'

He picked up her lute.

'While you were away, I wrote a song for you. I have had it in my head ever since, and gladly, for it conjured your image constantly. I've been longing to play it for you, my darling.'

'I long to hear it,' she said. She was now adept at leading Henry to believe that she was as ardent as he was. But the song was moving, and he poured all his feelings into it as he sang in his true tenor voice:

> *Adieu madame, et ma maîtresse,*
> *Adieu mon solas et ma joie!*
> *Adieu jusque revoie,*
> *Adieu vous dis par grand' tristesse!*

One day, Anne hoped, she might come to feel real love for Henry, the kind of emotion she felt for Norris. When she saw Norris in attendance the next day, she would not allow herself to acknowledge him, lest she betray her feelings. Yet she was aware of his eyes on her and the warmth emanating from him.

Anne was still disturbed about George and his marriage, and wanted to see if she could help. She sought out Jane, her sister-in-law, and invited her to supper in her lodging. They began with pleasantries, but there was a new wariness in Jane. No doubt she thought that Anne would take George's part, or that the Boleyns were all tainted with the same vices. Anne resolved to disabuse her of those notions.

'George confessed to me that he had been unfaithful,' she said.

There was a silence.

'I suppose he told you that I have too,' Jane said, her pouting lips pursed in resentment.

'He did. Dear sister, why are you both so unhappy together?'

'He is a beast!' Jane burst out. 'I could not, for shame, tell you what he has done to me, for I doubt you would believe it.'

'Try me,' Anne said, wondering if she wanted to hear this. 'What you say will go no further.'

'He has a . . . a sensual appetite.'

'I know. It is no secret. He has always been one for the ladies, but I hoped he would settle down when you married.'

'I am not talking about adultery,' Jane said, beginning to weep. 'I am talking about his unlawful vices. He made me . . . Shame restrains me from saying it . . . Oh, God, it was vile and detestable – an abomination!' She buried her face in her hands.

At the court of France, Anne had heard of many sexual practices, but she had no idea what Jane was talking about. Maybe her sister-in-law was naive and did not understand what was normal and what was not. Yet George had called her vicious.

'In faith, I am at a loss,' she said.

'You should rejoice in your ignorance,' Jane replied. 'It is an odious sin against God, what George did to me, several times.'

Anne was even more perplexed.

'Unless you are more specific, I cannot help.'

Jane reddened. 'It was like the beasts do!' she burst out.

Anne sagged with relief, remembering erotic drawings she had seen in France. 'Then it is not unnatural,' she said.

'Since when has sodomy been natural?' Jane hissed.

She did not confront George. She consigned what she knew to a hidden part of her mind, where she did not have to face it. She knew she ought to hate him as the worst man alive, but she could not.

She had tried to show sympathy to Jane, but Jane was having none of it. After her initial outburst, she had refused to be drawn further, and soon afterwards had taken her leave. Since then, on the rare occasions they encountered each other – because, Anne suspected, Jane was avoiding her – Jane had seemed more distant, even resentful. It was as if she blamed Anne for having forced the confidence.

Anne had more pressing things to think about. Queen Katherine was still presiding over the court. The Queen was polite enough when they came face to face, but being under the same roof was embarrassing for them both.

'It renders my own position anomalous,' Anne complained to Henry one evening, as they were supping with the Cardinal. 'I am neither maid-of-honour nor wife. There is no real place for me at court.'

'It would be more in keeping with propriety, Mistress Anne, for you to have an establishment of your own,' Wolsey said. Those who did not know better would have thought, these days, that she and he were best friends, so effectively had Anne feigned affection for him, and gratitude for all he was supposedly doing to push forward the Great Matter.

'That would be best,' Henry said. 'I could visit you there, darling. We must find a house for you.'

Anne considered for a moment. 'Since your Grace is so often here at Greenwich, I should very much like one nearby.' Norris had a house near Greenwich. What bliss – and what torment – it would be to be near neighbours.

'Perhaps, sir, I could investigate what is available,' Wolsey suggested.

'Excellent!' declared Henry. 'The sooner this can be arranged, the better it will be for everyone.'

'I thank you both,' Anne smiled, 'but you will not object, sir, if I go home to Hever until my house is ready?'

Henry groaned. 'Not again! I swear I'll raze that place to the ground.'

'If you do, I will just have to go to my father's house at Norwich, which is much further away,' Anne said sweetly.

It would be wonderful to have her own house and her own establishment. It would be like having her own court. The best thing about it was that Katherine would not be there.

Anne was impressed to receive a letter from Henry just two days after she arrived at Hever. A suitable lodging near Greenwich was not to be had, but the Cardinal had found another for her – Durham House on the Strand, by London. And Henry had already ordered her father to see to its refurbishing.

Anne travelled up to London immediately and went with Father to see it. The place was huge, its great empty chambers spacious and echoing. Through the windows she could see gardens and lawns sweeping down to the river. Then she entered what must once have been a bedchamber and stopped. A portrait of a young Queen Katherine hung on one wall.

'She lived here before her marriage to the King,' Father said.

'That has to go,' Anne insisted. 'I want no reminders of her.'

They spent an otherwise happy hour drawing up lists of the furniture, wall hangings and household stuff Anne would require.

'The King has authorised me to requisition from the Royal Wardrobe whatever necessities and furnishings you need,' Father said.

'Then I shall live like a queen!' Anne cried, and twirled around in the middle of what would soon be her own great chamber.

'Indeed you will. His Grace's express instructions were that you are to have a house fit for his bride-to-be.'

An army of servants and ladies-in-waiting was engaged to serve Anne, so that she could keep as much state at Durham House as if she were queen already. Among her new maids was a sweet, fair-haired girl called Nan Saville, who endeared herself to Anne by her delight in serving her future Queen. Anne had invited her sister Mary to serve her as lady-in-waiting, but Mary had refused. She had her children to think of, she said. So did most of her ladies, but it didn't stop them coming to court, Anne thought, annoyed at having her olive branch spurned.

Within three weeks all was ready and she moved in. Courtiers came flocking to pay their respects and proclaim their allegiance, George and Father were to prove constant visitors, and on the first evening the King arrived, with Norris in attendance, keeping a discreet distance. Anne suppressed her delight at seeing Norris. Not seeing him daily was the only thing she disliked about living at Durham House.

As soon as they were alone, Henry kissed her, and Anne could sense a suppressed excitement about him.

'I had word today,' he announced. 'Cardinal Campeggio will soon be arriving in England. An end is in sight.'

'That's marvellous news!' Anne cried.

'I have no doubt of the outcome, no doubt at all. God and my conscience are perfectly agreed on the righteousness of my case.' And he pulled her to him again, pressing his lips to hers. 'Soon you will be mine!' he breathed.

She took great pleasure in showing him and Norris around Durham House, feeling intensely conscious of Norris's nearness, but Henry was busy expressing hearty praise for the improvements that had been made, and her taste in furnishings.

They dined in private, off silver plate that had once graced his father's table.

'You serve a good venison pasty,' Henry complimented her, wiping his mouth with his napkin. There was a knock and an usher entered with a letter.

'It'll be from the Duke of Suffolk,' Henry said, dismissing the man with a gesture. 'I sent him to Paris to welcome Campeggio and escort him to England.' He broke the seal, read it, and frowned.

'What is it?' Anne asked sharply.

'A lot of nonsense. He says that Campeggio's mission will be mere mockery. I won't believe it. That legate hasn't come all this way for nothing.'

Henry was away hunting, for it was now the grease season. Anne remained at Durham House, fretting about the legate and waiting for Henry to send her news.

His next letter was joyous. The legate would be in Calais within the week. From there, it was but a short journey to England, weather permitting. And then, he wrote, 'I will look soon after to enjoy that which I have so longed for, to God's pleasure, and both our comforts. No more to you at this time, my own darling, for lack of time, but that I would you were in my arms, or I in yours, for I think it long since I kissed you.'

Henry was unable to stay away from Anne for long. He sent to her, asking her to come to him secretly at Easthampstead Park, his hunting lodge in Windsor Forest. It was more like a palace, actually, and with only Norris and the King's riding household in attendance, the place seemed empty, but it did afford them some privacy. Yet Norris's presence was a torment for Anne.

Apart from being overjoyed to see her, Henry was in a good mood. The hunting was proving excellent – they dined on the venison he had killed – and he was optimistic about the coming hearing.

He had started writing another book, *A Glass of the Truth*, which he was eager to show her. In it he was setting forth – very cogently – his arguments against his marriage and against a female succession. Anne was tempted to dispute the latter, but of course it would not be in her own interests to do so.

It was much later when Henry picked up a beautifully bound volume with a silken marker in it, and handed it to her.

'I would show you this, sweetheart. I found it in my choirbook.' She opened it and saw an exquisitely painted Tudor rose and the date 1515, then turned to the page he had indicated. The text was in Latin, and entitled *Quam pulchra es*.

'I do not know Latin,' she said, and gave the book to Henry.

'I will translate for you, then,' he said, and read the words, his voice resonant with emotion:

How beautiful you are, my love,
How beautiful and how comely you are;
How beautiful are your cheeks;
Your breasts are more excellent than wine;
Your neck is like a jewelled necklace;
Your eyes are those of doves.
Your lips, your throat, your hands,
Your belly and your face are as ivory.
O my love, lay yourself bare for me, for I am faint with love.

He looked up at her, his eyes aflame with desire. Never before had he used such erotic language to her. She was amazed that the passage had been included in a choirbook, although she knew it paraphrased the sensual, seductive Song of Solomon in the Bible.

'I am become a monk, Anne!' Henry complained. 'I ache for you, God only knows how much! You know I am resolved to wait until we are wed before making you mine completely, but darling, there is so much we can enjoy to assuage our desire.' Always he assumed that her need for him was as fervent as his for her. And he kissed her as if he would have devoured her, his insistent hands clutching at her waist, her hips and her thighs. Gently she disengaged them, but his fingers were soon at her low-cut bodice.

'No!' she whispered, prising them away. She had never permitted him to undress her in any way. And she was thinking about that date in the book. It had been made for him when he was young and happily married to Katherine. Had he shared those very same lyrics with her?

'Oh, you are cruel,' he groaned, his lips at her neck. She could smell the sweat on him, mingled with the scent of herbs, feel the hot tousle of his hair against her cheek, the rasp of his beard on her skin. She drew his face up to hers and kissed him, hoping to deflect his baser intentions, but he was too set on his course, moving his lips to her breast, pulling the stiff fabric down and taking her nipple in his mouth, teasing it with his tongue. Desire shot through her, shocking her, thrilling her. She had never expected to feel this with Henry.

He must not think he had conquered her. From here it was only a small step to greater liberties – and then what? Would he force her to submit wholly to him, as Mary claimed he had done to her? She was aware of his strength, his power. That arm that was holding her so tightly could wield a broadsword effortlessly. She was slender and much smaller than he was – he could overcome her with ease.

She sat up, gently but firmly pushing him away, and quickly adjusted her bodice.

'No!' he protested, looking at her with longing. 'Do not be cruel, Anne!'

'I am thinking of us both,' she said. 'The closer the embrace, the greater the frustration. We must be patient a little longer, my love. Besides, we dare not risk any scandal now.'

'No, you are right,' Henry sighed, letting her go. 'But I do not know how much longer I can stand this.'

When she returned to Durham House, there was already a letter waiting for her.

Mine own sweetheart,
    This is to tell you of the great loneliness that I feel since your departing, for I assure you I think the time longer this time than I used to do when we were apart for a whole fortnight. I think your kindness and my fervent love have caused this, for otherwise

I would not have thought it possible that it should so have grieved me. But now that I am coming towards you, I think my pain will be half cured, and also there is comfort in that my book keeps me busy. I have spent above four hours writing it today, which has caused me to write the shorter letter to you now, because of some pain in my head. Wishing myself, specially of an evening, in my sweetheart's arms, whose pretty dugs I trust shortly to kiss.

Written by the hand that was, is, and shall be yours, by his will, H.R.

He could not endure to be without her – and the legate would shortly be here!

'I have offered Cardinal Campeggio a state welcome in London,' Henry told Anne, as they glided along the Thames in his barge one evening early in October, to the sound of lutes and shawms. 'But he has refused it. I've put Bath Place by Temple Bar at his disposal. He'll be comfortable there, and it will be convenient for the Black Friars' monastery, where the hearing will be held.'

Anne drew in her breath. It was nearly upon them now, this judgement for which they had yearned for so long.

But when the good Cardinal did arrive, three days later, he immediately took to his bed.

Henry, discreetly visiting Anne at Durham House that afternoon, was exasperated. 'It seems he has gout, which was what delayed his journey.'

How clever of Clement to send a cardinal whose progress would inevitably be slow. She did not say, *I told you so.* Instead she began girding herself to face the likelihood that Campeggio's only instructions were to keep stalling and delay judgement for as long as possible. Already it had taken him five months to reach England – a journey that would normally take about three weeks in summer.

'Well, I'll give him tonight to rest,' Henry was saying, 'and I'll send Wolsey to talk with him tomorrow.'

*

223

The next evening, Henry stalked into her chamber, flushed with anger.

'Wolsey spent *hours* discussing the case with Campeggio today,' he fumed, 'and do you know what this legate said? He said the best solution would be a reconciliation between me and the Queen. But Wolsey, give him his due, stood his ground, and urged the expediting of the business with all possible dispatch. He told Campeggio that the affairs of the kingdom are at a standstill, as indeed they are. This Great Matter has ousted all else, and needs to be resolved.'

Anne said nothing. It was all happening as she had feared. They had put all their faith in this Pope, and for what?

'Don't look so despondent, darling,' Henry enjoined her. 'Wolsey will prevail. There's no statesman to touch him.'

'I wish I could believe it!' she cried. Only yesterday her father and Uncle Norfolk had again expressed concern about the Cardinal's true motives. They suspected him of secretly supporting the Queen. And if that were true, he would welcome the legate's stalling tactics.

'Why, sweetheart!' Henry was all concern. 'You are distraught, I understand that. This waiting has been too distressing. I assure you, no man has worked harder than the Cardinal on our behalf.'

'Then I must accept your Grace's assurances,' Anne conceded.

Henry kissed her. 'It is a joy to me to see you so wise and sensible. Try to rein in these vain thoughts and fantasies with the bridle of reason. Good sweetheart, continue in this resolve, for by Wolsey's means there shall come, both to you and me, the greatest quietness in this world.'

Anne only hoped that Henry's confidence in the Cardinal would be repaid.

They fell to talking of other matters. The court was moving to Bridewell Palace, by the Black Friars' monastery, and Henry, anticipating a speedy outcome to his case, was arranging for apartments at Bridewell to be prepared for her.

'But the Queen will be there,' Anne said.

'Fear not, darling, she won't trouble you,' Henry told her, his eyes taking on that steely glint that spelled danger. 'I am determined to make her heed my doubts about our pretended marriage, and take them seriously, which she has always refused to do. It irritates me, when I am very pensive, worrying about this hearing, and she goes about with a smile on her face, encouraging her people to dance and make music – all out of spite for me. And there is more . . . In truth, I am persuaded by her behaviour that she does not love me.'

Anne tried not to laugh – or cry. Why should Henry care if Katherine loved him? And why should the Queen love a man who was doing his best to repudiate her? If she was not his lawful wife, he could expect no wifely devotion. But he wanted it both ways.

'What has she done, besides look cheerful?' she asked.

Henry grimaced. 'She has not shown, in public or private, as much love for me as she ought. She shows herself too much to the people too, and tries to steal their affection from me. What else can I conclude but that she hates me?' He paused, looking very sorry for himself. 'My Council has received a secret report of a design to kill me and the Cardinal.'

'No!' Anne cried, alarmed. Without Henry, she was nothing, and the wolves would be waiting to pounce . . .

'Be at peace, sweetheart,' Henry soothed, 'for I am assured there is no real danger. But if it could be proved that the Queen had any hand in this conspiracy, she must not expect to be spared.'

There was no real danger. Anne suspected that there was no real conspiracy.

Henry was waxing indignant. 'My Council have advised me to separate from her, both at bed and board, and to take the Princess Mary from her.'

Anne did not believe that Henry would ever go so far, or not for long. If he did, she knew it would break Katherine. Momentarily she felt a sharp pang of sympathy for the Queen, but quickly reminded herself that Katherine did not need to be in this situation. It was her own fault that she was. Aloud, she said, 'It might make her capitulate. She should not be courting popularity at such a time.'

'No, she should not,' Henry growled. 'There is already too much sympathy for her. The common people, being ignorant of the truth, especially the women, say that I mean to take another wife for my own pleasure; and whoever speaks against it is much abhorred and reproved. Katherine has been warned that she must show herself less in public and adopt a more sober demeanour at this time – at the risk of my displeasure. And so, darling, when you come to Bridewell, you will not be troubled by her.'

He stood up. 'I must go. I am seeing Cardinal Campeggio myself in the morning. And he had better not suggest that I return to the Queen!'

Henry arrived the next afternoon in a jubilant mood. He kissed Anne and led her through to the garden, where they seated themselves on a stone bench facing the Thames.

'It did not begin well,' he related. 'At first the legate argued that I should return to the Queen. You can imagine my reaction. But then he showed me a Papal bull authorising him to give judgement on my case. He said his Holiness had granted it, not to be used, but to be kept secret, as he desired to demonstrate the goodwill he has towards me. Truly, Anne, I think Pope Clement means for judgement to be given, but he dare not make that bull public for fear of the Emperor.'

It is just a sop to keep you sweet, Anne thought. *What good is this bull if it cannot be used?* But she went on smiling.

'I showed him,' Henry said, 'that I have studied this matter with great diligence, and probably know more about it than any theologian or jurist. I told him in the plainest terms that I want nothing but a declaration whether my marriage is valid or not, although I said there could be no doubt that it is invalid. And then he came up with the ideal solution. Katherine should be persuaded to enter a nunnery. She's pious, and would make a wonderful abbess. Then the Pope can issue a dispensation allowing me to remarry, and the Emperor could not possibly object. We can be married, and England will have hopes of an heir.'

It was the best, the perfect answer. Anne's spirits soared.

'Do you think the Queen will agree?'

'I see no reason why not. She stands to lose only my person by entering religion; she knows I will not return to her, however things fall out. She could still enjoy any worldly comforts she desires, and I will allow her whatever she wishes, and above all I will settle the succession upon Mary, after any children we have, darling.' His eyes narrowed in that menacing way that betokened a steely determination to have his will. 'Besides, she, of all people, will wish to preserve the peace of Europe and the spiritual authority of the Holy See.' He was growing bullish now. 'Because if Clement ruled in her favour, I would lose all faith in his office, and so would many others. And I've made it very clear to Campeggio that if this divorce is not granted, I will annihilate the authority of the Pope in this kingdom.'

Anne felt as if she had been winded. Her heart began beating furiously. Did he really mean what he had just said? Would he overthrow a thousand years of England's obedience to the Church of Rome to free himself? And for her?

For a moment she was speechless. Then she found her voice.

'You would do that?'

'Without hesitation!' Henry declared. 'I could not countenance a corrupt Pope wielding spiritual authority over my realm. But it won't come to that. Katherine will see reason.'

Henry's words had left Anne thoughtful. That evening, as they dined and the conversation moved on to other matters, her thoughts kept straying to the momentous prospect he had opened up. It *was* a scandal that the Pope could not bring himself to pronounce on Henry's case. But, as she had known since her days at the court of the Regent Margaret, there was a lot else that was scandalous in the Church. The sale of indulgences; priests who charged the poor for the sacraments necessary for attaining Heaven, and who flouted their vows of chastity by taking mistresses. And these were the men chosen to interpret the Scriptures for lay people! Look at the fabulous wealth of the Church, which enabled popes, cardinals and bishops to live in sybaritic luxury. Look at Wolsey! Look at those clergy who, like him, acquired parishes and benefices simply for their revenues, and never even visited them. Was this the Church that Christ had founded? Surely He had never intended it to be like this.

Small wonder that reformers like Martin Luther had spoken out against the abuses. Faith, Luther had said, should be based on Scripture alone. Man is justified through his faith in Jesus Christ. And in the eleven years since he had nailed his list of protests against the abuses to a church door in Germany, thousands had come to agree with him, even though the Church branded them heretics.

Henry had castigated Luther, yet this Church he had defended so vigorously was now showing itself to be rotten to the core. And it was the same Church to which Queen Katherine and the Emperor and countless other orthodox Christians rendered unquestioning devotion, regarding any criticism of the corruption within as an attack on faith itself. It was the Church of which Anne saw Wolsey as the living embodiment.

She had read some of the Lutheran tracts that had reached England from abroad. People circulated them surreptitiously at court, and discussed them in secret, for they were officially banned. She had spoken about them with Father and George, who both saw some wisdom in them. But her traditional upbringing in the old faith was sufficiently deep-rooted for her to believe that one could get to Heaven through good works, not just through faith alone, as the Lutherans claimed. She could not accept Luther's rejection of five of the seven holy sacraments, leaving only baptism and communion. But in recent months she had been questioning the probity of the Church and even of the Pope himself. Why was it, she had begun to wonder, that those who were ordained were the only people allowed to interpret the Scriptures? And why did the Bible have to be in Latin? Why could not people read the word of God for themselves? It seemed that the enlightened days when Erasmus could freely translate the Scriptures were long gone, swept away by a reactionary fear of heresy. How could people come to a God they could not know properly? Some ignorant priests did not even know Latin!

Reform had to come. And she was uniquely placed to make it happen. Every word that fell from her lips had Henry spellbound. She could make him listen to her. She would lay the foundations of reform now, and build on them when she was queen. A sense of exaltation filled her. She would be a queen such as Esther had been in the Bible.

The Jewish Esther had become the beloved second wife of the pagan King Ahasuerus of Persia, after he had set aside his first Queen. His overmighty chief minister, Haman, had tried to massacre the Jews, but Esther had interceded and saved her people. And it would be said of Anne, as it had been said to Queen Esther, 'Who knoweth whether thou art come to the kingdom for such a time as this?'

'Darling?' Henry said plaintively. 'Did you hear what I said? You were miles away.'

'I'm sorry,' Anne excused herself, coming back to reality with a jolt. 'I must confess I am tired tonight.'

'Then you must rest, sweetheart,' he said, and took a loving leave of her.

She was glad to be alone to think, and in bed an hour later, she lay wakeful, conscious of the enormity of what Henry had said, and what she was planning. She was honest enough with herself to know that her aims were not purely grounded in principle. Taking a stand against the Church would enable her to stake out the high moral ground against Wolsey and the Queen. But had Henry really meant what he said about annihilating the Pope's authority, or had he threatened it in a fit of pique?

When Father and George visited two days later, Anne made them sit down.

'The King has said that if Clement does not grant this divorce, he will annihilate the authority of the Holy See in England,' she told them.

For a moment they were speechless. Their faces registered their astonishment at the enormity of what she had just said.

'Father, you agree the Church needs reforming. This might be the golden opportunity for it.'

'Reform, aye. But severing England from the Holy See?' Father frowned. 'Is this what the King really means to do?'

'He said so. I think he meant it.' Anne rose and began walking up and down the gallery. 'He is determined to have what he wants, by whatever means. And if it comes to a break with Rome, that will be our moment.'

229

'By God!' George exclaimed. 'If anyone can seize the day, it's you, Anne. I'm almost hoping that the Pope *will* declare the King's marriage valid, just to see what follows.'

'Don't be flippant,' his father reproved him. 'This is no light matter. It's the weightiest one to be raised in England in a thousand years. The King must be powerfully moved if he's making such threats. He's a conservative at heart when it comes to religion. He attends Mass faithfully and creeps to the Cross on Good Friday. He might waver in his resolve. That's where you come in, Anne. No one is better placed to lead him the right way. If Clement says yes to him, well and good, and we'll all go on telling our beads and asking the saints to intercede for us. But if not – I say thank God for you, daughter! You can lead us to the Promised Land.'

Anne stared at him. Never had Father revealed that he had such confidence in her, or encouraged her to use her power to its uttermost. He was virtually conceding supremacy to her, and acknowledging that she, not he, was now the head of her faction – and her family.

Reform was a favourite topic in the darkening autumn evenings, when she sat with Father and George by the fire in the great chamber at Durham House.

'We, the laity, should be able to make our own minds up about what the Bible says,' George declared.

'Give me one good reason why it should not be in English and freely available,' Father challenged, draining his goblet.

'They fear we will find out that the Scriptures don't offer any grounds for the corruption in the Church,' George said. 'Remember how the Bishop of London ordered all copies of William Tyndale's translation to be burned? Then Cardinal Wolsey condemned Tyndale as a heretic.'

'It's as well for him that he's living in Germany,' Anne said, getting up to fetch more wine.

'Tyndale was right,' Father stated. 'He said that nowadays no man may look on the Scriptures until he has had eight or nine years of indoctrination and become armed with false principles, by which time he is incapable of understanding them.'

'The Church wants to stay in control by censoring what the laity know,' Anne declared. 'Does it fear that if we could all read the Scriptures for ourselves, we might start questioning its authority?'

'We already are,' George observed.

'It's not just the Scriptures that we can't read,' Father said. 'Wolsey keeps a long list of the books he's banned.'

'What books?' Anne asked. 'Lutheran tracts?'

'I don't know all the titles, but only last week he was clucking about one called *A Supplication for the Beggars*. It's by an Englishman, Simon Fish, who lives in exile in Antwerp. Wolsey called it vicious and subversive, and said it would incite heresy, murder and treason.'

'It sounds like my kind of book,' Anne smiled. 'If Wolsey hates it, I am bound to like it. Where can I get a copy?'

Father and George stared at her. 'Are you mad, daughter?' Father barked. 'Do you want to be accused of heresy?'

'It's a long time since anyone was burned at the stake in England,' Anne retorted.

'The law is still in force,' he reminded her.

'But Anne is not subject to the same laws as the rest of us,' George said, grinning. 'I'll wager that her influence with the King is such that she could with impunity read any book that was banned.'

'I wouldn't like to put that to the test,' Father retorted.

'Never fear, I will not risk my skin,' Anne assured him.

Her interest was piqued, though. She could not be seen to be seeking out a copy of *A Supplication for the Beggars*. Instead, she sent one of her servants abroad to Antwerp, ostensibly to buy diamonds, but with secret instructions to procure the book. Within a week it was in her hands. She stored it under a floorboard, only taking it out to read at night, and was impressed. Simon Fish argued the case for translating the Scriptures into English. He appealed to King Henry, to whom his work was dedicated, to help the poor and the needy, since the Church only increased their miseries through its rapacity. Half of England's wealth was in its hands – a disproportionate amount, given that fewer than one person in a hundred was in holy orders. He accused the monasteries of corruption and heaping taxes on the poor, whom they were supposed to succour. Their wealth was obscene! What Fish really wanted to see was its redistribution, to the greater benefit of the realm.

But it was not just the Church's riches that he was targeting. The clergy, he asserted, had usurped sovereign power in England and cleverly subverted laws restraining them. The ancient kings of Britain had never been subject to Rome or paid taxes to the Holy See, a foreign power. But now the kingdom was in bondage, thanks to the many clerical parasites infesting it.

The book was strongly argued and provocative, explosive even, but it hit the core of the matter, and it was like a revelation. No wonder Wolsey had banned it!

Henry should see this, Anne resolved. It would give him much to think about. It was so apposite for the times that it would be worth her taking the risk. She did not think he would punish her.

She pushed it across the table when next they were dining together.

'Your Grace ought to read this,' she urged.

She knew by his frown that he had heard of it. 'The Cardinal banned it,' she said, 'but Master Fish makes some cogent arguments.'

Henry raised an eyebrow. 'Where did you get this?'

'From Antwerp.' She would not lie to him. 'Master Fish fled there for fear that the Cardinal would persecute him. I can see why Wolsey would object to it, but Henry, I would really value *your* opinion. Have you read it?'

He shook his head, turning over the pages, intrigued.

'Sir, are you content to leave it to the Cardinal to decide which books should be banned? He does it in your name.'

'I trust Wolsey,' Henry said. Did she detect a note of doubt in his voice?

'You might think differently when you have read Master Fish's book.'

'Very well, I will do so,' he said, and took it away with him. He had not uttered one word of reproof to her for procuring a heretical work.

Some days later he told her that he had read it, and that it had made him very pensive. But he would not give the order for it to be struck from the banned list. Nevertheless, Anne told herself, she had sown seeds that might ripen.

Katherine would not see reason. She refused, time and again, to enter a nunnery. Instead, she repeatedly asserted to the two cardinals that she was the King's true wife. Their begging, cajoling and bullying had not the slightest effect.

The November skies were lowering when a furious Henry stamped off to see Katherine himself, shouting, 'I'll make her go! I'll ram the veil on her head!' Anne did not see him for hours, and when he did come to her late that evening, he was in a foul mood.

'What did the Queen say?' Anne ventured.

'She is adamant. It is against her soul, her conscience and her honour.'

'So are you forcing her?'

'If it comes to it, I will. Campeggio is all for it. I'll let him put the pressure on.'

You're still afraid of her, Anne thought. *You'll leave others to do the confronting.*

'You'd think she'd be pleased to retire to a nunnery and leave all this behind,' she said. 'She would avoid the embarrassment that might arise if the case goes to trial. A lady of her sensibilities must shrink from the intimate details of her married life being exposed to public scrutiny.'

'*I* shrink,' Henry retorted. 'But nothing daunts her.'

Even Uncle Norfolk had praised Katherine's courage. But her refusal to face the reality of the situation was infuriating, as was the way that the commons continued to espouse her cause.

'Sir, the people seem to express their love for her ever more loudly, now that the legate is here. And they cry out against me.' Anne knew what they called her. 'Strumpet!' 'Whore!' 'Jezebel!'

'I know,' Henry said, pacing up and down, a lion ready to pounce. 'I will not have these foolish rumours and demonstrations. I shall invite the Lord Mayor and my lords, councillors, judges, aldermen, sheriffs, masters of the city guilds, and anyone else who cares to come here, and I will tell them so!'

And he did. Anne was not present in the great hall at Bridewell Palace when he addressed his leading subjects, but there were plenty to tell her how majestic the King had appeared, standing in his robes of state in front of the canopied throne, and how commandingly he had spoken, reminding everyone that he had so ordered affairs during his nineteen-year reign that no enemy had oppressed them, and of the necessity for preserving that peace by securing the succession. He praised the Queen, and said that, if she were judged his lawful wife, nothing would be more pleasing to him, and if he were to marry again, he would choose her above all women. Anne blenched at that, but she told herself it was only policy that dictated Henry's fair words.

But then he had declared his doubts of conscience and his fear that he had lived in adultery for so long. He had had them all nodding in sympathy. Only at the last did he declare that he would brook no opposition to a divorce, saying there was never a head so dignified but that he would make it fly. It was all bluster, of course – Anne did not believe he would ever go that far.

The King's speech was the sole topic of conversation in the court. Some expressed compassion for his plight, some remained mute, their silence eloquent, and a few bold souls expressed the view that he should never have raised the matter in public. But there were several whose hostility was replaced by understanding, and when reports of the speech spread to the streets of London, people spoke more soberly about the Great Matter than they had done before.

Anne decided it was best to stay at Durham House until things had quietened down. She did not want to undermine the good work Henry had done in calming his people. Let him visit her secretly, his unmarked barge mooring silently away from inquisitive eyes. She would miss seeing Norris, but she did not need any more turmoil in her life just now.

Anne had long accepted that, for the sake of outward appearances, Henry must visit Katherine from time to time, dine with her and even share a bed with her. He had assured her that on the rare occasions he visited the Queen at night, he never touched her. But why sleep with her at all? That he still did angered and disturbed Anne more and more. Did he truly want to separate from Katherine? The Queen had some hold over him that he seemed unable to shake off. Was it that she was older than he, a mother figure? Was she the link to his lost youth, the living reminder of happier, more carefree times, before the loss of his sons? Or was he just a moral coward, reluctant to provoke a scene – or the Emperor's wrath – by depriving Katherine of his company altogether?

Eventually Anne could bear it no more. 'The legate is here!' she cried, when, after a quiet afternoon spent making music together in her chamber, Henry had announced that he was going back to Bridewell Palace to have supper with the Queen. 'The case will soon be tried, yet you still have but one bed and one table!'

Henry hastened to placate her. 'Sweetheart, be at peace. It is for form's sake only. But I would not upset you, darling. I promise you, I will never bed with Katherine again. I am well aware of the moral danger that may ensue to me by it. From now on, she shall sleep alone. And soon, my dear love, we shall be together.'

'I do pray so!' Anne said, not entirely mollified.

She insisted on staying at Durham House, deaf to Henry's protests, while the court moved to Greenwich without her. Henry would not leave her be, of course, and in December she finally gave in to his pleas, closed up the house, and joined him at court. There she was delightfully surprised to be assigned a finer, more spacious lodging than before, near his own. He himself had chosen the furnishings, which included the costliest bed-hangings and tapestries, and a great oak buffet laden with gold and silver plate. The rooms were fit for a queen!

It was gratifying when the highest in the land came paying court to her, obviously anticipating that she would soon be marrying the King. It was noticeable that few were making their devoirs to the Queen, who wore her usual smile in public, bearing the snubs with dignified patience and staying firmly at Henry's side, to Anne's fury.

Anne was still uncomfortably aware of the hostility beyond the palace walls. When she had come here by river, they had watched her sullenly from the banks, and some had shouted, 'Nan Bullen shall not be our Queen! We'll have no Nan Bullen!'

It was intolerable! And Henry, for all his threats, was powerless to silence them.

There was still no sign of the two cardinals setting up the hearing. Christmas was approaching, and nothing would be done until afterwards. Anne was beginning to think it never would.

She learned only after it had happened – and then by overhearing one of Henry's councillors mentioning it to someone else – that Dame Isabel Jordan had been quietly installed as Abbess of Wilton after all. Her anger burned. That would have been Wolsey's doing. Did Henry know that the Cardinal had defied him? Or had Wolsey persuaded him to give his consent, both of them hoping she would not find out? Either way, Wolsey would soon learn that she was not to be trifled with.

Anne was furious when Henry invited Wolsey and Campeggio to keep Christmas with him at Greenwich, as his guests of honour, and resolved to stay in the empty splendour of her rooms.

Henry was distraught. 'But darling, I have laid on jousts, banquets, masques and disguisings. I am keeping open house. Come and join me, please!'

'Not while the Queen is presiding with you over the festivities,' she said. It was true, but it was not the whole truth. Yet Henry was growing weary of her complaints about Wolsey.

He looked helpless. 'I hate to think of you all alone here. How can I make merry, knowing you are not?'

'It will not be merry for me with those cardinals there.' She knew she was being unduly peevish, but she could not help herself. She was bursting with frustration and resentment.

He left her then, but he came back late at night, after the revelry had ended, and brought with him jewels: diamonds for her hair, gold bracelets set with true lovers' knots, a flower brooch, borders of gold for her sleeves, buttons crafted with rubies, roses and hearts. She accepted them as no less than her due; after all, had she not been kept waiting for the crown an unconscionably long time?

Chapter 16

1529

The gifts kept coming, as that seemingly endless winter gave place to spring. When they were together in public, Henry caressed Anne openly, as if she were already his wife, holding her hand, touching her cheek, putting his arm about her waist, not caring who saw. Yet still she would not be mollified. She held aloof, and took herself back to Durham House, angry at yet more delays.

'Why?' she kept demanding. 'Can they not just hear the case and be done with it?'

In private with George, she vented her frustration, and then ended up laughing hysterically. 'What an extraordinary situation we find ourselves in!' she gasped. 'Who could have foreseen it?'

She kept thinking of the parallels between herself and Queen Esther.

'I will be a second Esther,' she told her brother. 'I will be the champion of pure religion and save the Church in England from corruption. Let them call me a heretic! I know what people say about me. They think I follow Luther's teachings.'

'They think me and Father more Lutheran than Luther himself,' George grinned.

'I will never be a Lutheran,' Anne declared, 'and everyone will realise that in time. Until then, like Esther, I must tread carefully with the King in matters of religion.' And yet, she reflected, even Henry's staunch orthodoxy was being worn down by Clement's handling of the Great Matter.

She had managed to obtain a copy of another forbidden book, William Tyndale's *The Obedience of a Christian Man, and how Christian*

Kings ought to Govern. In it, Tyndale openly challenged the authority of the Pope and his cardinals, and asserted that the head of the Church in each realm ought to be the King, rather than the Pope, because the King, by virtue of his having been anointed with holy oil at his crowning, was next unto God anyway, and invested with divine wisdom, unlike ordinary mortals.

Several of Anne's maids, taking their lead from her, had become interested in the cause of reform, and she lent the book to one, Nan Gainsford, warning her to keep it hidden. But one day Nan came to her, weeping, and confessed that her lover, George Zouche, had seized it from her in a playful scuffle, then carried it off to read himself.

'But the Dean of the Chapel Royal came upon him and confiscated the book and gave it to the Cardinal,' Nan wailed.

'Do not fear,' Anne reassured her, and called for her barge. When it moored at Greenwich, she went straight to the King, whom she found relaxing in his privy chamber among his gentlemen. He looked astonished as she entered, curtseyed, and knelt before him.

'Do not kneel to me, sweetheart,' he said, and, dismissing his companions, would have raised her, but she stayed on her knees and told him what had happened, begging him to help her retrieve the book. 'For the Cardinal will think I dabble in heresy. All I sought was to understand why Master Tyndale is regarded as a heretic, when in fact his arguments make sense to me. Sir, I do beseech your Grace for your protection.'

Henry took her hands and pulled her to her feet. 'And you shall have it. Leave this with me.'

She emerged from his apartments triumphant. Again he had not censured her for reading a banned book. She was even more gratified when Wolsey came in person to Durham House that evening.

'This is yours, I believe, Mistress Anne,' he said, handing the book to her as if it were as innocent as a child's first primer.

'I thank you, my lord,' she said, and invited him to take some wine with her. As they were drinking and making polite conversation, Henry himself was announced, and after they had chatted a while, Wolsey left, bowing obsequiously.

'You have my undying gratitude,' Anne told Henry. 'I could see myself up before the church courts!'

'Do you think I would have allowed that to happen?' he asked, taking her in his arms and kissing her fervently.

'I hope not! But here is the book, and I urge you to read it. You will be surprised – and maybe impressed.'

He was. When she saw him next, he was full of it. 'These are compelling arguments, darling. This is a book for me and all kings to read.'

'But if the Cardinal has his way, no one would be able to read it,' Anne pointed out. 'Sir, is it right that the Church should wield universal control?'

Henry looked pensive. 'It's a good question, one I have asked myself several times recently.'

Anne sat up straight and braced herself, clearing her throat. Here was the moment she had been waiting for. 'The Church is in great need of reform,' she began, 'and a king who was unhampered by the dictates of Rome would be able to stamp out abuses. You have already said you will annihilate the Pope's authority in England if he does not satisfy your conscience.'

Henry stared at her. As she'd suspected, it had been mere bluster. 'You think I should break with Rome?'

'Sir, you yourself say you are disillusioned with the Church of Rome. You have said there is great need for reform.'

'Reform is one thing; breaking with Rome quite another. Besides, Rome may yet prove our champion in this Great Matter.'

'It *may*. I dare not allow myself to hope, because I have been having my hopes dashed for so long. I am sick to the teeth of living my life in suspense.' Tears were threatening, and as ever Henry hastened to comfort her. As he held her against his gem-studded doublet, she allowed herself the luxury of weeping. Sometimes she felt she could strive no more, but she was not one to give up easily. She was a fighter, and tonight she had planted another seed – in fertile ground, she thought. If the Great Matter was not resolved soon, radical action would be necessary. Henry would see that.

The King was no longer as friendly towards Wolsey as he used to be. The long delay in hearing the case was making him tense and short-tempered. One evening at supper at Durham House, Anne was jubilant to hear him voice his suspicion that the Cardinal was secretly opposing the dissolution of his marriage.

'We have feared that all along, sir,' Norfolk leapt in.

'He works against Your Grace because he thinks a decision in your favour will undermine the authority of the Holy See,' Anne said softly. 'The Pope can do no wrong, or so we are told, but you have asked his Holiness to undo what his predecessor did. If the Pope is infallible, then the dispensation allowing you to marry the Queen must be valid. But we know it was at variance with Scripture, and so by bringing this case, your Grace has exposed the flaw in the Pope's judgement. And that can only do damage to the Church.'

The men were all looking at her, clearly impressed.

'Now your Grace must see why you cannot trust Wolsey,' she concluded. 'He owes a greater allegiance to Rome.'

The next day, she went to Greenwich and sought out the Cardinal, demanding to know what was holding up the hearing.

He looked flustered. 'We are awaiting documents, Mistress Anne.'

'Documents?'

'Yes, for the Queen to produce in evidence.'

'My lord,' Anne bristled, 'this delay is caused by you and, I doubt not, Cardinal Campeggio. The King is not pleased. I am not pleased. No doubt the Queen wants the matter settled too.'

'I am doing my best!' Wolsey protested, reddening with anger.

'I think you are doing your best to delay matters!' Anne flung back. 'But I am watching you – and the King is too!'

All government business had now ground to a halt. Nothing was spoken of but the Great Matter. The Queen had lodged an appeal in Rome against the authority of the legatine court, but no one in England was taking any notice. Anne was becoming ever more incensed at the delays. The kingdom could not remain in suspension for ever.

'Soon you shall have all you wish for,' Henry assured her, but the weeks and months were passing and still the court had not been convened. And now it was Easter.

On Good Friday, Anne took her place in the royal pew above the Chapel Royal at Greenwich and watched as Henry, barefoot in token of his humility, crept to the Cross on his knees before an awed congregation of courtiers. She listened as Archbishop Warham invoked the Virgin Mary's blessing on his sovereign: 'Pray your sweet Son Jesus for our renowned King, Henry VIII, and beg for longed-for joys and never-failing glory to be granted him always.' *Amen!* Anne prayed vehemently.

After the service, as Henry had instructed, she rose and descended the stair to the nave, taking her place before a velvet-covered bench on which lay a great quantity of gold and silver rings. Everyone was staring, and there were indignant gasps and murmurs, but she tried to ignore them. It was normally the custom for the Queen to perform the ceremony of blessing the rings, which were distributed every Easter to people suffering from cramp, but this year Henry had insisted on Anne doing it. It was a great honour to receive one, he had explained. She knew that it was just another gesture to placate her for all the delays.

As she blessed the rings, she sensed the hostility around her, and realised that Henry had miscalculated badly. She was not yet crowned and anointed, and thus not invested with the spiritual power to be doing this, and everyone knew it. But she would not show her detractors that she was cowed by their disapproval. Having curtseyed to the altar and to the King, she went back to her place with her chin held high.

Henry was increasingly on edge. He had received letters from Rome, but would not tell Anne what was in them. Wolsey was walking around as if he had the weight of the world on his back. Anne felt like climbing the walls in frustration. But at last, at long, long last, all the preliminaries for deciding the Great Matter were concluded, and there could be no more cause for delay. At the end of May, Henry formally licensed the legates to convene their court in the great hall of the monastery of the Black Friars and hear his case.

The court moved to Bridewell Palace. There was a flurry of preparations. Never before had a king and queen of England been summoned before a court, and great care was taken to ensure that everything was done properly. And all the while the people murmured against the King and Mistress Anne Boleyn.

Anne was jittery and nervous, veering between tears and temper. Henry did his best to reassure her, staying late into the night with her, trying to allay her fears – and of course there was gossip about that. She knew that most people believed she was now his mistress in very truth, and raged at how unfair that was, because for nearly four years now she had jealously guarded her virtue – and for what? She was twenty-eight, almost middle-aged! Every time she looked in her mirror, she seemed to look older. There were faint lines of discontent around her mouth, the hint of a furrow in her brow. She was aware of how poor her reputation was, both in England and abroad. Such power and influence as she enjoyed had no basis in law; it rested only on the King's great love for her. Without him, she was nothing. Unlike Katherine, she had no powerful emperor to back her.

Henry had told her that once his case came before the legates, she would have to leave London. The prospect terrified her, because she would be leaving him open to the machinations of Wolsey and her enemies. She hung on at Durham House for as long as possible, delaying her departure until the very last moment.

Henry was as miserable as she at the prospect of another separation.

'But you must go, sweetheart,' he urged. 'It would not be fitting for you to appear at court until the verdict is given.' And so, when the June clouds were scudding across an azure sky, and all the world was tinged with the gold of summer, she bade him a tearful farewell and set off for Hever with a few servants and a royal escort.

She was so agitated that as soon as she arrived home, she wrote to Wolsey, who would probably be astounded to read her extravagant courtesies and protestations of her continuing love and favour towards him. But he would surely realise that she meant them to spur him to the right judgement. He knew her well enough to know that she would not be forgiving if he failed.

She sought respite in the innocent company of Mary's children, but Mary herself was tart. 'The King has set this realm in an uproar for you, but you don't look very happy about it.'

'One day,' Anne countered, 'we will all be grateful that he did so.'

'Don't count your chickens!' Mary retorted.

Fortunately Father soon arrived with a buoyant letter from Henry, who was missing her grievously, but optimistic.

The drawing near of that time which has been so long deferred so rejoices me that it is as if it were already come. Nevertheless it cannot be accomplished until the two persons most concerned come together, which I desire more than any earthly thing. For what joy in this world can be greater than to have the company of her who is the most dearly loved, knowing that she, by her choice, feels the same, the thought of which greatly delights me.

But she didn't feel the same, Anne thought. And that must always be her secret, it seemed. For her, the goal was a crown, a thing of cold metal, but infinitely alluring. She had had a taste of power and found it as heady as being in love. What would she not be able to do with that crown on her head! And she would be grateful to Henry, and loving, as would be her duty once they were married. He would never have cause to doubt her.

Her father was to return to court with her reply, so she hastened to pen a warm response, urging Henry to be of good cheer. Soon they would be together for always, she assured him.

The legatine court was now sitting. Messengers winging their way back and forth between Bridewell Palace and Hever Castle kept Anne abreast of developments. She was dismayed to hear that the Queen had refused to acknowledge the competence of the court to try the case, protesting that it would not give an impartial judgement. Katherine had even gone on her knees before Henry in the Black Friars' hall and made a deeply emotional appeal to him, begging him to spare her the extremity of the hearing and protesting publicly that she had come to him a virgin. Then she had walked out and refused to heed the crier calling her back.

Thankfully the hearing was proceeding without her, but it was clear that the long-drawn-out sessions of the court, most of which Henry did not attend, were trying his patience to the limit. Anne was gratified to hear that he had summoned Wolsey and vented his frustrations for over four hours.

It was in the fourth week of July that he summoned her back urgently to court, for Cardinal Campeggio was expected to give judgement imminently. Henry sounded confident, as if he knew it would be in his favour.

She had her maids pack immediately, and made all speed to Bridewell Palace, where Henry was impatiently awaiting her in his privy chamber.

'It cannot be long now,' he said, as they embraced. 'It could even be tomorrow. And then, my darling, we can start planning our wedding and your coronation. And you will be mine at last!'

She did not dare allow herself to hope. She wished she could go to the Black Friars to be present with him when the verdict was given, but that would not be politic. So, after Henry had kissed her farewell and departed in the company of the Duke of Suffolk, she stayed in the grand apartment he had assigned her, sipping wine to steady her nerves and trying not to dwell on what might be happening in the monastery just a few yards across the Fleet River.

Henry stormed into her chamber, his face thunderous. He was trembling with rage.

'Revoked to Rome!' he seethed.

She had known it in her bones. That faint-heart of a pope would never set him free. Henry had been tricked, hoodwinked! It had all been carefully planned to keep him sweet while Clement did the Emperor's bidding. If ever there was proof of corruption in the Church, this was it!

'What did Campeggio say?' she asked, her voice like stone.

'He said he would give no hasty judgement until he had discussed the case with the Pope. He said the truth is difficult to find.' Henry spat the words out. He would not look at her. 'My case is sound, I know it

244

and he knows it. But it has now been adjourned indefinitely. I tell you, Anne, this is a political decision. No matter what theological arguments I marshal, they will not be heard.'

Suffolk, who had followed Henry into the room, was just as furious. 'Mistress Anne, I shouted at those legates. I said, "England was never merry while we had cardinals among us!" His handsome, dissolute face – so like the King's – was set in a snarl. Anne knew him to be hot for reform; he would have enjoyed venting his contempt on Wolsey and Campeggio. But his wife, Henry's sister, who loved the Queen, would no doubt be delighted at the adjournment. This decision would not make for marital harmony.

Henry sat down, looking defeated. His voice was hoarse. 'It's the summer recess now. The Papal Curia won't sit again till October, and I know of old that it moves slower than a snail, so it could be months, if not years, before the Pope reaches a decision – and even then, the wait might be in vain, for with Clement hand-in-glove with the Emperor, judgement will probably be given in the Queen's favour anyway.' He cradled his head in his hands, weeping in despair.

Anne felt chilled to the marrow. She was looking ahead, seeing her youth disappearing as year after frustrating year passed. No! She would not endure it. There must be a better way than this. Her anger burned against Wolsey. He had played along with Campeggio and the Pope, while giving Henry fair words and false promises.

'We have the Cardinal to thank for this!' she burst out.

Even now, she feared, Henry would not see the truth. But she was wrong.

'Yes, and he will answer for it,' he snarled, raising his head. 'Before I left the Black Friars, I told him to inform my ambassadors at the Vatican that my royal dignity would not permit my being summoned to appear at the Papal court, nor would my nobles and subjects allow it. I said they were to tell his Holiness that if I went to Rome, it would be at the head of an army, not as a supplicant for justice.'

He got up and began pacing. 'I will not be bested, Anne! I'll have my divorce if I have to break with Rome to do it!'

It was their only hope. He meant what he said, she was sure of it.

She would have her revenge on Wolsey, she swore it! And on obstinate, infuriating Katherine, who was stubbornly clinging on to what she had already lost, and making life impossible for everyone. But it was Wolsey, base, ungrateful Wolsey, who was the greater culprit. He was a traitor to his King.

She had to vent her fury or she would burst. Wolsey must be told how deeply he had wronged her. As soon as Henry had gone to consult with his Council, she called for writing materials and took up her pen, scribbling furiously.

My lord, although you are a man of great understanding, you cannot avoid being censured by everybody for having brought on yourself the hatred of the King, who has raised you to the highest degree to which an ambitious man can aspire. I cannot comprehend, and the King still less, how your reverend lordship, after having misled us by so many fine promises about divorce, can have reneged on them, and how you could have done what you have in order to hinder the achieving of our wishes. What, then, is your mode of proceeding? Having given me the strongest marks of your affection, your lordship abandons my interests to embrace those of the Queen. I have put my confidence in your promises, in which I find myself deceived, but for the future I shall rely on nothing but the protection of Heaven and the love of my dear King, which alone will be able to set right again those plans which you have broken and spoiled, and place me in that happy situation which God wills and the King so much wishes, which will be entirely to the advantage of the kingdom. The wrong which you have done me has caused me so much sorrow, but I feel infinitely more in seeing myself betrayed by a man who only pretended to further my interests. Believing you sincere, I have been too precipitate in my confidence. It is this which has induced, and still induces, me to be more moderate in avenging myself, not being able to forget that I have been your servant, Anne Boleyn.

Let that strike dread into his heart! Let Wolsey quake in his shoes! He knew that her will was law to the King. There would be no more hypocrisy. She had declared her enmity openly, and felt better after dispatching the letter. But she still felt brittle and bruised, and when she was by herself, lying in the dark that night, she gave way to a storm of weeping.

As Anne moved about the court, she heard the buzz of speculation everywhere. The great Cardinal, who had all but ruled England for the past twenty years, was out of favour and had prudently retired to his manor of the More in Hertfordshire, plainly acknowledging that he had been to blame for the court's failure to deliver a favourable verdict.

Henry let him go. 'I do not want to set eyes on him,' he fumed. 'He has betrayed me.'

To make matters worse, the Emperor and the King of France, those two great enemies, had just made peace.

'It leaves me isolated and devoid of support abroad,' Henry told Anne, crestfallen, looking like a man who had been winded. There was no talk of marching on Rome with an army now, so when the Pope's brief citing the King to appear there was served on him, all he could do was erupt in impotent fury and order Katherine to leave court for one of her dower houses, freeing him to take Anne with him on his summer hunting progress.

Leaving London helped to lift Anne's depression. It was good to ride in the warm August sun along the pretty, leafy lanes and heat-baked roads of England, and see the verdant countryside rolling away to either side as they made their leisurely ways to Waltham, Tittenhanger and Windsor. The air was purer away from the city, and it rejuvenated her. Henry was calmer now, determined to find a way forward. He was even speaking of bringing about the divorce by declaring his own absolute power. With this in mind, he had summoned Parliament for November. The seeds Anne had planted were finally flowering.

The worst thing she had to contend with right now were the hostile crowds who had come running to see their King pass and were outraged to find him parading his mistress in public. They made their outrage felt, loud and clear. Where was the good Queen? they cried, again and again. 'We'll not have the Bullen whore!' There were even calls for Anne to be stoned for the adulteress they believed she was. In the end, Henry had to summon the Queen to join the progress at Woodstock. Anne's pleasure in it immediately evaporated.

With Katherine restored to her place at Henry's side, regally smiling and no doubt enjoying her small triumph, Anne found herself once more relegated to discreet obscurity. Nothing had changed. Would it always be this unhallowed triumvirate of herself, Henry and Katherine, doomed to be shackled together for ever?

Chapter 17

1529

On the feast of the nativity of the Virgin Mary, the royal train arrived at Grafton Regis, where Henry owned an old hunting lodge deep in the Northamptonshire countryside. It had been arranged that Cardinal Campeggio would come here to take his formal leave of the King before returning to Rome.

Anne had just left the lodging allocated to her when she heard the unmistakable sounds of a party of horsemen arriving in the courtyard. Looking out of a window in the gallery, she saw Cardinal Campeggio alighting stiffly from a litter. She watched as ostlers and grooms ran to see to the horses and the Cardinal's luggage, and the Knight Harbinger came bustling importantly forward to conduct His Eminence to the rooms that had been prepared for him. And then she saw that someone else was climbing out of the litter on the opposite side. It was Wolsey.

He had aged by about a hundred years. Gone was the air of self-importance, the urbane assurance; there was only an old, sunken man looking warily around the courtyard, plainly uncertain of his welcome – and with good reason, for the Knight Harbinger was seemingly blind to his presence, leading Campeggio away. Soon there was no one else in sight.

Anne stiffened. After the Cardinal's departure from court, Henry had hardly mentioned him. Out of sight, out of mind, she had hoped. And how lucky that was for Wolsey, for in his anger Henry had threatened to have his head.

A thickset man in black came along the gallery, bowed courteously to her, and peered out of the window, following her gaze. When he saw Wolsey, he recoiled suddenly.

'Your old master, Master Cromwell,' Anne said. She had sometimes seen this bull of a man with his porcine features in attendance on the Cardinal, and knew him for a respected lawyer, but they had never spoken. 'I wonder that he has the temerity to turn up here unannounced.'

'If I had been in his shoes, Mistress Anne, I would have deemed it a gross discourtesy to Cardinal Campeggio not to. Had he stayed away, it would have looked like an insult. But it seems he was not expected.' Wolsey was still standing alone, looking at a loss.

'After deceiving the King, he should have known he would not be welcome,' Anne replied.

'He did not deceive the King,' Thomas Cromwell said. 'I worked closely with him, and I know how hard he tried to secure a divorce. No man could have done more.'

That could not be true! 'I think you are yourself deceived,' she retorted.

He shrugged. 'I can only speak the truth as I see it, Mistress Anne.' Then he smiled, revealing a very different face to her. 'I should be soliciting your kindness towards him. He is ailing, and he has given his life to the King's service. To me, he was a good master, a man I respected. You could not know how grieved he is that he has failed you. He sent me this letter.' He reached in the leather scrip he carried and handed it to her.

'This very night I was as one that should have died,' she read. 'If the displeasure of Mistress Anne is somewhat assuaged, as I pray God, then I pray you to exert all possible means of attaining her favour.'

She looked up. 'Master Cromwell, you are a loyal servant, and to be commended for it, but I am far from convinced that the Cardinal was working in the King's cause. The evidence points to him working against it.'

Cromwell's shrewd features registered irritation. 'What evidence? Rumours put about by his enemies? There *is* no evidence. I was there. I saw what he did. I saw him run himself into the ground to give His Grace what he wanted.'

Anne was indignant. 'He bore me much malice, Master Cromwell!

He did everything he could to prevent my becoming queen, for he knew I would destroy him.'

'Not so, Mistress Anne, not so. But I see that you have been worked upon by those envious persons who seek the Cardinal's ruin. I pray you will think on what I have said.' And with that Master Cromwell bowed and walked on. She stared after him, furious. He had not listened to anything she had said.

She turned back to the window, simmering. Below, Norris had appeared. As ever, the sight of him, handsome and debonair, made her catch her breath. Often she thought she had conquered her feelings, but then she would see him and realise that she had deceived herself.

She could not believe her eyes when she saw Norris greet Wolsey and point towards the opposite range of lodgings. They spoke for a few moments, then Norris led the Cardinal away. Clearly accommodation had been found after all. But Wolsey had yet to face Henry, and she was confident that the King would give his former friend short shrift.

It wanted two hours until the supper hour, so Anne rested a little, then sat down to write to her mother. But suddenly Father and Uncle Norfolk were at her door, demanding to speak with her, and they were seething.

'The King has received Cardinal Wolsey,' Norfolk spat.

'And as warmly as he ever did,' Father added, grimacing. 'The entire court was watching to see if he would disgrace Wolsey publicly, and some had even laid wagers on it, but no – it was as if the Cardinal had never been out of favour.'

Norfolk's face was puce. 'When he and Campeggio came in and knelt before the King, he raised them both with fair words, and led Wolsey by the hand to a window, where he talked with him. No one could believe it. Then I heard the King say quite clearly that Wolsey should go to his dinner, and afterwards he would speak with him again.'

'Over my dead body!' cried Anne, who had heard all this with mounting rage. 'Wolsey thinks to have his foot in the door, but I'll not have it. He has wrought enough trouble.'

'Niece,' Norfolk said, 'you are in a position of unique influence.

Work on the King. It should not be difficult to re-arouse his anger towards Wolsey. Remind him of how the Cardinal deceived and failed him. Use your wiles.'

'I don't need any advice on that!' Anne retorted. 'The King is dining with me here later. I will put paid to Wolsey!'

The table in the panelled dining chamber was set for two with snowy napery, gleaming silver and crystal goblets. Candles flickered in their sconces and there was a fire in the hearth to take the edge off the chilly September evening. Anne had dressed carefully. The full skirts of her black velvet gown accentuated her tiny waist, and its low neckline, trimmed with a pearl-braided biliment, looked enticingly seductive. A crimson damask kirtle added colour. Her hair she wore loose, as a reminder to Henry that she was *still* unwed and a virgin.

She was cool towards him when he arrived, and while the first course was served.

'I hear that you gave Cardinal Wolsey a warm welcome this afternoon,' she challenged, looking him directly in the eye, and was gratified when he would not meet her gaze. She laid down her knife. 'If any nobleman in this realm had done but half so much as the Cardinal has done, he would have lost his head.'

Henry looked grieved. 'Why then, I perceive that you are not the Cardinal's friend,' he said.

How could he be so devastatingly naive?

'I have no cause,' Anne said quietly, 'nor any other that loves your Grace, if you consider well what he did.'

'Darling, I have spoken with him, and I do believe that he is as distressed as we are at the verdict of the court. He assured me he had done everything possible to ensure that it went our way, and I believe him.' Henry's tone was plaintive.

'Lies, all lies!' she flung back. 'He is hand-in-glove with that apology for a pope!'

Henry reached across and tried to take her hand, but she pulled it away. 'You cannot receive him back into favour, you cannot,' she insisted.

'Anne, Wolsey is clever—'

'Too clever for you!'

'Hear me out, please. He is the one man who can find a solution to our problem.'

'Is that what he's been telling you? Well, it's strange that this one man who can help has not found a solution in over two years of trying. And whatever he does, his influence in Rome does not exceed the Emperor's.'

'Anne, I will hear what he has to say,' Henry said, in the voice that had silenced many an importunate petitioner.

They ate on in silence, Anne seething at his refusal to heed her, and horrified at the very real prospect of Wolsey returning to prominence. Really, the situation was laughable, if it hadn't been so appalling. First Katherine had returned to court, and now Wolsey looked like doing so. They were all back where they had begun! It was hard to stop herself from bursting into tears – not that that would help in Henry's present mood.

When he had eaten his last mouthful, the King put down his napkin. 'Sweetheart, be reasonable,' he said. 'I am only trying to do what is best, and it is worth listening to what Wolsey has to say if it leads to our being together.'

She did not answer. He rose, pressed his hand on her shoulder and left.

They were meant to be going hunting in the morning, but Henry spent a long time closeted with Wolsey, and now it was afternoon. Anne was pacing the gallery, convinced that the Cardinal was worming his way back into favour. As soon as Henry emerged, she pounced.

'You promised we would leave after breakfast,' she complained. 'It's one o'clock already.'

Henry capitulated. 'Very well. I will tell the Cardinal to continue our discussion with the lords of my Council,' he said, and went to put on his riding clothes.

Anne had a mission of her own to accomplish. Her task completed, she met Henry, booted and spurred, in the porch, as the courtyard filled with men, horses and dogs. And there stood Wolsey and Campeggio, who were to depart after supper that evening. Anne, standing at Henry's side, smiled at them.

Henry mounted his steed. 'I will be back before you leave,' he said. The two men bowed, and he wheeled the horse around. Anne adjusted her feathered riding bonnet and followed close behind on her palfrey, thankful that Katherine never hunted these days. She did not look back. With luck, she would never have to see Wolsey's face again.

When they were a few miles from Grafton, riding abreast, she turned to Henry.

'I have a surprise for you,' she told him.

'For me?' He looked so humbly grateful. 'May I know what it is?'

'Later!' she teased. If she told him now, he might countermand her instructions.

He laughed, and then the quarry was sighted and the chase began.

It was nearing six o'clock when the afternoon's sport ended, and the carcasses of six deer were being loaded on to a cart. It was a beautiful evening, with the lowering sun's rays casting a golden light on the landscape.

'It's perfect weather for dining out,' Anne said.

'Dining out?' Henry echoed.

'Yes. That's my surprise. I have ordered an open-air dinner to be prepared in Hartwell Park. It's only a few miles in that direction.'

Henry hesitated. She could see him warring with himself. Would he continue to placate her and do as she wished, or would he risk angering her by insisting on returning to Grafton in time to see Wolsey before he left?

Belatedly he smiled at her. 'Darling, you think of everything,' he said. 'Nothing would please me better. Come, let us make haste! All this sport has given me an appetite.'

She had won the battle, if not the war. Now she must make sure that Henry saw the truth about Wolsey and was persuaded never to receive him again.

*

Two days later, Henry welcomed the new Imperial ambassador at Grafton. The Emperor had withdrawn his previous representative before the Black Friars hearing, in protest that it was biased in the King's favour. Now that the case had been revoked to Rome, Charles had relented and sent this new man.

Anne watched as Eustache Chapuys approached the dais and bowed low. He was dark-haired, with patrician features, and wearing a sober lawyer's gown. She saw the King receive him cordially, and the Queen's warmer welcome. Afterwards, at a reception, Henry introduced Anne to Messire Chapuys. He was courtesy itself as they exchanged pleasantries, but he knew who she was, and she sensed that he did not approve of her – how could he, when she was set to supplant his master's beloved aunt? And it was clear from his cultured conversation that he thought highly of the Queen. Anne realised that, for all his civility, he would be no friend to her.

'His instructions are to bring about a reconciliation between me and Katherine,' Henry told her later. 'He didn't say so outright, but it was implied. Well, he'll have his work cut out!' He gave a mirthless laugh.

The next day, Thomas Boleyn sought Anne in her lodging, looking concerned. 'This Chapuys is clever,' he warned. 'He has already made it plain to the Council whose side he is on, and I fear he could make trouble for us. He has the might of the Empire and Spain behind him. Be watchful.'

In October, the court returned to Greenwich, and Anne took herself off, with her mother for company, to Durham House. It was good to be away from the court for a while, and even to have some respite from wrangling with Henry over Wolsey, but she fretted constantly about what was happening in her absence. Would the Cardinal find some way to outsmart her? And what was this new ambassador, Chapuys, about? She missed Norris, as always, even though she was still annoyed with him for receiving Wolsey at Grafton. She had shown herself cool after that, and now regretted it. She should really be at court, and yet here she was talking about embroidery with Mother and her maids!

It was while she was rummaging around for red and blue silks that she discovered that the casket in which she kept some of Henry's love letters was empty. The lock had been broken!

She questioned the servants who had been left in charge during her absence, but they all showed themselves nonplussed, and none knew of any stranger breaking in or intruding.

When Henry arrived that evening, she told him that the letters were missing.

'Someone must have stolen them,' she said, thinking of Wolsey. 'Who would do that?'

He frowned. 'Cardinal Campeggio, I suspect. Perhaps one of his people bribed someone to search for evidence that we have committed criminous conversation, as the church courts like to put it. That, darling, as I need not remind you, could prove highly damaging to my case.'

'I know the Church is corrupt, but would a cardinal really stoop to theft?'

'If it were to get such evidence, yes. You and I know that we have not sinned, but anyone reading those letters might draw other conclusions – if it served them well. If Clement reads them, there's little hope of him deciding in my favour.'

Anne shuddered. It was horrible envisaging the consistory of cardinals poring over the letters, exposing her intimate secrets and drawing the wrong conclusions. It was even more horrible to think of the consequences.

'There is no time to lose!' Henry declared, jumping up and summoning an usher.

'Take a message to Dr Gardiner. Have him send soldiers to Dover to intercept Cardinal Campeggio and search his luggage, even his saddlebags. Tell him that letters belonging to the Lady Anne have been stolen, and we need to find them.'

The usher hurried away.

Henry sat down. He was fidgeting in agitation. 'I hope I can trust Gardiner to order an efficient search. Wolsey would have known just what to do. He'd have tracked down those letters.'

Oh, no, Anne thought. *This must not be your excuse for recalling the Cardinal.*

She had to prevent Henry from sending for Wolsey. The next morning, she summoned her father, her uncle of Norfolk and the Duke of Suffolk.

Dr Gardiner had been extremely efficient, but to no avail. Two days later, Anne received a note from Henry informing her that no trace of the letters had been found, despite a thorough search of the baggage of Campeggio and his suite.

She strongly suspected that Wolsey had them, and might use them against her. It was now more imperative than ever that Wolsey be brought down.

Father and Norfolk were exultant.

'The King has agreed to charge the Cardinal under the Statute of Praemunire, with the offence of allowing a foreign power to interfere in the affairs of the realm. We did not have to look far to find evidence against him. Accepting the office of Papal legate alone renders him guilty.'

'The penalty is forfeiture of all his lands and goods,' Norfolk added, gleeful. 'And it serves him right.'

They had done their work well. The relief was overwhelming. Anne had looked to harden Henry's heart against his former friend, but she had never expected him to go this far. Banishment had been the best she had hoped for. That evening she and her mother danced around her chamber in exultation.

Eight days later, Henry stripped Wolsey of his office of Lord Chancellor.

'My lord of Suffolk and I are off to demand that he surrender the Great Seal of England,' Norfolk came to tell her. 'He is to remain at his house at Esher while a bill of indictment is drawn up against him.'

The great Cardinal was finished, his stranglehold on the King broken. And it was she, that foolish girl yonder in the court, as he had called her, who had brought it to pass.

Henry came to see her, furious about Wolsey, yet pleased to be in possession of all the property that had belonged to the Cardinal.

'York Place is mine now,' he declared. 'For years, since Westminster burned down, I have lacked a great house in London. Now I have one! I am renaming it Whitehall, and darling, it will be our palace. I am having it renovated for you. It will be like those palaces of the Netherlands you often speak of. Tomorrow we will go and see it, and you shall decide what improvements you wish to make.'

She listened avidly as he spoke of the improvements he would make. Whitehall, being an archbishop's residence, had no lodging suitable for the Queen, and he had no plans to create any for Katherine. Anne was to have her own court and preside over it as queen in all but name.

Mother, who was still staying with her, attended her as chaperone when she viewed the palace with Henry. He was waiting for them there at ten o'clock in the morning, with just Norris in attendance. As usual, Anne's heart skipped a beat, but she would have to be especially careful not to betray her feelings today, for Mother knew her too well and had eyes like a hawk.

Henry kissed her hand on greeting, and she asked after Norris's health. She had noticed that he was clad entirely in black.

'I am well enough, Mistress Anne,' he told her, his light blue eyes meeting hers, 'but you find me in sorrow. My poor wife has died.'

The news struck her like a thunderbolt. 'I am so sorry, Sir Henry,' she managed to say, remembering fair-haired Mary Fiennes as a merry young girl in France, fourteen years ago now.

As Henry led the way through chamber after chamber, speaking enthusiastically of his plans for the palace, Anne followed slowly, barely seeing the breathtaking splendour. From the jocular way he was talking with the King, Norris did not seem too saddened by his wife's death. An arranged marriage, no doubt, made for convenience, as most were. All she could think about was that he was now free.

He could be hers.

But it was Henry who could give her the crown she so desperately wanted.

Above them the painted beams of the great hall soared, and Henry was saying that the first thing he'd do would be to have Wolsey's coats of arms removed – they were everywhere, uncomfortable reminders of the Cardinal's greatness. But Anne was asking herself why becoming queen mattered so much, when the chance of true love was hers for the seizing. And always she came back to the argument that the crown was hers for the seizing too.

She had never seen marriage alone as an especially fulfilling estate for women. She had always wanted more in life – and more than she had ever dreamed of would soon, God willing, be in her grasp. There was so much that she could accomplish as queen, and her children would be royal. That mattered very much indeed. To think that a child of her blood, a Boleyn, would one day sit upon the throne of England, and that her descendants would rule for centuries to come. It was a kind of immortality.

She realised that the prospect of the power she would wield as queen, and as the mother of the heir, was headier than the prospect of marriage with Norris. She looked at Henry and Norris standing together on the dais, and it dawned on her that love was not the most important thing in life. For her, power was more important than pleasure. And although she loved Norris far more than she could ever love Henry – and, yes, lusted after him – she knew that, in truth, they could never be together. She was Henry's, and he would never let her go. What was it Wyatt had written? '*Noli me tangere*, for Caesar's I am!'

It would suit her very well, she told herself, to go on loving Norris from afar. It would add some spice to her life, supplying the excitement that Henry could rarely inspire.

Resolutely, she turned to the King and smiled.

'These curtains will have to go!' she said.

Even now, it was proving difficult to get rid of Wolsey. Acquiring the Cardinal's property had gone a long way towards dispelling Henry's anger and resentment, and when, at the end of October, Wolsey threw himself on the King's mercy, Henry took him under his protection and graciously permitted him to remain Archbishop of York, second only to the Archbishop of Canterbury in the English church hierarchy.

'Not to be borne!' snarled Uncle Norfolk, when Anne, barely

containing her own anger, broke this news. 'We will fix this knave once and for all.'

Norfolk, Father, George and the Duke of Suffolk, with others who bore a grudge against the Cardinal, began meeting at Durham House, with Anne at their head, to plot Wolsey's final downfall. There was no time to be lost, for Parliament was soon to meet, and they were hoping to force through an Act of Attainder that would see the Cardinal deprived of his life as well as his possessions.

Henry was jubilant. Before he had even been announced at Durham House, he had burst into Anne's chamber, surprising her as she was practising on her lute while her mother sat sewing.

'Foxe and Gardiner are back from Rome, Anne, and they have news.'

'The Pope has ruled in your favour?' she asked, rising to her feet, hardly daring to hope.

'No, not that, darling.' His face clouded a little. 'They are both of the opinion that we can hope for nothing from Clement. But' – and he brightened again – 'they have met someone who has put forward a brilliant solution to my Great Matter. His name is Dr Thomas Cranmer, and they met him by chance when they lodged overnight at Waltham Abbey on their way here. He was seeking refuge from some sickness that is raging in Cambridge. He is a fellow at the university, and they've both known him for years.'

He drew her to a window seat overlooking the river. 'It was a friendly reunion, and Gardiner stood them all a good dinner. Then they fell to talking, and he and Foxe asked this Dr Cranmer his opinion on my case. And he said he had not studied the matter in depth, but believed that the validity of my marriage should be judged by doctors of divinity in the universities, not by the Pope.'

Anne stared at Henry, light dawning. It was indeed a stroke of brilliance, and might well be the best way forward. And, given that university men often held radical and forward-thinking views, it surely could not fail.

'And if the universities find in your favour, what would happen then?' she wanted to know.

'Ask Dr Cranmer, sweetheart. I've brought him here to meet you.' He rose and walked to the door. 'Come in,' he commanded.

The doctor was about forty, a soberly clad cleric with mournful eyes, dark stubble on his chin and a nervous smile. But it soon disappeared as he warmed to his subject.

'There is but one truth in the matter,' he said in his quiet voice, 'and it will be revealed in the Scriptures when they are correctly interpreted by learned scholars trained for such a task. And that, your Grace, may be done as well in the universities as at Rome. Had they been sounded first, you might have made an end of the matter long since.'

'But what authority would their decision have, if they decided for His Grace?' Anne asked.

'Mistress Anne,' Cranmer said, 'this case should be decided according to divine law, not canon law, therefore the Pope's intervention is unnecessary. If the divines in the universities decide that the King's marriage is invalid, then invalid it must be, and all that is required is an official pronouncement by the Archbishop of Canterbury to that effect, leaving the King free to remarry.'

'It sounds so easy,' she breathed.

'Dr Cranmer,' purred Henry, clamping an arm around the man's shoulders, 'you have the sow by the right ear! And I want you to set all other business aside, and write a treatise expounding on your views.'

Cranmer looked pleased and worried at the same time, but he agreed. That very day, Henry asked Anne's father to prepare accommodation for the doctor at Durham House, so that he could write in comfort. Father, of course, was delighted to comply. Never were rooms furnished so quickly! And so Cranmer got down to work.

On the occasions when he emerged to dine or sup with her, Anne found her new guest to be both learned and reassuring. He was interested in humanism and passionately vocal in the arguments for church reform that were so often aired at her table. Before long, Father made Cranmer their family chaplain, and the lugubrious cleric became very much a part of the Boleyn households. Indeed, Anne had come to account him a friend.

*

'I am thinking,' Henry said, staring fiercely into the flames dancing on the hearth, 'that I really would be better off without the Pope. My kingdom certainly would, and my people should be overjoyed at not having to pay tithes to Rome.' He punched his palm. 'Why should we owe spiritual allegiance to a man who denies me an annulment for political reasons? Does he not realise that I need an heir, desperately?' He was working himself up into a fury. His temper was becoming more volatile these days.

'Why won't Katherine set me free?' he ranted. 'Why must she be so stubborn? I'm not getting any younger, Anne – I'm thirty-eight. Do you realise I have not bedded with a woman in years?' He looked at her in anguish, longing in his eyes.

'We dare not risk—' she began.

'I'm not asking!' he interrupted. 'We are so close to success now. I can wait. God knows, I've had enough practice.'

'How much longer will it take to canvass the universities?' Anne asked.

'A few weeks, months, maybe. This time next year you could be carrying my son under your girdle. Think of it, Anne!'

'And what of the Pope?' she asked.

'I mean to be absolute ruler in my own realm,' Henry declared. 'I'll not be in tutelage to anyone, and I'll brook no interference from foreigners.'

She smiled, rejoicing to see that he was at last discovering the full extent of his strength and his power. There would never be another Wolsey.

The King had appointed Sir Thomas More to replace Wolsey as Lord Chancellor.

Anne had heard much about More's probity as a lawyer, and his outstanding scholarship. She had met him on several occasions, for Henry prized him as a friend. He was an upright man, but a dangerous one, for when More spoke, the whole world listened. His opinions were heeded and respected, because he held them without fear or favour.

Henry had for some time been earnestly persuading Sir Thomas to agree that his marriage was invalid.

'If he agrees to support me, it will add great weight to my case,' he had told Anne. 'Even the Pope will listen.'

But always, after seeing More, Henry came back dejected. 'I still cannot induce him to agree with me,' he lamented, as they walked through the gardens, cloaked and gloved against the November chill. The fact that he was sad rather than angry was a measure of his love for More.

'What did you say to him?' Anne asked, more sharply than she had intended.

'I told him I did not wish him to do or utter anything that went against his conscience; I said he must first look to God, and after God to me.'

And this was meant to be inducement!

'At least he has accepted the chancellorship,' Henry went on. 'He didn't want it, but I told him I needed men like him.'

Anne could not agree. 'Is it wise to appoint a man who is opposed to you in the most important matter of all?' she asked.

'Darling, fear not. Thomas and I have agreed that I will leave him out of my Great Matter, and he will not interfere. And I have made it clear to him that, because of that, his power as chancellor will be limited. Your uncle of Norfolk, as President of the Council, will be in overall charge, and my lord of Suffolk will be his deputy.

That at least was good news. And above them all would be – herself! She had the King's ear, so Norfolk and Suffolk would have no influence except what it pleased her to allow them. With this in mind, she found it possible to put on a smiling face when Henry invited Sir Thomas More to dine with them in his privy chamber to celebrate his friend's advancement. More greeted her very affably, considering that he had long been a friend of the Queen and must have sat at this same table with Katherine and Henry on several occasions. If he was discountenanced to find Anne here, he did not show it. At dinner he displayed a merry wit, and such a wise and learned grasp of affairs that she could see why he drew people to him and was universally liked and admired.

Anne wanted to know where this great man stood in relation to the cause of religious reform. 'Sir Thomas, have you ever read William Tyndale's translation of the Bible?' she asked.

'I have, Mistress Anne,' he said. Turning to Henry he added, 'Your Grace knows that Bishop Tunstall gave me permission to read heretical books.'

'You are the one man I would trust to do so,' Henry smiled. 'Thomas is hot on heresy,' he told Anne.

'Tyndale's Bible is not heresy, sir,' Anne declared. 'It puts forth the truth for ordinary people to read in their own tongue.'

'I'm afraid that's not quite the case,' More said gently. 'Tyndale did not scruple to change the text to conceal the truth. It pains me to say it, Mistress Anne, but he and that firebrand, Robert Barnes, are constantly pouring out abuse against the Church, the Sacraments and the Mass. And if they are allowed to continue, and books like theirs are made freely available, heresy will spread unchecked, make no mistake, and confusion and misery will overwhelm this kingdom. We are seeing the greatest attack on the Church that England has ever known.'

She supposed she should have anticipated such an answer. It was no secret that More held conservative views. 'But would you not agree that everyone should have the right to read the Scriptures – properly translated, of course – in English?' she persisted.

'I'm afraid not. Mistress Anne, would you have the word of God interpreted by ignorant folk?'

'I would rather a simple ploughman could read it and make up his own mind than see the Church continue to manipulate the Bible to its own ends.'

'My companion here has become a theologian,' Henry jested.

Anne simmered. She would not be patronised!

'And a very good one,' More said kindly. 'They could do with such rhetoric in Rome.'

'I spoke from the heart,' Anne said, her voice like steel. 'These are things that matter to many people.'

'Indeed they do,' More replied, 'but it is perhaps better to leave such matters to those who understand them best. His Grace here is greatly learned in theology. He would never let anyone fall into heresy.'

'Am I a heretic, then, for wanting the Bible to be read in English?'

'Darling, Thomas did not mean that,' Henry pacified her.

Oh, but he did, she thought. It was no secret that he loathed heretics. He would burn them all if he could.

'Not at all,' More smiled, but his eyes had grown cold. 'Yet you should know that it is heresy to read the Scriptures in English.'

'It is,' Henry agreed, 'and I mean to stamp out heresy in my realm.'

'In that your Grace will have my full support,' More said.

Anne subsided. The men had taken over the conversation. There was no point in her saying anything. But she would have her moment. She might have made an enemy of More this day – she was not deceived by his friendly manner – but she would triumph in the end. And to do that, it was all the more important that Henry make her his Queen – and soon.

Whitehall Palace was crawling with a great army of workmen, but Henry insisted on moving in at the beginning of November, in time for him to open Parliament. Some of the magnificent apartments he had assigned to Anne were already habitable – he had been visiting the palace almost daily and harrying the builders – and she was able to occupy them, with her mother there to deflect any gossip.

Many more ladies and servants had been engaged to attend her. Anne had felt obliged to ask George's wife to serve her, and was surprised when she accepted. From now on, she resolved, she would watch Jane for any signs of loose behaviour, but there were none. Jane was just her usual withdrawn self, especially when George was visiting. You could feel the animosity between them.

From the grooms and ushers who now served her, Anne selected men she could trust to be her eyes and ears at court. Out of livery, they could mingle unobtrusively in the throng of courtiers and servants, listen to gossip, engage in outwardly idle conversation, and keep her informed of things she ought to know.

Her wardrobe was now packed with sumptuous gowns, her caskets brimming with jewels worth a royal ransom. Petitioners flocked to her door. Save for the crown, she was a queen already. And the best thing was that Katherine was not here to overshadow her – she was at Greenwich, and would soon, God willing, be leaving court for good.

A queen, Anne had always been told, should be the model of virtue. It was bitterly unfair, she felt, that, having zealously guarded her virtue for years, she should be the butt of so much slanderous gossip. But she would confound her critics. She would openly pursue the cause of religious reform, make her views known and be an instrument for change. She spent a lot of time these days reading devotional books, and had taken to carrying with her always a copy of the letters of St Paul, so that all might see how righteously and virtuously she lived.

She was furious to hear Henry say that he had interceded with his justices for a priest who had been sentenced to death for clipping coins.

'You do wrong to speak for a priest!' she reproved him later. 'There are too many already, and all of them supporting the Queen!'

'Calm down, sweetheart,' he countered. 'All this will soon be behind us.'

She could not help being on edge and lashing out on occasion. The endless delays were unbearably frustrating, and the self-control she had struggled to maintain for so long was beginning to fray. It was Henry who was increasingly on the receiving end, and he showed remarkable patience as matters continued to progress at a snail's pace. Even Cranmer was taking a long time to finish his treatise. He had to get it absolutely right, he kept saying. Anne just wanted her future settled. She hated the person she was becoming. It was hard to remain alluring and detached when she was screaming inside. She did not want to feel vindictive towards those – Katherine and Wolsey and Clement – who were the cause of her present untenable situation, but she did. Sometimes she wished them dead. She feared their power to thwart her and wreck her plans.

Time, she felt, was passing her by.

'How long will you keep me waiting?' she would wail at Henry during one of her unreasonable moods. 'I might have contracted some advantageous marriage, and had children!' That, of course, was guaranteed to galvanise him. He would prod Cranmer to hurry up, harry Katherine, and snarl at his Council for not doing enough to relieve his situation. He came, contrite, to Anne with gifts – a length of purple velvet for a gown, a French saddle of black velvet fringed with silk and gold, a matching footstool to use as a mounting block, a white pillion saddle for when they shared a horse. He spent hundreds of pounds on keeping her sweet.

What he could not give her was security. She remained intolerably aware that everything she was and everything she hoped for depended entirely on his great love for her. Without it, the wolves would be at her door. Yet, for all that, she was often ill-tempered with him. Take the matter of the shirts.

Anne could sew, and she could embroider. Her needlework, in which she took great pride, was exquisite. So when Henry casually mentioned that he had ripped his shirt playing tennis, and sent it to the Queen for mending, she exploded with rage.

'If she is not your wife, she has no business to be mending your shirts!'

He looked at her, puzzled. 'But she's always mended them, and embroidered them.'

How could he be so dense? Almost she could have killed him. 'That's beside the point, you fool! You shouldn't encourage her by acting as if you were her husband! In future, you can send your shirts to me. *I* will mend them – and embroider them.'

Anyone else who'd dared speak to the King like that would doubtless have ended up in the Tower, but at that moment Anne was past caring. And Henry just stood there, shamefaced.

'I'm sorry, sweetheart, no slight was intended. You're right. I will send the shirts to you.'

It galled her that Henry was still at pains to convince everyone that he and the Queen remained on good terms, and kept Katherine constantly with him when they were in public. In fact, they were displaying so much courtesy to each other that anyone aware of the true situation would have considered their conduct heroic. But Henry assured Anne that, whatever happened in public, in private he left Katherine to her own devices.

She soon found out that that was not always the case, for one cold, dark night late in November, a downcast Henry arrived at Whitehall and slumped in a chair in her apartment.

'What's wrong?' she asked, concerned to see him so dejected.

'Katherine!' he barked. 'I dined with her – for form's sake, so please don't look like that – but I wish I hadn't bothered. She did nothing but complain about how she was suffering the pangs of purgatory on earth, and that I was treating her badly by refusing to visit her privately. I told her she had no cause to complain. I said I hadn't dined with her as I was busy, the Cardinal having left the affairs of government in great confusion. And as to visiting her in her apartments, and sharing her bed, I told her she ought to know that I am not her husband, and reminded her that I had been assured of this by many learned doctors.'

'I can imagine her response,' Anne said wearily.

'She insisted that my case has no foundation. So I told her that I was canvassing the universities, and would not fail to have their opinions forwarded to Rome. And if the Pope did not declare our marriage null and void, I would denounce him as a heretic and marry whom I please.'

'And did that shut her up?'

Henry looked defeated, as he often did after confronting Katherine. She always remained calm and resolute, while he just lost his temper and uttered threats.

'She said that, for every doctor or lawyer of mine, she could find a thousand to hold our marriage good.'

Anne shook her head. 'Did I not tell you that whenever you argue with the Queen, she is sure to have the upper hand?' She sighed bitterly. 'I see that some fine morning you will succumb to her reasoning, and cast me off! And alas! Farewell to my time and youth, spent to no purpose at all!'

'By God, Anne, you are cruel!' Henry protested. 'You know I will never forsake you. You are my whole life! And you should know that I keep my promises!'

He got up and strode to the door. Raised as royalty, and with two decades of kingship behind him, he would never understand how insecure she felt.

'Farewell,' he said, and he did not even try to kiss her. 'I'm going back to Greenwich to seek some peace and quiet.'

Within hours, he was all contrition. To make up for his outburst, he announced that he was creating her father not only Earl of Wiltshire, but also Earl of Ormond. Piers Butler had died, and that coveted title was to be Thomas Boleyn's at last. As Anne thanked Henry, lovingly, gratefully, she was thinking of what this elevation would mean for her and her family, and realising that he was also preparing her for greater things. The daughter of a belted earl was a far more fitting mate for the King of England than the daughter of a viscount.

A week later, she watched the ceremony of ennoblement, sitting there proudly, near the throne, as her father knelt to receive the trappings of his new rank, which made him one of the chief peers of the realm. George, as Father's heir, was now Lord Rochford, and Anne would henceforth – for a short space, until she was queen – be the Lady Anne Boleyn. Instead of the Boleyn bulls, they would all adopt the black lion of Ormond as their heraldic emblem.

The next day, to celebrate Father's elevation, the King hosted a feast at Whitehall, insisting that Anne sit at his side, in the chair of estate that Wolsey had kept for Katherine, and take precedence over all the ladies of the court. She saw Eustache Chapuys, the Emperor's ambassador, watching her disapprovingly, but paid him no heed. Soon he would be bowing his knee to her.

There would be such a feast when she was married, Anne decided. In fact, given tonight's festive air, the rich food and her virginal gown of white and silver, it seemed as if nothing was wanting but the priest to give away the nuptial ring and pronounce the blessing. If only this could have been her marriage day!

Henry had promoted George to the Privy Council. He was to follow in his father's footsteps and pursue a career as a diplomat, for which – being Father's son – he had considerable talent. Already he enjoyed great influence at court. But his private life was a mess. Anne knew that he and Jane were virtually estranged. Anne had tried to get the resentful Jane to confide in her, but with no success.

When Anne saw George at court these days, he was sometimes in company with a young man who was very handsome – a little rough-spoken, with a strange accent, yet gifted on the lute and keyboard.

She asked Norris who he was.

'Mark Smeaton,' Norris said, his eyes warm. She knew that, had she given him the slightest encouragement, he would have been at her feet, for all he was still in mourning. 'Why do you ask?'

'George seems to like him, but he seems of lowly birth to me.'

'He's recently been appointed a groom of the Privy Chamber. His father, apparently, was a carpenter.'

'I should not sneer at that.' Her smile was wry. 'Our Lord was a carpenter's son too. Yet there is something coarse about Mark Smeaton.' Something sly, too. She did not like the appraising way he looked at her, for one thing.

'I think he's Flemish. He was in Wolsey's household. He's come far because of his talent for music. Give him any instrument and he'll play it.'

He could dance, too. He was often in the throng, showing off, when there was dancing in the presence chamber. Anne noticed that his shirts, hose, shoes and bonnets were of the finest quality. Henry obviously paid him well.

Smeaton once sang, at Henry's behest, for the entertainment of the court, but he overdid the dramatics.

'Even honey, if taken too much, becomes sickly,' Father murmured at Anne's side. 'Who is that oaf?'

George, however, was increasingly with Mark, and they were often joined by Francis Weston, another young gentleman of the King's Privy Chamber. He was a likeable young man with fair hair, blue eyes and an extravagant taste in dress, who was also skilled on the lute. Sometimes Anne and her closest attendants – her cousin, beautiful Madge Shelton, and Norfolk's daughter, Mary Howard – would join them, along with Norris, Bryan and other gallant gentlemen. One day Anne picked up a manuscript of poems someone had brought along. She recognised it as a book that George had once treasured. It was inscribed: 'This book is mine. George Boleyn 1526', but below it was written: 'Mine, Mark S'.

It perturbed her. How come George liked Mark so much that he had given him that precious manuscript? Was Mark worthy of a nobleman's friendship? Was it because of George that he was always aping his betters? He not only dressed well, but kept several horses at court and had servants who wore his livery. How did he afford it all?

At the French court, Anne had heard of men who loved other men. In England, such things were never spoken of. She could not believe it of her brother and Mark. She had seen Mark ogling ladies of the court – she herself had been the recipient of his bold stares (and God only knew what Henry would do if he noticed) – and George, by his own admission and reputation, was a womaniser.

No, the common bond had to be music.

Parliament had been in session for a month when, three weeks before Christmas, the Lords and Commons presented the King with a list of forty-four charges against Wolsey. Anne rejoiced: all those weeks of working to bring Wolsey down had borne fruit. And Henry had agreed to consider the accusations. She was annoyed, therefore, when he seemed reluctant to lift his hand against his old friend, and even refused to discuss the matter.

The thought of Christmas depressed her. She could not face another season of keeping it in solitary state while Katherine queened it over the court, so she had resolved to go to Hever with her family. Next Christmas, God willing, things would be different, and it would be her presiding over the Yuletide festivities.

Henry begged her to stay. He was concerned to see her so low. She would stay low, she was determined, until he saw sense over Wolsey. But Henry was not subtle enough to get the message. Even so, he was moving closer towards pushing through radical changes. Before she left court on Christmas Eve, while they were inspecting the ranks and ranks of silver-gilt cups that he would present as gifts to favoured courtiers on New Year's Day, he turned to her.

'You know, darling, if the Pope pronounces sentence against me, I will not heed it. I prize the Church of Canterbury as much as people across the sea prize the Church of Rome. And so I will tell Katherine. She must not put her hopes in the Pope.'

'England would be better off unshackled from Rome,' Anne observed.

I am coming to believe it,' Henry said. 'The only thing that would make me change my mind is a judgement in my favour.'

Chapter 18

1530

At Hever, Anne could think only of what she was missing at court, and fretting at the thought of Henry being with Katherine and their daughter, sharing in the festivities, while she was left out. As soon as Twelfth Night was over, she hastened back to London.

She found Henry despondent. 'It has been hellish without you,' he told her. 'When I think of how long I have waited for a ruling, I confess that I find myself in such perplexity that I can no longer live in it.'

Anne rested her hand on his. 'Let us put our faith in the universities.'

Henry hesitated. 'If there remains a chance that the Pope will judge in my favour, I will not look for a solution elsewhere.'

Anne gave way to despair. He had been a good son of the Church for too long, and its champion against heresy. He might bluster and threaten, yet his heart was orthodox. But what was Henry's loyalty to the Church worth against Clement's fear of provoking the Emperor? One day he would finally accept that the man beneath the triple crown was as weak and fallible as the rest of mortality.

Anne hastened to Henry's privy chamber, wondering why he wanted to see her so urgently.

'His Grace is upset,' Norris warned, admitting her. Their eyes met for a moment, and there was that old, familiar recognition. She looked away and joined Henry, who was with Dr Butts. The doctor bowed at her approach.

'The Cardinal is very ill,' Henry said, lifting a stricken face. 'I sent Dr Butts to see him, and in truth, I am very sorry to hear what he has to say. God forbid that Wolsey should die, for I would not lose him for twenty thousand pounds!'

Anne stiffened. He would never stop loving Wolsey. She had feared it all along. But it mattered little now, if Wolsey was dying.

Dr Butts spoke. 'I fear, Lady Anne, that he could be dead within four days if he receives no comfort from His Grace and you.'

There were tears in Henry's eyes. 'I am sending him this ring.' He took it off his finger and gave it to the doctor. 'He knows it well, for he gave it to me. Tell him that I am not offended with him in my heart. Bid him be of good cheer. God send him life!' He seized Anne's hand. 'Good sweetheart, I pray you, as you love me, send the Cardinal a token with some comfortable words.'

It could not hurt, not now. And one must show charity to the dying, even to one's enemies. She detached a small gold tablet book from her girdle, and handed it to Dr Butts. 'I wish him well too,' she said.

Whether it was down to the comfortable words and tokens, or the skill of Dr Butts, Wolsey mended daily, and Anne's brief flowering of sympathy withered. Again she began reminding Henry that the Cardinal was responsible for their present intolerable situation, insinuating his offences into their conversations whenever possible, stoking the King's anger. He was not receptive at first, but soon she realised she was making headway. Recalling how Wolsey had duped him, his resentment festered. And Anne seized her moment.

'Your Grace's sympathy for the Cardinal is laudable,' she said, 'but he is not worthy of your forbearance. I beg of you not to see him. I know you could not help but pity him, but it would not be fitting for a traitor like him to come into your presence.'

'But darling—' Henry began.

'Don't darling me!' she interrupted, furious. 'Sometimes I think you love him more than you love me! Well, you will have to choose between us. I have endured this waiting long enough.'

'Sweetheart,' he begged, leaping up to embrace her, 'be reasonable! Is not my displeasure enough punishment for him?'

Anne fended him off. 'Others, committing lesser offences, would have gone to the block! But you need not go so far, Henry. I will go and pack.'

'No!' he shouted, as she moved towards the door. 'No, Anne. Do not leave me! What would my life be without you? I love you! And I promise you, I will not receive the Cardinal. I will do whatever you wish, if only you will stay with me.'

And then, of course, she relented, and all was harmonious between them again. If Henry resented having been forced to capitulate, he did not betray it. His ardour was inflamed all the more by the thought of losing her.

Norris escorted her out.

'You heard what the King said?' she asked.

He smiled at her. 'I could not help overhearing, my lady Anne.'

'I will put paid to this Cardinal once and for all,' she murmured, 'even if it costs me twenty thousand crowns in bribes!'

'It will not,' he assured her. 'There are many who will do much to prevent his return to power.'

She did not tell him that she had sent a spy, in the guise of a servant, to infiltrate Wolsey's household, with instructions to seek out anything remotely incriminating. George had been most helpful in setting that trap, and the spy had been dispatched with a pouch full of gold.

Soon the Cardinal's physician was overheard telling a colleague that his master had been corresponding with the Pope. Naturally the servant who heard him, being loyal to the King, came hurrying to report this to the Privy Council. The physician was arrested.

Henry, relating this to Anne over supper that evening, was incensed.

'The Cardinal has asked the Pope to excommunicate me and lay an interdict on England if I do not dismiss you and treat the Queen with proper respect.'

Anne's rage was genuine. 'Now you see him for what he is! The vilest traitor. When I think of all the years he has caused us to waste – all lost – and how my honour has been defamed.' She was weeping now. 'In truth, I cannot go on like this. I am weary of it all. Often I think it would be best to end it now, then we can both get on with our lives.'

Henry was crying too. 'Darling, please do not speak of leaving me!'

'You have no idea how it is for me,' she sobbed. 'The world thinks I sleep with you, and some even say I have borne you bastards. My reputation is in ruins, thanks to Wolsey and that weakling Clement. How do you think that feels? Wolsey should pay for what he has done! You should have him arrested.'

'But I can't do that,' Henry shouted, dabbing at his eyes and recovering himself. 'That letter the physician spoke of cannot be found, and without it there is a poor case against the Cardinal. I would do anything for you, Anne, but this would be against my honour, and against all justice.'

'Is the man's testimony not enough?' she cried, frantic. 'Men have been beheaded on the strength of witness depositions.'

'More depositions than we have in this case,' Henry argued.

She would not push him further. She had failed, but tomorrow was another day. 'Forgive me if I seemed vehement,' she said, drying her tears. 'It was the thought of your having been deceived and betrayed.'

'You don't know how you twist the knife, Anne,' Henry told her.

Anne strode through Whitehall to the King's apartments, pushing past Norris without waiting to be admitted. Henry had pardoned Wolsey! What was he thinking of?

'You should have had him arrested instead!' she cried, upbraiding him for his folly, but he was immovable as a rock.

'You would not have me pervert the justice that is carried out in my name?' he challenged.

'You don't have to show him such favour!' she flung back. And so it continued, back and forth, in a vicious cycle that left her feeling drained and ragged.

She could no longer control her fears or her temper. She lived in trepidation that Henry would welcome Wolsey back, and that Wolsey, knowing her enmity, would do his best to destroy her. She knew she was trying Henry's patience to the limit, but she could not curb her tongue. Entering his privy chamber one day, she came upon him talking to Sir John Russell, a courtier with a distinguished career behind him, and heard Sir John urging the King to show kindness to the Cardinal.

'He is a consummate statesman, sir, and no one served you more loyally, even if he did fail you in the end—'

'Sir John,' Anne said, interrupting, 'I marvel that you should praise such a man to the King's own face, when he has been accused of so many offences against His Grace. A pardon does not mean that they have been forgotten.'

She did not wait for the astonished Sir John to reply. Aware that Henry was glowering at her, she walked away. She would not speak to Sir John again, she vowed.

But Henry came after her. 'Anne, I love you very much, but I will not have you ill-treating a gentleman of my household in my presence,' he reproved her, as courtiers standing nearby watched, smirking. 'And yes, a pardon does mean that a man's offences are forgotten – by me, and it's my opinion that matters.'

'Then *I* beg your Grace's pardon,' Anne said scathingly, sweeping a graceful curtsey and moving away before he could say any more.

He came to her, of course, as soon as he could – all contrite, and terrified lest she threaten again to leave him – and she graciously accepted his apology. As usual, after a quarrel, he was more ardent than ever, so she let him kiss and caress her.

It worried her that she could so easily let her tongue run away with her. But she could not help herself. It seemed that she was always fighting her demons. And chief of them, right now, was Wolsey.

The bickering continued, fuelled by Henry's reluctance to act on Cranmer's treatise, which was now finished. Soon it was spring, and now it was summer, and still he hesitated, loath to take that final leap that might well bring him into schism with Rome. And no amount of urging or nagging could move him.

'You were so fired up by Dr Cranmer's solution,' Anne reminded him.

'Yes, but I have thought about what might ensue if I take that course. I mean now to have all my lords, spiritual and temporal, petition the Pope to decide the case in my favour.'

'And you think that will move him?' Anne was scornful. 'Henry,

I am twenty-nine, and not getting any younger. If you hope for sons, you must do more than send petitions.'

'Anne, if I take any course other than seeking the Pope's judgement, the Emperor may declare war. Do you realise how many enemies I have made in pursuing our marriage? Not just abroad, but here in my realm, in my court! Do you have any idea what I am risking for you? My popularity, England's security, even my very throne!'

'That matters not,' she countered passionately, knowing she had to stop him from seeing her as part of the problem. 'What matters is us and our marriage. Do you know, I read of an ancient prophecy that at this time a queen shall be burned. That could be me! I know I am hated, and I grieve for it. But even if I were to suffer a thousand deaths, my love for you would not abate one jot!'

He kissed her then, his anxieties forgotten for a space. But he had given her a jolt, and she resolved to show a little more deference to him from now on – and to try to be the person he had fallen in love with in the first place.

Henry was to visit his daughter, the Princess Mary, at Hunsdon. She was fourteen now, and had rarely been at court since the Great Matter had arisen, since both her parents wished to protect her from its consequences.

'I miss her,' Henry told Anne, 'and I would reassure myself that she has not been infected by Katherine's obstinacy.'

He came home in a foul mood.

'It's a fine thing when a man's own daughter starts telling him he is in error,' he growled. 'Never mind the duty she owes him! Katherine's got at her – Mary is repeating the same old arguments. I told her I would visit her again only when she has accepted the truth. The little minx said that she was ready to obey me in all things save what was against her conscience.'

'Has she no respect for her father and King?' Anne asked, indignant.

'She has never defied me before, ever,' Henry mourned, deeply upset. Anne could remember often seeing him with Mary in Katherine's chamber. He had adored the child, and she him.

*

The lords' petition had been sent to Rome. In Henry, hope sprang anew, but Anne expected nothing. Weeks went by with no word in response. Then, in September, Clement, still avoiding pronouncing sentence, suggested that the King might be allowed two wives.

'*Two wives!*' Henry erupted. 'Does the Church now sanction bigamy?'

'How can he justify it?' Anne gaped, shocked to her core.

'He says he can permit that with less scandal than would be caused by granting an annulment.'

Secretly, she was pleased. In stooping so low, Clement had lost all credibility with Henry – and, if there was any justice, with the world at large.

'I'm finished with him,' Henry said, his eyes steely. 'I should have relied all along on my conscience, which is a higher court of justice than the corrupt court of Rome. God, I know, is guiding my actions. Clement has kept me waiting for three tortuous years, and now he shall know that my patience has worn out. Send for Cranmer!'

Thomas Cromwell came upon Anne as she was strolling along the riverside at Greenwich, wondering how long it would be before they could expect the universities to give their opinions. Cromwell was now a member of the King's Privy Council, and Henry spoke highly of him, being impressed by Cromwell's zeal in his cause. Anne did not much like the man personally, but they shared a common desire for reform and the translation of the Bible, and if he was willing to use his considerable talents to help secure an annulment, she was more than ready to give him the benefit of the doubt.

She doubted that Henry would ever again rely on a counsellor as much as he had relied on Wolsey – he had become too much his own man for that – but she knew that Cromwell's influence was growing. As long as he realised that her will was law to the King, they would get along very well.

Cromwell bowed. 'Lady Anne, I thought you would wish to know. New evidence has been laid before the Council about the Cardinal.'

'*New* evidence, Master Cromwell?'

He looked about him. There was no one within earshot on this cold first day of November. Most courtiers were indoors, huddled by fires and braziers. He lowered his voice. 'We have letters proving that Wolsey has written to the Emperor and the King of France, asking them to intercede with the King on his behalf. A foolish move, is it not, Lady Anne, on the part of a man who was charged under the Statute of Praemunire? It is being construed as treason, and he is to answer for it.'

'The King believes it?' Only a few days ago, she had heard Henry say that Wolsey was a better man than any of his councillors, and praise him for the way he was carrying out his spiritual duties in Yorkshire.

'Yes. Even as we speak, a warrant is being drawn up for his arrest.' Cromwell's porcine eyes fleetingly registered emotion.

'You are sorry for your old master,' she said.

'He was a good master,' he observed thoughtfully, then his mouth set in its familiar bullish line. 'But I would not want anyone to think I have any love for a man who has committed treason. You might like to know that the Earl of Northumberland has been deputed to arrest the Cardinal in the King's name.'

Harry Percy, now come into his father's estate! There was a kind of justice in it.

'It is fitting, is it not?' Cromwell said softly, and suddenly Anne remembered being in Harry's arms under that lime tree near the Observant Friars' house, and a man in black watching them.

'You saw us!' she exclaimed. 'You knew!'

'I had the ear of the Cardinal. I know what happened. There was no betrothal to Mary Talbot. It had been discussed, true, but Wolsey pushed it through. It was his way of being revenged on you Boleyns for sneering at him. Be grateful he stopped at that. He brought that fool Buckingham to the block.'

Anne stared at him. 'So Harry and I were lawfully betrothed after all?'

'Yes, you had witnesses. But the Cardinal had it formally annulled. Percy had no choice but to agree or face the King's displeasure. I am sorry for you, Lady Anne. It was a cruel way to treat you. But now you will have your revenge.'

'You think I am wrong to want that?' she asked, appalled. She had been right all along about Wolsey.

'No one would blame you,' Cromwell said.

Despite the grey weather, Anne was outside, watching Henry shooting at the butts at Hampton Court – that great sprawling palace that Wolsey had built and later given to him, as an extravagant gesture of loyalty. He had just scored a bullseye when Wolsey's gentleman usher, George Cavendish, approached and bowed low.

'Your Grace, the Cardinal is dead,' he announced.

Henry turned ashen. 'Dead?' he echoed.

'Yes, sir. He had been ailing for months, and being brought to London, he was taken ill at Leicester, where the monks of the abbey gave him shelter. He died that night.' Cavendish was near to tears. He had been devoted to his master. He would not look at Anne.

Henry swallowed. 'Did he speak of me at the end?' His voice was hoarse.

Cavendish looked uneasy.

'What did he say?' Henry asked. 'Tell me!'

'Sir, forgive me. He said that, if he had served God as diligently as he had your Grace, He would not have abandoned him in his grey hairs.'

There was a tense silence.

'I wish he had lived!' Henry burst out, and stalked off.

Anne left him alone. She was waiting until he had had time to absorb the news. But it was he who came to her.

'God will judge him,' he said. He looked as if he had been weeping for hours.

'You would have had him face an earthly judge,' she reminded him. 'He must have known he was bound for the Tower.'

'Was he a traitor?' he asked, troubled.

'You know he was.'

'I know only what his enemies said about him.'

'You had proof! In those letters he sent.'

'But was his intention treasonous?' He was racked with doubt.

'What else could it have been?'

He looked at her then, his eyes misting, then his expression hardened.

'Yes, he was a traitor, in the pocket of Rome. You might say that God has given judgement.'

She wondered if Henry really would have gone so far as to execute a cardinal of the Church. When it came to it, he would probably have forgiven Wolsey, as he had so many times before. He had loved him.

Not so the rest of the court. The Cardinal had been virulently envied and resented, and there was much rejoicing at his death. Having barely suppressed her jubilation when she was with Henry, Anne knew a huge sense of relief that never again could Wolsey return and confound her.

Father and George were triumphant.

'Good riddance!' spat Uncle Norfolk.

George and the debonair Francis Weston grabbed Anne's hands and pulled her in the direction of the office of the Master of the Revels.

'I've an excellent idea for a masque,' George explained. 'Francis agrees.'

'A masque? Now?'

'There will never be a better time. I'm calling it *The Going to Hell of Cardinal Wolsey.*'

Anne wondered what Henry would say, but their excitement was infectious, and they had certainly captured the prevailing mood of the moment. And so she dressed up as a particularly beguiling devil, and joined the others in celebrating Wolsey's end, prodding the actor playing the Cardinal with pitchforks as he disappeared into the fiery pit, while musicians played discordant notes and the court roared its approval. And Henry, surprisingly, raised no protest, but laughed with the rest, hiding whatever grief he was feeling. It was Cromwell, she noticed, who turned away.

Anne was deeply saddened to hear that Margaret of Austria had died of a fever. Only last year Margaret had skilfully negotiated what had become known as the Ladies' Peace between France and Spain, herself representing the Emperor Charles, and Madame Louise King François.

'She was a great lady,' Henry said.

'She was an inspiration,' Anne replied. And she had proved, as Isabella had, that a woman could rule as successfully as any man – as Anne intended to do herself.

Katherine lay gravely ill at Richmond. It seemed wrong to hope that she would follow Wolsey to the grave, and so resolve the Great Matter at a stroke, yet Anne could not but do so. Henry, whose patience with Katherine had all but run out, showed little sympathy and stayed with Anne at Hampton Court.

'I'm not risking infection,' he declared. 'There is plague in Richmond.' He contented himself with sending Katherine hectoring letters, urging her to enter religion. Weak as she was, she persisted in her refusal.

Soon, Anne knew, the universities would speak. In a few short months – weeks, even – she might be queen. She knew there would be criticism that her lineage was nowhere near as impressive as Katherine's or most of the queens of England who had gone before her. It was not enough to be descended from ancient royalty through the Howards on her mother's side; it was who your father was that counted, and there would be plenty to point the finger and say that she was too lowly to be queen. But there had been talk in the family, doubtless passed down for generations, that the Boleyns were descended from a Norman lord who had settled in England in the twelfth century.

She discussed the matter with a herald from the College of Arms, and commissioned him to draw up a family tree. To her delight, he traced her lineage back to a great lord, Eustace, Count of Boulogne, who had married into the English royal family and whose granddaughter had wed King Stephen.

Henry scanned the impressive chart showing all the generations of Boleyns, and frowned.

'Who is the knave that did this?' he asked, to her dismay. 'It's an invention. The sons of this Eustace became kings of Jerusalem.' Henry was well informed on his royal pedigree.

'There was another son from whom my family descends.'

'Hmm,' he murmured, not convinced. 'Best not trumpet this about.'

'But it's the truth!' Anne protested.

'I said no, Anne. I would not have you a laughing stock.' And he was immovable.

He was equally displeased by the motto she had chosen and had embroidered on the new liveries she had bought for her servants – 'Thus it will be, grudge who grudge'. It was a message for anyone who dared challenge her right to be queen.

But Henry put his foot down. 'Do you really want to attract ridicule, Anne? You of all people should know that the Emperor's device is "Grudge who grudge, long live Burgundy". You were at his aunt's court. Already people are making jests. I saw Chapuys smiling at one of these badges yesterday.'

Anne felt her cheeks flaming. She had not consciously remembered the device from her days in Burgundy, but now she was mortified. Immediately she gave the order for the offending badges to be removed.

Katherine did not die. For His own mysterious reasons, God let her live. She joined Henry at Greenwich, with the Princess Mary, for Christmas – and once again Anne found herself celebrating (if that was the word) the season at Hever. Another year wasted! But it would be the last. Henry had assured her that their marriage would undoubtedly be accomplished in the new year.

Chapter 19

1531

The Spanish Lady Willoughby looked down her aristocratic nose at Anne. Of all Katherine's ladies, she was the one who had shown the most contempt. An outspoken woman, she had made no secret of her opinion on the King's case. So when Anne encountered her in a gallery on the day she returned from Hever to Greenwich, the air became as frosty indoors as it was outside.

'Oh, Lady Anne,' the Baroness said, as she moved aside to let Anne and her baggage-laden attendants pass, 'we had hoped you would stay at Hever.'

'And I,' Anne countered, 'wish that all Spaniards were in the sea!'

'Such language is disrespectful to our good mistress the Queen,' Lady Willoughby reproved.

Anne was determined to discountenance this unpleasant woman. 'I care nothing for her,' she retorted. 'She is no true queen, and I would rather see her hang than acknowledge her as my mistress!' And she sailed on, not giving her tormentor a chance to reply.

As always, Henry welcomed her back to court with open arms, and they dined together alone in his privy chamber.

'I wish you had been here for Christmas, darling,' he said. 'The festivities were marvellous and the court was crammed. The best thing was having Mary to spend it with me. She is quite the young lady now, and very learned and accomplished.'

Anne felt her anger rising. 'This *is* the same Mary who has defied you and supported her mother?' she lashed out. 'I marvel that you should praise her so, when she has forgotten her duty to you!'

Henry stared at her, that dangerous flush rising from his neck.

'Sometimes I think you forget yourself,' he said. 'We have been apart for days, and I had been longing to see you again, but already you are upbraiding me.'

'I *was* overjoyed to see you,' Anne cried, 'but you seem to be deluding yourself – or has the Princess now changed her opinion and become obedient?'

'No, but Anne, she is my daughter, and I love her dearly. She will see sense in time. She is young and lacking in the wisdom to deal with such matters. Really, you could be a little kinder. Katherine never in her life used such ill words to me.' There were tears in his eyes.

'Well, I'm sure she'd be delighted to have you back!' Anne said tartly.

Henry reached across the table and took her hand. 'Let's not quarrel, darling, please. I will deal with Mary, I promise, but in my own way. I don't need any more unpleasantness at this time. Clement has cited me to appear in Rome to defend my case.'

'Will you go?' She squeezed his hand back, to let him know she had forgiven him. Always, these days, she found herself pushing him to the brink, then realising that she must let him see her softer side.

'No! And I intend to ignore also the brief he has issued, ordering me to send you away and forbidding my subjects to meddle with my case. Truly, Anne, I am becoming convinced that the English Church would be better off with me, the King, as its head.'

Don't just keep talking about it! she fumed inwardly. *Do something!*

'I have thought that for a long time,' she said, 'and you know that others think it too.'

'Cromwell for one,' he told her. 'We've been having some interesting discussions. He thinks there would be many advantages to severing the Church of England from Rome. But he can tell you himself.'

He sent for Cromwell there and then, and invited the big bull-necked man to join them at table, calling for more food and wine to be brought.

'This is an unexpected honour, sir,' Cromwell said, smiling, 'and what a pleasure to have the company of the Lady Anne.' He bowed his head in her direction.

'Tell her what you said to me,' Henry commanded, as they tucked into venison pasty and jugged hare.

Cromwell turned to Anne. 'The Pope delays in judging His Grace's suit. Why wait for his consent? Every Englishman is master in his own house, so why should the King not be so in England? Ought a foreign prelate to share his power with him? I have told him, with no disrespect intended, that he is but half a king, and we are but half his subjects.'

An impressive argument! And Henry was lapping it up greedily, by the look of him.

'I could not have put it better myself,' Anne declared, warming to Cromwell.

'The Church of Rome owns great wealth and estates here,' he went on, then looked at Henry. 'Given a free hand, I could make your Grace the richest sovereign that ever reigned in England.'

Henry's eyes gleamed. 'I do believe that breaking with Rome would be a popular move,' he said. 'True Englishmen resent having to pay Peter's Pence to Rome. It is a burdensome levy.'

'Your Grace could stamp out corruption the more easily if you were head of the English Church,' Anne pointed out.

'By God, I could!' Henry agreed, fired up at the prospect. 'I should be governing my kingdom without interference from Rome or any other foreign power.'

She thrilled to hear him say it. But, on past experience, how far was he really prepared to go?

He surprised her. At the end of January, he summoned the convocations of the clergy of Canterbury and York to Westminster. It was apparent to everyone that something momentous was in the air, for it was only with the assent of Convocation that important church reforms could go forward.

A week later, the King stood up in Parliament and demanded that the Church of England recognise and acknowledge him as its sole protector and supreme head.

'Neither Parliament nor Convocation will defy me!' he told Anne afterwards.

Daily he granted leave of absence to those Members of Parliament who supported the Queen. And then the elderly Archbishop Warham announced that the Convocations were prepared to acknowledge the King as Supreme Head of the Church of England – as far as the law of Christ allowed.

'They insisted on that qualification,' Henry told Anne, somewhat disgruntled, when he visited her at Whitehall that evening. 'Tempers got a little frayed as we negotiated. But the thing is accomplished, darling. Henceforth the English Church will no longer recognise the Pope, or the Bishop of Rome, as I would have him called now. Nor may he receive allegiance from my bishops or enjoy any spiritual jurisdiction in England.'

Anne felt dizzy with joy. It was far more than she had ever hoped for. She was sure that no king of England had ever undertaken so daring an enterprise. Her respect for Henry soared. He was showing great courage in pushing ahead with what was effectively a revolution. England had been subject to Rome for a thousand years, and now all that would be overturned. It was a magnificent, if daunting, prospect. The ramifications could be never-ending.

'Together, Anne, we can build a new Church!' Henry said, his eyes shining. And in that moment she loved him, truly loved him.

Parliament wasted no time in approving the King's new title, and the momentous news was proclaimed all over England. Henry's subjects were told that he was now effectively king and pope in his own realm, with jurisdiction over his subjects' material and spiritual welfare.

Anne was beside herself when the announcement was made at court, and threw her arms around Henry in full view of everyone. 'I feel as if I have gained Paradise,' she cried. She caught Chapuys's hostile stare and smiled challengingly at him.

Father and George were ecstatic. And when, at the reception afterwards, the venerable John Fisher, Bishop of Rochester, insisted that it was against God's law for the King to be head of the Church of England, Father's blood was up.

'Bishop, I could prove to you, by the authority of Scripture, that when God departed this world, He left no successor or vicar,' he asserted.

'Who then said to His disciple, "Thou art Peter, and upon this rock I will build my Church; and the gates of Hell shall not prevail against it"?' the old man countered.

'Let us have no dissent today,' the King said, intervening. 'As you will see, my lord Bishop, most of the nobility have come to rejoice with me – and not a few of your fellow clergy. Come, my lord of Wiltshire, and drink with me.' He and Anne left Fisher to ponder on that and joined Cromwell.

'My chancellor is not here,' Henry said, looking around in vain. 'I had hoped to see him.'

'Thomas More will not countenance this,' Cromwell said. 'It has probably upset his stomach.' But there More was, hurrying into the presence chamber with a great stack of papers under one arm. Joy and relief shone in Henry's face.

'Thomas!' he cried, and embraced More before he could bow.

'I crave your Grace's pardon. I was detained in Chancery, and then I had to wait at Westminster for a barge.' His smile was pleasant, but his eyes were wary.

Norfolk joined them. 'By the Mass, Master More, I did not look to see you here!' he exclaimed, clapping More on the shoulder. They had long been friends.

'I am the King's good servant,' More said. 'My place is here.'

'What does your lordship think of the King's new title?' Cromwell challenged Norfolk. As Henry fixed his gaze on her uncle, Anne drew in her breath. Everyone knew that Norfolk, a devout Catholic like all the Howards, was against reform.

'Don't ask me!' the Duke snorted. 'I leave all that business to those with brains in their heads, like His Grace here.'

Henry laughed. 'Spoken like a true Englishman! I hope that all my subjects will prove as wise as you, my lord. Unlike that fool Fisher.' He turned to Anne, her father and Cromwell, leaving Norfolk and More conversing together. 'He has to be stopped,' he said in a lower voice.

'I will have a quiet word with him,' Cromwell said.

'That wretched Bishop was bloody rude to me,' Father chimed in.

'He could be a dangerous opponent,' Anne warned. 'People respect him as a great theologian. He defended the Queen without fear or favour, remember.'

'He's still writing books defending her,' Henry fumed. 'Her supporters see him as saintly. My grandmother did too – he was her chaplain. But there's steel beneath that air of sanctity. See he keeps his mouth shut, Cromwell.'

Fisher was just one dissident. 'There could be legions of them,' Anne burst out to George the next morning, as they braved the February winds to walk in the gardens.

'Last night, even after the King tried to silence him, the Bishop was airing his views to whoever was listening,' George told her. 'Spreading sedition, no less. And some did listen, especially those who favour the Queen.'

'He must be silenced!' Anne cried. 'No one can be allowed to challenge the King's supremacy. I will speak to His Grace.'

'He can now have him defrocked,' George reminded her. Yes, she *would* speak to Henry.

Henry's face was grave.

'There has been an attempt to poison Bishop Fisher,' he told Anne one afternoon after he had been in Council. 'We've arrested the culprit, a knave called Richard Rouse, the Bishop's cook. He added some powders he says he was given to the gruel that was to be served to my lord and his guests and servants. Two of them have died, and seventeen are seriously ill. It beggars belief that anyone could do such a thing. Poisoning is a horrible crime, and worthy of severe punishment.' His lips were pursed primly in outrage.

'And Bishop Fisher? Was he poisoned?' Anne asked, thinking – God forgive her – that it *would* be convenient to have the saintly prelate confined to his bed, mute, for a space.

'No, I thank God. He had decided to fast. But there's no doubt that the poison was meant for him. Rouse said at first that he thought the powders were laxatives, and that he'd done it for a joke, but then he changed his story and said he had been given to understand that they would do no more than make people sick and would not cause any real harm. What he won't say is who told him that. Someone gave those powders to him.'

Anne had a chilling thought. *They will point the finger at me! The Bishop is known to be against the divorce. People will say I tried to have him murdered.*

'Have you pressed this Rouse to name who sent him?' she asked aloud.

'Yes, he has been interrogated. He is to be examined again today, a little more rigorously.' Henry's eyes narrowed. 'I think he will talk.'

After Henry had left for the council chamber, Anne hastened to confide her anxieties to George. He listened with increasing anger.

'Rouse is being questioned again as we speak,' she told him. 'So far he has taken all the blame upon himself.'

'Maybe he's telling the truth. He could have bought those powders and been told about their effects by the apothecary, or used too much.'

'Or maybe he was warned that, if he talked, it would go worse for his family. George, this was a deliberate attempt on the Bishop's life – it must have been, for it is so timely. And I can't help but think that one of our friends was behind it – someone powerful enough to frighten this Rouse into silence.'

George slid an arm around her. 'Sister, *I* think you are letting your imagination run away with you.'

'But what motive did Rouse have to do such a thing?'

'A grudge against someone?'

Anne stood up. 'I wish I believed that.' A bell sounded in the courtyard outside. 'I must go. Henry will be out of Council soon.'

'Let me know if Rouse talks,' George said.

A horrible germ of a suspicion crept into Anne's mind. Father had waxed hot against Fisher. He had exploded later, after the reception, calling the Bishop all manner of nasty names. And she had confided to

George her fears that Fisher was dangerous. Henry himself had said he should be stopped. But not like this! And really, she could not credit that Father would have stooped so low as to commit murder – and by poison, too, a woman's weapon, given that no brute force was needed. Of course he would not!

Surely George had not done this dreadful thing. Did he love her so much that he would commit murder for her? Was he so stupid not to think of the consequences?

George was a mercurial character, a law unto himself. By his own admission, he had committed rape. And, of all her family, he was the one whom fame and advancement had touched the most. He had grown more ambitious even than she and Father were. Had he done this in the mistaken belief that it would smooth her path? No, she could not believe it.

Rouse did not talk. He still would not name the person who had given him the powders.

Henry came to Anne a few days later. He spoke reluctantly, as if dragging the words out. 'Lord Chancellor More has told me that there are seditious rumours that you, sweetheart, your father and your brother were involved in that poisoning attempt.' His tone was contemptuous.

'It's all wicked lies!' Anne cried, alarmed. 'I would never—'

'Darling, *I* know that,' Henry comforted her. 'By God, I'll still their tongues if I have to cut them out! None shall slander you. I told More – I said you were being blamed unfairly for everything, even the weather.'

Someone, Anne was sure, was trying to frame her. The very use of poison had been intended to put her, a woman, in the picture. For which other woman had a motive to want Fisher silenced?

'There will be no trial,' Henry told Anne, after Rouse had been interrogated for the fourth time.

'But you said—'

'Anne, I must divert suspicion from you and yours.'

'I would see Rouse questioned in open court, to have my name cleared,' Anne demanded. 'He must admit his guilt.'

Henry sat there immovable. He would not look at her.

'What did he say today?' she demanded to know.

'He said little more, despite being pressed. He is adamant that he was acting alone.' Still Henry would not meet her gaze, but sat there toying with the bases of his doublet. 'Darling, the rumours proliferate. Parliament, the supreme court in this realm, will pass an Act of Attainder against this wretch, demonstrating how seriously I regard his crime. And because I utterly abhor such an abominable offence, I am having Parliament pass a new law, making wilful murder by poison high treason, for to me it is equal to it, and should attract similar odium. Those who offend will be boiled to death – a dreadful punishment for a dreadful crime.'

Anne's hand flew to her mouth. It was barbarous. The agony was unimaginable. And that Henry could sanction it! But she could see why he was being so ruthless. The punishment must be a deterrent to others. She hoped, how she hoped, that Rouse was not to suffer it as a scapegoat for someone else.

Sir Francis Bryan went to Smithfield to witness Rouse's execution, and came back sickened. 'They hung him up in chains from a pulley and dipped him in and out of a cauldron,' he related. 'He roared mighty loud, and some women who were big with child fainted. It took him a long time to die.'

Anne shuddered. Her eyes met George's. He was as horrified as she was.

At last the universities of Europe had all spoken. The final determination arrived as Henry and Anne were playing cards in her chamber.

'That makes twelve for me, and four for the Queen,' Henry said, jubilant. 'It's cost me a fortune, but it was worth it.'

Anne hoped they had not all been susceptible to bribes, and that their determinations were honest, but really it did not matter. The outcome was what they had both desired.

'Darling, think on it,' Henry was saying. 'The finest and most learned minds in Europe have pronounced my marriage to be incestuous and against the law of God – and so it *must* be null and void. Pope Julius had no business in the first place to dispense with it.'

'So our marriage can go ahead?' she asked.

'In a little space,' Henry said. 'I'm hoping that Clement will pay heed to these verdicts and grant my annulment, so that this breach can be healed.'

Anne wondered if she had understood him correctly. Was he, even now, ready to be reconciled to Rome? He had made himself head of the English Church! Did he really think that the Pope would welcome him back into the fold with open arms now? She despaired of him, she truly did. At heart, he was still a good son of the Roman Church.

Henry had the verdicts of the universities read out in Parliament and published. Inevitably there was an outcry.

'The most vocal in opposition seem to be women, who are more wilful than wise or learned,' Cromwell reported. 'They accuse your Grace of having corrupted the learned doctors. It would be wise to let the clamour settle down before proceeding further.'

'My book should still their tongues,' Henry declared. *A Glass of the Truth* was about to be published. 'Or we might have to find better ways of doing it.'

The book was greeted largely with derision, and Anne had never been so unpopular. The rumours surrounding the Rouse affair had not been forgotten. People hissed 'Murderess!' when she went out in public.

Anne's misery deepened. She had thought that once the universities had spoken, Henry would instruct the Archbishop of Canterbury to declare his marriage invalid, and they would be wed. But Henry was still, even now, casting about for a more conventional means of bringing that to pass. At present, he was doing his best to provoke Katherine into giving him grounds for a divorce by deserting him. When the Princess Mary fell ill and Katherine was desperate to see her, he told her she might go to her if she wanted, and also stop there. But Katherine, no fool, decided to stay at court. She told him she would not leave him for her daughter or anyone else in the world. Oh, she was clever!

Henry tried a different strategy. When a letter from the Vatican informed him that his case could be tried only in Rome and nowhere else, he shouted that he would never consent. 'And I care not a fig for Clement's excommunications!' he stormed, stumping off to confront Katherine, determined to force her to withdraw her appeal to the Pope.

'I told you she would refuse,' Anne said wearily, when he returned in a foul temper.

'She will rue it,' Henry replied. 'I am sending a deputation from the Privy Council to tell her to be sensible.'

But Katherine refused to be sensible. She insisted that she would abide by no decision save that of Rome. Anne wanted to shake the infuriating woman.

'This cannot go on!' she flared. 'Always she defies you.'

'I agree,' Henry said. 'But the Emperor is powerful. Chapuys watches all that I do. I must not provoke war.'

'The Emperor is busy with fighting the Turks in the east,' Anne pointed out. 'He has little leisure to make war on England.'

'I know that, but be sure he takes a close interest in what happens here. And I do wonder what he would do if Katherine asked him to intervene. Remember, his domains are vast. Think of the armies he could raise. But you are right, darling – this situation cannot continue.'

That summer, they divided their time between Windsor and Hampton Court, riding out to the chase every day, fishing in the Thames and enjoying the good weather. Katherine and Mary came with them to Windsor, but they kept to the Queen's apartments, to Anne's relief. After Katherine had called her a shameless creature in front of the whole court before they left Greenwich, she did not trust herself to be civil.

At the end of June, Henry turned forty. Something of the vigour of youth still clung to him, even if he was broader in person these days and his hair was receding under his bonnet. Maturity suited him. Tall, elegant, muscular and graceful, he yet drew all eyes. Some considered him a perfect model of masculine beauty, but not Anne. She was not dazzled by his majesty – she had long been familiar with the man beneath.

Turning forty made Henry conscious of time flying by. At his age, a man should have a son old enough to wield a sword in battle. He often spoke of his desire to go on a new Crusade against the Turks, but dared not commit himself until the succession was assured. His desire for a male heir was a constant theme – so much depended on it that Anne began to fear it might be too late for her to bear children. She was thirty now, old to be contemplating motherhood for the first time. Another thing to fret about!

'I've had enough,' Henry murmured one evening in July, as he led Anne into the presence chamber at Windsor and saw Katherine already seated there. 'I'm separating from her for good.'

As she went through the farce of curtseying to the Queen and moved to her place further down the high table, Anne dismissed Henry's words as more bluster, thinking there was no point in rejoicing. But he proved her wrong.

'Her obduracy is making a mockery of my scruples, and thanks to her my Great Matter is now talked about through all Christendom,' he grumbled later. 'She has brought shame and dishonour on me. By God, I will not endure her defiance any longer. When we move to Woodstock two days hence, I'm leaving her behind.'

'You really are leaving her for good?' Anne could not quite believe it.

'Yes, darling. I should have done it long ago.'

At last! At last!

'You will tell her beforehand?'

Henry shook his head. 'I can't face another confrontation. When we've gone, I'll send a messenger to say it is my pleasure that she vacate the castle within a month and go to a house of her own choosing. She will understand.'

Yes, she would – but Anne could not help thinking that this was a rather cowardly way of handling the matter. If she had been Henry, she'd have had a few choice words to say! But then he always had been frightened of Katherine and her mighty relations.

*

Early morning, on a beautiful summer's day, and they were riding away from Windsor, leaving Katherine behind and unaware of the momentous step that Henry had taken.

Two days later, Henry's messenger stood nervously before him and recounted how, informed that the King had left her, the Queen had bidden him to convey a message of farewell. The man cleared his throat. 'Your Grace, she said, "Go where I may, I remain his wife, and for him I will pray."'

Henry was furious. 'Go back. Tell the Queen I do not want any of her goodbyes! She has caused me no end of trouble by her obstinacy. She depends, I know, upon the Emperor, but she will find God Almighty more powerful still. Let her stop it and mind her own business. I want no more of her messages.' The messenger departed, visibly quaking.

But the thing had been done, and in Anne optimism burgeoned. With Katherine out of the way – and a blessed relief that was – it was time to establish a queenly household. She asked Edward Foxe to be her almoner, and appointed other officers. Henry was still lavishing gifts on her – often the genial Sir William Brereton, a gentleman of his Privy Chamber, still handsome in his fifties, would be at her door with some new offering – and now visiting ambassadors always brought presents too. The world was aware that in three or four months she could be queen.

'You had best watch your step, niece,' Uncle Norfolk grumbled, sitting down next to Anne as she watched a game of tennis. 'You grow too arrogant.'

'I think you had best watch yours!' she retorted.

'I'm doing just that,' he told her. 'I see the way you treat His Grace; I hear how you speak to him. You think you can rule him, but you forget that he is the King. It's folly to see him as just a man like any other. Go on like this and you'll be the ruin of all your family.'

'Don't be ridiculous, uncle,' Anne retorted. 'His Grace loves me. He has no complaints.'

'He's complained to me of the words you use to him.'

That stung. 'He has said nothing to me.'

'He's afraid of you, Anne – and the day will surely come when he hates himself for it. So be warned. Temper your arrogance with a little respect.'

'You should talk!' she flung after him.

Sir Henry Guildford, Comptroller of the King's Household, was holding forth to his friends in Henry's near-deserted privy chamber when, nursing her resentment both at Norfolk and at Henry, Anne arrived to tax the King for complaining about her. Sir Henry had long shown himself friendly to her, and was well liked by Henry, so she was astonished to hear him saying to Norris that he was sorry, but he could not countenance a divorce without the Pope's sanction, and that he admired the Queen for holding steadfast. Norris, seeing Anne, nodded a warning to Sir Henry, who spun around.

'My lady Anne,' he said, bowing.

She was in no mood to be forgiving. Such talk was subversive and must be stopped.

'I am sorry to hear such disloyal sentiments expressed in His Grace's own chamber,' she snapped. 'If I ask the King, he will dismiss you from your office.'

'You need not wait so long,' Sir Henry retorted angrily. 'I do not like what is happening in this kingdom. When His Grace returns, I am offering him my resignation.'

'What's going on here?' interrupted a familiar high voice, and there loomed Henry, sweating in his tennis slops and short velvet coat, racquet in hand.

'Sir Henry is resigning,' Anne said.

'No!' Henry said. 'I will not allow it. Come, Guildford, and talk with me,' and he led the comptroller into the closet that served him as a study.

Anne stood looking after them. As the door closed, she heard Henry say something about taking no notice of women's talk. She could have breathed fire.

She turned to Norris and tried to fill the silence. 'I hear that the King has made you chamberlain of North Wales and a wealthy man. They are saying that you are richer than many of the nobility. I congratulate you!' She knew her voice sounded brittle.

'You are unhappy,' he said in a low voice. 'Is it all worth it, Lady Anne?'

She was biting back tears now; to have the man she loved show her compassion was almost too much. 'I pray God it is,' she said, aware that this conversation was teetering dangerously on the intimate. 'I should go. I will see the King another time.'

She did not like to go out these days. The hatred of the people was palpable, an obscene thing. Hearing them yelling insults terrified her as much as it enraged her. Wherever she went she was accompanied by an escort of the King's guards. It did not help that Bishop Fisher and other friends of Katherine – a dwindling yet vocal minority – were constantly writing and spouting against the divorce.

As the next session of Parliament loomed, Anne sent a terse message to Fisher warning him not to attend in case he should suffer a repetition of the sickness he had suffered in February. After the messenger had left, she realised that what she had meant to sound sarcastic actually sounded incriminating. But it was too late now to recall the message. Oh, God, let them think what they liked!

She rarely visited Durham House now, but some of her belongings were still there, and in November she went to see what she would need when she became queen. That prospect still seemed some way off. She had been urging Henry to get Parliament to sanction asking Archbishop Warham to declare his marriage invalid, but he was reluctant. Warham was an old man now, and wanted a quiet life in his declining years. Henry thought he could not last much longer, and was loath to put pressure on him, but oh, Anne thought, why could not the bumbling old fool either write the declaration or shuffle off to his Maker?

She was going over and over all this in her mind as she sat in her great chamber in solitary splendour, eating the dinner that had been prepared for her, when she became aware of shouting in the distance. It grew louder and louder.

'What's that?' she asked one of the servitors who were standing, impassive, behind her chair.

'I do not know, my lady,' he said, looking perturbed, for the din was becoming more menacing by the moment. Voices, lots of them, and they sounded very angry.

There was the sharp splinter of breaking glass, and Anne jumped up. 'Summon the guard,' she ordered, trying not to give way to panic. And then she heard, among the shouting, 'Kill the whore!' 'Burn the whore!'

Suddenly the royal guards came thundering into the room, brandishing their ceremonial pikes.

'Make haste, Lady Anne, make haste! There's a mob out there, seven or eight thousand strong, coming for you. We must leave now. Follow me!'

Shaking uncontrollably, Anne ran after them on legs that seemed to have turned to jelly, down to the service quarters and out into the kitchen garden that led to the river. And all the time she expected the mob to catch up, with the lust of violence in their eyes, and set upon her. They would tear her apart, she knew. Her breath was coming in short, harsh gasps, but they were nearing the jetty now, where her barge was moored. Pray God her legs would carry her that far.

The shouting was much louder now, and closer. They were in the gardens already! With no one guarding the house, they must have surged through unchallenged. She dared not look back.

'Hurry!' the guards were urging, and in one final spurt they reached the boat. Picking up her skirts, Anne leapt in, followed by the guards, and the bargemen pushed away – just in time. As the great mob came to a halt at the shore, jeering and shaking their fists, their quarry was out of reach in the middle of the Thames.

'Sirs, I thank you,' she panted. 'Without your help, I would be dead.' She was trembling as if she had the ague, shuddering at the thought of what might have happened.

'Lady Anne, we answer to the King for your safety,' one guard said, a tall, strong fellow in his splendid red livery embroidered with the King's initials. 'We are sworn to protect you with our lives.'

The crowd stayed there, gesticulating and yelling, as the barge was steered around in the direction of Greenwich. 'Look at them – they're like animals,' one of the boatmen said.

Anne fixed a basilisk stare on the rabble on the bank. 'Why, most of them are women! But one has a beard under her coif. Look, there are men there dressed as women!'

'Cowards, the lot of them,' the guard said. 'The King shall hear of this.'

Henry was incandescent when Anne reached Whitehall and threw herself, still pale and trembling, into his arms.

'They shall pay! Every last one of them!' he bawled, holding her tightly to his breast as if he would never let her go. But by the time his soldiers got to Durham House, the mob had long dispersed and there was no way of tracing them. Anne's spirits plummeted when she heard. For ever after, she knew, whenever she went abroad in London, she would wonder if any of those fiends was lying in wait for her.

She had been due to return yet again to Hever for Christmas, a Christmas she had expected to keep as queen, but she was so shaken by her narrow escape that she decided to go now. Henry protested, of course, but she told him she did not feel safe in London, and needed time to recover. Reluctantly, he let her go.

Chapter 20

1532

Hever, for once, felt like a refuge. In the peace of the snowbound Kent countryside, Anne began to recover her equilibrium. It had been a horrible year, and she would be glad to see the end of it.

By Christmas, she was bored, and fretting about missing the celebrations at court. Next year, please God . . .

By the end of December, boredom had outweighed any fears she had about returning to court. Henry would protect her. She could have all the armed might of his guards behind her if she wished. On New Year's Day, she set off for Greenwich.

Henry, apprised of her coming, was waiting for her, and embraced her passionately.

'I have a surprise for you, darling,' he said, and escorted her, to her astonishment, to the Queen's apartments.

'These are yours now,' he declared, with a flourish of his hand.

Waiting for her in the sumptuous presence chamber were her ladies, their numbers now increased, waiting to attend her as if she were queen. Henry was watching her, eager for her response.

'This is a great honour,' she said, thinking, *If only I could be entering here as queen!* 'Your Grace is more than good to me.' She looked about her in wonder and resolved to be kinder to Henry in the future. Maybe Uncle Norfolk had spoken sense.

'And is prepared to do more for you when I can,' Henry promised. 'Now open that door.' It was the door to the Queen's privy chamber, made of solid oak. 'This is my New Year's gift to you,' he said.

She gasped. The whole room was newly hung with cloth of gold and silver, and heavy embroidered satin.

'Here you shall hold court, just like a queen,' Henry told her.

She was choked, filled to the brim with warring emotions, overwhelmed by the apartment and the magnificent gift – but why, oh why must she always be *like* a queen!

'It makes my gift to you seem paltry,' she apologised. 'It is some ornamented spears for hunting the wild boar that King François shipped over. And Mary has sent you a shirt she embroidered herself. When my gear is unpacked, you shall have them.'

'How very kind! I shall look forward to both gifts,' Henry said gallantly.

'May I have Mary to be my lady-in-waiting?' Anne asked. 'I really should ask her.'

'Of course,' Henry agreed. But it was clear that he wasn't keen, and to be honest, Anne wasn't either. Yet it would have looked odd not to have her sister serve her. Whatever Father and Mother said, she could not leave Mary hidden away at Hever.

As they wandered through the spacious rooms, from which all trace of their previous occupant had been removed, Anne could not help but think of Katherine. And when they came to the bedchamber, with its great bed hung with green silk, she thought of Henry spending his wedding night with Katherine here, and the many nights he would have lain in her bed thereafter. Judging by the awkward silence between them, he was remembering too.

'Katherine sent me a gold cup,' he said at length, 'but I sent it back with a message commanding her not to give me gifts in future, since I am not her husband, as she should know.'

'Do you think that this new year will see us wed?' Anne asked anxiously.

'By God, I hope so!' Henry replied, and kissed her hand with fervour.

It seemed, however, that the opposition just would not lie down and be quiet.

Henry's cousin, Reginald Pole, the son of Katherine's beloved Lady Salisbury, had until recently been supportive of the King's case, and had used his influence to ensure that learned opinion was in Henry's favour at the University of Paris. But now, persuaded doubtless by his mother, he suddenly turned his coat.

'He warned me that dangers would ensue upon our marriage, and said I was in error to seek a divorce,' Henry raged. 'After all I've done for him, paying for his education and advancing his family! I ordered him to explain himself, but he refused, and now he's bolted off to France. It beggars belief. My own blood deserting me!'

Archbishop Warham now entered the fray. His unease about the Great Matter had been no secret, but the King's supremacy was a step too far. That February, the Archbishop made a formal protest in Parliament against all Acts that were derogatory to the Pope's authority.

'Evidently he fears the judgement of God more than he fears me,' a grim Henry observed to Anne.

'He is your Archbishop of Canterbury. You should censure him.'

'He is dying, Anne. I'll let him be. It cannot be long.' And he would not be moved. It was infuriating, because without the Archbishop's co-operation, there could be no formal declaration that Henry's marriage was invalid. And there Anne was, still unwed, still a queen-in-waiting, and still the target of widespread hatred. It was no use Henry commanding that those who called her a common whore and worse be hauled before the justices – it did not silence her ill-wishers, or the mad Nun of Kent, who had continued to shout out in public her vile prophecies against the King.

'She is in league with Bishop Fisher,' Cromwell told Anne. 'My agents are watching her. Fear not, she will condemn herself out of her own mouth.'

There was criticism closer to home, too. On Easter Sunday, Anne was seated beside Henry in the royal pew of the Chapel Royal at Greenwich when the Princess Mary's confessor, Friar William Peto, ascended the steps into the pulpit and directed his hawk-like gaze at Henry.

'O King, hear what I say to you: I tell you truly that this marriage you intend is unlawful. Take great heed lest, being seduced into error, you merit Ahab's punishment, who had his blood licked up by the dogs.'

Henry had gone purple with rage. He rose to his feet before the friar had finished, grabbed Anne's hand and stalked out. The following week he had one of his own chaplains preach a sermon denouncing Friar Peto.

'He is a dog, a slanderer, a base and beggarly rebel and traitor!' the chaplain thundered. 'No subject should speak so audaciously to his Prince!'

'What if his Prince has the audacity to put away his lawful wife?' cried a voice in the congregation. It was another friar.

'Silence!' roared Henry.

'Have that man and Friar Peto brought before my Council,' he ordered Cromwell afterwards. Later that day, Anne heard that Friar Peto had been imprisoned. His friend had escaped with a reprimand – too lightly, she thought angrily.

Now here was Father, come to supper with her and Henry, and looking unusually worried. 'In truth, sir,' he said, breaking his bread, 'I wonder if this is all worth it.'

Henry frowned. 'Is *what* all worth it?'

'Your Grace's determination to marry Anne, flattering though it is.'

'Father!' Anne burst out, shocked. 'Have you gone mad?'

'Sometimes I think all this will drive me to insanity,' Thomas Boleyn confessed. 'We are forever in your Grace's debt for the great honour you have shown us, but it's a pretty nest of vipers that's been stirred up.'

To Anne's astonishment, Henry reached over and patted Father on the shoulder. 'Have patience, man,' he encouraged. 'What I have resolved, I will carry out. My marriage is invalid whoever I choose to make my next Queen. And the English Church is sorely in need of reform. My Great Matter has merely exposed the corruption in Rome. And by God, sir, I will have Anne to wife, whatever the opposition!'

'Bravely said, your Grace,' Father applauded, rallying. 'You must forgive my concern for my daughter. All these delays cause unbearable strain.' So he had noticed. Anne had thought him too preoccupied with the glories to come. 'And that business at Durham House,' he was saying, shaking his head. 'It shook us.'

'It shook me, too,' Henry said, signalling for more wine to be brought, 'but you may rest assured that I will never allow anyone to harm Anne. She will always be under my special protection. Yet the delays weary me too. I have waited five years now to marry her, and still I do not have a son to succeed me. And, as I told Parliament, I am nearly forty-one years old, at which age the lust of man is not so quick as in lusty youth.'

Anne stared at him. She had wondered if her own juices were drying up at thirty-one; it had never occurred to her that Henry, with those great embroidered and bejewelled codpieces he wore protruding from the bases of his doublets, and his ardent importunings for some kind of sexual satisfaction, was anything less than energetically virile. But there he sat, looking sorry for himself, and Father was commiserating.

'Fear not,' Anne told them. 'That which we have so long wished for will soon be accomplished.'

That spring, the clergy in Convocation formally renounced their allegiance to the Pope, and Henry exacted a steep fine as a penalty for their past misplaced loyalty to Rome.

The very next day, pleading ill health, Sir Thomas More resigned from his office of Lord Chancellor.

Henry was cast into gloom when he joined Anne in her great chamber later that day. 'There is nothing wrong with his health. It's his conscience that bothers him. He says he can't uphold my case.' He sighed. 'I would have given much to have his support.'

'He has retired from public life?' Anne asked, hopeful.

'Yes, he's gone home to Chelsea, to his family and his books. I'm appointing Sir Thomas Audley Chancellor in his place. He can't hold a candle to More, but he's staunch in my cause.'

He leaned over and kissed her. 'Be of good cheer, darling. We cannot have long to wait now. Warham is at death's door, and as soon as he's gone, I'm having Cranmer in his place. And then, Anne, you'll see, things will move quickly.'

As if in earnest of that, he summoned his tailors, who appeared with their arms laden with beautiful garments.

'My Queen shall have only the best,' Henry declared, as one held up a gown of rich gold-figured fabric. There was another of black velvet edged with pearls, with a matching French hood, and a third of royal purple. Yet what delighted Anne the most was a sumptuous nightgown of black satin trimmed with black velvet.

'For our wedding night,' Henry murmured in her ear. 'You need wear nothing under it.'

That spring, through clever diplomacy, Henry managed to lure King François away from the Emperor, and in the summer, England and France signed a treaty of alliance against Charles V.

'Now I can count on François's support in my Great Matter,' Henry rejoiced. 'I'm meeting with him in the autumn at Calais to discuss it. And you, darling, are coming with me.'

Henry's patience with Katherine had almost run out. Exiled from the court, yet living in great state, she had remained resolute. He had thought to weaken her resolve by depriving her of the company of their daughter, but that had provoked a public outcry, so he had relented and allowed the Princess to pay her mother a widely publicised visit.

Yet still Katherine insisted that she was his true queen, and it was clear that she had further infected Mary with her obstinacy.

'I'm keeping them apart in future,' Henry growled. 'Mary is growing older and might be persuaded to intrigue with the Emperor against me.' And, of course, he wanted to punish Katherine. It would serve her right, Anne thought.

The prospect of returning to France delighted Anne. She set about choosing the ladies she wanted to wait on her. Her sister Mary, who had now joined her household, would be one of them.

But then – was there no end to the obstacles that had been placed in her way? – Mary Talbot, Countess of Northumberland, petitioned Parliament for a divorce from Harry Percy. Henry stumped into Anne's chamber with the news. 'The Countess says there was a precontract between you and her husband,' he told her, watching her jealously. 'Was there?' They had never spoken of her affair with Harry Percy.

'We made a foolish promise, not really knowing what we were doing,' she admitted. 'I understood that the Cardinal had dealt with it. He told me that Harry Percy was already betrothed.'

Henry said nothing for a few moments. 'Did you love him?' he asked at length, his piercing eyes intense.

'It was a youthful infatuation,' Anne lied. 'I did not love him in the way I love you.' That, at least, was the truth.

'Well, the matter needs to be resolved,' Henry said, apparently satisfied, and getting up to leave. 'I'll have Warham and the Archbishop of York question the Earl.'

'You don't believe me?' Anne asked.

'Of course, darling, but if I am to marry you, I have to ensure that you are free from all previous entanglements, for I dare not risk compromising the legitimacy of our children. So I will have the Earl questioned in the presence of the Duke of Norfolk and my lawyers, just to be on the safe side.'

Harry denied any precontract. He even swore it on the Blessed Sacrament, perjuring himself. Of course, it would have been dangerous admitting to having loved the King's future wife. '*Noli me tangere*, for Caesar's I am!' And Parliament refused his wife's petition. Anne felt sorry for them both. The Countess must have been unhappy in her marriage to take such a drastic step. Anne hated the thought of Harry trapped in a loveless, acrimonious wedlock. He was a good man, and he did not deserve that.

It was August when the news came that Archbishop Warham had died.

'I should be mourning the old man, but he's of more use to God than he ever was to me,' Henry said, clasping Anne and whirling her around in his joy. 'No one can say no to us now, darling! I'm nominating Cranmer to the See of Canterbury this very night. I'm going through the motions with Rome, so that none in Christendom can challenge my new Archbishop.'

Anne could hardly believe it all. When Henry let her go, she stood there trying to grasp the implications of Warham's death. It really would be only a matter of weeks now before her marriage. For Cranmer would not hesitate to declare Henry's union with Katherine invalid; and he was the one man who would zealously push through the religious reforms that were so important to him and Anne.

Henry was looking at Anne as if he might devour her. She met his gaze and read in it years of pent-up desire. Outside the open window behind him, the sun was descending behind the trees, casting soft, radiant light on an enchanted world and on his red-gold hair. They were alone on this balmy summer evening. Henry took a step towards her and she went into his arms.

'I love you, Anne.' His voice was heavy with passion. 'Be mine, darling! There is nothing to stop us now.'

Why not? she thought, her cheek against the rough gold thread of his doublet, her arms twined around his broad torso. We have denied ourselves for so long! And if I do not love him as he loves me, I have at least been aroused by him. Suddenly she was shaken by a longing to be at one with him, to give something back for all the long years of a very one-sided wooing – and for not loving him enough.

'Would your Grace like to see me in that beautiful nightgown?' she murmured, looking up into his eyes. They were blazing with his terrible need of her.

'Darling!' His voice trembled.

'Wait here. I will not be long,' she promised.

She lay in her tumbled bed, sore but triumphant. Outside, the watch was crying two o'clock, but otherwise all was quiet. She stretched and looked across to where Henry had lain. The pillow still bore the indentation of his head, the sheets were stained with his seed, which was leaking out of her. He had gone, kissing her lovingly good night, to write Cranmer's nomination, promising to return as soon as he had done it. He'd wanted to get it off to Rome at first light.

Their coming together had not been quite as she had expected. It had hurt a little, but there had been no pleasure, just the sweaty fusion of two bodies. She had never seen a man naked and erect before, though she had imagined it after hearing many jests and giggling confidences, yet the reality of Henry did not quite match up to her mental vision of what he would be like. His member was smaller than the codpiece had led her to believe.

He had himself slid the nightgown from her shoulders, then held

309

her away so that he could gaze on her body, revealed to him for the first time. Then he'd pulled her down on the bed, his eyes dark with desire. And yet – she was sure she had not imagined this – he had been nervous. He kept touching his manhood and squeezing it. And then he entered her, painfully, breathing heavily and thrusting frantically back and forth – and it was all over very quickly.

Was that it? she asked herself, as they lay together afterwards with his strong arms around her, his face buried in her hair. Was that what the poets and lyricists made such a song about? What men languished or killed for? What Henry had broken with Rome for? If so, it must be very different for men! Yet she was not unduly disappointed, apart from wishing that it could have happened after the wedding. What mattered was power and founding a dynasty and pushing through reforms. Sex was a means to an end, and now all those things were within her grasp. She was Henry's; they might even have conceived the son who would crown all their blessings. Within her, triumph burgeoned.

Henry had held her for a long time after they made love. He told her several times that he loved her, and thanked her for letting him possess her. He had kissed her hand when he left the bed to write his letter, and murmured a fond farewell. He had done all the right things. So why was it that she was left with the disconcerting feeling that something was out of kilter? Was this culmination of all the years of waiting and denial? Had she done something wrong? She had played a passive part, letting him take the initiative; wasn't that what women were supposed to do? And then she remembered things from her days at the French court: the reliefs on that golden bowl; the very paintings on the walls; those lewd books that had been passed around. No, she had it all wrong. Women *were* meant to take an active role. That was the way to keep a man interested, once he had conquered you.

She tried to imagine doing those things to, and with, Henry. It made her realise how little she knew him. What would make love special for him? Should she ask, or should she surprise him? Just do it, she told herself, smiling.

Then, unbidden, came a treacherous thought, of how much more wonderful love would be with Norris. If he were in her bed, she would feel something, she knew it. But that could never be; she must never think of it. And yet, when Henry returned an hour later, claimed her once more and climaxed again in her arms, she let herself imagine that he was Norris – and then desire did stir in her.

The next morning, Anne was hoping that Henry would lie abed with her so that she could pleasure him as she had planned, but he was up and pulling on his nightgown as she awoke. He bent and kissed her.

'Good morning, sweetheart!'

'Good morning, your Grace,' she smiled, stretching luxuriously.

'I wish I could stay, but I must go,' he said, reaching for his nightcap. 'I ride to Hunsdon this morning.'

'To Hunsdon? Why?'

'I had planned to visit Mary.'

Anne sat up, her good mood evaporating. 'I marvel that you show her such favour, considering how disobedient she has been.'

Henry bent to put on his slippers. He had his back to her. 'At heart she is a good child, and loving. I would bring her around with gentle words.'

'It's more than she deserves!' Anne retorted. 'She's sixteen and should know her duty better. If I were her father, I would have her whipped, and put an end to this nonsense.'

'Darling, give me a chance. I would speak with her.'

'You've spoken with her before, to no effect! I had thought you would spend this day, of all days, with me.'

Henry turned and squeezed her hand. 'I promise I will not stay long. I'll be back by evening, and then, sweetheart, we can be together again.' His eyes were alight with promise.

'Very well,' she conceded, 'but see you do bring her to heel. She could prove every bit as dangerous as her mother.'

'I am her father,' Henry said. 'She will obey me, you'll see.'

That morning, after Henry had kissed her lovingly and ridden off to Hertfordshire, Anne joined George to watch a game of bowls in the palace gardens.

'You heard about Warham?' she asked, as they sat on the grass a little away from the others.

'I did! Things are moving speedily your way, sister.'

'I know. But still the King is being too lenient with the Princess. He's gone to visit her today to make her see sense, but he won't succeed. That little madam is moulded from the same clay as her mother. God help me, but I could strangle her! When I am queen – and it won't be long now – I'll have her in my own train and give her too much dinner! Or I'll marry her to some varlet!'

'Would that I were in want of a wife!' George teased. 'I'd teach her!'

'Would that you were,' Anne agreed, wishing that he could be released from his unhappy marriage to sour-faced Jane.

When Henry returned that evening, he embraced her absent-mindedly. Who would have thought that they had become lovers only the night before? He was tense and morose.

'Don't tell me,' Anne sighed, as she poured him some wine. 'The Princess proved difficult.'

Henry sighed. 'She's as stubborn and opinionated as her mother. I warned her she had better look to her future, for big changes were coming. But darling, I don't want to dwell on her unnatural behaviour. I've decided that, in advance of our visit to France, I am raising you to the peerage. You will accompany me as my lady Marquess of Pembroke. It is a royal title; my Uncle Jasper bore it. No woman has ever before been granted a peerage in her own right in England, so consider yourself very special.'

Anne hugged and kissed him heartily. 'Sir, it is a great honour.' And a reward, of course. 'I thank your Grace.' Her mind was racing through the implications. Such a title not only elevated her status for the coming trip: it also conferred nobility on Henry's future queen.

'I want you to see the wording on the patent of creation,' Henry said, and handed her a paper on which he had scrawled some sentences. It began, 'A monarch ought to surround his throne with many peers of the worthiest of both sexes, especially those who are of royal blood.' She liked that reminder of her descent from Edward I. But she was perturbed to see that something was missing from the passage relating to any children to whom her new title might one day descend.

'Shouldn't it say "lawfully begotten issue"?' she asked.

'I thought about that, but we need to ensure that any child we conceive is provided for in the event of my dying before I can marry you,' Henry explained, coming up behind her to nuzzle her neck. She relaxed in relief. For a horrible moment she had feared that, having possessed her, he was thinking of pensioning her off and providing for any bastard she might bear him. And that, she knew, was what others might think when they heard the patent read out at the ceremony of ennoblement. But they would soon find out how wrong they were.

It was at Windsor, on the first day of September, that Anne received her peerage. A fanfare sounded as, preceded by Garter King of Arms carrying the patent of nobility, and her cousin Mary, Norfolk's daughter, bearing a robe of state of crimson velvet furred with ermine and a gold coronet, she entered the presence chamber, flanked on either side by the countesses of Rutland and Sussex, and followed by a great train of courtiers and ladies. For this ancient ceremony she had been given the traditional robes of nobility, in a style dating from centuries ago: a short-sleeved surcoat of crimson velvet trimmed with ermine, with a close-fitting long-sleeved gown beneath it; like a queen, she wore her glossy hair loose about her shoulders.

Ahead of her the King sat enthroned, attended by Norfolk, Suffolk, the French ambassador and the lords of his Council. She curtseyed three times as she approached him, then knelt as the Letters Patent conferring her new title were read out by Stephen Gardiner, who had been made Bishop of Winchester as a reward for all his hard work in Rome. Henry rose, smiling at her. He placed the mantle of estate about her shoulders and lifted the coronet on to her head, then presented her with her patents.

'I thank your Grace most humbly,' she murmured, then rose and curtseyed again, before leaving the chamber to another burst of trumpets. Afterwards, Henry joined her for Mass in St George's Chapel, where the *Te Deum* was sung in her honour.

How could she ever have thought there was something wrong? She had imagined it. Henry was as loving as ever – more so now that they were lovers in every way, every night. It was as if he could not leave her alone for an hour.

There were now only a few weeks to go before the visit to Calais. Henry had high hopes of it.

'I have never desired anything as much,' he declared. 'François hopes to meet with the Pope early next year, and I'm glad of this chance to see him first and tell him in person of the determinations of the universities. That will make Clement sit up and think!'

Even now, he was hoping that, at the last minute, Clement would decide in his favour.

'Darling, I want you to wear the Queen's jewels in France,' he told her. Anne had seen those jewels many times when she served Katherine. She knew they had been handed down from consort to consort, and that some were centuries old and had great historical or sentimental value. When she was queen, they would be hers, but the prospect of having them now – and of Katherine being made to realise that she had no right to them – suddenly assumed prime importance.

'It will show the world that our marriage is as good as made,' Henry said, and sent a messenger to Katherine demanding that she deliver up the jewels to him.

But the messenger came back empty-handed: Katherine had refused to surrender them without the King's express command in writing, because he had commanded her not to send him anything. Anne stood in the privy chamber, her cheeks burning, as the messenger repeated what Katherine had actually said: that it was offensive and insulting to her, and would weigh upon her conscience, to give up her jewels for such a base purpose as that of decking out a person who was a reproach to Christendom and was bringing infamy on the King through his taking her to France.

'I'll write the order now!' Henry shouted, enraged.

Within two days, the jewels were in Anne's possession. But they were not compensation enough for her humiliation. That still smarted.

314

'If I may have the Queen's jewels, might I have the Queen's barge as well?' she asked. It would be gratifying to be rowed up and down the Thames in that ornate, gilded vessel, and have everyone know that the future Queen sat therein.

Henry agreed, but after Anne gave the order for Katherine's coat of arms to be burned off the barge and replaced with her own, his smile slipped.

'That wasn't very tactful,' he reproved her, looking weary after a long meeting with the Imperial ambassador. 'Chapuys is complaining that the barge has been shamefully mutilated. He hopes that you will content yourself with the barge, the jewels and the husband of the Queen. For God's sake, Anne, don't provoke him unnecessarily.'

'No offence was intended,' she replied, 'but some damage was unavoidable. They had to break up the arms first, and then burn off the rest. And, for the record, I'm very contented with the husband of the Queen!' She put her hands up to Henry's cheeks and kissed him.

'Sweetheart, we have encountered a problem,' Henry said, looking embarrassed as he sat down on the bed beside Anne. 'For some weeks now my envoys have been discussing which royal lady will receive you in France. François's new queen, Eleanor, is the Emperor's sister, and naturally her sympathies are with Katherine. François felt he could not command her; besides, I'd as soon see the Devil as a lady in Spanish dress!'

He reached for her hand. 'I asked that the honours be done by François's sister, the Queen of Navarre, whom you once served.'

Marguerite! How she would love to see clever, spirited Marguerite again after all these years. 'That would be wonderful,' she said.

Henry hesitated. 'I'm afraid she refused. I wouldn't tell you this for the world, but you may hear it from others in France. She said she would have nothing to do with one whose behaviour was the scandal of Christendom.'

Anne could have wept. And this was the same Marguerite who had held such enlightened views and advocated the reign of the virtuous woman? The same Marguerite who had shown herself so friendly to Anne?

Henry lay down and put his arm around her. 'Things have changed in France since you were there,' he said.

'I know. The King is no longer as tolerant as he was in matters of religion.' Marguerite, she was aware, had had to abandon her forward-thinking views. Three years ago, a protégé of hers had been burned for heresy in Paris with all his books. She had been powerless to protect him. She had even been questioned herself. It seemed that she had changed in other ways, too. But Anne had still thought her a friend.

'Without any lady of rank to receive me, I cannot leave Calais and go into France,' she pointed out.

'I know, darling, and François has been at pains to find a solution that will please everyone. He even suggested that the Duchess of Vendôme do the honours.'

'But she is his mistress!' Anne cried.

'I'm aware of that, and I told him it would be a disgrace and an insult to you and our English ladies. I'm sorry, darling, but reluctantly I've decided that you must remain in Calais when I go to meet François.'

She was trembling with rage and disappointment.

'Don't be too disappointed. François is going to visit us in Calais afterwards,' Henry comforted her. 'And we will be together for much of the time. It will be like a honeymoon.' His hand moved down to her breast. 'Cromwell says people are speculating that we will marry in France.'

'You do not want that, surely?' she asked.

'No, darling,' he reassured her.

'I would never consent to it. I want our wedding to take place here in England, where other queens have been married and crowned.'

'It will, I promise,' he murmured, drawing her to him.

They enjoyed a smooth crossing to Calais, having departed from Dover at dawn's first light in a fine ship called the *Swallow*. In the great cabin, Mark Smeaton entertained Henry, Anne and favoured courtiers with some virtuoso playing on his lute. Anne, standing by the latticed window with her sister Mary, watching the coast of England receding, was aware of Tom Wyatt regarding her dispassionately across the crowded space. When their eyes met, he looked away. She marvelled at how desire could turn to indifference.

They arrived in Calais at ten o'clock that morning, and were greeted by a thunderous royal salute. There was a civic reception hosted by Lord Berners, the Governor of Calais, after which Henry and Anne were conducted in procession to the church of St Nicholas to hear Mass. Later they proceeded to the Exchequer Palace, where Anne was impressed with her suite of seven fine rooms, with a bedchamber adjoining Henry's. While her attendants were unpacking, she and Mary explored the palace, a large residence with a long gallery, a tennis court, and extensive gardens on both the King's and Queen's sides. Anne had not told Mary that she and Henry were now lovers, but let her draw her own conclusions from the sleeping arrangements.

That night, Henry came to her. Always, since their first night together, he had taken the initiative in their lovemaking, and she had not yet ventured to do so herself. But now that they were in France, with that carefree sense of being on holiday, she decided that it was time to be more adventurous. And so, when Henry reached for her, she pressed him back on the bed and began trailing light kisses down the length of his body, using her mouth to pleasure him. He gasped and spent himself almost at once. As he lay there panting, she cuddled up by his side.

'I wanted to please you,' she whispered.

He did not answer. Was he asleep already? But no, in the flickering flame of the single candle they had left burning, she could see him looking at her, frowning slightly.

'Where did you learn how to do that?' he asked.

'At the French court there were books in circulation, showing people making love in different ways,' she said, realising he'd thought some past lover had taught her, and that she was not as virginal as she'd led him to believe. 'I have never done it, Henry! I just remembered, and thought to please you.'

There was a silence, during which she realised, to her horror, that she had not pleased him at all. Of course, Katherine would never have . . . But there had been mistresses . . .

'Darling,' Henry said, 'if we are to get a son, that is not the way to go about it. And the Church frowns on practices like that. But I appreciate your wanting to please me. You do that best when you allow me inside you.'

'Then I am your Grace's to command,' she said lightly, knowing she had miscalculated badly. Never again would she take the lead in bed with him.

Henry kissed her. 'Remember that!' he said, his tone warmer.

It was frustrating being left behind at Calais when Henry sallied forth to Boulogne to spend four days with King François. But Anne made the most of her time, going hawking, gambling at cards and dice, and feasting on delicacies sent by the French King – carp, porpoise, venison pasties, choice pears and grapes. She also did her best to evade Mary's blatant curiosity about the exact state of her relations with Henry.

The King returned in a jubilant mood.

'François is sympathetic to us,' he told Anne. 'I've invited him here on Friday.'

Anne was not especially eager to welcome François, that great lecher, and Mary – who had thought not to see him – flinched at the news, but she agreed to attend Anne with the other ladies, there being safety in numbers. Anne made them all practise for a masque to be performed before François. She expressed delight in the costly diamond he sent her by the Provost of Paris.

A three-thousand gun salute was fired in the French King's honour when he arrived. For two days, at Henry's request, Anne kept out of sight, but on the third evening she graced the high table at a lavish supper and banquet given by Henry in the great hall of the Staple Inn, where François was staying. The hall looked magnificent, hung with gold and silver tissue and gold wreaths glittering with pearls and precious stones, which reflected the light from the twenty silver candelabra, each bearing a hundred wax candles. A dazzling display of gold plate on a seven-tier buffet proclaimed Henry's riches, as did his suit of purple cloth of gold, his collar of fourteen rubies, and his two great ropes of pearls, from one of which hung the famous Black Prince's ruby. They feasted on one hundred and seventy dishes, with a lavish variety of meats, game and fish prepared from both English and French recipes.

Afterwards, Anne led Mary, Jane Rochford and four other ladies in the masque, attired in a costume of cloth of gold slashed with crimson satin, puffed with cloth of silver and laced with gold cords. All wore masks. After the ladies had danced before the two kings, Anne went up to François, curtseyed, and led him out to the floor, at which Mary and her companions invited King Henry and the other lords to join them.

'These ten years have not changed you, my lady Marquess,' François said gallantly. 'We have missed you at the French court.' He himself had put on weight, and his saturnine features had coarsened. It repelled her to hold his hand, but she kept smiling and set herself to charm him, for he was willing to be a friend to Henry and could prove very helpful. This new alliance would counterbalance any threat from the Emperor.

Henry was laughing, going about the dancers and pulling off the ladies' masks. He stopped before Anne and removed hers. 'Now you may see how beautiful my lady is!' he said to François.

Anne accepted the compliment graciously, as Henry led her into the next dance. She noticed that Mary was talking animatedly to her partner, a young man Anne did not know.

'Who is that?' she asked Henry.

'Young Stafford, a distant cousin of mine. He's here in my train.'

They seemed to be getting on very well together. Anne watched Mary flirting with Stafford, who looked some years younger than her. It was good to see her enjoying herself after being a widow for so long.

After the French had left, with François promising to do all in his power to bring about a reconciliation between Henry and the Pope, violent storms blew up in the English Channel, which meant that Henry and Anne had to stay on at the Exchequer for another fortnight. It did not matter. Henry welcomed his enforced break from state duties, and gave himself up entirely to Anne. They ate long, leisurely meals, rode out beyond the town walls to see the rolling countryside of the Calais Pale, a little part of England on the edge of France, and made love every night and morning. Anne even donned a pair of breeches and beat Henry at tennis. She felt closer to him than ever before.

Their idyll came to an end one midnight in the middle of November, when Henry decided that they should seize the opportunity afforded by a favourable wind to sail home to England. The voyage was appalling, twenty-nine hours of hell in roiling seas, and Anne, usually a good sailor, was more than grateful to see the cliffs of Dover ahead at last.

They took their time enjoying a sedate progress eastwards through Kent. They lodged at Leeds, a fine castle that seemed to rise out of a lake, and then rode on to Stone Castle, where they stayed as guests of an old friend of Anne from Hever days, Bridget, Lady Wingfield. After a good dinner, Henry and Anne joined their hostess, Sir Francis Bryan and Francis Weston in their favourite card game, Pope Julian, and a groaning Henry lost heavily to Anne.

Afterwards, they all sat by the fire and talked, as spiced wine was served. Weston spoke of the happiness he had found in his recent marriage to Anne Pickering, and how much he was looking forward to seeing her.

'You mean Weston the wanton has finally settled down?' Bryan joked.

'I long to get home to Sutton Place,' Weston sighed.

'I hear the house is beautiful,' Anne said.

'It's magnificent,' Henry told her. 'It was my gift to Francis's father for his good service to me. He must be very proud of you, Francis.'

'He is, sir, apart from when he's telling me off for beating your Grace at cards.'

'He has a point there,' Henry grinned. 'Come on, then, since Mark is abed, give us a song on your lute, Francis.'

Weston picked up the instrument. 'Here's one for your Grace and the Lady Anne.' And he sang in his rich baritone voice:

> Whoso that will for grace sue
> His intent must needs be true,
> And love her in heart and deed,
> Else it were pity that he should speed.

But love is a thing given by God,
In that therefore can be none odd;
But perfect indeed and between two,
Wherefore then should we it eschew?

Henry's arm stole around Anne and he looked down at her with one eyebrow raised.

'It's your own song,' she said. 'No one surpasses you when it comes to the perfect marriage of music and lyrics.'

'Never mind that,' he muttered in her ear. 'Just come to bed, as soon as he's finished.'

They were at Whitehall Palace, preparing for Christmas, when Anne found a thin volume lying on the table in her privy chamber. It was a book of prophecies containing crude drawings, and it had been left open at a lurid one depicting a woman with her head cut off. As she looked closer, she realised it was meant to be her. The caption warned that this would be her fate if she married the King. Nan Saville, coming up behind her and seeing it, was horrified.

'If I thought it true, I would not have him, were he an emperor,' she declared.

Anne slammed the book shut. 'Tut, Nan, it's just a bauble, and I am resolved to have him, so that my children may be royal, whatever becomes of me.'

For all her bravado, the drawing had upset her, and she consigned the book to the fire. Who had left it for her to find? Access to her privy chamber was restricted to approved servants and those who were close to or approved of by her. She wondered if Jane Rochford had done it. She mentioned the book to Jane, but got no reaction.

As the days passed, she forgot about the incident. Christmas was coming, and this year, God be praised, she would not be spending it in exile at Hever, but presiding over it at court, by Henry's side.

Part Three

'The Most Happy'

Chapter 21

1533

Anne felt excitement mounting as she came from her close stool and washed her hands. She was a week overdue, her breasts were tender, and today she had felt nauseous on rising. She was with child, she was sure of it.

She hastened to find Henry, but he was in Council. She waited in the gallery, fidgeting, for him to emerge. When he did, she hurried up to him as the lords following in his wake stared curiously.

'I must speak to your Grace,' she murmured, barely able to contain herself. What would he say when she told him that the heir to England slept under her girdle?

'Of course, sweetheart,' he agreed. 'Gentlemen, we shall meet again at the same time tomorrow.'

And by then everything would have changed!

He led her into the nearby chapel and looked at her questioningly.

'I'm with child!' she burst out.

His face was transfigured; it burst into a radiant smile. 'Thanks be to God!' he breathed, bowing to the crucifix on the altar. He turned to her. 'You know what this means, Anne? It is a vindication of all I have done. Heaven has smiled on us both. Our marriage will be truly blessed. Oh, my darling, I am so proud of you!' And he took her in his arms, very tenderly, and kissed her gently. 'You must take care,' he urged. 'You carry a precious burden. Thank you, Anne, thank you! You cannot know how much this news means to me.' He laid his hand on her belly. 'A son – an heir to England, and her saviour, no less. Now we will be free from the threat of civil war.'

'I am the happiest of women!' Anne exulted. 'I shall choose "The

Most Happy" for my motto as queen, to remind me of this precious moment.'

'We must be married without delay,' Henry said. 'I'll go and talk to Cranmer now.'

He returned to her chamber rejoicing. 'Cranmer says there is no impediment, and that my union with Katherine is unquestionably null and void. He says he will confirm everything formally in his court. Darling, there is no need to wait, and no time to be lost. People must believe that our child was conceived in lawful wedlock. We must be married now.'

It was still dark when Anne rose on the feast of the conversion of St Paul, the twenty-fifth day of January. Anne Savage was dressed already, and waiting to attire her for her wedding. Around them the palace slumbered on.

She had chosen to wear white satin, with her hair loose, in token of the symbolic virginity of a queen. The gown was beautiful, with its low square neckline, hanging sleeves, pointed stomacher and heavy skirts. It was a gown made for display, but this wedding had to take place in secret, so she suffered her ladies to conceal it under a voluminous black velvet mantle lined with fur.

With Anne Savage bearing her train, she hastened silently up a deserted spiral staircase to a little oratory in a high tower. There, awaiting them in the sanctuary, stood Henry's chaplain, Dr Lee, in full vestments. Then Henry arrived, tall, eager and imposing in cloth of gold, accompanied by his gentlemen, all sworn to secrecy: Norris, who met Anne's eyes with a slight but poignant frown; Thomas Heneage of the King's Privy Chamber, and William Brereton. Anne Savage divested her mistress of her mantle. Anne curtseyed gracefully to Henry, who took her hand and kissed it. 'You look beautiful,' he said, his eyes drinking her in.

They knelt together before the altar, and Dr Lee began intoning the words of the Holy Sacrament of marriage. The King's eyes never left Anne's as they spoke their vows.

'I, Henry, take thee, Anne . . .'

'I, Anne, take thee, Henry . . .'

326

'Those whom God hath joined together, let no man put asunder!'
Dr Lee commanded, and pronounced them man and wife.

Anne could barely contain herself. She wanted to shout out to
the world that she was Henry's wife and Queen, but she controlled the
impulse. It could not be long before their marriage was proclaimed, for
in a few weeks her pregnancy would start to show. She contented herself
by telling her friends that she was now as sure that she should be married
to the King as she was of her own death.

Now that Anne was his wife, Henry was utterly resolved to brook
no opposition. In anticipation of that, he banished Katherine to
Ampthill Castle, forty-six miles from London, determined to break her
resistance.

Gladly Anne battled the nausea that had plagued her from the first.
The only thing that helped was eating apples, for which she had
developed a sudden craving. One day, coming out of her chamber with
a host of courtiers, she saw Tom Wyatt approaching along the gallery.
He stopped and bowed stiffly, avoiding her gaze. She would teach him
to be distant, he that had once been so hot in pursuit!

'Tom, do you have any apples?' she asked mischievously. 'I have a
wild desire to eat apples, such as I never had in my life before! The King
tells me it is a sign that I am with child, but it is nothing of the sort.' At
the look on Tom's face, she burst out laughing.

He turned on his heel and walked away. She looked for him all day,
intending to apologise, but he did not return.

'I think I might go on pilgrimage to Our Lady of Walsingham after
Easter,' she told Henry. '

'And I think you should rest and not go gallivanting around the
country,' he told her. 'Go and give Our Lady thanks after you've been
delivered. She will understand.'

'But I'm feeling very well, apart from this nausea in the mornings,'
she protested.

'No, darling,' Henry commanded. 'You will not take any risks with
our son.'

His insistence brought home to her, for the first time, the fact that,

327

as his wife, she was now bound to obey him in all things. When she had been his mistress, she had had the mastery of him, and he could only have commanded her as her King, which he had rarely done, having always played the role of devoted servant. But now that they were married, he seemed to think he could be master of her as he had been master of Katherine. Well, he must think again! This pilgrimage was a small issue; she would let it go. But she was not about to let any man, be he king or husband, order her about.

Together they hosted a great banquet in Anne's presence chamber at Whitehall, and anyone might have guessed it was a wedding feast, for Henry was behaving like a bridegroom, fawning upon Anne, unable to refrain from caressing her. By the end of the evening he was so drunk that most of what he said was incomprehensible, but Anne's aunt, the Duchess of Norfolk, gave him a sharp look when he began waving his hands at the sumptuous furnishings and asking her, 'Has not the Lady Marquess got a grand dowry and a rich marriage, and all that we see? And the rest of the plate belongs to the lady also.'

So much for discretion! Anne nudged him sharply to make him shut up.

Henry sent George to France discreetly to inform King François that he had married Anne. Soon after George had sailed, the unsuspecting Pope's bull confirming Cranmer as Archbishop of Canterbury arrived in England, speedily followed by the good doctor's consecration in Canterbury Cathedral. Henry and Anne had privately feared that Clement would reject Cranmer, but whatever he might have heard about him, he too seemed keen to avoid an irrevocable breach between Henry and Rome.

George returned to court early in April, whereupon Henry summoned his Council and informed them that he had married Anne two months before, and that she was carrying the heir to England.

'You should have seen their faces!' he recounted, joining her for dinner afterwards. 'Stunned silence – then a belated rush to congratulate me. They have advised me to inform Katherine at once. I'm sending Norfolk and Suffolk to Ampthill the day after tomorrow.'

'I don't envy them,' Anne said. 'You know how she will take it.'

'I don't care how she takes it! I'll not have her making any more trouble. She must accept that I am married, and that henceforth she is to abstain from the title of queen and be called the Princess Dowager of Wales, as Arthur's widow.'

Neither of them was surprised when the two dukes returned and reported that Katherine had defied them. As long as she lived, she had declared, she would call herself queen.

'By God, I'll silence her!' Henry raged.

'What can she do?' Anne asked. 'She is isolated from her friends, a lone woman protesting in vain. No one hears her.'

'The whole of Europe hears her!' Henry stormed. 'That weasel of an ambassador has his agents in her household, be sure of it. And although the Emperor is busy fighting the Turks, we cannot be certain of what he will do when he hears of our marriage. It could mean war. Darling, I'm not jesting.'

Anne paused as the implications of their marriage began to sink in.

'It could happen,' Henry said, 'especially if Katherine appeals to Charles. And the worst of it is, she'd have a lot of my ignorant subjects on her side.'

'If she is the true wife she claims to be, then her first duty is to you, and she would surely never do anything to your hurt,' Anne reassured him.

'Yes, but what if she considers that her first duty is to persuade me that my conscience is in error?'

'Henry, she's been doing that for years. And the Emperor has his hands full.'

'I know, but he could still make trouble. Why doesn't Katherine just accept things? I'm never going back to her. Let's hope that Cranmer's judgement makes that plain.'

The very next day, Henry instructed Cranmer to proceed to the examination, final determination and judgement of his Great Matter.

Henry had decided that on the eve of Easter Sunday, Anne would appear as queen in public. On that Saturday morning, wearing robes of

329

crimson velvet and decked with diamonds and other precious stones, she walked through Greenwich Palace in royal state to hear Mass in her closet, with sixty maids of honour following her, escorted by servants in liveries bearing her new motto, 'The Most Happy'. In all the royal palaces, stonemasons, carpenters, glaziers and seamstresses were even now at work replacing Katherine's initials with hers, and the pomegranate of Spain with the crowned falcon, the badge she had chosen for herself. As she made her way slowly to Mass, past the astonished courtiers crowding into the halls and galleries, she made a point of cradling her hands over the slight swell of her stomach, hinting at the prince that lay within her.

Some of those watching looked shocked, others as if they did not know whether to laugh or cry. Most made obeisance as Anne passed by, but others just stared.

After Mass, Henry was waiting with Cromwell when Anne returned to her privy chamber. She was relieved to see him. It had been an ordeal.

'Were you well received?' he asked.

'I think that some of your nobles are less than enthusiastic about their new Queen,' she told him.

'I was listening in the privy gallery,' Cromwell said. 'Some were saying that His Grace has gone too far and that the Princess Dowager is the rightful Queen.' He turned to Henry. 'A few, if they dare, will offer all possible resistance to this marriage. Men like Bishop Fisher.'

'Have him placed under house arrest,' Henry ordered. 'I want him out of the way when Cranmer gives judgement.' He bent down and kissed Anne. 'Do not fret, darling. I will suggest that my lords and gentlemen come and pay court to you, and tell them that I intend to have you solemnly crowned after Easter.'

That was the moment, the supreme triumph, that Anne had been longing for. 'This is the best news you could have given me,' she smiled, her spirits soaring.

'It will be the greatest public celebration since my own coronation,' he beamed. 'It will sweeten my subjects and proclaim my esteem for you to the world. I'm having you crowned as Queen Regnant, Anne, not just as my consort, and all eyes will be on you alone, for I would not draw attention from you. But I shall be in Westminster Abbey, watching behind a lattice.'

'Was ever woman so honoured?' Cromwell smiled.

Anne embraced Henry with tears in her eyes. 'Your Grace's kindness to me is boundless. I am utterly beholden to you. Thank you, thank you!'

'I cannot do sufficient honour to the mother of my son,' he declared.

The Queen's chair of estate was smaller than the King's. It stood beside it beneath the ornate canopy of estate emblazoned with the royal arms of England. Wearing her robes of estate again for this first occasion on which she would preside as queen over the court, Anne seated herself beside Henry, arranging her heavy skirts around her. The presence chamber was crowded with courtiers and petitioners, craning to see how she conducted herself.

She was dismayed to see that the first person who came forward and bowed was Chapuys.

'I promised him an audience,' Henry muttered. 'I can't send him away without giving offence.'

Chapuys did not look once in Anne's direction. When Henry beckoned him forward, he spoke in a low voice. 'Sir, I cannot believe that a prince of your Majesty's great wisdom and virtue has consented to the putting away of the Queen. Since your Majesty has no regard for men, you should have some respect for God.'

Henry's face flushed an angry red. 'God and my conscience are on good terms,' he retorted. 'You sting me!'

'Then I beg your Majesty's pardon,' Chapuys apologised.

Henry glowered at him. 'If the world thinks this divorce so extraordinary, then it should find it strange that the Pope granted me a dispensation without having the power to do so. Moreover, messire, I wish to have a successor to my kingdom.'

'Your Majesty has a daughter endowed with all imaginable goodness and virtue, and of an age to bear children,' Chapuys reminded him. 'Nature obliges your Majesty to leave the throne to the Princess Mary.'

'I wish to have male children,' Henry growled, really riled now.

'Your Majesty is not sure of having them?' Chapuys asked boldly. Anne was holding her breath.

'Am I not a man like other men?' Henry barked, incensed. 'You are not privy to all my secrets!'

Chapuys bowed, but persisted. 'I must warn your Majesty that the Emperor will never recognise the Lady Anne as queen. Any annulment you might procure in England can have no validity in law.'

'It was no marriage!' Henry snarled.

'But your Majesty has often confessed that the Queen was a virgin when you married.'

'Hah! A man when he is jesting and feasting says a good many things that are not true.' He leaned forward menacingly. 'All your remonstrances are useless. The Lady Anne, as you call her, *is* my Queen. The Emperor has no right to interfere. I shall pass such laws in my kingdom as I like. And now, Messire Chapuys, this audience is at an end.'

As Chapuys bowed himself out, Henry whispered to Anne, 'Don't let him upset you, sweetheart. He is all threats and hot air, and I've heard it far too many times before.'

After the officers and members of Anne's household had all sworn their oaths of allegiance, she summoned them to attend the first meeting of her council. Looking around at them as she sat in her great chair at the head of the table, she reflected that Henry had done her proud. The household he had assigned her was worthy of the greatest of queens. It was packed with Boleyn connections, all eager to serve her, and as officers he had appointed able men who were congenial to her.

Her great train of ladies was headed by the King's own niece, Lady Margaret Douglas, who had served the Princess Mary as lady-of-honour, but seemed happy to fill the same post under Anne. Margaret was half Scots, the daughter of Henry's older sister Margaret; she was a great beauty and a poet. Anne was also delighted to have Elizabeth Browne, Countess of Worcester, who was a good friend, despite her half-brother, Sir William FitzWilliam, the treasurer of the King's household, having shown himself hostile towards her. Her old friend from Hever days, Lady Wingfield, had come up from Stone Castle to join Anne's retinue.

Anne was not keen on having her overbearing Aunt Elizabeth among her ladies, but as her uncle, Sir James Boleyn, had come all the way from Norfolk to be her chancellor, she could not very well refuse. And then of course there was the resentful Jane Rochford, another whose appointment could not be avoided. Mary would be there to counteract her antipathy, for Mary did not like Jane either, but Anne was uncomfortable having her sister in her household. She now saw that her parents had been right, and that Mary would be an ever-present reminder that Anne's marriage to Henry might be considered by some to be as incestuous as Katherine's. Anne had felt obliged to invite her, feeling she could not do otherwise, but she would have preferred to keep her out of sight. God grant that no one knew or found out about Mary and the King.

Among her bevy of maids-of-honour were her lively, learned cousins, Lady Mary Howard and Madge Shelton, pretty Nan Saville, demure Nan Gainsford and pert Frances de Vere, daughter of the Earl of Oxford. The matronly Mrs Stonor was Mother of the Maids, and Mrs Orchard had come up from Hever to assist her.

Anne knew it was important, now that she was queen, to overcome the slurs of her detractors and her undeserved poor reputation. People must see her as a patron of religion and learning, the living embodiment of virtue. She had this in mind when she addressed her household.

Her voice rang out. 'My lords, ladies and gentlemen, while you are in my service, I expect you to conduct yourselves virtuously. Gentlemen, you are to resist frequenting brothels, on pain of instant dismissal, to your utter shame. You shall set a godly standard to others by attending Mass daily and displaying an irreproachable demeanour. Ladies, you too must be above reproach. I want you to have these, to hang from your girdles at all times.' She nodded to her chamberlain, who handed out exquisite little books of prayers and psalms to each woman in the room.

From that day onwards, Anne decreed, she and her ladies would spend several hours daily making garments for the poor.

There were a few murmurs and downcast looks, but after only a week, Anne's old silk-woman, who had served two queens before her, turned to her and said, 'Madam, I've never seen better order among the ladies and gentlewomen of the court!' That pleased her no end. She hoped her enemies had noticed.

Her new life was not all sewing and charitable works, although these occupied her for much of the time. For years she had been forging friendships with courtiers of wit, charm and intelligence, who could be relied upon to ensure that the days were never dull, and they now formed the core of her inner circle. George, Norris, Weston, Brereton, Bryan and other gentlemen of the King's privy chamber flocked to the Queen's apartments to enjoy stimulating conversation and flirt with her ladies and maids. Anne loved nothing more than to lead the repartee and banter, and she insisted on informality in the privacy of her chamber. Sometimes, when his duties permitted, Henry would join them. He would bring his lute and play for them, or dance with the ladies, or show a keen interest in the book of love poems that Margaret Douglas, Mary Howard and Madge Shelton were compiling.

When he was absent, the atmosphere was more relaxed. Couples were pairing off: Nan Gainsford with George Zouche; Frances de Vere with Anne's cousin, Henry Howard, Earl of Surrey, Norfolk's heir; and Margaret Douglas with another cousin, Norfolk's young brother, Thomas Howard. Anne hoped that Henry would consent to their marrying; it would reinforce the bond between her blood and the royal house. She had no doubt that she could persuade him to consent to Surrey marrying Frances.

Surrey sometimes brought with him his great friend, Henry's bastard son, the Duke of Richmond, a tall, gangling youth with his father's looks but not his charm, for he was proud, insufferable and resentful of his bastardy. He was showing an interest in Mary Howard. Anne thought she might talk to Henry about them too. It would be a feather in her cap to marry her cousin to the King's son.

Madge Shelton was doing her best to attract the attentions of Norris, but without success. Anne suspected that he came to these gatherings for her alone. There was still that unacknowledged frisson between them, but things had changed. She might indulge in innocent flirtations with him and the men in her circle, but she was Caesar's wife now, and must be above reproach. And her advancing pregnancy seemed to have unsexed her. Henry was still sharing her bed every night, but showing heroic restraint. He caressed her, kissed her, asked her to use her hands to pleasure him, but he would not enter her, fearing to harm the child.

George was the foremost member of her court, and the person in whom she confided most. Henry had showered him with preferments: he was now Constable of Dover and Master of the Buckhounds, and was often away on diplomatic missions. It would only be a matter of time, Anne was sure, before Henry gave him a peerage in his own right.

She had grown to like William Brereton since he had come one day with a greyhound puppy for her.

'My bitch had a litter, and he's the best. His name is Urian,' he told her as she took the pup in her arms, exclaiming in delight.

'A little devil,' she teased, for in Burgundy Urian had been another name for Satan.

'Your Grace, he is named for my brother, who serves as groom in His Grace's privy chamber. Believe me, he *is* a little devil!'

Soon Anne and Urian were inseparable. He was forever at her feet or at her heel.

She knew there was another side to Brereton. He was a lot older than most of those who frequented her chamber, and a man of some standing, being the Duke of Richmond's deputy as Steward of the Welsh Marches, where he exercised great power. Anne had heard Cromwell, who didn't like him, refer to Brereton as an overmighty subject, but she was determined to see that Brereton continued to enjoy the King's favour. It was upon loyal supporters like him that she depended.

Her marriage had now been proclaimed all over England, but it had not been generally well received. There was still a great swell of love for Katherine and the Princess Mary, and there were very vocal complaints that Anne's elevation to queenship would mean war with the Emperor and disaster for the lucrative trade that England enjoyed with the Empire.

Henry's Council was dealing with a torrent of public protests against her marriage. He spared her the details, but they were notorious at court, and there were those, such as the half-Spanish Lady Exeter, a friend of Katherine, who seemed to take great pleasure in repeating them to Anne's ladies.

'What are they saying about me?' Anne pressed George, as they sat down to dinner in her chamber and the King's waiter arrived, punctual as usual, to wish her, on her husband's behalf, 'Much good may it do you.'

She smiled graciously at him. 'I thank His Grace.' When the waiter had departed, she turned to her brother. 'You can't just say there's seditious talk and not tell me what it is!'

'Do you really want to know?' he asked, his dark eyes concerned. 'The King would kill me if I told you.'

'And I will kill you if you don't!' she retorted. 'Forewarned is forearmed.'

He gave in. 'Some fools are greatly agitated about your marriage. A priest was hauled before the justices for calling you the scandal of Christendom and worse. Another priest commended you to his flock and was abused by the women among them. And when you were first prayed for, as queen, in the churches, a congregation in London walked out. The King has personally reprimanded the Lord Mayor. Do you want to hear more?'

Anne had listened with mounting dismay, but she nodded.

'The Dean of Bristol has lost his office for forbidding his priests to pray for you. One woman who cried out "God save Queen Katherine!" and called you – pardon me – a goggle-eyed whore has been sent to prison, as has Mrs Amadas.' Anne knew Elizabeth Amadas slightly, for her husband was keeper of the royal Jewel Tower.

'What did *she* say?' she asked, feeling a little faint.

'I hardly dare repeat it,' George replied. 'She predicted that you would be burned as a harlot. She accused Norris of acting as bawd between you and His Grace. And – I hesitate to say this – she alleged that the King had kept both Mother and Mary as his mistresses, and that Father acted as bawd to them and to you.'

Anne was horrified. The allegation about her mother was monstrous but ridiculous, yet far worse was the realisation that, somehow, Henry's affair with Mary had become public knowledge.

'How did Mrs Amadas know about Mary?'

'I have no idea,' George shrugged. 'What I can't forgive is the slur on our lady mother. Of course, she did have a bit of a reputation in her youth.'

'What do you mean?'

'She took lovers. Father told me. That's why they don't get on.'

'But to accuse her of sleeping with the King! Are they implying that I'm the fruit of their adultery? How could that be? He was ten when I was born! It's a vile slur on him. But he did have Mary, and if there is talk at court about his affair with her, everyone will soon know about it. George, this is serious. It could upset everything, because the world does not know that we had a dispensation.'

'From the Pope, whose authority is no longer recognised here. It might be of no more worth than the dispensation granted to Katherine.'

'I must speak to the King!' Anne cried. 'Never fear, I'll say I made you repeat all this.'

She flew through her apartments to her bedchamber, where a door led into Henry's lodging. Mercifully he was there, reading.

'Darling? What's wrong?' he asked, springing to his feet.

She burst into tears and repeated what George had told her. 'And now people will know that there is an impediment to our marriage!' she cried.

'I'm aware of that already,' he said, holding her to him as gently as if she were glass and might break. 'I've consulted Cranmer, who tells me that the granting of that dispensation could fatally undermine my cause against Katherine, and make me look a hypocrite. I said it was essential that the legality of our marriage be beyond dispute, and he recommended that the matter be dealt with by Parliament. As for these protests, they will be silenced. My subjects will accept you as queen. Now be at peace, sweetheart, and rest. You must think of our son.'

The passing of a new Act permitting marriage with the sister of a discarded mistress did not come a moment too soon for Anne. But it did not put a stop to the spreading gossip about Mary, which only served to exacerbate public disapproval of Anne's marriage. And after Parliament enacted that Katherine should be called Queen no more, but Princess Dowager, there were even more strident protests.

Henry appointed Whitsunday, the first day of June, for Anne's coronation. He himself wrote to the City of London commanding the Mayor and his brethren to prepare pageants for it, and summoned his nobility and clergy to attend.

Anne went about with a smile on her face. The sickness had eased, the child stirred lustily under her stomacher, and she had never felt better. Happily she selected the materials for the gowns and robes she would need for the river pageant that would conduct her from Greenwich to the Tower, her state entry into London, and her crowning itself. She could not wait. Being crowned would invest her with a regal sanctity and set her apart from ordinary mortals – and might silence her enemies.

Meanwhile, Cranmer had been summoning various divines and canon lawyers to a special ecclesiastical court in Dunstable Priory, just four miles from Ampthill. Katherine had been cited to appear before this court.

Henry was convinced that Chapuys was doing his utmost to incite the Emperor to war and persuade Katherine that it was the best way to get her husband back.

'Cranmer pronouncing judgement against her might give Charles the pretext he needs,' he said anxiously.

'He never calls me queen,' Anne seethed.

'He will!' Henry blustered. 'I can't lock Chapuys up, but I can muzzle him!'

Chapuys was summoned before the Privy Council and warned not to meddle further in Katherine's affairs. Anne doubted it would have any effect, although it might keep him quiet for a while. But Henry could not silence the outcry in Europe at the news of their marriage. Throughout Christendom voices were raised, protesting that Katherine was the rightful Queen of England, and Anne an upstart adulteress.

Dining with her and Henry one day, Cromwell showed his exasperation. 'Everywhere there is derision. One of my correspondents in Antwerp has informed me that – saving your Graces' presence – a painting of Her Grace was pinned inappropriately to one of you, sir. In the Netherlands and Spain they take great pleasure in jesting about your Grace and the Queen. In Louvain, lewd and malicious students have scratched scurrilous verses on doors and street corners. I will spare you the details.'

Henry threw down his napkin. 'Have my ambassadors abroad briefed as to how to counter such calumnies. Tell them they must insist that Anne is the true Queen, and refuse to speak to anyone who gives Katherine that title.'

'You think that will silence the protests?' Anne asked.

'Maybe not, but Cranmer's judgement assuredly will.'

It could not come soon enough. It was now May, and her condition was evident to all.

'Soon I will look like an elephant,' she grumbled to her father. 'I've had to add a panel to my skirts. All my gowns are too tight.'

'You should stop complaining and thank God to find yourself in such a condition,' he retorted.

Her temper flared. 'I'm in a better state than you wanted last year! You were wondering if it was all worth it.'

'I spoke out of weariness with the situation and concern for you,' Father placated her. 'God be praised, you did not heed me. I am glad to see you looking so well.'

'I will be better still when this court has declared my marriage valid,' she told him.

'You know that Katherine has utterly refused to obey Cranmer's summons and says she will have no other judge but the Pope? Cranmer has declared her contumacious, and is proceeding without her, thank God!'

'Amen to that,' Anne said.

On the twenty-third day of May, Cranmer pronounced Henry's union with Katherine absolutely null and void and contrary to divine law.

'Free at last!' Henry shouted, tossing his bonnet in the air and kissing Anne heartily. 'Thank God! Thank God!' Immediately he ordered the distribution of a tract he had written himself to inform his loving subjects of the truth about his marriages. 'I'll make sure Katherine gets one,' he added wickedly.

A deputation of the Privy Council was sent to inform the Princess Mary of Cranmer's judgement.

'Well?' Anne demanded of Henry when he came to her that evening. She had seen, from her window, the councillors returning.

'She defied them,' he admitted, looking crestfallen. 'She said she would accept no one for queen except her mother, upon which, on my orders, they forbade her to communicate in any way with Katherine until she had come to her senses.'

Rage welled up. 'How very dutiful of her! You have nurtured a viper in your bosom.'

'Let us hope that being cut off from her mother brings her to her senses,' Henry muttered, his mouth set in a grim line.

Five days after he had judged Katherine's marriage invalid, Cranmer announced that the King's marriage to the Lady Anne was good and lawful.

'Six years it has taken!' Henry exclaimed. 'Six long years! But darling, finally, we have what we have most desired. You are now lawfully mine, and our son will be born in undisputed wedlock.'

Anne surrendered joyfully to his embrace. The ruling had been timely, for on the morrow she was to make her progress by river to London for her coronation. The hour she had dreamed of was almost upon her.

Uncle Norfolk, as Earl Marshal of England, had been put in charge of the arrangements, but he and she were now barely on speaking terms after she had heard him praising Katherine's courage to Chapuys. His ingratitude stung, because she had just persuaded Henry to agree to the marriages of Norfolk's daughter to the Duke of Richmond and his son to Frances de Vere – *and* she had got Henry to waive a dowry in Mary Howard's case. But, for all her uncle's animosity and constant tut-tutting, he did plan everything with superb efficiency.

The Lord Mayor of London and the aldermen and sheriffs were coming to Greenwich to escort Anne by barge to the Tower, where she would spend the night before her state entry into London.

'You look gorgeous,' Henry told her, when she appeared before him in her cloth-of-gold finery; but as they waited for the city fathers to arrive, he was fretting about Thomas More.

'I sent him an invitation to the coronation, and money for a new gown,' he brooded. 'I hope he will come. I've dispatched three bishops to Chelsea this morning to persuade him. If he recognises our marriage by attending, it will go a long way towards quelling the opposition.'

For Henry's sake, Anne prayed that More would say yes. But when she saw the glum faces of the bishops on their return, she knew their mission had been hopeless.

'What did Sir Thomas say?' Henry asked anxiously.

'He will not come, sir. He said there are those who are desirous to deflower us, and when they have deflowered us, they will not fail soon after to devour us. But he would provide that they shall never deflower him.'

Henry bristled. 'So this is how he repays me for my friendship! Well, no matter, we will not spoil your day, darling, for an ungrateful knave!'

It was three o'clock. The Lord Mayor was here. There was no more time for talk. Henry kissed her farewell. He would travel to the Tower by covered barge.

She stepped into the barge she had appropriated from Katherine, followed by Mary and her other ladies, her father and a group of privileged nobles. Out on the Thames bobbed the gaily decorated crafts of the London guilds, many of them filled with minstrels playing sweet music. Anne was gratified to see huge crowds lining the banks as her barge began making its stately way along the river, its cloth-of-gold heraldic banners fluttering in the breeze. On a boat to her left a water pageant was being staged, with terrible monsters and wild men casting fire, which made her maidens squeal. But there was little cheering from the eerily silent crowd, apart from when the monsters ended up in the water, and she was relieved to catch sight of the Tower of London ahead.

As she alighted at the Queen's Stairs, the Lord Chamberlain greeted her and escorted her to the King, who was waiting just inside the postern gate in the Byward Tower.

'Darling!' he cried, and kissed her lovingly, as trumpets and shawms sounded her arrival and the canons on Tower Wharf fired a resounding salute.

Anne thanked the waiting Mayor and citizens for their kindness in arranging such a wondrous pageant, and then Henry led her to the old royal apartments.

'I've had Cromwell refurbish them in your honour,' he told her. 'He's spent over three thousand pounds on repairs and improvements so that you can be accommodated in suitable splendour.' They entered the Queen's lodgings and she looked around, impressed. The walls and ceilings had been decorated in the antick style, with plaster friezes of gambolling cherubs, all gilded, and costly new tapestries portraying the story of Queen Esther, which Henry had commissioned in acknowledgement of her zeal for reform.

'This is your great chamber,' he told her, 'and that closet over there will serve as a private oratory.' He ushered her into a dining chamber embellished with a great fireplace and fine wainscoting. Beyond it was a bedchamber with a royal bed hung with red velvet, and a privy set into the wall.

'These were my dear mother's lodgings,' Henry told her, looking around wistfully. 'She died here. Of course, they look very different now. I do hope you are pleased with them.'

Anne took his hands. 'They are superb, and I will thank Master Cromwell for the good work he has done.'

They spent the next day resting in the Tower, and in the evening Henry dubbed eighteen Knights of the Bath, explaining to Anne that this ancient ritual was normally performed only at the coronations of reigning monarchs, but that a special exception was being made for her. Francis Weston was one of those he honoured.

In the morning, Anne rose early to be made ready for her ceremonial entry into London. For this she had chosen a traditional surcoat and matching mantle of shimmering white cloth of tissue furred with ermine. On her head she wore a coif surmounted by a circlet studded with rich stones. Her hair was loose, in token of her symbolic virginity as a queen, but beneath the white gown the mound of her belly swelled.

Her ladies assisted her into a horse litter of white cloth of gold, to which were harnessed two palfreys caparisoned in white damask. Sixteen knights of the Cinque Ports took up their positions around it, bearing a canopy of cloth of gold on gilded staves, attached to which were silver bells that tinkled above Anne's head. Already the great procession of lords, clergy, officers and courtiers was leaving the Tower, bound for the City of London. As her litter was borne up Tower Hill behind it, a great train of ladies followed in chariots and on horseback. Crowds were gathering, but they mostly just stood there watching, some of them palpably hostile.

The City of London had spared no expense in honouring her. She passed along newly gravelled streets, beneath triumphal arches, past buildings hung with scarlet and crimson cloth. Every window was crammed with ladies and gentlewomen, eager to catch a glimpse of her. Music played, children made speeches, and free wine splashed in the conduits and fountains, that all might celebrate this day. Choirs raised their voices in sweet harmony in her honour:

> Anna comes, the most famous woman in all the world,
> Anna comes, the shining incarnation of chastity,
> In snow-white litter, just like the goddesses,
> Anna the Queen is here, the preservation of your future.

'Honour and grace be to our Queen Anne!' the singers chorused. 'For whose cause an angel celestial descends, to crown the falcon with a diadem imperial.'

In Cornhill, the Three Graces wished Anne hearty gladness, continual success and long fruition. 'Queen Anne, prosper, go forward and reign!' they cried.

In a pageant in Cheapside, an actor playing Paris, asked to choose the most beautiful of the three goddesses, Juno, Pallas and Venus, took one look at Anne and declared that, having seen her, he could not call

343

any of them fair. In St Paul's Churchyard, the choristers sang an anthem that recalled the coronation of the Virgin: 'Come, my love, thou shalt be crowned!'

Verses recited by a little child reminded Anne of the fruitfulness of her saintly namesake, St Anne, mother of the Virgin Mary. One banner bore the legend, in Latin: 'Queen Anne, when thou shalt bear a new son of the King's blood, there shall be a golden world unto thy people.'

'Amen!' Anne said loudly, smiling.

Within the city walls, the crowds had turned out in their thousands, but as before they were largely silent and their welcome was cold. As Anne passed by, turning her face from side to side to greet the people, she saw few caps removed and hardly ten people who cried, 'God save your Grace!' She heard her fool, capering along a little way ahead, cry angrily, 'Ye all have scurvy heads and dare not uncover!' Worst of all, wherever the intertwined initials of the King and Queen appeared in the decorations, the mob jeered, 'HA! HA!' Remembering what had happened at Durham House, Anne prayed fervently that the citizens would confine their hatred to verbal abuse. She felt horribly exposed in her open litter, a sitting target for anyone who might make an attempt on her life.

She began to relax only when her procession left the City by Temple Bar, wending its way towards Westminster. When her litter drew up inside Westminster Hall, she alighted and ascended the great staircase to the high dais, where she seated herself beneath a cloth of estate and was served a banquet of subtleties, wines and hippocras, which she waved away and sent down to her ladies.

She should have been enjoying her moment of triumph, but she felt so strung up and nauseous that she could barely touch the food, and by the time the banquet ended, and she was thanking the Lord Mayor and all the lords and ladies, she was utterly exhausted. It was a huge relief to withdraw with her ladies to the White Hall in the Palace of Westminster, where Mary and Jane Rochford relieved her of the heavy mantle before she was escorted out of the palace to a waiting barge, which took her swiftly to York Place.

Here Henry was waiting for her, eager to hear how the day had gone.

'How liked you the look of the City, sweetheart?'

'Sir, the City itself was well enough,' she replied, sinking into a chair, 'but I saw many caps on heads and heard but few tongues.'

Henry swore under his breath.

'You can't make them love me,' she said. 'If you could stop them hating me I'd be happy, but you can't tell people what to feel.' She did not tell him that she had felt frightened. 'Henry, I must go to bed. I'm worn out and your son is very active. I have a big day ahead tomorrow.'

He was all anxious solicitude. 'Of course, darling. I'll send for your women. You must take care of yourself.'

Chapter 22

1533

Anne stood at the great west door of Westminster Abbey, her ladies fluttering around her, checking that her ermine-trimmed surcoat and her robe of purple velvet were arranged perfectly over the kirtle of crimson velvet. Mary adjusted the rich coronet with its caul of pearls and stones, while Madge Shelton gave one final sweep of the comb to Anne's long hair.

She was ready, and Archbishop Cranmer and the assisting bishops and abbots, richly coped and mitred, moved forward to receive her and support her in procession along a carpet of cloth of ray that stretched to the high altar. She walked beneath a glittering canopy of cloth of gold, with Suffolk going before her carrying the precious glittering crown of St Edward the Confessor, and the Dowager Duchess of Norfolk bearing her train, which was so long that Anne's chamberlain had to support it in the middle. Following behind were her ladies-in-waiting, all attired in scarlet, after whom came a great entourage of lords and ladies, the Yeomen of the King's Guard, the monks of Westminster, and the children of the Chapel Royal, who were to sing during the ceremony.

A platform had been erected between the high altar and the choir, and at its centre stood a rich chair, in which Anne seated herself. Around her stood the nobility of the realm, and she caught sight of her parents, watching her with undisguised pride, and George, smiling encouragement. As she rose to go to the altar, she looked around for Henry, and espied a movement behind a lattice set into a pew at the side of the sanctuary. It was comforting to know that he was nearby.

With some difficulty, for she was in her sixth month now, she prostrated herself on the mosaic pavement before the altar while the collects were said, and then she was helped up and raised into her chair, and Cranmer came forward and anointed her on the head and breast with holy oil. Then he lifted St Edward's crown – with which every English sovereign had been invested since time immemorial – and placed it on her head. It weighed heavily, but it was a burden she was happy to bear.

It was done, accomplished! She was the Queen of England.

As she received into her hands the sceptre of gold and a rod of ivory surmounted by a dove, she was thinking of the words of Christine de Pizan. How appropriate they were now. As the wife of a powerful man, she would ensure that she was highly knowledgeable about government, and wise. Knowledge was power; she must learn to understand everything, and make her influence felt. Moreover, she must have the courage of a man. *I have that courage!* she told herself. Exultation filled her heart.

The choir burst into song with the *Te Deum*, after which Cranmer came forward and lifted the great diadem from her head, replacing it with the new crown that had been made for her, a gorgeous golden circlet studded with sapphires, balas rubies and pearls, with crosses of gold and fleurs-de-lis around the rim. She sat there, crowned and enthroned, while Mass was celebrated.

She had joined the ranks of great queens and women rulers, and she vowed to herself that, in her rule, she would honour the memory and inspiration of Margaret of Austria and Isabella of Castile, and make herself as widely respected as they had been.

A fanfare of trumpets signalled the end of the ceremony, and Father stepped forward with Lord Talbot to support her on either side as she processed slowly out of the abbey. 'Now the noble Anna bears the sacred diadem!' sang the children of the Chapel Royal.

In Westminster Hall, Anne's ladies brought rose water to refresh her, straightened her skirts and adjusted the crown so that it was comfortable. Ready for her coronation banquet, she seated herself in solitary splendour at the centre of the high table on the dais, with the countesses of Oxford and Worcester standing behind her, ready with a napkin and fingerbowl, and two maids sitting at her feet. She was so tense from the overwhelming excitement of the day that she could not eat. In fact she was nauseous, and the countesses had to shield her from view, holding a fine cloth in front of her when she needed to vomit. Archbishop Cranmer, sitting at the end of the high table at the Queen's right hand, looked at her with concern.

'Is your Grace all right?' he enquired.

'Never better!' she assured him. 'It's just a case of too much emotion and too much rich food. Not a good combination for me, in my condition. Oh, no, more food!' she grimaced, as the trumpets sounded and the new Knights of the Bath brought in the next lavish course.

'Would your Grace like some wine?' It was Tom Wyatt, acting as chief ewerer. He too looked concerned about her, and there was in his expression something of the old Tom she had liked so much.

'No, Tom, but is there any barley water?'

'I will get you some,' he said, and hastened away.

Two hours later, she was still sitting there, sipping barley water. At the long tables below her, the guests were still indulging themselves, and there was a deafening clamour of chatter and laughter. She had managed just three dishes out of the eighty she had been offered, and even though she had admired the subtlety of her own falcon badge, which was made entirely of sugar and carried in and presented to her with much ceremony, she waved it away.

She caught sight of Mary at the first table on her right, leaning back and talking to a gentleman standing behind her. Anne knew his face. It was William Stafford, with whom her sister had flirted in Calais. They seemed to be getting on very well, for she could hear Mary giggling. In contrast, George and Jane were ignoring each other, chatting to their neighbours.

It was late when the banquet ended and the order was given for the guests to stand until Anne had washed her hands and descended to the floor of the hall. Here she was served wine and comfits, and when she had nibbled at a couple, she beckoned the Lord Mayor over and gave him a gold cup, thanking him and the citizens once more for their efforts on her behalf. The barons of the Cinque Ports were waiting with their canopy to escort her to the door of her chamber, and thus she left the hall, tired but exhilarated. It had, she reflected, been the most extraordinary day of her life.

The festivities continued for some days more. There were dances, tournaments, hunts and sports, all in her honour. Henry had made his pleasure clear, and his courtiers were outdoing each other to honour their new Queen. She suspected that it was not because they wanted to, but because they were aware of him watching like a hawk. But it was gratifying to have everyone striving to be as attentive as possible to her.

Henry had decided that his heir was to be born at Greenwich, his own birthplace, and presented Anne with one of the richest and most sumptuous beds she had ever seen for her confinement. It was French, ornately carved and gilded; years before, it had been part of the ransom for a royal duke, and it had been languishing in the Royal Wardrobe ever since. Surely it was the most wondrous bed any queen had ever owned, Anne thought, luxuriating in its splendour.

News of the death of her great critic, Mary Tudor, did not move her, but Henry was upset at losing his sister, and full of regret that she had died unreconciled to him.

As the summer continued, and Anne grew heavy with her precious burden, she stayed mostly in her apartments resting, or enjoying pastime in her chamber with her favoured courtiers, who exerted themselves to entertain her with music, verse, cards or dice, and flirted outrageously with her ladies.

'I feel sorry for Tom Wyatt and his fellow envoys, having to be overseas at this time,' Norris said, sitting down beside Anne and watching the amorous couples with amusement.

'If they thought that these ladies favoured them, and hated parting with their faithful servants, they should see them now,' Anne laughed.

He turned to her and gave her that sweet smile she loved. 'And how is your Grace? I trust that all is well with you.'

'I shall be glad to be delivered,' she said. 'I am becoming very cumbersome! Soon I must think about taking to my chamber.'

'If there's anything I can do to bring your Grace comfort, do not hesitate to command me,' Norris invited.

'That's very kind. And how are you these days, Norris?'

He shrugged. 'I do well enough. My work in the Privy Chamber keeps me busy.'

'You should marry again,' she teased.

'Alas, madam, my heart is given to a very special lady, whose name I may not say, for she is wed.' He looked meaningfully at her with eyes full of devotion.

Her heart stirred. How different her life would have been if she had given herself to this loyal, honourable and gentle man. She could have loved him as she had never loved Henry. But she could not regret choosing the crown. It was enough to have Norris's friendship and bask in the warmth of his kindness.

'You are wise, sir,' she told him, 'for, being married, she must guard her reputation, whether she loves you or not. And some husbands can be very jealous.'

A deputation of lords of the Council had informed Katherine of Cranmer's judgements.

'She refuses to recognise them,' Henry snarled, stalking up and down beside the bed where Anne was resting. 'I told them to tell her that I cannot have two wives, or permit her to persist in calling herself queen. It was made clear to her that my marriage to you is irrevocable, and has the consent of Parliament, that nothing that she can do will annul it, and that she will only incur my displeasure and that of Almighty God if she persists in her obstinacy. And what did she do? She took the parchment laying out my terms for her submission, and wherever she found the name of Princess Dowager, she struck it out, insisting she is my true wife and queen.'

'Will she never desist?' Anne cried. 'She has lost you. What more do you have to do to convince her of it?'

'I'm sending her to Buckden, which is further north, with a reduced household. The tower there is fifty years old, and damp. That should make her see sense.'

'I hope so!' Anne said fervently. 'You should ban all visitors.'

'I've already given the order. There will be no letters, either. We don't want Chapuys cooking up mischief with her.'

'Or the Princess,' Anne said. 'I heard today that when Mary went abroad in the countryside recently, the people came hastening to greet her as if she were God Himself descended from Heaven. Henry, you should stop her from inciting demonstrations like that, and punish the demonstrators.'

'I don't think Mary would have incited them,' Henry said. 'They just turned up to see her.'

'Will you never see the truth?' Anne flung back. 'She's playing a clever game, building up sympathy for herself. Poor sweet little Princess, parted from her mother . . . Henry, she's seventeen! I was parted from my mother at the age of twelve, and didn't see her for six years. Mary should count herself lucky.'

Henry subsided. Where his daughter was concerned, he was weak, but Anne was determined that he take a firmer stand with her. Let Mary put another foot wrong, and there'd be a reckoning.

In July, the King took Anne to Hampton Court to rest in the final weeks of her pregnancy. They spent the balmy days taking slow strolls in the beautiful gardens, picnicking in the little banqueting houses that Henry had built in the grounds, reading companionably together in Anne's privy chamber and making merry at supper. He no longer came to her bed, for he did not wish to disturb her rest, and in truth, the size she was, she preferred to sleep alone. She felt well, and had never seen Henry so happy.

It was only in these last weeks of her pregnancy that she began to worry about the possibility of her baby being a girl. Henry had always referred to it as a son, and she too had come to think of it as a boy. But what if it wasn't? Henry had done all that he had sworn to do: he had broken with Rome to marry her, and had her crowned with as much pomp as if she were a reigning monarch. It was now up to her to seal her part of the bargain by presenting him with the son that, at forty-two, he needed more desperately than ever, not only to ensure the succession, but also to justify the risks he had taken on her account. The blessing of a male heir would show the world that God smiled on their union, and would undoubtedly bring many waverers and dissidents over to their side – and it might silence, once and for all, that infuriating woman at Buckden!

So much hung on the sex of the child. That it might not be a son did not bear thinking about. And so she grew daily more anxious, when she should have been enjoying the calm euphoria of these last weeks before the birth.

The wretched Nun of Kent had chosen the day of Anne's coronation to prophesy doom for the King and his new Queen. This time the authorities had pounced, and Elizabeth Barton had been brought before Cranmer to be examined.

'He should not have let her go with just a warning,' Anne complained. 'She's already ignored it.'

'Sweetheart, do not excite yourself,' Henry exhorted, all concern, as they sat down to cold chicken, a raised pie, salad and a dish of cherries in the banqueting house that stood on the hillock overlooking the privy garden. 'I had her re-arrested this morning, and Cranmer examined her again. She's admitted that she never had a vision in her life.'

'What will you do with her?'

'Let her go. She's been discredited, out of her own mouth.'

'That won't deter her. Mad or not, she's never held her peace before.'

'If she spouts more sedition, she will feel the full force of my displeasure,' Henry declared. 'But let's not speak of unpleasant things. You do not want to agitate the babe. I am of the belief that what a woman thinks or feels can affect the child in her womb – it stands to reason.'

'I don't know about that,' Anne smiled, 'but this one leaps about as if it's practising for the joust! Feel!' She guided Henry's hand to her belly.

'By God, here's a future king to be proud of!' he chuckled. 'Darling, I know I can't be there with you when our son is born, but I want to be near at hand. I'm not going far on my hunting progress this year; I'm keeping near to London.'

'That is a great comfort to me,' Anne said, reaching across and squeezing his hand.

He smiled at her. 'I'm ordering that prayers for your safe delivery be offered up in every church, and I will ask my loving subjects to pray to Jesus, if it be His will, to send us a prince. I've consulted the physicians, and they all assure me that the child will be male.'

How did they know? They had never examined her, merely enquired how she was feeling and exhorted her to take care of herself. Childbirth was women's work! She had already engaged a midwife, who was even now in residence at court, guzzling rich food and idling away the days in luxury. But she had come highly recommended by Lady Worcester.

After they had finished their meal, Henry took Anne to see an astrologer he had summoned. She had heard of William Glover, for he was celebrated throughout the land for foretelling the future. He was not the first of the seers Henry had consulted; he was as anxious as she was about the baby's sex. Of course, they had all assured him that it would be a boy, but the pronouncement of this Glover, with his great reputation, would carry special weight.

He was a raven-haired, thin-faced man with bushy brows, completely immersed in a world of his own. He showed them charts of celestial configurations, then looked into his glass and paused for a very long moment before turning to Anne.

'I see your Grace bearing a woman child and a prince of the land.'

She was shocked.

'*Two* children?' Henry barked. 'A prince and princess?'

'No, your Grace. I see only one child.'

'How can a woman child be a prince?' Henry countered.

'My vision does not reveal that.'

'You're a charlatan!' Henry accused him. 'Everyone else says it will be a son!'

'Lord King, I know only what my glass tells me,' Glover insisted.

Henry dismissed him, glowering.

'Don't let him upset you, darling,' he said to Anne, when the man had gone. 'He's a knave!'

'Indeed he must be,' she agreed, wanting to forget the episode.

'Henry, I have been thinking about the Prince's baptism. Are there special christening robes and bearing cloths in the Royal Wardrobe?'

'Maybe. Katherine used a very rich triumphal cloth she brought from Spain to wrap up our children for baptism.'

'Do you think she still has it?' It would be sweet revenge to wrap her son in that cloth.

'Probably,' said Henry.

'Will you ask her for it?'

He grinned wolfishly. 'It will be my pleasure.'

Back came the prompt answer. It had not pleased God that Katherine should ever be so badly advised as to assist in a case as horrible as this.

'How dare she!' Anne raged.

'Darling, as she rightly says, the robe is her personal property. I don't think I can press the point.' As usual, Henry was hopeless in the face of Katherine's malice.

'But it's a snub.'

To her astonishment, he rounded on her. 'We should not have asked in the first place. Anne, I have more pressing matters to worry about. I've just heard that the Pope has annulled all Cranmer's proceedings and declared our marriage null and void, making it appear to all Christendom that we are living in adultery. Worse still, he has threatened me with excommunication if I do not put you away by September.'

'You must ignore him!' Anne cried. 'You don't need him now!'

'I intend to ignore him!' Henry shouted. 'God, who knows my righteous heart, always prospers my affairs.'

But she could see the fear that belied his bullish words. In the eyes of the faithful, he was a schismatic adulterer who might soon be cut off from God. And his enemies would be waiting to pounce . . . It was more imperative than ever that she bear him a son, to show that God smiled upon him.

'The King danced many times with Lady Carew last night,' Jane Rochford said.

'They are old friends,' Anne replied, handing the basket of silks across to Nan Gainsford. Gossip had it that Lady Carew had bedded with Henry before her marriage to Sir Nicholas Carew, but that was long ago, even before Bessie Blount's time. Yet Jane was looking at Anne with a sly, gloating expression, as if to say, *I know something you don't.*

'What is it you wish to tell me, Jane?' she asked briskly.

Jane seemed reluctant to speak, but Anne suspected that she was enjoying this. 'I did not like to say anything – after all, it probably means nothing, but . . . well, with your Grace being with child . . .'

'What, then?' Anne demanded to know. The other ladies and maids were looking from one to the other.

'I saw him kiss her,' Jane said.

It was like a punch, winding her. 'Kiss her? What, beyond what is courteous?'

'It looked more than courtesy to me,' Jane replied.

Anne searched the shocked faces around her. 'Did any of you see this?'

Nan Saville looked guilty. 'Yes, your Grace.'

'Just the once?'

'I saw him kiss her three times,' Jane said.

'Well, well,' Anne retorted, 'probably it was just a courtly flirtation. Now, what design shall we embroider on this altar frontal?'

How she got through the afternoon and behaved as if all was normal she did not know, but by five o'clock she could stand it no longer and dismissed them all, saying she needed to rest. Then she sent for Norris, the person she trusted best. He, of all people, would know if Henry was being unfaithful.

'What can I do for your Grace?' he asked, standing before her, with Mary, for propriety's sake, just out of earshot in the bedchamber beyond.

'Sir Henry, can I ask you something in the strictest confidence?' Anne asked, trying not to cry.

'Of course, madam.' His face was all concern.

'Is the King being unfaithful to me with Lady Carew?'

Norris looked embarrassed. He hesitated.

'Your face says it all,' she said, and then the tears did fall.

'Oh, my dear lady,' Norris said, and in an instant was on one knee before her, holding her hands. 'I would not for the world cause you any distress.'

'But I must know!' she sobbed. 'If my ladies are talking about it, the whole court will be. And he has never been unfaithful before. For eight years he has been true to me.'

Norris looked into her eyes. He was still holding her hands, and she would have given anything for him to take her in his arms and comfort her properly. Nothing else would make her feel better. It was her pride that was hurt, far more grievously than her heart, for it had never been truly Henry's. But he adored her, surely: she was special, not like Katherine, whom he had deceived many times.

It was his deception, and his making her an object of ridicule before the whole court – especially her enemies, who would be laughing up their sleeves, or not so discreetly – that was unforgivable.

She resisted the impulse to melt into Norris's strong arms and seek oblivion. She would not stoop to Henry's level.

'Are they lovers?' she asked, disengaging her hands and finding her handkerchief.

'You are asking me to break my oath of service. I owe discretion to the King in all matters.'

'I must know!' Anne insisted. 'Just indicate yes or no. The gossip will be rampant anyway, so I could have heard it anywhere. Has he slept with her?'

Norris's nod was barely perceptible. His eyes were full of compassion.

'Thank you. Please go and ask the King if he will visit me when he is free. And Norris – no hint of this to him, please.'

Henry arrived within the hour, in a high good humour and with a bowl of choice apples for her.

She greeted him cordially, then sent her women into the next room. When the door had closed behind them, she turned on him.

'Is it true what my ladies are saying about you and Lady Carew?' she asked.

Henry's good mood evaporated. His eyes narrowed.

'I danced with her, that's all. What do you take me for?'

'You were seen kissing her!' she cried fiercely. 'And the gossip I heard accuses you of more than that. Do you deny it?'

'I do deny it!' he flared, that menacing flush rising from his neck.

'Then you are lying,' she accused. 'I have it on good authority that you have bedded with her. Some ladies cannot keep a still tongue.'

'You would believe gossip rather than the word of a king? By God, Anne, you try me!'

'I have good cause – admit it!' she shrieked, beside herself with fury, feeling the poor babe leap in distress in her womb. 'You pride yourself on your honour, but what price honour when your rod governs your royal will?'

'Remember who I am!' Henry flung back. 'When I think of what I have done for you – how I fought the whole world to have you, and honoured you with my marriage. How I have showered you with gifts – look at that great bed I gave you. By God, Anne, you would not have it now, having used such words to me. You are my wife, and you must shut your eyes and endure as more worthy persons have done.'

'Then you admit it,' she hissed.

Henry's face was like thunder, his voice icy. 'Madam, you ought to remember that it is in my power to humble you again in a moment, more than I have raised you.'

He walked out, leaving her stunned. Never had he spoken to her like that. And to compare her unfavourably to Katherine! How *could* he? She collapsed in a storm of weeping, and her ladies came running. They made her rest, fearful for the babe. If only its father had been, she thought bitterly.

It was all bluster, she told herself. At heart Henry was a spoilt child who expected to have whatever he wanted and not be gainsaid. He would come around, begging her forgiveness, she was sure.

But he did not. For three endless days he did not visit her, and when, taking the air with her ladies, she came upon him practising his archery at the butts, he greeted her coldly. She waited until he had finished and then walked back with him to the palace, their attendants following behind. She guessed he would have preferred not to have her with him, but did not want to argue in public.

'A year ago you were my loving servant,' she said, low. 'That man would never have spoken to me the way you did the other day.'

'We are married now,' he said. 'A husband is not a servant. As my wife, you owe me obedience, and it is not your place to criticise me. I will not brook it!'

Anne walked on in silence, appalled at his words. Was this the man who had defied all Christendom to marry her? They had been wed but six months, and already he had been unfaithful. And he expected her to maintain a dignified silence! Well, silent she would be. At the door, she curtseyed and went alone to her apartments. He did not come after her.

When they arrived at Greenwich, an uneasy truce between them, Anne took to her chamber to await the birth of her child.

Henry had thawed a little. In the barge that brought them from Hampton Court, he had told her he was planning a pageant and tournament to mark the birth, and on the morning before she disappeared from public view, he kissed her for the first time since their quarrel.

'I will come to see you, and I will pray constantly that God will send you a happy hour,' he said.

She could feel her eyes brimming with tears. It wasn't meant to be like this.

'All will be well,' Henry reassured her.

'What will you do while I'm in seclusion?' she asked.

'I'll be hunting hereabouts. I won't be far away. I meant to say, I've had letters to the nobility prepared, announcing the birth of a prince.'

She wished he had waited. It was tempting Fate.

'Anne,' he said, tilting her chin up. 'I love you. Never forget that.'

Her heart lighter, she went to hear Mass, in company with her household. Afterwards she went in procession to her presence chamber, where she sat beneath her canopy of estate and was offered spiced wine and little cakes. Then her chamberlain required all her people to pray

358

for her, that she might be safely delivered. As the trumpets sounded, she withdrew into her privy chamber and then to her bedchamber – the Chamber of the Virgins, so called because it was hung with tapestries depicting St Ursula and her eleven thousand virgins. There, dominating all, was the great French bed. She sank down on it thankfully as her ladies drew a heavy curtain across the door. They had most of them been appointed household officers, for no man save the King and her chaplain might enter her chamber while she was in seclusion.

They brought her, along with the choicest food and anything else she fancied, all the latest gossip. The Duke of Suffolk was about to marry his son's betrothed, a girl of fourteen – and he nearly fifty! Anne laughed aloud when she heard the name of his bride, for young Kate Willoughby was the only child of the Princess Dowager's staunchest friend, that dragon, Lady Willoughby! She could foresee fireworks, for Suffolk had long supported the King . . .

Early in the morning of the seventh day of September, Anne's pains began and the midwife was sent for. All was progressing well, she pronounced, even when the contractions became unbelievable agony, with little respite in between. It seemed to go on for hours, but around three o'clock in the afternoon, just as Anne thought she could endure no more, the midwife told her the babe was coming.

'Chin down on your chest, your Grace, deep breath, and push!'

Anne pushed – and pushed, and pushed. Travail was rightly named!

'I can see the head!' the midwife cried. 'Not long now!'

Around the bed, the ladies were crying encouragement. She strained again, and felt the child slither out between her thighs. There was silence – then a lusty wail.

A girl. She was devastated, racked with disappointment and fear of what Henry would say. He had set such store by all the doctors and astrologers who had predicted it would be a boy. Only William Glover had seen the truth.

Would Henry lay the blame for this at her door? Would he see it as a sign of divine displeasure?

He had been sent for. She lay tense in her grand bed, washed, refreshed and clad in a clean lawn shift with a pretty embroidered neck-line, waiting with dread for his coming. Beside her, in the vast gilded cradle bearing the arms of England, the sleeping babe lay swaddled, robed in crimson velvet, with an embroidered satin bonnet on her head. Anne had held her once, surprised at how tiny she was. She had looked down and seen the Tudor red hair, Henry's Roman nose and her own narrow face and pointed chin. It was an old face for so young a child.

'She's strong and healthy,' the midwife had said. All the women had praised the child, saying that her safe arrival presaged a long line of sons. And the wet nurse had exclaimed at how quickly the babe had latched on the breast and taken suck. But Anne felt strangely detached from her. She had heard that mothers experienced a great rush of love for their newborns. It had not happened to her. She was too disappointed, too gripped by a strong sense of failure. The tiny creature in the cradle would be a constant reminder of it.

There was a muffled commotion outside, then the curtain was drawn back, the door opened, and Henry strode in, wearing his hunting clothes and bringing with him the scent of the open air.

'Darling!' he said. 'Thank God you are come through this safely.' He bent over the bed and kissed her, then peered into the cradle. 'Hello, little one,' he said, and picked up the sleeping infant, tenderly kissing the tiny head. 'May God bless you.'

'Sir,' Anne whispered, 'I am so sorry I did not bear you a son.'

He looked up. She could see no reproach in his eyes.

'You have given me a healthy child,' he said. 'You and I are both lusty, and by God's grace, boys will follow.'

She could not help herself. The relief was so great that she began weeping.

'Darling,' Henry said, handing the baby to the midwife and taking Anne in his arms, 'I am proud of you. I would rather beg from door to door than forsake you.'

'Thank you!' she sobbed, laughing and crying at the same time.

He let her go and reclaimed the infant. 'We will call her Elizabeth, after my mother,' he said.

'By a happy coincidence, it's my mother's name as well,' Anne said. 'The perfect choice.'

'She has my nose,' Henry remarked, kissing the child and laying her back to sleep, beckoning the rockers to come forward. 'Now I will leave you to rest, darling. I have the christening to arrange.'

'What of those letters you had prepared?' Anne asked.

'There is room to amend "prince" to "princess",' he said. 'They will go off tonight.'

'When will you hold the tournament?'

'I've decided not to.' For the first time, Henry looked a little downcast. 'But we will have a splendid christening. Until we have a son, Anne, Elizabeth is my heir, and all must recognise her as such.'

When Elizabeth was three days old, Anne watched her being wrapped in a purple mantle with a long train furred with ermine. Then she was borne off in the arms of the Dowager Duchess of Norfolk to be taken in a stately procession to her baptism in the chapel of the Observant Friars. Father would be supporting his granddaughter's long train and George was one of those carrying the canopy of estate above her head.

Anne lay on her grand French bed, an ermine-trimmed mantle of estate about her shoulders. Henry, wearing cloth of gold, had come to sit beside her to await their daughter's return. They would not attend the christening; it was the godparents' triumph. Henry had chosen four: Archbishop Cranmer and the Dowager Duchess, and, two supporters of Katherine, the Marchioness of Dorset and the Marquess of Exeter. 'It will look as if they approve,' he gloated.

As they waited, Henry described for Anne the tapestries that had been hung on the outer walls of the palace and all along the processional route; the font of solid silver, set on a platform three steps high beneath a crimson satin canopy fringed with gold; the ceremonial to be observed; the noble guests. She listened approvingly. No honour had been scanted.

Presently, in the distance, they heard a fanfare.

'They're bringing her back,' Henry said. Soon the Princess was carried into the Queen's chamber and placed in the King's arms. He gave her his blessing, then passed her to Anne, who gave hers and called the child by her baptismal name for the first time, as was a mother's privilege. Refreshments were served to the godparents and chief guests, and then Henry directed Norfolk and Suffolk to convey his thanks to the Lord Mayor and aldermen for attending.

'Will there be fireworks tonight?' Anne asked Henry.

'I haven't ordered any,' he replied, looking uncomfortable. She knew he would have done had a prince been christened. She was upset to learn, the next day, that there had been no celebratory bonfires in the streets of London either, and appalled when George, visiting her and his niece, told her that two friars had been arrested for saying that the Princess had been christened in hot water that was not hot enough.

'How can they say that of an innocent babe?' she asked.

'Ignore them,' he counselled. 'Chapuys told me to my face that we should not have expected the people to celebrate. He said there was little love for you or any of our race.'

'I trust you told him to go hang himself,' Anne seethed.

'Something of the sort!' George snorted.

Henry had not visited her very often. For all his brave words at Elizabeth's birth, she was convinced he felt she had failed him. Was he asking himself why he had risked so much for her, and – more crucially – why God had denied him a son? Yet he had made it implicit to Anne that he was determined not to lose face, and was as adamant as ever that he had been right to put away Katherine and marry her.

As if to prove this, he suddenly had the Nun of Kent and her supporters arrested and imprisoned.

'What will happen to her?' Anne asked, sitting up in her chair for the first time since giving birth.

'She will be tried. She has said enough and more to incriminate herself of high treason.'

This was one aspect of the new Henry of which Anne could approve. He had been too patient, too forgiving, towards his opponents. She rejoiced now to see him so resolute.

He was more resolute in bed, too. As soon as she had recovered from the birth and had been churched, he appeared at her bedchamber door.

'Let's make that son you promised me,' he said, bearing down on her, lust in his eyes.

She was reluctant to let him make love to her so soon. She had lost the weight she had put on in pregnancy, but her belly and breasts were slack, and on her hips there were silvery marks where the skin had stretched. She did not want him to see her like this. She feared being penetrated so soon after giving birth, and she really did not want to be pregnant again yet. She had also been tormenting herself with thoughts of him cavorting with Lady Carew. Was he still swiving her? She did not dare to ask. She was maintaining the dignified silence he had enjoined.

But she knew her wifely duty, and she was well aware of the urgent need for her to bear a son. So she opened herself to him, and was surprised by the force of his desire. Maybe he *had* been celibate since August. At least it proved one thing: he still wanted her.

It worried her that she could not love Elizabeth as she ought. She was quite content to leave the child to her nurses, in her elaborate nursery. Sometimes, out of guilt, she commanded that the Princess be brought to her chamber and laid on a cushion at her feet, so that all could see how devoted a mother she was, and not guess at the heavy sense of failure she carried.

She often wondered if she could have loved Elizabeth had she been a boy. Would she love a son who had that old face and seemed such a self-contained infant, as her daughter did? Margaret, Lady Bryan, who had efficiently run the Princess Mary's nursery and had been appointed by Henry to preside over Elizabeth's, reported that the Princess was a good baby generally, but was given to roaring tantrums when denied something she wanted. 'But she's very forward for her age, madam, and takes her milk well.'

Anne salved her conscience by buying the child pretty toys – a rocking horse, a cloth doll, a wooden stump babe for teething – and commissioned jewellery for her: a bracelet for the tiny wrist, a miniature string of pearls and a golden girdle book of psalms for when she was older. She did all the things she thought a good mother should do. And she suffered in silence, because she did not want anyone thinking her unnatural and unfeeling.

Late in November, the Nun of Kent was found guilty of treason, and an example was made of her and the Observant Friars and priests who had abetted her. All did public penance, walking through the streets of London to Paul's Cross, where they were made to stand on a scaffold, holding lighted tapers, while a sermon was preached against them.

But the sympathies of the watching crowds were with the 'Holy Maid of Kent', as they called her, shouting out their encouragement. It was gratifying that the evidence for her treason had sounded suitably damning when blasted from Paul's Pulpit, and that the crowd had witnessed the accused being hustled to the Tower to await sentencing. Henry was trying to persuade his reluctant Council to agree to Parliament passing an Act of Attainder condemning them. He did not want them sentenced in open court because he feared there would be demonstrations.

By then, Anne was nursing a secret. She was sure she had conceived again. She had seen just one flowering of her courses since Elizabeth's birth, in the middle of October. By late November, her hopes were high.

'I am with child already,' she informed Henry.

'Darling!' He was ecstatic. 'That is the best news I've had in ages!' He folded her in his arms, pressing his lips to hers. 'When will it be?'

'In the summer – probably in July.'

'It cannot be soon enough.' Henry's eyes were shining. 'How are you feeling?'

'Very well,' she assured him, elated and relieved. If he had had any doubts that God approved of their marriage, this must allay them.

In December, when Elizabeth was three months old, Henry established a household for her at Hatfield, which was convenient for London, yet well away from its noisome, often plague-infested air. In the capable arms of Margaret Bryan, and attended by an army of nursemaids, laundresses, officials and servants, the Princess was taken north from Greenwich by a roundabout route, the better to be seen by the people and impress on them her status as the King's heir.

Watching her daughter depart, Anne felt that familiar ache of relief and guilt. When she had a son, she would love Elizabeth better, she assured herself.

Among Elizabeth's maids was nine-year-old Catherine Carey, Mary's daughter by Henry, who was new to court. Despite her looking so like him, he had never acknowledged her, and she knew nothing of their blood tie. Anne was fond of her niece, and pleased that she had secured the place for her. Catherine was thrilled to be serving the Princess.

Unlike Henry's other daughter, Mary, who had impudently refused to recognise Elizabeth's title. From Hertford, where she was lodging with her household, she wrote to the Council that she would call Elizabeth 'sister', nothing more.

Henry was incandescent. 'She shall be stripped of the title and trappings of princess!' he shouted. 'She is not my lawful daughter, and therefore she cannot be my heir. She is my bastard, nothing more. From henceforth she must be called the Lady Mary.' Without hesitation, he sent a deputation of the Council to inform her of her demotion. Anne inwardly applauded him for being firm with Mary at long last.

The councillors returned to Greenwich grim-faced. Mary had insisted that she alone was the King's true daughter, born in lawful matrimony. She'd said she would say nothing to the slander of her mother, the Holy Church and the Pope, and declared she would dishonour her parents if she falsely confessed herself a bastard. She had written a letter to her father, beseeching his blessing.

'I will curse her rather!' he snapped, reading it. 'She trusts I was not privy to the Council's message. She doubts not that I take her for my lawful daughter, born in true matrimony.'

'You will not let this pass?' Anne challenged. He could not. Mary was popular, while her own child was seen by many as a bastard. With Katherine out of sight at Buckden, she could see Mary becoming a focus for those who opposed the King. Mary's resolve must therefore be broken, by fair means or foul.

'I will write to her, never fear,' Henry growled. 'I will leave her in no doubt that it was my will that she was deprived of the title of princess. And I will tell her that I'm giving her palace of Beaulieu to your brother Rochford.'

'That is most bountiful of Your Grace,' Anne said, lowering her eyes so he would not see the triumph in them. 'I would like her jewels for Elizabeth.'

'You shall have them. A bastard cannot be permitted to wear what rightfully belongs to the lawful heir.'

An idea occurred to Anne. 'Would it not be a good thing to have Mary in Elizabeth's household, where she can be under the eye of people loyal to us?'

Henry was still simmering. 'An excellent solution. Her household shall be disbanded. That troublemaker, Lady Salisbury, can go to the Devil, and Mary can go to Hatfield and serve Elizabeth. That'll teach her to defy me. I'll force her to bend the knee to my true heir.'

Jubilation mingled with relief. 'And who shall be her lady mistress in place of Lady Salisbury?'

'Who in Elizabeth's household would be most suitable?'

'My aunt, Lady Shelton. She is utterly loyal.'

'So be it. I will give the order.'

Anne was happily nursing her triumph over Mary when a message arrived from Katherine asking if the King would let her move to a healthier house, as her lodging at Buckden was damp and cold, winter was descending, and her health was beginning to suffer.

She had brought it on herself. If she had seen sense, she could have been living in luxury with her daughter at her side. But maybe Henry's harsh measures were beginning to achieve results. No doubt the ever-industrious Chapuys had informed Katherine of what was planned for Mary. It was one thing to suffer yourself, another to see a loved child suffer unnecessarily. And if the mother broke, the daughter would too.

Anne did not want to hound Katherine to her death, although she kept thinking that Katherine dying would solve everything. But a little more of the same medicine might teach the stubborn woman what was good for her.

Cromwell was the man to ask. He seemed to know everything. She summoned him to her privy chamber.

'Tell me,' she said, 'do you know of any great houses that are in poor order yet habitable?'

'Is this for the Princess Dowager?' he asked.

'You must have read my mind,' she smiled.

'No, madam, I read her letter to the King.' Nothing, it seemed, escaped him.

She explained her strategy, and Cromwell thought for a bit.

'The Bishop's Palace at Somersham near Ely is surrounded by deep water and marshes,' he said. 'Your Grace might like to suggest that to the King.'

Anne went straight to Henry and told him that Cromwell had suggested a house for Katherine.

'How long she stays there is up to her,' she said. 'When she arrives at Somersham and sees that her situation is not going to improve unless she obeys your orders, she may capitulate.'

'Darling, I fear you want hope to triumph over experience,' Henry observed. 'I think she would go into the fire rather than admit she is wrong.'

'It's insane, when she could be having a good life in retirement.'

'If she remains obstinate, I'll have her declared as insane as her sister Juana,' Henry said. 'There's madness in that family. People will believe it.'

Chapuys, unusually well informed, protested of course.

'He complains that Somersham is the most unhealthy and pestilential house in England,' Henry huffed. 'He'll be telling tales to the Emperor if I don't send Katherine somewhere else. I thought of her castle of Fotheringhay. It was a royal palace fifty, sixty years ago, and after I granted it to her she tried to restore it. But it was already decaying, and despite the works she had carried out, it's now in an even worse condition than Somersham.'

'Send her to Fotheringhay,' Anne urged.

But Katherine, it seemed, was well apprised of the state of Fotheringhay. Back came the answer from Buckden: she would not go there.

'Then she must go to Somersham,' Anne decreed, and Henry issued the order.

Again Katherine refused to go.

'I'll teach her to defy me!' Henry stormed, and ordered the dismissal of all but the most necessary of her servants, insisting that those remaining must not address her as Queen, but as Princess Dowager. To enforce her obedience to these commands, and escort her to Somersham, the Duke of Suffolk was sent to Buckden with a detachment of the King's guards. He was reluctant to go. Anne guessed he would infinitely have preferred to spend Christmas at court with his young bride. But north he marched, and she held her breath, hoping that this show of armed force might persuade Katherine to give in.

'Sir John Seymour begs that you will accept his daughter into your service.' Henry handed Anne a letter. 'She served the Princess Dowager at court, and was with her at Buckden until Sir John summoned her home.'

'I remember Jane Seymour,' Anne said, recalling a quiet-spoken, fair girl with a pale complexion, watchful eyes and a prim mouth.

'Her father clearly regrets sending her to Katherine, and is worried about losing my favour because of it – and about not finding her a husband. But, as he explains, it's not been easy to obtain another place for her. No one wants someone who was associated with Katherine.'

'Is Jane Seymour a friend to her?'

'As I remember, she's a little mouse who wouldn't say boo to a gnat. Sir John is loyal. He has served me well. She'll do as he bids her.'

'Very well. I'll have her as a maid-of-honour,' Anne agreed.

Jane Seymour was twenty-five, demure and dutiful. She performed her duties efficiently, behaved with circumspection and decorum, and gave no cause for complaint. But Anne could not like her. Her friendly overtures had been received with courtesy, not warmth, and Jane seemed to exist alongside the life of the Queen's household, rather than as a part of it. When there was pastime in Anne's chamber, she was rarely to be seen. She kept her head down and herself to herself. No doubt she still nursed an affection for her previous mistress. Yet Anne could not sense hostility, only detachment. She did her best to make the young woman feel welcome, but it was hard work.

She was more preoccupied with the nausea of early pregnancy and what was happening at Buckden. In Suffolk's first letter, he had reported that Katherine had shut herself in her chamber and refused to open the door. Neither threats nor entreaties could persuade her. The Duke dared not use force, and had contented himself with dismissing her servants, leaving only a few to care for her needs. In his second letter, he described how he had stood outside Katherine's door and pleaded with her to come out. Against all reason, she had refused, saying she would not go to Somersham unless he bound her with ropes and took her by violence. 'She is the most obstinate woman that may be!' he complained, adding that he had found things at Buckden far from the King's expectations, and would explain further when he returned to court.

The next they heard was that a hostile mob of yokels, armed with scythes and billhooks, had encircled Buckden and were just standing there watching menacingly. Suffolk feared that, if he tried to force Katherine to leave, they would pounce.

Exasperated, Henry instructed Suffolk to return to court.

'There's nothing he can do,' he explained to Anne. 'I cannot risk an ugly confrontation. Imagine if Katherine was hurt. We'd have the Emperor here at the head of an army in ten minutes, never mind the Turks!'

Chapter 23

1534

As soon as Suffolk returned to Greenwich, he asked to see the King in private. Anne was present when Henry welcomed back his old friend, warmly assuring him that he did not blame him for what had happened. 'The Princess Dowager is best left to her obstinacy,' he declared.

'Your Graces, there is more to the situation than that,' Suffolk said, gratefully taking the chair Henry indicated.

'Leave us, please,' Anne ordered the servants. 'I will pour the wine.' She handed out the goblets and the Duke took his gratefully. He looked exhausted. No longer was he the dashing hero of the lists of Tournai, but a middle-aged man running to fat, his once-handsome face showing lines of strain, his hair grizzled. Beside him, Henry, his mirror image, was a paragon in his prime.

'So tell me, Charles, what is the true situation at Buckden?' Henry asked.

'The Princess Dowager is a sick woman, sir. I hardly recognised her. Her chamberlain told me she has dropsy and will not live much longer. I can well believe it.'

Anne realised she had been holding her breath. Maybe God was smoothing the way for her son to be born as the undisputed heir to England. Because, once Katherine was dead, no one could deny that she, Anne, was the true Queen.

'She's not so ill that she can't defy me.' Henry's voice was peevish.

'Her spirit is undaunted,' Suffolk conceded. 'I do not think she will ever give way.'

370

'Then the sooner God Almighty takes her to Himself, the better,' Henry muttered. 'Her obduracy only encourages Mary. Did you know that Mary made a scene when they came to escort her to Hatfield? Norfolk told her plainly that she was unnatural and, if she was his daughter, he would knock her head against the wall until it was as soft as a baked apple.'

'I can imagine him doing it,' Suffolk observed.

'He's right,' Henry said. 'She's a traitor and deserves punishment, and so he told her.'

'Lady Shelton will treat her as she deserves,' Anne said. 'I have every confidence in her.' Mary must be brought to heel. Anne had come to hate and fear her more than she hated and feared Katherine. Elizabeth was the King's true heir and, however deficient her own qualities as a mother, Anne was determined that her blood should sit upon the throne. It was Mary who posed the deadliest threat to Elizabeth's future.

Mary had been at Hatfield for two weeks when Henry received a letter from her, begging leave to see him.

'You won't say yes, will you?' Anne flared.

'No,' he said, after the barest hesitation. 'But darling, she is my daughter, and for all her disobedience, she has many good qualities. I would not be too harsh on her.'

She stared at him. What an about-turn! 'She is a traitor – you said so yourself. We deal harshly with traitors in this realm, and quite rightly!'

Henry sighed. 'I will ignore the letter. I would not have you upset at this time.'

As she well knew, the bonds of parenthood could be strong; look how fiercely protective she herself was of Elizabeth's rights. It would be a struggle to make Henry see Mary as the subversive rebel she really was. When he announced one morning that he was going to visit Elizabeth at Hatfield, she fell into a frenzy of anxiety lest he decide to see Mary too and be moved by her youth and his fatherly pity to treat her better and restore her title. That Anne could never allow.

After he had gone, she summoned Cromwell and commanded him to ride after Henry and prevent him, at any cost, from seeing or speaking to Mary. Cromwell looked at her askance. His expression said that, as Chancellor of the Exchequer, Master of the Jewel House and Master of the Rolls, he was too busy to act as her messenger, but he pursed his lips, made no comment and left.

Whatever he said to Henry had the desired effect – to begin with. Probably he had warned him of the need to keep Anne calm while she was breeding. But, as he explained later, all his persuasions were for nothing.

'When the King was mounting his horse, ready to leave, the Lady Mary appeared on the terrace at the top of the house, and knelt with her hands joined in supplication. His Grace turned around and saw her. He bowed to her and put his hand to his hat. None of the rest of us had dared to raise our heads, but, following His Grace's lead, we had to salute her.'

Anne could not contain her rage.

'How could you do it?' she screamed at Henry when he arrived a few minutes after Cromwell had left.

'Do what?' he countered, but she could see from his face that he knew.

'You saluted your bastard, as if she had done nothing wrong.' She was in tears now.

'It was but a courtesy,' he said defensively.

'She does not deserve your courtesy,' she snapped, and sank into her chair in a storm of weeping.

'Darling, please!' Henry begged, kneeling down and embracing her. 'Think of the child.'

'The child! The child! All you think of is the child! What of me?'

'You know very well how precious this child is,' he said coldly, standing up. 'I will send your ladies to you.' And he was gone.

She could not rest, could not calm her agitation. She was sick to the teeth of Mary's defiance, and Henry's failure to deal with it. It galled her to think that that proud, obstinate girl was universally loved by the people, whereas if she herself went out in public, they still cried 'Whore!' 'Heretic!' 'Adulteress!' And it was not just the common people who slandered her.

One day, hearing voices below her window, she had peered out to see Harry Percy talking to Chapuys.

'The Queen is a bad woman,' she had heard Harry say. 'I am certain that she is determined to poison the Princess.'

Anne leaned back against the wall, shaking. That even Harry, that good man who had once loved her, should say such things of her was shocking. She had never dreamed of poisoning Mary!

In desperation, she resolved to change her tactics and use kindness to win over her stepdaughter. If the girl was seen to be friendly to her, it would give the lie to what Harry – and no doubt others – were thinking, and make the people love her.

It was time to pay a visit to Elizabeth.

All was in pristine order in the royal nursery at Hatfield. The baby – how she had grown in two months – slept serenely in her cradle, lulled by the young maids rocking her, and all around there was an atmosphere of peaceful activity.

'Her Highness is doing so well, Madam,' the plump and motherly Lady Bryan told Anne. 'I do believe we had a smile today! And she takes suck lustily.'

As Anne bent over the cradle, Elizabeth opened her blue eyes and blinked at her, regarding her solemnly. Then she went red in the face, opened her tiny mouth and roared.

'She'll need her clouts changed,' the wet nurse smiled. 'Come along, my poppet.' And she picked up the baby and bore her off to the adjoining bedchamber.

'I will come back later,' Anne said to Lady Bryan. 'Do you know where I can find the Lady Mary?'

'She's with Lady Shelton in the schoolroom, Madam.'

When Anne appeared at the door, both ladies rose, but Mary threw her a look of such venom that she almost forgot her resolve.

'Your Grace.' Lady Shelton curtseyed, and Anne embraced her.

'Dear aunt, I trust you are well.' She turned to the thin, red-haired, snub-nosed girl who stood glowering at her.

'My lady Mary,' she said, forcing herself to smile, 'I would speak with you, as a friend.'

'Lady Anne' – and Mary would not acknowledge her as queen – 'you can be no friend to me.'

'But I would be,' Anne said. 'You have had a difficult time, but things can change for the better. I urge you, for the sake of your future happiness, to visit me at court and honour me as queen.'

'Never!' Mary spat, her plain features – so like her mother's – contorted in hatred.

'Hear me out,' Anne insisted, trying not to lose her temper. 'It would be a means of reconciliation with the King your father, who is as unhappy about this estrangement as you are. I will intercede with him for you, and then you will find yourself as well or better treated than ever.'

Mary looked at her as if she were a clod of dirt she had just scuffed from her shoe. 'I know of no queen in England save my mother,' she said, 'but if you would do me that favour with my father, I would be much obliged.'

Would the girl never see sense? 'I exhort you to accept my offer, which was made out of kindness and in the interests of us all,' Anne challenged.

'It would serve your cause well to have me on your side, Madam Boleyn. Don't think I'm so innocent that I don't understand the game you are playing. Thanks to you, I had to grow up very quickly.'

'Speak to me like that, and you could find yourself in a worse case than you are now,' Anne warned. 'But accept my offer of friendship, and you shall find me zealous to protect your interests.'

Mary snapped. 'You can protect them best by taking yourself and your bastard off to some distant land and leaving my father free of your bewitchment, so that he can return to my mother, the true Queen!'

'Don't speak to the Queen like that!' Lady Shelton cried.

'The Queen is at Buckden,' Mary rounded on her.

This was intolerable. 'Trust me, I will bring down the pride of your

374

unbridled Spanish blood,' Anne warned. 'As for having you at court, I will not now hear of it. You have made your bed, now you must lie on it.'

'Now see what you have done, you foolish girl,' Lady Shelton hissed.

Mary shrugged. 'It is labour wasted to press me, and you are deceived if you think that ill-treatment, or even the threat of death, will make me change my determination.'

'We shall see,' Anne retorted, and swept from the room.

Lady Shelton hurried after her.

'Your Grace, she is not a bad girl at heart. She is confused and frightened, and deeply grieved at being separated from her mother. And she is at a difficult age, when the young are wont to be rebellious. She should never have spoken to you like that, but she is her own worst enemy.'

'I care not,' Anne said. 'I'm washing my hands of her.'

But she did care. All the way home, as the litter rumbled along, she was in despair. Henry would be angry when he heard how Mary had spoken to her, but he was vulnerable where his daughter was concerned, and she did not believe he would punish her severely enough. And there was Mary, defiant and sure of her rights, popular, beloved and pitied – and there was the Emperor, who might decide to use armed force to support her. What would then become of herself and Elizabeth? Would they indeed be banished to some distant land – or worse?

Henry erupted in fury as Anne had anticipated; he erupted again when Mary refused to accompany Elizabeth's household when it moved to the More in Hertfordshire and had to be manhandled into her litter. His patience was wearing out.

'I will so order it that she will never defy me again – her or anyone else!' he roared. 'Parliament shall see to it!'

That spring, he ordered that an Act be passed naming Anne as regent of the realm and absolute governess of her children in the event of his death. Another Act deprived Katherine of the lands she had held as queen, and returned to her the lands that she had once held as Prince Arthur's widow. The Queen's estates were now assigned to Anne. An

Act of Attainder was passed against Bishop Fisher, condemning him to imprisonment in the Tower. Cromwell had learned that the Bishop had interrogated the Nun of Kent about her prophecies, but had failed to tell the King about it, and Henry was ready to believe that this signified treasonable involvement. But Fisher was too ill to travel to London.

The Nun herself and four of her acolytes were attainted for high treason. But the piece of legislation that meant the most to Anne was the Act that vested the succession to the crown of England in her children by Henry. Better still, this new Act required all the King's subjects, if so commanded, to swear an oath acknowledging Queen Anne as the King's lawful wife and the Princess Elizabeth as his legitimate heir. Those refusing to swear would be accounted guilty of abetting treason and sent to prison.

The prospect of her enemies being forced to acknowledge her calmed Anne's nerves. But on a sunny day in early April, Henry burst into her chamber.

'That whoreson Pope!' he spluttered, seething with fury. He looked so puce in the face she feared he might have an apoplexy. Rising quickly from her curtsey, she made him sit in the chair she had vacated.

'What has he done?' she asked.

Henry looked ill. 'The French ambassador has just informed me that Clement has found for Katherine. He said that our marriage always had been, and still stands, firm and lawful, and Mary is its legitimate issue.'

Anne felt sick. This judgement might rally many waverers to Katherine and her daughter, and the Emperor might now decide that making war in his aunt's cause was worthier than crushing the Turks. The Act of Succession had been passed not a moment too soon.

'But he has ignored all the determinations of the universities!' she exclaimed. 'Plainly the opinions of the finest minds in Europe are of no consequence to him. He is a disgrace to his office, and should be defrocked!'

Henry nodded in vehement agreement. 'He has ordered me to resume cohabitation at once with Katherine. I'm to hold and maintain her as becomes a loving husband and my kingly honour. If I refuse, I will be excommunicated. And – this is the final insult – I am to pay the costs of the case!'

He was visibly shaken, and Anne realised that even after all he had done to break with Rome, he had been hoping, right up until the last minute, that the breach could be healed. But Clement, by this judgement, had wrecked all hope of that. If England was in schism, it was the Pope's fault.

'This was a political decision,' she said.

'Aye, but that's been Clement's approach these seven long years. He cares not a fig for the Scriptures, or the theologians, who are far more learned in these matters than he is. But he shall rue the day he gave this judgement. The sentence of this Bishop of Rome no longer carries any weight in England. I will have sermons preached in every church in the land declaring his perfidy.'

The order went out. On Easter Day, congregations all over England were informed of the wickedness of Pope Clement, and true subjects were commanded to pray every week for King Henry VIII as being, next unto God, the only and Supreme Head of the Church, and Anne his wife, and Elizabeth their Princess. It did not prevent public celebrations being held in some places in anticipation of Katherine's expected return to favour.

Henry now sent out commissioners to all parts of the realm to administer the new oath upholding the Act of Succession to all who held public office and anyone else whose loyalty was in question. Anne was tense, waiting for reports of disaffection to come pouring in, but her fears were soon allayed, because most people, even members of the religious orders, were swearing it without demur. Only a few refused. She was not surprised to hear that Bishop Fisher, whose sentence had been commuted to a fine, was among them – and Sir Thomas More. He had refused the oath twice, and no amount of pressure could persuade him to say why.

Henry was deeply hurt. 'I accounted him my friend,' he said. 'This will go against me with the people because he is so universally respected. My commissioners advise that he should be left alone.'

'You mean they would collude in his breaking the law?' Anne was amazed. 'Henry, this man should be made an example of. If others see him defying you and getting away with it, they will refuse the oath too.'

Henry had his head in his hands. 'How can I proceed against More? I have loved him, Anne. And I would bring much hatred on myself by punishing him.'

'Whatever he is, he should not be exempt from your laws. By allowing it, you undermine the oath and the Act and our marriage.'

'Very well,' Henry capitulated. 'I will have the oath put to him again.'

He sent More to the Tower for defying him a third time. Anne had not thought him capable of it, but he surprised her. She suspected he had done it as much for fear of her reaction if he had not, as out of anger and righteousness. He would not risk upsetting her while she carried his child.

As Henry had predicted, there was much murmuring at More's imprisonment, which would no doubt soon reverberate all over Europe. And there was a lot more murmuring when the Nun of Kent and her associates were drawn on hurdles to the gallows at Tyburn, where, before huge crowds, she was hanged until dead, then beheaded and the men suffered the horrors of a traitor's death: hanging, drawing and quartering. Theirs, Anne realised, was the first blood that had been spilt on her account. Well, it would serve as an example to the people, and a warning that they must obey their King or it would go worse for them.

Cromwell, she was aware, was becoming very powerful. That April he was advanced to the office of Principal Secretary to the King. He had risen above everyone except herself, and had more credit with his master than ever the Cardinal had.

'There is now no one who does anything except Cromwell,' George said, sitting with Anne in the window seat in her chamber. 'He is become the most influential of the King's ministers. You had best watch out, sister.'

'Henry heeds me more than he heeds Cromwell,' she insisted, but her brother's words had chilled her. What would happen if she bore another daughter? Would Cromwell creep closer into the King's counsels and oust her? He could prove a formidable rival. 'Cromwell is on our side,' she declared. 'He is still my man, and we owe much to him for implementing the changes Henry has made and promoting the royal supremacy.'

George frowned. 'I'm just asking you to be watchful. This man thrives on power. He controls access to the King. He uses a host of paid informers and grateful clients anxious to do him service. Knowledge is power, Anne, and Cromwell has seen to it that he occupies a position of enormous influence. He could try to undermine you.'

'Henry would not let him,' she assured him. 'He doesn't love Cromwell as he loved Wolsey. And Cromwell and I share common aims. We both support reform and the King's supremacy.'

'Well, just make sure that you keep him on your side,' George warned. 'He's already unhappy with what Brereton did.'

Brereton had accused a man of killing one of his Welsh retainers, but when a court in London acquitted the fellow, Brereton had taken matters into his own hands and hanged him.

'Master Secretary is most put out, with Brereton, and apparently with you. Father heard him say it was done out of sheer malice, and that he had liked the man and tried to save him.'

'Brereton says he was a villain,' Anne replied. 'He told me how justice had failed him, and *I* authorised him to have the fellow re-arrested and re-tried.'

'That explains why Cromwell mentioned your name.'

'Well, he'll have to get over it,' she said. 'Justice has now been done.'

Norris joined them, lute in hand.

'I hear you are to be congratulated,' George said, clapping him on the back. 'Keeper of the King's Privy Purse and Master of the Hart Hounds and Hawks! And Black Rod in the Parliament House.'

'It is thanks only to the gracious favour of your Grace and the King,' Norris protested. 'I fear I am not worthy of your goodness to me.'

'Nonsense!' Anne smiled. 'The King loves you as he loves no other man. And I – I have every confidence in you.'

Norris went down on one knee, took her hand and kissed it. 'I am blessed to serve such a loving mistress,' he declared fervently.

Anne drew her hand away. She had seen George looking at them curiously.

'Mary is ill,' Henry said, arriving late for supper. 'Chapuys has begged me to let her go to her mother, but I do not trust him – or them. Don't say anything, Anne – I would never consent to it. Cromwell recommends that I send my own physician to Mary.'

Pray God that this child is a son, Anne was beseeching inwardly, as she sat down at the table and her napkin was placed over her shoulder. Until she had borne a prince, she would feel – and, indeed, be – insecure on her throne. In her most desperate moments, in the still watches of the night, she fretted that Henry would cease to love her if she gave him another daughter. Her worst nightmare was that he would heed the Pope's sentence and return to Katherine.

A few days later, news came that Mary had recovered from her illness, and Anne could not stop herself from thinking it would have been better if Mary had died, and her mother, too. It would resolve everything.

Henry was considering making a state visit to France. She would not be accompanying him, because of her condition, but that suited her perfectly.

'If Mary is taken ill while he's away, I'll not be sending my own physician,' she told George when they were relaxing in her chamber that afternoon. 'I'd as soon do away with her. I might starve her to death.' She was bursting with angry frustration.

George frowned. 'I wouldn't answer for how the King might react if you did.'

'I wouldn't care, even if I was to be burned alive for it afterwards,' she cried, feeling herself becoming hysterical.

'Hush, sister, you must not say such things.'

'But she is a threat to me, George, and to Elizabeth. I wish she were dead!' She was near to tears now.

'Soon she will be silenced,' he soothed. 'The King said today that

380

the oath is to be administered to the Lady Mary and the Princess Dowager. He's sending the Archbishop of York, who won't stand for any nonsense. He'll visit the Princess Dowager first.'

'Thank God!' Anne exulted, relief flooding through her. 'If they take the oath, well and good. If they refuse it, Henry *must* proceed against them. Whatever they do, we have them!'

Katherine had refused the oath. She had stated that, if she was not the King's wife, as he maintained, then she was not his subject, and could not be required to take it.

'But since she has always insisted that she *is* your wife, she must know that she is laying herself open to punishment,' Anne observed to Henry as they rode at the head of their cavalcade, through lanes made festive with spring blossom, on their way to visit Elizabeth at Eltham Palace.

'They will persevere with her,' Henry promised.

The Princess's household made obeisance in unison as the King and Queen entered the nursery and found their daughter on her lady mistress's lap.

Elizabeth was seven months old now and talking already.

'Come to your father,' Henry said, scooping her out of Lady Bryan's arms and dandling her on his knee.

'Papa!' the infant crowed, pulling at his beard.

'Ouch! You've a strong hand there, sweetheart,' Henry told her. 'She is as goodly a child as I've ever seen, don't you agree, Anne?' he asked.

Anne bent down and kissed Elizabeth on her downy head. 'Indeed,' she said, feeling the familiar emptiness. All would right itself, she hoped, when her son was born. Then Elizabeth would not be a living and breathing reminder of her failure to bear a prince.

They left her with her nurses and went to inspect the nursery that was being prepared for the Prince. Well satisfied with its gilded splendour and luxurious furnishings, they proceeded to the chapel for Vespers.

As they came out, Lady Rochford approached Anne. 'Madam, I

must tell you. The Lady Mary was in chapel, and curtseyed to your Grace as you left.'

'Would that I had seen it!' Anne exclaimed, as Henry beamed. 'If I had, I would have done as much to her. Where is she?' She looked eagerly around the crowded gallery, and espied Mary's back, disappearing through the door at the far end.

'Go after her, Jane,' she said, all her ill intentions towards Mary forgotten. 'Tell her that I salute her with much affection, and crave pardon, for if I had seen her make a curtsey to me, I would have done the same to her. Tell her I desire that this may be the beginning of a friendship between us, which will be warmly embraced on my part.' Lady Rochford hastened away.

When Henry and Anne arrived in the soaring great hall and seated themselves at the high table for supper, Anne saw her stepdaughter at one of the long tables set at right angles. Not so long ago, Mary would have occupied the place of honour by the King.

She was aware of the girl watching her as the first course was served. And then, as the company began eating and there was a lull in conversation, she heard her address Lady Rochford in a carrying voice. 'It is not possible that the Queen can have sent me such a message, Her Majesty being so far from this place. You should have said it was the Lady Anne Boleyn, for I can acknowledge no other queen but my mother. I curtseyed in chapel to the Lady Anne's Maker and mine, so they are deceived, and deceive her, who tell her otherwise.'

It was humiliating and it was offensive. Henry flushed angrily, but before he could speak, Anne turned to him and in tones as ringing as Mary's declared: 'I swear I'll bring down this high spirit!'

'I will deal with her,' he muttered. 'Let be for now.'

Before they left, he took Mary aside into a closet, and kept her there for several minutes. But when he emerged, Anne could tell, from the look on his face and the tears in his eyes, that his daughter had bested him yet again.

She had a high belly now and tired easily. In three months, God willing, she would bear a son, a living image of his father. Henry fussed over her constantly. He had Archbishop Cranmer warn preachers that they must not weary her by over-long sermons in chapel. He gave her, for her delight, a peacock, and a pelican that had come all the way from a far-off country called Newfoundland. But the best gift of all was his sanctioning the translating of the Bible into English, in response to a petition from his clergy, which had been driven by the seven reformist bishops who had been appointed, thanks to Anne's good offices, since she had become queen. A reformist scholar, Miles Coverdale, was undertaking the translation, and his work was going to be dedicated to Henry and to her. Anne had hugged and kissed Henry when he told her.

She was delighted to receive from Lady Lisle, wife of the Governor of Calais, a brace of dotterels for her table, a singing linnet in a cage and an adorable little dog. Of course, Lady Lisle had daughters she no doubt hoped to place at court, and wanted to ingratiate herself, but with well-wishers thin on the ground, the gesture was heartening. The dog was the sweetest thing. It gazed up at her with soulful, enquiring eyes, and she thought of a name for it at once.

'I shall call you Little Pourquoi, because you look as if you are always asking me why!'

Heartening too was Henry's decision to punish Katherine for not taking the oath by sending her under house arrest to Kimbolton Castle, which was further from London than Buckden. Then he sent out heralds to warn all his subjects that anyone slandering his beloved Queen or his lawful heirs would be guilty of high treason, for which the penalty was death.

In the second week of July, George, now Lord Warden of the Cinque Ports, was sent on an embassy to France, leaving Anne feeling depressed. She wished he did not have to go away when her child was soon to be born and she needed him most to allay her fears, or just listen to them. Mary had gone home to Hever – not that she would be much comfort anyway. Even the antics of Little Pourquoi, or the docile loyalty of the greyhound Urian, failed to cheer Anne.

A week later, Henry broke the news that his daughter had refused the oath. When he had gone, growling about making her pay for her defiance, Anne took up her pen and wrote to Lady Shelton: 'Give her a good beating, for the cursed bastard she is.' She would see to it that Mary got her just deserts, even if Henry baulked at it.

George was soon home.

'It's been agreed that I won't go to France this year,' Henry told Anne. 'Katherine and Mary bear you no small grudge, and might in my absence make mischief.'

'Thank God,' Anne said. 'I feel much safer when you are with me.'

Henry caressed her cheek. 'It will not be long now, darling. The doctors say it is often easier the second time.'

It *was* easier – in fact it was all over within two hours. The baby came sooner than she had expected: she had not even taken to her chamber. But her pains were for nothing.

As the midwife wrapped the tiny babe in a cloth and covered his dead face, Anne lay racked with sobs. 'Why? Why?' she kept crying out. 'Other women have sons – why not me?'

Her women tried to soothe her, but when they heard that Henry was coming, they drew back nervously, warning, 'The King! The King!'

Anne twisted in the rumpled bed. She knew she must look dreadful, her face raw from weeping, her body sweaty from her travail, as yet unwashed and still clothed in her bloody shift. She pulled the sheets and counterpane around her. Little Pourquoi leapt up and snuggled next to her, as if sensing her distress.

Henry's gaze was wounded and accusing. There was no doubting that this was her fault.

'I am so sorry!' she sobbed. 'He came too early.'

'Where is he?' Henry demanded.

'Here, your Grace.' The midwife nervously handed him the shrouded bundle. Henry pulled the covering aside. 'Oh, God, my son, my little son,' he murmured brokenly, tears streaming down his face. 'Take him.' He thrust the body back into the midwife's arms, mastered himself with an effort, then bent his gaze on every soul in the room.

'You will not speak of this to anyone,' he commanded. 'If you are asked, you must say that the Queen miscarried. Do not say it was a boy.

Do you all understand?' Anne knew he would not look a fool in the eyes of Christendom.

The women nervously nodded assent.

'I will leave you to rest,' Henry said to Anne. 'See to the Queen, ladies.'

Anne lay there weeping silently. This wasn't how it was meant to be. What of her dreams of power and of the reign of virtuous women? It was all an illusion, dependent on the will of men. Because, when it came down to it, power depended only on a woman's body not letting her down.

She mended quickly, and by the end of July she was ready to accompany Henry on his annual summer hunting progress. But her spirit was crushed, for he had been cold to her since she had lost their son. It was cruel of him, for she was grieving too, for her baby, for herself, and what this tragedy might mean for her.

If she had been depressed before the birth, she was in despair now. It was hard to rise above it and be the sophisticated, witty woman with whom Henry had fallen in love. And yet she must win him again. He too had suffered a bitter disappointment, but underneath the distant exterior, his heart still beat with love for her – she must believe it.

She could not find in herself much appetite for lovemaking, but Henry returned to her bed, almost with an air of doing what he had to do. She submitted willingly, knowing that conceiving another son was the only way to keep him hers. She did not deceive herself: it was a joyless experience.

And soon she found out why. Apparently it was no secret that he was betraying her – with her own maid-of-honour, too! Joan Ashley was seventeen, a pretty girl whom Anne had thought shy, but a more apt word would be sly. With her own credit with the King lower than it had ever been, there was no shortage of people to drop hints. She had even come across Jane Rochford gossiping about the affair, and been met with an embarrassed silence. It seemed it had been going on for some time.

Rage consumed her. When Henry next came to dine, she dismissed the servants and stood with her back to the door.

'Why are you wasting your seed on that worthless little cow Joan Ashley?' she challenged him. 'You're *my* husband and you're old enough to be her grandfather!'

'You forget yourself, Anne,' Henry barked, his voice icy. 'I am your King, and you have good reason to be content with what I have done for you – which I would not do now if I were to begin again.'

'That's rich! You're the one who commits adultery, yet you have the gall to censure me!'

'Stand aside!' Henry commanded, red with anger. 'I'm dining elsewhere, where I'm sure of a welcome.'

'Go to your whore, then!' she hissed, and let him push past her. When he had gone, she collapsed, whimpering, to the floor. How had it all gone so wrong? Why had God withheld the blessing of a son? And where was the adoring servant who had so passionately courted her? How had he turned into this cruel and thoughtless man?

For three days she did not see Henry. She longed for someone to confide in, someone she could trust. George was at Dover, presiding over the warden's court, and Mary was still at Hever. She should be back any day now. She was not George, but she was loyal at heart.

That evening, there was to be a feast in the presence chamber in honour of some visiting envoys from France. Anne took her place beside Henry, who inclined his head but would not look at her. She was aware of his stern profile, mostly turned away from her towards her father and his other guests. His displeasure with her was plain for all to see. Father was frowning. He knew about the tragedy that had befallen her.

Afterwards there was dancing, and Henry rose, bowed and led her out to the floor. She did her best to dance alluringly and gracefully, knowing that all eyes were on her, but to little effect, because afterwards Henry escorted her back to her seat and took himself off to partner Joan Ashley. Watching the silly bitch with her triumphant simper, Anne trembled with anger. People were staring at her, some with pity, some smugly. She would endure it no more, she decided. When the dance was over and everyone milling around, she would slip away.

And then she saw her sister enter the hall: Mary, with a ripe swell to her belly, blooming with fruitfulness, drawing all eyes. Mary, proclaiming her condition for all the world to see, and the courtiers, even the King, staring in shock or glee . . .

Anne rose at once and went to greet her sister, putting on a smiling face, then she curtseyed to the King and hustled Mary away as quickly as she could. Hot on their heels came Father with a face like vengeance. He followed them into Anne's apartments and, before she could speak, rounded on Mary.

'Have you been whoring again, daughter?'

Mary faced up to him. 'No! I am married.'

'Married?' he repeated. 'Without my permission?'

'Or mine!' Anne chimed in. 'I am your Queen! Who is he?'

'William Stafford,' Mary said with a defiant flourish. 'I met him in Calais and again at your coronation. He has been visiting me at Hever.'

'He's been doing more than that!' Father bellowed.

'Forgive me,' Mary pleaded, 'but we love each other.'

'Stafford of the Calais garrison?' Father thundered, his pug face puce. 'A man of little status and no fortune! You could at least have contrived to marry to our family's advantage.'

'He is a dozen years younger than you,' Anne added, disgusted.

'William loves me! He was eager to marry me.' Mary was prouder than Anne had ever seen her.

'Love, bah!' Father spluttered. 'Marrying for love offends God, good order and all. It's wayward and foolish. It's bad enough neglecting to ask *our* permission, but you had not the courtesy to ask the King! What of your mother? Did you have the grace to inform her?'

Mary shook her head. The bravado had vanished. 'We paid a clerk in Tonbridge to wed us. Mother was so angry when we told her. She's written to you. That's why we had to come here.' She was weeping now.

Father was implacable. 'You just went ahead regardless of us, and the King's likely displeasure. You're the Queen's own sister! Did it never occur to you that the scandal this marriage will cause will do nothing for her reputation?'

'You did not think of me,' Anne said, near to tears herself. 'A scandal is the last thing I need at this time.'

There was the sound of footsteps outside. The door flew open and the King was announced. Henry strode in, his face dark with fury.

'Mistress Carey, the whole court is talking about you,' he snapped. 'A fine show you put on for my guests.'

Mary curtseyed, shaking, tears running down her cheeks.

'She has secretly married William Stafford of the Calais garrison,' Anne said.

'Really?' Henry replied. 'I'm surprised that one of your blood has married so cheaply. And to someone whose name is tainted by treason. I have not forgotten that this Stafford's kinsman Buckingham lost his head for plotting my ruin, or that the Staffords have supported the Princess Dowager.'

'Sir, William is loyal, and he is your Grace's loving cousin,' Mary said, finding her voice. 'He is a good man and he loves me.'

'Be that as it may, you should have asked permission before marrying him. You have scanted your respect and the obedience you owe to my lord your father here, and to your Queen. They have every reason to be angered by this misalliance.'

'Sir,' Mary pleaded, 'all the world set so little store by me. I was in bondage. My family are ashamed of me. But Master Stafford was kind, kinder than anyone has ever been – and kindness means more than lineage or standing.'

How true that was, Anne realised jealously. It was dawning on her how favourably Mary's situation compared with her own. Mary had a husband who adored her and was kind to her, whereas Henry was unfaithful and could be cruel; Mary had hopes of a child when Anne's had just been brutally dashed. Through her folly, Mary had landed the world, while she herself, who had longed and schemed and prayed for years, had yet to experience true love and the security of holding a son in her arms. Her anger burned against her sister.

'You never appreciated me,' Mary accused her. 'You always had to be the successful one, whereas I had compromised my reputation and stained the family honour, even though it was not my fault.'

Anne was aware of Henry stirring uncomfortably beside her. *Serves him right!* she thought. *Let him squirm!*

'You would do well not to speak thus to your sister,' Henry warned Mary. 'She is not at fault. What matters is this misalliance you have made. Was this child conceived in wedlock?'

Mary blushed. 'No, sir.'

'Then you'll get not a penny from me,' Father snorted. 'And I'm sure His Grace will agree that I'm justified in stopping your allowance.'

'It is your husband's duty to support you now,' Henry agreed.

'And I don't want you under my roof!' Father barked.

'But where shall we go?' Mary wailed.

'That's no concern of mine,' he replied.

'I don't want you at court,' Anne said. Scandal aside, she did not need a constant reminder of what she herself lacked. Seeing Mary with the doting Stafford would be more than she could bear. She turned to Henry. 'They deserve banishment for their offence, sir.'

Henry nodded. 'I agree. Mistress Stafford, you have brought this upon yourself through your own foolishness. You will leave court and not return until summoned.'

'No! Please!' Mary cried, but Henry had turned to leave, and Anne followed after him.

'See that she goes tonight, Father,' she said before the door closed behind her.

The autumn leaves were thick on the ground when news came from Rome that Pope Clement had died.

'The great devil is dead!' Cromwell observed, breaking it to Anne. 'They've elected a successor, Paul III. Already he has made it clear that he will not countenance what he likes to call the King's disobedience. He has threatened to put into effect a sentence of excommunication that Clement drew up but never published. His Grace, of course, intends to ignore this threat, but we must be wary. If the Bishop of Rome decides to publish the sentence and incites the Emperor to war, the King, as an excommunicate, would stand alone, and could not expect aid from other Christian nations.'

'Do you think the Bishop of Rome will carry out his threat?' Anne asked, envisaging Katherine and Mary being borne back to Whitehall in triumph, and herself . . . Oh, God, what would they do to her?

'We must not be complacent,' Cromwell said, 'but I think it may just be political bluster.'

Although Henry had supported Anne in her stand against her sister, and was gradually thawing towards her, gossip informed her that he was still dallying with Joan Ashley. It ate at her. In desperation, she determined to put an end to the affair.

Jane Rochford had taken pleasure in gossiping about it, so Jane could compensate for that by helping her. Anne had never liked her sister-in-law, and the antipathy was mutual, but that did not matter. Jane would pay for her gloating.

'I want to get rid of Joan Ashley,' Anne told her. 'I need a pretext to send her away. Maybe we could contrive an urgent summons home?'

Jane's wide eyes gleamed. Anne suspected that, lacking excitement in her own life, she enjoyed it vicariously at one remove, hence her willingness to be involved in this intrigue.

'Far better if she merited dismissal,' Jane said.

'She certainly does,' Anne agreed. 'If it could be put about that she is making herself available to all and sundry, then I would have every justification – and the King would be angry with her for sharing her favours. He will brook no rival. Jane, you know all the latest gossip. Who better to spread the word?'

Within days, the entire court was whispering about the King's mistress, and how strange it was that he was paying his addresses to one who was so promiscuous. Anne smiled inwardly. Revenge was sweet! She would give it a day or so, and then she would send the girl packing.

But that very afternoon, Jane Rochford came to her in tears of rage. 'I have been banished from the court!' she cried. 'I am to leave at once, and it's all your fault!'

'On what grounds are you banished?' Anne demanded to know.

'For spreading gossip! I've been before Master Secretary. He told me that several people had testified that I had made it all up so that you could get rid of Joan Ashley. I think I've been watched. I wish I had never helped you in your foolhardy scheme!' And, omitting her curtsey, she flounced off to the lodging she shared with George.

Good riddance, Anne thought. But she was disturbed to think that Jane thought she had been watched, because if she *had* been, then Anne herself might be under surveillance too. Jane was right. She had indeed been foolhardy.

'I'm sorry,' she hastened to say, when George came to her chamber and told her that Jane had gone home to Grimston.

'I'm not!' he grimaced. 'I'm relieved to see the back of her. She makes my life a misery with her constant barbs. I wish I'd never set eyes on her.' His steely expression softened. 'I'm more concerned about you, sister. How has the King taken this?'

'I don't know,' Anne said, chilled at the thought of Henry's reaction. 'I haven't seen him.'

'When you do, show yourself loving but remorseful. Say you acted only out of despair at the thought of losing him.'

'I will do that,' she agreed, quailing at the thought.

Henry did not come to upbraid or question her, but his displeasure was soon made manifest.

She went to visit Elizabeth at Richmond, suffering a guilty conscience, as she had not seen her daughter on her first birthday. With her went Uncle Norfolk and the Duke of Suffolk and a train of lords and ladies. She spent some time playing with the child, who was quite a babbler and full of curiosity, toddling around in her velvet skirts and beribboned bonnet, and pouncing on a long-suffering Little Pourquoi as Lady Bryan and her nursemaids stood by, ready to catch her if she fell. She regarded Anne with curiosity, reaching a pudgy hand to her face and pinching it.

'Pretty lady,' she said.

The two dukes, having bestowed the requisite praise on the Princess, were getting fidgety.

'I will not be long,' Anne said. 'The nights are drawing in now. We will leave by four o'clock.'

Norfolk then shocked her. 'Your Grace, the King has ordered us to visit the Lady Mary while we are here, and convey his greetings,' he said, in a tone that brooked no argument.

'You will not go!' Anne flared, unable to believe that Henry had done this.

'It is His Grace's command,' Suffolk told her. 'We dare not disobey.' And with that they walked out, the other lords and even some of her ladies following in their wake.

Anne stood up and shooed Elizabeth towards Lady Bryan. She was shaking, shocked by the realisation that her power was waning and that everyone knew it. Could it be that Henry, even now, was contemplating restoring Mary to the succession? If so, where would that leave her and Elizabeth?

She must do something. If only she were pregnant! But Henry had not visited her bed since she had upbraided him about Joan Ashley — and that little bitch was still at court.

As she was rowed back to Whitehall, she sat in her cabin with the curtains drawn. She would not speak to those who had betrayed her. When she reached the sanctuary of her chamber, she lay on her bed and cried hot tears of despair.

Feeling a little restored, she decided it would be politic to do as Henry wanted. If she too showed herself friendly to Mary, it might go a long way towards restoring her to his good graces. And so she wrote warmly to her stepdaughter, bidding her be of good cheer.

There was no reply. But she suspected that Henry had heard about her letter, for he began visiting her again at night. He was still distant, and stayed long enough only to do what was necessary to impregnate her, but it was enough for now. Once she was with child, he would come back to her, as he used to be, and Joan Ashley could go hang herself! And when she herself had a son, none would dare touch her.

The Admiral of France was in England on a state visit, his purpose being to promote friendly relations between the two kingdoms. Henry arranged a great banquet in his honour and invited many beautiful ladies to court to take part in the festivities. Anne was to preside, and took great care in choosing her attire. A glance in her mirror told her that she was looking strained, miserable and every one of her thirty-three years. She pinched her cheeks and compressed her lips to redden them. It was essential that she look her best beside the other ladies. She wanted to impress the Admiral, who was a great friend of the French King and very powerful in France. She needed to convince him that there was no better bride for King François's youngest son, Charles, Duke of Angoulême, than the Princess Elizabeth. François's agreement to their marriage would amount to a public recognition of her as queen, and Elizabeth as Henry's legitimate heir. And once Elizabeth was betrothed to his son, he would surely prove as powerful a friend to Anne as the Emperor had been to Katherine.

Anne was making this approach with Henry's blessing. He himself had suggested the match some time before. He had not said as much, but she'd guessed that he had been thinking forward to a time when Elizabeth was Queen of England. Marrying a younger son, who had no obligations to his country and could live here, would prevent England from becoming a mere dependent of France.

A thousand candles lit the great hall, the plate on the buffets glinting in their glow. During the banquet, the Admiral, a cultivated and rather handsome aristocrat, listened courteously to Anne's arguments. He gave nothing away. Seeing there was no more to be gained from persuasion, she asked if he had ever met Leonardo da Vinci, and he told her he had, and that the old man's beloved portrait of Monna Lisa was now hanging in King François's bathroom.

She was reminiscing about her time at the French court and watching the dancing when Henry joined them.

'My lord Admiral, I am just going to fetch your secretary and present him to the Queen,' he said. Anne watched him go, weaving between the swirling couples, and saw him suddenly stop and bow before a lady. It was Joan Ashley! Seconds later, they were dancing together. The shock made her laugh out loud.

The Admiral looked offended. 'Madam, do you laugh at me?' he asked.

Hastily she shook her head and pointed across to where the King was standing.

'He went to fetch your secretary,' she said, 'but he ran across a lady, and she has made him completely forget what he went for!' She laughed again, but the tears were welling. The Admiral looked away, embarrassed.

Mary had now been rusticating in the country for three months. George had learned that she and William had gone to stay with the Stafford family.

'I'm still furious with her,' Anne told him. 'She'd better not show her face here!'

But now here was Cromwell, showing Anne a letter from Mary in which she had begged him to intercede for her. Anne read it, then thrust it back at him in disgust.

'She does herself no favours!' she snapped. 'I have never heard a petitioner use a more defiant, unrepentant tone. How come she thinks her plight is more deserving of pity than anyone else's? Master Cromwell, she makes too many demands of you. If she is really hoping for a reconciliation with me, she is going the wrong way about it.'

She did not say how sharply Mary's words had stung. *For well I might have had a greater man of birth, but I assure you I could never have had one that loved me so well. I had rather beg my bread with him than be the greatest queen christened.* The taunt went too deep. It laid bare Mary's jealousy and underlined the bitter irony of their respective situations.

'Never again will I receive her at court,' she told Cromwell. 'It is useless to plead for her.'

'I had no intention of doing so, madam.' His smile was wry. 'I could perceive the venom in that letter. My advice to her will be to go with her husband to Calais and stay there.'

Christmas was approaching, and Anne and her ladies were sewing smocks for the poor when Henry arrived looking unusually solemn.

'You may go,' he said, and the ladies scattered.

He took the chair opposite Anne, then stood up again and, coming over to her side of the fire, went down on his haunches before her and took her hands. She was so overcome by the gesture that when he seemed to be struggling to speak, she thought he was about to say that it was all over between them. That was what had happened with Katherine.

'I know you set much store by Little Pourquoi,' he said at last. 'Anne, I'm sorry to tell you that he fell from a window within this last hour. There was nothing anyone could do to save him.'

'Oh, no!' she cried, desolate. Henry hesitated, then she felt his arms go around her, and, despite her grief over Little Pourquoi's terrible end, it was so good to feel him close and being kind to her after so long. For a precious moment she felt safe.

'No one dared tell you,' he said against her hair. 'My good niece Margaret came to me and asked if I would do it. I am very sorry. It must have been instantaneous.'

He drew back and her eyes searched his. In them she could read only pity.

Christmas was awful. Harry Percy was at court, and when they came face to face in a gallery, he threw her a look of utter contempt and walked on, not even bothering to bow. She felt as if she had been slapped.

'Cheer up, niece!' Uncle Norfolk chided her at dinner that day. 'You won't entice the King to your bed with that whey face!'

'Why don't you just go and swive yourself?' she flung back, and everyone stared. Norfolk stood up, flung down his napkin and stalked out. 'I can see why they call you the great whore!' he spat as he reached the door of her chamber.

At that very moment, the King arrived. Norfolk almost collided with him. Henry looked at the Duke and then at Anne. She waited for him to explode and censure her uncle for speaking so foully to her – he must have heard him – but he said nothing and, no doubt deciding that his mistress would be more congenial company, went away again. Anne was near to despair. Once he would have taken exception to such a gross insult to her, but not any more.

Chapter 24

1535

In the depths of January, Henry joined Anne for supper one evening. His mood seemed lighter, conciliatory.

'This will please you,' he said. 'I have appointed Cromwell Vicar General, with the power to arrange visitations to every religious house in my kingdom. Like you, I am concerned to root out abuses within my Church, and there have been too many reports of irregularities in the monasteries. Moreover, Cromwell tells me that some of the smaller houses lack the wherewithal to support themselves.'

Anne's spirits soared. 'You are reforming the monasteries?'

'I wish to evaluate their wealth and expose any shortcomings in their practices.'

'You will close any that are poor or corrupt?'

Henry hesitated. He poured himself some wine and drank deep. 'I intend, in time, to close all of them.'

'All?' She had not expected this.

'It's nothing new, Anne. Henry V was doing it a hundred years ago. Wolsey closed some minor or corrupt houses. Do you know, there were only two new foundations in England in the last century?'

'But the monasteries succour the poor. They look after the sick—'

'They are hotbeds of popery!' Henry interrupted. They're subversive and disloyal. And they grow fat on wealth that should be mine, as head of the Church. It will give me the wherewithal to buy support for my reforms – the reforms you wanted, Anne. I can sell off monastic land to those who defend my stand against Rome, and the rest can go towards replenishing my treasury. It is all but empty.' She knew it. He had squandered his father's fortune on pleasure and fruitless wars.

In many respects she approved of his plans, and his aim to stamp out popery. But what of the consequences for all the monks and nuns who would be turned out on the streets, the sick who had no one else to care for them, the beggars who would starve, but for the bounty they received at the monastery gates, and the travellers who would find no lodgings for the night? Almost as bad would be the tragic loss of houses renowned for their excellence in learning and teaching, and as repositories of knowledge and great libraries.

This was Cromwell's doing, she had no doubt. Hadn't he promised to make Henry the richest sovereign who ever reigned in England? But had he thought this scheme through? Surely there was a better way?

'I have no doubt that your Grace will do all for the best,' she said, resolving to see what transpired and what she could do to achieve a compromise.

Henry stayed with her that night. He took his pleasure briskly, and was just donning his night robe before returning to his own apartments when she caught at his hand.

'Do you think François will agree to Elizabeth's marriage?' she asked, hoping he would not see how much store she set by it.

He sighed and loosed his hand. 'I don't know, Anne. François has become a good son of the Church, stamping out heresy and free thinking. He may baulk at marrying his son to the daughter of one whose marriage has so often been called into question.'

Icy shards pierced her heart. That Henry, who had been so zealous in ensuring that everyone acknowledged her as his true Queen, should say such a thing to her! Did *he* now doubt that she was? Was he thinking of divorcing her too?

Lying there alone, she told herself that, even if he did regret marrying her, she was still safe, for Katherine's supporters would see any sign of his abandoning her as an admission that he had been wrong all along, and urge him to take Katherine back. And that she was certain Henry would never do.

It was not until February that Palmedes Gontier, secretary to the Admiral of France, asked for an audience with them both.

'It must be about Elizabeth's marriage!' Anne cried.

'If he has asked for you to be present, it must be,' Henry smiled. 'It is proper for a queen to be consulted when her daughter is to be married.'

She sat beside him on the dais in the crowded presence chamber and smiled at the advancing Gontier. He bowed and presented her with a letter from the Admiral. She devoured it, but her spirits plummeted when she saw that it contained no word of Elizabeth's betrothal.

Henry took the letter and read it, then scowled at Anne as if it were her fault. 'If you will excuse me, I will confer with my Council,' he said, and leaving her with Gontier, he strode over to his waiting lords.

Anne beckoned Gontier forward. Something had to be said. Ignoring the proposal was tantamount to rudeness on the part of King François.

She realised that the lords and courtiers in the presence chamber were watching her closely, some with ill-concealed hostility. Henry was watching her too. As the envoy drew near, she lowered her voice. 'Tell your master, sir, that this long delay in sending an answer about the proposed marriage has engendered in the King my husband many strange thoughts, for which there is great need of a remedy. I hope the King my brother does not wish me to be driven mad and utterly lost, for I find myself near to that, and in more pain and trouble than I have been since my marriage.'

Gontier flinched, obviously embarrassed by her outburst. She knew it was an unforgivable breach of diplomatic etiquette, but she did not care. She was fighting for her daughter's future and her own. 'I pray you, speak to the Admiral on my behalf,' she begged. 'I cannot speak as amply to you as I would like, for fear of where I am and of the eyes that are watching me. I cannot write, I cannot see you again, and I can no longer talk with you.'

She rose, leaving the astonished secretary staring at her, and joined Henry, who took her hand and led her out to the hall.

'I told him how eager we are for the marriage,' she said lightly.

*

For several days now, Anne, ever watchful, had seen Joan Ashley going about with a long face.

'I think, or rather, I hope, that the King has tired of her,' she said to Madge Shelton, as they sat at a table with Mary Howard and Margaret Douglas, looking through the poems Madge and her friends had collected for their book.

'He has,' Madge said. 'She was weeping about it this morning.'

'He was ever fickle!' Anne's laugh was bitter. 'To be plain, Madge, I've given up expecting him to be faithful. What I couldn't bear was the arrogance of that little bitch.'

'She's not arrogant any more.' Madge grinned.

'You are lucky having Norris for a suitor,' Margaret said. 'He's a good man. He would never be untrue.'

Anne froze. Norris was courting Madge? That could not be. He loved *her*, she knew it. But she was forbidden to him . . . and he was a man, with a man's needs. She should be glad that he was seeking happiness elsewhere. Yet that did not allay the pain of the wound she had just been dealt.

Madge was watching her curiously. Their eyes met. 'He can never be true to me,' Madge whispered. 'He loves another.'

If she had guessed, others might.

'Nonsense!' Margaret smiled at Madge. 'He told me he hoped you would marry him.'

'Well, I won't,' Madge declared. 'And if the King must take a mistress, your Grace should push in his path one who loves you and will win his sympathy for you.' Their eyes met again.

'Are you offering?' Anne asked after a long pause.

'I have taken lovers before,' Madge shrugged. 'Between the sheets, even the King is a man like other men.'

'You would do that for me?' Anne asked, deeply affected.

'You are my blood. Of course I would. We all owe you so much.'

'Are you sure you want to do this?' Anne asked. 'What of the risk?'

'There are ways to prevent pregnancy,' Madge laughed. 'A woman has to experience pleasure to conceive. I'll think of something gruesome if I find myself getting carried away!'

It felt bizarre plotting the seduction of Henry, her own husband, like this. What had she come to? But if Madge could persuade him to treat her more kindly, it might be worth it.

'It worked!' Madge whispered two days later, as she followed Anne to Mass.

Anne did not know what to feel – pleased or jealous. She should be grateful to Madge, but she couldn't help feeling wronged. Henry was probably making efforts to please her cousin. With Anne, he no longer bothered.

Two days later, though, Madge was despondent. 'He's not interested in talking, and when I mentioned you, he told me we had better things to do.'

After a week, it was over. 'I don't know how you stand it, Anne,' Madge said, sorting through the Queen's jewel box as Urian tried to nuzzle her hand. 'He's the most boring lover I've ever had. Thank God he's tired of me.'

The Lady Mary was ill again. Henry found Anne in her closet, writing letters.

'The doctors fear she might die,' he told her, looking utterly miserable and torn. 'Chapuys has urged that she be sent to her mother to be nursed, but I daren't allow it. What if she escapes abroad, as she might easily do if she were with Katherine? The Emperor might well aid her, then hold me to ransom.'

He sat down, his head in his hands. 'If Katherine was to take Mary's part, she could wage against me a war as fierce as any her mother Isabella ever waged in Spain.'

'They are rebels and traitors, deserving of death,' Anne declared, 'and while they live, they will always make trouble for you.'

'If you gave me a son, they could do nothing!' he cried.

'Heaven knows I have tried,' she flung back. 'I pray for a son daily, but I fear it is in vain. I had a dream the other night, in which God revealed to me that it will be impossible for me to conceive children while Katherine and Mary live.'

Henry looked at her with distaste. 'Sometimes I wonder if God approves of this marriage. You should look to your duty, madam, and not invent excuses.' And without another word, he got up and left her.

She could not have felt more wretched or insecure. It did not help that Father kept telling her about those who slandered her. A woman was in prison for calling her a whore and a bawd, a priest for saying she stank worse than a sow in her fornication. Worse still, a monk had been hauled before the Council for asserting that young Henry Carey was the King's son by her sister. Fortunately, the boy, who had been in her charge since Mary and William Stafford had departed for Calais, was at Hever with his grandmother, protected from the gossip.

These were the little people, their crime mere sedition. The defiance of influential persons was more threatening. Whatever Henry had said to Anne in private, in public he would not lose face. All must acknowledge that he had been right to set aside Katherine and marry her, that Elizabeth was his rightful heir, and that he was Supreme Head of the Church of England. When it came to those who had denied the oath, he was savage.

In May, the Prior of the London Charterhouse, two Carthusian priors and a monk of Syon were hung, drawn and quartered at Tyburn. Norris was there, watching, and told Anne afterwards that, far from being terrified, these monks went joyfully to their deaths. He spared her the grim details, and she could barely imagine what it had been like to be dragged on hurdles through the streets, hanged until they were half dead, then cut down to suffer the horrors of castration, disembowelling and decapitation. At least they had been unaware of their bodies being hacked into quarters, to be publicly exhibited.

'How did the people react?' she asked.

Norris winced.

'They blamed me,' she whispered. His nod was imperceptible, his eyes full of compassion. She turned away. She must not think of what Norris meant to her. If she did, she might break.

*

That week, Henry had the oath put again to Fisher and More, and again they refused to take it.

'They are traitors and deserve death,' Anne reminded him, again and again, desperate for their voices to be silenced for ever.

'They will be tried,' he told her, his expression grave. 'The law will take its course.'

'No one must challenge the legitimacy of our son,' she said.

He looked at her, his eyes widening. 'Our son?'

'Sir, I am with child!' she told him triumphantly, barely sure of it herself, but so desperate to be restored to his love and esteem that she could not contain herself.

He took her hand and kissed it. 'I thank God,' he declared. 'You must look after yourself, Anne. We dare not risk losing this one.' It was not quite the reaction she had wanted, but it signalled a new beginning, she hoped.

Luck was again with her, she told herself. She was looking daily for George's return from another embassy to France, hoping that he had managed to persuade King François to agree to Elizabeth marrying the Duke of Angoulême. But one glance at his face when he arrived at Greenwich told her that he had failed.

'How dare François slight me like this!' she seethed.

She would not let her disappointment spoil her joy in the coming child. She arranged feasts and sports and dancing, and as her mood lightened, so did Henry's. The change in him she had prayed for was dawning. And while she danced, ten Carthusian monks, having refused to acknowledge the royal supremacy, were chained, standing upright, to posts and left to die of starvation, by the King's order.

Let that serve as an example to her enemies. It was a pity Henry had not chained Fisher and More to die with them. But she would have her way. She laid on a lavish banquet for Henry at the grand house he had given her at Hanworth, twelve miles from London. The fine sweet wine of Anjou that he loved was poured in abundance, and soon he was drunk, throwing his arm about her, kissing her heartily and patting her belly in front of the company.

'There are those who would have me put away,' she murmured in his ear. 'While they live, spreading their vile sedition, this little fellow I carry will never be secure in his title.'

'Of whom do you speak, darling?' Henry asked, slurring his words.

'Bishop Fisher and Sir Thomas More! For the sake of our son, sir, I beg of you, put them to death. Silence those who have the power to destroy us!'

'It shall be done,' Henry promised. 'I can deny the mother of my son nothing.'

Two days later, Bishop Fisher was tried at Westminster Hall and condemned to suffer as a traitor. Soon afterwards, news came from Rome that Pope Paul had made Fisher a cardinal, and was sending his red hat to England.

'Afore Heaven,' Henry raged, 'he shall wear it on his shoulders, for by the time it arrives he shall not have a head to put it on!'

When three more Carthusian priors died bloodily at Tyburn, and there was public outrage at the prospect of the same sentence being meted out to the seventy-six-year-old Fisher, Henry promptly commuted it to beheading. The Bishop died on the scaffold on Tower Hill, and his head was set up on London Bridge as an example to others. On the day he suffered, Anne went to Mass, fighting unexpected feelings of guilt, and ordered her chaplains to offer prayers for the repose of his soul. She did not sleep that night.

The next day, she told herself firmly that the execution had been justified. Fisher had been a dangerous enemy. Smothering her qualms, she ordered a masque to be staged for the King's pleasure, showing God sitting in Heaven, signifying His approval of the recent executions. Henry sat there beaming, roaring with laughter as he watched himself cutting off the heads of the clergy. Was he laughing a little too loudly? Was he feeling as troubled as she was? She thought not when he told her that she ought to arrange for the masque to be repeated on the Eve of St Peter, a day on which the Pope had used to be honoured in England.

What really chilled her was being told that Fisher's head had not decayed. Some were calling it a sign of sanctity, which disturbed her even more, because if God approved of the Bishop, then assuredly He could not approve of her. She was heartily relieved therefore to hear that the head had been tipped into the Thames and lost.

The announcement that Anne was soon to bear the King a child made all the difference. No one dared slight her now, her opinions counted once more, and her patronage and favour were eagerly sought by all. When Henry's fool, in an ill-judged jest, cried, 'Anne is a ribald, the child is a bastard!' the King was so angry that Anne thought he would kill him, and the fool was obliged to go into hiding.

By late June she was unlacing her gown to accommodate the growing infant, and feeling extraordinarily well. But one morning, while watching Norris play Weston at tennis, she felt nagging twinges of pain in her lower back. When she returned to her apartments for dinner, the pain had seated itself in her womb. It came and went, and steadfastly she tried to ignore it. It was nothing. It would go away soon. But as she stood up, she felt dampness between her legs, and when she moved towards the stool chamber, she was dripping spots of blood on the floor. Soon she was bleeding quite heavily, passing clots, and the cramping pains became severe. Shaking with fear, she screamed, and her women came running.

Shortly afterwards she delivered a tiny, perfectly formed dead boy.

Henry sat by her bedside, stricken. 'Why does God deny me sons?' he cried. His sorrow was harder to bear than the anger he had not displayed.

Anne lay there, too shocked to weep. It had all been so sudden. She made a supreme effort.

'We can try again, Henry,' she said.

'How many times do we have to try?' he flung back. 'Many men I know have a whole clutch of sons. I lead a righteous life; I love God; I put away my unlawful wife, so why is that blessing withheld from me?'

'I do not know! I took care of myself, I ate sensibly, exercised carefully, rested. It just happened, and I am so sorry, so very sorry.'

'It is not your fault,' Henry conceded. 'But if it were known that you have borne me two dead sons, our enemies would say that God has cursed us, and that this is my punishment for what I have done. I dare not proclaim another failure to the world, so see that your ladies do not speak of it – on pain of my heavy displeasure.' He got up wearily, looking every one of his forty-four years. 'I will come to you when you are well.'

She reached out and caught his hand. 'Henry, *you* do not believe that God has cursed us?'

'I no longer know what to believe,' he muttered.

On the first day of July, Sir Thomas More was tried for treason in Westminster Hall and condemned to death. Six days later, he was due to mount the scaffold on Tower Hill and die by the axe.

Anne got up early to wait for news with Henry in his privy chamber. She watched him becoming more restless and agitated as the time passed. At nine, the hour appointed for the execution, he summoned his Master of the Cellar, one of his favoured opponents, for a game of dice, and they sat down to play. Anne looked on, barely concentrating.

Norris entered and bowed. 'Your Grace, Thomas More is dead.'

Henry threw down the dice. The Master of the Cellar bowed his head.

'Did he speak on the scaffold?'

'He declared that he died your Grace's good servant, but God's first.'

Henry was trembling. 'What have I done?' he asked faintly. 'There was an outcry at Fisher's death; how much louder will the outcry be now? And it won't just be in England – it will be heard all over Christendom.' Tears were streaming down his face.

'Leave us!' he commanded. Anne made to go, but he caught her wrist. 'Stay.'

When the others had left, he rounded on her in fury. 'This is because of you!' he shouted. 'The most honest man in my kingdom is dead!'

She reeled in the face of his wrath, as great tearing sobs burst forth from him. 'And you are also to blame for all the other terrible things that have happened recently in this kingdom!'

That was unfair! 'Sir, you are more bound to me than any man can be to a woman,' she countered. 'Have I not delivered you from a state of sin? Have I not been the cause of reforming the Church, to your own great profit and that of all the people?'

'You hounded me to have these good men put to death!'

'You were fierce to have them punished!' she retorted.

'Go away!' Henry roared. 'The sight of you sickens me.'

That month, the King's commissioners began visiting the monasteries and submitting their reports, which Cromwell was collating in a great book.

In private, in her chamber, Anne confided in George. 'I have concerns about this plan to close the monasteries. I'd rather see their wealth used to good purpose.'

'I think the King would see replenishing his coffers as a good purpose,' George observed. 'And I'd rather see all monks and nuns rot in Hell.' She knew that at heart he was a Lutheran, and that many thought she was too. Certainly she had become the hope of those who had secretly embraced Luther's precepts. Men like the firebrand Robert Barnes, who had fled England for fear of persecution, but had been able to return four years ago, thanks to her protection, and preach openly in London, unmolested. Henry had granted her every wish in those days. Even last year he had agreed to release a convicted heretic, and four months ago he had approved the appointment of another reputed Lutheran, Matthew Parker, as her chaplain.

'No one could say I am not a friend to true religion,' she said to George. 'I see myself as a zealous defender of Christ's Gospel. But it seems wrong to use the wealth of the monasteries to buy the support of individuals for the King's supremacy. I feel strongly that the confiscated riches should be used for educational and charitable purposes that would benefit everyone.'

'And you think the King will agree with that?'

'I'll do my best to persuade him.' It wouldn't be easy when he was barely speaking to her.

George snorted. 'Cromwell certainly won't. He would make His Grace rich, and buy himself further into his good graces.'

'Cromwell has too much power,' Anne said.

'More than you, I fear.'

'Until I get pregnant again,' she was quick to say.

'You mean there is a chance of your getting pregnant? Anne, I have seen how things stand between you and the King.'

She would not weep. 'I can make him return to me, never fear. And then Cromwell had best look to his back, for I will have my way over this!'

'Go to, sister!' George applauded.

Laying up treasure in Heaven, and hopefully with Henry, she was now spending her days doing the good deeds that would earn her salvation and increase her store with the Almighty. She gave alms weekly to the poor, with the piles of clothing she had sewn with her ladies. She provided for widows and impoverished householders, giving money for the purchase of cattle or other livestock. Braving those who shouted abuse, she visited towns and villages, sending her almoner ahead to find out from the parish authorities if there were any needy families in the district. When she arrived, she made grants of money towards their support.

She aided poor scholars, providing money for their education. She even helped Wolsey's bastard son when he returned penniless from the University of Padua. She wrote to King François and secured the release of a French humanist, Nicholas Bourbon, who had been imprisoned for heresy. When Bourbon arrived in England, she made him tutor to her nephew, Henry Carey. Bourbon could not sufficiently express his undying gratitude. 'Your Grace is one whom God Himself loves,' he told her. She wished she could believe it. For all her charities and good works, she knew she was still hated.

It was rare for Henry to visit her these days, but when he came to her chamber to tell her that he had at last persuaded King François to enter into negotiations for the marriage of Elizabeth to his son, she was overjoyed and took courage from it, assuring herself that he would not have pressed for the match if he had been planning to divorce her.

But then, relaxing with a book in her privy garden one day, with

Urian sleeping at her feet and her ladies chattering and laughing in a circle on the grass, she heard voices beyond the high box hedge behind her.

'It's the Lady Mary people look to when they consider the future.' That was Cromwell! 'The Princess Elizabeth is not yet two, and if anything should happen to the King, Mary would have a far more realistic chance of gaining and holding the throne. I've decided that it's in everyone's interests if I lend Mary my support.'

'I am gratified to hear that, Master Secretary,' she heard Chapuys reply. 'Someone should stand up for the Princess's rights. Many do not recognise the Lady's child as legitimate.'

'I'm well aware of that. I'm looking into the possibility of altering the Act of Succession with a view to naming Mary the King's heir.'

How *dare* he! This was treason! Anne leapt up, threw down the book and raced out of the garden. At the sight of her bearing down on them vengefully, both men stared in dismay, then Cromwell hurriedly bowed low and Chapuys walked away without acknowledging her.

'You are a traitor!' she accused Cromwell, shaking with fury. 'I will have your head off your shoulders! I heard what you said about supporting the Lady Mary. It's treason, as you should know, to deny my daughter's title.'

Cromwell appeared unperturbed. 'Madam, as the King's chief minister, I have to take a pragmatic view. God forfend, but should the King die, a two-year-old girl could not rule.'

'His Grace has provided that, in that event, I should be absolute mistress of the realm during Elizabeth's minority. You seem to have forgotten that.'

He regarded her dispassionately. 'And your Grace thinks that the lords will accept you as regent? Madam, you would not last a quarter of an hour, and I say that as a friend who wishes you well.'

'Is working to have my daughter dispossessed an act of friendship?' she flung at him. 'You overreach yourself, Master Secretary. The King shall hear of this!'

He shrugged. 'I think you will find that he too will take a pragmatic view. He knows I have this kingdom's interests at heart.'

408

'We shall see!' Anne cried, and left him standing there.

She found Henry in his privy chamber, rummaging through his cupboards. A pile of dog leads, tennis balls and rolled-up maps lay on the floor.

'Wait a moment, Anne,' he said. 'I'm looking for a plan of the Calais fortifications. I want to go over and inspect them soon.' He stood up at last, holding a large scroll. 'Well?'

She told him what Cromwell had said. 'He is a traitor and should be punished as such,' she demanded.

Henry sat down wearily, stroking his beard. 'He is the ablest man in my kingdom, and very useful to me. I should be loath to lose him. If he has said these things to Messire Chapuys—'

'*If?*' she interrupted. 'I heard him, as clearly as I hear you!'

'Madam!' His look silenced her. 'I am in no doubt that Master Cromwell spoke from an earnest desire to ensure the future security of this realm. After all, you have failed to bear me a son.'

'That was not my fault. And I can't believe you are turning a deaf ear to his treason.'

'Madam, you are in no position to complain. Now go, and leave me in peace. I have business to attend to.'

She fought back the tears. 'How can I give you a son when you never come to my bed?'

'I will come to you later,' Henry said, making it sound more like a threat than a promise.

He came, as he had said he would. She tried to be as alluring and welcoming as she could, wearing an almost transparent shift and lying with her long hair spread out over the pillows. He grunted a greeting, took off his robe, climbed into bed still wearing his nightshirt, and did what was necessary to get her with child without one word spoken. After he had lain beside her for a space, recovering his breath, he rose to leave. By then, she had turned away, weeping helplessly, not caring if he heard.

Suddenly she felt his hand on her heaving shoulder. 'Anne? I apologise if I was abrupt with you. It may not be your fault that our sons have died, but is it mine? Have I offended God in some way? In faith, I am so angry, so confused, and so frustrated. I am a plain man, and sometimes a rough one.' He sighed. 'I wonder what has happened to us. Where we lost each other.'

Anne turned to face him. She sat up in the bed, wiping her eyes. 'I thought you blamed me for the loss of our sons, that I had forfeited your love because of it. And when I saw that you loved others, my heart broke.' He must believe that it was her heart, not her pride, that had been wounded.

'You are still my lady,' Henry said, looking at her more tenderly than he had done in months. 'I am determined to show the world that I was right to marry you. Pray God this night's work will bear fruit. I will come to you tomorrow, and again after that, to make sure.' He was actually smiling at her.

Relief flooded through her. She still had power over him!

This new kindness between them proved to be no fleeting thing. When Henry went away on his annual progress, to the West Country this year, he took Anne with him. Her presence was important, he said, his purpose not just to get her with child.

'I am determined to see that my reforming policies are being enforced,' he told her. He would be inspecting monasteries, talking to bishops and clergymen, favouring with a visit those who supported his policies, as well as traditionalists whose goodwill he wished to retain. The aim was to rouse support for the coming closure of the religious houses. Cromwell, who was travelling separately, would be ensuring that the King's laws were being observed and valuing the assets of the monasteries he visited. Anne was to be visibly supporting Henry's policies.

He was looking forward to the progress. He liked to be seen by his subjects, to bask in his popularity, and to win more by listening to what they had to tell him and redressing their grievances. Above all, he loved the good hunting to be had in this grease season. Anne caught his mood. She was happier than she had been in months.

The great procession set off from Windsor, and she rode at Henry's side. In their wake lumbered a long train of lords, ladies, officials, servants, carts and sumpter mules bearing the rich furnishings that always accompanied the King when he was on progress.

Late in July, they arrived at Winchcombe in Gloucestershire, where they were to stay at Henry's castle of Sudeley, in the magnificent apartments built by his great-uncle, Jasper Tudor, Duke of Bedford. Anne sent George and some officers of her household to inspect Hayles Abbey, where there was a famous phial of the Holy Blood – Christ's own life blood, spilt on the Cross – which people had flocked for centuries to venerate.

'It's the blood of a duck,' George informed her on their return. 'The monks regularly renew it.'

'And they charge pilgrims to see it?' she asked, outraged. 'Tell them in my name that they must remove it from public view or face my displeasure.'

George saw that the monks obeyed, but when Henry and Anne were on their way to Tewkesbury, they were annoyed to hear from Cromwell that the phial had been put back.

'Soon they won't have four walls in which to house it,' Henry growled.

The progress continued. They stayed near Gloucester, at Painswick Manor, then moved on to Berkeley Castle, Thornbury Castle, a fine but unfinished palace confiscated from the late Duke of Buckingham, and Acton Court, where Sir Nicholas Poyntz, a reformist and friend of Cromwell and Tom Wyatt, had built a lavish new lodging, with the latest in antick decoration, especially for their visit.

Early in September, they arrived at Wulfhall, a manor house on the outskirts of Savernake Forest in Wiltshire. It was the residence of Sir John Seymour, Sheriff and Justice of the Peace for Wiltshire, whose daughter Jane was in Anne's train. She had been proudly telling the other maids about her family seat, which was nowhere near as grand as she had given them to believe.

What Anne saw before her was a substantial timbered manor house. They rode into a cobbled courtyard, where Sir John and his lady were waiting, their strapping sons and pale-faced daughters drawn up in a line behind them, all bowing and curtseying. Henry greeted his host affably, and kissed the hand of Lady Seymour. Then, when Jane had been embraced by her parents, the King and Anne were shown by their effusive host to the comfortable lodgings that had been prepared for them. On the way, Sir John took great pleasure in pointing out the impressive long gallery he had had built, and the tapestry-hung family chapel.

It had been a long ride, so Anne dismissed her ladies and lay down on her bed to rest. Presently Henry joined her, and soon they were making love, feeling the warm September breeze drifting through the open window and caressing their entwined bodies.

Afterwards Henry poured some of the wine that Sir John had thoughtfully left for them.

'He's an old rogue,' he said. 'A capable administrator, and something of a diplomat, but a scoundrel with the ladies.'

'What? He must be at least sixty!' Anne sat up in the bed and took the goblet from Henry.

'He's an old Priapus! You met his son, Edward – the tall, serious one, not that buffoon, Thomas, or the rustic, Henry. Edward's been at court for years, ever since he was my page. He was young when his father found him a bride. She bore him two sons, and then I heard that she'd been packed off to a convent. She died last year and Edward married again. When I gave my permission, he told me that his father had seduced his wife and had probably sired her sons too.'

'My God!' Anne exclaimed.

'He has disinherited them now, and do you blame him? Did you not notice the frostiness between Sir John and Edward Seymour?'

'I didn't. I was more interested to meet Lady Seymour, because my mother served with her in the Duchess of Norfolk's household when they were girls. The poet Skelton dedicated verses to them both.'

'My old tutor,' Henry said. 'I know one of those poems: "To Mistress Margery Wentworth". The poor lady has had a lot to put up with.'

'And yet she seems cheerful enough. How awful for her, having her husband dally with their son's wife – and probably under her very roof.'

'We will not mention it. It's best forgotten.'

'It doesn't seem fair,' Anne pondered.

'What doesn't?' Henry stroked her hair.

'If Lady Seymour had fornicated with her daughter's husband, all hell would have been let loose. But let a man commit incest, and he gets away with it.'

'There will be a greater reckoning, Anne. God, who knows all, will judge him.'

'I rather think an earthly power would have judged Lady Margery – and harshly.'

'That is because a wife must not compromise the issue she bears. Her husband must be sure it is his, or all the laws of inheritance will be in jeopardy.'

Anne sat up. 'True. But I think Sir John should have been called to account.'

'No doubt he has – by his wife!'

Anne pointed to the great silver-bound ivory hunting horn resting on brackets on the wall of the Broad Chamber, where they were having an abundant and delicious dinner, all prepared under the supervision of Lady Seymour.

'That's an impressive horn,' she said.

'It's been in our family for generations, your Grace,' Sir John told her proudly. 'We Seymours are hereditary rangers of Savernake Forest, and that is the symbol of our office.'

'There's good hunting to be had hereabouts,' Henry beamed, helping himself to another custard tart. 'These are excellent, Lady Margery.'

'We're in for a good season, sir,' their host said. 'We'll ride out tomorrow and show your Grace some lively sport. But I fear that's all that's lively in these parts. This year's harvest has been ruined due to the bad weather.'

'So I heard,' Henry replied, his good mood wavering. Anne knew that the common people blamed him – and her, naturally – for the rains and the poor harvest, seeing them as a sign of God's displeasure with them both. There were still murmurs of disapproval about the executions that had taken place earlier in the year.

Sir John turned to Anne. 'Your Grace, I trust that Jane is giving satisfaction.'

Anne smiled at Jane, who was sitting demurely further along the table and gave a faint smile in return. 'I have no complaints,' she said. *Except that she never says anything but what she has to for courtesy's sake, and that I have a strong feeling that she doesn't like me, and I don't really like her much either.*

'She is a good girl,' Lady Margery said.

'You have a fine family,' Henry told her, looking wistful.

'Ten I've borne, sir, and buried four, God rest them. We count ourselves lucky.'

'Oh, to be a country gentleman and have a houseful of children and a good table like this!' Henry mused. It pleased him to entertain such fancies.

When did she first notice that Henry was paying too much attention to Jane Seymour? Was it when she saw them standing together in the garden, Henry looking down at Jane as she pointed out the various plants in the herb bed she had made? Or was it when Henry leaned over Jane's chair on the third evening of their visit and praised her needlework? She had looked up and given him a rare smile.

These incidents could have meant nothing, but when they arrived in Winchester, Anne noticed that Henry seemed to be in Jane's vicinity more and more – and that Jane seemed to have acquired a new confidence.

She decided to ignore her suspicions, and made an effort to be merry and enjoy the daily hawking expeditions that had been arranged. She came to love Winchester, as Henry did. He was fascinated by King Arthur's Round Table, which hung in the great hall of the castle. Sometimes Anne thought he fancied himself as the reincarnation of the hero King.

In the evenings, they feasted, and afterwards Anne's ladies and some of the King's gentlemen gathered in her chamber to play cards or make music. It hurt her to watch Madge flirting with Norris, yet she was pleased to see that Norris was not responding, possibly out of consideration for her presence, or that of Nan Saville, who was seated on his other side. One evening, she sent for Mark Smeaton, who was in Henry's train, to play the virginals for them. George insisted on accompanying him on the lute, and Anne watched them covertly, relieved to detect no sign that they were anything other than friends. But Smeaton kept throwing her bold glances that made her feel uncomfortable. In the end she dismissed him, saying that it was late and the music would disturb the King in his chamber below. She would not call on Smeaton again, she resolved.

They were still making the most of the good hunting that Hampshire had to offer, and were following the beaters one day when Cromwell arrived, his clothes mud-stained, his horse lathered.

'Your Grace, I must speak with you urgently. Tunis has fallen to the Emperor, and the Turks have lost a great naval base.' He looked unusually perturbed. 'Effectively they've been crushed, for this will halt their encroachment upon the eastern reaches of the Empire.'

The holiday mood melted away. Anne began to tremble. Henry's face drained of colour. 'That leaves Charles free to make war on England, if he chooses,' he said hoarsely, after a long pause.

'Indeed it does. Does your Grace want me to look into the state of the kingdom's defences?' Cromwell asked.

Henry nodded. 'I've inspected many myself, although Dover may need reinforcing. Yes, get surveyors out.'

He could not sleep that night. He lay restlessly, turning this way and that.

'Can't you get comfortable?' Anne asked.

'No. I have too much on my mind.' He got up, lit the candle and used the stool chamber in the corner of the room. Then he sat down heavily on the bed, rubbing his leg. Of late, an old wound from a fall from his horse years before had started to give him pain. 'I doubt that Charles would make war now on Katherine's behalf, for he must know she is always ailing, but he might decide to enforce what he sees as Mary's rights.'

'If you had proceeded against them both when they defied you, you would not be suffering this anxiety,' Anne said.

415

'If I had done as you urged me, I'd have had Charles and his army on my doorstep long ere this.' He sighed. 'All we can do now is wait and see what he will do – and pray that the Turks find some means of fighting back, although, God knows, I never thought I'd hear myself saying that.'

By the time they reached the Vyne, the fine residence of the King's chamberlain, Lord Sandys, Anne had begun to fear that Henry had again distanced himself from her. Since receiving the news about Tunis, he had been preoccupied and sometimes abrupt, and for the last two nights he had not come to her. He must be distracted by the very real prospect of war, a war that might lose him his throne. God knew, it struck terror into her too. But could there be a reason closer to home, in the person of quiet Mistress Seymour?

Soon, though, it might not matter! She was cherishing the secret hope that she was with child, waiting until she was absolutely sure before she told Henry. If only God would look kindly on her this time!

She prayed alone in the Vyne's chapel for the great blessing of a son. The room was gloomy, the windows above the altar shrouded in canvas sheeting. Lord Sandys, apologising profusely, had said that they were being repaired, but the work had taken longer than promised. But if any glaziers had been working in the chapel, there was no trace of them now, no tools, nothing. Curious, Anne entered the sanctuary and lifted the canvas – and there, in all the glory of their jewelled colours, were exquisite stained-glass portraits of a young Henry and Katherine. No wonder Sandys had hidden them – and no wonder he had no intention of destroying them, for they were very fine indeed.

Should she tell Henry? The possession of that glass could be seen as evidence of disloyalty, and yet she knew Sandys to be wholeheartedly the King's man. No, she would hold her peace and let him keep this great treasure.

The next day, as they were preparing to mount their horses for the chase, Henry beckoned George over.

'Lord Rochford,' he said, very stern, 'you should look to your wife.'

416

George grimaced. 'What has she done now, sir?'

'I've just been informed that, when the Lady Mary lately left Greenwich, a great crowd of women – unknown to their husbands, I have no doubt – were waiting for her, weeping and crying that she was their true Princess, notwithstanding my laws to the contrary. Some were poor women, some the wives of citizens and a few were of gentle birth. One, my lord, was your wife.'

'God's blood!' George swore, shaking his head. 'She is a born troublemaker.'

'Certainly she is in trouble now,' Henry told him. 'She is among the chief offenders, for she persists in her opinions, and to teach her the error of her ways I have sent her to the Tower. Your aunt, Lady William Howard, is there too.'

George winced. 'I can only apologise for my wife's conduct. Your Grace knows that ours has been a miserable marriage. We see as little of each other as we can; she has lived at Grimston since your Grace banished her. Had it been otherwise, I would have curbed her treacherous folly.'

'She should have stayed there!' Henry's eyes narrowed. 'It seems strange to me that your wife should support the Lady Mary.'

'It is not so strange when your Grace considers that her father, Lord Morley, loved the Lady Mary from her childhood, and that Jane herself was brought up at court in the household of the Princess Dowager. She always held the Lady Mary in great esteem.'

'She hates our family,' Anne told Henry, 'but she has never until now been disloyal.'

'I think there is a reason for this protest,' George explained. 'Lord Morley once served your Grace's grandmother, the Lady Margaret Beaufort. He was a great friend of her confessor, the late Bishop Fisher. I think it must have been the Bishop's execution that turned Jane.'

'That may be so,' Henry said, severe, 'but I am charging you to ensure me of her good behaviour in future. Do that, my lord, and you shall see her released.'

'I will stand surety for her,' George promised, his tone implying that it would be the most unwelcome task in the world.

At last! At last! The thing she had prayed for, which might save her and render her invincible, had come about.

'I am with child,' Anne murmured to Henry as they came from Mass on the first Sunday of December.

'Truly? God be praised! It is the answer to all our prayers.' He seized her hand and raised it to his lips in full view of the courtiers. Anne smiled at them in triumph, ignoring the thinly veiled hostility in many faces. Soon they would have cause to regret their enmity.

She was horribly sick with this pregnancy. Henry was all solicitude in public, sending for delicacies to tempt her, urging her to rest, concocting remedies to soothe her nausea. Outwardly he did everything a concerned husband should do, but she had a strong sense that he shrank from her in private.

Looking out of her window one day, she saw Jane Seymour surrounded by a small crowd of people. Sir Francis Bryan and Sir Nicholas Carew were there, talking animatedly with Jane's brothers, Edward and Thomas, who seemed rapidly to have risen high in the King's favour of late. And with them, to her surprise, was Chapuys.

The sight filled her with a sense of foreboding. It was disconcerting to see these men making so much of plain little Jane.

And now Henry came into view, wrapped in furs against the cold, his entourage at a respectful distance. As if on cue, Jane's admirers bowed and dispersed. Anne watched as she curtseyed and Henry raised her, took her hand and kissed it fervently. And then, to her surprise, Jane drew it away, said something, curtseyed again, and hastened back towards the palace, leaving him standing there looking utterly discountenanced.

It was true: he was chasing Jane. And she, the sly bitch, was playing a clever game, one that Anne herself had played in her time. For, once denied something he wanted, Henry would move Heaven and earth to have it.

Anne had to sit down, she felt so faint. She must think of the child. She would not reproach Henry. Jane was powerless while she, Anne, carried the heir to England in her womb. By the time this babe arrived,

Jane Seymour would probably be a distant memory, a passing irritation, no more.

What was more worrying was the possibility of the Emperor bearing down vengefully on England.

'I cannot tell you how it terrifies me to think that, if we are invaded, our children might be excluded from the throne for the sake of the Lady Mary,' she told Henry when he came to pay the daily duty visit he felt due to his gravid wife. 'Because, if the Emperor has his way, that is what will happen.'

'You must stop worrying, Anne,' Henry comforted her. 'If he invades these shores, we will be ready for him.' His bravado sounded a little forced.

'Sir!' – and she was vehement, desperate – 'The Lady Mary will *never* cease to trouble us. Her defiance of your just laws has only given courage to our enemies. I pray you, let the law take its course with her! It's the only way to avert war. What profit can Charles gain when there is no one to fight for? He needs our trade and our friendship.'

Henry's solicitous expression had turned into a scowl. 'You are asking me to send my own daughter to the scaffold.'

'She is a traitor, and a danger to you. While she lives, our son will never be safe!'

He was looking at her with distaste. 'Maybe my *threatening* to have her executed would serve as a sufficiently effective warning to the Emperor.'

She said nothing. It was enough for now, and as a strategy it might work. She would bide her time until her son was born.

But then Henry spoke again. 'You're right. I am resolved. It shall be done.'

The next day, he visited her before dinner.

'I have just come from the Privy Council,' he told her. 'I declared to them that I would no longer remain in the trouble, fear and suspicion that Katherine and Mary are causing. I said the next Parliament must release me by passing Acts of Attainder against them or, by God, I will not wait any longer to make an end of them myself!'

'What did they say?'

'They looked shocked, but I told them it was nothing to cry or make wry faces about. I said that, even if I lose my crown for it, I would do what I have set out to do.'

Would he? Still she wondered.

'It was well done, Henry,' she congratulated him. 'It is the only way to secure the future of our children.'

'Yes, but, by God, at what a price!' he cried. Already he was wavering.

Later she sent for George and told him what Henry had threatened.

'Even if he weakens now, when I have a son, he will not deny me. But it is now that I worry about. I fear that my enemies are poised to destroy me. Already they pay court to that wench Seymour.'

'They cannot touch you if you bear the King a son,' George reassured her.

'No, but what if God denies me that blessing?'

'Pray that He will grant it.'

Anne bit her lip. 'I cannot help fearing that while Katherine lives, I will never bear a living son. And even if I did, there would always be those to call it bastard. If only I could be the true *and* undisputed Queen!'

George said nothing. He just sat there, pensive.

'Katherine is my death and I am hers,' she said. 'I will take good care that she shall not laugh at me after I die.'

'And how do you mean to do that?' he asked.

'I will think of something.'

He looked at her sceptically. He knew her too well. Of all the things people called her, they were unjust in naming her 'murderess'. She did not have it in her.

And then it seemed that God Himself intervened. Katherine, Henry was informed, had fallen seriously ill. It seemed like the answer to all Anne's prayers. Her son might be indisputably legitimate.

But the next report informed them that Katherine had rallied.

'I beg of you,' Anne said to Henry, desperate, 'put an end to her and her daughter! For our child's sake!'

Henry rounded on her. 'Such sentiments do not become a woman.' His tone was scathing.

'You will never know security until you are freed from these traitors!' she cried. 'I will never be satisfied until they are dead.'

'Then you will be satisfied soon, at least in part. Reading this report, I suspect I need do nothing to hasten Katherine's end. Peace be, Anne. Let Nature take its course.'

Chapter 25

1536

'Chapuys wants to see me,' Henry told Anne. It was a week into the new year, and mercifully the nausea of early pregnancy was abating. And Chapuys might be bringing the news she needed to hear, having just returned from Kimbolton. Believing that Katherine was dying, Henry had at last permitted him to go to her.

'It cannot do any harm now,' he had said.

Anne took her place beside Henry in the presence chamber, which was packed with courtiers anticipating a drama. Father was there, and George, eager to hear that she was now the undoubted Queen of England.

Chapuys was announced. He came wearing unrelieved black, his face grey and solemn.

'Your Majesty,' he said, rising from his bow, 'I have great sorrow in telling you that the Queen is dead.'

The Angel Gabriel had hardly brought better news. 'Now I am indeed a queen,' Anne declared.

'God be praised that we are free from all suspicion of war!' Henry said jubilantly.

Chapuys threw him a fleeting, withering look. 'I bring you this, her last letter.' He handed over a folded paper sealed with the arms of England and Spain. Henry broke the seal and read, with all eyes upon him. Suddenly he was very still, and Anne saw a tear trickle down his cheek. But he recovered himself. 'God rest the Princess Dowager,' he said, crossing himself.

Anne heard her father muttering that it was a pity the Lady Mary did not keep company with her mother.

Afterwards, when she was resting in her chamber, hardly able to believe that her great rival was finally no more, George came to see her.

'It has fallen out the way you wanted it,' he observed. 'You should be pleased.'

'I cannot thank God sufficiently,' she said. 'If we needed proof that He smiles on us, this is it.'

'Sometimes He needs a little assistance in working His will,' George observed.

'What do you mean?' she asked sharply, sitting up to face him.

'He helps those who help themselves.'

Horror gripped her. 'Brother, what are you trying to say to me?'

'I think you know, Anne.' He smiled at her. 'A few well-chosen herbs . . . But never fear, all is well now. And she would have died anyway. We could not risk her living until your son is born.'

She was in turmoil. That George, her beloved George, should have done this terrible thing – and for her! And worse that, out of her own mouth, she had unwittingly said the words that had driven him to it. Yes, she had wanted Katherine dead – but by the just process of the law, not by the hand of a murderer. For that was what he was now, her brother – a murderer. God had had no part in this at all.

'I did not ask it!' she hissed. 'It was not done in my name! How could you? Now we will all be cursed. How can God smile on me now?'

Breaking down, blinded by tears, she stumbled from the bed and fled to the little oratory that led off her chamber. Ignoring George's pleas to listen to him, she locked the door.

'Go away!' she cried. 'You have done me an evil that can never be mended.' And she slid to her knees, weeping copiously. God would surely punish her for this, even though she had not intended it. Her son, if it was a son, was cursed. And if he was born dead, like the others, there was little hope for her. Henry would get rid of her as he had Katherine, and her enemies would waste no time in finding him another wife. He was highly suggestible, as she well knew, and – she must face it – his passion for her had died. She realised suddenly that, while

Katherine had lived, he would not have contemplated abandoning her. It would have been tantamount to admitting that he had been wrong to marry her, and that Katherine was his true wife. But with the Princess Dowager dead, all that stood between Anne and disaster was her unborn child.

She had calmed down by the time Henry joined her for supper that evening, but she was still in shock about what George had done, and Henry noticed.

'Why so serious?' he chided. 'You should be rejoicing tonight. I've ordered my cellarer to bring a good Burgundy to celebrate.' She realised he had not donned black.

She collected herself. 'I can't stop worrying that the Emperor might invade on Mary's behalf.'

'Don't fret. I spoke to Chapuys before Vespers. I told him I wanted Charles to withdraw his support from Mary and get the Papal judgement revoked. He said he didn't think such things would be possible, but I said I was confident that Mary can be brought to submission now that her mother is dead, and that I hoped the Emperor would be willing to offer friendship now that the real cause of our enmity no longer exists. I gathered from Chapuys's demeanour that he knows Charles would prefer us to be allies. His merchants are suffering as ours are. So be of good cheer.'

She tried to smile. She could never tell Henry the truth. How could she condemn George to the dreadful death that had been meted out to Richard Rouse? And he being her brother, people would point the finger at her as his accomplice, or even the begetter of his crime. They thought the worst of her anyway, so few would doubt it. They would be baying for her blood.

Thinking of Rouse brought to mind the attempt to poison Bishop Fisher. Had George been behind that after all? She dared not ask him, for she did not want to know.

No, silence was imperative. She must bear this burden alone.

Henry sent for the Princess Elizabeth to be brought to Greenwich, and the next morning he carried her triumphantly to Mass with the trumpets sounding a fanfare and the child – she was two and a half now – sitting solemnly in his arms. The message was clear to all: she was his undoubted heir. She sat between her parents, very well behaved, a cushion on her chair so that she might see over the edge of the pew. Already, Anne noticed, her daughter knew when to make the responses in the service.

Anne spent the rest of the morning playing with Elizabeth, getting to know and like her better, this little stranger whom she had hardly seen. She was extraordinary, with her quicksilver wits and eternal curiosity; she spoke as well as a four-year-old and could read all the letters on the horn book she wore at her girdle. She was so self-contained, so poised, so much her own mistress already, that Anne began to feel less guilty about not loving her enough. Elizabeth did not need her. Lady Bryan was, clearly, far more important to the child. What mattered was that Anne did her best for her and defended her rights. And soon she could take pleasure in preparing for Elizabeth's marriage to the Duke of Angoulême.

In the afternoon, Henry arrived in the hall where Anne and her ladies were dancing. He was dressed defiantly, from head to foot, in yellow, the colour of joy, hope and renewal, with a white feather in his cap, and brought in his wake a company of gentlemen.

'Ladies, let us celebrate England's liberation from the threat of war!' he cried, and took Anne by the hand. She danced as she had not danced in a long time, the other couples swirling around her as he led her in measure after measure. If she gave herself up to pleasure, she might forget the dreadful secret that overshadowed her.

After an hour, Henry departed for his apartments, urging everyone to carry on with the revelry. Minutes later, he reappeared with Elizabeth in his arms, and proudly showed her off to everyone present, with the gentlemen kissing the tiny imperious hand and the ladies cooing at her. Anne looked on, gratified and relieved that Henry had chosen to emphasise Elizabeth's importance. Following his example, she herself donned yellow for the banquet he hosted that evening, and showed the world a triumphant face, but later, when her ladies were preparing her for bed, her fears returned.

'Is anything the matter, madam?' Madge ventured, looking concerned.

'Is your Grace feeling unwell?' Margaret asked, in her pretty Scots accent.

'It's not that,' Anne replied. 'I keep thinking that, throughout Christendom, most people will now regard His Grace as a widower. And if I do not bear a son, I am afraid they may do with me as they did with the Princess Dowager.'

'Nonsense!' Margaret exclaimed. 'You only had to see how proud of you the King looked today, and how he favours the Princess, to know that there is no danger of that.'

'But if this child is a girl, or . . .' She could not voice it.

'His Grace loves you,' Madge assured her.

'He pursues Jane Seymour,' Anne said.

There was a silence. 'I know by your faces that it is true,' she told them. 'But as long as he respects me as the mother of his heir, and does not publicly slight me, I am content.'

In the second week in January, Henry came to Anne's chamber after supper and sent her attendants away.

'I've received the report of the chandler who examined the Princess Dowager's body,' he said, his face grave. 'I wanted to talk to you in confidence.'

Anne's heart began thudding against her chest. The child must not be affrighted. She had to calm down.

'Why?' she asked, trying not to sound as if it mattered much.

'Because I'm concerned, and Chapuys is asking questions,' Henry said. 'They found all the internal organs sound except the heart. It had a black growth, hideous to behold. The chandler washed it, but it did not change colour, and it was all black inside. I don't know what to think, Anne, but I'm doing my best to keep the report secret. Already people are saying that Katherine was murdered. They're even accusing me of sending a messenger to hold to her lips a poisoned gold cup. Chapuys is very suspicious.'

'No doubt some hold me responsible,' she said, inwardly shuddering to think how close Henry had come to guessing the truth. He might yet guess it, she thought, the hairs on her neck prickling with fear.

'I didn't like to tell you,' Henry admitted. 'Some blame you and your family. They say you had the most to gain. Do not heed them, Anne – they are ignorant. But I came to warn you what is being said, so that you won't heed any gossip. We have to think of the child.'

She did not like the way he was looking at her, as if he was remembering all the times she had urged him to proceed against Katherine, and wondering if the gossips were right.

That month, the Lady Mary fell dangerously ill at Hunsdon. She had taken the news of her mother's death grievously, and was in a desperately sad condition.

It was time, Anne felt, to give lie to rumour and extend the olive branch. Hate Mary as she did, she could yet feel pity for a girl who had lost a beloved mother, and now that Katherine was no more, Mary might feel able to recognise her as queen.

She sent a message asking Lady Shelton to tell Mary that, if she would obey her father like a good girl, she, Anne, would be the best friend in the world to her and, like another mother, would try to obtain for her all that she wanted. And if she would come to court, she would be exempt from carrying the Queen's train and would always walk by her side, as an equal. She couldn't have offered more.

Mary's reply was like a slap in the face. To comply with Anne's terms would conflict with her honour and conscience.

Well, she had had her chance. Infuriated, Anne informed Lady Shelton that her pleasure was that she attempt no more to make the Lady Mary obey the King's Grace. 'What I have done,' she wrote, 'has been more for charity than because the King or I care what course she takes. When I have a son, as soon I look to have, I know what will come to her. Remembering the word of God, that we should do good to our enemies, I have wished to give her warning before then, because I know the King will not value her repentance, or the cessation of her madness and unnatural obstinacy, when she no longer has power to choose. Lady Shelton, I beseech you, do not trouble yourself to turn her from any of her wilful ways, for to me she can do neither good nor ill.'

She entrusted the letter to a messenger and went to lie down. The effort of dealing with her stepdaughter had exhausted her.

She was awakened by Urian barking and the acrid smell of burning. The Turkey rug in front of the hearth was afire. She leapt up and ran into the outer chamber, yelling for help. Her grooms and ushers came running, and smothered the flames before they could spread.

No harm had been done. The floor had been scorched, nothing more, and the room needed a thorough airing. She sat in her presence chamber, cuddling the dog, shuddering at the thought of what might have befallen her. She could not get out of her head one of the seditious prophecies that had been reported to the Council: 'When the Tower is white, and another place green, then shall be burned two or three bishops and a queen.' It was a prediction that had been openly – and hopefully – recited by her detractors, and now it had so nearly come true. She was badly shaken. It had been Katherine who had been meant to suffer martyrdom, not herself. She remembered that other prophecy, which had accompanied the horrible drawing of herself with her head cut off. It was frightening to think that there were those who sought her death.

A few days later, she received another nasty jolt. Uncle Norfolk came to her – a rare occurrence these days, for they did not speak to each other – and, in as gentle a manner as that brusque martinet was capable of, informed her that the King had taken a fall in the lists. 'He fell so heavily that everyone thought it a miracle he was not killed, but mercifully he sustained no injury. Even so, madam, he gave us all a fright, for those of us who saw it thought his fall would prove fatal.'

Again she found herself trembling, and even Norfolk looked concerned.

'Niece, are you all right?' he barked.

'Yes, Uncle. I am just so relieved. It is dreadful to think of what might have happened.' For an instant she had glimpsed the fearful prospect of a future without Henry there to protect her from a hostile world; of herself and Elizabeth cast adrift, swept up in the maelstrom of civil war, and worse . . .

'I must go to the King,' she said, standing up on legs that threatened to buckle beneath her.

'There's no need,' Norfolk said. 'He doesn't want a fuss. He's quite cheerful and is being divested of his armour right now. Then he is going in to dinner.'

'I thank God to hear it,' Anne replied, calmer now, the spectre of a sudden violent widowhood receding.

Henry had decided that Katherine should be buried in Peterborough Abbey with all the honours due to her as Princess Dowager of Wales. He spared no effort to afford her a magnificent state funeral, at which a great train of ladies was to follow the coffin, and provided black cloth for their apparel.

Chapuys suggested that it would well become his greatness to rear a stately monument to her memory, at which he declared that he would build Katherine one of the goodliest monuments in Christendom. Now that she was dead, he could afford to be generous, and gave the command for a tomb and effigy to be made. But he confiscated all Katherine's personal effects to meet her funeral expenses.

'I've ordered a day of solemn obsequies,' he told Anne. 'I and all my servants will attend, wearing mourning. It is fitting that I pay tribute to the memory of my sister-in-law.' It was a sentiment with which she could fully agree.

On the morning of the funeral, Anne had an impulse to accompany Henry to the obsequies. It would give her credit in the eyes of the Imperialists and smooth the path to friendship with the Emperor. She had her ladies dress her in black, but when she arrived at the King's apartments, the presence chamber was deserted. The guards saluted her as she walked through to the privy chamber. Not a gentleman to be seen. They must all be in chapel already. Then she heard a woman giggle in a nearby closet, the one Henry used as a study. With every sense on high alert, Anne strode over and opened the door. There was her husband, in mourning attire, with Jane Seymour on his knee, his hand on her breast.

Of all the shocks she had received lately, this was the worst. It was one thing to know he was being unfaithful, another entirely to catch him in the act.

'How could you?' she screamed, almost hysterical, all her worst fears coming to the fore. Jane was herself, nine years before, and she, by some diabolical alchemy, was in Katherine's place. Fortune's wheel had turned completely.

Henry pushed Jane, none too gently, off his knee and leapt up.

'Go,' he said to her, and she scuttled away, smirking at Anne, who would have smacked her had she not disappeared so quickly.

'Darling, I am sorry,' Henry said, spreading his hands helplessly.

Anne was crying uncontrollably now. 'Have you any idea how you have hurt me?' she sobbed. 'The love I bear you is greater than Katherine's ever was, and my heart breaks when I see that you love another.'

He had the grace to look abashed. 'It meant nothing,' he said.

'Nothing? I saw you with my own eyes.' Suddenly she felt a cramping pain in her womb. Her hands flew to her belly, as if to protect the child.

Henry looked alarmed. 'What is it?'

The pain had ceased. 'It is the distress you have caused me!' she cried.

'Just be at peace, sweetheart, and all will go well with you,' he soothed. 'Think of our son.'

'It's a pity you didn't!' she flung back, and left him standing there, open-mouthed.

No sooner had she reached her apartments than the pain came again.

Henry loomed over her. In his face she could read bitter disappointment and grief.

'A boy!' he wept. 'A stillborn foetus of fifteen weeks' growth, they tell me. This will be the greatest discomfort to all my realm.' He was in agony.

'I was in peril of my life,' Anne murmured, remembering the pain and the blood. *I have miscarried of my saviour*, she thought. Never had she felt such extreme misery.

'And I have lost my boy!' Henry wailed.

'It was because of your unkindness!' she burst out. 'You have no one to blame but yourself, for it was caused by my distress of mind over that wench Seymour.'

Henry stood up. 'I will have no more boys by you,' he said icily.

'What do you mean?' she cried.

His look silenced her. 'I see clearly that God does not mean to give me male children. I do not wish to discuss it now. I will speak to you when you are up.' And he left, glowering, looking very ill-done-by.

His words had struck fear into her, and it took all her courage to smile at her weeping ladies. 'It is for the best,' she told them, 'because I will be the sooner with child again, and the son I will bear shall not be doubtful like this one, which was conceived during the life of the Princess Dowager.' Nan Saville took her hand and squeezed it.

For two days she lay there brooding, wishing that Henry would come to her, terrified lest she had lost him for good. When she finally rose from her bed and looked in her mirror, she was appalled to see a thin, drawn, pinched old woman looking back at her. She was thirty-five, no longer the captivating young maiden who had ensnared a king – and never would be again.

Many times she repented of her hasty words of reproach. She was in great fear, for Henry might now consider her as barren of sons as Katherine had been. Was he even now looking for a pretext to have their marriage annulled and their daughter declared a bastard? She did not have Katherine's powerful friends – she had not very many friends at all – so there would be few to champion her cause. Without Henry, she would be an object of derision, calumny and hatred; some would want her blood.

Early in February, she was informed that the King had gone to London for the Shrovetide celebrations and to attend Parliament.

He left her behind. It proved that he was still angry with her. She wept when she remembered the time when he had been unwilling to leave her for an hour. Her only consolation – if it could be called that – was that he had been unable to take that bitch Seymour with him. With the Queen's household remaining at Greenwich, he had been obliged, for propriety's sake, to leave Jane there too. She was skulking about, keeping out of Anne's way.

Anne's only companions were her ladies, who could talk of nothing, it seemed, but Madge's betrothal and forthcoming wedding. For Norris had succumbed to her blandishments and asked her to marry him. Their families approved, and Madge, who seemed to have forgotten her reservations, was luminous with happiness. Anne felt like screaming. Norris did not love Madge. He loved her. It was in his eyes every time he spoke to her. Jealousy was like a sharp knife piercing her vitals.

Every day she mourned her losses: her baby, Henry's love, and Norris. Security and happiness had been almost within her grasp. Now she lived with fear and an overwhelming sense of failure.

Messengers bearing packages and letters kept arriving from York Place.

'They're for Jane,' Madge whispered. Anne's jealousy was a torment. She watched Jane continually, and lashed out at her for the slightest dereliction of duty – but it did not wipe the complacent smile off Jane's face. One day the woman was brazen enough to wear a new jewelled locket. Guessing who had sent it, Anne confronted her.

'That's a costly piece. Let me see it,' she demanded.

Jane stared at her mutinously, clearly unwilling, whereupon Anne lost her temper and ripped the locket from Jane's neck with such force that the chain cut into her hand. With blood welling in drops from the wound, she prised the locket open with unsteady fingers, to find inside a miniature portrait of Henry. Tears blurred her eyes.

She thrust the locket back into Jane's hands. 'Take it, and him! You are welcome to him!'

The relief was indescribable when George arrived to tell her that Parliament had assigned her two royal manors.

'Then I am not entirely out of favour,' she said, trying to forget what George had done, and to remember that he was her brother, whom she loved.

'The King approved the grant. It seems that his anger is spent and that he is determined to continue in your marriage.'

'So Mistress Seymour is just another passing fancy. Thank God! She has caused me such grief, flaunting her presents from His Grace.'

'Anne, hearken to me.' George was regarding her with unusual compassion. 'Take stock. I am shocked to see how you have grown so thin and sad. Eat for your health. Look to your hair and your dress. Put a brave smile on your face. You can fight back! None knows better how to. You won the King once; now win him back.'

'It's not easy when he is in London and I'm here,' she said.

'I will persuade him to summon you,' George promised. 'Leave it to me.'

Days later, the summons came. George had played his part, and now she must play hers. She had herself garbed in a sumptuous gown of black velvet with oversleeves of fur and a low neckline edged with black embroidery and pearls. Around her neck, to proclaim her pride in her queenship and her family, she hung a pendant in the shape of a B – one of several initial jewels she favoured. She was still too slim, but the black gown flattered her. Her hair she left loose in token of her rank, threaded with jewels as she had used to wear it.

Henry received her courteously, looking her up and down with approval, yet failing to meet her eye.

'It is a joy to me to see your Grace again,' she said.

'I trust you are fully recovered.' Still his manner was distant.

'I am very well, sir.'

'Your brother told me that you were unhappy at Greenwich, and so I thought you would like to join me to celebrate the feast day of St Matthias.'

'I shall be honoured and delighted,' she told him. She was also delighted to find that Jane was nowhere to be seen on the feast day.

Henry was being kind to her. He came to her bed most nights, and she began to believe that all was not lost. It was clear from the petitions she received that others still believed she had influence with him. She took care to be charming to all.

Resolving to be a good mother, she sent for Elizabeth and spent lavishly on clothing for her, dressing the little girl up in caps of purple, white and crimson satin, cauls of gold, ribbon for her plaits, and miniature court gowns of velvet and damask. She taught her how to manage a train. Watching her daughter toddling along, head held high, swathes of damask trailing behind her, Anne almost loved her.

The signs were that the Emperor was hoping for an alliance with Henry.

'And if he approaches me – so the terms be acceptable – I will be willing,' Henry told Anne. 'I've heard from my agents in Rome that Pope Paul is ready to proclaim my excommunication. Charles's friendship might prevent that. Not that I care a fig for what the Bishop of Rome does, but the rest of Christendom will. They may not deal with me honestly if I am cast out of the fold.'

But what of me? she wondered. *The Emperor hates me. I am a stumbling block to this alliance.* She did not say any of this; it was for Henry to deal with, or rather Cromwell. Instead, she asked how François would take it.

'Our relations have been unstable lately,' Henry said, 'and I fear there is little hope of Elizabeth's marriage being concluded. François is as slippery as an eel, and he's ill of the pox and in a bad humour. All that fornication is catching up with him.' Henry's lips were prim. *You can't talk!* Anne thought. 'He and Charles are at odds,' he added. 'Soon they'll be at war. Friendship with the Emperor offers us the greatest hope for the future security of this realm.'

Yes, she thought again, *but what of my security?*

'Sir Edward Seymour has been appointed to the Privy Chamber,' Father announced one evening when they were supping alone in his lodgings. 'I warn you, Anne, the influence of these Seymours increases daily.'

Rage welled in her. 'What can I do?' she stormed. 'He flaunts her almost under my nose.'

Father snorted. 'I shouldn't need to tell *you* what to do to win him back.'

'That's unfair!' she snapped.

'You could bloody well cheer up.'

'You lose three sons in a row, see your husband chasing other women and sense your enemies ready to pounce – you'd be cheerful, I'm sure! But Father, I do try. And maybe God will give me a son now that my marriage is not in doubt. When that happens—'

'Anne, be realistic. Katherine lost five children. You've lost three. Is that telling you something?'

Her hand flew to her mouth as the possibility of Henry being in some way at fault dawned on her. 'But if that's true, what can I do?'

Father shrugged. 'Nothing but pray. And be watchful. Those Seymour brothers are greedy, ruthless and cunning, and they are in daily contact with the King. And there's another thing you should know. Our friend Cromwell has willingly obliged your husband by vacating his chambers so that Sir Edward Seymour and his wife can lodge there. The King can access these chambers from his own apartments by certain galleries without being perceived. You can imagine what his purpose is.'

'You mean Cromwell is encouraging this infidelity?' That chilled her to the bone.

'He has been accommodating. What worries me more is that the wench and her family are insisting that His Grace pay his addresses to her only in the presence of her relatives. It's supposed to be a discreet arrangement, but it's being bruited about the court as if the town crier had announced it.'

'Dear God!' Anne whispered, sinking back in her chair. 'If she's playing that game, what end to it can there be but marriage? Unless he tires of her, which I pray he will. But this preservation of her virtue smacks to me of preparing her for queenship. I, of all people, know that! And if Cromwell has readily facilitated this, then he obviously takes it seriously. I have long suspected that he had become my enemy – now I know. Well, he shall hear about this from me!'

Angrily she summoned Cromwell to her closet. He bowed low before her.

'Your Grace. This is a pleasant surprise.'

'Don't cozen me, Master Secretary. I've just learned that you have readily given up your lodging to the Seymours, so that my husband can dally with his mistress.'

'Your Grace must not call her that,' Cromwell said. 'Mistress Seymour is a most virtuous lady. Had she been otherwise, I would not have agreed to it.'

'Virtuous or not – and I beg leave to doubt – trying to steal her mistress's husband is not edifying behaviour.'

'No, madam, it is not.' He looked pointedly at her. By God, he went too far! 'May I give you a word of advice?' he went on. 'Do not meddle in state affairs. The King doesn't like it.'

This was outrageous! 'You mean, Master Secretary, that you don't want me interfering with your plans for the monasteries. Now that Parliament has approved their closure, you will make the King rich and grateful. But he listens to me too – I am not so far out of favour as you might like – and I mean fiercely to oppose the wealth of these houses being sold off wholesale to buy support for the royal supremacy. I think the King would be shocked if he knew that, under the guise of the Gospel and religion, you are advancing your own interests.'

'Not so!' Cromwell protested. She could sense him becoming riled. It was satisfying to pierce that urbane facade.

'So you *don't* plan to put everything up for sale? You don't accept bribes to confer ecclesiastical property and benefices upon the enemies of true doctrine?'

'I am the King's good servant,' he replied coldly.

'I think Sir Thomas More said much the same thing, and look what happened to him! I tell you, Master Secretary, other reformists support me. My almoner, John Skip, is one of them. We are determined to see a substantial portion of the confiscated riches used for educational and charitable purposes that can benefit everyone.'

'And you think the King will agree with you?' Cromwell smiled patronisingly, as if she were an ignorant fool. 'The treasury is empty. He is a man who likes to live lavishly. I don't see him turning down this unique opportunity to make himself rich.'

'The King is virtuous too,' she countered. 'He loves learning. I know I can persuade him to listen to me – and you know it too.'

Cromwell continued to smile at her. 'We shall see, madam,' he said.

'We shall!' The gauntlet had been flung down. 'In the meantime, don't encourage Mistress Seymour, or you will find yourself in the greatest trouble.' And with that she dismissed him.

When Henry came to supper with her the following evening, Anne brought up the subject of the monasteries. 'Sir, I know you need money, but would it not be a worthy thing to divert some of their wealth to education and charity? I can think of so many deserving causes. Henry, you could become renowned for founding schools and supporting scholars. You could establish chairs at the universities, set up a fund for the poor who are in desperate need and will be more so when the monasteries are gone.'

Henry was looking at her with fresh admiration. 'I like your ideas, Anne.'

'You would be remembered in centuries to come as the King who gave the gift of learning to his people along with the Bible in English. And that would be a greater achievement than any victory in battle.'

'By St Mary, you speak truth,' he declared. 'The religious houses have riches beyond imagining, so I am told, enough to do all these things *and* fill the treasury.'

'These causes would be more noble than selling off the land to buy the opinions of your lords.'

'I might have to offer some inducements, Anne, but you are right. Some of the money should be used for worthy causes.'

They spent a happy hour discussing those causes in detail, and it felt like old times. There was an intimacy in shared aims. Above all, he had heeded her. Her influence was still a force to be reckoned with. How she would love to see Cromwell's face when Henry enthusiastically outlined his new schemes. He would know that she had bested him!

And she wasn't finished with him yet. Like Queen Esther, she would rid the kingdom of corrupt ministers – and at the same time she would show Henry that she would not tolerate any infidelity. She was fighting back.

*

On Passion Sunday, she had her almoner preach a sermon in the Chapel Royal on the text 'Which among you accuses me of sin?'

She sat next to Henry as Father Skip ascended the pulpit.

'A king needs to be wise and resist evil counsellors who tempt him to ignoble actions,' he began. 'A king's counsellor ought to take good heed of what advice he gives in altering ancient things.' He paused, glaring fiercely at the congregation below him, leaving them in no doubt as to whom he was referring. Anne glanced at Henry, who was looking pensive – exactly what she had hoped for. Cromwell was frowning.

'Look at the example of King Ahasuerus, who was moved by a wicked minister to destroy the Jews,' Skip continued. 'That minister was Haman, who had tried to destroy Ahasuerus's queen, Esther. But after Esther exposed his evil plot and saved the Jews from persecution, Haman was justly hanged. And thus triumphed this good woman, whom King Ahasuerus loved very well, and put his trust in, because he knew she was ever his friend.'

Henry was nodding sagely. He knew the story well. He had commissioned those tapestries depicting it.

Skip now got to the pith of the tale. 'Among his evil deeds, Haman had assured Ahasuerus that eliminating the Jews would result in ten thousand talents being appropriated for the royal treasury, and for the King's personal gain.' Anne felt Henry stir beside her. 'So, in our own day, we have cause to lament that the Crown, misled by evil counsel, wants the Church's property, and will have it. We can only lament the decay of the universities and pray that the necessity for learning will not be overlooked.'

All eyes were now on Anne; Cromwell's were full of menace – and, she was gratified to see, fear. He could be in no doubt now. She was setting herself up in opposition to his policies. The swords had been unsheathed.

Now it was Henry's turn to squirm. Skip was looking sternly on his flock. 'But it is not only in fleecing the Church that corruption lies. Look at the example of Solomon, who lost his true nobility through his sensual and carnal appetite, and taking too many wives and concubines.'

Henry's breathing quickened. He looked as mad as a bull about to charge. Only recently, his painter, Hans Holbein, had portrayed him as Solomon, the fount of all wisdom. It was as well that Skip had finished, and was exhorting the congregation to kneel in prayer. For all his fury, Henry had to obey.

After the service, he grabbed Anne's hand and pulled her into one of the holy-day closets behind the royal pew.

'Did you put him up to that?' he asked angrily. 'Or did he take it upon himself to preach sedition and slander me, my councillors and my whole Parliament?'

Before she could answer, Cromwell, forgetting his place, barged into the closet. He did not acknowledge Anne.

'Your Grace will surely not let that pass!' he hissed. Anne had never seen him so exercised.

'I intend to have my Council reprimand this priest, and warn him that he had best mind his tongue if he wishes to remain in the Queen's service.'

'But your Grace agrees with him,' Anne said. 'Only the other night you were saying what a worthy thing it would be to divert the wealth of the monasteries into education and charity. It is not *you* who seeks personal gain.'

'He made it appear that it was me,' Henry growled.

'That was not his intention, I'm sure, and your Grace need not worry, for the world will soon know the truth.'

'Your Grace, I must speak to you in private,' Cromwell insisted.

'*Must?* Master Secretary, it is the King you address,' Anne reminded him.

'I will see you later, Cromwell.' Henry said.

'We are going to dine now,' Anne said sweetly, and swept out.

At table, Henry did not mention Skip's attack on his infidelity. He could neither deny it nor risk another quarrel. But his mood was sour for the rest of the day, and the unfortunate almoner received a verbal lashing from the Council. Anne did not know what had been said between Henry and Cromwell. It did not matter. She was about to stir up public opinion again.

Hugh Latimer, a fiery reformist who preached regularly before the King, had agreed to take up the struggle on her behalf the next day of that Holy Week.

'Think on the parable of the tenants who refused to pay rent to the owner of a vineyard,' he enjoined in his homily in the chapel royal. 'Once the tenants have been evicted, the vineyard will pass to more worthy persons, who may convert it to some better use.' There could be no doubt in anyone's mind that he was referring to the dissolution of the monasteries.

Henry made no comment. After the service, he threw Anne a withering look and stumped off, so she immediately enlisted the assistance of Archbishop Cranmer, who agreed to defend her in any argument with the King, and to write to Master Secretary in support of her views. Soon, thanks to Cranmer, Anne was gratified to find that Henry's enthusiasm for her plans – and her bed – had revived. But while they had reached common ground and were getting on better than they had in a long time, it did not prevent him from dallying with Mistress Seymour. Anne saw them playing bowls together on Maundy Thursday, smiling at each other with that special intimacy of lovers, and she felt like weeping and raging as she performed the traditional queenly function of distributing money to beggars and washing their feet (which had been thoroughly scoured beforehand) in memory of the Last Supper. Was that little bitch always to be a malign presence in her life?

'We are moving closer towards friendship with the Emperor,' Henry told her that night, as they lay in bed. 'There are still obstacles to be overcome. I am determined to get Charles to recognise you as Queen, and to that end I have asked Chapuys to come to court on Easter Tuesday, to give him the opportunity of paying his respects to you.'

Relief and elation surged through her. This proved that Henry still respected her as his Queen, even if he did not love her as he used to.

'It's about time!' she said. 'Chapuys has never bent the knee to me as Queen, never kissed my hand.' How she would savour her triumph!

'He will do so now, and in public,' Henry growled, 'and he will know he is acknowledging that I was right all along to put away

Katherine and marry you. I will not sign an alliance with Charles on any other terms.'

Henry sent George to receive Chapuys at the gates of Greenwich Palace, so that the ambassador should be in no doubt that the hoped-for alliance was conditional upon his being cordial to the Boleyns. George had instructions to afford Chapuys a warm welcome, making it plain that Anne, her family and friends were in favour of a rapprochement with the Emperor.

Cromwell was to follow close behind, bearing a message from Henry inviting Chapuys to visit Anne and kiss her hand, a great honour conferred only on those in high favour. 'He will say that this will be a great pleasure to me,' Henry told her, rubbing his hands in satisfaction at the thought.

Anne followed Henry into chapel, and they seated themselves in the royal pew in the upstairs gallery. Below them, in the main body of the chapel, there was a great concourse of people. Word of Chapuys' visit had been spread, and everyone was curious to see what he would do. Some, she knew, were probably hoping that he would slight her.

When the time came to make their offerings, Henry made Anne descend the stairs to the altar first, keeping close behind her. At the bottom, she almost collided with Chapuys, who was standing behind the door. There was a pause, and then he bowed to her. She smiled graciously. No one could touch her now. The Emperor would soon be her friend.

Courtesy being the order of the day, she made a deep curtsey to Chapuys as his master's representative, and was surprised when he did her the kindness of handing her two candles to use in the ritual.

She emerged from the chapel feeling jubilant, and deeply relieved. As she walked along the gallery with Henry at the head of a long train of courtiers, she could not contain her euphoria. 'I am sorry that Spain is at war with France,' she said loudly, so that all could hear, 'but I am firmly on the side of the Emperor. I have abandoned my friendship with King François. It seems to me that, tired of life on account of his illness, he wants to shorten his days by going to war.'

'He can't shorten them quickly enough for me,' Henry murmured.

He escorted her to dinner in her apartments, as was his custom after Mass; often he invited honoured guests.

'Will Chapuys be joining us?' Anne asked.

'I have asked him to come,' Henry said, as they sat down at the high table. The room was filling up, but there was no sign of the ambassador. She looked in vain among the group of foreign envoys waiting at the door to be announced. Had Chapuys repented of his gesture already?

'Why does not Messire Chapuys enter?' she asked Henry.

'No doubt he has a good reason,' he answered. 'His courtesy to you will have excited much comment, especially among the Imperialists, some of whom who will be angry with him for acknowledging you.'

'They had better get used to it,' she said, and sent her usher to find Chapuys. He returned to say that he was dining with her brother and the chief nobles of the court in the King's presence chamber. She smiled at Henry, satisfied.

The next day, George told her that there had been a furious row between Henry and Cromwell about the negotiations with Spain. From what he could gather from those within earshot, Cromwell had exceeded his instructions. George had seen him slumped on a coffer outside Henry's presence chamber with sweat running down his face, looking as if he'd just escaped from the hounds of Hell.

'It looks very much as if he is out of favour,' he said gleefully.

Anne smiled. 'I will take full advantage of that.'

The following morning, Henry told her that Cromwell was ill and had gone home to his house at Stepney to recuperate.

Good riddance! she thought. She was more concerned about the imminent annual chapter meeting of the Order of the Garter, for a vacancy had arisen for a new Garter knight, and she had asked Henry if George might fill it. Although it was the knights who voted, she hoped that he would make his wishes known.

She was highly displeased to hear that they had chosen Sir Nicholas Carew, whom she had come to despise for his friendship with the

Seymours. She knew what people would be whispering: that she lacked sufficient influence to secure this most prestigious honour for her brother.

'But darling,' Henry protested when she took him to task in private, 'I promised François years ago that I would remember Sir Nicholas, whom he loves, when a Garter vacancy arose, so I felt bound to put his name forward.'

Yes, and because he is known to be close to the favourite, he got the vote. But she could not say that to Henry. It was galling to have to accept that her enemies had scored this small triumph.

Walking into her chamber the next day and coming upon Francis Weston flirting with Madge, Anne's patience snapped. It offended her to see Norris being made a fool of. Madge should not have encouraged it. She did not deserve such a good man.

'Go to my chamber and finish those smocks!' she ordered. Madge fled.

Weston looked at her sheepishly. 'Your Grace wouldn't deny me a little innocent pleasure, surely? She is such a comely wench.'

'If she's so comely, I wonder why Norris has not yet married her,' she retorted.

The smile vanished from Weston's handsome face. 'Does your Grace want the truth?'

'What do you mean?' she asked warily.

'We all know that Norris comes more to your chamber for you than for Madge.'

Her heart sang, but she must not show it. 'Nonsense!' she snapped. 'You just want Norris discountenanced because *you* love Madge and you don't love your wife.'

Weston's gaze was bold. 'I love one in your household better than them both.'

'Who is that?'

'It is yourself.' There was a silence. Weston loved her? It was the first she had known of it. He was just chancing his luck at the old courtly game!

'I defy you to tell the King that!' she retorted, and left him standing there.

'I'm taking you with me to Calais,' Henry said, as he watched Anne raise her bow to shoot at the butts.

The visit had been arranged some weeks before, and she had assumed he was going alone. It was gratifying to hear that he wanted her with him. It was the physic she needed, after receiving news from Hever that her mother was ill with a cough that grieved her sorely. It had come on in the winter and seemed to be getting worse. Anne had written, promising to visit as soon as she returned from Calais, and prayed fervently that Mother would soon be restored to health.

'Bull's eye!' Henry applauded. The courtiers clapped.

'We'll make a progress of it,' he told her, reaching for his bow. 'We'll go via Dover, as I want to inspect the new harbour and fortifications.'

'You're not planning to meet with François this time?' she asked warily.

'I've not decided. I have to choose whether to ally myself with Charles or François. Charles is insisting that Mary be restored to the succession before Elizabeth, but I've told my envoys to oppose his demands.'

'I do not want Elizabeth's rights overturned,' she said, alarmed.

'I will never allow it,' Henry assured her.

The last week of April was mellow and warm with the blossoming of spring. Anne walked daily in the gardens at Greenwich with her ladies, often accompanied by George, Norris and the other gentlemen she favoured. While Henry was busy with state business, she watched tennis matches, played bowls and ordered baskets of food to be eaten outdoors. Whenever she encountered Jane Seymour, she threw her an icy glance and walked on. Her position seemed once again secure. She would not let Jane bother her.

One fine evening, as dusk fell on a golden sunset, she climbed to the very top of the hill behind the palace to Mireflore, an old tower that had been part of the original palace of Placentia, which Henry had had refurbished but rarely used.

'Come on, you snails!' she yelled at her ladies, who were puffing along some way behind her. 'Oh, wait there then!' she laughed, and they gratefully collapsed on to the grassy slope.

The tower stood four-square before her, looming up imposingly against the darkening sky. Close to, it looked eerie and forbidding, but Anne was not one to be frightened by phantoms. Using the key the sergeant porter had given her, she unlocked the iron-barred door and pushed it open. Inside she found herself in a dim vaulted chamber covered in wall and ceiling paintings. There was something repellent in the stark black outlines of the people portrayed in them.

It seemed that no one had been here in a long time. Cobwebs trailed across the pointed windows, and a musty smell pervaded the still air. Anne climbed the spiral staircase in the corner. It led to a bedchamber, but the tester bed had been stripped bare. On the floor lay a dusty lady's stocking.

There was nothing of interest here. She was about to leave when she heard a footfall above. Her heart began to race. What if someone who wished her ill had seen her coming, raced ahead and hidden, determined to kill her?

The footsteps were coming down the stairs now. Her instincts told her to run down to the ground floor as fast as she could, but then a man appeared in the doorway.

'Norris!' she cried in relief.

'Anne!' he exclaimed delightedly. In his surprise he had not used her title.

'I came to explore this place,' she said. 'And you?'

'I . . . had to collect some things.' She noticed he had nothing in his hands.

'What's up there?'

'Another bedchamber. There's not much to see.' He seemed reluctant to move, so she sidled past him and ran up the stairs. She was astonished to enter a sumptuous apartment with a bed made up as richly as her own, three tapestries and some fine pieces of furniture. On the floor lay a costly Turkey carpet.

Norris had ascended the stairs behind her.

'This is a room fit for a king!' she exclaimed.

'His Grace uses it occasionally,' he said.

'For his trysts with Jane Seymour? Don't worry, Norris, I know about that.' Her voice was bitter. 'But I didn't know that they were making the beast with two backs.'

Norris hesitated again. 'Jane Seymour has not been here,' he said.

Understanding dawned. 'But he has brought others.'

He did not answer.

'In my time?' She turned to face him.

'Don't make me hurt you,' he begged, choked. 'I love you too much.'

It would have been so easy to go into his arms, to feel – for a magical moment – safe and cherished. Kissing him would come as naturally as breathing, and feel beautiful and right. She had never experienced anything like that with Henry. She cared not whether he had brought a hundred women in here. He had never had her heart.

Yet she was his Queen, and – which mattered more – she did not want to forfeit Norris's respect. She was no wench to be tumbled on that luxurious bed, although for a wicked instant she had been tempted. It would be the perfect revenge to cuckold Henry on the very bed in which he had betrayed her. But this precious thing that existed between her and Norris must not be sullied by revenge or any baseness.

Her voice was gentle but firm. 'You cannot know how much I have longed for you to hold me,' she told him, as he looked at her yearningly. 'But we can never be lovers.'

'I am ashamed of declaring myself,' he confessed. 'The King accounts me his friend. He has been good to me. But I was overcome at the sight of you. I thought, we're alone here and no one will know.'

'Nor shall they. What we have said shall be our secret. It will be enough to carry in my heart. You have Madge. Be happy.' She felt tears threatening. Thank goodness it was growing dark. She did not want Norris to see her cry. 'I must go back.' She led the way down the stairs. 'My ladies might come looking for me. I'll go ahead, you go after.'

He caught her hand as she hastened to the door, lifting it to his lips and kissing it. 'You are the sweetest lady that ever drew breath, Anne, and if I can ever be of service to you, you have only to crook your little finger.'

'I will remember that. Now farewell. Give me a few minutes.' She slipped through the door and almost ran down the hill, her heart heavy with a poignant sadness.

Her conscience would not let her rest. She wondered if Henry felt the same urge to confess to sinning with his mistresses. And *her* infidelity was only in her heart!

She sought out Father Skip and unburdened herself. He absolved her and imposed a light penance, since he felt she had truly repented.

Feeling as if a weight had been lifted from her soul, and resolving never to be alone with Norris again, she called for Elizabeth to be brought to court from Hatfield, summoned her tailor, and had the child fitted for more new clothes. Because Elizabeth was so adventurous, darting off without warning, she ordered two leading reins with big buttons and long tassels, then decided that her daughter would look very pretty in a new cap of taffeta with a caul of damask gold. Henry was not forgotten. She bought silver and gold fringe and buttons for his saddle.

She became aware that day of a sense of unease pervading her household. There was nothing tangible, just the feeling that everyone was approaching her a little warily. Over the past week, some had absented themselves inexplicably, with no excuses offered. Today, a few others briefly disappeared. One was Jane Seymour. Was it her imagination, or was something going on? It was like being the only one left out of a secret.

All her old insecurities surfaced again. She felt as if some unknown disaster was looming. But that was nonsense. All was well. Henry was behaving much more kindly towards her; he had defended her rights and Elizabeth's; he was taking her to Calais soon. So what could she have to fear?

Father came to see her and spent a few minutes admiring Elizabeth and grinning at her antics. But Anne could tell he was preoccupied.

'Your uncle of Norfolk and I have been appointed to the Middlesex Grand Jury,' he told her.

'Why look so miserable about it? It's an honour, surely.'

'I don't know,' he admitted, as Elizabeth threw her ball at him. He tossed it back. 'We are to sit on a commission that will enquire into all kinds of treasons, but I don't know anything more, and I'm not supposed to talk about it. But you're the Queen; I can tell you.'

'Henry has probably decided to silence his opponents once and for all,' Anne speculated. 'He might even be thinking of proceeding against the Lady Mary.'

Father shook his head. 'That really would scupper his *entente* with the Emperor. No, it can't be that.'

'Maybe he is planning to make a case against Cromwell.'

Father's eyes gleamed. 'Maybe! Cromwell is still at Stepney. That would be a surprise for him, hah!'

'No more than he richly deserves,' Anne said.

It was only when she was lying in bed alone in the dark that a dreadful thought came to her.

Suppose Henry had determined to marry Jane Seymour? The Emperor would far prefer Jane, who was known to be a good Imperialist. Yet Henry, surely, would not want to go through another divorce. Could he be plotting some other way to get rid of her? Oh, God, had she and Norris been observed? Had it been a trap? And had her father been appointed to that jury to lull her into a false sense of security while her enemies plotted a case against her?

They were legion. Cromwell, the Seymours, Chapuys, the Papists, Francis Bryan, Nicholas Carew . . . A disparate group with one thing in common.

She must calm down. These were night thoughts. She would feel better in the morning. She must remember that Henry had shown no sign of displeasure towards her – rather the opposite.

But she did not feel better in the morning. She still had a terrible feeling of nameless dread, that something awful was about to happen. She wished that Henry was there so that she could unburden herself to him. If anyone could make her feel safe, he could. But Henry had not visited her bed for three nights now, and that in itself seemed ominous.

What if something evil befell her? It would leave Elizabeth so vulnerable. What could she do to protect her?

She sent for her chaplain, Matthew Parker, a good reformist and a great preacher. Henry liked him as much as she did, and would heed what he said.

'I am afraid!' she told him. 'I hope I'm mistaken, but I fear I might be accused of treason.' She was weeping now. The young chaplain waited until she had composed herself, his blunt features creased in concern. He tried to reassure her, saying it was all in her imagination, but she would not be comforted.

'You must help me!' she insisted. 'If the worst happens, will you look to the care of my child? There is no one I trust more.'

Father Parker regarded her with compassion. 'Your Grace may count on me,' he vowed. 'I give you my word.'

She sat with her women, trying to concentrate on her sewing, but hemming smocks for the poor did not offer much distraction. Furtively she glanced at Madge, and Mary Howard, and Margaret Douglas and all the rest. Did they know what was going on? What about those unexplained absences? Dare she confront them? They might think she was mad. For the first time, she found herself missing her sister. There had been no letters exchanged between them in nearly two years. Mary was still in Calais. George kept in touch. He said she sounded very happy. Lucky Mary!

Still Henry had not visited Anne. He had been in Council every day until late in the evening.

Anxiously she asked George if there was anything afoot.

'There's trouble with France, I think,' he said. 'Certain letters have been brought by the French ambassador. There's no need to look so worried.'

Maybe François had threatened war. If so, Henry's visit of inspection to Calais was timely. They were due to leave three days after the traditional May Day jousts. Anne distracted herself by planning her wardrobe, choosing her most flattering gowns. Maybe the passion Henry had shown during their first sojourn at the Exchequer Palace would be rekindled. And maybe she would send for Mary and forgive her.

Leaving her maids and chamberers to pack the gowns in her travelling chests, she returned to her presence chamber, where she found Weston playing on a lute, Margaret Douglas deep in conversation with Thomas Howard, and Mark Smeaton standing in the oriel window looking miserable.

'Why so sad, Mark?' she asked briskly, disliking the bold, haughty mien he always adopted. She had avoided him since he had stared at her too familiarly in Winchester.

'It is no matter,' he said, and leered at her. By God, he was trying to play the game of love with her – and he but a lowly musician.

Her voice was icy. 'You may not look to have me speak to you as I should do to a nobleman, because you are my inferior.'

He was still smiling at her. 'No, no,' he said, 'a look suffices me.' He bowed. 'Farewell, your Grace.' And he sauntered out of her chamber, the insolent knave.

Well! she said to herself. Any more of that kind of conduct and Henry would hear of it.

After Mass on the last Sunday morning in April, Anne took Urian for a walk in Greenwich Park and stopped to watch a dog fight. She laid and won wagers, and returned to the palace feeling a little more cheerful.

After dinner, she gathered her ladies and favoured gentlemen and led them into her privy garden, to make the most of the sunshine. Norris was of the company, and she guessed he was trying as hard as she to make it appear that there was nothing more between them than friendship – not so easy now they had declared their feelings.

She bade him sit next to her on the stone bench in the arbour, keeping a safe distance between them. A few feet away, well within sight, the others were strolling along paths, chattering away, laughing and even kissing.

'Why have you not gone through with your marriage to Madge?' Anne asked.

Norris paused. 'I've decided to tarry a time.'

She lowered her voice. 'You look for dead men's shoes, for if anything evil befell the King, you would look to have me.'

There was another silence. 'No,' Norris murmured. 'If I had any such thought, I would wish my head off. Madam, this is dangerous talk. To speak of the King's death, even in jest, is no light matter.'

She knew it. It was treason to imagine or plot the death of the sovereign, and probably even to speak of it.

'Yes, but I can trust you,' she said. 'Remember, I can undo you if I so please!' It was said in jest, but Norris was looking at her in horror.

'Madam, I pray I can trust you too,' he said, standing up and bowing.

'Don't go,' she whispered.

'I have duties to attend to in the King's privy chamber,' he said. 'Good day to your Grace.'

As he walked away, she saw Lady Worcester's brother, Sir Anthony Browne, enter the garden. He bowed in her direction and went to speak to his sister. They were looking at her curiously. She realised with a shiver of fear that he would have approached her garden by the path that skirted the arbour. Oh, God – he hadn't heard what she and Norris had said? Sir Anthony was close to Henry and much respected by him. If he told the King about their conversation, Henry might well believe him. She would be condemned out of her own mouth, and Norris too. It might be inferred, from what she had said, that they shared a guilty secret. Violating the King's wife was high treason. Any man convicted of it would suffer the unthinkable horrors of hanging, drawing and quartering.

Not Norris! Not loyal, good, devoted Norris, who had done nothing wrong apart from love her hopelessly from afar.

She must warn him! Bidding her attendants stay, she hastened into the palace, heading for Henry's apartments. She caught up with Norris in the pages' chamber, where he was administering a rebuke to some wretched boy for idleness. When the page had gone, goggling at the sight of the Queen standing there, she closed the door. Norris stared at her in dismay.

'I think we were overheard,' she said, as he looked at her with horror. 'Sir Henry, I pray you, go to my almoner now and swear that, whatever he hears of me, I am a good woman.'

'Anne, is this wise?' Norris asked, profoundly agitated. 'It smacks of protesting too much. I could swear it myself, should the need arise.'

'Go!' she shrilled. 'There is no time to be lost!'

'Madam, the King wishes you to attend him,' her chamberlain announced.

Having spent the past two hours agonising over what had happened with Norris, Anne was expecting the worst. This was the retribution she had been expecting. Henry had found out. Well, she would not go down without a fight! For ammunition she picked up Elizabeth – with her child, so unmistakably the King's, in her arms, she would appeal to Henry as a wronged mother.

She found him staring through an open window at the courtyard below. He was frowning, restless. She curtseyed, still clutching the child, and he turned.

'I have been hearing strange things of you, Anne,' he said, his eyes like steel. 'Your almoner told your chamberlain that you felt the need to send Norris to protest your virtue to him.'

'Sir,' she cried, 'it was to counteract horrible gossip about me, that I am a loose woman, and I did not want Father Skip believing it. I thought it would come well from Norris, because he is known for an upright man and loyal to you.'

Henry did not answer. 'If I thought you had played me false, I would never forgive you,' he said.

'How could you think that?' she asked. 'I love *you*, Henry. This child was born of our love. I could never forsake you for another.'

His gaze bore down on her. 'Never let it be said that you made me a cuckold, madam!'

'Why is Papa cross?' Elizabeth asked as Anne carried her away.

'It is nothing to worry about,' Anne assured her, fighting tears and praying that was true. 'All will be well, sweeting.'

*

That evening there was a banquet, and Henry was once more his usual self, courteous and companionable. His anger, to Anne's relief, had burned itself out. They led the dancing, and he admired her gown, a new one of grey damask with a crimson kirtle. He left at ten o'clock, pleading the need to attend to urgent state business.

When he had gone, she became aware of an undercurrent of speculation in the presence chamber. Around eleven o'clock, someone said that the Council was still in session. Clearly some deep and difficult question was being discussed. Was war imminent?

She waited until the meeting of the Council broke up, and caught her father as he emerged from it. His face was grey and he looked as if he was bearing the weight of the world on his shoulders.

'What is it?' she asked urgently.

'I cannot tell you, Anne,' he croaked. 'We are all sworn to secrecy. But the King's visit to Calais is to be postponed for a week. They're announcing it shortly.'

'Does this concern me?' She could hear the fear in her voice.

'It concerns us all. Now I bid you good night.'

If it concerned everyone, it must be war.

Part Four

'I Have Not Sinned'

Chapter 26

1536

Anne had always loved May Day and the annual court festival celebrating the coming of spring, which was customarily marked by a great tournament. This year it was to be held in the tiltyard at Greenwich. It was a warm day, and pennants fluttered in the breeze as she took her seat at the front of the royal stand, her ladies clustering behind. Presently Henry arrived, to a great ovation. He greeted her cordially, but seemed preoccupied as he took his seat. He had been meaning to compete himself, but the old wound in his leg was still giving him trouble, and did not seem to be healing.

They watched as the contestants ran their chivalrous courses, lances couched, armour gleaming. George led the challengers, thrilling the crowd by his skill in breaking lances and vaulting on horseback. Norris headed the defenders, but his temperamental mount refused to enter the lists, whereupon Henry called down that Norris could ride his own horse as a token of his esteem. Anne was thankful that Henry seemed to harbour no suspicions of his old friend.

Tom Wyatt excelled himself, surpassing all the rest, although Norris, Weston and Brereton all performed great feats of arms, and Henry was loud in his applause and appreciation. Anne smiled down encouragingly on all the gallant knights.

Halfway through the contests, a page appeared and handed a folded piece of paper to Henry, who read it, flushed a dangerous red, then got up and stalked off, nearly overturning his chair. Father and George were among the lords who hastened after him.

Anne could not credit that Henry was leaving. There was a hubbub of comment. What had happened? Had the French invaded? He had not troubled to say farewell to her – he who rarely scanted in his courtesy – so it must be serious. She could not help but read something ominous into his hasty departure.

She signalled for the jousts to resume, but she was aware of the whispers and the speculation. When, bewildered and fearful, she returned to the palace a few hours later, and was told that the King had gone to Whitehall, she knew that some great catastrophe was at hand. And there was no one she could ask about it. As soon as the jousting ended, Norris had hurried to join the King. All her powerful protectors were gone.

She slept fitfully that night. In the morning, hoping and dreading that the day would bring Henry's return, or at least some news of what was going on, she had her women dress her in a sumptuous gown of crimson velvet and cloth of gold, and then tried to divert herself by watching her household officers playing tennis. Her champion won, which lifted her spirits a little.

'I wish now I had placed a wager on him,' she said to Madge, who was sitting next to her in the viewing gallery. Madge nodded, indicating that there was someone behind her. Anne turned to see an usher in royal livery standing waiting.

'Your Grace, I am come to bid you, by order of the King, to present yourself before the Privy Council at once,' he said. The Privy Council was here at Greenwich? She had thought it with the King at Whitehall.

'Very well,' she replied, trying to stem the tide of panic that gripped her. For a queen to be thus summoned was strange indeed, and she was in deep trepidation as she entered the council chamber.

There were three grave-faced men seated at the council board: Uncle Norfolk, looking implacable; Sir William Fitzwilliam, whom she had never liked, the feeling being mutual; and Sir William Paulet, the King's comptroller, who alone greeted her with gentle courtesy as they all rose to their feet.

Norfolk came to the point without preamble. 'Madam, by the powers granted by the King's Grace to us as royal commissioners, we are formally charging you with having committed adultery with Sir Henry Norris, Mark Smeaton and one other.'

Anne was overcome with faintness. This was her worst nightmare coming true. How could they believe such things of her? And with *Smeaton*? How could they even think she would stoop so low? And Norris – they *had* been overheard! But she had done nothing wrong. Trembling, she opened her mouth to protest, but Norfolk raised his hand and stilled her.

'Before you say anything, you should know that Norris and Smeaton have admitted their guilt.'

'Then they are lying, since there is nothing to admit! I am the King's true wife, and no other man has ever touched me.'

'Tut, tut, tut! We have the depositions of witnesses, madam. Are they all lying?'

'Someone is making an occasion to get rid of me!' she countered, in great fear.

'You have given them the occasion by your evil behaviour,' Norfolk sneered.

'Oh, you are cruel, uncle, to believe such calumnies of an innocent woman – and your own blood at that!'

His face was like granite. 'I serve the King, madam. My first loyalty is to him, and he has ordered your arrest. These crimes laid against you are grave and, if proved, will merit just punishment.'

Henry had sanctioned this travesty of justice! Did he really believe the worst of her? It terrified her that he had preferred to heed the accusations of others, rather than give her a chance to refute them. What hurt most was that an investigation must have been going on all these past days, yet he had said not a word of it. Oh, her enemies had been busy!

'What is to happen to me?' she asked. 'I must see the King. He will listen to me.'

'He won't see you,' Fitzwilliam snarled. 'He is the Lord's anointed: he won't be tainted by associating with a traitor.'

'A traitor?' She feared her knees would buckle. 'I am no traitor.'

'Compromising the royal succession is treason, madam,' he barked, as Norfolk tutted sorrowfully.

'We will escort your Grace back to your apartments,' Paulet said.

'Dinner will be served to you, and you will remain there until further notice. Your chamberlain has informed your household that you have been charged with treason.'

It was a nightmare walk back from the council chamber to her lodging, with the lords walking stone-faced either side of her and the King's guards keeping pace in front and behind. News of her disgrace must have spread quickly beyond her household, for everywhere there were people staring at her, most of them hostile or disapproving. They were ready to believe anything of her, it seemed.

It was no great relief to get back to her chamber, for she was greeted by the ominous silence of her ladies, and servants struggling to conceal tears, which further unnerved her, as did the presence of guards outside her door, their halberds crossed to prevent any unauthorised person from entering. They raised them to allow in her servitors, who brought her the usual choice of delicious dishes, but she was so upset when the King's waiter failed to appear with his customary greeting – a poignant reminder of the awfulness of her situation – that she could not touch the food. She could only sit there, making stilted conversation with her ladies about children and dogs and tennis. She thought of sending for Elizabeth, but feared that, seeing and holding her child, she might break down, which would distress the little one. And probably they wouldn't let her see Elizabeth anyway; there would be more nonsense about the taint of treason.

At two o'clock, she was still at table, seated under her canopy of estate, when Norfolk returned with Cromwell, Lord Chancellor Audley and several other Privy councillors. Norfolk had in his hand a scroll of parchment.

She rose to her feet in alarm. 'Why have your lordships come?'

'This, madam,' Norfolk waved the paper, 'is the warrant for your arrest. By the King's command we are to conduct you to the Tower of London, where you will abide during His Highness's pleasure.'

The Tower! Her flesh shrank from the prospect of being incarcerated in that grim fortress. She had only ever visited at the time of her coronation, when the Queen's apartments had been refurbished at huge expense for her, but she knew the rest of the Tower was grim by comparison. Thomas More had been in prison there for a year. They said he had emerged an old man . . . And about fifty years ago, two little princes had disappeared in the Tower, done to death, it was bruited, by their wicked uncle. Would she disappear too?

She made a huge effort to muster her courage. 'If it be His Majesty's pleasure, I am ready to obey,' she said. 'What may I take with me?'

'You must come as you are,' Norfolk said.

'In this?' She looked down at her gorgeous royal gown.

'There is no need to change.'

'All necessities will be provided,' Paulet told her. It sounded ominous, until she remembered hearing that prisoners in the Tower had to pay for their own keep and any comforts they wanted.

'What of my household?'

'They must remain here. New attendants await you in the Tower.'

'You will wait here until the tide changes,' Norfolk told her. We expect to leave at half past four.'

They left her then, and she spent the afternoon trying to hold herself together, going over and over in her head what she could possibly have said or done to lead people to think she had given an ounce of encouragement to Smeaton. Norris she could understand, although they were guilty only of indiscreet banter and that brief acknowledgement that there was more between them than could ever be fully said. But Smeaton – the very thought turned her stomach! How could Henry have believed it of her? And how could he have done this to her, whom he had passionately loved, and who had borne his children?

If she had not known that Cromwell was ill at Stepney, she would have sworn that his hand was in this. His enmity had been made clear, and she had threatened him. Maybe he was not ill at all: maybe it was a front for plotting her ruin. The more she thought about this, the more she believed it. Anything was better than believing it of Henry.

Her ladies offered some words of comfort to her in her distress, but they were keeping a wary distance. That taint of treason again! Anne picked up her embroidery, but her hands were not steady enough to wield a needle and thread. She wondered if she would ever finish it.

Towards four o'clock, by which time her heart was thumping in anticipation of what lay ahead, the Countess of Worcester, suddenly emitted a moan. She had had her hands on her pregnant belly for some time.

'The child does not stir,' she said, her face tragic.

'How long have you noticed this?' Anne asked, as the ladies clustered around.

'Since they came for you,' the Countess whispered. 'It was the shock.'

'You should lie down,' Mary Howard urged her, and helped her away to her bed.

Again Anne felt faint.

The lords came for her soon afterwards, accompanied by a larger detachment of the King's guard and Sir William Kingston, the Constable of the Tower, a tall, distinguished knight in middle age who had long served Henry well and was high in his favour.

'Madam,' he said, bowing, 'I am to have charge of you during your stay at the Tower. You must come with me now.' His grey eyes were not unkind or devoid of humanity, and his grizzled head was respectfully bowed. Although Anne knew he had been a friend of Cardinal Wolsey, and had been rumoured to be an admirer of the late Princess Dowager, she sensed that he had some sympathy for her.

She bade a brief farewell to her attendants, gave Urian a last pat – poor boy, he was looking at her so soulfully, perhaps sensing her distress – then walked with her custodians through the palace to where her barge was waiting. Passing between the ranked stone statues of heraldic beasts, she descended the privy stairs and stepped on board, as the lords climbed into the vessel behind her. Norfolk indicated that she should enter the cabin, then sat down heavily beside her on the cushioned bench and himself drew the curtains so that she should not be seen from the shore. It was one small mercy.

As the barge began its journey, she tried to ignore his sanctimonious tut-tutting.

'You should remember that your paramours have confessed their guilt,' he said.

She flared. 'I am innocent! I have had no paramours! I beg of you, take me to see His Grace.'

'Tut, tut!' Norfolk repeated, shaking his head, until she thought she would scream.

'We're nearing the Tower now,' he said presently, and she started as a deafening burst of cannon fire almost rocked the barge. 'They're announcing your arrival. It's done when a person of high rank is brought here under arrest.' There was the sound of shouting and loud voices from outside, and the Duke peered through a chink in the curtains. 'People are running to see what's happening.'

Anne looked out too, and at the sight of the great fortress looming up in front of her, her courage almost failed her. She remembered that More and Fisher and the Nun of Kent had left this place for the scaffold.

She waited as the oarsmen steered the vessel towards the Queen's Stairs, which led up to the Court Gate, the postern entrance where she had entered at her coronation. The difference between that day and this was too monumental to bear thinking about. Back then, Henry had been waiting here to welcome her; he had kissed her in front of everyone. Now she was alone – and terrified of what he might do to her.

Sir William Kingston appeared at the door of the cabin. 'Please come with me, madam.' She rose and clambered along the footway behind him, between the rows of staring oarsmen, Norfolk and the other lords bringing up the rear. She could hear the roar of the crowd on Tower Hill as she ascended the Queen's Stairs. Waiting at the top was Kingston's deputy, Sir Edmund Walsingham, the Lieutenant of the Tower, flanked by a detachment of guards.

When she reached the dark passage below the ancient Byward Tower, Anne faced the stark reality of her situation. It was rare, she realised, for anyone accused of treason to escape death. She felt so ill with fear that she thought she might collapse. As her stoutly maintained composure disintegrated, she sank to her knees. 'Oh, my God, my God, help me, as I am not guilty of those crimes of which I am accused!' she wailed. The councillors stood there looking down on her pitilessly.

'Sir William, we commit the Queen, here prisoner, to your custody,'

Norfolk said to Kingston, then he turned to his colleagues, nodded, and made to depart.

Anne struggled to her feet, despairing. 'My lords, I pray you, beseech the King's Grace to be good to me!' Her voice rose on a sob, but still they ignored her and headed back through the postern – to freedom. They knew not how blessed they were!

'Sir William, may I write to the King?' she begged.

'You may not write to anyone, madam,' he told her.

'Please! He is my lord and husband.'

'Orders is orders,' grunted Sir Edmund Walsingham.

'Come this way,' Kingston said. The guards surrounded Anne and she followed the Constable along the outer ward of the Tower that led towards the royal lodgings.

'I was received with greater ceremony the last time I entered here,' she recalled. 'Master Kingston, do I go into a dungeon?'

He looked at her in surprise. 'No, madam, you shall go into the lodging that you stayed in at your coronation.'

The relief was indescribable. Henry, for reasons she could not fathom, was doing this to teach her some sort of lesson. They did not house traitors in palaces. But then no queen had ever been accused of treason in England . . .

She thought of Norris, of how nearly she had sinned with him, had indeed sinned in her heart. He did not deserve to be caught up in this.

'Where are those accused with me being held?' she asked.

'I am not allowed to discuss them with you, madam,' the Constable said.

'They are in dungeons – you don't need to tell me.'

'We cannot say,' Sir Edmund barked. 'Orders is orders.'

'Then this lodging is too good for me!' she cried, imagining Norris in chains, and veering back from optimism to terror. What did they intend to do with her? 'Jesu, have mercy on me!' she cried out, and fell helplessly to her knees on the cobbles, great sobs racking her body. Kingston and Sir Edmund stared down at her in dismay, but neither ventured to help her up. It was not done for a lesser mortal to lay hands on the Queen of England. At the thought, she burst out laughing hysterically. They might be preparing to put her to death, but they dared not lift her up!

With an effort, she rose, and they continued past the Lieutenant's House to the entrance to the palace, where Kingston preceded her up the stairs to her lodgings. It was as if three years had melted away. The rooms smelt musty, but they were just as she had left them to go in triumph through the City. It seemed like yesterday that she had admired the spacious chambers, the great mantel and the mischievous *putti* gambolling along the antick frieze.

Those who had been chosen to attend her were waiting for her. She was dismayed to see that chief among them were four ladies she disliked. There was her Aunt Boleyn, the wife of her Uncle James, who had recently incurred Anne's enmity by switching his allegiance to the Lady Mary. There too was Lady Shelton, who greeted Anne with undisguised venom.

Lady Kingston came forward and curtseyed. She too was a friend of the Lady Mary, and had once served the Princess Dowager. Anne did not expect her to be sympathetic. Lastly, there was Mrs Coffyn, the wife of her Master of Horse.

Was this some added refinement of cruelty on Henry's part, forcing upon her the company of four women who hated her? How could he! But he had sent her old nurse, Mrs Orchard, who was shaking her head in sorrow, and the amiable Mrs Stonor, her Mother of the Maids. These two ladies, Kingston explained, would serve as her chamberers and sleep on pallet beds in her bedchamber at night.

'Madam, it is customary for prisoners of rank to take their meals at my table,' he said. 'Supper is ready, and I should be pleased if you would join me and my wife.'

Anne was surprised by this unlooked-for courtesy, and allowed herself to be escorted to the Lieutenant's House, a crumbling old building facing Tower Green and the chapel of St Peter ad Vincula. A table was set with linen and silver, and good fare was placed before her. Heartened, she managed to eat a little, under the watchful eyes of her host and hostess, but the conversation was awkward, punctuated by tense silences. There was so much she wanted – nay, needed – to know, but dared not ask, for fear of what she might hear.

Above all, she had a burning need to proclaim her innocence, and that of Norris and Smeaton. She also craved spiritual comfort. 'Master Kingston, will you please move the King's Highness to agree to my having the Blessed Sacrament in my closet, so that I might pray for God's mercy?' she asked.

'I can arrange for that, madam,' he told her, dabbing his mouth with his napkin. 'Would you like me to ask one of the Tower chaplains to give you Holy Communion after supper?'

'I should like that very much,' she faltered, trying not to cry. 'God will bear witness that there is no truth in these charges, for I am as clear from the company of man as from sin, and I am the King's true wedded wife. Master Kingston, do you know why I am here?'

Kingston looked troubled. 'If I did, I would not be allowed to discuss it with you.'

'When did you last see the King?' she persisted.

'I saw him in the tiltyard on May Day.'

'I pray you tell me where my lord my father is,' she begged. Father had influence. Surely he could intercede for her.

'I saw him before dinner at court,' Kingston replied. Had Father been aware of what was happening? He was a member of the King's Council – and he had been appointed to that Grand Jury. She remembered how distracted he had been when she saw him last. Had he known about this and not warned her? And George? If George knew, he would move Heaven and earth to save her. *He* would speak to the King on her behalf and fearlessly defend her. She could not bear to imagine his distress when he heard of her arrest.

'Where is my sweet brother?' she cried desperately.

'I left him at York Place,' Kingston said.

Lady Kingston reached across and touched her arm. 'Madam, there's no use working yourself up into a frenzy,' she said. But Anne was lost in terror, deeply agitated, and remembering that someone unnamed had also been charged with committing treason with her. Who could it be?

'I hear that I am accused with three men,' she said, 'and I can say no more but nay, I have done nothing wrong, unless I should open my body to prove it!' So saying, she pretended to hold wide her bodice, and then found herself laughing hysterically again at the absurdity of what she had just said, until Kingston reminded her that Norris and Smeaton had testified against her. She could believe it of Smeaton, for he was no gentleman, but not of Norris. Surely he would not betray her?

'Oh, Norris, have you accused me?' she burst out, laughter turning to weeping. 'You are in the Tower with me, and you and I shall die together. And Mark, you are here too,' she lamented, remembering that he too was innocent. Then she thought of her mother, still lying sick at Hever, and how badly the news of her arrest, with all its shocking implications, would affect her. 'Oh my mother, you will die for sorrow!' she cried. The thought of her mother was too much to bear, so she quickly changed the subject and spoke of her fears for Lady Worcester, whose child might have died inside her.

'What caused it?' Lady Kingston asked.

'It was for the sorrow she felt for me,' Anne told her. There was a silence.

Anne turned to the Constable. She desperately needed to know if she was to face trial. 'Master Kingston, shall I die without justice?'

'The poorest subject of the King hath justice,' he replied.

She laughed at that. She could not stop herself.

It was ten o'clock. The chaplain had long gone, and Anne was completing her light penance in her closet when she heard Lady Kingston, in the outer chamber, say to her aunts that Smeaton had at last been found a lodging in the Tower, and that it was meaner than Norris's. Would to God she knew where Norris was lodged. But as she fell, exhausted, into her bed, at the close of what had been the most dreadful day of her life, it was a small comfort to know that he could not be far away.

Sleep was impossible. She had suffered night terrors before her arrest, but they were a hundred times worse now. Henry, she was convinced, wanted to be free to take a third wife who could give him sons, but without the trouble that had ensued when he had tried to set Katherine aside. But she, Anne, would go quietly, if only she were given the chance – and she would say so as soon as the opportunity arose. It might be her only hope of saving herself. Unless, of course, he was just trying to frighten her into submission. How many times had his threats proved to be mere bluster? He did not really mean to put her to death, not after all she had meant to him. She tried not to imagine herself kneeling before the block, waiting for the axe to fall – the thought was too terrifying. And she had thought rape was the worst thing a man could do to a woman! Her thoughts kept revolving, an endless, convoluted torment, until she saw another bright May morning dawn outside her window.

A few hours later, she was allowed to sit in the Queen's garden, a walled enclosure with an unkempt lawn and poorly tended flower beds. Her four guardians had to accompany her, and she realised that Lady Kingston, who was ostensibly busy with her sewing, was watching her closely. Lady Shelton's overt hostility was unmitigated. It hurt, especially after Anne had done her the honour of appointing her to Elizabeth's household.

'Why are you so angry with me, aunt?' she challenged.

'You should know!' Lady Shelton hissed. 'Not content with bringing disgrace on our family, you have ruined my Madge's reputation! Do you deny that you pushed her into the King's path? Or that Norris, the man she loved, betrayed her with you? Thanks to you, her good name is gone and her happiness destroyed.'

'None of that is true,' Anne protested. 'I have brought no disgrace on our family, for I have been true to the King. Those charges are all lies. I never betrayed him or Madge with Norris. And it was Madge who offered to seduce His Grace.'

'You lie!' Lady Shelton spat. 'My daughter would never do such a thing.'

'I beg to correct you, but she did. Ask her.'

'I know what her answer will be. But your wickedness did not end there, as I well know. You forced me to make the Lady Mary's life a misery; that poor girl, that good girl, lived in fear that you would do

468

away with her. How would you like someone to treat your daughter like that? Think on it, madam, for soon you may not be here to protect her.'

'Lady Shelton, I think you have said enough,' Lady Kingston said, as Anne sat there trembling. She might indeed be facing death, and if there was anything that should trouble her conscience, it was the vile way she had treated Mary.

Lady Kingston was looking at her with pity in her eyes. 'I suggest you refrain from making wild threats,' she told Lady Shelton, 'as we don't know what is to happen to the Queen here. We await the King's orders.'

So there was cause for hope after all. Anne did not know how much longer she could live with the uncertainty, the wild veering between optimism and despair. But she was resolved that, if Henry did spare her, she would be truly kind to Mary and make up to her for all the misery she had inflicted.

Mrs Coffyn, who had been feeding the birds with crumbs from the breakfast table, now sat down beside Anne. 'I am most sorry for your present trouble,' she said. 'I cannot imagine why you are in this situation. I'm told it is because of something your chamberlain said. Why would Sir Henry Norris tell Father Skip that he would swear you were a good woman? Why should he even speak of such a matter?'

It dawned on Anne that Mrs Coffyn, and the others, had been set to spy on her and get her to incriminate herself out of her own mouth. No doubt every word she said was being reported back to Kingston – and Henry!

'I bade him do so,' she said, deciding that telling the truth was the best course. 'We had exchanged some remarks in jest, no more, that we feared had been overheard and misconstrued.' She recounted the conversation she had had with Norris.

'You should know that, even now, Sir Francis Weston is being questioned by the Privy Council about his relations with your Grace,' Mrs Coffyn revealed, watching her closely.

Weston too! She had wondered if he was the third man. 'I fear him talking more than anyone else,' she admitted. 'He thinks that Norris is

469

in love with me.' And she related her exchange with Weston about Norris being reluctant to marry Madge. 'And that,' she said, glaring at Lady Shelton, 'was all there was to this so-called treason.'

She turned back to Mrs Coffyn. 'I will not be convicted,' she declared. 'There is no evidence they can produce against me. If they are twisting silly talk like this, they must be groping around in the dust for a means to get rid of me. But my brother will speak for me, and Norris will declare my innocence, as must Weston and Smeaton.'

'Lord Rochford has been arrested too,' Lady Kingston revealed. 'He is here in the Tower.' She would not meet Anne's horrified gaze.

George too? It did not make sense. Why should he be imprisoned on her account? God forbid, had his part in Katherine's death been discovered? If Chapuys knew of it, Henry would need to make an example of her brother to satisfy the Emperor, whose friendship he desired. And she, Anne, for all Charles's fair words, remained an obstacle to that. Were they also trying to make out that she and her friends had been accomplices in murder, so that the alliance could go ahead? Was this about adultery or murder?

'This is becoming farcical,' she declared. 'I pray you, Lady Kingston, send for your husband so that I might speak to him.'

Sir William, duly summoned, was soon standing before her, hat in hand.

'I hear that my lord my brother is here,' she said.

'It is true,' he confirmed.

'But why?' she asked.

'You know I cannot discuss that with you.' ·

She sighed. 'I am very glad that we are so near each other.' It struck her that, without George and Norris to speak for her, she really was utterly friendless.

Kingston cleared his throat. 'Madam, I may also tell you that four other gentlemen are in the Tower on your account: Sir Francis Weston, Sir William Brereton, Sir Thomas Wyatt and Sir Richard Page.'

That made six men beside her brother! Wyatt she could perhaps understand, for he had loved her once, but she barely knew what Page looked like. What sort of sexual predator did they suppose her to be?

Or were they trying to suggest that, being so desperate to get a son, she had resorted to lover after lover in the hope of filling the royal cradle? It was ridiculous. Had they not remembered that she had had no trouble at all making sons with Henry? Or were they trying to imply that those sons – and even Elizabeth, God forfend – were not Henry's?

Something *was* becoming clear. This whole stinking matter was not just Henry's doing: it was Cromwell's, of that she had no doubt. He had feared her enmity, and he had counterattacked. The arrest of Brereton proved it. Cromwell had a score to settle with him. The hand of Master Secretary was becoming all too evident in this business. This was not about adultery or murder!

Well, she would deal with him!

'Master Kingston, I desire you to bear a letter from me to Master Secretary,' she said.

'Madam,' he replied, 'tell it me by word of mouth, and I will do it.'

'I beg you, say to him that I much marvel that the King's Council does not come to see me. They have not questioned me at all, and yet they have arrested these seven gentlemen. I should like an opportunity to explain everything and clear my name.'

Kingston said nothing.

Anne looked up at the cloudless sky. 'If good men will do nothing to remedy my situation, God will make manifest His displeasure. I'll wager we shall have no rain till I am delivered out of the Tower.'

'Then I pray it will rain soon, because we need fair weather for the crops,' Kingston said, and left her.

When he had gone, Lady Kingston gave her a frame, some fabric and some silks, and she tried to concentrate on embroidery. As she stitched, she warmed even more to her theory about Cromwell. None of her women had been arrested for abetting adultery, and it would have been impossible for her to have indulged in a succession of liaisons without the collusion of at least one trusted maid. In accusing her of whatever crime she was supposed to have committed, Cromwell had taken a breathtaking risk, which showed how desperate he must be.

But Cromwell was no fool – whatever proofs he had shown Henry would have had to be convincing, or the consequences for Master Secretary could be horrific.

By the following evening, Anne had grown so sick of the unwelcome vigilance and barbs of her attendant ladies that she could stay silent no longer. At dinner, when they were all present, she turned to Kingston.

'The King knew what he was doing when he placed my aunts and Mistress Coffyn about me, for they tell me nothing about anything.'

Lady Boleyn snorted. 'Your love of intrigue has brought you to this, niece.'

'I have never intrigued against the King,' Anne declared.

There was a silence. Mrs Stonor filled it. 'You know Mark Smeaton is the worst treated of all the prisoners here, for he wears irons.'

Anne was disturbed to hear it. 'That is because he is no gentleman,' she observed. 'I know of no wrong he has done. He was only ever in my privy chamber at Winchester, when I sent for him to play for the company. I did not speak with him after that till the Saturday before May Day, when I found him standing in the window in my presence chamber.' She related what had happened. 'Is it for this he was arrested?'

The ladies said nothing. She hoped they would report her defence of Smeaton.

After dinner, her spirits sank again at the thought of another night spent agonising about her situation. When Kingston was preparing to escort her back to her lodging, she broke down. 'My lord my brother will die!' she wailed.

'That is by no means certain,' he said.

'I have never heard of a queen being so cruelly treated,' she told him. 'I think the King does it to prove me.' And suddenly she was laughing again. It was the thought of Henry, who had been constantly unfaithful, testing her devotion. With an effort, she controlled herself. 'I shall have justice.'

'Have no doubt of that,' Kingston assured her.

'And if any man accuses me, I can say nothing but nay, for they can bring no witness. I wish, though, that I could have made some statement of my innocence. If I had done so, my case would be won. I would to

472

God I had my bishops with me, for they would all go to the King for me if they knew the truth.' It appalled her to think that those who had known her as a friend to true religion might now believe the worst of her.

Kingston was looking sceptical, which aroused her anger.

'I think the most part of England must be praying for me,' she said, 'and if I die, you shall see the greatest visitation of divine punishment that ever came to England. But I shall be in Heaven, for I have done many good deeds in my days.' And, at the thought, she wept again.

She had been in the Tower nearly a week when a deputation of councillors visited her.

'Make a full confession of your crimes and it will go better for you,' they exhorted her.

'What crimes?' She faced them boldly, holding herself regally, as their Queen. 'My lords, I have no further hope in this world, but I will confess nothing, certainly not to things I have not done. All I want now is to be delivered from this purgatory on earth, so that I can go and live in Heaven. I no longer care about dying.' It was true. She was calmer now, resigned to the worst. Her life had become such a living hell that death would come as a welcome release.

They stared at her, astonished. Had they expected tears and pleading?

She returned their gaze. 'I can confess no more than I have already spoken.'

Two days later, Kingston stood before her. 'I am to tell your Grace that I have this day received orders that I am to bring up the bodies of Sir Francis Weston, Sir Henry Norris, Sir William Brereton and Mark Smeaton to Westminster Hall to be tried for treason on Friday next.'

Two days hence.

'And what of Lord Rochford and myself?'

'I have received no instructions about that, madam.'

'This is outrageous!' she flared. 'We should all be tried at the same time. The outcome of the one trial may prejudice the other.'

'Madam,' Kingston said patiently, 'these men are commoners and will be heard by the commissioners who brought the case against them. You and Lord Rochford have the right to be tried by the peers, your equals, in the court of the High Steward of England.'

She knew that whoever tried whom the law was heavily weighted against anyone suspected of treason. She had heard of only one person ever being acquitted.

'What of Master Wyatt and Master Page?' she asked.

'Again, I have received no instructions,' Kingston said.

She was on a dagger's edge on the day the men were tried, and kept sending to know if Kingston had returned. The sight of his grave face when, late in the afternoon, he appeared before her made her fear the worst.

'Tell me!' she begged. 'Were they found guilty?'

'All,' he said, swallowing.

'Of what?' she cried.

'I may not discuss the indictments with your Grace.'

'Tell me at least if they protested my innocence,' she pleaded.

'Only Smeaton pleaded guilty,' Kingston told her, 'but the verdict was unanimous.'

This was a worse nightmare than any she had suffered in the hours of darkness. 'What will happen to them?' she whispered, dreading the answer.

Kingston looked distressed. 'They will suffer the death meted out to traitors.'

Not Norris! her heart cried out. Not that true, loyal man. Nor Weston, who was young and full of life, or Brereton, whose only crime had been to offend Cromwell, or Smeaton, for all his insufferable pride! This could not be happening. And what did it portend for her and for George? They were all doomed.

The next day, Kingston returned. 'Madam, I have received the King's writ commanding me to bring your Grace and Lord Rochford before the Lord High Steward on Monday for trial here in the King's Hall.'

So she was not to go out of the Tower. No doubt they feared demonstrations on her behalf – or more likely, against her.

'But I have not been told what has been alleged against me!' she cried. 'How can I prepare my defence?'

'You will hear the indictment in court, madam, where they will also read out the depositions of any witnesses.'

'May some lawyer be appointed to speak for me?'

Kingston was looking increasingly uncomfortable. 'Madam, legal representation is forbidden to those charged with treason. Nor may you call witnesses on your own behalf.'

She laughed bitterly at that. 'It is doubtful that any would dare come forward anyway. So how *can* I defend myself?'

'You may dispute with your accusers.'

'You told me I would have justice!' she snapped. 'This sounds like a travesty of it.'

Kingston lowered his guard, and she could see the compassion in his eyes. 'As my good friend Cardinal Wolsey once said to me,' he observed, 'if the Crown were prosecutor and insisted on it, justice would be found to bring in a verdict that Abel was the murderer of Cain.'

The realisation that she was in the same plight as she had intended for Wolsey stung. 'Then I am brought to fight without a weapon,' she whispered.

Kingston hastened away, saying there was much to be done, leaving her to her frustration and her fears. She spent much of the rest of that day, and all day Sunday, watching from her window as the courtyard of the inmost ward below became the scene of frantic activity, with workmen carrying wood and scaffolding poles into the adjacent King's Hall, a flustered Kingston directing them, and Tower officials running back and forth to do his bidding. Looking at the rich furnishings being borne in – a great gilded board bearing the arms of England, tables, Turkey rugs, upholstered chairs and a chest of silver goblets – she realised that she was to be tried with an appropriate degree of state and ceremonial. She was, after all, the Queen of England.

Chapter 27

1536

She waited in the porch with Kingston, Sir Edmund Walsingham, her four female warders and – a welcome surprise – four of her former maids-of-honour: Nan Saville, Margery Horsman, Mary Zouche and Norris's sister, another Mary, all of whom it was a comfort to see. She was near tears as she embraced them, although the evident distress in their faces alarmed her. They would have heard the gossip at court. Did they know something she did not?

At least, as queen, she would be properly attended, but this was no court ceremonial. The Gentleman Gaoler of the Tower waited with her, and there were guards before and behind her.

From inside the hall she could hear a great hubbub of conversation. The place must be packed. She had seen the common folk queuing from before dawn to get in. At least she was to be tried in the sight of the people.

She heard a voice crying for silence, then the gruff tones of Uncle Norfolk, who – Kingston had told her – was acting as Lord High Steward on this occasion, calling, 'Gentleman Gaoler of the Tower, bring in your prisoner.'

An usher appeared at the door, and at his nod, Anne held her head high, as became a queen, and followed him into the vast aisled hall, aware of a thousand eyes upon her. The benches and the stands that lined the length of the walls were packed with spectators. She knew she cut a regal figure in her gown of black velvet, worn over a kirtle of scarlet damask, and a small bonnet sporting a black-and-white feather. They had been among the items of apparel that had been bundled into a chest and delivered to the Tower shortly after she arrived.

476

She was heartily thankful that the uncontrollable hysteria of her first week in captivity had abated, leaving her calm, dignified and ready to face whatever Fate – or Henry – had in store for her. God, she felt, walked by her side, and from Him she would gain her strength.

She tried not to look at the Gentleman Gaoler of the Tower, who walked beside her carrying his ceremonial axe, its blade turned away from her to signify that she was as yet uncondemned. Ahead of her was Uncle Norfolk, enthroned under a cloth of estate bearing the royal arms, for he represented the King. He leaned on the long white staff of his office, and on a chair at his feet sat his son, her cousin Surrey, grasping the golden staff that Norfolk wielded as Earl Marshal of England. At the Duke's right hand sat Lord Chancellor Audley, and at his left the Duke of Suffolk, who could both be trusted to do the King's bidding.

On either side stood the peers who had come to try her – two dozen and more of them, all familiar faces, many belonging to men she had once called her friends. Some were staunch partisans of the Lady Mary, others relations or favourites of the King. She could not look for much help there. She noticed Harry Percy, looking drawn and ill. And, God save her, *Father* was there too, red-faced and not meeting her eye. At the sight of him she faltered for a moment. What kind of monster would command a father to judge his own children? Had Henry sunk so low? Or did she have Cromwell to thank for this?

He was there, Master Secretary, looking important and smug. His eyes bore down on her in triumph. He had won, he was telling her. He had nothing more to fear from her. She resolved to expose him for the villain he was.

Her gaze took in the Lord Mayor of London with his aldermen, sheriffs and guildsmen. There was the French ambassador and other foreign diplomats; but Chapuys – whose derision she had dreaded – was nowhere to be seen.

A great platform had been raised in the centre of the hall. She stepped up to it, walked to the bar and curtseyed to her judges, her eyes raking them all. She would not show them any sign of fear. To a man, they bowed, and Norfolk invited her to be seated on the fine chair that stood on the platform. She sat down, arranging her skirts elegantly about her. Next to the chair was a small table on which had been placed her crown, as if to remind those watching of her exalted rank. They would have brought it over from the Jewel House next door.

With much flourishing of papers and clearing of his throat, Sir Christopher Hales, the Attorney General, rose to read the indictment. His voice rang out. 'Whereas Queen Anne has been the wife of King Henry VIII for three years and more, she, despising the solemn, most excellent and noble marriage between our lord the King and her, and having in her heart malice against our lord the King, and being seduced by evil and not having God before her eyes, and following daily her frail and carnal appetites, did falsely and traitorously procure, by base conversations and kisses, touches, gifts and other infamous inducements, many of the King's close servants to be her adulterers.'

Anne put up her hand. 'Not guilty,' she said firmly. 'This is all lies.'

Sir Christopher glared at her. 'Madam, you shall have your say. Pray allow me to finish. Ahem. Several of the King's servants yielded to her vile provocations.' He named Norris, Weston, Brereton and Smeaton, then read out a long list of the dates on which adultery was supposed to have taken place. She listened in growing amazement that whoever had compiled it could have been so careless.

It was shameful having to listen to descriptions of herself enticing, by sweet words, kisses, caresses and worse, her co-accused to violate her, and having illicit intercourse. But it was the dates that, above all else, drew her attention. They were many of them impossible, because either she or the gentleman in question had not been in that place at that time, or not together. And yet it had been made impossible for her fully to refute the charges because of the frequent assertion in the indictment that adultery had been committed on many occasions before and after the date listed. This, as she had feared, was a travesty of justice.

'Not guilty,' she said again.

She was wondering what part George was supposed to have played in all this, and when Sir Christopher would get to the charges of conspiracy, when she heard his name.

'Also' – and here the Attorney General paused for effect – 'that the

Queen procured and incited her own natural brother, George Boleyn, knight, Lord Rochford, to violate her, alluring him with her tongue in the said George's mouth, and the said George's tongue in hers, and also with kisses, presents and jewels, against the commands of Almighty God, and all laws human and divine. Whereby he, despising the commands of God, and all other human laws, violated and carnally knew the said Queen, his own sister.'

She could have died of shame. She was trembling so violently that she thought she would die. This was outrageous! It was bad enough that they had made her out to be the basest and most wanton monster, but they could not seriously be suggesting that she had bedded George? It was foul, abominable and sickening, and if her cheeks were flaming, it was because she was revolted by such filth.

'Not guilty!' Her voice rang out loudly.

But Sir Christopher had not finished. 'Furthermore,' he continued, 'the Queen and the other traitors compassed and imagined the King's death; and the Queen frequently promised to marry one of the traitors whenever the King should depart this life, affirming she would never love the King in her heart.'

'Never!' she declared. 'This is utter calumny.'

Sir Christopher, in full flight, was not to be deterred. 'My lords, think of the effect of all this upon our sovereign lord the King. Having come only a short time ago to hear of these false and detestable crimes, vices and treasons committed against himself, he has suffered such inward displeasure and heaviness that certain harms and perils have befallen his royal body, to the scandal, danger and detriment of the heirs of the King and Queen.'

Henry was suffering? What about her, having all these vile, unjust accusations flung at her in public? It was hard to sit there patiently, listening to them, while trying to look like the innocent person she was. She felt dirty, sullied, almost as if she *were* guilty.

At last Sir Christopher stopped speaking. 'You may answer the charges now, madam,' he told her.

It was important to stay calm and not protest too much, but this was the moment she had longed for. She looked around the hall at all the people staring at her expectantly. 'I have never been false to the King,' she insisted. 'I remember well that, on about half of the days on which I am charged with adultery, I was not even in the same house as the gentleman concerned, or I was with child, or had recently given birth. Ask your wives, my lords, what woman wants dalliance with a man at such a time?' There was a murmur of laughter. Good. She had some of them, at least, with her.

'But think: what does charging me with adultery on these dates imply?' she went on. 'It is a foul slur on my issue with the King, a hint that he did not sire my children, and I find that shocking. Impugning the royal succession is treason – and in making these charges my accusers are guilty of it! And on at least one of the days I am supposed to have seduced my paramours, I knew myself to be under constant surveillance. My lords, I am not that much of a fool.' There was more laughter.

She waited until it had died down. 'But now I must refute the serious charge of conspiring the death of the King. It is the most heinous of them all, and high treason of the first order. If I were guilty of it, then I should say that I deserved to die. But when I allegedly first plotted this treason, the Princess Dowager was yet alive, and what would it have availed me? For if the King had died then, there might well have been a rising in favour of the Lady Mary, or even civil war.' She paused to let that sink in. 'What would it have profited me to kill my chief protector and ally myself in marriage with any of those men? None of them could have given me what the King gave me.'

She braced herself to go on. 'As for the charge of incest, it is plain that my enemies have conjured it purely to arouse outrage and revulsion against me. And in regard to all the accusations of adultery, committing that crime would have been impossible without the connivance of the ladies waiting on me, who are witnesses to my private doings. And yet none have been charged with misprision of treason.' She looked defiantly around the court, gratified to hear some murmurs of assent. 'Moreover,' she went on, emboldened, 'I knew I stood in danger from my enemies. I could not have been more wary and wakeful, for I knew their eyes were everywhere upon me, and that their malicious hearts were bent on making some mischief where they found none. What halfwit would commit misconduct knowing they were so closely watched?'

The Attorney General and Cromwell stood up.

'Admit it, the charges are all justified,' Sir Christopher barked.

'I refute them utterly,' she insisted.

Cromwell spoke. 'There was a promise, was there not, between you and Norris to marry after the King's death, which you hoped for?'

'No, there was not.' She would not deign to look at him.

'You danced in your bedchamber with gentlemen of the King's Privy Chamber?'

'I danced with them in my privy chamber, and my ladies were always present.'

'You were seen kissing your brother, Lord Rochford.'

'My lords, I do protest!' Anne cried. 'Which of you have wives, sisters and daughters who do not kiss their brothers from time to time?'

Cromwell ignored that. 'You cannot deny that you wrote to your brother, informing him that you were with child?'

'Why should I not? I informed all my family. Since when has it been a crime?'

'Some might see it as proof that your brother had fathered your child.'

She responded to that with the contemptuous silence it merited, raising her eyebrows.

Sir Christopher returned to the attack. 'You and your brother laughed at the King's attire and made fun of his poetry.'

She would not deign to answer that either. They really were raking for muck.

'You showed in various ways that you did not love the King and were tired of him. My lords, is this not shocking conduct in a woman whom the King had honoured by marrying her?' The lords nodded sagely.

'I love my lord the King, as I am by honour and inclination bound to do,' Anne protested in a loud voice. 'I have maintained my honour and my chastity all my life long, as much as ever queen did. This case you have constructed against me is nothing but calumny!'

That set many to murmuring, and she sensed that they were expressing doubts and suspicions in regard to the prosecution's case. Some were looking at her and nodding approvingly.

'But your paramours have confessed.'

'Four of them pleaded not guilty,' she reminded them. 'That leaves the wretch Smeaton. One witness is not enough to convict a person of high treason.'

'In your case it is sufficient,' Cromwell said. 'Besides, we have the witness depositions. Let them be read.'

They added nothing new to the Crown's case, but Anne was deeply hurt to hear that Lady Worcester had testified to her alleged relations with George and Smeaton, and Lady Wingfield had confided to a friend that the Queen was a loose woman.

'But Lady Wingfield is dead,' Anne objected, 'so her testimony can only be hearsay, which I believe is inadmissible as evidence. I repeat, everything you have alleged against me is untrue. I have committed no offence.'

The Attorney General looked at her as if she were speaking in a foreign tongue. 'That concludes the case for the Crown,' he intoned. 'My lords, will you consider your verdict?'

The lords nodded their assent, and began conferring with each other. Hardly able to bear the tension, Anne watched as several walked over to commune with their fellows on the other side of the hall. She searched their faces for some sign of what they were thinking, but it was impossible to tell. They were giving nothing away. Her mouth felt dry and her hands clammy. All she wanted now was for this ordeal to be over.

Eventually Suffolk signalled to Sir Christopher Hales.

'My lord of Surrey, I call upon you first to give your verdict,' the Attorney General said.

'Guilty!' Surrey declared.

'My lord of Suffolk?'

'Guilty!'

'My lord of Worcester?'

'Guilty!'

'My lord of Northumberland?'

Harry Percy stood up. His face was deathly pale, but his voice was strong. 'Guilty!'

And then – what else had she expected? – every other earl and baron among them stood up, each in his turn, and said the same, until Sir Christopher came to her father, who looked like a broken man.

'My lord of Wiltshire?'

Father rose slowly to his feet. He was struggling to speak.

'My lord?'

'Guilty,' he muttered.

They had forced him to this, Anne knew, even as she was horrified that he had condemned her. He had bought his safety by betraying his children. That was more terrible to her than her own peril. And yet he had Mother to think of. He was salvaging what he could of his life – but he would have to live with what he had done.

Sir Christopher Hales was regarding Anne sternly. 'Prisoner at the bar, you will stand to receive judgement.'

She stood up. Everything seemed unreal. She was barely aware of the speculative murmurs rippling along the benches.

Suffolk came to the bar and addressed her. 'Madam, you must resign your crown into our hands.'

By that she knew the worst. She lifted the crown and gave it to him, aware that in this symbolic act she was ceremonially divesting herself of the trappings of her rank. All her power had come to this.

'I am innocent of having offended against His Grace,' she declared, but Suffolk remained impassive.

'In the name of the King, I degrade you from your title of lady marquess,' he proclaimed.

'I give it up willingly to my lord my husband who conferred it,' she replied, aware that the title of queen had not been mentioned. They could not take that away – at least, not now. It was hers under the Act of Succession, which had named her Queen by statutory right, not just by right of marriage to the King.

A hush descended as Norfolk sat up straight in his chair. She was astonished to see tears streaming down his cheeks. No doubt they were for his family's lost honour and status, and the jeopardising of his own career by this scandal, rather than for her.

He fixed his martinet gaze on her. 'Because you have offended against our sovereign lord the King's Grace in committing treason against his person, the law of the realm is this, that you have deserved death; and your judgement is this: that you shall be burned at the stake here within the Tower of London on the Green, or you will have your head smitten off, according to the King's pleasure.'

There was a shriek from the back of the stands, and Anne glimpsed Mrs Orchard in a state of unspeakable distress. The justices were muttering indignantly, clearly unhappy about the sentence. 'It should be one thing or the other,' she heard one say. 'It is unfair on the prisoner.' Norfolk glared at him. Suddenly Harry Percy slumped in his chair, apparently unconscious. The lords nearby moved to help, and ushers came hastening to carry him out. Had it been too much for him, knowing that the girl he had once loved was the woman he had just condemned to a terrible death?

They were waiting for her to speak now. She still felt calm. She could not connect these dread events to herself. It was as if the whole trial had taken place in a dream. She looked down at her skirts, wondering if they would expect her to go royally garbed to her burning. What a waste of good clothes that would be.

And then the awful realisation of what lay in store for her sank in.

'O Father, O Creator, Thou who art the way, the life and the truth knoweth whether I have deserved this death,' she cried out, raising her eyes to Heaven. She looked desperately at her judges. 'My lords, I will not say your sentence is unjust, nor presume that my defence can prevail against your convictions. I am willing to believe that you have sufficient reasons for what you have done; but they must be other than those which have been produced in court, for I am clear of all the offences laid to my charge. I have ever been a faithful wife to the King, though I do not say I have always shown him that humility which his goodness to me merited. I confess I have had jealous fancies and suspicions of him, which I had not discretion and wisdom enough to conceal at all times.'

She paused, bowing her head in humility, then her voice rang out strong and true. 'But God knows, and is my witness, that I have not sinned against him in any other way. Think not I say this in the hope to prolong my life, for He who saves from death has taught me how to die, and He will strengthen my faith. I know these, my last words, will avail me nothing but for the justification of my chastity and honour.' She looked directly at her father, who would not meet her eye. 'As for my brother and those others who are unjustly condemned, I would willingly suffer many deaths to deliver them, but since I see it so pleases the King, I shall willingly accompany them in death, with this assurance, that I shall lead an endless life with them in peace and joy, where I will pray to God for the King and for you, my lords.'

Silence greeted her impassioned words. The peers had the grace to look chastened. She wondered if, in their hearts, they believed her guilty. It did not matter. It was Henry, clearly, who had been convinced of it, and once his will had been made plain, no one would dare contravene it. She looked at her accusers again, her gaze taking in Hales and Cromwell. 'The Judge of all the world, in Whom abounds justice and truth, knows all,' she reminded them, 'and through His love I beseech that He will have compassion on those who have condemned me to this death.' She paused. 'I ask only for a short space of time for the unburdening of my conscience.' She could hear more than one person sobbing. Norfolk was weeping again. Even Cromwell had pity in his eyes.

The court rose. Anne curtseyed to the peers, then Kingston came forward to escort her from the hall, with Lady Kingston following. The Gentleman Gaoler walked alongside, his ceremonial axe now turned towards her, to show the waiting crowd outside that she had been condemned to death.

She had been told that her brother's trial was to follow, and was praying that she might catch a glimpse of him and even offer him some words of comfort, but there was no sign of him. As she left the hall, a buzz of conversation erupted behind her.

Back in her chamber, she was relieved to learn that only Lady Kingston, Aunt Boleyn, Mrs Orchard and her four maids were to attend her from now on. Lady Shelton and Mrs Coffyn had been dismissed.

She sank down on her bed, and it was only now that she gave herself up to terror, shrinking in her mind from the heat of the flames, the scorching of her flesh and the unimaginable agony and horror of being burned to death. She stuffed the sheet in her mouth to stop herself from screaming.

George had been condemned too – in his case to a traitor's death.

'But because he is a nobleman, the King will almost certainly commute it to beheading,' Kingston said, his tone gentle. He had been treading warily around Anne since she had emerged, drained and fragile, from her bedchamber.

'Did he deny the charges?' She was desperate to know.

Now that judgement had been passed, the Constable seemed willing to talk.

'He did, and he answered them so prudently and wisely that it was a marvel to hear. He never confessed to anything, but made himself clear that he had never offended. Sir Thomas More himself did not reply better.'

Brave George! He had not played the craven and let her down.

'It was his wife who deposed against him in regard to the incest,' Kingston told her. Jane, that little hellcat! What a vile revenge she had wreaked for George's base use of her, and for Fisher's death.

'It seems that it was more out of envy and jealousy than out of love towards the King that she betrayed this accursed secret,' Kingston added.

'Why should she be jealous?' Anne cried.

'It seems she thought her husband loved you more, madam.'

'That's what she wants the world to think. No, she is for the Lady Mary. She means to destroy me and my blood.'

'I think many agreed with your Grace,' Kingston revealed. 'Some said much money would have been won, at great odds, if Lord Rochford had been acquitted.'

'How did my brother take the sentence?' she asked.

'Bravely. He observed that every man was a sinner and that all merited death. Then he said that, since he must die, he would no longer maintain his innocence, but confess that he had deserved to die.'

Anne was about to protest that George would never have incriminated them both by saying such a thing, and then it dawned on her. He had not been talking about incest, but about murder.

Mrs Orchard, who had stayed in the hall to watch George's trial, came to offer comfort.

'He won't let them kill you,' she said, holding Anne to her ample bosom, just as if she were a child again. 'When it comes to it, you'll get a reprieve, you'll see.'

'Yes,' Anne sobbed. 'I pray you are right.'

'Something strange happened at your brother's trial,' Mrs Orchard told her.

Anne sat up. 'What?'

'They accused him of putting it about that you had told Lady Rochford something secret about the King. They wouldn't say what it was, but wrote it down and showed it to Lord Rochford, ordering him not to repeat it. But he did. He read out that you had told Lady Rochford that the King wasn't able to copulate with a woman, for he had neither potency nor vigour.'

'I never said that!' Anne flared. 'It's not true, so why would I say it?' But she knew the answer. If Henry could not have sired her children, because of impotency, some other man must have done. And there might be another, more sinister, explanation, for all the world knew that impotency was caused by witchcraft. That might explain Sir Christopher's strange claim that harms and perils had befallen the King's body. Were they really implying that she herself had cast an enchantment on Henry to make him incapable of siring the sons she had so desperately longed for? It defied all reason.

'That's what your brother told them. He said, "I did not say it!" He insisted he would never arouse any suspicion that might prejudice the King's issue.' No, *he* would not – but others were striving their best to do just that. Anne dared not think of what the consequences would be for Elizabeth. In fact, she dared not think of Elizabeth, for that way lay madness.

On the day after the trial, Kingston informed Anne that he was going to Whitehall to see the King. A little hope sparked in her, especially when he told her that the condemned men were to die the next day, but no instructions had been sent, nor any date set, for her own execution.

'Sir William, have you been told how . . . how I am to die?' she faltered.

'No, madam. Today I mean to discover the King's pleasure concerning you, in regard to your comfort and what is to be done with you.'

'I pray he will put me out of this misery. It's not knowing what will happen that torments me the most. If I know my fate, I can prepare myself to face it.'

Kingston's grey eyes were full of sympathy. She suspected he had grown to like her, and that he did not believe what they said of her. 'I will do my best for you,' he promised.

That afternoon, Archbishop Cranmer was ushered into her presence chamber. She fell to her knees weeping when she saw him, seizing the hem of his surplice and kissing it. 'Oh, my dear friend! It is such a comfort to see you.'

Cranmer knelt beside her, his heavy features contorted with emotion. 'The King has appointed me your confessor,' he told her. 'Oh, Anne! I am exceedingly sorry that the charges have been proved against you. I told them I could not believe it of you. I said I never had a better opinion of a woman, and that I loved you for the love you bear to God and the Gospel – but the things they told me!'

'All lies,' she assured him. 'My enemies have united to get rid of me, and they have turned the King against me. Tell me, does he really believe it all?'

Cranmer looked miserable. 'I fear he does. But I have hardly seen him. No one has. He has shut himself away, and will see only me and

Cromwell. When I saw His Grace today, he was in a pensive mood. But you know him of old, Anne. It's impossible to know what he is thinking. He spoke of the succession. He said that the Princess Elizabeth cannot stand in the way of any heirs he might have with a future wife.'

'Then he really does mean to be rid of me,' she whispered, feeling again the rising terror she had fought so hard to control. He meant to make Jane Seymour queen. A fine queen she would be, who was sly, deceitful and never had a word to say for herself!

'All I can say is that he has charged me with finding cause to dissolve your marriage,' Cranmer said.

'The marriage you found to be good and valid just three years ago!' Anne retorted bitterly. 'And what will that make my daughter – a bastard?'

'I fear so,' Cranmer admitted, wringing his hands.

Anne stood up. 'Has anyone pointed out to Henry the absurdity of charging me with adultery if I was never lawfully his wife?' She laughed mirthlessly. 'Of course, it makes little difference, for they cleverly added that charge of plotting the King's death, which is high treason by anyone's reckoning!'

She regarded Cranmer. He loved her, but his admiration for her counted for little against his desire to please the King, his sense of self-preservation, and his zeal for reform. She would be a hindrance to that now, with her reputation in tatters. But she must be fair. Cranmer was in a difficult position. Her fall might well have an adverse impact on him, the man who had facilitated her marriage to the King. He needed to survive to fight for the cause another day.

'So what is it to be?' she asked. 'Consanguinity? A precontract with Harry Percy? Insanity? By the way, how is Harry Percy?'

'Mortally ill, I fear,' Cranmer said, rising to his feet. 'Madam, I cannot argue that the King's union with the Princess Dowager was lawful after all. We'd all be a laughing stock. And Percy has again denied that there ever was a precontract. That leaves the impediment raised by the King's relations with your sister. Now I know that the Bishop of Rome issued a dispensation covering that, but the recent Dispensations Act provides that it cannot be held as valid because it is contrary to Holy Scripture and the laws of God. Thus your marriage may be deemed null and void. I have come to summon you and the King to appear before my court at Lambeth Palace to hear my judgement. I advise you not to contest it.'

All she could think of was that she would see Henry. She would have this one last chance of convincing him she had never betrayed him, and of telling him she would make no fuss if he divorced her, but would go abroad and disappear into a nunnery. Anything would be better than facing the flames.

'The King will be there?' she asked eagerly.

'Neither of you will be there,' Cranmer said. 'You will both be represented by proctors.' It was crushing to hear that, but then hope sprang again. If Henry meant to have her executed, why go to the bother of annulling their marriage? Sadly, the answer was plain. He must ensure an undisputed succession.

'My daughter was born before the Dispensations Act was passed, when the King and I believed we had entered into marriage in good faith. Surely she must be deemed legitimate?'

'Anne, this is no time for legal niceties,' Cranmer warned her. 'I am come to obtain your admission of the impediment to your marriage, and your consent to its dissolution, which will mean the disinheriting of your child. In return for that, I am authorised to tell you that the King promises you the kinder death. Already, out of pity, he has sent to Calais for an expert swordsman to do the deed swiftly. Madam, I urge you to consider well and accept the offer. If you do, I am hopeful that you might be spared the extreme penalty altogether.'

There could be no contest. The prospect of a reprieve was too compelling. Even if Henry did not pardon her, it would be easier for Elizabeth to grow up in the knowledge that her mother had died by the sword rather than by fire. The child was sharp, with her wits about her and had it in her to fend for herself. Yet Henry loved her, there was no doubt of it; he would protect her. As his bastard, she would be safer than if she was a contender for the succession. Look at the misery that had befallen the Lady Mary. Anne thanked God now that, for all Mary's treason, Henry had never carried out any of his threats. His fatherly love went too deep, and Anne trusted that Elizabeth too would be safe from his anger against her mother. Anyway, who would take up the cudgels on Elizabeth's behalf now?

'I accept,' she said. 'Thomas, will you hear my last confession?'

Cranmer hesitated. Naturally, he did not want to carry the burden of her innocence. But he surprised her. 'Of course,' he said. 'I will return.'

At supper, she felt more cheerful than she had in days. She had wondered all along if Henry would actually send her to her death, and now she was becoming convinced that he would not.

'I believe I will go to a nunnery,' she said. 'I am hoping that my life will be spared.'

They were all looking at her with pity in their eyes.

'The gentlemen are to die tomorrow, madam,' Kingston said gently.

She realised she had been cruelly deceived. Henry had meant all along for her to die. There would be no reprieve. She had been tricked, by the lure of a mercifully quick end, into sanctioning the disinheriting of her child. She kept her composure, although her stomach was churning at the thought of what lay ahead of her days, hours perhaps, hence. 'I do hope that those poor gentlemen will not suffer traitors' deaths,' she said.

'I have just had word, madam. The King has been pleased graciously to commute the sentences to decapitation.'

'Thank God!' she breathed.

'That is a great clemency to Smeaton,' Lady Kingston observed. 'He is a lucky fellow. Only persons of rank get their sentences commuted.'

'Maybe it is because he confessed to something they knew he had not done,' Anne said, remembering how Cranmer had bargained with her.

'Master Kingston, I desire very much to be shriven of my sins,' she said. 'His Grace of Canterbury promised to return to hear my last confession.'

'I will send for him,' Kingston said, 'when the time comes.'

'He told me that a French swordsman had been summoned.'

'Not French, Madam. It is one of the Emperor's subjects, from Saint-Omer.'

She managed a smile. 'That will please Messire Chapuys.'

'The King is paying the headsman handsomely to ensure you are dispatched humanely,' Kingston told her. 'This "Sword of Calais" is of some renown for his swiftness and skill.'

How could the severing of someone's head be humane? 'That is one mercy,' she said aloud, feeling the panic rising again. 'At least it will be quick. But it is a pity he could not get here in time to dispatch my brother and the others.'

'It is, alas. But they are all ready and, I trust, at peace with God. They shall have good warning in the morning.'

She shuddered. She could not bear to think of George and Norris dying for her sake. This time tomorrow, she would be the only one left, and then it could only be a matter of hours . . .

In the morning, Mrs Orchard woke her early.

'Madam, Lady Kingston is here. Orders have come. You are to witness the executions.'

Anne was instantly awake. 'No! I cannot!'

'My dear lamb, you have to. It is the King's wish.'

Oh, that Henry would go to Hell and be eternally damned! Had he not done enough to her? This was purely vindictive.

She suffered them to dress her in the black gown she had worn at her trial, and emerged to face the waiting Kingston.

'I am very sorry for this, madam,' he apologised, 'but I have my orders.'

'I understand,' she said shakily.

He led her, with Lady Kingston following, across the inmost ward, through the Coldharbour Gate and back to Water Lane, which they followed some way around the outer ward to one of the ancient towers. He unlocked the door and they mounted the stone stairs to an empty and very dusty round chamber.

'Your Grace will be able to see from that window,' Kingston said. 'I regret I cannot remain with you, but I must attend the prisoners to the scaffold.' He bowed and hastened away.

It was a small window, set in the thickness of the wall. Although Anne shrank from looking out, her attention was drawn by the vast crowds on Tower Hill, beyond the walls of the fortress. They were being contained by soldiers ranked around a high scaffold, and in the front she recognised many courtiers she knew. After a few minutes, the crowd quietened, and every head was turned in the direction of the entrance to the Tower. The ranks of people parted and Anne could see George, surrounded by guards, then Norris, followed by Weston, Brereton and Smeaton. All appeared calm except the musician. Even from here he looked terrified.

At the sight of her brother and the man she loved, Anne started weeping uncontrollably, and Lady Kingston put a motherly arm around her. Beneath her stolid, taciturn exterior, she had a kindly heart.

'I pray they make good ends,' she said. 'It is a pity we cannot hear their farewell speeches, but no doubt my husband will tell us what they said.'

Anne cried out as George mounted the scaffold. She sobbed as she watched him, cool and confident as ever, speaking to the crowd for a long space in a loud voice, which she could just hear. It tore her apart to think it was for the last time. In minutes that loved voice would be stilled for ever.

She watched as he knelt before the block and lay down. She saw the public executioner raise his axe.

'No!' she screamed, and buried her face in her hands.

'It is over, it is over,' Lady Kingston soothed. 'Nothing can hurt him now.'

'Oh, my God, have mercy on his soul!' she wept. 'Is it safe to look?'

'Wait . . . Yes, they have taken him away.'

Anne opened her eyes. She was trembling violently, bowed by grief. She peered through the window to see the block, and the executioner's assistant chucking water from a bucket over the scaffold. It was dripping pink with blood – George's blood. She felt sick at the sight. Soon, her own blood would be flooding a scaffold.

Through the blur of tears she saw Norris addressing the people. He was brief, so she had little chance to gaze for the last time upon those loved features. When he knelt, she sank to the floor, howling, not caring what Lady Kingston made of it.

She stayed there, keening and sobbing, mourning for the only two men who had loved her genuinely and unconditionally. She did not want to live in a world without them. Her only comfort lay in knowing that she would not be far behind them. Somehow she would get through the hours until she could join them.

She did not see the other men die. Lady Kingston did not press her. When it was all over, she helped Anne to her feet, turned her away from the window, put an arm around her and supported her down the stairs, for she was shaking so much that she could not have stood alone.

Kingston came within ten minutes. His face was grim, and he frowned when he saw Anne.

'They all died very charitably,' he said. Lady Kingston was shaking her head warningly. They helped Anne back to her lodgings in silence.

When they got there, Kingston turned to her. 'It is my heavy duty, madam, to inform you that you are to die tomorrow morning.'

All she could feel was relief. 'This is joyful news to me,' she declared. 'I long only to keep company with my brother and those other gentlemen in Heaven.'

There was one thing she had to know. 'Tell me, please, did any of them protest my innocence at the last?'

'Lord Rochford said he had deserved to die shamefully, for he was a wretched sinner and had known no man so evil.' Anne closed her eyes. She was the only person who knew what he meant. 'He prayed us all to take heed of his example, and exhorted us not to trust in the vanity of the world, especially in the flattery of the court. He said, if he had followed God's word in deed, as he read it, he had not come to this, and prayed that he might be forgiven by all whom he had injured. It was strange, madam. He admitted he deserved a heavier punishment for his other sins, but not from the King, whom he had never offended.'

494

'He spoke truth,' Anne whispered. 'He has proclaimed our innocence.'

Kingston nodded almost imperceptibly. He could not, of course, openly agree with her.

'What did Norris say?'

'He said he did not think that any gentleman of the court owed more to the King than he did, and had been more ungrateful than he had. He also declared that, in his conscience, he thought your Grace innocent of the things laid to your charge. He declared he would die a thousand times rather than ruin an innocent person.'

He too had vindicated her, with his last breath. Had ever woman been so blessed in the men that loved her?

Kingston was finishing his account. 'The others said little, madam. Smeaton, being of low degree, was last. He acknowledged that he was being justly punished for his misdeeds. He cried out, "Masters, I pray you all pray for me, for I have deserved the death."'

'Has he not then cleared me of the public infamy he has brought me to?' Anne cried. 'Alas, I fear his soul now suffers for it, and that he is being punished for his false accusations, for his words will give rise to many reflections. But I doubt not but that my brother and those others are now in the presence of that great King before whom I am to be tomorrow.'

The time could not come quickly enough.

Later that day, Kingston reappeared to tell Anne that Archbishop Cranmer had declared her marriage to the King invalid. She smiled at that. There was a certain irony in the fact that it had taken minutes to dissolve the marriage that Henry had striven and schemed for six years to make. And look where it had brought her! She had been falsely accused of the vilest of crimes, and she had lost nearly everything that had mattered to her: her husband, her child, her brother, her status, her friends, her wealth and her reputation. Her daughter had been branded a bastard and there was nothing she could do about it. Five men had died on her account. Her father had abandoned her. Her mother's grief was unimaginable. And now she faced a violent death. The husband who had won her so dearly had carried out his threat to lower her as much as he had raised her. There was nothing left to live for.

She did not regret losing Henry. He had become a monster and did not deserve her love and loyalty. She felt no sadness for the ending of their wedlock. When she thought back over the three years it had lasted, she could remember only the quarrels, the dreadful insecurities that had driven her to be so cruel to Katherine and Mary, her desperation over not bearing a son, and the slow death of Henry's love. She was glad to have all that behind her. But she wept to think that innocent young Elizabeth was now branded a bastard, and would grow up believing her mother an adulteress and a traitor. That haunted her.

That evening, Father Skip came to offer her ghostly comfort in her last hours. They prayed together deep into the night. She could not have slept anyway, for the distant hammering and sawing of wood, echoing across the deserted tournament ground and Tower Green, was a constant reminder that they were building a new scaffold on which she was to die in the morning. Not for her the public scaffold on Tower Hill. She did not want to sleep, for soon she would be asleep in Christ, enjoying eternal rest. Her remaining time on Earth could be used more profitably for the repose of her soul.

She was still up and praying when dawn broke and Cranmer arrived, as he had promised, to hear her final confession and to celebrate Mass and give her Holy Communion. She asked Kingston to be present when she took the sacrament. She wanted him to hear her declare her innocence before God.

She prepared to receive the good Lord with fervent devotion, knowing that she would shortly be in His blessed presence. 'I desire to go to Him,' she declared. 'I would that I had suffered yesterday with my brother, that we might have gone to Paradise together. But we shall be reunited today. And now I take God to be my witness that, on the damnation of my soul, I have never offended with my body against the King.' It was the truth. That she had strayed in her heart was another matter, one covered by the general confession of all her sins.

Cranmer then administered the Holy Sacrament, and afterwards she again affirmed her innocence, so that Kingston, the Archbishop and all her attendants could see there was nothing on her conscience. Hopefully word would be carried back to Henry and Cromwell. Let them look to their own consciences.

When Kingston left to make the final preparations for her execution, Anne sank to her knees again in prayer. Now that the hour was almost upon her, she was thinking constantly about the moment of death. It was not the dying she feared, but the means of it. It would be quick, she knew, but it would be brutal.

Have courage! she told herself. It would be over in an instant, and then she would be lifted up out of this miserable world and know eternal joy.

As nine o'clock, the appointed hour, approached, she was ready – frightened, but braced for her ordeal. And then Lady Kingston arrived.

'I am sorry, madam, but your execution has had to be postponed until noon.'

'Oh, no!' Anne gasped. Three hours was a horribly long time to prolong this agony of waiting. 'Why?'

'My husband has just received orders to have foreigners conveyed out of the Tower, and has had to send for the Sheriff of London to see that this is done. He knows you will be upset by the delay, but he cannot help it.'

'Indeed I am! Pray send him to me when he has a moment free.'

Anne summoned Father Skip. She had never felt more in need of spiritual support, and she gripped his hands tightly as they knelt and prayed in her closet, she beseeching God to sustain her courage for a little longer.

Kingston came to her not long afterwards. By then, she was becoming agitated and panicky.

'Master Kingston,' she addressed him, 'I hear that I shall not die before noon, and I am very sorry for it, for I thought then to be dead and past my pain.'

'There should be no pain, madam,' Kingston reassured her. 'It is so subtle a blow.'

'I have heard you say the executioner is very good, and I have a little neck.' She put her hands around it, and laughed nervously.

'I have seen many men and women executed,' he told her, 'and they have all been in great sorrow, but I can see that your Grace has much joy and pleasure in death.'

'There is nothing left for me in this world,' she told him. 'I do long to die, but my poor flesh shrinks from it, so I am heartily glad it will be over quickly.'

'It will be,' he said, and reached out to squeeze her hand.

This unexpected and unorthodox kindness nearly broke her. 'I should be grateful if no one would trouble me when I make my devotions this morning,' she said, blinking back tears. Kingston promised she would be left alone with her almoner, and departed.

Time dragged. Throughout that dreadful morning she found herself constantly striving for calm. Noon came and went. She was now in an agony of suspense.

Belatedly Kingston arrived. 'I am so very sorry, madam. Your execution has now had to be postponed until nine o'clock tomorrow morning. We need more time to give people notice to attend.'

'Oh, Master Kingston, I am deeply sorry to hear that,' Anne lamented, tears welling in her eyes. 'I entreat you, for the honour of God, to beg the King that, since I am in a good state and disposed for death, I might be dispatched immediately. I had thought myself prepared to die, and fear that the delay might weaken my resolve.'

Kingston looked deeply distressed. 'Madam, I have my orders. I can only exhort you to pray for the strength to endure longer.'

It was her strong will and her faith that sustained her through those terrible final hours. Again she sought fortitude in prayer. The hardest times were when her ladies and maids burst into tears and she had to console them.

'Death is not a thing to be regretted by Christians,' she reminded them. 'Remember, I shall be quit of all unhappiness.'

It seemed strange to be doing all the normal things – eating meals, or rather, picking at them, going to the stool chamber, sipping wine –

when the dread and horribly final event of the morrow approached ever nearer. After dinner, as they all sat together around the table sewing, Anne finished her embroidery, the last she would ever complete, laid it down, and did her best to make cheerful conversation with her attendants. She even attempted a jest.

'Those clever people who invent names for kings and queens will not be hard put to it to invent one for me. They will call me Queen Anne Lackhead!' She laughed nervously, and the ladies gave a weak response.

'You know,' she told them, 'I never wanted the King. It was he who pursued me all along.'

They did not answer – it was too dangerous a subject for them.

'There is one thing I really do regret,' she said. 'I do not consider that I have been condemned by Divine Judgement, except for having caused the ill-treatment of the Lady Mary and having conspired her death. I would make my peace with her. Lady Kingston, would you carry a message for me?'

'Yes, I can do that,' Lady Kingston agreed.

'Then come with me into my great chamber,' Anne bade her. 'I would unburden myself in private.'

She led Lady Kingston into the next room and locked the door behind them. Her chair of estate was still there, under the canopy. Neither had been removed.

'Please sit there.' Anne indicated the chair.

Lady Kingston looked shocked. 'Madam, it is my duty to stand, and not to sit in your presence, especially upon the Queen's seat of estate.'

'I am a condemned person,' Anne said, 'and by law have no estate left me in this life, but for the clearing of my conscience. I pray you sit down.'

'Well,' Lady Kingston replied, 'I have often played the fool in my youth, and to fulfil your command I will do it once more in my age.' And she sat down.

Anne knelt humbly before her and held up her hands in supplication, as the good lady looked down at her, astonished. 'I beseech you, Lady Kingston, as you will answer to me before God and His angels when you appear at His judgement seat, that you will fall down in my place before the Lady Mary's Grace and, in like manner, ask her forgiveness for the wrongs I have done her, for until that is accomplished, my conscience cannot be quiet.'

'Be assured, madam, I will do it,' Lady Kingston promised. 'Now, madam, please get up and let us join the others.'

As darkness fell, Anne sat at table, writing farewell letters to Mother and Mary, begging forgiveness from the latter.

She laid down her pen and thought back over all she had achieved in her time. What would posterity say about her? Future generations should say that she had influenced monumental change, and for the better. She had helped to free England from the chains and corruption of Rome, and to make the Bible available to ordinary Englishmen in their own tongue – no mean achievement, that. Without her, none of it might ever have happened.

But few would acknowledge that debt to her now. All her achievements had been eclipsed by her disgrace, and no doubt she would be remembered more for that, and a bloody scene on a scaffold. Her daughter would grow up living with that horror, thinking ill of her.

She shuddered. In a few short hours . . .

To take her mind off her fate, she set herself to composing a poem. It helped to get her thoughts down on paper. The words flowed.

O Death, rock me asleep,
Bring me to quiet rest,
Let pass my weary, guiltless ghost
Out of my woeful breast.
Toll on, thou passing bell,
Ring out my doleful knell,
For the sound my death doth tell.
Death doth draw nigh,
There is no remedy.

Farewell, my pleasures past,
Welcome, my present pain,

I feel my torments so increase
That life cannot remain.
Cease now, thou passing bell,
Rung is my doleful knell,
For the sound my death doth tell.
Death doth draw nigh;
Sound the knell dolefully,
For now I die.

*

That night, sleep was impossible, so she got up, tiptoed through the dark chambers to her closet, and tried to focus on God and the hereafter. 'Give me strength to bear my ordeal!' she beseeched Him.

The first golden streaks of a May dawn were lightening the sky when she rose and returned to her bedchamber. She sat down on the bed and waited. God had been merciful. She was calm and composed, her courage high. She was ready.

Chapter 28

Friday 19 May 1536

Her maids dressed her in a beautiful night robe of grey damask. Beneath it was the low-necked red kirtle she had worn on the night before her arrest. Then Aunt Boleyn placed a short white ermine cape around her shoulders.

'In case it is chilly outside,' she said. A change had come over Aunt Boleyn since Anne's condemnation. She had become kinder, more respectful, and now she looked quite emotional.

'Lady Kingston and I will not be attending you,' she said. 'The young ladies are to have that honour.' They looked terrified.

She bound up Anne's hair, piling the plaits high above her neck, and placed a gable hood on her head. Then she handed a white linen coif to Nan Saville. 'Put it in your pocket,' she said. 'You know what it is for.'

'Do I look presentable?' Anne asked. 'I am told that the people are being allowed in to watch.'

'You look every inch the Queen!' Aunt Boleyn told her.

Father Skip came soon afterwards to celebrate Mass. After receiving the sacrament, Anne toyed with her breakfast, nibbling on a piece of manchet bread to please her ladies, but she had no appetite. She kept having to visit the stool chamber. Nerves had made her bowels run to water. She felt light-headed after having had so little sleep.

At eight o'clock, Kingston appeared at the door.

'Madam, the hour approaches,' he said, his voice hoarse with emotion. 'You should make ready.'

'Acquit yourself of your charge,' she told him, 'for I have long been prepared.'

He gave her a purse. 'It contains twenty pounds for you to give in alms.' It would be her last queenly act.

He cleared his throat. 'Madam, a word of advice. When you are asked to kneel, you must stay upright and not move at all, for your own sake. Do you understand me? The executioner is skilled, but if you move, the stroke may go awry.'

'I will stay still,' she vowed, trying desperately not to think about it.

'We must go now,' he said.

Lady Boleyn hugged her tightly. 'God be with you,' she said fervently.

Lady Kingston patted her arm as she passed. She was so obviously trying not to cry. As Anne descended the stairs, she could hear the four young ladies behind her weeping and bewailing bitterly her fate.

In the inmost ward, two hundred Yeomen of the King's Guard were waiting to conduct her to her execution. She had not expected such ceremony. As soon as she appeared, they began their slow march towards the Coldharbour Gate, followed by the officers of the Tower. Kingston walked with Anne behind them, and the maids-of-honour and Father Skip brought up the rear.

As she passed between the massive twin towers of the Coldharbour Gate, Anne could see the waiting crowds around the scaffold ahead of her, which stood on the Green before the House of Ordnance. It had been built high, and it was draped in black material.

A great murmur rose from the crowd when they saw her walking slowly towards them. Although her instinct was to run, she took care to carry herself in a queenly fashion. It suddenly occurred to her that, even now, Henry might grant her a reprieve. This whole macabre charade might have been staged for the purpose of allowing him to make a grand gesture of mercy and so win credit with his people.

As she distributed the alms she had been given to the poorest-looking spectators, she could hear her maids still weeping in her wake, and turned round several times to hush them. Her ears remained alert for the sound of a royal messenger galloping into the Tower with a pardon. But there was nothing. She knew in her heart there would be no reprieve.

There must have been a thousand people waiting on the tournament ground. Nearing the front, she saw Lord Chancellor Audley and Master Secretary Cromwell standing with Henry's bastard, the Duke of Richmond – come to report back to his father, no doubt. Well, Henry should hear only of her courage. She would not criticise him or his justice – she had made her peace with God, and she wanted no retribution to fall upon her family.

She caught young Richmond smiling at her maliciously. Norfolk and Suffolk were there, with many nobles, and the Lord Mayor of London with the aldermen and sheriffs – but she looked in vain for her father.

They had reached the scaffold now. Sawdust had been strewn over it, and several men were standing on it awaiting her. They wore ordinary dress, so she could not tell which one was the executioner. She could see no sign of his sword. On the ground to the far side she glimpsed a wooden chest. Sweet Jesus, it was her coffin! She forced herself to stay calm. She did not have to be brave for much longer.

Kingston offered her his arm and assisted her up the five wooden steps, her four maids following. She stood on the scaffold, looking down on the crowd, trying hard to smile and show them that she felt no fear.

She turned to Kingston. 'May I have leave to speak to the people? I promise I will not say anything contentious. And I beg you not to hasten the signal for my death till I have spoken that which I have a mind to say.'

He nodded. 'Please speak now, and be brief.'

She turned back to the crowd, breathless with nerves. 'Good Christian people, I am come here to die, according to the law, for by the law I am judged to die, and therefore I will speak nothing against it. I come here only to die, and to yield myself humbly to the will of the King, my lord. And if, in my life, I did ever offend the King's Grace, surely with my death I do now atone.' She bowed her head, her heart racing, for when she finished speaking, only death awaited her. She forced herself to continue, praying that her voice did not betray her fear.

'I come here to accuse no man,' she declared, 'nor to speak anything of that of which I am accused. I pray and beseech you all, good friends, to pray for the life of the King, my sovereign lord and yours, who is one of the best princes on the face of the earth, who has always treated me so well that better could not be found, wherefore I submit to death with a goodwill, humbly asking pardon of all the world. If any person will meddle with my cause, I require them to judge the best. Thus I take my leave of the world, and of you, and I heartily desire you all to pray for me.'

At a nod from Kingston, her young ladies stepped forward, but they were in such anguish that she had to help them remove her cape, her night robe and her hood, leaving her standing there in her red kirtle. Nan Saville drew the linen coif from her pocket and gave it to her. She pulled it over her head, making sure that all her hair was tucked in, and was dismayed to find that one plait kept sliding down. She pushed in the clips and prayed it would stay in place. Nothing must be allowed to impede the sword.

'Pray for me!' she beseeched her maids. 'I beg your pardon for any harshness I have shown towards you, for while I lived, you have always showed yourselves diligent in my service, and now you are present at my last hour and mortal agony; as in good fortune you were faithful to me, so even at this, my miserable death, you do not forsake me.' They were looking pitifully at her, tears streaming down their cheeks. Anne smiled faintly at them. 'As I cannot reward you for your true service to me, I pray you take comfort for my loss,' she said. 'Be not sorry to see me die. Forget me not, and always be faithful to the King's Grace and to her whom with happier fortune you may look to have as your Queen and mistress. And always esteem your honour far beyond your life, and in your prayers to the Lord Jesus forget not to pray for my soul.'

A big, brawny man in a sober but well-cut suit of clothes stepped forward and knelt before Anne. As he spoke, in heavily accented English, she realised it was the executioner. Her heart began pounding furiously.

'Madam,' he said, 'I crave your Majesty's pardon, for I am ordered to do my duty.'

'I give it willingly,' she told him.

'Madam, I beg you to kneel and say your prayers,' he instructed.

This was the moment. She knelt in the sawdust, taking care to remain upright, as Kingston had exhorted her.

'Please allow me a little time for prayer,' she asked, arranging her skirts modestly about her feet, so that when her body fell, it would not be exposed.

'O Christ, receive my spirit!' she entreated, over and over again. Below her the Lord Mayor cried, 'All kneel in respect for the passing of a soul!' The crowd fell to its knees. Only Suffolk and Richmond remained standing. Anne tried to pray, but she was frightened that the blow would come when she was not ready, and kept looking fearfully around her.

'Madam, do not fear. I will wait till you tell me,' the executioner said.

She touched her coif, checking that her plait was still in place, as she continued her prayers. Nan Saville came forward, weeping uncontrollably, with a linen cloth to blindfold her, but her fingers were trembling so much that Anne took the cloth from her. She looked for a final time upon the world and the sea of faces gazing up at her, then covered her eyes. The last thing she saw before doing so was the sunny sky above the Tower roofs.

'Jesu, have pity on my soul! My God, have pity on my soul!' she prayed fervently. 'To Jesus Christ I commend my soul.' She heard the executioner quietly bid her maids stand out of the way, and there was a shuffling and a fresh outbreak of loud weeping. It was terrifying not being able to see what was happening around her.

'Strike now!' she cried, her heart hammering so hard and painfully in her chest that she thought there might be no need for any headsman. 'O Lord God, have pity on my soul! To Christ I commend my soul!'

She heard the executioner say, 'Bring me the sword!' There was a movement in the direction of the scaffold steps, and she blindly turned her head that way.

She had believed Kingston when he had said there would be no pain, and prayed that the blow would be instantaneous and bring immediate oblivion, but when it came there was a choking explosion of searing agony and a dreadful warm gush of blood. She was aware of tasting it in her mouth and of its flooding her nostrils as she felt her head, horribly light now, hit the scaffold with a painful thud and the blindfold fell away. She would have cried out, yet no sound came apart from a terrible, silent gurgling, and she wanted to clamp her hands to the mortal wound that had been dealt her, yet she had no hands any more. They were attached to the dark, bloodied, crumpled thing that lay on the scaffold next to her. She blinked and tried to look away. Through her torment she could still see the blurred shapes of people around her on the scaffold. And then her eyes dimmed and the merciful darkness descended.

Author's Note

I could write another book on how this novel was constructed from the historical sources. Over the course of my years of study, I have seen perceptions of Anne Boleyn change substantially. I am aware that in some circles, particularly on the Internet, she has acquired celebrity status, and that she has become many things to many people and, in the process, controversial. During the writing of this book, an admirer of Anne Boleyn expressed the hope that I would portray her accurately, to which I answered that historians might well differ when considering what 'accurately' might mean. There is so much room for conjecture.

The problem facing any historian or novelist writing about Anne Boleyn is that, in some ways, she is unknowable. We do not have a wealth of her letters, unlike with Katherine of Aragon, whose inner thoughts were often passionately expressed. Much of the material on Anne Boleyn comes from a hostile source, the Imperial ambassador, Eustache Chapuys. Yet recent research on Chapuys shows that he was an observant, well-informed witness, close to the centre of affairs, who cited his sources, so we can usually judge how accurate they are likely to have been. This presents those wishing to see Anne Boleyn in a sympathetic light with another problem: how does one get beyond the sometimes damning testimony of Chapuys?

In writing this novel from Anne's point of view, I have tried to reconcile conflicting views of her, and to portray her as a flawed but very human heroine, a woman of great ambition, idealism and courage who found herself in an increasingly frightening situation.

It has become fashionable to see Anne Boleyn as a feminist heroine, a concept that, until recently, I would have dismissed as anachronistic, arguing that feminism was unknown in Tudor England. That much is true, but in early sixteenth-century Europe, where Anne spent her formative years, there was an intellectual movement and debate that questioned traditional concepts of women and looked forward to an era in which they would enjoy more power and autonomy. This was an age of female rulers and thinkers, and Anne had two shining examples before her: Margaret of Austria and Marguerite of Valois. (Two sources mention her serving Marguerite of Valois, but no dates are given; I have placed her in Marguerite's household from 1520 to 1522.) I have set Anne in this European context and focused on the cultural influences to which she was exposed. So yes, it is legitimate to see her as a feminist long before her time: it is a concept she would have understood, it underpinned her ambitions and self-image, and it was this Renaissance cultural background, not just the French fashions and manners, that would have made her stand out at the English court.

Anne spent seven years at the French court, serving Queen Claude, the wife of François I, and Marguerite, but there are no contemporary French sources that mention her. I thought it would be helpful to track, as far as possible, the movements of her mistress, Queen Claude, who imposed an almost conventual rule on her ladies and shunned the court whenever she could, preferring the palaces of Amboise and Blois on the Loire. There is no doubt that Anne would have known these palaces well. But she probably travelled more widely in France too. In 1515, during a campaign to win Milan, François I won the Battle of Marignano. Lingering in Italy, he was introduced to the great artist Leonardo da Vinci, and the following year we find Leonardo installed, at the King's expense, in a house, Le Clos Lucé, near the chateau of Amboise. Leonardo remained in France and died in that house in 1519.

Early in 1516, Queen Claude travelled with François's sister, Marguerite of Valois, and his mother, Louise of Savoy, down to Provence to meet up with the returning hero and accompany his triumphal progress back through France. Anne Boleyn would almost certainly have been with them. It is likely too that she knew – at least by sight – Leonardo da Vinci, for she was often at Amboise, and he had close links to the court. The scenes in this novel are imagined, but they are not improbable.

509

Legend links Anne Boleyn with the chateau of Briis-sous-Forges south of Paris. There are all sorts of theories as to how the Donjon Anne Boleyn came to be so named, and I evolved a new one for this book. It proved, however, to be too long, and will be the subject of an e-short to be published separately. Did you pick up the hints in these pages as to what that story might be about? The novel stands alone without it, but in the e-short you can read a slightly different version of that chapter in Anne's story.

Apart from a few fictional attendants at the courts of Burgundy and France, the characters in this book all lived. I have kept closely to the historical record, but have taken occasional minor liberties, so as not to slow the flow of the narrative. Given the sometimes awkward syntax of Tudor sources and letters, I have modernised the language in places to make the meaning clearer. Some quotes have been taken out of context or put in the mouths of others, but the sentiments are appropriate for the character or situation. The poetry is all authentic.

One can only understand the courtships of Anne Boleyn in the context of the game of courtly love, which is explained in the book and is an ongoing theme that dominates the relationships between the male and female characters.

Seventeen of Henry VIII's love letters to Anne survive in the Vatican library. Given the couple's long separations – I was struck afresh by how long they actually were – I am convinced that there must have been more letters, and I have invented or referred to others in this novel. Anne's replies are lost. If we had them, we would have more insights into her character and her feelings for Henry VIII. In her indictment, it was alleged she had said she had never wished to choose the King in her heart, and while that was an accusation against her, along with other accusations that can be proved false, I think it might have been true. It chimes with what we know of their relationship. It made writing this book from that angle a more seamless task than portraying Anne as being in love with Henry. I think it was all about power on her side. Of course, this is only a theory, and no doubt some will disagree with it, but it was interesting to tell the story from this perspective. It makes it even more poignant.

To add further poignancy, there is the unacknowledged – until near the end – attraction between Anne and Norris. This was suggested by the wording of her last confession. From her insistence that 'she had never offended *with her body*' against the King, it might be inferred that she had offended in her heart or her thoughts, and that she had secretly loved another but had never gone so far as to consummate that love. The evidence suggests that, of the men accused with her, Norris was the likeliest object of her affections. Again, it's just a theory, but a compelling one. Norris did confess to something after his arrest – we don't know what – but later retracted it.

Sources hostile to Anne mention her sixth fingernail, but it is also mentioned in a laudatory memoir by George Wyatt, grandson of the poet Thomas Wyatt. George Wyatt spent his life researching Anne Boleyn, drawing on his family traditions and the first-hand reminiscences of people who had known her, among them Anne Gainsford. He should be accounted a generally reliable source.

There is evidence, discussed in my biography *Mary Boleyn: 'The Great and Infamous Whore'*, that Mary Boleyn was forced to become Henry VIII's mistress. In that same book, I argued the case for Elizabeth Howard having a poor reputation. Some have inferred, from passages in *The Heptameron*, her collection of novellas, that Marguerite of Navarre was raped, although others have seen this as a literary conceit. The man, who is not named in the text, was Guillaume Gouffier, Sire de Bonnivet.

The rivalry between Anne and her sister Mary is implicit in the letter Mary wrote to Thomas Cromwell in 1534. The attitudes towards sodomy expressed in the book reflect the contemporary opinion, for it was then held that sexual intercourse was intended for procreation, and that preventing conception was sinful.

Studying Henry VIII's love letters to Anne, it struck me that they fall into three categories: those importuning her to be his mistress in the physical sense, which belong to the initial phase of his courtship; those urging her to be his mistress in the courtly sense; and those in which he is longing to marry her and consummate their relationship, in which he is importuning her no more. It has long been asserted, by me in earlier books, and by many others, that Anne held Henry off for seven years, but this reading of the letters strongly suggests that it was Henry who made the decision not to sleep with her lest she become pregnant, which would have caused an embarrassing scandal at a time when he was trumpeting her virtue to the Pope.

I do not think the wording of the dispensation issued in 1528, specifically allowing Henry, whenever he was free to marry again, to take to wife any woman, 'in any degree [of affinity], even the first, *ex illicito coito* [arising from illicit intercourse]', implies that Henry had already had intercourse with Anne; rather, it refers to his illicit intercourse with Mary Boleyn. There is nothing in Henry's letters to Anne to suggest that they had briefly become lovers in the fullest sense.

There is no doubt that Anne Boleyn was an unpopular queen. The state papers contain many libels or slanders. All those mentioned in the novel come from contemporary authentic records.

The identity of the mistresses Henry VIII took in 1533 and 1534 remains unknown. It's been conjectured that Elizabeth Carew was the first, and I've speculated here that Joan Ashley was the second. She was unmarried, and did serve Anne Boleyn as a maid-of-honour.

Much has been made of Anne leaving behind a motherless child of two years and eight months. In fact, Anne saw very little of her daughter, the future Elizabeth I. Elizabeth had her own separate household from the age of three months, and Anne visited infrequently, while Elizabeth was at court only on rare occasions. Tudor queens were not required to be hands-on mothers, although in the novel, we see Anne interesting herself in Elizabeth's marriage, as was expected of her. We have a record of items of clothing she bought for Elizabeth. Her involvement in her daughter's life doesn't amount to much, which suggested to me that, disappointed by Elizabeth's sex, Anne found it hard to bond with her or love her. In the novel, this only adds to her unhappiness.

Some readers may wonder at my suggestion that Jasper Tudor built the banqueting hall range at Sudeley Castle, which has traditionally been said to have been the work of Richard III; but while Richard did own the castle, there is no evidence that he ever visited. Jasper Tudor held it from 1486 to his death in 1495, so it's more likely that he was responsible.

There is no historical evidence linking George Boleyn to Katherine of Aragon's death. Readers who are interested in reading more of this tale might enjoy my e-short, *The Blackened Heart*, which continues a story thread only hinted at in the first novel in this series, *Katherine of Aragon: The True Queen*. There were rumours of poison after Katherine's autopsy, the report of which was suppressed. There *was* a poison attempt on Bishop Fisher (although Richard Rouse was actually a friend of the Bishop's cook), and the Boleyns were suspected of having been behind it. Anne Boleyn did warn the Bishop not to attend Parliament in case he should suffer a repetition of the sickness the poison had caused. Certainly Katherine's death was timely, given the need for Anne, who was pregnant, to bear an indisputably legitimate heir. On hearing of Katherine's death, Anne did weep in her oratory. But the sum of these parts does not amount to good evidence that the Boleyns poisoned Katherine.

The compromising conversations of Anne Boleyn with Norris, Weston and Smeaton, and her conversations in the Tower, are based on Sir William Kingston's detailed reports to Cromwell. Some of these conversations seem disjointed and make little sense in parts, and I suspect that not every utterance was recorded; therefore, using the creative freedom of a novelist, I have tried to make better sense of them.

The quotation 'Orders is orders' is what Sir Edmund Walsingham, Lieutenant of the Tower, famously said to Sir Thomas More.

Some sources mention Anne's father being among the peers who condemned her. I have discussed the evidence for this in my book *The Lady in the Tower: The Fall of Anne Boleyn*.

George Boleyn's scaffold speech went way beyond the conventional acknowledgement of sins expected of those about to die, suggesting he was carrying a burden of guilt for some heinous deed(s). I have outlined the evidence for his sexual relationships in *The Lady in the Tower*.

I do not subscribe to the view that Henry VIII suffered from impotence during his marriage to Anne, as alleged at George Boleyn's trial. The fact that Anne became pregnant four times in three years rather counterbalances it. Nor do I subscribe to the popular theory that Henry VIII suddenly changed character after a fall from his horse in January 1536; the source that states he lay without speaking for two hours is an unreliable one.

Writing the final scenes of Anne's life was a gruelling experience that stayed with me for days, and in case anyone wonders about my portrayal of her actual beheading, I must point out that a judge, Sir John Spelman, who witnessed her execution, recorded seeing 'her lips moving and her eyes moving' afterwards. There is a discussion about the survival of consciousness after decapitation in *The Lady in the Tower*. In 1983, a medical study found that 'no matter how efficient the method of execution, at least two to three seconds of intense pain cannot be avoided'. Research undertaken in the late nineteenth century suggested that most victims of the guillotine died within two seconds, but a more modern estimate would be an average of thirteen seconds. In 1905, a French doctor observed a decapitated criminal taking twenty-five to thirty seconds to die.

Severing the spinal cord causes death only when the brain has been completely deprived, through massive haemorrhaging, of the oxygen in the blood that nourishes it. In 1956, two French doctors concluded: 'Death is not instantaneous: every element survives decapitation. It is a savage vivisection.' Anne Boleyn did possibly experience a few dreadful moments in which she was aware of what was happening.

As has been the case before when I've written historical novels, telling the fictional version of Anne's story from her point of view has afforded me new insights into what might have happened. I feel I understand better what shaped her into the person she was, her enmity towards Cardinal Wolsey and Thomas Cromwell, what went wrong in her marriage to Henry VIII, and why she was so unkind to Katherine of Aragon and the Lady Mary. This has made it possible for me to portray her in a more sympathetic light than I could as a historian keeping within the confines of the sources and credible speculation.

I wish to express huge appreciation of my editors, Mari Evans at Headline and Susanna Porter at Ballantine, for their inspiring enthusiasm and

514

creative support. Warm and grateful thanks go also to my agent, Julian Alexander, who has been the guiding force, and a tower of strength, throughout my literary career.

I owe a huge debt of gratitude to Sarah Gristwood for taking the time to read this novel when she was under great pressure to finish her own marvellous book, *Game of Queens*. I'm indebted to Sarah for generously sharing her research on feminist thought in Renaissance Europe and on the female rulers of the period, and for her creative suggestions. She conjures unique insights and has a huge talent for joined-up and lateral thinking, which, coupled with the emotional intelligence that underpins her work, makes for a new and vivid understanding of all the subjects about whom she writes. This book has benefited greatly from that expertise.

I'd like also to extend my warm thanks to the fantastic, supportive team at Headline: my brilliant editor, Flora Rees, for suggesting so many ways of enhancing the book; Caitlin Raynor, Deputy Publicity Director, for being such a wonderful publicist; Jo Liddiard, Head of Marketing, for her enthusiasm and technical assistance; Siobhan Hooper, Senior Designer, and Patrick Insole, Art Director, for making my books look so beautiful; Louise Rothwell, Production Manager, Sara Adams, Editorial Assistant, Frances Doyle, Digital Strategy Director, Barbara Ronan, Sales Director, Jane Selley, copy-editor, and Sarah Coward and Caroline Pretty, proofreaders, for all their hard work behind the scenes; and the amazing Balbusso Twins for their glorious artwork. Last, but by no means least, a huge thank you to Pete Rendeiro, who suggested the subtitle.

Finally, heartfelt thanks to my wonderful husband, Rankin, who, despite a difficult year following surgery, has remained an enormous support and struggled manfully through his recovery to sustain and encourage me in my work.

Dramatis Personae

In order of appearance or first mention. Names in italics are fictional characters.

Anne Boleyn, younger daughter of Sir Thomas Boleyn.

Mary Boleyn, elder daughter of Sir Thomas Boleyn.

Margaret Butler, Lady Boleyn, daughter of Thomas Butler, Earl of Ormond; paternal grandmother of Anne.

Elizabeth Howard, Lady Boleyn, daughter of Thomas Howard, 2nd Duke of Norfolk; mother of Anne.

George Boleyn, later Viscount Rochford; youngest brother of Anne.

Sir Thomas Boleyn of Hever Castle, Kent, later Viscount Rochford, and afterwards Earl of Wiltshire and Ormond; father of Anne.

Father Davy, musician, tutor to the young Boleyns.

Thomas Boleyn, eldest brother of Anne.

Edward Stafford, Duke of Buckingham, the Boleyns' neighbour at Penshurst, Kent.

Henry Boleyn, middle brother of Anne.

Margaret, Archduchess of Austria, Duchess of Savoy, Regent of the Netherlands; daughter of the Holy Roman Emperor Maximilian I.

Henry VIII, King of England, second monarch of the Tudor dynasty.

The Wyatt family, neighbours of the Boleyns at Allington, Kent.

The Sackville family of Buckhurst Park, Sussex, kinsfolk of the Boleyns.

The Haute family of Ightham Mote, Kent, neighbours of the Boleyns.

Desiderius Erasmus, renowned Dutch scholar, humanist and man of letters.

Master Johnson, merchant.

John Skelton, poet laureate, former tutor to King Henry VIII.

The Howard family, earls of Surrey and dukes of Norfolk, powerful kinsfolk of the Boleyns.

Thomas Butler, 7th Earl of Ormond, Irish peer; paternal great-grandfather of Anne.

Henry VII, King of England from 1485 to 1509, first monarch of the Tudor dynasty, father of Henry VIII.

Sir Geoffrey Boleyn, paternal great-grandfather of Anne.

Edward I 'Longshanks', King of England from 1272 to 1307.

William the Conqueror, King of England from 1066 to 1087.

Thomas Howard, Earl of Surrey, afterwards 2nd Duke of Norfolk; maternal grandfather of Anne.

Thomas Howard, Earl of Surrey, afterwards 3rd Duke of Norfolk; maternal uncle of Anne.

Anne of York, daughter of King Edward IV, first wife of Thomas Howard, 3rd Duke of Norfolk; aunt of Henry VIII and Anne Boleyn.

Edward IV, King of England from 1461 to 1483; maternal grandfather of Henry VIII.

Elizabeth of York, daughter of King Edward IV, Queen of Henry VII, mother of Henry VIII and sister of Anne of York.

Katherine of Aragon, daughter of Ferdinand V, King of Aragon, and Isabella I, Queen of Castile; first Queen of Henry VIII.

Mrs Orchard, nurse to Anne.

Sir John Broughton, a knight of Westmorland.

Maximilian I, of the House of Habsburg, Holy Roman Emperor.

Mary, Duchess of Burgundy, first wife of the Emperor Maximilian I, mother of Philip the Handsome and Margaret of Austria.

Philip the Handsome, Archduke of Austria, Duke of Burgundy and King of Castile; son of the Emperor Maximilian I by Mary of Burgundy.

Juana I, Queen of Castile, daughter of Ferdinand V, King of Aragon, and Isabella I, Queen of Castile; wife of Philip the Handsome; mother of Charles V, Holy Roman Emperor and King of Spain.

Ferdinand V, King of Aragon, formerly King of Spain; father of Juana

I, Juan, Prince of Asturias, and Katherine of Aragon, first wife of Henry VIII.

Charles of Habsburg, Archduke of Austria, Infante of Castile, later Charles I, King of Spain, and Charles V, Holy Roman Emperor.

William Caxton, publisher; set up the first printing press in England in 1476.

Monsieur Semmonet, tutor to Anne in Burgundy.

Isabeau, fille d'honneur to Margaret of Austria.

Christine de Pizan (1364–c.1430), Italian writer at the French court; early feminist.

Isabella I, Queen of Castile and Spain; mother of Juana I, Juan, Prince of Asturias, and Katherine of Aragon.

Philibert II, Duke of Savoy; third husband of Margaret of Austria.

Gerda, Anne's maid in Burgundy.

Charles, Dauphin of France, later Charles VIII King of France from 1483 to 1498; first husband of Margaret of Austria.

Juan, Prince of Asturias, son and heir of Ferdinand V, King of Aragon, and Isabella I, Queen of Castile; second husband of Margaret of Austria.

Etiennette de la Baume, *fille d'honneur* to Margaret of Austria.

Charles Brandon, Viscount Lisle, later Duke of Suffolk, friend and jousting partner of Henry VIII.

Jacoba, lady-in-waiting to Margaret of Austria.

Mary Tudor, daughter of Henry VII, sister of Henry VIII, third Queen of Louis XII, King of France; first wife of Charles Brandon, Duke of Suffolk.

Louis XII, King of France.

François of Valois, Count of Angoulême, Dauphin of France, afterwards François I, King of France.

Louise of Savoy, Countess of Angoulême, mother of François and Marguerite of Valois.

Madame d'Aumont, *dame d'honneur* to Mary Tudor, Queen of France.

Jeanne of Valois, Queen of France, first wife of Louis XII.

Lady Elizabeth Grey, sister to the Marquess of Dorset, maid-of-honour to Mary Tudor.

Florence Hastings, maid-of-honour to Mary Tudor.

Mary Fiennes, maid-of-honour to Mary Tudor; later wife of Sir Henry Norris.

Claude of Valois, daughter of Louis XII, King of France, first Queen of François I, King of France.

Elizabeth Grey, Viscountess Lisle; betrothed to Charles Brandon, Viscount Lisle.

Jane Bourchier, maid-of-honour to Mary Tudor.

Cardinal Thomas Wolsey, Archbishop of York, Lord Chancellor of England, chief minister to Henry VIII.

Marguerite of Valois, sister of François I, wife first to Charles IV, Duke of Alençon, and later to Henry II, King of Navarre.

Louise of Valois, daughter of François I and Claude of Valois.

Leonardo da Vinci, Italian artist and inventor.

Jeanne de Lautrec, lady-in-waiting to Claude of Valois.

Madame de Langeac, lady-in-waiting to Claude of Valois.

Mary Tudor, daughter of Henry VIII and Katherine of Aragon; later Queen Mary I.

François, Dauphin of France, son of François I and Claude of Valois.

Monna Lisa Gherardini, the subject of Leonardo da Vinci's portrait.

William Carey, cousin of Henry VIII, Gentleman of the Privy Chamber; first husband of Mary Boleyn.

Jane Parker, daughter of Henry Parker, Lord Morley; later wife of George Boleyn.

Henry Parker, Lord Morley, humanist aristocrat.

Piers Butler, 8th Earl of Ormond, distant cousin of Thomas Butler, 7th Earl of Ormond, Anne's great-grandfather.

James Butler, later 9th Earl of Ormond; son of Piers Butler, 8th Earl of Ormond.

Sir Henry Norris, Groom of the Stool, Head of the Privy Chamber, and trusted friend of Henry VIII.

Margaret Plantagenet, Countess of Salisbury; cousin to Henry VIII, lady-in-waiting to Katherine of Aragon, and governess to the Princess Mary.

William Cornish, musician, Master of the Revels to Henry VIII.

Elizabeth 'Bessie' Blount, maid-of-honour to Katherine of Aragon;

mistress of Henry VIII and mother of his bastard son, Henry Fitzroy.

Henry Fitzroy, Duke of Richmond and Somerset, bastard son of Henry VIII by Bessie Blount.

Henry (Harry) Percy, heir to Henry Percy, 5th Earl of Northumberland; later 6th Earl of Northumberland.

Thomas Cromwell, later Secretary of State and chief minister to Henry VIII.

James Melton, gentleman to Cardinal Wolsey; friend of Harry Percy.

Cuthbert Tunstall, Bishop of London.

George Cavendish, gentleman usher to Cardinal Wolsey.

Lady Mary Talbot, daughter of the Earl of Shrewsbury; wife of Henry Percy, 6th Earl of Northumberland.

Catherine Carey, daughter of Mary Boleyn by Henry VIII.

Sir Thomas Wyatt, poet and diplomat.

Sir Francis Bryan, Gentleman of the Privy Chamber to Henry VIII.

Margaret Wyatt, sister of Sir Thomas Wyatt; wife of Sir Henry Lee.

Henry Carey, later Lord Hunsdon, son of William Carey and Mary Boleyn; ward of Anne.

Elizabeth Brooke, wife of Sir Thomas Wyatt.

Sir Henry Wyatt of Allington Castle, Kent; father of Thomas and Margaret Wyatt.

Sir Nicholas Carew, Master of the Horse to Henry VIII.

Gabriel de Grammont, Bishop of Tarbes, French ambassador to England.

Matilda, Roman Empress, Lady of the English for a brief period in 1141.

Arthur Tudor, Prince of Wales (1486–1502), eldest son of Henry VII, brother of Henry VIII; first husband of Katherine of Aragon.

John Longland, Bishop of Lincoln; confessor to Henry VIII.

William Warham, Archbishop of Canterbury.

A goldsmith of Tonbridge.

Pope Clement VII.

Maria de Salinas, Lady Willoughby, lady-in-waiting to Katherine of Aragon.

Maud Green, Lady Parr; lady-in-waiting to Katherine of Aragon; mother of Queen Katherine Parr.

Sir Thomas More, Privy Councillor, later Lord Chancellor of England; renowned scholar, humanist, man of letters, martyr and saint.

Dr William Knight, secretary to Henry VIII.

Cardinal Lorenzo Campeggio, Papal Legate.

Edward Foxe, chaplain to Henry VIII.

Dr Stephen Gardiner, secretary to Henry VIII; later Bishop of Winchester.

Elizabeth Barton, nun and visionary, the 'Holy Maid of Kent'.

Dame Isabel Jordan, Prioress of Wilton.

Eleanor Carey, sister of William Carey; nun at Wilton Abbey.

Dr William Butts, physician to Henry VIII.

Dr John Chambers, chief physician to Henry VIII.

Nan Saville, maid-of-honour to Anne.

Martin Luther, monk of Wittenberg, Germany, religious reformer and founder of the Protestant religion.

William Tyndale, reformer and martyr; author of *The Obedience of a Christian Man*, and translator of the Bible into English.

Simon Fish, reformer and author of an influential heretical book, *A Supplication for the Beggars*.

Anne (Nan) Gainsford, maid-of-honour to Anne.

Sir George Zouche of Codnor, future husband of Anne Gainsford.

Eustache Chapuys, Spanish/Imperial ambassador to England.

Dr Thomas Cranmer, reformer and martyr; chaplain to the Boleyns; later Archbishop of Canterbury.

Robert Barnes, reformer and martyr.

Mark Smeaton, musician; Groom of the Privy Chamber to Henry VIII.

Sir Francis Weston, Gentleman of the Privy Chamber to Henry VIII.

Mary (Madge) Shelton, daughter of Sir John Shelton and Anne Boleyn, sister of Sir Thomas Boleyn; maid-of-honour to Anne; briefly mistress to Henry VIII.

Mary Howard, daughter of Thomas Howard, 3rd Duke of Norfolk, and wife to Henry Fitzroy, Duke of Richmond and Somerset; lady-in-waiting to Anne.

Dr Augustine, physician to Cardinal Wolsey.

Sir John Russell, Gentleman of the Privy Chamber to Henry VIII; later Lord Privy Seal and Earl of Bedford.

Eustace, Count of Boulogne (d.c. 1087), possible ancestor of Anne Boleyn.

Stephen, King of England from 1135 to 1154.

John Fisher, Bishop of Rochester; martyr and saint.

Richard Rouse, cook to John Fisher, Bishop of Rochester.

Pope Julius II.

Sir William Brereton, Gentleman of the Privy Chamber to Henry VIII.

Sir Henry Guildford, Comptroller of the Household to Henry VIII.

Reginald Pole, son of Margaret Pole, Countess of Salisbury; later Cardinal Pole and Archbishop of Canterbury.

Friar William Peto, confessor to the Princess Mary.

Sir Thomas Audley, Lord Chancellor of England.

Jasper Tudor, Earl of Pembroke, Duke of Bedford; uncle of Henry VII.

Elizabeth Lovell, Countess of Rutland; lady-in-waiting to Anne.

Margaret Stanley, Countess of Sussex; lady-in-waiting to Anne.

Eleanor of Austria, daughter of Philip the Handsome and Juana of Castile, sister to the Emperor Charles V, and second Queen of François I of France.

Françoise, Duchess of Vendôme, reputedly the mistress of François I.

John, Lord Berners, Governor of Calais.

William Stafford, distant kinsman of Edward Stafford, Duke of Buckingham; second husband of Mary Boleyn.

Bridget, Lady Wingfield, friend and lady-in-waiting to Anne.

Anne Pickering, wife of Sir Francis Weston.

Sir Richard Weston of Sutton Place, father of Sir Francis Weston.

Anne Savage, later Lady Berkeley, lady-in-waiting to Anne.

Rowland Lee, chaplain to Henry VIII; later Bishop of Coventry and Lichfield.

Thomas Heneage, Gentleman of the Privy Chamber to Henry VIII.

Lady Margaret Douglas, daughter of Archibald Douglas, Earl of Angus, by Margaret Tudor, sister of Henry VIII; lady-of-honour to Anne; later married Matthew Stuart, Earl of Lennox, and became the mother of Henry, Lord Darnley, second husband of Mary, Queen of Scots.

Elizabeth Browne, Countess of Worcester, lady-in-waiting to Anne.

Sir William Fitzwilliam, Treasurer of the Household to Henry VIII.

Elizabeth Wood, Lady Boleyn, wife to Sir James Boleyn; lady-in-waiting to Anne.

Sir James Boleyn of Blickling, brother of Sir Thomas Boleyn; uncle and chancellor to Anne.

Frances de Vere, daughter of the Earl of Oxford, and later wife to Henry Howard, Earl of Surrey; lady-in-waiting to Anne.

Margaret Foliot, Mrs Stonor, Mother of the Maids to Anne.

Henry Howard, Earl of Surrey, son and heir of Thomas Howard, 3rd Duke of Norfolk; cousin of Anne.

Lord Thomas Howard, younger brother of Thomas Howard, 3rd Duke of Norfolk.

Urian, Anne's greyhound.

Gertrude Blount, Marchioness of Exeter, wife of Henry VIII's cousin Henry Courtenay, Marquess of Exeter.

Elizabeth Amadas, wife of Robert Amadas, Keeper of the Jewel Tower.

St Edward the Confessor, King of England from 1042 to 1066.

Anne Howard, Dowager Countess of Oxford; lady-in-waiting to Anne.

William Glover, astrologer.

Elizabeth Bryan, Lady Carew, wife of Sir Nicholas Carew; reputedly a mistress of Henry VIII.

Katherine Willoughby, daughter of William, Lord Willoughby d'Eresby, and Maria de Salinas; second wife of Charles Brandon, Duke of Suffolk.

Elizabeth Tudor, daughter of Henry VIII and Anne Boleyn; later Queen Elizabeth I.

Agnes Tilney, Dowager Duchess of Norfolk, widow of Thomas Howard, 2nd Duke of Norfolk; step-grandmother to Anne.

Margaret Wotton, Dowager Marchioness of Dorset, widow of Henry Grey, 2nd Marquess of Dorset.

Margaret, Lady Bryan, mother of Sir Francis Bryan; lady mistress, in turn, to the Princesses Mary and Elizabeth.

Anne Boleyn, Lady Shelton, sister of Sir Thomas Boleyn, wife of Sir John Shelton, mother of Madge Shelton, and aunt to Anne.

Sir John Seymour of Wulfhall, Ranger of Savernake Forest; father of Jane Seymour, maid-of-honour to Anne.

Jane Seymour, maid-of-honour to Anne.

Miles Coverdale, reformist scholar, translator of the Bible into English.

Honor Grenville, Lady Lisle, wife of Arthur Plantagenet, Viscount Lisle, bastard son of Edward IV, and Governor of Calais.

Little Pourquoi (or Purkoy), Anne's dog.

Joan Ashley, maid-of-honour to Anne.

Pope Paul III.

Philippe de Chabot, Admiral of France.

Charles of Valois, Duke of Angoulême, third son of François I of France.

Palmedes Gontier, secretary to Philippe de Chabot, Admiral of France.

John Houghton, Prior of the London Charterhouse; Robert Lawrence, Prior of the Beauvale Charterhouse; Augustine Webster, Prior of the Axholme Charterhouse: Carthusian martyrs.

Richard Reynolds, monk of Syon Abbey; martyr.

Humphrey Middlemore, William Exmew and Sebastian Newdigate: Carthusian monks and martyrs.

Matthew Parker, chaplain to Anne; later Archbishop of Canterbury.

Nicholas Bourbon, French humanist scholar, tutor of Henry Carey.

Sir Nicholas Poyntz of Acton Court, reformist courtier.

Margaret (Margery) Wentworth, wife of Sir John Seymour and mother of Edward, Henry, Thomas and Jane Seymour.

Sir Edward Seymour, eldest son of Sir John Seymour and Margaret Wentworth; later Earl of Hertford, Duke of Somerset and Lord Protector of England.

Sir Thomas Seymour, son of Sir John Seymour and Margaret Wentworth; later Baron Seymour of Sudeley and Lord High Admiral.

Henry Seymour, son of Sir John Seymour and Margaret Wentworth.

Katherine Fillol, repudiated first wife of Sir Edward Seymour.

Elizabeth Tilney, Duchess of Norfolk, first wife of Thomas Howard, 2nd Duke of Norfolk; maternal grandmother to Anne.

William, Lord Sandys, Chamberlain to Henry VIII.

Margaret Gamage, Lady William Howard, wife of Lord William Howard, younger son of Thomas Howard, 2nd Duke of Norfolk; aunt of Anne.

Lady Margaret Beaufort, Countess of Richmond and Derby; mother of Henry VII and grandmother of Henry VIII.

John Skip, almoner to Anne.

Hugh Latimer, performist cleric, later Bishop of Worcester and martyr.

Sir Anthony Browne, courtier and diplomat.

Sir William Paulet, Comptroller to Henry VIII.

Sir William Kingston, Constable of the Tower of London.

Sir Edmund Walsingham, Lieutenant of the Tower of London.

Mary Scrope, Lady Kingston, wife of Sir William Kingston.

Margaret Dymoke, Mrs Coffyn (or Cosyn), wife of William Coffyn, Anne's master of horse.

Sir Richard Page, Gentleman of the Privy Chamber to Henry VIII.

Margery Horsman, maid-of-honour to Anne.

Mary Zouche, maid-of-honour to Anne.

Mary Norris, sister of Sir Henry Norris; maid-of-honour to Anne.

The Gentleman Gaoler of the Tower.

Sir Christopher Hales, Attorney General.

Henry Somerset, 2nd Earl of Worcester.

The Sword of Calais, executioner.

Timeline

1485

- (August) Battle of Bosworth. Henry Tudor defeats Richard III, the last Plantagenet King, and becomes Henry VII, first sovereign of the royal House of Tudor

1491

- Birth of Henry VIII

1499?

- Birth of Mary Boleyn

1501?

- Birth of Anne Boleyn

1503?

- Birth of George Boleyn

1509

- (April) Accession of Henry VIII
- (June) Marriage and coronation of Katherine of Aragon and Henry VIII

1513

- Anne sent to Burgundy to serve Margaret of Austria, Regent of the Netherlands

1514

- Marriage of Henry VIII's sister, Mary Tudor, to Louis XII of France

1515

- Death of Louis XII; accession of François I of France
- Anne arrives at the French court to serve Mary Tudor
- Marriage of Mary Tudor to Charles Brandon, Duke of Suffolk
- Anne transfers to the household of Queen Claude, wife of François I

1516

- Birth of the Princess Mary, daughter of Henry VIII and Katherine of Aragon

1517

– Martin Luther publishes his ninety-five theses in Germany and inspires the Protestant Reformation

1519

– Birth of Henry Fitzroy, bastard son of Henry VIII by Elizabeth Blount

1520

– The Field of Cloth of Gold: lavish diplomatic summit meeting between Henry VIII and François I

1522

– War breaks out between England and France; Anne returns home to serve Katherine of Aragon, and makes her debut at the English court

1523

– Anne is forbidden to marry Henry Percy and is banished from court

1525

– Henry Fitzroy created Duke of Richmond and Somerset
– Henry VIII starts paying court to Anne

1526

– Henry VIII in pursuit of Anne Boleyn

1527

– Henry VIII questions the validity of his marriage to Katherine of Aragon and asks the Pope for an annulment
– Henry VIII resolves to marry Anne

1528

– Anne recovers from the sweating sickness
– Cardinal Campeggio, the Pope's legate, comes to England to try the King's case

1529

– The legatine court sits at the monastery of the Black Friars in London, where Katherine of Aragon appeals to Henry VIII for justice; the case is referred back to Rome
– Cardinal Wolsey falls from favour; Sir Thomas More appointed Lord Chancellor
– Eustache Chapuys appointed Charles V's ambassador to England
– Thomas Boleyn created Earl of Wiltshire and Ormond

1530

- Henry VIII begins canvassing the universities for their views on his case
- Death of Cardinal Wolsey

1531

- Katherine of Aragon banished from court
- Thomas Cromwell emerges as Henry VIII's chief minister

1532

- Sir Thomas More resigns the office of Lord Chancellor
- (August) Death of William Warham, Archbishop of Canterbury, paving the way for the appointment of the radical Thomas Cranmer
- Anne becomes Henry VIII's mistress
- (September) Anne created Lady Marquess of Pembroke

1533

- (25 January) Henry VIII secretly marries Anne
- (April) Parliament passes the Act in Restraint of Appeals (to the Pope), the legal cornerstone of the English Reformation
- (April) Anne Boleyn appears at court as Queen of England
- (May) Cranmer pronounces the marriage of Henry VIII and Katherine of Aragon incestuous and unlawful, and confirms the validity of Henry's marriage to Anne Boleyn
- (1 June) Coronation of Anne Boleyn
- (7 September) Birth of the Princess Elizabeth, daughter of Henry VIII and Anne Boleyn

1534

- (March) The Pope pronounces the marriage of Henry VIII and Katherine of Aragon valid
- Parliament passes the Act of Supremacy, making Henry VIII Supreme Head of the Church of England, and the Act of Succession, making the children of Queen Anne the King's lawful heirs
- Imprisonment of Sir Thomas More and John Fisher, Bishop of Rochester, for refusing to swear the oath of supremacy
- Anne bears a stillborn child

1535

- Anne bears a second stillborn child

- Executions of John Fisher, Bishop of Rochester, Sir Thomas More and several Carthusian monks

1536
- (7 January) Death of Katherine of Aragon
- (29 January) Anne miscarries a son
- (2 May) Anne arrested and imprisoned in the Tower of London
- (15 May) Anne tried and condemned to death for treason
- (17 May) Anne's marriage to Henry VIII dissolved
- (19 May) Anne beheaded in the Tower of London

Reading Group Questions

- From the opening scene of *A King's Obsession*, Anne Boleyn is impatient for change – for something new and exciting to happen. She is a capricious child, highly aware of her mother's ancestry on one hand, and her father's ambition on the other. How do you think her character is influenced by this family background? How does Thomas Boleyn's tendency to value his children in terms of their use to the Boleyn name affect Anne's actions throughout her life?

- By including Anne's education in the courts of Margaret of Austria, Queen Claude and Marguerite of Valois, Alison Weir explores a fascinating world of high culture and intellect. What key lessons does Anne learn at each court, and how is her outlook changed by these three women? Does she manage to emulate them once she has the crown? Did anything Anne learned surprise you?

- George Boleyn is a complicated and interesting character. He has a similar craving for power as Anne, but has to find different ways to gain it. How are he and Anne alike, and how do they differ? On the surface he has far greater freedom, but is he also trapped into achieving the Boleyn family's ambitions as firmly as she is?

- Every scene in *A King's Obsession* is shown from Anne's point of view, so the narrative is shaded by her thoughts and emotions. How does this technique develop the 'Anne Boleyn' Alison Weir has chosen to portray, and does sharing Anne's viewpoint increase your empathy for her actions?

- The behaviour of powerful men towards women, including Mary Boleyn, causes Anne grief and anger. The shocking moments of discovery that a king's sister is not protected, nor a favourite brother innocent, have a profound effect on Anne. How does she attempt to overcome this? How does she try to exercise her own control over others, and was there a scene when you felt she finally achieves this? When she does have power, does she ever use it well?

- *"'You don't love him, do you?'" Mary challenged. "You just want to be queen.'"* Henry's feelings for Anne are described by many as an obsession – something emphasised even in the book's title. Alison Weir's interpretation shows Anne herself motivated by a desire for power rather than by love. Does this match with your idea of their relationship before reading the book and, if not, did Alison convince you? What is it about becoming queen that Anne finds so seductive?

- Henry and Anne's relationship is dominated by Katherine of Aragon, both in presence and absence. How does Anne reconcile her early affection for the Queen with her need to remove and replace her, and justify her cruelty towards Katherine and Mary? Do you feel she starts to identify more with Katherine's situation once she has won this battle, and when is this most starkly shown?

- Anne's role in encouraging Henry's stance against the Church of Rome is an intriguing part of the novel, and she isn't afraid to express her desire for change. How much do you feel this is through a powerful personal belief in the need for Reformation, and how much expedience to reach her own goals? How do Alison Weir's descriptions of this period of history bring its turbulence to life?

- *A King's Obsession* is the second of six novels about the queens of Henry VIII. Anne's impression of Henry is very different to that of her rival, Katherine. How does Alison Weir show Henry through Anne's eyes, while retaining the character she developed in *The True Queen*, where Katherine of Aragon sees her adored husband very differently? How would you compare the voices of the two queens in the first two books in the series?

- '"Strike now!" she cried, her heart hammering so hard and painfully in her chest that she thought there might be no need for any headsman.' The ending of *A King's Obsession* is visceral and perhaps shocking but very vivid. How did you feel reading Anne's last moments, and how effective did you find Alison Weir's narration of her final experience on the block?

- Alison Weir's background as a historian means that she has distilled a huge amount of research into this novel, creating a rich and vivid background to the characters' lives. However, as a novelist, she has had to choose a version of Anne's story to tell. Do you agree with the journey Alison has given her, and did you discover a new angle on Anne's life through *A King's Obsession*?